VOLUMES 1 & 2

WHAT MIGHT HAVE BEEN

WHAT MIGHT HAVE BEEN

VOLUMES 1 & 2

ALTERNATE EMPIRES
ALTERNATE HEROES

EDITED BY
Gregory Benford &
Martin H. Greenberg

SPECTRA

BANTAM BOOKS
NEW YORK • TORONTO • LONDON • SYDNEY • AUCKLAND

CONTENTS

VOLUME 1

ALTERNATE EMPIRES

CONTENTS

INTRODUCTION

Perhaps there is no more poignant theme than *if only* . . .

Certainly writers of many stripes and persuasions have wondered what might have been and attempted to rewrite history. This practice has been termed many things, some ambiguous, such as *parahistory* and *metahistory*. Academics have offered *uchronia*, by analogy with *utopia*. Some suggested *allohistory* and *alternative history*.

Whatever the term, this volume begins a series of stories devoted to refashioning history in a logical manner to explore what could or might have been. Other volumes will follow.

The theme has a considerable history itself. The first use of it was Louis-Napoleon Geoffroy-Chateau's *Napoleon and the Conquest of the World, 1812–1823*. This nationalist vision, published in 1836, told how a crucial decision to not tarry in Moscow as winter drew on saved the French forces. Napoleon then had the entire planet on the run and established the first world empire. In 1931 J. C. Squire gave the theme great momentum by assembling *If: or History Rewritten*. This volume was not fiction, but rather speculative essays by such luminaries as Winston Churchill, G. K. Chesterton, and Hilaire Belloc.

In a scholarly afterword to *Alternative Histories* (edited by Charles G. Waugh and Martin H. Greenberg), Gordon B. Chamberlain and Barton C. Hacker gave a rough count of which ideas have been most popular. The most common theme is World War II, Hitler, and the atomic bomb. We edited an entire volume of such stories, *Hitler Victorious*. The second most popular theme is the survival of Rome or Byzantium. Third is the American War of Secession and Lincoln. Then comes changes in the Spanish Armada and the Reformation, followed by switches in the lot of the Aztecs and other Native Americans. A bit less common are different outcomes for Napoleon and altered American Revolutions.

This series explores these and other avenues. We commissioned tales from writers we thought would most ingeniously use the great freedom the idea allows. We imposed one further constraint: the changed history had to be a failed event. This is a way to explore the fragility of human action. Can small tweaks and tunings wrench history onto utterly different tracks? Historians themselves have no clear answer to this question. The appeal of the notion lies in our suspicion that some crucial events have great leverage, yet seeming inconsequentialities can be the fulcrum. (My novel *Timescape* argues for the sensitivity of great events to minor changes, and that is my bias. I could not resist the impulse to take that view in my own story here. But in consulting with authors, we resisted imposing any of our opinions.) In science fiction alternative histories often arise from the device of time travel, where causal paradox can play a role. Within limits, this too was an allowed option for our contributors.

Given the theme of what might have been and asked to dwell upon grand events that failed to come about, our authors could write whatever they liked. Interestingly, three stories deal with changes in the great religions of the world, which then alter empires and world society with great effect. Others treat recent changes, some military.

We cajoled Larry Niven into writing the closing story as a homage to Robert Heinlein—and Heinlein read and approved it with real pleasure only a month before his death in the spring of 1988. The thought that a science fiction writer could prove crucial to history seems both amusing and, after reflection, quite plausible.

A later collection will treat the Great Man idea and explore the importance of individuals in the great sweep of history. We hope you will find this range of imaginative experiments thought-provoking and perhaps even unsettling.

—GREGORY BENFORD
OCTOBER 1988

IN THE HOUSE OF SORROWS

SORROWS

Poul Anderson

That is a very old land, full of wrongs that will not die. They weighted me like the noontime heat, and with the same stillness, but the names of many of them I had never known. My horse's hoofs made the loudest noise, beneath it now and then a creak of saddle leather, once the twitter of a shepherd boy's pipes. Dusty green orchards and kitchen gardens dappled summer-brown hills. Dwellings, mostly sun-baked brick, strewed themselves likewise. They grew thicker along the road as it wound upward. Men in shabby caftans stared at me from doorways, women and children from deeper inside, speaking no word. A few times I met laden camels, donkeys, oxcarts. The lips of their drivers closed when I came in sight.

It had been thus for the past day. Some news had flown abroad. Riding, I had glimpsed restlessness in the villages and between them. No longer did anybody hail me, rush forth to offer wares or beg for alms. Thrice I stopped to water my mount, my remount, and myself, and sought to ask what went on, but those I spoke to gave short, meaningless answers and slipped away. That was easy for them. I had little of either the Aramaic or the Edomite tongue.

That night I deemed it best not to seek a caravansary, but rolled up in my saddle blanket in a field well off the highway. At sunrise I ate what cheese and pita bread were left me, and quenched thirst with the last water in my flask. It's hard for a Marklander to be without his morning coffee, but dead men can't drink anyhow.

Now the walls of Mirzabad rose before me. Afar, they had shimmered hazy through the heat. Close, I saw the pockmarks of former wars in their gray-white stone. A flag drooped from a cross-armed staff above the gate. The Lion and Sun of Persia slackened a little the tightness in me. At least that much abided. My gaze sought after the hues of Ispanya and did not find them. However, I told myself, belike they were not seeable from here.

Lesser buildings, shops and worksteads, crowded the roadsides. They should have been alive with the racket of the East, hammers on iron, hooves thudding, wheels groaning, beasts lowing and braying, fowl cackling, folk shrilling. Smells should have thickened the heat, smoke, sweat, dung, oil. Instead, what drifted to me seemed eerily loud and sharp in its loneliness. Some traffic did move. Dust from it gritted my eyelids, nostrils, mouth. My horses must push their way among walkers, wagons, huge burdens on hairy backs. Yet this was scant, and all outbound. Faces were grim. The looks I got ran from sullen to hateful. Often men spat on my shadow.

A score of warders stood by at the gate. Sicamino itself posted only four at any inway. These were also Persians, also wearing striped tunics, breeches bagged into half-boots, turbans on bearded heads. They also bore old-time, muzzle-loading rifles and curved short-swords. They slouched with the same slovenliness, soldiers of what was today an empire in name only. But their wariness came to me like a stench of fear, and it was no astonishment when their overling shouted in bad Ispanyan, "Ho, you, Westman, stop! Haul over!"

I obeyed, careful to hold my hands on the reins, well away from pistol and broadsword. A paved space under the wall was kept clear. The head warder beckoned me to it and snapped, "Get off."

Such a bearing toward a newcomer whom they must deem a European boded ill. I swung down from the stirrups and stood before them, hoping I looked neither too haughty nor too lowly. My years among the Magyars and Turks had given me some understanding of warlike men whose kingdoms have lost greatness. "Ahura-Mazda be with you, sirdar," I greeted in my best Persian.

The overling blinked, then turned and bowed low as another man trod from a door in the gateway. This was not an Ispanyan gunnaro, such as should have been on call. He was another Persian, tall and lean, grizzle-bearded, in white turban and flowing black robe. The soldiers dipped their heads and touched their breasts. To them, I saw, he was a holy man; but that was no outfit of an orthodox murattab. "Who are you and what would you, Frank?" he asked with a deadly kind of softness.

I laid palms together above my heart. "Venerable one, I am no Frank," I said cat-footedly. "Nor, as you have perceived, am I an Ispanyan." Sometimes a man of that kingdom is fair-haired and much taller than most are in Lesser Asia; but on the whole, the Visigothic blood has long since lost itself in the Iberian. "May it please you, I am a humble messenger, bringing a letter to the Mirzabad factor of the Bremer Handelsbund."

The dark eyes smoldered against mine. I thought, though, that underneath, he was taken aback. Tales of the Saxonian strength off the Persian shores must have reached him, too. "Do they not trust our postal riders?" he asked slowly; and I saw wrath flare in the faces behind him.

Of course they didn't. "I bring, as well, certain words from the consul of the Hauptmannsreich in Sicamino to the factor Otto Gneisberg here in Mirzabad, such words as go best by mouth. Your reverence will understand." At least, he would be unsure whether I lied or no.

"Hm. Show me your papers."

He muttered over my passport. "Ro Esbernsson from . . . New Denmark?" I could barely tell what sounds he was trying to utter.

I pointed to the notation and seal "Not a Saxonian myself, true, but in the service of the excellent consul, as bodyguard and courier."

The letter itself was in a packet addressed to Gneisberg from von Heidenheim in the Latin, Greek, and Persian alphabets. This priest, or whatever he was, must feel a clawing wish to cut the thongs and take the writing to someone who could read it. For a heartbeat I thought he might, and wondered if I could shoot my way free, leap on my horse, and outgallop pursuit. Then he gave the things back to me, and my breath with them. The sweat prickled below my shirt. Not yet did anybody want to risk *that* war. He spoke a curt command and withdrew, his dignity gone stiff.

The soldiers took their time ransacking my baggage. Passersby stared; some jeered. In the end, they left me my papers and packet, money, a handbag with clothes and other everydayness, and my sword. The last was unwillingly, only because my being a consul's handfast man gave me the standing of warrior and to take my steel would have been to blacken him. They kept my firearms, horses, and wayfaring gear. I got no token of claim, but was not about to question their honor.

Nor did it seem wise to ask what had happened. I was glad enough to leave them behind me and pass on into the city.

A bazaar lay just beyond the gate, booths around a square whose flagstones should have been decked by spread-out rugs, metalware, crockery, fabrics, farm produce, all the goods that vendors chanted the wonders of, while the crowd milled and chattered. Today it brooded well-nigh empty beneath the hard blue sky, between the hot blind walls. A few folk, so few, went among such dealers as still dared be there. Mostly they were after food. I kenned the women: Aramaics and Edomites loosely and fully clad, low-rank Persians in long, close-fitting gowns and flowing scarves, Turks short and sturdy in blouses and breeks. Most had a man of her breed at her side, who must be warding her.

The street bore a little more upon it than the market did: sandals, boots, slippers, shoes, hooves, wheels a-clatter over bumpy cobbles. Those all belonged to men. Among townsfolk and hinterland peasants I spied some from far parts of the Shahdom, Kurds, Syrians, Badawi, with here and there an outlander, Greek, Egyptian, Afghan —but no Turk of the Sultandom, no Russian or other underling of the Grand Knyaz, no Frank or Saxonian or Dane—and with a chill in the white sunlight, I saw no Ispanyan either, be he tradesman or soldier of the Wardership. I was the one Westerner in that whole thin swarm.

"Master! Lord! Effendi!" A hand plucked my sleeve.

I looked down at a boy of maybe nine years, Edomite, all grime and rags, shock hair and big eyes. "Glorious master," he cried in bad but swift Persian, "I am your servant, your guide in the name of the heavenly Yazata to safe lodging, fine food and wine, pleasure, everything my lord desires." He jumped to worse Ispanyan: "Mestro, I show you good inn, eat, drink, beautiful girls."

Such urchins ought to have overrun me, each eager to win a coin for bringing in me and my money. Now this one alone had the pluck. I liked that. Not that I was about to go where he hoped to take me. From my own childhood I remembered the stave that begins, "Gang warily in where wolves may lair." Still, I could use a guide. The map that had been given me showed an utter tangle of streets. It did not mark at all that stead which I had decided I had better seek first. Let the lad earn his copper from me.

"Take me to the Mithraeum," I said in Persian.

"Ah, to the house of your god, sirdar? I leap at your order, I, Herod Gamal-al-Mazda. In the Street of Ulun Begh it lies, near the Fountain of Herakles, and we shall go there swift as the wind, straight as the djinn, most glorious master. Only come!"

He tried to take my bag for me, but I didn't trust him that much and he skipped ahead, doubtless happy not to have the weight dragging at his thin shoulders. The ways that he took twisted downward. The houses that hemmed them were shut. I had a feeling that the dwellers crouched within like hares in a burrow when the fox is a-prowl. The few men we met drew aside and watched me in the same wise. I saw from their neck rings that they were slaves, and from scrawniness and whip scars that they were worth little. The good ones their owners kept indoors, sending the trash out on such fetch-and-carry tasks as could not wait for a better time.

"You lead me widely about, do you not?" I said at last.

Herod threw an eye-glint backward. "My lord is shrewd," he said. "The main thoroughfares are dangerous."

As if to bear him out, a growl and mutter reached me. The walls and crooked lanes in between faintened it, but I knew that noise of old, and the hair stood up on my arms. It was the mouthings of a crowd adrift and angry.

Herod bobbed his head. "Many like them today."

"What has happened here?" I blurted.

"It is not for an alley rat to speak about the mighty," he said fast, and scuttled onward. Indeed so, I thought, when he did not know whose man I was. I bore a sword, and death walked under this hot heaven.

Well, but at the Mithraeum, once I had shown myself to be initiate in the Mysteries—I have reached the rank of Lion—its Father would tell me the truth. Then I could plan how best to bring Otto Gneisberg the word of his motherland. Merely fumbling to his house, I might well meet some foolish doom.

The ground canted sharply. Either the rubble that elsewhere underlay the city, yards deep, had never been piled here, or else an overlord had had it cleared away a few hundred years ago because there were things worth salvaging.

Housefronts showed workmanship of kingdoms long dead. In the basin of a dry fountain stood a statue that I reckoned was of Hercules and the Hydra, though as battered as it was, it might as well have been Thor and the Midgard Worm. Nearby crumbled a Roman temple or basilica, with columned portico and a frieze gone shapeless. The Turks in their day had made it over for their own worship, and their great-great-grandchildren still used it; through the doorless inway I saw the Warrior Buddha, sword in left hand, right hand lifted in blessing, the bronze of him turned green.

How many breeds had owned this town? The Persians of now, on whom the Ispanyans had laid wardship lest other Europeans do more than that; Edomites; Turks; Syrians; Mongols; Old Persians; Romans; Greeks—and how many before them, dust that scuffed up from my boots?

Wondering ended when Herod trilled, "Master, behold your sacred goal." I could hardly have mistaken it. Nonetheless, it was not such as my fathers knew.

Mithraists have been few hereabouts since the last West Roman legions withdrew. The Ispanyan garrison surely had its own halidoms, though those would also be strange to me. They look on our Northern godword as heretical. Asiatic Mithraisms are at odds with both, but hold that different roads may lead to the same truth. In this, if naught else, the East is wiser than the West.

The building and its sister beside it bore shapes of their land. Both stood taller than any in Europe or Markland, whitewashed, roofs swelling into domes, red on the Mithraeum, blue on the Shrine of the Good Mother. Easterners celebrate the Mysteries in windowless rooms rather than underground. Mosaics above the doors glowed with his Bull, her Rose. That much spoke straight to my heart. No matter any otherness. On a narrow and rough-stoned street, pressed between dingy blanknesses of walls, these houses reared upright as the faith itself.

But— Suddenly, spear-sharp, came back to me the halidoms of my boyhood. They stand a little outside of Ivarsthorp, on a grassy bank where the Connecticut River gleams past farmsteads, shaws, meadows marked off by stone walls and flowering hedges; they are low beneath their three-tiered roofs, but the wood of them is richly carved, and dragons rear skyward from the beam ends. Within the Mithraeum, when you have gone by lionheaded Aeon and the holy water bowl, Odin and Thor flank the altars of the Tauroctony: as I was told Frigg and Freyja honor our forebears at the Mystery of the women.

Here in Mirzabad, the land I had forsaken hunted me down, dogwood white in springtime, yeomen in summer fields that had been rock and bramble when the Trekfolk first came, the blazing hues of New Denmark fall, winter starlight that seemed to ring as it struck the snow—outings to fish and swim in Lake Winnepesaukee, days in jouncing wains and nights in old inns till we came to Merrimack Haven and saw the masts of the ships at dock lift their yards like the boughs of Yggdrasil— What unrest had driven me overseas? Why had I drifted from land to land, calling to calling, master to master, war to war, while my years spilled out of me and left only emptiness behind?

None of that, I barked at myself. There was work to do. "Wait," I told Herod. "I think I shall want you to guide me elsewhere." To Gneisberg's trading post, if I was lucky, and thence back to the western gate and away from this lair of Ahriman. I strode to the door of the Mithraeum and turned its handle.

The iron-bound timber stayed fast. It was locked.

This should not be. If naught else, a Raven or an Occult should be on watch inside, to help whatever brothers might come in need of help and to keep the holy of holies untrodden by the unhallowed. He could tell me where the Father lived, which was bound to be close by. I grasped the serpent coil of the knocker and clashed it on the plate. The noise fell hollow into the furnace day.

Herod squeaked at my back. I turned to see. The door had opened in the Shrine of the Good Mother and a woman had come forth.

She halted a few feet off. Beneath a blue gown of Persian cut, slenderness stood taut, ready to take flight. Young, she was likely of no more than Damsel rank in her Mysteries. Tresses astray from under her scarf shone obsidian black. Her face was finely molded and light-skinned, with the great gazelle eyes of the Sunrise Lands.

Persian women have never been as muffled in spirit as Hindi. Just the same, she astounded me with a straightforwardness well-nigh Frankish, if not quite Danish: "Wayfarer, you knock in vain. The Mithraeum is shut. The Father and the Courier of the Sun are both departed, and at their wish, all lower initiates have likewise sought what safety may be found."

Dismay smote me. "What, what is awry?" I stammered.

"You know not?"

Numbly, I shook my head. If the thanes of Mithras must flee, then Loki was loose. "I am but now come here, my lady."

Her look searched me. "Yes, you are a foreigner; and not a Frank, but from farther away." Even then, I knew keenness when I met it, and somehow that put heart back in me. "A believer, a warrior." Fire leaped in her voice. "By the faith, I require your help!"

"What? My lady, I have a mission."

"As do I. Mine will not wait, and yours can scarcely be done at once. This is for the Light, against the Chaos. Mithras will bless you."

She offered escape from bewilderment and uselessness. Also, she was fair to behold. "What is the task, my lady?"

"The Shrine holds certain treasures," she said crisply. "I came to save them before the city explodes and the throngs go rioting, looting, burning. Wait while I fetch them out, and give me escort to the Basileum." She flashed a smile that would have been lovely were her mood not so bleak. "You'll gain a den for yourself, and thus outlive the night—we may hope."

In a whirl of cloth, she sped back. I almost followed, but stopped myself at the threshold men may not cross. "The Basileum?" I mumbled. "What is that?"

"I think the noble lady must mean the House of Sorrows, lord." Herod's voice startled me; I had forgotten him. He tugged at my cloak. "Take me along. Should my lord and lady meet danger along the way, I know many a bolthole."

"We are in a powder keg, then," I said slowly.

"And sparks dance everywhere, my lord," the boy told me. "I should be glad of a snug hiding place too, where I may heed my master's every bidding."

"Better you go home to your mother."

He shrugged. The sigh of an old man blew from the wizened small face. "She will have enough to do keeping herself alive, my lord. I have heard that when men go wild in the streets, they go mad in the joyhouses."

"What in the name of evil has befallen?"

"I am only an alley rat, master. How shall I eavesdrop on the councils of the mighty?" He drew breath. "However, the word flying about is that yesterday the *rais* was overthrown by a follower of the Prophet Khusrev who had smuggled men and arms into this city. The Ispanyans have all drawn back into their fortress, and other Europeans have taken refuge there as well. So, perhaps, have the high priests and priestesses of these twin *dewali*. Far be it from me to call them craven. It was simple prudence. But I do not think my lord and lady could now shelter behind those gates and guns. This morning from a rooftop, I saw how armed men stand thick around every portal of the compound, and they wear the yellow sash of the Prophet."

Hard news was this. Yet the past hours had somewhat readied me for it. If only the powers, any of the powers, had foreseen! It would have been easy enough twenty years ago to send a small host into the Zagros Mountains and root Khusrev out. The Shah could have said little against it, might well have given it what feeble help was his to give. Did not this self-made Prophet cry that the Zarathushtran faith was fallen into corruption and idolatry, and that to him alone had come the saving revelation? Already then he spoke not simply of cleansing the belief and the rites, but of slaying everyone who would withstand him.

However, the Shahdom was a ghost, barely haunting the inland tribes, while the Ispanyan Wardership kept troops only in those provinces that bordered the Midworld Sea. Khusrev had seemed merely another among untold mullahs who had sprung up in the backlands lifetime after lifetime, preached, died, and blown away in dust.

Too late now, I thought, when the Puritans did as they would throughout Isfahan, Laristan, Kerman. and their flame went across

Mesopotamia and down the Arabian Peninsula. In every other province of the empire, too, it was breaking loose. Fleetingly I wondered if somehow, something of it had overleaped the ocean. Was it just happenstance that half of South Markland was in uprising, and the latest news told how the Inca of Tahuantinsuyu had ended fellowship with the Ispanyan crown? Oh, the inborns yonder called on their own gods, but—

Be that as it may, Ispanya had scant strength left for this part of the world. Day by day, the garrisons thinned, the grasp weakened, and men also scorned the law of the Shah.

I stared at Mithraeum and Shrine. Even the orthodox Zarathushtrans have always looked on Mithraists as fallen halfway back into heathenism, the more so after our cult linked itself to that of the Good Mother. To the Puritans we are worse than that, worse than infidels, the very creatures of Angra Mainyu.

Thoughts of the past went from me in a cold gust as the woman came back out the door. In her arms she carried two leatherbound books and several parchment scrolls. Mottlings and crumbly edges bespoke great age. "Let us begone," she said.

"Treasure—" I gulped.

"These are the treasures." She tossed her head. "Looters may have the vessels of gold and silver if they must."

Herod bounced around us. "Will my lady go to the House of Sorrows?" he twittered. "I know the safest ways, if any be safe. Give me leave to guide you!"

The woman cast me a look. I spread my hands and half smiled. "We could have a less canny leader," I said. "I have often met his kind. Shall I carry those?"

She shook her head. "You already have a bag. Better you keep your sword hand free."

We set forth, quick-gaited. Blue shadows slithered at our heels, over the cobblestones. They had lengthened a bit. The heat had waxed. To run in it would have been berserk. As was, my tongue stirred thick and dusty: "We have no names for each other, my lady. I am Ro Esbernsson. From North Markland."

Her eyes widened. "Across the Western Sea? What brings you to this place of woe?"

"An errand. What else? Perhaps you can counsel me."

She was bold for a Persian woman, but a shyness was built into her that she must overcome before she said: "I am Boran Taki. A votary of Isis." Thus they call the Good Mother in these parts. "As I trust you are of Mithras," she finished in haste.

I nodded. "Tell me what is going on, I pray you."

She swallowed hard. "Yesterday— But let me first say that Zigad Moussavi, a nobleman in the Jordan Valley, was converted to the New Revelation of Khusrev some years ago. His agitation against the Shah and the Ispanyans who uphold the Shah became so fierce, an outright call for insurrection, that his arrest was ordered. He fled with his followers into the desert. Since then their numbers have swelled, the countryside is often in turmoil, and if you traveled here alone without trouble, Mithras himself must have been watching over you."

My sword and pistol had something to do with it, I thought. Moreover, I went forewarned, wary, using those roads and inns that von Heidenheim had told me were likeliest to be still safe. He had eyes and ears everywhere in the province. Nonetheless, he had not looked for an outbreak this soon.

Boran went on in her scholarly, step-by-step way: "He must long have conspired with persons in the city, officers of the governor among them. Yesterday we suddenly heard gunfire, shouting—we saw people flee from the markets like sheep from a lion—rumors grew ever more frightening—then toward sundown, the noise dwindled away. Presently criers went through the streets, guarded by riflemen who wore yellow sashes. We were all commanded on pain of death to remain indoors until morning. During the night there were more shots and screams. Today a vast silence has fallen. But it seethes."

I nodded again. "Clearly, this Moussavi has seized the governor's palace and quelled whatever resistance the royal troops made. Did the Ispanyans do nothing?"

"It went too fast for them, I think, when they had no unequivocal orders," she answered. Yes, I thought, she might have led a sheltered life hitherto, but it had not dulled her wits. "They seem to have drawn back into their stronghold at the Moon Tower and prepared to stand siege if necessary. I suppose the Europeans among us have taken refuge with them, as well as Persians and other Easterners who have special reason to fear the new masters. As yet there has been no attack on the compound, and perhaps there will not be. Placards have gone up in public places, directing people to continue their daily lives in orderly fashion. Of course they do not heed that."

"You have read such a proclamation, then? What does it say?"

"It declares that Zigad Moussavi, servant of Ahura-Mazda, has overthrown the corrupt and idolatrous governor of the Shah and taken command of Mirzabad in the name of the Prophet. It promises a great beginning to the work of purifying the faith and restoring the ancient glory of Persia. Foreigners shall be expelled and infidels brought to justice."

"Hm. He's far from Khusrev country. Does he imagine he can hold this single city, all by himself?"

"He is no dolt. A madman, perhaps, but not stupid. I have studied his career as it progressed. Surely he expects by his example to ignite the entire province. To that end, although he calls for public order, he does nothing to enforce it. His warriors have not replaced the police patrols they drove off. More and more people are taking to the streets. They mill to and fro, they quarrel, they listen to ranting preachers and to songs of blood. Anything at any moment may bring on the eruption. After that is over, the city will have no choice but to heed Moussavi: because if the Shah's rule comes back, so will his headsmen."

"But I thought— Are the Persians in this city not largely orthodox Zarathushtrans?" I remembered those I had met in Europe, and the few who have made their way to Markland. They keep much to themselves, but are soft-spoken, good-hearted, hard-working folk with a high respect for learning.

Her tone was stark: "They too have things to avenge."

Well, yes, I must allow. In most countries of Europe, Zarathushtrans may not own land; in some, they are made to live in wretched, crowded quarters of the towns. Also, here at home they have seen foreigners swaggering where once their kings rode under golden banners.

"True. And many will not dare sit still, whatever their inward feelings," I foretold. "They will think they also must show zeal, so that afterward the Puritans will let them get on with their lives. Moreover, the bulk of the dwellers, Aramaics and Edomites and all the rest, will snatch at this chance to take out old grudges against each other, or simply to wreck and plunder."

Her look rested awhile on me. "You know the world well, Ru Esbernsson," she said low.

"And you seem wise beyond your years," I began. That and my smile died.

Herod heard first, and halted. Half a minute later the sound reached our older ears. It grew as we stood stiff, a racking growl through which sawed screams, the sound of a man-pack unloosed.

"The Mother help us, it has begun," Boran whispered.

"They are bound this way," Herod said. He cast about as a dog

does, then he beckoned and his slight form shot on down the street.
We loped after.

Where a slipper painted above a doorway marked the house of a
shoemaker, and it shuttered and barred, the boy darted aside. We
followed, into the sudden gloom and half-coolness of an alley. Flies
buzzed over the offal that made its cobbles slick. It twisted among
windowless buildings, more lanes joined it, Herod took us through a
maze and brought us out in a court. This too was filthily littered,
though vines trailing over one of the walls around it told that the
garden of somebody well-to-do lay on the other side.

Herod stopped. "I think we will be safe here for a while, if we are
quiet," he said. The calm of a seasoned man had fallen over him.
"Yonder is the home of Haidar Aghasi, the wine merchant. He'll be
with strong, well-armed hirelings to guard his wealth. The rioters
ought to know that and pass by."

"Might he take us in?" I wondered.

"No, master, he would be witless to link himself with a European,
today. Would he not?" Herod replied, and I felt myself rebuked for
my childishness.

Boran clutched the books to her breast. "Besides, I must bring these
to my father," she said.

Well, if they meant so much that she dared go forth after them—I
settled myself to wait. The grisly racket loudened.

Herod yelped, Boran gasped. I swung on my heel. The sword
sprang into my hand. A man stumbled into the court.

For a moment he stood panting. We glared at each other. He was
burly, red of hair and beard, freckled of snub-nosed face. His skin had
once been fair, but Southern sun had made leather of it. The shirt was
half ripped off him and blood oozed from three shallow wounds. He
gripped a staff, long and heavy, in a way that said that to him this was
a weapon. In his left hand gleamed a sheath knife.

I knew such features and shape of blade. My sword lowered. "You
are from Eirinn," I murmured in Danish such as they speak in England. A Gaelic sailor would be bound to understand me.

He swallowed a few more draughts of air, grinned, and said with
the lilt of his folk, "Sure and this is an unlikely place to be meeting
the Lochlannach."

"Hush," Herod begged. The man and I nodded. Without need to
plan it, we turned back to back, covering both sides from which attack might come.

It snarled on by. Inch by inch, we reached the knowledge that we
would live a bit longer.

The man and I faced around again. He put away his knife, took staff in left hand, and held out his right. "A good day to ye, your honor," he said merrily. "Ailill mac Cerbaill I am, from Condacht through Markland, China, and points west. My greetings to the little lady. If only I could speak her tongue, I'd be paying her the compliments that luckier men certainly do."

I smiled and clasped the hand. It was thick, hard, from years of fisting canvas and winding capstans. I gave him our names and asked what brought him so far from the sea.

"Och, it's not many miles," he said.

Herod jittered about. "My lord, my lord, we should begone," he urged. "The pack—I think they will smash and loot in the Street of the Comfit Makers, who are mainly Turks, but they may not, and whatever they do, they will shortly return this way."

"Come," I agreed. A thought struck me. "Ailill, are you astray?"

"I am that," the seaman said. "The landlord at my inn sent me off this morning for an outland unbeliever, and never counted what bedbugs of his I took with me. Then as I wandered the streets, that gang swept about a corner and set upon me. I thought I heard the wings of the Morrigan beat overhead, but Lug Long-Arm strengthened mine enough that I broke free."

For a heartbeat I envied him his gods, that to a Gael are still real beings. What are the gods of our forebears to us Mithraists, save names in the rites? Mithras himself is no longer the embodiment he once was. At that, we are better off than the Saxonians, who never had a higher religion and whose olden sacrifices are now no more than a show of loyalty to the Hauptmann.

"Join us," I offered. "We're bound for shelter, where I daresay they can use another doorkeeper."

He was glad to. Herod led us out and thence widely roundabout. Boran looked askance at the uncouth newcomer, though when I gave her my thought she said that I was right, *if* he was trustworthy.

Therefore I sounded Ailill out. It was easy. He had gotten drunk in Sicamino and missed his ship. On the beach, he learned of a venture that needed men, smuggling tobacco down from Turkey and past the Persian customs. The stuff came in at Joppa, which has a bad harbor and so is not much watched. Because unrest in the countryside had aroused banditry, inland shipments wanted guards. Ailill chose to go along with the camels headed for Mirzabad; he had heard of its time-gnawed wonders. I gathered he was not altogether a deckhand and roisterer; he had a touch of the skald in him like many among his folk.

"Well, there I was, stumping down the Street of the Magi—What bit you, my friend?"

I clamped my jaw. The Bremer Handelsbund kept its warehouse, shop, quarters for the factor and his workers, on the Street of the Magi. "Was anything . . . plundered, burned . . . there?" I asked.

"It was not. I think the violence had only just begun. But those are some grand houses, and when the weasels have been at easier chicken coops and tasted blood, they will be back, I think."

I nodded. "We may have a few hours."

"Eh? . . . What might this port be that you're steering for?"

My lips bent upward. "I wish I knew."

Our course wound onward and onward, like a nightmare. Amid the squalor, I spied remnants, a fluted column, a slim spire, a wall slab that bore the worn-down carving of a winged bull with a man's head. The downslope grew ever more steep, lanes turned into flights of stairs hollowed out by uncounted footfalls, and ahead of us, above the flat roofs, I saw turrets and battlements four-square athwart eastern hills. A few times a ragged form scuttled around a corner or into a lane. My skin crawled with the feeling of eyes that peered through slits in the shouldering walls.

"Where do you take us?" I asked Boran, forgetting that she had told me.

"To the House of Sorrows," Herod piped up.

The woman winced. "A horrible name," she said. "It is rightfully the Basileum."

The Greek word stood forth in the Persian. "And what might that mean, my lady?"

"It is the archive of archives," she answered. "There repose the chronicles, the records, the tablets and letters and . . . whatever whispers to us of the past. Such things are no longer of use to the state, but precious to what scholars remain alive."

I searched my mind. "Basileum? That which a king built? Should the word not be—m-m—no, I suppose not 'biblioteka'—'museum'?"

Her tone softened. "You are no barbarian, Ro, are you?"

"I have read books." Maybe they were what first called me outward from my homeland.

"This was founded by Julian the Second, Augustus in Byzantium, when the East Romans still held the Syriac lands. He established others where he could, though I know of none else that have endured. Rome itself had lately fallen. He foresaw a dark age. How else might the heritage of the ancients be saved, even a little?"

I shivered. That was fifteen hundred years ago, was it not?

We passed a monument. A muffled shriek from Boran tore me out
of my thoughts. Two deathlings sprawled before us. They were pulp,
splinters, huge splashes and pools of blood flamingly red under the
sun. Flies blackened the simmering air.

I caught her elbow. "Come along," I said. She moaned once, but
swallowed her sickness.

"Turks, by what's left of their clothes," Ailill muttered. "One quite
young, a girl."

Their kin must have dwelt in Mirzabad since the Sultans ruled it,
when white men were barely setting foot on the shores of Markland;
but today they had become outlanders, unbelievers, and a gang that
caught them had stamped them into the stones. After all my wanderings I should have been able to shrug off a sight like this, but it
saddened me anyhow. "May their Buddha take them home," I said.

"Hurry, hurry," Herod chattered.

"You ought never to have gone forth, Boran," I told her.

"I slipped away before my father could forbid it," she answered. It
did her good to speak. "The Basileum is in his care."

Since he was surely a Mithraist, I knew he had a Zarathushtran
above him; but that was belike a eunuch of the governor's, who did
scant more than draw large pay and pass half of it on to his lord. It
was no wonder that the New Revelation was taking hold in souls
from the Caspian to the Midworld Sea.

"These are genealogies and annals that the Shrine kept," she went
on, holding them tightly to her. "Often has my father longed to study
them. I saw his anguish when it seemed they might be lost, and—"

"Behold!" Herod crowed.

We had reached a small square, in whose faded and patched paving
dolphins rollicked. Across from us lifted a building of no great size.
Age had pitted and blurred it. Gracefulness lingered in the pillars of
the portico, the golden rectangle and low gable of the front; the marble was the hue of wan amber beneath tiles that had gone dusky rose.
As we drew nigh, I saw Greek letters above the columns, and they
were clear. Lifetime by lifetime, somebody had renewed them as they
wore away.

"What does that mean?" I asked, pointing.

Boran's voice was as hushed as mine: " 'Polla ta deina' Wonders are
many, and none more wondrous than man."

We mounted the stairs and must have been seen through a slotted
shutter, for the door opened before us. Him who came out in a white
robe I knew by his gray-bearded handsomeness to be Boran's father.
He reached his arms toward her. "Oh, my dearest," he called.

She caught her breath, stumbled forward, and blurted, "I b-brought you the books from the Shrine."

"You should not have, you should not have. I was terrified when I found you were missing. Madness runs free."

"That is why I had to go." She shook her head as if to dash the tears from her lashes.

The man looked across her to me. "Ro Esbernsson of Markland, learned sir," I named myself, "with Ailill mac Cerbaill of Eirinn and, and Herod. We met your daughter and escorted her."

"That was nobly done of you," he said with renewed steadiness. "The Lord Mithras will remember when your souls depart for the stars. I am Jahan Taki, in charge of the Basileum now that . . . others have abandoned it. Enter, I pray you."

He stood aside. We walked through an anteroom into a broad chamber of mosaic murals. I knew Athene, foremost among the figures. Tinted glass in a clerestory softened light. Air was blessedly cool. Half a dozen men stared at us. Two were old, three young but thin and stoop-shouldered. The only one that might be worth anything in a fight was a big black African whose garb said that he did the rough work.

Boran set the books down on a table of ivory-inlaid ebony. Gold glowed in the robes of gods and philosophers on the walls. What a house to sack, I thought.

Jahan Taki might have heard that. "I am not sure how safe a refuge this is," he said. "For excuse, raveners can scream that the books are full of wicked falsehoods and should be destroyed."

"They get by me first," growled the African. He saw my startlement and gave me a harsh smile. "I work for low wages because wiseman Taki lets me read."

"And these among my colleagues and students would not flee either." The pride in Jahan faded. "We can only pray that none will come until peace has been restored."

"That may take days," I warned. "Have you food and drink on hand?"

Boran nodded. "I reminded them when we first gathered here," she said, "and the cistern already held sufficient."

"Good," I answered through the dust in my throat. "Let us have some of that water, and we'll look to your defenses."

The African hastened off. Meanwhile Jahan took me over the ground floor. The books and relics were in vaults beneath. There were two doors. I told him they should be barricaded as well as bolted. "At the front, leave a space for going in and out, but narrow enough for a single man to hold. If you have nothing better, pile up your furniture."

Jahan winced. "It will hurt like fire, but rather that than lose the books. Most have never been printed. I think many are the last copies that survive anywhere."

It struck me as strange, this love of learning for its own sake, a Greek thing I had thought died with Rome like the avowed love of men for boys. The Zarathushtrans study their holy writ but add nothing new. The rest of us give ourselves to the worldly arts. Oh, we measure the earth and the stars in their courses because that helps navigation, but to wonder about them, that is something children outgrow. We keep old books if they are useful or enjoyable, but otherwise, why should we care? In this house I felt as though I stood among ghosts. Had they a right to spook through the life of young Boran?

The African brought the water. I swished mine about in my mouth before swallowing it. The mummy dryness began to go away. "Can you make the place secure according to what master Taki has heard from me?" I asked him.

"As well as the Yazata will have it, my lord," he answered. So he was a Zarathushtran himself.

"I know a wee bit about such things too," Ailill put in. "But ye'll be foreman over us, Ro, won't ye?"

I shook my head. "No, the task had better not wait till I get back. Which I may not."

He blinked. "What? Why, sir, here we've stumbled into an anchorage as snug as any outside the Ispanyan fort—"

Boran caught our drift. Her hand fell on my arm. For an Eastern woman to do thus gave away, more than any words, how shaken she was. "Ro, you would leave us? You must not!"

"I go without joy," I told her, "but honor requires it. I am in the service of a man. As long as I take his pay, I do his bidding."

"Where do you seek, my son?" Jahan asked.

"To the Saxonian factor. I bear a message."

Sharply to me came the room overlooking Sicamino harbor where I had been given that word. Through its window I saw the schooners, barks, square-riggers, dhows, feluccas, the trade of half a world. The bay opened out to a sea that shone like quicksilver. Against the dazzle, at the edge of sight, I could just make out three tall vessels. Light struck little sparks off their guns. I knew that at their mastheads flew the falcon banner of the Hauptmann of Saxonia.

My look returned, crossed the desk, came to rest on Konrad von Heidenheim. The consul sat sweating, as so fleshy a man does in such heat. The beard spilling down his chest was wet with it. His right hand wielded a fan, his left cradled a fuming pipe. But the eyes were like chips of ice, and when he spoke it was a drumroll from the depths.

"Ro, boy, I do not myself like the job I have for you. However, need is for several couriers I can trust to bring a word from me and keep it quiet. I think you will go to Mirzabad. The Handelsbund has a good-sized post there. It is of more than economic value. It has strategic potential."

I leaned back, crossed shank over knee, and waited.

He chuckled dourly. "Ach, always you play the lynx-calm soldier of fortune. As you like. Now listen close. I have a lecture prepared.

"You think you know why Saxonia has brought ships and troops offshore. This crazy Prophet and his Puritans are tearing the interior of the Shahdom in pieces. The trouble will spread farther before it is put down, if it can be put down. Maybe it cannot. Maybe the Prophet will enter Persepolis. That will mean the Ispanyans depart. Their wardership is shaky, they have ample grief overseas, they will not protest an order from a new government for their expulsion. A wave of religious persecution will sweep through the footprints they leave.

"The Russians may then move in. The Grand Knyaz in Kiev is not willing for such a risk. Too many of his boyars are, though. If they prevail, the Russian armies may march 'to the rescue of their Turkish coreligionists,' as the mealy-mouths will say. Saxonia can ill afford such a threat to its Balkan flank. We have brought strength into the eastern Mediterranean and are marshaling troops in Greece as a warning to the Russians not to attempt this, no?"

"That's what I've been given to understand, herr," I said, not unthankful for hearing it again. It was new to me and less than clear. I was lately back from two free months in Egypt, a land so lost in mysticism that, once well up the Nile, you hear hardly a whisper from outside.

Von Heidenheim puffed smoke that stung my nostrils. "Well, you should know and keep it to yourself, matters are more dangerous still. They have intelligence reports in Hamburg that they have relayed to their agents abroad, like me. Frankland will not let the Russians take over Persia. If they try, it means war, general war, with my poor Saxonia caught between Franks to the west and Russians to the east. At the same time, Frankland has not yet mustered the strength to forestall those hot-headed boyars.

"*We* have it. Wotan with her, Saxonia can interpose herself. The Russians should feel much less eager to move, knowing they shall fight us while the Franks make ready. It is risky, yes, that is obvious; but the risks of inaction look worse. Of course, we take this action only if we must. Perhaps things will not explode after all, and everybody can go home. But I have my doubts.

"So." He leaned forward. "This is my message to our various factors throughout the maritime provinces of the Shah. Come trouble, come the breakdown of royal authority and the Wardership, they should not flee. If at all possible—and their buildings are stout—they should hold fast and call for help. Most of them keep carrier pigeons that will make for Sicamino. I tell them that we will land troops at once and come straight to their rescue.

"Do you see? This demonstration of will and power should give even the Puritan fanatics pause. It could perhaps be the one added push that keeps the Shah from falling down. But we must have proper cause for intervention—landsmen of ours and their valuable goods to save, as is our right. Else it looks too much like collusion between us and the Franks, and may touch off the very war we hope to prevent.

"Therefore, go to Mirzabad and tell Otto Gneisberg to ready his establishment for a possible siege."

We had not known I would be too late.

Or was I?

A small voice at my elbow: "Where now would my master fare?"

I looked down. Herod had tiptoed wide-eyed through what he might well believe were the splendors of a djinni's hall. "Best you stay behind, lad. You've done well, but it's dangerous out there." I reached for my purse. "First I'd better pay you. Uh, learned Taki, may he remain?"

"Of course," Boran answered softly. "He has made himself our child." Her father nodded.

Herod straightened his thin body. "I am not a babe," he said. "Have I not led men? Master, let me prove my worth beyond doubting. Then perhaps I can be your servant always."

I thought I knew what went on in that shock head. Money, a good berth, a way out of the trap that held his mother—for him, if not for her. But the big eyes sought mine with more than reckoning behind them. I knew that hope, that he had found himself a lord to live for and die at the feet of. I never would.

It touched me more than I might have awaited. Also, I could in truth use his guidance. "If you will have it thus, Herod," I told him. "Your pay shall be three gold royals."

He sprang up and down for joy.

"Go with Mithras and Isis," Boran whispered. "Return to us. Oh, return, Ro."

I found I was unable to speak further. Instead I lifted my hand and made the sign of the Hammer. They did not ken it, but maybe they would guess that it stood for the strongest wish I could offer.

Swiftly, the boy and I left. When we were out on the square he chirped, "Where shall I take you?"

"To the house of the Saxonian traders," I said. "Do you know? They are in the Street of the Magi, where the red-haired man was set upon."

He pondered, finger to chin, laughed, and slipped off.

Thrice we heard prowling packs. He drew me into side lanes and we waited until he felt we could go on. Again he brought me widely around; but belike I would not have arrived without him.

Above the massive door of a building that was a stronghold, its few outside windows iron-shuttered, hung a sign, as signs hang in Western lands. It showed an olden galley sailing on the red-black-red of Bremen. I knocked and shouted. The noise rattled between neighboring walls. "None here," I mumbled at last.

"They went to the Ispanyans," Herod guessed.

"So must we."

"My lord, I told you I have seen the men in yellow sashes outside that place. They will not let us through. Else everyone they mean to kill would flock there."

"Go back to . . . the House of Sorrows."

"Lord!" He sounded downright angry. "I am your servant."

I smiled a little. "Well, lead me as you did before."

We snaked our way onward, though only once needed we go to earth. We were getting back to the upper town, which the rebels must have under some control. Trudging down the sky, the sun had begun to glare in my eyes. I saw vultures wheeling aloft.

The garrison besat a steading much like the one in Sicamino, though smaller. From the city wall, where a tower reared, jutted three of brick. The compound within held barracks, officers' quarters, arsenal, whatever else the peacekeeping force needed—and, now, fugitives crammed together. A broad open space ringed the defenses. From its far side I saw the three gates shut. Watchmen stood tautly on the parapet. Below them squatted warriors posted by Moussavi. Those were mostly Edomites, in threadbare djellabas and burnooses;

but yellow was around every waist and a firearm at every shoulder. Townsfolk who felt themselves safe and, I supposed, were glad the Puritans had come, milled and babbled before them.

"Wait here," I told Herod, and strode forward. It would not help me to have such a ragamuffin in tow. I looked neither right nor left, walking as if I were the conqueror. Men scowled, snarled, spat, but habit was strong in them. They gave way, a roiling bow wave that closed in a wake of curses and shaken fists. My sweat reeked. I would not let myself think how easily a knife could slide between my ribs.

"Hold!" cried a man who seemed in charge on the east side. "None may pass."

I halted and gave him my haughtiest stare. "May none come out?" I asked. "This will surely be of interest to him who gave you your orders."

Uneasy, he tugged his greasy beard. "We are here . . . to keep the law of the Prophet," he growled. "What do you want, Westman?"

"To convey a message of the greatest moment, desert runner," I snapped. "If I may not pass through, you shall let someone out to hear me. Else I will report this, and after that your camel will know you no more."

Before he could think, I filled my lungs and shouted in Ispanyan. The sentries above leaned over the battlements. For a moment I was unsure whether I would live. A real soldier would at the least have had me seized. But these were simple peasants and nomads, unused to chains of command. I won my bet. The headman let me finish, he waved back followers who sidled near with rifles cocked, he even bade them hold off the crowd that pressed close and threatened me.

Nonetheless, that became a long wait in the heat and the reaching shadows.

It wasn't really. They were able men inside, who knew they must act at once. Otherwise the folk might get out of hand, or a true officer of the Puritans happen by. The doors creaked ajar. A lean, dark-haired man in blue tunic, white breeks, and headcloth marched forth. He looked about and went to me.

"Speak so I can understand you," said the Edomite.

"This is not for the likes of you to hear," I told him. He flushed. I looked into the hatchet face of the Ispanyan and said in his tongue: "Quickly, do you know if the Saxonian Otto Gneisberg and his household are with you?"

"They are," he answered. "What do you want? We stand on a volcano."

"I have a word of hope, mestro." I gave him my name.

"Reccaredo de Liria," he gave back, "hiltman in His Gothic Over-lordship's Valencian Grenadiers."

I told him what von Heidenheim had told me. He gnawed his lip. "The Saxonians, the pagan Saxonians—"

"They are Europeans too," I said.

His pride snatched at that. "By the Bull, good enough in these miserable times! What would you have me do?"

"Tell Gneisberg. We must move fast. If we have everything ready before Zigad Moussavi hears of it, we can hope he will overlook the matter, set it aside, because he will not know what it means and he has his hands full already. But if first he gets any hint— They have an art in Persia of flaying a man alive and showing him his stuffed skin before he may die, do they not?"

"They will buy mine dearly," de Liria snorted. "Very well, I will go straight to Gneisberg." Luck had been with me. Many a young officer would first have sought the garrison commander. We had no time for that. I should think the *chefe del hirdo* would later be happy to learn that a few refugees had gone out from under his ward.

If they did.

De Liria flipped me a Roman salute and went back. The gate shut. "He is to bring forth certain men who have need to return to their home," I told the Edomite overling.

He glowered. "What plot is this?"

"None. How can an unarmed spoonful menace the triumph of the New Revelation? If anything, they become hostages to it. This is a simple business of perishable goods that have just arrived and require care. You have already shown that you may let people leave the com-pound."

"Ey-yah, what you Westmen will do for money!" he fleered.

I shrugged. "The lord Zigad Moussavi is a man of wisdom. He will wish to keep their goodwill, when it costs him nothing, and take taxes from them afterward."

I waited. These warriors were ignorant of much, and their heads were afire with their faith, but they were not stupid. Give them time, only a short time, and they would begin to wonder. Then I would be done. I tried to dwell on things far away, ice skating in New Den-mark, a girl in London, a moonlit night off the Azores; and I waited.

After some part of endlessness—but the sun was still above the tower—the gate opened anew. A man came out beside de Liria. Though he was short and bald, he walked briskly. Behind them were another half-score, both European and inborn, who must belong to the trader's staff. My heart knocked.

They stopped before me. "I am Otto Gneisberg," said the short man in Saxonian.

"Mithras, could I go with you!" de Liria breathed.

"Hold fast where you are," Gneisberg said. "That will be your service."

Our band thrust into the crowd. It yielded surlily. "You're doing well to heed me, herr," I said.

Gneisberg's smile was wry. "Hiltman de Liria said something about preserving civilization. But we have left wives and children with him. If the compound comes under attack, it cannot hold out more than a few days."

"Do you think your post can do as well?"

"No. A while, though, yes, a while. We have firearms and provisions in the cellar, a cistern on the roof. I understand why it is critical that we be in possession of the place."

Herod tagged after us. We walked unhindered to the Street of the Magi.

Beneath the sign of the Handelsbund, Gneisberg unclipped a key from his belt. "I will now send a pigeon with this news, and the Saxonians offshore will make ready," he said. "If we are then bestormed, and I think we shall soon be, I will send the next message, and a relief expedition is justified under the Law of Kings, that the Russians honor too. It will put down these rebels, which should dampen insurrection elsewhere in the province."

For a time, I thought.

"You will join us?" he asked. "You have done well. If I live, I will see to it that you get a commendation."

I forebore to say I would rather have a cash reward. "No, I must be off."

He raised his brows. "What? This is not the most secure spot in the world, I grant you, but surely your chances are better here than anywhere else outside the compound, and your presence will improve them. Or are you leaving Mirzabad?"

"Not yet. I have unfinished work."

"The gods be with you," he sighed. "Or, in my philosophy, may you gain by the principles of righteousness."

"Mithras be with us both," I said, and left. Herod trotted at my side.

"Do we go back to the House of Sorrows?" he asked.

"We do," I answered, "and there we stay till the danger is past."

"Oh, good, good!" he warbled. "It is misnamed. I never knew how wonderful it is inside."

The real wonders you do not know about, I thought. I hardly do, myself. Maybe we can learn something together.

This time he took me by the straightest way, as nearly as I could tell from the westering sun. Alike his ears and whatever inward senses his life had whetted must be saying that rage had rolled elsewhere. Or had calm already begun to fall throughout the city? Hope flickered in my breast.

It died when he stopped, lifted a bird-frail hand, strained forward. After a moment he stared back at me. "Lord, I fear bad men are at the House," he whispered.

Otherwise I heard only the seething in my ears. Drawing breath, I told him, "Bring me there unbeknownst."

"It is deadly," he said. "What oath have you given them?"

None. If anything, my duty was to keep myself hale for whatever von Heidenheim wanted next. Yet something in me without a name refused me the right to sheer off. At least I must see if there was any way of helping. "I am a man," was all I could think of to say.

Herod squared his shoulders. "And I am the man of my man," he said, red in the cheeks, so gravely that I almost laughed.

As fast as would keep stillness, we ran. Soon the noise reached me, yelp, clatter, thud. By houses we had passed earlier, I knew it came indeed from the Basileum. At the end, Herod took me into an alley and pointed upward. The building alongside was low; the grate over a window gave a hold for fingers and toes. I boosted him to the flat roof and scrambled after. On our bellies we glided to the other side and peered across the dolphin paving.

I counted nine men on the stairs. They seemed inborn here. The rags and the dirt could have been anybody's, but they yelled in Aramaic—street scourers, day laborers, stunted and snag-toothed. However, their thews were tough; they carried knives, clubs, an ax; once they got inside, Ailill and the African could slay two or three at most before going under. Then Jahan, his scholars, his daughter were booty. The gang had gotten a balk of timber. Again and again they rammed it against the door. Bronze groaned. Hinges began to give way.

"Too many, lord," Herod breathed in my ear.

"We shall see," I murmured back. "Surprise and a good blade have much to do with fate. Wait here, small one. If I fall, remember me."

I crouched and sprang. As I fell, it flashed through me that I had not given him his pay.

I landed loose-kneed on stone, drew sword while I sped forward, wrapped end of cloak about left forearm. The robbers were lost in their work, sweating, slavering, a-howl with glee. I bounded up the stairs.

The heart is a fool's target, hard to find and fenced by the bones. My point went into the nearest scrawny back. I twisted to gash the liver, pulled my steel loose, and got the next man in the neck. Blood geysered, dazzling red. He rolled down the steps to lie crumpled.

"Out, out!" I roared in Danish. "Give me a hand, you scuts!"

The seven who were left let go the beam and whirled around. I caught a thrust on my basket hilt and slashed downward. There is a big artery in the thigh. The six yammered around me. I stopped a stab with the padding on my left arm.

The door swung wide. Ailill's staff whirred and crashed. In skilled hands, that is a fearsome weapon. I heard him sing as he fought, a song of wild and keening mirth. The African had found a mace among relics of old, proud days. I saw a skull splinter beneath it.

The axman came at me. He knew his trade. I withdrew before the battering weight. It could tear the sword out of my grip. Down the stairs we went. My friends had enough else to do.

A little form darted from nowhere. Catlike, Herod swarmed up the axman's back and clawed at his eyes. He shrilled and spat. The axman reached around, pulled him off, dashed him to the ground. Meanwhile I had the opening I needed. I stepped in and freed my foe's guts.

Two of the gang were still on their feet. They fled. "After them!" I bawled. "Let them not get away!"

I overtook the closest and hewed. Ailill and the African crushed the other.

They came panting to me. "Make sure of them all," I said. Ailill's knife slid forth. Soon the disabled stopped screaming.

I went back to Herod. The axman had fallen across him. I dragged the carcass off and knelt to see. In the pinched face, mouth gaped and eyes stared blind. The limbs were dry sticks. I lifted his head. He had landed on the back of it, hard. I lowered it again and rose.

Ailill and the African sought me anew. "Let's haul these corpses away," I ordered. My look went to the portico. Jahan and his folk clustered on it. They seemed well-nigh as drained of blood. "You," I called to the scholars. "Fetch mops and water. Scrub these stones as best you can. Take that timber inside. Be quick."

Nobody stirred. "Ahriman in hell," I snarled, "we've need to hide that anybody ever was here. Else we'll soon have others, more than we can handle."

Boran trod forward. "We heed you," she said softly. To the scholars: "Come."

It is folklore that a man is heavier dead than alive, but he does feel thus, and we three were wearied, shaken. Remembering how Herod had led me, I found an alley off a side street about a quarter mile away, narrow and already choked with rubbish. We ferried ours to it. Surely eyes watched from behind walls, but those that saw this end of our trip did not see the other. Nobody showed himself, nor questioned us from within. I had counted on that. The main wish of most folk is to be left in peace. They seldom get it. Witnesses would do and say naught. If these wretches we'd rid ourselves of had kin or friends, it was unlikely that those knew what had happened or where. Only a second mischance would bring the Basileum again under attack.

By the time we were done, the sun was behind westward walls. Streets brimmed with shadow. Jahan met us on the stairs. In the dimming light he looked ill, and his voice came faint. "We have washed the stones, as you see. I pray you, go not straightway inside. Go to the back door and down into the storage room. We have brought soap, water, fresh garb. Cleanse yourselves."

"Of course, venerable one," said the African.

Jahan's words stumbled onward. "We are grateful to you beyond measure. Never think us otherwise. But it is not fitting to track blood over these floors."

"Sure and it's glad I'll be to get the stickiness off," laughed Ailill when I had explained.

Jahan shivered. "How can he be merry after . . . what was done?"

"It is nothing uncommon, you know," I answered.

Bewilderment crossed his face. "But this has been horrible."

"Few lives are like yours. Today you have glimpsed the world as it is."

For another heartbeat I stood still, while the dusk rose around us beneath a sky turning green in the west, violet-blue in the east. "Before I myself wash, I have one more thing to do," I said. "Where is the nearest Fire Temple?"

Jahan gave me directions. It wasn't far. The scholars had laid Herod Gamal-al-Mazda on the portico, folded his hands and closed his eyes. When I picked his light form up, it felt colder than it really was. Nonetheless I held it close to my breast as I walked.

The Zarathushtran priest was aghast at sight of me and my burden, but stood his ground like a man. I smiled through the dusk. "Be at ease," I said. "This is a believer whom I bring home to you. Give him the rites and take him to your Tower of Silence."

To make sure of that, I handed over the three gold royals I had promised. Then I returned to the Basileum.

Thereafter we abided in our lair. Every day we heard a few shots. Thrice, somebody close by screamed. But none beat on our doors, and we dwelt day and night, day and night, as if outside of creation.

"Why do they call this the House of Sorrows?" I asked Boran.

She winced and frowned. "The commoners are superstitious," she said, and went on to speak of something else.

Later I talked with the African. Rustum Tata, his name was. Like me, he had come from afar to Mirzabad, knowing little, soon enthralled by the witchcraft that lay in the books. In some ways he was a better guide to them than Boran. She knew so much, her mind was so swift, that I was apt to find myself groping for what she meant. Thus she and I became likeliest to talk of homely things when we were together, our own lives and dreams.

"Why do they call this the House of Sorrows?" I asked Rustum.

He shrugged. "It holds whatever chronicles and relics of the city are left after more than three thousand years," he said. "That gives time for much weeping."

Me, I took happiness out of the vaults. Suddenly around me, speaking, loving, hating, striving, not dead but merely sundered from me in time, were the builders, the dwellers, the conquerors, Persians, Turks, Mongols, Romans, Greeks, Phoenicians, Babylonians, Assyrians, Peleshtim, Egyptians, endlessly manyfold. In their sagas I could lose myself, forget that I was trapped and waiting for whatever doom happened to be mine.

Oh, yes, it was beyond me to read what stood on the crumbling paper, parchment, papyrus, clay. The scholars misliked my even touching them with my awkward fingers. But they would unfold a text for me, and put it into words I kenned, and we would talk about it for hours, down in those dim cool caves. The lesser men are now wan in my mind. I remember bluff Rustum, wise Jahan, Boran the lovely.

What I learned is mostly lost too, flotsam in my head. How shall a wanderer carry with him the dynasties of the Shahs, the Khans, the Caesars, or the Pharaohs? Here a face peers from the wreckage, there a torch glimmers in the distance, a word echoes whose meaning I have forgotten, ghost armies march to music long stilled. It was with a wry understanding of each other that Boran and I said farewell.

One voice is clear. That may seem odd, for belike it mattered the least of all. But it lingers because it was the last that came to me.

Jahan had been my guide through time that day. We were down in

the deepest crypt where the oldest fragments rested. A lantern on a
table cast a light soon eaten by the shadows around. The air was cold,
quiet, with a smell of dust.

Under our gaze was a Babylonian tablet. Beside it lay a sheet of
papyrus that must have been torn off a scroll. The inked letters were
well-nigh too faded to read, but they looked like far kin to Edomite or
Arabian. I pointed and asked idly, "What is that?"

"Eh?" said Jahan. He bent over the case and squinted. "Oh . . .
oh, this. I have not thought about it for years. A fragment of an
ancient lament."

"What does it mourn?"

"That is unclear. For see you, the language is long extinct. A prede-
cessor of mine puzzled out a partial translation, by comparing related
words in languages that he could read. Um-m." Jahan stroked his
beard. His tone quickened. "I studied it once. Let me try whether I
can still decipher it."

He opened the case and carefully, carefully took the papyrus out.
For a while he held it close to the lantern. His lips moved. Then,
straightening, he said:

"It is by a man of an obscure people who held this city and hinterland for a while in the remote past. Sennacherib of Assyria captured
it and dispersed them through his empire. The many races within it
blotted theirs up. A similar fate had already befallen a sister kingdom
of theirs. This poet was, I believe, an aged survivor, looking backward
and bewailing what had come to pass."

He peered again at the sheet and word by slow word rendered into
Persian, not the everyday tongue but the stately speech of old:

*"Jerusalem hath grievously sinned; therefore she is removed. . . . for she
hath seen that the heathen entered into her sanctuary. . . . For these things I
weep; mine eye, mine eye runneth down with water, because the comforter that
should relieve my soul is far from me: my children are desolate, because the
enemy prevailed."*

He glanced at me. "I skip over lines that are illegible or that I
cannot well make out," he explained.

"Was Jerusalem the name they gave this city?" I asked.

He nodded. "They appear to have been a peculiar people, always
questioning things, even their gods, always driven toward a perfection they should have known is impossible. Certainly they had some
ideas unique to them." He read onward:

"Thou, O Lord, remainest for ever; thy throne from generation to genera-
tion. Wherefore dost thou forsake us for ever, and forsake us so long time?
Turn thou us unto thee, O Lord, and we shall be turned; renew our days as of
old.

"But thou hast utterly rejected us—"

Boran's shout flew down the stairs. Jahan put the dead man's cry
back in the case before he followed me. By then I was on the ground
floor. Through the walls I heard the rumble and crash of the Saxonian cannon.

REMAKING HISTORY

Kim Stanley Robinson

The point is *not* to make an exact replica of the Teheran embassy compound." Exasperated, Ivan Venutshenko grabbed his hair in one hand and pulled up, which gave him a faintly Oriental look. "It's the *spirit* of the place that we want to invoke here."

"This has the spirit of our storage warehouse, if you ask me."

"This *is* our storage warehouse, John. We make all our movies here."

"But I thought you said we were going to correct all the lies of the first movie," John Rand said to their director. "I thought you said *Escape From Teheran* was a dumb TV docu-drama, only worth remembering because of De Niro's performance as Colonel Jackson. We're going to get the true story on film at last, you said."

Ivan sighed. "That's right, John. Admirable memory. But what you must understand is that when making a film, *true* doesn't mean an absolute fidelity to the real."

"I'll bet that's just what the director of the docu-drama said."

Ivan hissed, which he did often while directing their films, to show that he was letting off steam, and avoiding an explosion. "Don't be obstructionist, John. We're not doing anything like that hackwork, and you know it. Lunar gravity alone makes it impossible for us to make a completely realist film. We are working in a world of dream, in a surrealist intensification of what really happened. Besides, we're doing these movies for our own entertainment up here! Remake bad historical films! Have a good time!"

"Sure, Ivan. Sure. Except the ones *you've* directed have been getting some great reviews downside. They're saying you're the new Eisenstein and these little remakes are the best thing to hit the screen since

Kane. So now the pressure is on and it's not just a game anymore, right?"

"Wrong!" Ivan karate-chopped the air. "I refuse to believe that. When we stop having fun doing this"—nearly shouting—"I quit!"

"Sure, Sergei."

"Don't call me that!"

"Okay, Orson."

"JOHN!"

"But that's *my* name. If I call you that we'll all get confused."

Melina Gourtsianis, their female lead, came to Ivan's rescue. "Come on, John, you'll give him a heart attack, and besides it's late. Let's get on with it."

Ivan calmed down, ran his hands through his hair. He loved doing his maddened director routine, and John loved maddening him. As they disagreed about nearly everything, they made a perfect team. "Fine," Ivan said. "Okay. We've got the set ready, and it may not be an *exact* replica of the compound—" fierce glare at John—"but it's good enough.

"Now, let's go through it one more time. It's night in Teheran. This whole quarter of the city has been gassed with a paralyzing nerve gas, but there's no way of telling when the Revolutionary Guards might come barreling in from somewhere else with gas masks or whatever, and you can't be sure some of them haven't been protected from the gas in sealed rooms. Any moment they might jump out firing. Your helicopters are hovering just overhead, so it's tremendously noisy. There's a blackout in the compound, but searchlights from other parts of the city are beginning to pin the choppers. They've been breaking like cheap toys all the way in, so now there are only five left, and you have no assurances that they will continue to work, especially since twice that number have already broken. You're all wearing gas masks and moving through the rooms of the compound, trying to find and move all fifty-three of the hostages—it's dark and most of the hostages are knocked out like the guards, but some of the rooms were well-sealed, and naturally these hostages are shouting for help. For a while—and this is the effect I want to emphasize more than any other—for a while, things inside are absolutely chaotic. No one can find Colonel Jackson, no one knows how many of the hostages are recovered and how many are still in the embassy, it's dark, it's noisy, there are shots in the distance. I want an effect like the scene at the end of *The Lady From Shanghai*, when they're in the carnival's house of mirrors shooting at each other. Multiplied by ten. Total chaos."

"Now hold on just a second here," John said, exaggerating his Texas accent, which came and went according to his convenience. "I like the chaos bit, and the allusion to Welles, but let's get back to this issue of the facts. Colonel Jackson was the hero of this whole thing! He was the one that decided to go on with all them helicopters busting out in the desert, and he was the one that found Annette Bellows in the embassy to lead them around, and all in all he was on top of every minute of it. That's why they gave him all them medals!"

Ivan glared. "What part are you playing, John?"

"Why, Colonel Jackson." John drew himself up. "Natch."

"However." Ivan tapped the side of his head, to indicate thought. "You don't just want to do a bad imitation of the De Niro performance, do you? You want to do a new interpretation, don't you? Besides, it seems to me a foolish idea to try an imitation of De Niro."

"I like the idea, myself," John said. "Show him how."

Ivan waved him away. "You got all you know about this affair from that stupid TV movie, just like everyone else. I, however, have been reading the accounts of the hostages and the Marines on those helicopters, and the truth is that Colonel Jackson's best moment was out there in the desert, when he decided to go on with the mission even though only five helicopters were still functioning. That was his peak of glory, his moment of heroism. And you did a perfectly adequate job of conveying that when we filmed the scene. We could see every little gear in there, grinding away." He tapped his skull.

"De Niro would have been proud," Melina said.

John pursed his lips and nodded. "We need great men like that. Without them history would be dead. It'd be nothing but a bunch of broken-down helicopters out in a desert somewhere."

"A trenchant image of history," Ivan said. "Too bad Shelley got to it first. Meanwhile, the truth is that after making the decision to go on with the raid, Colonel Jackson appeared, in the words of his subordinates, somewhat stunned. When they landed on the embassy roof he led the first unit in, and when they got lost inside, the whole force was effectively without leadership for most of the crucial first half-hour. All the accounts of this period describe it as the utmost chaos, saved only when Sergeant Payton—*not* Colonel Jackson; the TV movie lied about that—when Payton found Ms. Bellows, and she led them to all the hostage rooms they hadn't found."

"All right, all right." John frowned. "So I'm supposed to be kind of spaced out in this scene."

"Don't go for too deep an analysis, John, you might strain something. But essentially you have it. Having committed the force to the raid, even though you're vastly undermanned because of the damned helicopters breaking down, you're a bit frozen by the risk of it. Got that?"

"Yeah. But I don't believe it. Jackson was a hero."

"Fine, a hero, lots of medals. Roomfuls of medals. If he pinned them on he'd look like the bride after the dollar dance. He'd collapse under their weight. But now let's try showing what really happened."

"All right." John drew himself up. "I'm ready."

The shooting of the scene was the part they all enjoyed the most; this was the heart of the activity, the reason they kept making movies to occupy their free hours at Luna Three. Ivan and John and Melina and Pierre-Paul, the theoreticians who traded directing chores from project to project, always blocked the scenes very loosely, allowing a lot of room for improvisation. Thus scenes like this one, which were supposed to be chaotic, were played out with a manic gusto. They were good at chaos.

And so for nearly a half-hour they rushed about the interior of their Teheran embassy compound—the base storage warehouse, with its immense rows of boxes arranged behind white panels of plywood to resemble the compound's buildings and their interiors. Their shouts were nearly drowned by the clatter of recorded helicopters, while intermittent lights flashed in the darkness. Cut-outs representing the helicopters were pasted to the clear dome overhead, silhouetted against the unearthly brilliance of the stars—these last had become a trademark of Luna Three Productions, as their frequent night scenes always had these unbelievably bright stars overhead, part of the films' dreamlike effect.

The actors playing Marines bounded about the compound in their gas masks, looking like aliens descended to ravage a planet; the actors playing hostages and Revolutionary Guards lay scattered on the floor, except for a few in protected rooms, who fought or cried for help. John and Pierre-Paul and the rest hunted the compound for Melina, playing Annette Bellows. For a while it looked as if John would get to her first, thus repeating the falsehood of the De Niro film. But eventually Pierre-Paul, playing Sergeant Payton, located her room, and he and his small unit rushed about after the clear-headed Bellows, who, as she wrote later, had spent most of her months in captivity planning what she should do if this moment ever came. They located the remaining comatose hostages and lugged them quickly to the plywood helicopter on the compound roof. The sound of shots punctuated the helicopters' roar. They leaped through the helicopter's door, shafts of white light stabbed the air like Islamic swords.

That was it; the flight away would be filmed in their little helicopter interior. Ivan turned off the helicopter noise, shouted "Cut!" into a megaphone. Then he shut down all the strategically placed minicams, which had been recording every minute of it.

"What bothers me about your movies, Ivan," John said, "is that you always take away the hero. Always!"

They were standing in the shallow end of the base pool, cooling off while they watched the day's rushes on a screen filling one wall of the natatorium. Many of the screens showed much the same result: darkness, flickering light, alien shapes moving in the elongated dancelike way that audiences on Earth found so surreal, so mesmerizing. There was little indication of the pulsing rhythms and wrenching suspense that Ivan's editing would create from this material. But the actors were happy, seeing arresting images of desperation, of risk, of heroism in the face of a numbingly loud confusion.

Ivan was not as pleased. "Shit!" he said. "We're going to have to do it again."

"Looks okay to me," John remarked. "Son of Film Noir Returns From the Grave. But really, Ivan, you've got to do something about this prejudice against heroes. I saw *Escape From Teheran* when I was a kid, and it was an inspiration to me. It was one of the big reasons I got into engineering."

Pierre-Paul objected. "John, just how did seeing a commando film get you interested in engineering?"

"Well," John replied, frowning, "I thought I'd design a better helicopter, I guess." He ignored his friends' laughter. "I was pretty shocked at how unreliable they were. But the way old De Niro continued on to Teheran! The way he extricated all the hostages and got them back safely, even with the choppers dropping like flies. It was great! We need heroes, and history tells the story of the few people who had what it takes to be one. But you're always downplaying them."

"The Great Man Theory of history," Pierre-Paul said scornfully.

"Sure!" John admitted. "Great Woman too, of course," nodding quickly at the frowning Melina. "It's the great leaders who make the difference. They're special people, and there aren't many of them. But if you believe Ivan's films, there aren't any at all."

With a snort of disgust, Ivan took his attention from the rushes. "Hell, we are going to have to do that scene again. As for my theory of history, John, you both have it and you don't. As far as I understand you." He cocked his head and looked at his friend attentively. On the set they both played their parts to the teeth: Ivan the tormented, temperamental director, gnashing his teeth and ordering people about; John the stubborn, temperamental star, questioning everything and insisting on his preeminence. Mostly this was role-playing, part of the game, part of what made their hobby entertaining to them. Off the set the roles largely disappeared, except to make a point, or have some fun. Ivan was the base's head of computer operations, while John was an engineer involved in the Mars voyage; they were good friends, and their arguments had done much to shape Ivan's ideas for his revisionist historical films, which were certainly the ones from their little troupe making the biggest splash downside —though John claimed this was because of the suspenseful plots and the weird low-gee imagery, not because of what they were saying about history. "*Do* I understand you?" Ivan asked curiously.

"Well," John said, "take the one you did last time, about the woman who saved John Lennon's life. Now that was a perfect example of heroic action, as the 1982 docu-drama made clear. There she was, standing right next to a man who had pulled out a damn big gun, and quicker than he could pull the trigger she put a foot in his crotch and a fist in his ear. But in your remake, all we concentrated on was how she had just started the karate class that taught her the moves, and how her husband encouraged her to take the class, and how that cabbie stopped for her even though she was going the other direction, and how that other cabbie told her that Lennon had just walked into his apartment lobby, and all that. You made it seem like it was just a coincidence!"

Ivan took a mouthful of pool water and spurted it at the spangled dome, looking like a fountain statue. "It took a lot of coincidences to get Margaret Arvis into the Dakota lobby at the right time," he told John. "But some of them weren't coincidences—they were little acts of generosity or kindness or consideration, that put her where she could do what she did. I didn't take the heroism away. I just spread it around to all the places it belonged."

John grimaced, drew himself up into his star persona. "I suppose this is some damn Commie notion of mass social movements, sweeping history along in a consensus direction."

"No, no," Ivan said. "I always concentrate on individuals. What I'm saying is that all our individual actions add up to history, to the big visible acts of our so-called 'leaders.' You know what I mean; you hear people saying all the time that things are better now because

John Lennon was such a moral force, traveling everywhere, Nobel Peace Prize, secular pope, the conscience of the world or whatnot."

"Well, he *was* the conscience of the world!"

"Sure, sure, he wrote great songs. And he got a lot of antagonists to talk. But without Margaret Arvis he would have been killed at age forty. And without Margaret Arvis's husband, and her karate instructor, and a couple cabbies in New York, and so on, she wouldn't have been there to save his life. So we all become part of it, see? The people who say it was all because of Lennon, or Carter, or Gorbachev—they're putting on a few people what we *all* did."

John shook his head, scattering water everywhere. "Very sophisticated, I'm sure! But in fact it was precisely Lennon and Carter and Gorbachev who made huge differences, all by themselves. Carter started the big swing toward human rights. Palestine, the new Latin America, the American Indian nations—none of those would have existed without him."

"In fact," Melina added, glancing mischievously at Pierre-Paul, "if I understand the Margaret Arvis movie correctly, if she hadn't been going to see Carter thank his New York campaign workers for the 1980 victory, she wouldn't have been in the neighborhood of the Dakota, and so she wouldn't have had the chance to save Lennon's life."

John rose up like a whale breaching. "So it's Carter we have to thank for that, too! As for Gorbachev, well, I don't have to tell you what all he did. That was a hundred-eighty degree turnaround for you Russkies, and no one can say it would have happened without him."

"Well—he was an important leader, I agree."

"Sure was! And Carter was just as crucial. Their years were the turning point, when the world started to crawl out from under the shadow of World War Two. And that was their doing. There just aren't many people who could've done it. Most of us don't have it in us."

Ivan shook his head. "Carter wouldn't have been able to do what he did unless Colonel Ernest Jackson had saved the rescue mission to Teheran, by deciding to go on."

"So Jackson is a hero too!"

"But then Jackson wouldn't have been a hero if the officer back in the Pentagon hadn't decided at the last minute to send sixteen helicopters instead of eight."

"And," Melina pointed out quickly, "if Annette Bellows hadn't spent most of a year daydreaming about what she would do in a rescue attempt, so that she knew blindfolded where every other hostage was being kept. They would have left about half the hostages behind without her, and Carter wouldn't have looked so good."

"Plus they needed Sergeant Payton to find Bellows," Ivan added.

"Well shit!" John yelled defensively, which was his retort in any tight spot. He changed tack. "I ain't so sure that Carter's reelection hinged on those hostages anyway. He was running against a flake, I can't remember the guy's name, but he was some kind of idiot."

"So?" Melina said. "Since when has that made any difference?"

With a roar John dove at her, making a big splash. She was much faster than he was, however, and she evaded him easily as he chased her around the pool; it looked like a whale chasing a dolphin. He was reduced to splashing at her from a distance, and the debate quickly degenerated into a big splash fight, as it often did.

"Oh well," John declared, giving up the attack and floating in the shallow end. "I love watching Melina swim the butterfly. In this gravity it becomes a godlike act. Those muscular arms, that sinuous dolphin motion . . ."

Pierre-Paul snorted. "You just like the way the butterfly puts her bottom above water so often."

"No way! Women are just more hydrodynamic than men, don't you think?"

"Not the way you like them."

"Godlike. Gods and goddesses."

"You look a bit godlike yourself," Melina told him. "Bacchus, for instance."

"Hey." John waved her off, jabbed a finger at the screens. "I note that all this mucho sophisticated European theorizing has been sunk. Took a bit of Texas logic, is all."

"Only Texas logic could do it," Pierre-Paul said.

"Right. You admit my point. In the end it's the great leaders who have to act, the rare ones, no matter if we ordinary folks help them into power."

"When you revise your proposition like that," Ivan said, "you turn it into mine. Leaders are important, but they are leaders because we made them leaders. They are a collective phenomenon. They are expressions of us."

"Now wait just a minute! You're going over the line again! You're talking like heroic leaders are a dime a dozen, but if that were true it wouldn't matter if Carter had lost in 1980, or if Lennon had been killed by that guy. But look at history, man! Look what happened when we did lose great leaders! Lincoln was shot; did they come up with another leader comparable to him? No way! Same with Gandhi, and the Kennedys, and King, and Sadat, and Olof Palme. When those folks were killed their countries suffered the lack of them, because they were special."

"They *were* special," Ivan agreed, "and obviously it was a bad thing they were killed. And no doubt there was a short-term change for the worse. But they're not irreplaceable, because they're human beings just like us. None of them, except maybe Lincoln or Gandhi, was any kind of genius or saint. It's only afterward we think of them that way, because we want heroes so much. But we're the heroes. All of us put them in place. And there are a lot of capable, brilliant people out there to replace the loss of them, so that in the long run we recover."

"The *real* long run," John said darkly. "A hundred years or more, for the South without Lincoln. They just aren't that common. The long run proves it."

"Speaking of the long run," Pierre-Paul said, "is anyone getting hungry?"

They all were. The rushes were over, and Ivan had dismissed them as unusable. They climbed out of the pool and walked toward the changing room, discussing restaurants. There were a considerable number of them in the station, and new ones were opening every week. "I just tried the new Hungarian restaurant," Melina said. "The food was good, but we had trouble, when the meal was over, finding someone to give us the check!"

"I thought you said it was a Hungarian restaurant," John said.

They threw him back in the pool.

The second time they ran through the rescue scene in the compound, Ivan had repositioned most of the minicams, and many of the lights; his instructions to the actors remained the same. But once inside the hallways of the set, John Rand couldn't help hurrying in the general direction of Annette Bellows's room.

All right, he thought. Maybe Colonel Jackson had been a bit hasty to rush into the compound in search of hostages, leaving the group without a commander. But his heart had been in the right place, and the truth was, he had found a lot of the hostages without any help from Bellows at all. It was easy; they were scattered in ones and twos on the floor of almost every room he and his commandos entered, and stretched out along with the guards in the rooms and in the halls, paralyzed by the nerve gas. Damn good idea, that nerve gas. Guards and hostages, tough parts to play, no doubt, as they were getting kicked pretty frequently by commandos running by. He hustled his crew into room after room, then sent them off with hostages draped

over their shoulders, pretending to stagger down the halls, banging
into walls—*really* tough part to play, hostage—and clutching at gas
masks and such; great images for the minicams, no doubt about it.

When all his commandos had been sent back, he ran around a corner in what he believed to be the direction of Annette Bellows's
room. Over the racket of the helicopters, and the occasional round of
automatic fire, he thought he could make out Melina's voice, shouting
hoarsely. So Pierre-Paul hadn't gotten to her yet. Good. Now he
could find her and be the one to follow her around rescuing the more
obscurely housed hostages, just as De Niro had in the docu-drama. It
would give Ivan fits, but they could argue it out afterward. No way of
telling what had really happened in that compound twenty years
before, after all; and it made a better *story* his way.

Their set was only one story tall, which was one of the things that
John had objected to; the compound in Teheran had been four stories
high, and getting up stairs had been part of the hassle. But Ivan was
going to play with the images and shoot a few stair scenes later on, to
achieve the effect of multiple floors. Fine, it meant he had only to
struggle around a couple of narrow corners, jumping comatose Revolutionary Guards, looking fierce for the minicams wherever they
were. It was really loud this time around; *really* loud.

Then one of the walls fell over on him, the plywood pinning him to
the ground, the boxes behind it tumbling down and filling the hallway. "Hey!" he cried out, shocked. This wasn't the way it had happened. What was going on? The noise of the helicopters cut off
abruptly, replaced by a series of crashes, a whooshing sound. That
sound put a fine electric thrill down his spine; he had heard it before,
in training routines. Air leaving the chamber. The dome must have
been breached.

He heaved up against the plywood. Stuck. Flattening himself as
much as possible he slithered forward, under the plywood and out
into a small space among fallen boxes. Hard to tell where the hallway
had been, and it was pitch-dark. There wouldn't be too much time
left. He thought of his little gas mask, then cursed; it wasn't connected to a real oxygen supply. That's what comes from using fake
props! he thought angrily. A gas mask with nothing attached to it.
Open to the air, which was departing rapidly. Not much time.

He found room among the boxes to stand, and he was about to run
over them to the door leading out of the warehouse—assuming the
whole station hadn't been breached—when he remembered Melina.
Stuck in her embassy room down the hall, wouldn't she still be there?
Hell. He groped along in the dark, hearing shouts in the distance. He

saw lights, too. Good. He was holding his breath, for what felt like minutes at a time, though it was probably less than thirty seconds. Every time he sucked in a new breath he expected it to be the freezing vacuum, but the supply of rushing, cold—very cold—air continued to fill him. Emergency supply pouring out into the breach, actually a technique he had helped develop himself. Seemed to be working, at least for the moment.

He heard a muffled cry to one side, began to pull at the boxes before him. Squeak in the gloom, ah-ha, there she was. Not fully conscious. Legs wet, probably blood, uh-oh. He pulled hard at boxes, lifted her up. Adrenaline and lunar gravity made him feel like Superman with that part of things, but there didn't seem to be anywhere near as much air as before, and what was left was damned cold. Hurt to breathe. And harder than hell to balance as he hopped over objects with Melina in his arms. Feeling faint, he climbed over a row of boxes and staggered toward a distant light. A sheet of plywood smacked his shin and he cried out, then fell over. "Hey," he said. The air was gone.

When he came to he was lying in a bed in the station hospital. "Great," he muttered. "Whole station wasn't blown up."

His friends laughed, relieved to hear him speak. The whole film crew was in there, it seemed. Ivan, standing next to the bed, said, "It's okay."

"What the hell happened?"

"A small meteor, apparently. Hit out in our sector, in the shuttle landing chambers, ironically. But it wrecked our storage space as well, as you no doubt noticed."

John nodded painfully. "So it finally happened."

"Yes." This was one of the great uncontrollable dangers of the lunar stations; meteors small and large were still crashing down onto the moon's airless surface, by the thousands every year. Odds were poor that any one would hit something as small as the surface parts of their station, but coming down in such numbers. . . . In the long run they were reduced to a safety status somewhat equivalent to that of mountain climbers. Rockfall could always get you.

"Melina?" John said, jerking up in his bed.

"Over here," Melina called. She was a few beds down, and had one leg in a cast. "I'm fine, John." She got out of bed to prove it, and came over to kiss his cheek. "Thanks for the rescue!"

John snorted. "What rescue?"

They laughed again at him. Pierre-Paul pointed a forefinger at him.

"There are heroes everywhere, even among the lowest of us. Now you have to admit Ivan's argument."

"The hell I do."

"You're a hero," Ivan said to him, grinning. "Just an ordinary man, so to speak. Not one of the great leaders at all. But by saving Melina, you've changed history."

"Not unless she becomes president," John said, and laughed. "Hey Melina! Go out and run for office! Or save some promising songwriter or something."

Ivan just shook his head. "Why are you so stubborn? It's not so bad if I'm right, John. Think about it. If I am right, then we aren't just sitting around waiting for leaders to guide us." A big grin lit his face. "We become the masters of our fate, we make our own decisions and act on them—we choose our leaders, and instruct them by consensus, so that we can take history any direction we please! Just as you did in the warehouse."

John lay back in his bed and was silent. Around him his friends grinned; one of them was bringing up a big papier-mâché medal, which vaguely resembled the one the Wizard of Oz pins to the Cowardly Lion. "Ah hell," John said.

"When the expedition reaches Mars, they'll have to name something after you," Melina said.

John thought about it for a while. He took the big medal, held it limply. His friends watched him, waiting for him to speak.

"Well, I still say it's bullshit," he told Ivan. "But if there is any truth to what you say, it's just the good old spirit of the Alamo you're talking about, anyway. We've been doing it like that in Texas for years."

They laughed at him.

He rose up from the bed again, swung the medal at them furiously. "I swear it's true! Besides, it's all Robert De Niro's fault, anyway! I was *imitating* the real heroes, don't you see? I was crawling around in there all dazed, and then I saw De Niro's face when he was playing Colonel Jackson in the Teheran embassy, and I said to myself, well hell, what would he have done in this here situation? And that's just what I did."

COUNTING POTSHERDS

Harry Turtledove

The ship clung close to land, like a roach scuttling along a wall. When at last the coast veered north and west, the ship conformed, steering oars squealing in their sockets and henna-dyed wool sail billowing as it filled with wind to push the vessel onto its new course.

When the ship had changed direction, the eunuch Mithredath summoned the captain to the starboard rail with a slight nod. "We draw near, then, Agbaal?" Mithredath asked. His voice, a nameless tone between tenor and contralto, was cool, precise, intelligent.

The Phoenician captain bowed low. The sun sparked off a silver hoop in his left ear. "My master, we do." Agbaal pointed to the headland the ship had just rounded. "That is the cape of Sounion. If the wind holds, we should be in Peiraieus by evening—a day early," he added slyly.

"You will be rewarded if we are," Mithredath promised. Agbaal, satisfied, bowed again and, after glancing at his important passenger for permission, went back to overseeing his crew.

Mithredath would have paid gold darics from his own purse to shorten the time he spent away from the royal court, but no need for that: he was come to this western backwater at the royal command, and so could draw upon the treasury of Khsrish, King of Kings, as he required. Not for the first time, he vowed he would not stint.

The day was brilliantly clear. Mithredath could see a long way. The only other ships visible were a couple of tiny fishing boats and a slow, wallowing vessel probably full of wheat from Egypt. Gulls mewed and squawked overhead.

Mithredath tried to imagine what the narrow, island-flecked sea had looked like during those great days four centuries before, when the first Khsrish, the Conqueror, had led his huge fleet to the triumph that subjected the western Yauna to Persia once for all. He could not; he was not used enough to ships to picture hordes of them all moving together like so many sheep in a herd on their way to the marketplace of Babylon.

That thought, he realized with a wry nod, showed him what he was most familiar with: the baking but oh-so-fertile plain between the Tigris and Euphrates. He also knew Ektabana well, the summer capital of the Kings of Kings, nestled in the shade of Mount Aurvant, though he had never suffered through a winter there. But until this journey, he had never thought to travel on the sea.

Yet to his surprise, Mithredath was finding a strange sort of beauty here. The water over which he sailed was a blue deep enough almost to be wine-purple, the sky another blue so different as to make him wonder how the same word could apply to both. The land rising steeply from sea to sky was by turns rocky and bare and shaggy with green-gray olive trees. The combination was peculiar but somehow harmonious.

True to his promise, Agbaal brought Mithredath to his destination with the sun still in the sky. True to his, the eunuch pressed a pair of goldpieces into the captain's palm. Agbaal bowed almost double; his swarthy face glowed with pride when Mithredath offered him a cheek to kiss, as if the two of them were near in rank.

The docks swarmed with the merchant folk of the Western Sea: Phoenicians like Agbaal in turbans, tunics, and mantles; Italians wearing long white robes draped over one shoulder; and, of course, the native Yauna or, as they called themselves, Hellenes. Their slightly singsong speech was heard even more than Aramaic, the Empire's common tongue understood everywhere from India to the edges of the Gallic lands.

Mithredath's rich brocaded robes, the gold bracelets on his wrists, and the piles of baggage his servants brought onto the docks drew touts—as a honeypot draws flies, he thought sourly. He picked a fellow whose Aramaic had less of a Hellenic hiss to it than most, said, "Be so good as to lead me to the satrap's palace."

"Of course, my master," the man said, but his face fell. He would still get his fee from Mithredath, but had just had his hopes dashed of collecting another from the innkeeper upon whom he would have foisted Mithredath. Too bad, Mithredath thought.

He was used to Babylon's sensible grid of streets; these small western towns had their narrow, stinking lanes running every which way —and sometimes abruptly petering out. He was glad he had hired a guide; no one not familiar with these alleys from birth could have found his way through them.

Though larger than its neighbors, the satrap s residence—palace, Mithredath discovered, was far too grand a word—looked like any other house hereabouts. It presented a plain, whitewashed front to the world. Mithredath sniffed. To his way of thinking, anyone who *was* someone should let the world know it.

He paid the guide—well enough to keep him from sneering, but not extravagantly—and rapped on the door with his pomegranate-headed walking stick. A moment later, a guard opened the little eye-level observation window to peer out at him. "Who comes?" the fellow demanded fiercely.

Mithredath stood where the man could see him clearly, and answered not with the accented Aramaic in which he had been challenged but in pure, clear Persian:

"I am Mithredath, *saris*"—somehow, in his own tongue, *eunuch* became almost a word of pride—"and servant to Khsrish King of Kings, king of lands containing many men, king in this great earth far and wide, son of Marduniya the king, an Achaemenid, a Persian, son of a Persian, of Aryan seed. May Ahuramazda smile upon him and make long his reign. I am come to the satrapy of the Yauna of the western mainland upon a mission given me from his own royal lips. I would discuss this with your master, the satrap Vahauka."

He folded his arms across his chest and waited.

He did not wait long. He heard a thump on the other side of the door, and guessed the guard had dropped his spear in surprise. Mithredath did not smile. Years at the court of the King of Kings had schooled him against revealing his thoughts to a dangerous world. His face was perfectly composed when the guard flung the door wide and shouted, "Enter, servant of the King of Kings!"

The guard bowed low. Mithredath walked past him, returning the courtesy with a bow barely more than a nod. Some people, he thought, deserved to be reminded from time to time of their station.

As he had intended, more folk in the satrap's residence than the door guard heard his announcement. A majordomo came rushing to greet him in the outer hall. He wore the rectangular mantle of a Hellene over Persian trousers. His bow Mithredath returned in full; he would be a power in this miniature court.

The majordomo said, "Excellent *saris*"—he was a cautious one too, Mithredath thought, again not smiling—"his highness Vahauka, great satrap of the Yauna of the western mainland, now dines with the secretary, with the *ganzabara* of the satrapy, and with the general of the garrison. He bids you join them, if your long journey from the court of the King of Kings, may Ahuramazda smile upon him and make long his reign, has not left you too tired."

"The gracious invitation honors me," Mithredath said. "I accept with pleasure." He was glad to get the chance to meet the *ganzabara* so soon; the financial official was the one who would have to meet his tablet of credit from the court.

"Come this way, then." The majordomo led Mithredath out to the central courtyard where the satrap and his officers were dining. Here at last the eunuch felt himself among Persians again, for most of the courtyard was given over to a proper paradise, a formal garden of roses, tulips, and other bright blooms. Their fragrance, mingled with the odors of cookery, made Mithredath's nostrils twitch.

"Lord Vahauka, I present the *saris* Mithredath, servant of the King of Kings," the majordomo said loudly. Mithredath began to prostrate himself, as he would have before Khsrish, but Vahauka, a lean, gray-bearded Persian of about fifty, stopped him with a wave. The satrap turned his head, presenting his cheek to the eunuch.

"My lord is gracious," Mithredath said as he stepped up to Vahauka and let his lips brush the satrap's beard.

"We are both the King of Kings' servants; how can our ranks greatly differ?" Vahauka said. His fellow diners nodded and murmured in agreement. He went on. "Mithredath, I present you to my secretary, Rishi-kidin"—a perfumed, sweating Babylonian in linen undertunic, wool overtunic, and short white cloak—"the *ganzabara* Hermippos"—a clean-shaven Hellene who, like the majordomo, wore trousers—"and the general of this satrapy, Tadanmu"—a Persian with a no-nonsense look in his eyes, dressed rather more plainly than suited his station.

Mithredath kissed more cheeks. After the satrap's example, his aides could hardly show the eunuch less favor. The feel of Hermippos's face was strange; only among his own kind was Mithredath used to smooth skin against his lips. Not being the only beardless person present made him feel extraordinarily masculine. He laughed at himself for the conceit.

"Here, sit by me," Vahauka said when the introductions were done. He shouted for his servants to bring Mithredath food and wine. "Refresh yourself; when you have finished, perhaps you will favor us by telling what business of the King of Kings, may Ahuramazda smile upon him and make long his reign, brings you to this far western land."

"With pleasure, my lord," Mithredath said. Then for some time he was busy with food and drink. The wines were excellent; the satrapy of the Yauna of the western mainland was known for its grapes (one of the few things it was known for) even in Babylon. The food pleased Mithredath less. Vahauka might be used to salted olives, but one was enough to last Mithredath a lifetime.

Servants lit torches as twilight gave way to darkness. Insects fluttered round the lights, whose smoke was sweet with frankincense. Every so often, a nightjar or bat would dive into view, snatch a bug, and vanish again.

The majordomo led in three flutegirls wearing only wisps of filmy cloth. Vahauka sent them away, saying, "Our distinguished guest's news will prove more interesting than their songs and dances, which we have all seen and heard before, and surely he will not miss them in any way."

Mithredath glanced at the satrap from under lowered brows. Was that a sly dig at his condition? If so, Vahauka was a fool, which might account for his governing only this undistinguished satrapy. Eunuchs' memories for slights were notoriously long, and Mithredath soon would be far closer to the ear of the King of Kings again than Vahauka could dream of coming.

For the moment, of course, Mithredath remained the soul of courtesy. "As my lord wishes. Know then that I am come at the command of the King of Kings, may Ahuramazda smile upon him and make long his reign, to learn more of the deeds of his splendid forefather the first Khsrish, called the Conqueror, that those deeds may be celebrated once again and redound to the further glory of the present King of Kings, who proudly bears the same name."

A brief silence followed, as the officials thought over what he had said. Vahauka asked, "This is your sole commission, excellent *saris?*"

"It is, my lord."

"Then we will be pleased to render you such assistance as we may be capable of," the satrap said fulsomely. His aides were quick to echo him. Mithredath heard the relief in their voices. He knew why it was there: No misdeed of theirs had come to the notice of the King of Kings.

"You want to learn how the first Khsrish took Hellas, eh?" Hermippos said. Mithredath almost failed to recognize the King of Kings' name in the man's mouth; flavored by his native speech, it came out sounding like *Xerxes.* The *ganzabara* went on, "The ruins of Athens, I suppose, would be the best place for that."

"Aye!" "Indeed!" "Well said!" Vahauka, Rishi-kidin, and Tadanmu all spoke at once. Mithredath smiled, but only to himself. How eager they were to get him out of their hair! Perhaps they, or some of them, *were* up to something about which Khsrish should know.

Still, Hermippos had a point. As Mithredath had learned in Babylon preparing for this mission, Athens led the western Yauna in their fight against the Conqueror. The eunuch sighed. Having come so far already, he supposed poking through rubble could not make things much worse.

Hermippos said, "If you like, excellent *saris*, I will provide you with a secretary who reads and writes not only Aramaic but also the Hellenic tongue. It is still often used here, and in the ancient days of which you spoke would have been the only written language, I suppose."

"I accept with thanks," Mithredath said sincerely, dipping his head. He'd picked up a few words of the tongue of the Hellenes on his westward journey, but it had never occurred to him that he might also need to learn the strange, angular script the locals used. He sighed again, wishing he were home.

Vahauka might have been peering into his thoughts. "Tell us of the news of the court, Mithredath. Here in this distant land we learn of it but slowly and imperfectly."

Nodding, Mithredath gave such gossip as he thought safe to give: he had no intention of setting out all of Khsrish's business—or his scandals—before these men he did not know. He was, though, so circumspect that he blundered, for after he was through, Tadanmu observed, "You have said nothing, excellent *saris*, of the King of Kings' cousin, the great lord Kurash."

"I pray your pardon, my lord. I did not mention him because he has been seeing to his estates these past few months, and hence is not currently in attendance upon the King of Kings, may Ahuramazda smile upon him and make long his reign. Lord Kurash is well, though, so far as I know, and I have heard he has new sons by two of his younger wives."

"And likely hiked up the midwife's skirts after she came away from each one of them, to celebrate the news," Tadanmu chuckled; Kurash's prowess—and his zeal in exercising it—were notorious.

The general asked more of Kurash. Mithredath declined to be drawn out, and Tadanmu subsided. Mithredath made a mental note all the same. Kurash's ambitions, or rather the forestalling of them, were the main reason the eunuch had come to the satrapy of the Yauna of the western mainland. New glory accruing to Khsrish the Conqueror would also reflect onto his namesake, the present occupant—under Ahuramazda—of the throne of the King of Kings.

Mithredath drained his cup, held it out for more. A servant hurried up to fill it. The eunuch sipped, rolled the wine around in his mouth so he could appreciate it fully, nodded in slow pleasure. Here was one reason, anyhow, to approve of this western venture. He cherished such reasons. He had not found many of them.

"My lord?"

Mithredath looked round to see whom the young Hellene was addressing, then realized with a start that the fellow was talking to him. The ignorance of these provincials! "No lord I," he said. "I am but a *saris* in the service of the King of Kings."

He watched a flush rise under the young man's clear skin. "My apologies, my . . . excellent *saris,*" the Hellene said, correcting himself. "You are called Mithredath, though, are you not?"

"That is my name," the eunuch admitted, adding icily, "You have the advantage of me, I believe."

The fellow's flush grew deeper. "Apologies again. My name is Polydoros; I thought Hermippos would have mentioned me. If it please you, I am to be your guide to the ruins of Athens."

"Ah!" Mithredath studied this Polydoros with fresh interest. But no, his first impression had been accurate: the fellow was well on the brash side of thirty. Wondering if the *ganzabara* was trying to palm some worthless relative off on him, he said cautiously, "I had looked for an older man—"

"To be fluent in Aramaic and the Hellenic tongue both, you mean?" Polydoros said, and Mithredath found himself nodding. The Hellene explained, "It's coming from a banking family that does it, excellent *saris.* Most of the inland towns in this satrapy still cling to the old language for doing business, so naturally I've had to learn to read and write it as well as speak it."

"Ah," Mithredath said again. That made a certain amount of sense. "We'll see how things go, then."

"Very good," Polydoros said. "What are your plans? Will you travel up to the ruins each day, or had you planned actually to stay in Athens?"

"Just how far inland is it?" Mithredath asked.

"A parasang and a half, maybe."

"Close to two hours' walk each way? In the little time I'd have in the ruins, how could I hope to accomplish anything? I'd sooner pitch a tent there, and spend a much shorter while in a bit more discomfort. That will let me return to the east all the sooner."

"As you wish, excellent *saris*. After tomorrow, I shall be at your service."

"Why not go tomorrow?" Mithredath asked, rather grumpily. "I can send my servants out at once to buy tent cloth and other necessities."

"Your pardon, sir, but as I said, I am of a banking family. Tomorrow the monthly silver shipment from the Laurion mines south of here will arrive, and I'll need to be present to help with weighing and assaying the metal. The mines don't produce as they did when the great lode was found not long after Hellas came under Persia, but there will still be close to a talent of silver: forty or fifty pounds of it, certainly."

"Do what you must, of course," Mithredath said, yielding to necessity. "I'll look forward to seeing you morning after next, then." He bowed, indicating that Polydoros could go.

But the Hellene did not depart immediately. Instead he stood with a faraway expression on his face, looking through Mithredath rather than at him. The eunuch was growing annoyed when at last Polydoros said dreamily, "I wonder how the conquest would have gone, had the Athenians stumbled onto that silver before Khsrish's" —he pronounced it *Xerxes'* too—"campaign. Money buys the sinews of war."

A banker indeed, Mithredath thought scornfully. "Money does not buy bravery," he said.

"Perhaps not, excellent *saris*, but even the bravest man, were he naked, would fare badly against an armored warrior with a spear. Had Athens been able to build ships to match the Persian fleet, the Hellenes might not have fallen under the Empire's control."

Mithredath snorted. "All the subject peoples have their reasons why they should have held off Persia. None did."

"Of course you are right, excellent *saris*," Polydoros said politely, wise enough to hide his true feelings, whatever they were. "It was but a fancy of the moment." He bowed. "Till the day after tomorrow." He hurried off.

"I came to the proper decision." Mithredath lifted his soft felt cap from his head, used it to wipe sweat from his face. "I shouldn't care to have to make this journey coming and going each day."

"As you say, excellent *saris*." With broad-brimmed straw hat and thin, short Hellenic mantle, Polydoros was more comfortably dressed than Mithredath, but he was sweating too. Behind them, the eunuch's servants and a donkey bore their burdens in stolid silence. One of the servants led a sheep that kept trying to stop and nibble grass and shrubs.

Something crunched under Mithredath's shoe. He looked down, saw a broken piece of pottery and, close by it, half-buried in weeds, a chunk of brick. "A house stood here once," he said. He heard the surprise in his voice, and felt foolish. But knowing this wilderness had been a city was not the same as stumbling over its remains.

Polydoros was more familiar with the site. He pointed. "You can see a fragment of the old wall there among the olive trees."

Had he noticed it, Mithredath would have taken it for a pile of rocks. Now that he looked closely, though, he saw they had been worked to fit together.

"Most of what used to be here, I suppose, has been carried off over the years," Polydoros said. Mithredath nodded. Stealing already-worked stone would be easier for a peasant than working it himself. Polydoros pointed again, to the top of one of the hillocks ahead. "More of the wall around the akropolis—the citadel, you would say in Aramaic—is left, because it's harder to get the rock down."

"Aye," Mithredath said, pleased to find the Hellene thinking along with him. It was his turn to point. "That is the way up to the—the citadel?" At the last moment, he decided against trying to echo the local word Polydoros had used.

The Hellene dipped his head, a gesture Mithredath had learned to equate with a nod. "Of course, it will have been an easier ramp to climb when it was kept clear of brush," Polydoros said dryly.

"So it will." The eunuch's heart was already beating fast; he had endured more exertion on this western journey than ever before in his life. Still, he had a job to do. "Let us go up. If that is the citadel, the ruins there will be important ones, and may tell me what I need to learn of Athens."

"As you say, excellent *saris*."

On reaching the top of the akropolis, Mithredath felt a bit like a conqueror himself. Not only was the ancient ramp overgrown, it was also gullied. One of the eunuch's servants limped with a twisted ankle; had the donkey stumbled into that hole, it likely would have broken a leg. Mithredath was winded, and even Polydoros, who seemed ready for anything, was breathing hard.

Rank grass and weeds also grew on the flat ground on top of the citadel, between the stones of the wrecked wall, and over the lower parts of the destroyed buildings the Persians had sacked so long ago. One of those buildings, a large one, had been unfinished when Athens fell. Marble column drums thrust up from the undergrowth. Mithredath could still see scorchmarks on them.

In front of those half-columns stood a marble stele whose shape was familiar to the eunuch—there were many like it in Babylon—but which did not belong with the ruins around it. Nor was the inscription carved onto that stele written in the local language, but in Aramaic and in the wedge-shaped characters the Persians had once used and the native Babylonians still sometimes employed.

A thrill ran through Mithredath as he read the Aramaic text: " 'Khsrish, King of Kings, declares: you who may be king hereafter, of lies beware. I, Khsrish, King of Kings, having pulled down this city, center of the rebel Yauna, decree that it shall remain wilderness forevermore. You who may be king hereafter and obey these words, may Ahuramazda be your friend and may your seed be made numerous; may Ahuramazda make your days long; may whatever you do be successful. You who may be king hereafter, if you see this stele and its words and follow them not, may Ahuramazda curse you, and of your seed more may there not be, and may Ahuramazda pull down all you make as I, Khsrish, King of Kings, have pulled down this city, center of the rebel Yauna.' "

"A mighty lord, Khsrish the Conqueror, to have his decree obeyed down across the years," Mithredath said, proud to be of the same Persian race as the long-ago King of Kings, though of his own seed, of course, more there would never be.

"Mighty indeed," Polydoros said tonelessly.

Mithredath looked at him sharply, then relaxed. Polydoros was, after all, a Hellene. Expecting him to be overjoyed before an inscription celebrating the defeat of his forefathers was too much to ask.

The eunuch rummaged in one of the packs on the donkey's back until he found a sheet of papyrus, a reed pen, and a bottle of ink. He copied the Aramaic portion of Khsrish's inscription. He presumed the Persian text said the same thing, but could not read it. Perhaps some magus with antiquarian leanings might still be able to, perhaps not. The present Khsrish would only care about the Aramaic. Of that the eunuch was certain.

He looked at what he had written. He frowned, compared the papyrus to the text carved into the stele. He had copied everything written there. Still, something seemed to be missing.

Perhaps Polydoros could supply it; he was a native of these parts. Mithredath turned to him: "Tell me, please, good Polydoros, do you know the name of the king of Athens whom Khsrish the Conqueror overcame?"

The Hellene frowned. "Excellent *saris,* I do not. The last king of Athens whose name I know is Kodros, and he is a man of legend, from long before the time of Xerxes."

"I might have known this was going too smoothly," Mithredath sighed. Then he brightened. "It was to learn such things, after all, that I came here." He scratched his head; he did not approve of loose ends. "But how is it you know of this—Kodros, you said?—and not of the man who must have been Athens's last king?"

"Excellent *saris,*" Polydoros said hesitantly, "in the legends of my people, Kodros *is* the last king of Athens."

"Ridiculous." Mithredath snorted. "*Someone* must rule, is it not so? This Athens must have been an enemy worthy of Khsrish's hatred, for him to destroy it utterly and afterward curse it. Such an enemy will have had rulers, and able ones, to oppose the King of Kings. How can it have lacked them for all the time since the death of Kodros? Did not one lead it all those years? I cannot believe that."

"Nor I," Polydoros admitted.

"Very strange." Mithredath glanced over to the unhappy sheep his servants had urged—and dragged—up the overgrown ramp. "Here, before Khsrish's victory stele, seems as good a spot as any to offer up the beast." He drew the dagger that hung from his belt, cut a spray of leaves from a nearby bush. He put the leaves in his cap. "They should be myrtle, but any will do in a pinch."

Polydoros watched him lead the sheep over to the marble pillar, set the dagger against its neck. "Just like that?" the Hellene asked. "No altar? No ritual fire? No libation? No flute-players? No grain sprinkled before you sacrifice?"

"The good god Ahuramazda does not need them to hear my prayer."

Polydoros shrugged. "Our rites are different."

Mithredath cut the sheep's throat. As the beast kicked toward death, he beseeched Ahuramazda to help him succeed in his quest for knowledge with which to glorify the King of Kings. He was forbidden to pray for any more personal or private good, but with this sacrifice had no need to do so in any case.

"Does your god require of you any of the flesh?" Polydoros asked as the eunuch began the gory job of butchering the carcass and setting the disjointed pieces on a heap of soft greenery.

"No, it is mine to do with as I will. A magus should pray over it, but as none is here, we shall have to make do."

"Is that garlic growing over there? It will flavor the meat once it's cooked." Polydoros licked his chops.

Mithredath felt saliva flow into his own mouth. He turned to a servant. "You can get a fire going now, Tishtrya."

"What are you doing?" Polydoros asked the next morning.

"Looking through the notes I made before I left Babylon," Mithredath said. "Here, I knew there was something that would tell me who ruled here when the first Khsrish came. An old tablet says he led Dēmos of Athens into captivity. Who is this Dēmos, if Kodros was the last king here?"

" 'Dēmos' isn't a who, I'm afraid, excellent *saris*, but rather a what," Polydoros said. "Whoever wrote your tablet wanted to celebrate the King of Kings, as you do, but did not know the Hellenic tongue well. 'Dēmos of Athens' simply means 'the people of Athens.' "

"Oh." Mithredath sighed. "If you knew the trouble I had finding that—" He shuffled scraps of papyrus, briefly looked happy, then grew cautious again. "I also found something about 'Boulē of Athens.' Someone told me -*ē* was the feminine ending in your language, so I took Boulē to be Dēmos's wife. You're going to tell me that's wrong too, though, aren't you?"

Polydoros dipped his head. "I'm sorry, but I must, excellent *saris*. 'Boulē' means 'council.' "

"Oh." The eunuch's sigh was longer this time. "The people of Athens, the council of Athens—where is the king of Athens?" He glared at Polydoros as if the young banker were responsible for making that elusive monarch disappear. Then he sighed once more. "That's what I came here to find out, I suppose. Where are we most likely to find whatever records or decrees this town kept before it came under the rule of the King of Kings?"

"There are two likely places," Polydoros said after a visible pause for thought that made Mithredath very much approve of him. "One is up here, in the citadel. The other would be down there"—he pointed north and west—"in the agora—the city's marketplace. Anyone who came into the city from the countryside to do business would be able to read them there."

"Sensible," Mithredath said. "We'll cast about here for a while, then, and go down again later. The fewer trips up and down that ramp I take, the happier I shall be." When Polydoros agreed, the eunuch turned to his servants. "Tishtrya, Raga, you will be able to help in this enterprise too. All you need do is look for anything with writing on it, and let me or Polydoros know if you actually find something."

The servants' nods were gloomy; they had looked forward to relaxing while their master worked. Mithredath expected little from them, but did not feel like having them sit idle. He was surprised when, a few minutes later, one of them came trotting through the rubble and undergrowth, waving excitedly to show he had found something.

"What is it, Raga?" the eunuch asked.

"Words, master, carved on an old wall," Raga replied. "Come see!"

"I shall," Mithredath said. He and Polydoros followed the servant back to where his companion was waiting. Tishtrya proudly pointed at the inscription. The eunuch's hopes fell at once: it was too short to be the kind of thing he was seeking. He turned to Polydoros. "What does it say?"

"*Kalos Arkhias,*" the Hellene replied: "'Arkhias is beautiful.' It's praise of a pretty boy, excellent *saris,* nothing more; you could see the like chalked or scratched on half the walls in Peiraieus."

"Nasty buggers," Tishtrya muttered under his breath in Persian. Polydoros's eyes went hard for a moment, but he said nothing. Mithredath upbraided his servant; at the same time he made a mental note that the Hellene understood some Persian.

The search resumed. The citadel of Athens was not a large place; a man could easily walk the length of it in a quarter of an hour. But how many such trips would he have to take across it, Mithredath wondered, to make sure he missed nothing? Assuming, of course, he added to himself a moment later, anything was there to be missed.

Polydoros sat down in the narrow shade of an overthrown chunk of masonry, fanned himself with his straw hat. He might have been thinking with Mithredath's mind, for he said, "This could take forever, you know, excellent *saris.*"

"Yes," was all Mithredath cared to reply to that obvious truth.

"We need to plan what to do, then, rather than simply wandering about up here," the Hellene went on. Mithredath nodded; Polydoros seemed to have a talent for straightforward thinking. After more consideration, Polydoros said, "Let's make a circuit of the wall first. Decrees often go up on the side of a wall so people can see them. Is it not the same in Babylon?"

"It is," Mithredath agreed. He and Polydoros made their way back to the ramp up which they had come.

They walked north and east along the wall. Mithredath's heart beat faster when he saw letters scratched onto a stone, but it was only another graffito extolling a youth's beauty. Then, when they were about halfway along the northern reach of the wall, opposite the ruins of some many-columned building, Polydoros suddenly pointed and exclaimed, "There, by Zeus, that's what we're after!"

Mithredath's eyes followed the Hellene's finger. The slab Polydoros had spied was flatter and paler than the surrounding stones. As they hurried toward it, Mithredath saw the slab was covered with letters in the angular script the Hellenes used for their own language. If this was someone praising a pretty boy, he'd been very long-winded.

"What does it say?" the eunuch asked. He fought against excitement; for all he knew, the inscription had been ancient when Khsrish took Athens.

"Let me see." Polydoros studied the letters. So, in his more ignorant way, did Mithredath. He could see that the stone-carving here was more regular than the scratchings his servants and he and Polydoros had come upon before. That in itself, he suspected, marked an official document.

"Well?" he asked impatiently. He took out pen and ink and papyrus and got ready to transcribe the words Polydoros was presumably rendering into Aramaic.

"This is part of what you seek, I think," the Hellene said at last.

"Tell me, then!" Had he been a whole man, Mithredath's voice would have cracked; as he was what he was, it merely rose a little.

"I'm about to. Here: 'It seemed good to the council and to the people' . . . *boulē* and *dēmos* again, you see?"

"A plague on the council and people!" Mithredath broke in. "Who in Ahuramazda's name was the king?"

"I'm coming to that, I think. Let me go on: '—with the tribe of Antiokhis presiding, Leostratos serving as chairman, Hypsikhides as secretary—' "

"The king!" Mithredath shouted. "Where is the name of the king?"

"It is not on the stone," Polydoros admitted. He sounded puzzled. Mithredath, for his part, was about ready to grind his teeth. Polydoros continued. "This may be it: 'Aristeides proposed these things concerning the words of the prophetess of Delphi and the Persians:

" 'Let the Athenians fortify the citadel with beams of wood as well as stone to meet the Persians, just as was bid by the prophetess. Let the council choose woodsmen and carpenters to do this, and let them be paid from the public treasury. Let all this be done as quickly as possible, Xerxes already having come to the Asian Sardis. Let there be good fortune to the people of Athens.' "

"Read it over again," Mithredath said. "Read it slowly, so that I can be sure I have your Yauna names correct."

"Not all Hellenes are Ionians," Polydoros said. Mithredath shrugged—how these westerners chose to divide themselves was their business, and he did not care one way or the other. But Khsrish, back in Babylon, would think of them all as Yauna. And so, in his report, Yauna they would be.

Polydoros finished reading. Mithredath's pen stopped its scratching race across the sheet of papyrus. The eunuch read what he had written. He read it again. "Is, ah, Leostratos the ruler of Athens, then? And this Aristeides his minister? Or is Aristeides the king? The measure is his, I gather."

"So it would seem, excellent *saris,*" Polydoros said. "But our words for king are *anax* or, more usually, *basileus.* Neither of those is here."

"No," Mithredath said morosely. He mentally damned all the ancient Athenians to Ahriman and the House of the Lie for confusing him so. Khsrish and his courtiers would *not* be pleased if Mithredath had traveled so far, had spent so much gold from the King of Kings' treasury, without finding what he had set out to find. Nothing was more dreadful for a eunuch—for anyone, but for a eunuch especially—than losing the favor of the King of Kings.

Mithredath read the translated inscription once more. "You have rendered this accurately into Aramaic?"

"As best I could, excellent *saris,*" Polydoros said stiffly.

"I pray your pardon, good Polydoros," the eunuch said. "I meant no disrespect, I assure you. It's only that there is much here I do not understand."

"Nor I," Polydoros said, but some of the ice was gone from his voice.

Mithredath bowed. "Thank you. Help me, then, if you will, to put together the pieces of this broken pot. What does this phrase mean: 'it seemed good to the council and to the people'? Why does the stonecarver set that down? Why should anyone care what the people think? Theirs is only to obey, after all."

"True, excellent *saris,*" Polydoros said. "Your questions are all to the point. The only difficulty"—he spread his hands and smiled wryly—"is that I have no answers to them."

Mithredath sat down on a chunk of limestone that, from its fluted side, might once have been part of a column. Weeds scratched his ankles through the straps of his sandals. A spider ran across his instep and was gone before he could swat it. In the distance, he heard his servants crunching through brush. A hoopoe called its strange, trill-ing call. Otherwise, silence ruled the dead citadel.

The eunuch rubbed his smooth chin. "How is Peiraieus ruled? Maybe that will tell me something of Athens's ways before the Con-queror came."

"I beg leave to doubt it, excellent *saris*. The city is no different from any other in the Empire. The King of Kings, may Zeus and the other gods smile on him, appoints the town governor, who is responsible to the satrap. In the smaller towns, the satrap makes the appointment."

"You're right. That doesn't help." Mithredath read the inscription again. By now he was getting sick of it, and put the papyrus back in his lap with a petulant grunt. " 'The *people*,' " he repeated. "It almost sounds as if they and the council are sovereign, and these men merely ministers, so to speak."

"I can imagine a council conducting affairs, I suppose," Polydoros said slowly, "though I doubt one could decide matters as well or as fast as a single man. But how could anyone know about what all the people of a city thought on a question? And even if for some reason the people were asked about one matter, surely no one could expect to reckon up what they sought about each of the many concerns a city has every day."

"I was hoping you would give me a different slant on the question. Unfortunately, I think just as you do." Mithredath sighed and heaved himself up off his makeshift seat. "I suppose all we can do now is search further and hope we find more words to help us pierce this mystery."

The eunuch, the Hellene, and the two servants prowled the citadel for the next two days. Tishtrya almost stepped on a viper, but killed it with his stick before it could strike. Mithredath came to admire the broken statuary he kept stumbling over. It was far more restrained than the ebullient, emotional sculpture he was used to, but had a spare elegance of its own.

The searchers came across a good number of inscriptions, but none that helped unravel the riddle the first long one had posed. Most were broken or worn almost to illegibility. Twice Polydoros found the formula, "It seemed good to the council and to the people—" Each time Mithredath swore in frustration, because the rest of the stone was in one case buried beneath masonry it would have taken twenty men to move and in the other missing altogether.

"Enough of this place," Mithredath said on the evening of that second day. "I don't care any longer if the answer is right under my feet—I think it would run away from me like a rabbit from a fox if I

dug for it. Tomorrow we will search down below, in the marketplace.
Maybe our luck will be better there."

No one argued with him, although they all knew they had not
thoroughly explored the citadel—that would be a job for months or
years, not days. They rolled themselves in their blankets—no matter
how hot the days, nights stayed chilly—and slept.

The marketplace had fewer ruins than the citadel. "How do I know
this still *is* part of the marketplace?" Mithredath asked pointedly as
he, Polydoros, and the servants picked their way along through grass,
bushes, and brush. Before Polydoros could answer, the eunuch added,
"Aii!" He had just kicked a large stone, with painful results.

He pushed away the brush that hid it. It was a very large stone; he
felt like an idiot for not having seen it. In his anger, he bent down to
push the stone over. "Wait!" Polydoros said. "It has letters on it." He
read them and began to laugh.

"What, if I may ask, strikes you funny?" Glacial dignity,
Mithredath thought, was preferable to hopping up and down on one
foot.

"It says, 'I am the boundary stone of the agora,'" Polydoros told
him.

"Oh," the eunuch said, feeling foolish all over again.

The most prominent wrecked building was a couple of minutes'
walk north of them; its wrecked facade had eight columns, two of
them still standing at their full height and supporting fragments of an
architrave. "Shall we examine that first?" Polydoros asked, pointing.

Mithredath's throbbing toes made him contrary. "No, let's save it
for last, and wander about for a while. After all, it isn't going anywhere."

"As you wish," Polydoros said politely. Behind them, Mithredath's
servants sighed. The eunuch pretended he had not heard.

"What's that?" Mithredath asked a minute or so later, seeing another piece of stone poking up from out of the weeds—seeing it,
thankfully, before he had a closer encounter with it.

"By the shape, it's the base a statue once stood on," Polydoros said.
He walked over to it. "Two statues," he amended: "I see insets carved
for four feet. Ah, there's writing on it here." He pulled weeds aside,
read, "'Harmodios and Aristogeiton, those who slew the tyrant Hipparkhos.'"

"What's a tyrant?" Mithredath frowned at the unfamiliar word.
"Some sort of legendary monster?"

"No, merely a man who ruled a city but was not of any kingly line. Many towns among the Hellenes used to have them."

"Ah. Thank you." Mithredath thought about that for a moment, then said incredulously, "There was in the marketplace of Athens a statue celebrating men who killed the city's ruler?"

"So it would seem, excellent *saris,*" Polydoros said. "Put that way, it is surprising, is it not?"

"It's madness," the eunuch said, shuddering at the idea. "As well for all that Persia conquered you Yauna. Who knows what lunacy you might otherwise have loosed on the world?"

"Hmm," was all Polydoros said to that. The Hellene jerked his chin toward the ruined building, which was now quite close. "Shall we go over to it now?"

But Mithredath reacted to the Hellenic perversity exemplified by the ruined statue base with perversity of his own. "No, we'll go around it, see what else is here." He knew he was being difficult, and reveled in it. What could Polydoros do about it?

Nothing, obviously. "As you wish," the Hellene repeated. He then proceeded to skirt the ruins by an even larger margin than Mithredath would have chosen. Take that, the eunuch thought. Smiling behind Polydoros's back, he followed him north and west.

Still, enough was enough. "I'm certain *this* isn't the marketplace anymore," Mithredath said when the Hellene had led him almost all the way to Athens's overthrown gates.

"No, I suppose not," Polydoros admitted. "Are you ready to head back now?"

"More than ready." Mithredath caught Polydoros's eye. They grinned at each other, both of them a little sheepish. Mithredath glanced at his servants. They did not seem amused, and knew better than to seem annoyed.

Something crunched under the eunuch's foot. Curious, he bent down. Then, more curious, he showed Polydoros what he had found. "What's this?"

"An *ostrakon*—a potsherd," Polydoros amended, remembering to put the Yauna word into Aramaic.

"I knew *that,*" Mithredath said impatiently. "I've stepped on enough of them, these past few days. But what's this written on it?"

"Hmm?" Polydoros took a closer look. "A name—Themistokles son of Neokles."

"Why write on a potsherd?"

"Cheaper than papyrus." Polydoros shrugged. "People are always breaking pots, and always have sherds around."

"Why just a name, then? Why not some message to go with it?"

"Excellent *saris*, I have no idea."

"Hrmp," Mithredath said. He took another step, heard another crunch. He was not especially surprised to find another potsherd under his foot, as Polydoros had said, people were always breaking pots. He was surprised, though, to find he had stepped on two sherds in a row with writing on them. He handed the second piece of broken pottery to Polydoros, pointed at the letters.

"Themistokles Neokles' son again," the Hellene said.

"That's all?" Mithredath asked. Polydoros dipped his head to show it was. The eunuch gave him a quizzical look. "Good Polydoros, why write just a man's name—just his name, mind you, nothing else—on two different pieces of broken pottery? If one makes no sense, does twice somehow?"

"Not to me, excellent *saris*." Polydoros shifted his feet like a schoolboy caught in some mischief by his master. This time his sandal crunched on something. Mithredath felt a certain sense of inevitability as Polydoros looked at the sherd, found writing on it, and read, "Themistokles son of Neokles."

The eunuch put hands on hips. "Just how many of these things are there?" He turned to his servants. "Tear out some brush here. My curiosity has the better of me. Let's see how many sherds we can turn up."

The look Raga and Tishtrya exchanged was eloquent. Like any master with good sense, Mithredath pretended not to see it. The servants bent and began uprooting shrubs and weeds. They moved at first with the resigned slowness servants always use on unwelcome tasks, but even they began to show some interest as sherd followed sherd in quick succession.

"Themistokles Neokles' son," Polydoros read again and again, and then once, to vary the monotony, "Themistokles of the district Phrearrios." He turned to Mithredath, raised an eyebrow. "I think we may assume this to be the same man referred to by the rest of the sherds."

"Er—yes." Mithredath watched the pile of potsherds grow by Polydoros's feet. He began to feel like a sorcerer whose spell had proven stronger than he expected.

His servants had speculations of their own. "Who d'you suppose this Themis-whatever was?" Tishtrya asked Raga as they worked together to uproot a particularly stubborn plant.

"Probably a he-whore, putting his name about so he'd have plenty of trade," Raga panted. Mithredath, listening, did not dismiss the idea out of hand. It made more sense than anything he'd been able to think of. . . .

"Themistokles son of Neokles," Polydoros said, almost an hour later. He put down another sherd. "That makes, ah, ninety-two."

"Enough." Mithredath threw his hands in the air. "At this rate we could go on all summer. I think there are more important things to do."

"Like the ruin, for example?" Polydoros asked slyly.

"Well, now that you mention it, yes," Mithredath said with such grace as he could muster. He kicked a foot toward the pile of potsherds. "We'll leave this rubbish here. I see no use for it but to prove how strange the men of Athens were, and it would glorify neither Khsrish the Conqueror nor through him our Khsrish IV, may Ahuramazda make long his reign, to say he overcame a race of madmen."

The eunuch's servants laughed at that: they were Persians too. Polydoros managed a lopsided smile. He was on the quiet side as the four men made their way back to the ruined building in the marketplace.

Once they were there, the Hellene quickly regained his good spirits, for he found he had a chance to gloat. "This building is called the *Stoa Basileios*," he said, pointing to letters carved on an overthrown piece of frieze: "the Royal Portico. If we wanted to learn of kings, we should have come here first."

Chagrin and excitement warred in Mithredath. Excitement won. "Good Polydoros, you were right. Find me here, if you can, a list of the kings of Athens. The last one, surely, will be the man Khsrish overcame." Which will mean, he added to himself, that I can get out of these ruins and this whole backward satrapy.

Seized perhaps by some of that same hope, Raga and Tishtrya searched the ruins with three times the energy they had shown hunting for potsherds. Stones untouched since the Persian sack save by wind, rain, and scurrying mice went crashing over as the servants scoured the area for more bits of writing.

Mithredath found the first new inscription himself, but already had learned not to be overwhelmed by an idle wall scratching. All the same, he called Polydoros over. " 'Phrynikhos thinks Aiskhylos is beautiful,' " the Hellene read dutifully.

"About what I expected, but one never knows." Mithredath nodded, and went on looking. He had been gelded just before puberty; feeling desire was as alien to him as Athens's battered rocky landscape. He knew he would never understand what drove this

Phrynikhos to declare his lust for the pretty boy. Lust—other men's lust—was just something he had used to advance himself, back when he was young enough to trade on it. Once in a while, abstractly, he wondered what it was like.

Raga let out a shout that drove all such useless fancies from his mind: "Here's a big flat stone covered with letters!" Everyone came rushing over to see. The servant went on, "I saw this wasn't one stone here but two, the white one covering the gray. So I used my staff to lever the white one off—and look!" He was as proud as if he'd done the writing himself.

Mithredath plunged pen into ink, readied papyrus. "What does it say?" he asked Polydoros.

The Hellene plucked nervously at his beard, looked from the inscription to Mithredath and back again. The eunuch's impatient glare finally made him start to talk: " 'It seemed good to the council and to the people—' "

"What!" Mithredath jumped as if a wasp had stung him. "More nonsense about council and people? Where is the list of kings? In Ahuramazda's name, where if not by the Royal Portico?"

"I would not know that, excellent *saris*," Polydoros said stiffly. "If I may, though, I suggest you hear me out as I read. This stone bears on your quest, I assure you."

"Very well." It wasn't very well, but there was nothing Mithredath could do about it. Grouchily, he composed himself to listen.

" 'It seemed good to the council and to the people,' " Polydoros resumed, " 'with the tribe of Oineïs presiding, Phainippos serving as chairman, Aristomenes as secretary, Kleisthenes proposed these things concerning *ostrakismos*—' "

"What in Ahriman's name is *ostrakismos?*" Mithredath asked.

"Something pertaining to *ostraka*—potsherds. I don't know how to put it into Aramaic any more precisely than that, excellent *saris*; I'm sorry. But the words on the stone explain it better than I could, in any case, if you'll let me go on."

Mithredath nodded. "Thank you, excellent *saris*," Polydoros said. "Where was I? Oh, yes: '. . . concerning *ostrakismos*: Each year, when the sixth tribe presides, let the people decide if they wish to hold an *ostrakophoria*.' " Seeing Mithredath roll his eyes, Polydoros explained, "That means a meeting to which potsherds are carried."

"I presume this is leading somewhere," the eunuch said heavily.

"I believe so, yes." Polydoros gave his attention back to the inscribed stone. " 'Let the *ostrakophoria* be held if more of the people are counted to favor it than to oppose. If at the *ostrakophoria* more than six thousand potsherds are counted, let him whose name appears on the largest number of *ostraka* leave Athens within ten days for ten years, suffering no loss of property in the interim. May there be good fortune to the people of Athens from this.' "

"Exiled by potsherds?" Mithredath said as his pen scratched across the sheet of papyrus. "Even for Yauna, that strikes me as preposterous." Then he and Polydoros looked first at each other, then back the way they had come. "Raga! Tishtrya! Go gather up the sherds we were looking at. I think we may have a need for them, after all." The servants trotted off.

"I also think we may," Polydoros said. "Let me read on: 'Those who have been ordained to leave the city: In the year when Ankises was *arkhon*—' "

"*Arkhon?*" Mithredath asked.

"Some officer or other." Polydoros shrugged. "It means 'leader' or 'ruler,' but if a man only held the post a year, it can hardly have been important, can it?"

"I suppose not. Go on."

" 'In the year when Ankises was *arkhon*, Hipparkhos son of Kharmos; in the year when Telesinos was *arkhon*, Megakles son of Hippokrates; in the year when Kritias was *arkhon*—' " The Hellene broke off. "No one was exiled that year, it seems. In the next, when Philokrates was *arkhon*, Xanthippos son of Ariphron was exiled, then no one again, and then—" he paused for effect—"Themistokles son of Neokles."

"Well, well." Mithredath scribbled furiously, pausing only to shake his head in wonder. "The people really did make these choices, then, without a king to guide them."

"So it would seem, excellent *saris*."

"How strange. Did the *ostrakismos*"—Mithredath stumbled over the Yauna word, but neither Aramaic nor Persian had an equivalent—"fall upon anyone else?"

"Not in the next two years, excellent *saris*," Polydoros said, "but in the year when Hypsikhides was *arkhon*, the Athenian people chose exile for Xerxes son of Dareios, who can only be the King of Kings, the Conqueror. I would guess that to be a last gesture of defiance; the list of *arkhontes* ends abruptly with Hypsikhides."

"Very likely you are right. So they tried to exile Khsrish, did they? Much good it did them." Mithredath finished writing. The servants were coming back, carrying in a leather sack the sherds that had helped exile a man. Their shadows were long before them; Mithredath saw with surprise that the sun had almost touched the rocky western horizon. He turned to Polydoros. "It would be dark by the time we got back to Peiraieus. Falling into a pothole I never saw holds no appeal. Shall we spend one more night here, and return with the light of morning?"

The Hellene dipped his head. "That strikes me as a good plan, if you are satisfied you have found what you came to learn."

"I think I have," Mithredath said. Hearing that, Tishtrya and Raga began to make camp close by the ruins of the Royal Portico. Bread and goat cheese and onions, washed down with river water, seemed as fine a feast as any of the elaborate banquets Mithredath had enjoyed in Babylon. Triumph, he thought, was an even better sauce than pickled fish.

His servants dove into their bedrolls as soon as they finished eating; their snores all but drowned out the little night noises that came from beyond the circle of light around the campfire. Mithredath and Polydoros did not go to sleep right away. The eunuch was glad to have company. He felt like talking about the strange way the Athenians had run their affairs, and the Hellene had shown himself bright enough to have ideas of his own.

"No sign of a king anywhere," Mithredath said, still bemused at that. "I wonder if they settled everything they needed to decide on by counting potsherds."

"I would guess they probably must have, excellent *saris,*" Polydoros said. "All the inscriptions read, 'It seemed good to the council and to the people.' How would they know that—why would they write that —if they had not counted potsherds to know what seemed good to the people?"

"There you have me, good Polydoros. But what if something that 'seemed good to the people' was in fact bad for them?"

"Then they suffered the consequences, I suppose. They certainly did when they decided to oppose Xerxes." Polydoros waved at the dark ruins all around.

"But they were the leading Yauna power at the time, were they not? They must have been, or Khsrish would not have obliterated their city as a lesson to the others. Until they chose to fight him, they must have done well."

"A king can also make an error," Polydoros said.

"Oh, indeed." Being a courtier, Mithredath knew better than the Hellene how gruesomely true that could be. "But," he pointed out, "a king knows the problems that face his land. And if by some mischance he should not, why, then he has his ministers to point them out to him, so that he may decide what needs to be done. How could the people—farmers, most of them, and cobblers and potters and dyers—how could they even have hoped to learn the issues that affected Athens, let alone what to do about them?"

"There you have me," Polydoros confessed. "They would be too busy, I'd think, working just to stay alive to be able to act, as you say, more or less as ministers in their own behalf."

Mithredath nodded. "Exactly. The king decides, the ministers and courtiers advise, and the people obey. So it is, so it has always been, so it always will be."

"No doubt you are right." An enormous yawn blurred Polydoros's words. "Your pardon, excellent *saris*. I think I will imitate your servants." He unrolled his blanket, wrapped it around himself. "Will you join us?"

"Soon."

Polydoros did not snore, but before long was breathing with the slow regularity of sleep. Mithredath remained some time awake. Every so often his eyes went to the bag of potsherds, which lay close by Raga's head. He kept trying to imagine what being an Athenian before Khsrish the Conqueror came had been like. If the farmers and potters and such ruled themselves by counting sherds, would they have made an effort to learn about all the things Athens was doing, so they could make sensible choices when the time came to put the sherds in a basket for counting, or whatever it was they did? What would it have been like, to be a tavern-keeper, say, with the same concerns as a great noble?

The eunuch tried to imagine it, and felt himself failing. It was as alien to him as lust. He knew whole men felt that, even if he could not. He supposed the Athenians might have had this other sense, but he was sure he did not.

He gave it up, and rolled himself in his blanket to get some rest. As he grew drowsy, his mind began to roam. He had a sudden mental picture of the whole vast Persian Empire being run by people writing on potsherds. He had visions of armies of clerks trying to transport and count them, and of mountains of broken pottery climbing to the sky. He fell asleep laughing at his own silliness.

Third-rate town though it was, Pciraicus looked good to Mithredath after some days pawing through the ruins of dead Athens. He paid Polydoros five gold darics for his help there. The Hellene bowed low. "You are most generous, excellent *saris*."

Mithredath presented his cheek for a kiss, then said, "Your assistance has but earned its fitting reward, good Polydoros."

"If you will excuse me, then, I'm off to see how much work has fallen on my table while I was away." At Mithredath's nod, Polydoros bowed again and trotted away. He turned back once to wave, then quickly vanished among the people crowding the port's streets.

"And now we are off to the satrap's residence," the eunuch told his servants. "I shall inform Vahauka of the success of my mission, and draw from the *ganzabara*—" Mithredath snapped his fingers. "What was the fellow's name?"

"Hermippos, wasn't it, sir?" Tishtrya said.

"Yes; thank you. I shall draw from Hermippos the funds we need for our return journey to Babylon. After giving Polydoros his due, we are for the moment poor, but only for the moment."

"Yes, sir. I like the sound of going home fine, sir," Tishtrya said. Raga nodded.

"I wouldn't be sorry never to see this satrapy again, myself," Mithredath admitted, smiling.

The satrap's residence was busier in the early morning than it had been at nightfall. A couple of guards stood outside the entrance to make sure the line of people waiting to see Vahauka and his officials stayed orderly.

Mithredath recognized one of the guards as the man who had been at the door the evening he'd arrived. He went up to the fellow. "Be so good as to convey me to his excellency the satrap," he said. "I don't care to waste an hour of my time standing here."

The guard made no move to do as Mithredath had asked. Instead, he looked down his long, straight nose at the eunuch and said, "You can just wait your turn like anybody else."

Mithredath stared. "Why, you insolent—" He started to push past, but the guard swung up his spear. "What do you think you're playing at?" the eunuch said angrily.

"I told you, no-stones—wait your turn." The spearhead pointed straight at Mithredath's belly. It did not waver. The guard looked as though he would enjoy thrusting it home.

Mithredath glanced at his servants. Like any travelers with a shekel's weight of sense, he, Tishtrya, and Raga all carried long daggers as protection against robbers. Neither servant, though, seemed eager to take on a spear-carrying soldier, especially when the man served the local satrap. Seething, Mithredath took his place in line. "I shall remember your face," he promised the guard.

"And I'll forget yours." The lout laughed loudly at his own wit.

The line crawled ahead, but Mithredath was too furious to become bored. The revenges he invented grew more and more chilling as he got hotter and hotter. A soldier who thwarted one of the royal eunuchs—even a soldier so far from Babylon as this guard—was asking to have his corpse given to ravens and kites.

The eunuch had thought Vahauka would signal him forward as soon as he saw him, but the satrap went right on with his business. At last Mithredath stood before him. Mithredath started to prostrate himself, waited for Vahauka to stop him and offer his cheek. Vahauka did not. Feeling his stomach knot within him, the eunuch finished the prostration.

When he rose, he had his face under control. "My lord," he said, and gestured toward the bag of potsherds Raga held, "I am pleased to report my success in the mission personally set me by Khsrish, King of Kings"—he stressed the ruler's name and title—"may Ahuramazda make long his reign."

Vahauka yawned. Of all the responses Mithredath might have expected, that was the last.

Having to work now to keep his voice from stumbling, the eunuch went on. "As I have succeeded, I plan to draw funds from the *ganzabara* Hermippos for my return voyage to Babylon."

"No." Vahauka yawned again.

"My lord, must I remind you of my closeness to the King of Kings?" Only alarm made Mithredath's threat come out so badly.

"No-balls, I doubt very much if you ever have been—or ever will be—close to Kurash, King of Kings, may Ahuramazda smile upon him and make long his reign."

"Ku—" The rest of the name could not get through the lump of ice that suddenly filled Mithredath's throat.

"Aye, Kurash. A ship came in with the word he'd overthrown and slain your worthless Khsrish the day you left for the old ruined inland town. Good riddance, says I—now we have a real King of Kings again, and now I don't have to toady to a half-man anymore, either. And I won't. Get out of my sight, wretch, and thank the good god I don't stripe your back to send you on your way."

The satrap's mocking laughter pursued Mithredath as he left the hall. His servants followed, as stunned as he.

Even the vestiges of dignity deserted him as soon as he was out of sight of the satrap's residence. He sat down heavily, buried his face in his hands so he could not have to see the passersby staring at him.

Tishtrya and Raga were muttering back and forth. "Poor," he heard one of them say. "He can't pay us anymore."

"Well, to Ahriman with him, then. What else is he good for?" the other replied. It was Raga. He dropped the leather sack. The pot-sherds inside clinked. The sack came open. Some sherds spilled out.

Mithredath did not look up. Nor did he look up at the sound of his servants—no, his ex-servants, he thought dully—walking away.

They were some time gone when at last the eunuch began to emerge from his shock and despair. He picked up a sherd. Because one man had died, his own life, abruptly, was as shattered as the pot from which the broken piece had come, as shattered as long-ago Athens.

He climbed slowly to his feet. Perhaps he could beg one of his darics back from Polydoros. It would feed and lodge him for a couple of weeks. Then he could—what? At the moment, he had no idea. For that matter, he did not even know if the Hellene would give him the gold.

One thing at a time, he thought. He stopped a man and asked the way to the bankers' street. The man told him. Nodding his thanks, he tossed the potsherd on the pile and started off.

LEAPFROG

James P. Hogan

Fall had come to the northern hemisphere of Mars. At the north pole, the mean temperature had fallen to $-125°$ C—cold enough to freeze carbon dioxide out of the thin Martian atmosphere and begin forming the annual covering that would lay over the permanent cap of water-ice until spring. In the southern polar regions, where winter had ended, the carbon dioxide was evaporating. Along the edge of the retreating fields of dry ice, strong winds were starting to raise dust. During the short but hot southern summer, with Mars making its closest approach to the sun, the resulting storms could envelop the planet.

Edmund Halloran watched the surface details creep across the large wallscreen at one end of the mess area of Yellow Section, Deck B, of the interplanetary transfer vessel *Mikhail Gorbachev*, wheeling in orbit at the end of its six-month voyage from Earth to bring the third manned mission to the Red Planet. The other new arrivals sitting around him at the scratched and stained green-topped aluminum tables—where they had eaten their meals, played innumerable hands of cards, and talked, laughed, and exchanged reminiscences through the long voyage out—were also strangely quiet as they took in the view. Unlike the other views of Mars that they had studied and memorized, this was not being replayed from transmissions sent back from somewhere on the other side of millions of miles of space. This time it was really on the outside of the thin metal shell around them. Very soon, now, they would be leaving the snug cocoon with its reassuring routine and its company of familiar faces that they had come to know as home, to go down there. They had arrived.

The structure had lifted out from lunar orbit as a flotilla of three separate, identical craft, independently powered, each fabricated in the general form of a *T*, but with the bar curved as part of the arc of a circle, rather than straight. On entering the unpowered free-fall phase that would endure for most of the voyage, the three ships had maneuvered together and joined at their bases to become the equispaced spokes of a rotating *Y*, creating comfortable living conditions in the three inhabited zones at the extremities. The triplicated design meant that in the event of a major failure in any of the modules, everybody could get home again in the remaining two—or at a push, with a lot of overcrowding and at the cost of jettisoning everything not essential to survival, even in a remaining one. The sections accommodated a total of 600 people, which represented a huge expansion of the existing population of 230 accrued from the previous two missions. Some of the existing population had been distributed between a main base on Lunae Planum and a few outlying installations. The majority, however, were still up in MARSIANSKAYA MEZHDUN-ARODNAYA ORBITAL 'NAYA STANTSIYA, or "Mars International Orbiting Station," awaiting permanent accommodation on the surface. In the Russian Cyrillic alphabet this was shortened to MAPCMOC, yielding the satisfyingly descriptive transliteration MARSMOS in English, which was accepted as the standard international language.

The region coming into view now was an area roughly twenty degrees north of the equator. Halloran recognized the heavily cratered area of Lunae Planum and the irregular escarpment at its eastern edge, bounding the smoother volcanic plain of Chryse Planitia. Although he knew where to look, he could see no indication of the main base down there. He picked out the channels emerging from the escarpment, where volcanic heating had melted some of the underground ice that had existed in an earlier age, causing torrential floods to pour out across the expanse of Chryse, which lay about a kilometer lower.

An announcement from the overhead speakers broke his mood of reverie. "Attention please. The shuttle to MARSMOS is now ready for boarding. Arrivals holding disembarkation cards ninety-three through one hundred twenty should proceed through to the docking area. Ninety-three through one hundred twenty, to the docking port now."

Halloran rose and picked up his briefcase and a bag containing other items that he wanted to keep with him until the personal baggage caught up with them later. As he shuffled forward to join the flow of people converging toward the door, a voice spoke close behind him. "It looks as if we're on the same trip across, Ed." He looked

around. Ibrahim and Anna, a young Egyptian couple, were next in
line.

"I guess so," Halloran grunted. Ibrahim was an electronics technician, his wife a plant geneticist. They were both impatient to begin
their new lives. Why two young people like these should be so eager
and excited about coming to a four-thousand-mile ball of frozen
deserts, Halloran couldn't imagine. Or maybe he couldn't remember.

"We'll be going straight down from the station." Ibrahim gestured
toward Anna; she smiled a little shyly. "The doctors want her to
adapt to surface conditions as soon as possible."

Anna's pregnancy had been confirmed early in the voyage. Although the baby wouldn't be the first to be born on Mars, it would be
one of a very select few. The knowledge added considerably to
Ibrahim's already exuberant pride of first fatherhood.

"It may be a while before I see you again, then, eh?" Halloran said.
"But I wouldn't worry about not bumping into each other again. It's
not as if there are that many places to get lost in down there yet."

"I hope it won't be too long," Ibrahim said. "It was good getting to
know you. I enjoyed listening to your stories. Good luck with your
job here."

"You too. And take good care of Anna there, d'you hear."

They moved out through the mess doorway, into a gray-walled
corridor of doors separated by stretches of metal ribbing. Byacheslav,
one of the Russian construction engineers, moved over to walk beside
Halloran as they came to the stairway leading up to the next deck,
where the antechamber to the docking port was located. He was one
of the relatively few older members of the group—around Halloran's
age.

"Well, Ed . . . it would be two years at least before you saw Earth
again, even if you changed your mind today."

"I wasn't planning on changing my mind."

"It's a big slice out of what's left of life when you get to our end of
it. No second thoughts?"

"Oh, things get easier once you're over the hump. What happens
when you get over the top of any hill and start going down the other
side? You pick up speed, right? The tough part's over. People just look
at it the wrong way."

Byacheslav smiled. "Never thought about it that way. Maybe
you're right."

"How about you?"

"Me? I'm going to be too busy to worry much about things like
that. We're scheduled to begin excavating the steel plant within a

month. Oh, and there was something else. . . ." Byacheslav reached
inside his jacket, took a billfold from the inside pocket, and peeled out
Unodollar tens and ones. "That's to settle our poker account—before
I blow it all in the mess bar down at Mainbase."

Halloran took the money and stuffed it in his hip pocket. "Thanks.
. . . You know, By, there was a time when I wouldn't have trusted a
Russian as far as I could throw one of your earthmovers. It came with
the trade."

"Well, you're in a different business now."

"I guess we all are."

They entered the antechamber, with its suiting-up room and two
EVA airlocks on one side, and passed through the open doors of the
docking port into the body of the shuttle. To align with the direction
of the *Mikhail Gorbachev*'s simulated gravity, the shuttle had docked
with its roof entry-hatch mating to the port, which meant they had to
enter down a ladder into the compartment forward of the passenger
cabin. The seats were small and cramped, and Halloran and Byacheslav wedged themselves in about halfway to the back, next to a young
Indonesian who was keeping up a continuous chatter with someone
in the row behind.

"Do you know where you're going yet, Ed?" Byacheslav asked as
they buckled themselves in.

"Probably a couple of weeks more up in orbit, until the new admin
facility is ready down below," Halloran replied. "The director I'll be
working for from MCM is supposed to be meeting me at MARS-
MOS. I should find out for sure then. I guess it depends on you
construction people."

"Don't worry. We won't leave you stuck up here. . . ." Byacheslav
looked at Halloran and raised his eyebrows. "So, one of the directors
is meeting you personally, eh? And will they have a red carpet? If
that's the kind of reception an administrator gets, I think I'm starting
to worry already. I can see how the whole place will end up being
run. That was what I came all this distance to get away from. Hmm
. . . maybe I've changed my mind. Perhaps we will leave you up
here."

Halloran's rugged, pink-hued face creased into a grin. "I wouldn't
get too carried away if I were you. He's based up at MARSMOS most
of the time, anyway. I'm just here to take care of resource-allocation
schedules. Nothing special. They used to call it being a clerk."

"Now I think you're being too modest. There's a lot more to it than
scratching in ledgers with pens these days. You have to know com-

puter systems. And in a situation like this, the function is crucial. You
can't tell me you're not good."

"Don't believe a word of it. It's just Uncle Sam's way of retiring off
old spy chiefs in a world that doesn't need so many spies anymore."

Halloran sat back and gazed around the cabin. All of the passengers
were aboard and seated, and the crew were securing the doors. The
metaphoric umbilical back to Earth was about to be broken. It had
been over thirty years ago when he joined the Agency. Who would
have thought, then, that two months after turning fifty-five, he'd have
found himself at a place like this, starting with a new outfit all over
again?

And of all outfits to have ended up with, one with a name like
Moscow-Chase-Manhattan Investments, Inc., which controlled a development consortium headed by the Aeroflot Corporation, the
Volga-Hilton Hotels group, and Nippon Trans-Pacific Enterprises.
Similar combinations of interests had opened up the Moon to the
point where its materials-processing and manufacturing industries
were mushrooming, with regular transportation links in operation
and constantly being expanded, and tourism was starting to catch on.
If the U.S. space effort hadn't fallen apart in the seventies and eighties, America could have had all of it, decades ahead of the Soviets. As
it was, America was lucky to have come out of it, along with Europe
and some of the other more developed nations, as junior partners.
The Second Russian Revolution, they called it. Back to capitalism.
Many people thought it was better that way.

In the case of Mars, of course, the big obstacle to its similar development was the planet's greater distance from Earth, with corre-
spondingly longer flight times. But that problem would go away—
and usher in a new era of manned exploration of the outer Solar
System—when the race to develop a dependable, high-performance,
pulsed nuclear propulsion system was won, which would bring the
typical Mars round-trip down to somewhere around ten days. Although some unforeseen difficulties had been encountered, which had
delayed development of such a drive well beyond the dates optimisti-
cally predicted in years gone by, the various groups working feverishly around the world were generally agreed that the goal was now
in sight. That was the bonanza that MCM was betting on. Thirty
years ago, Halloran would have declared flatly that such a coordina-
tion of Soviet and Western interests under a private initiative was
impossible. Now he was part of it. Or about to be. . . .

He found himself wondering again if the Vusilov who would be
meeting him could be the same Vusilov from bygone years. Possibly

the KGB had its own retirement problems, too. But in any case, after all the months of wondering, it would be only a matter of minutes now before he found out.

The shuttle nudged itself away from the docking port, and Halloran experienced a strange series of sensations as it fell away from the *Mikhail Gorbachev*, shedding weight as it decoupled from the ship's rotational frame, and then accelerated into a curving trajectory that would carry it across to the MARSMOS satellite.

"MARSMOS has increased tenfold in size in the last six months," Byacheslav commented. "You'll probably have more places to discover there in the next couple of weeks than I'll have down on the surface."

"There'll need to be, with all these people showing up," Halloran said.

Even before the arrival of the two previous manned missions, a series of unmanned flights had left all kinds of hardware parked in orbit around Mars. In a frenzy of activity to prepare for the arrival of the third mission, the construction teams from the first two had expanded the initial station into a bewildering Rube-Goldberg creation of spheres, cylinders, boxes, and domes, bristling with antennas, laser tubes, and microwave dishes, all tied together by a floating web of latticeworks and tethering cables. And the next ship from Earth, with another six hundred people, was only two months behind.

There was a brief period of free-fall, and then more disorienting feelings of unbalance came and went as the shuttle reversed and decelerated to dock at MARSMOS. When Halloran unfastened his restraining straps, he found himself weightless, which meant that they were at the nonrotating section of the structure. Using handrails and guidelines, the newcomers steered themselves out through an aft side-door into an arrivals area where agents were waiting to give directions and answer questions.

After receiving an information package on getting around in MARSMOS, Halloran called Moscow-Chase-Manhattan's number and asked for Mr. Vusilov.

"Da?"

"Mr. Vusilov?"

"Speaking."

"This is Ed Halloran."

"Ah, Mr. Halloran! Excellent!" The voice sounded genial and exuberant. "So, you are arrived now, yes?"

"We docked about fifteen minutes ago. I've just cleared the reception formalities."

"And did you have a pleasant voyage, I trust?"

"It dragged a bit at times, but it was fine."

"Of course. So you are still liking the idea of working with us at MCM? No second regrets, yes?"

A reception agent murmured, "Make it brief, if you wouldn't mind, Mr. Halloran. There is a line waiting."

"None," Halloran said. "Er, I am holding up the line here. Maybe if I could come on through?"

"Yes, of course. What you do is ask directions to a transit elevator that will bring you out here to Red Square, which is a ring—a joke, you see, yes? This is where I am. It is the part of MARSMOS that rotates. First we have a drink of welcome to celebrate, which is the Russian tradition. You go to the south elevator point in Red Square, then find the Diplomatic Lounge. Our gentlemen's club here, comfortable by Martian standards—no hard hats or oily coverups. There, soon, I will be meeting you."

With no gravity to define a preferred direction, the geometry inside the free-fall section of MARSMOS was an Escherean nightmare of walls, planes, passages, and connecting shafts intersecting and going off in all directions, with figures floating between the various spaces and levels like fish drifting through a three-dimensional undersea labyrinth. Despite the map included in the information package, Halloran was hopelessly lost within minutes and had to ask directions three times to the elevator that would take him to the south terminal of Red Square. To reach it, he passed through a spin-decoupling gate, which took him into the slowly turning hub structure of the rotating section.

The elevator capsule ran along the outside of one of the structural supporting booms and was glass-walled on two sides. A panorama of the entire structure of MARSMOS changed perspective outside as the capsule moved outward, with the full disk of Mars sweeping by beyond, against its background of stars. It was his first close-up view of the planet that was real, seen directly with his own eyes, and not an electronically generated reproduction.

As the capsule descended outward and Halloran felt his body acquiring weight once again, he replayed in his mind the voice he had heard over the phone: the guttural, heavily accented tone, the hearty, wheezing joviality, the tortured English. It had sounded like *the* Vusilov, all right. Perhaps he had upset somebody higher up in the heap, Halloran thought—which Vusilov had had a tendency to do from time to time—and despite all the other changes, the old Russian penchant for sending troublemakers to faraway places hadn't gone away.

Direction had reestablished itself when he emerged at the rim. Halloran consulted his map again and found the Diplomatic Lounge located two levels farther down, in a complex of dining areas and social rooms collectively lumped together in a prize piece of technocratese as a "Communal Facilities Zone." But as he made his way down, austere painted metal walls and pressed aluminum floors gave way to patterned designs and carpeting, with mural decorations to add to the decor, and even some ornaments and potted plants. Finally he went through double doors into a vestibule with closets and hanging space, where he left his bags, and entered a spacious, comfortably furnished room with bookshelves and a bar tended by a white-jacketed steward on one side. On the other, vast windows looked out into space, showing Phobos as a lumpy, deformed crescent. Leather armchairs and couches were grouped around low tables with people scattered around, some talking, others alone, reading. The atmosphere was calm and restful, all very comfortable and far better than anything Halloran had expected.

And then one of the figures rose and advanced with a hand extended. He was short and stocky, with broad, solid shoulders, and dressed casually in a loose orange sweater and tan slacks. As he approached, a toothy grin broadened to split the familiar craggy, heavy-jowled face, with its bulbous, purple-veined nose—a face that had always made Halloran think of an old-time prizefighter—from one misshapen, cauliflower ear to the other.

Vusilov chuckled delightedly at the expression on Halloran's face. "Ah-hah! But why the so-surprised look, Edmund Halloran? You think you could get rid of me so easy, surely not? It has been some years now, yes? It's often I am wondering how they figure out what to do with you, Halloran. . . . So, to Mars, welcome I say to you, and to Moscow-Manhattan."

They shook hands firmly. It was the first time they had done so, even though they had met on numerous occasions as adversaries. "I wondered if it was you, Sergei . . . from the name," Halloran said.

"As I knew you would."

"You knew who I was, of course."

"Of course. I've seen your file. It wouldn't have been customary for them to show you mine."

"Who'd have guessed we'd wind up like this?" Halloran said. "Times sure change. It all seems such a long time ago, now. But then, I guess, it was literally another world."

"The axes are buried under the bridge," Vusilov pronounced. "And now, as the first thing, we must drink some toast. Come." He took Halloran's elbow lightly and steered him across to the bar. The bartender, young, swarthy, with dark eyes and flat-combed hair, looked up inquiringly. "This is Alfredo," Vusilov said, gesturing with a sweep of his hand. "The best bartender on Mars."

"The only one, too," Alfredo said.

"Well, what of it? That also makes you the best."

"I thought there was a bar down in the main surface base," Halloran said.

"Pah!" Vusilov waved a hand. "That is just a workman's club. Dishwashing beer from serve-yourself machines. This is the only *bar*. Alfredo is the source of all that's worth knowing up here. If you want to know what goes on, ask Alfredo. Alfredo, I want you to meet Ed Halloran, a good friend of mine who is very old. He has now come here to work with us."

"Pleased to meet you, Ed," Alfredo said.

"Hi," Halloran responded.

"Now, you see, from the old days I remember the files we keep on everybody. Your favorite choice to be poisoned with is a scotch, yes?"

"That would do fine."

"I refuse absolutely. Today you are joining us here, so it must first be vodka. We have the best."

"Okay. Make it on ice, with a splash of lime."

"And my usual, Alfredo," Vusilov said. "Put them on MCM's account."

Alfredo turned away and began pouring the drinks. After a few seconds, Halloran asked Vusilov idly, "When was the last time?"

Vusilov's beady bright eyes darted restlessly as he thought back. "In 2015, wasn't it? Vienna. Hah-hah! Yes, I remember." The Russian guffawed loudly and slapped the bar with the palm of his hand. "You paid a hundred thousand dollars to buy back the coding cartridge. But the truth, you never knew! It was worthless to us, anyway. We didn't have the key."

Halloran raised a restraining hand. "Now *wait* a minute. You may be the boss here, but I'm not gonna let you get away with that. We knew about the code. It was worth about as much as those hundred-dollar bills I passed you. Didn't your people ever check them out?"

"Hmph." The smile left Vusilov's face abruptly. "I know nothing about that. My department, it was not." Halloran got the impression that it was more a slight detail that Vusilov had conveniently forgotten. Alfredo placed two glasses on the bar. Vusilov picked them up.

"Come," he said. "There are two quiet chairs over there, by the window. Never before do you see so many stars, and so flammable, yes?"

"Don't change the subject," Halloran said as they began crossing the lounge. "You have to admit that we undid your whole operation in Bonn. When we exposed Skater and he got sent back to Moscow, it pulled the linchpin out of it."

Vusilov stopped and threw his head back to roar with mirth, causing heads to look up all around the room. "What, you still believe that? He was the decoy you were *supposed* to find out about. We were intercepting your communications."

"Hell, we knew that. We were feeding you garbage through that channel. That was how we kept Reuthen's cover. He was the one you should have been worrying about."

Vusilov blanched and stopped in midstride. "Reuthen? The interpreter? He was with you?"

"Sure. He was our key man. You never suspected?"

"You are being serious, I suppose?"

Halloran smiled in a satisfied kind of way. "Well, I guess you'll never know, will you?" It was a pretty tactless way to begin a relationship with his future boss, he admitted to himself, but he hadn't been able to resist it. Anyhow, what did career prospects matter at his age? Hell, it had been worth it.

Vusilov resumed walking, and after a few paces stopped by a chair where a lean, balding man with spectacles and a clipped mustache was reading what looked like a technical report of some kind, in French. "This is Léon, who you should know." Vusilov spoke stiffly, his joviality of a moment ago now gone. "Léon is with the European group here, who will build the launch base and make spaceships here."

" 'Allo?" Léon said, looking up.

"Please meet Ed Halloran," Vusilov said. "He comes here to work with us at MCM."

"A pleasure, Monsieur 'alloran." Léon half-rose from his chair to shake hands.

"Mine, too," Halloran said.

"They work very hard on the race for the nuclear pulse drive back home," Vusilov went on. He seemed to have smoothed his feathers, and lowered his voice in a tone of mock confidentiality. "They think they will be first, and when they get it, they are already out here at Mars ahead of us all to go deep-space. Isn't it so, Léon, yes?"

The Frenchman shrugged. "Anything is possible. Who knows? I

think we 'ave a good chance. Who else is there? Your prototype has problems. Rockwell and Kazak-Dynamik both admit it."

"Well, there is always the Chinese," Vusilov said, resuming his normal voice. He evidently meant it as a joke. For the past six months the Chinese had been constructing something large in lunar orbit, the purpose of which had not been revealed. It had provoked some speculation and a lot of unflattering satire and cartoons about their late-in-the-day start at imitating everyone else. "After all, what year is it of theirs? Isn't it the Year of the Monkey, yes?"

Vusilov started to laugh, but Léon cut him off with a warning shake of his head, and nodded to indicate an Oriental whom Halloran hadn't noticed before, sitting alone in an alcove on the far side of the room. He had a thin, droopy mustache and pointed beard, and was the only person in the room who was dressed formally, in a dark suit with necktie, which he wore with a black silk skullcap. He sat erect, reading from a book held high in front of his face, and showed no sign of having overheard.

Vusilov made a silent *Oh* with his mouth, in the manner of someone guilty of a faux pas, but at the same time raised his eyebrows in a way that said it didn't matter that much.

"Who's he?" Halloran murmured.

"The Chinese representative," Léon replied quietly.

"What are they doing here?"

"Who knows what they do anywhere?" Vusilov said. "We have many countries with persons at MARSMOS, whose reasons are a mystery. They do it for getting the prestige."

"That's why this is called the Diplomatic Lounge," Léon added.

"Anyway, we shall talk with you later, Léon," Vusilov said.

"I 'ope you enjoy your stay 'ere, Monsieur 'alloran."

Vusilov led the way over to the chairs that he had indicated from the bar, set one of the glasses down on the small table between them, and sat down with the other. Halloran took the other chair and picked up his drink. "So, here's to . . . ?" He looked at the Russian invitingly.

"Oh, a prosperous business future for us, I suppose. . . ." Vusilov's mood became troubled again. He eyed Halloran uncertainly as their glasses clinked.

But, just for the moment, Halloran was oblivious as he sipped his drink and savored the feeling of a new future beginning and old differences being forgotten. A portent of the new age dawning . . .

Until Vusilov said, "What else did Reuthen do for you?"

"Hell, why get into this?"

"A matter of professional pride. You forget that the KGB was the number-one, ace, properly run operation—not sloppy-dash slipshoe outfit like yours."

"Oh, is that so? Then what about the general who defected in 2012, in Berlin? We snatched him from right under your noses. That was a classic."

"You mean Obarin?"

"Of course, Obarin."

Vusilov tried to muster a laugh, but it wasn't convincing. "That old fart! We *gave* him to you. He knew nothing. He was more use to us on your side than on ours."

"Come on, let's get real. He'd been a frontline man ever since he was a major in Afghanistan back in the eighties. He was a gold mine of information on weapons and tactics."

"All of it out of date. He was an incompetent in Afghanistan. It saved us having to pay his pension."

"Let's face it. You were all incompetents when it came to Afghanistan."

"Is that so, now? And are you so quickly forgetting a little place called Vietnam? It was we who sucked you into that mess, you know, like the speedsands."

"Baloney. It was our own delusion in the early fifties over a global Communist conspiracy being masterminded from the Kremlin."

"Precisely! And where did the delusion come from, do you think? The misinformation-spreading was always one of our masterpiece arts, yes?"

They raised their glasses belligerently, looking at each other over the rims as they drank. Vusilov's mouth contorted irascibly. Clearly he was unwilling to let it go at that, yet at the same time he seemed to be having a problem over whether or not to voice what was going through his mind.

"It didn't do you a hell of a lot of good with China," Halloran said.

That did it. "But our greatest secret weapon of all, you never discovered." Halloran raised his eyebrows. Vusilov wagged a finger. "Oh, yes. Even today, you don't even suspect what it was. The Russian leaders we have today, they are young now, and even most of them forget."

"What are you talking about?" Halloran asked.

Vusilov gave a satisfied nod. "Ah, so, now I have got you curious, eh?" He paused to extract the most from the moment. Halloran waited. The Russian waved a hand suddenly. His voice took on a stronger note. "Look around you today, Ed Halloran, and tell me what do you see? Back on Earth, the Soviet space enterprises are supreme, and we are started already to colonize the Moon. And out here, you see we are the major presence in the nations who come to Mars. . . . Yet, now look back at the way the world was when it ends the Great Patriotic War in 1945, and you see it is America that holds the oyster in its hand, yes?" Vusilov shrugged. "So where does it all go down the pipes? You had it made, guys. What happened?"

Halloran could only shake his head and sigh. "These things happen. What do you want me to say, Sergei? Okay, I agree that we blew it somehow, somewhere along the line. We've got a saying that every dog has its day—and so do nations. Look at history. We had ours, and now it's your turn. Congratulations."

Vusilov looked at him reproachfully. "You think that's all there is to it, that the power plant which the USA had become all just goes away, like the dog who had a lousy day? You do us a disservice. Wouldn't you grant us that perhaps, maybe, we might just have a little piece to do with what happens?"

Now it was Halloran's turn to laugh. "You're not trying to tell me it was your doing?"

"But that is exactly what I am telling you." Vusilov stared back at him unblinkingly.

Halloran's grin faded as he saw that the Russian was being quite serious. "What the hell are you talking about?" he demanded. "How?"

Vusilov snorted. "While for years your experts in universities are busy preaching our system and idolizing Marx, we are studying yours. In Wall Street you have the yo-yo economy that goes up, then it comes down again like a flat face in what you call the depressions. Well, what is it that makes the depressions, do you think?"

Halloran shrugged. "They're part of the boom-bust cycle. It's an inevitable part of the price you pay with a market economy."

Vusilov shook his head, and his humor returned as he chuckled in the way of someone who had been suppressing a long-kept secret. "That's what most Americans say. But the joke is that most Americans don't understand how market economies work. A depression, you see, is what happens when malinvestments liquidate. A malinvestment is when capital and resources are poured into adventures for which there is no real demand. When the bubble goes bust, all the capital and labor and factory machinery and know-how that went in, nothing has any use for anymore, and so we have the depression."

Halloran nodded stonily. "Okay. So?"

"What you have been seeing ever since the one giant step for mankind is the depression in the American space program. It comes from the same reasons of which I have been telling you."

"I'm not sure I follow."

"It is nothing to do with any boom-bust bicycle that comes with capitalism. That was a fiction that we invented, and your 'experts' believed. In a truly free market, some decision makers might guess the wrong way, but they go out of business. It only takes a few who are smart to get it right, and the others will soon follow. If it is not interfered with, the natural mechanism of prices to telegraph information adjusts supplies and demands to give the best bodyguards against malinvestments that you can get. The depression happens when *all* the businesspeoples make the same mistakes at the same time, which can only be because they all get the same wrong information. And there is only one way that can happen to the whole economy at once." Vusilov paused and looked at Halloran expectantly. Halloran shook his head. "Government!" Vusilov exclaimed. "They're the only ones who have the power. Only government interference can distort the whole picture to make the same mistakes happen everywhere."

Halloran didn't look convinced. "What about the big crash of 1929? Wasn't that a classic case of the free market going belly-up?"

"You see, I told you that Americans don't understand their own economics. No, it was nothing of the kind. The boom busted directly because of the inflation of the money supply through the late twenties by the Federal Reserve because they thought that easy credit would stimulate business, but what it really does is encourage reckless investments. Also, they made huge, soundless loans to Europe, to make Germany into a roadblock for Russia."

Halloran didn't want to get into all that. "So what does that have to do with our space program fifty years later?" he asked.

Vusilov shrugged. "Think what I have been saying. What happened to your space program was a depression, which is when wrong investments liquidate. And the only force that can cause it is when government meddles into the business of people who know what they're doing." He left it to Halloran to make the connection.

Halloran frowned. "What, exactly, are you saying?"

"Well, you tell me. What was the biggest case of where your government went muscling in and took over directing the space program?"

"Do you mean Kennedy and Apollo?"

Vusilov nodded emphatically and brought his palm down on the arm of his chair. "*Da!* Apollo! You've got it!"

Halloran was taken aback. "But . . . that was a success. It was magnificent."

"Yes, it was a success. And I give you, it *was* magnificent. It did what Kennedy said. But what was that? You stuck a flag in the Moon —fine, very good. And you concentrated your whole industry for years on producing the Saturn V behemoth engine, which ever since has no other use than to be a lawn ornament at the Johnson Space Center. An expensive gnome for the garden, yes?"

"Hey, there was more than that."

"Oh, really?" Vusilov looked interested. "What? You tell me."

"Well . . ."

"Yes?"

"There was the spinoff . . . all kind of technologies. Big scientific discoveries, surely . . ."

"But what about the other things that *didn't* happen because of it?" Vusilov persisted.

"What do you mean?"

"Think of all the other things that would have come true if Apollo had never happened. In the late fifties, the U.S. Air Force wanted to go for a spaceplane—a two-man vehicle that would have pushed the explored frontier to the fringes of space, the natural step from the rocket aircraft you had been flying. We were terrified of it. It would have led to a whole line of evolution that would have seen commercially viable hypersonic vehicles by the end of the sixties—New York to Tokyo in two or three hours, say, with the same payload and turnaround time of an old 747. That would have led to a low-cost, reusable surface-to-low-orbit shuttle in the seventies, permanently manned orbiting platforms in the eighties, with all the potential that would attract private capital, which gives us a natural jump-off point for the Moon, say, maybe in the mid-nineties, yes—all lightning-years ahead of anything we could have done."

Halloran raised a hand and nodded glumly. "Okay, okay." It was all true. What else could he say?

Vusilov nodded. "Yes, Apollo was magnificent. But the truth was, nobody really needed it then, militarily, commercially, or scientifically. It was all twenty or thirty years too soon. It got you your flag and your lawn pixie. But beyond that, it put government geniuses in charge of your whole space program. And what did that get you? Dead-end after Apollo. Then Skylab fell down. By the eighties you'd sunk everything in the original shuttle, which already had old-age.

When that blew up there was nothing, because it was the only one you had. The program was so bankrupt that you'd been reduced to playing a public-relations shell game by switching the same set of flyable insides around between different skins. That was why it took ten thousand technicians three months to prepare for a launch, and why you had to shut the line down for two years to build another. And by then, everything was over. The design was already obsolete, anyway."

Halloran nodded wearily. Now that it was all spelled out, there was nothing really to argue about. He raised his glass to drink, and as he did so, he saw that Vusilov's eyes were watching him and twinkling mischievously. "What's so funny?" he asked.

The Russian replied softly, in a curious voice, "Well, surely you don't imagine that all of that just . . . happened, do you?"

Halloran's brow knotted. "You're not saying it was *you* who brought it about?" Vusilov was nodding happily, thumping his hand on the arm of his chair again with the effort of containing himself. "But how? I mean, how could you possibly have manipulated U.S. government policy on such a scale? I don't believe it."

Vusilov brushed a tear from his eye with a knuckle. "It was like this. You see, we had been operating with centralized government control of everything under Stalin for decades, and we *knew* that it didn't work. It was hopeless. Everything they touched, they screwed up. By the time we got rid of him after the war, we knew we had to change the system. But America was racing so far in front that we would never catch up. What could we do? Our only hope was to try somehow to get America to put its space program under government control and let them wreck it, while we were getting ours together. . . . And we did!"

Halloran was looking dumbfounded. "You're not saying that . . ."

"Yes, yes!" Vusilov put a hand to his chest and wheezed helplessly. "We strapped a bundle of obsolete missile-boosters together and threw *Sputnik 1* into orbit; and then we scratched the Gagarin flight together on a shoelace and put him up, too. . . . And hysterical American public opinion and your wonderfully uninformed mass-media did the rest for us . . . ha-ha-ha! I can hear it now, Kennedy: '. . . *this nation should commit itself to achieving the goal, before this decade is out, of landing a man on the Moon and returning him safely to Earth.*' He fell for it. It was our masterstroke!"

Halloran sat staring at the Russian, thunderstruck. Vusilov leaned back in his chair, and as if finally unburdened of a secret that had been weighing him down for years, laughed uproariously in an outburst that echoed around the lounge. Halloran had had enough. "Okay, you've had your fun," he conceded bitterly. "Suppose we concentrate on the present, and where we're going from here."

Vusilov raised a hand. "Oh, but that isn't the end of it. You see, it made for you an even bigger catastrophe on a national scale, precisely *because* it succeeded so well."

Obviously Halloran was going to have to hear the rest. "Go on," he said resignedly.

"The U.S. economy could have absorbed the mistake of Apollo and recovered. But you didn't let it end there. It gave you a whole generation of legislators and lawmakers who saw the success and concluded that if central control by government and massive federal spending could get you to the Moon, then those things could achieve anything. And you went on to apply it beyond our wildest hopes—when Johnson announced the Great Society program and started socializing the USA. You didn't stop with bankrupting the space industries; you bankrupted the whole country. Apollo was a bigger disaster for America than the Vietnam War. In Vietnam, at least you knew you'd gone wrong, and you learned something. But how can anyone argue with success?

"And what made it so hilarious for us was that you were doing it while we were busy dismantling the same constructions of meddling bureaucrats and incompetents in our country, because we knew how well they didn't work. *That* was our biggest secret—the discovery that made everything else that you see happening today possible. That was the secret that the KGB was there to protect. That was why it was such a big organization."

Despite himself, Halloran couldn't contain his curiosity. "What discovery?" he asked. "What secret are you talking about?"

"*Capitalism!* Free enterprise, motivated by individualism. That was why our defense industries and our space activities were so secret. That was how they were organized. If America wanted to waste the efficiency of its private sector on producing pet foods, laundry detergents, and breakfast cereals, while destroying everything that was important by letting government run it, that was fine by us. But we did it the other way around."

Halloran was looking nonplussed. "That was the KGB's primary task?"

"Yes. And you never came close to finding out."

"We assumed it was to protect your military secrets—bombs, missiles, all that kind of thing."

"Bombs? We didn't have very many bombs, if you wish to know the truth."

"You didn't?"

"We didn't need them. Washington was devastating your economy more effectively than we could have done with thousands of megatons."

Halloran slumped back in his chair and stared at the Russian dazedly. "But why . . . how come we've never even heard a whisper of this?"

"Who knows why? The leaders we have now are all young. They only know what they see today. Only a few of us old-timers remember. Very likely, most of history was not as we believe."

Halloran drew in a long breath and exhaled shakily. "Jesus . . . I need another drink. How about you? This time it's scotch, no matter —" At that moment a voice from a loudspeaker concealed overhead interrupted him.

"Attention, please. An important news item that has just come in over the laser link from Earth. The People's Republic of China has announced the successful launch of a pulsed-nuclear-propelled space vehicle from lunar orbit, which is now en route for the planet Jupiter. The vessel is believed to be carrying a manned mission, but further details have not been released. A spokesman for the Chinese government gave the news at a press conference held in Beijing this morning. The Chinese premier, Xao-Lin-Huong, applauded the achievement as tangible proof of the inherent superiority of the Marxist political and economic system.

"In a response from Moscow amid public outcry and severe criticism from his party's opposition groups, the new Soviet premier, Mr. Oleg Zhocharin, pledged a reappraisal of the Soviet Union's own program, and hinted of a return to more orthodox principles. 'We have allowed ourselves to drift too far, for too long, into a path of indolence and decadence,' Mr. Zhocharin said. 'But with strong leadership and sound government, I am confident that by concentrating the resources of our mighty nation on a common, inspiring goal, instead of continuing to allow them to dissipate themselves uselessly in a thousand contradictory directions, the slide can be reversed. To this end, I have decreed that the Soviet Union will, within ten years from today, send men out to the star system of Alpha Centauri and return them safely to Earth.' Mr. Zhocharin also stated that . . ."

Excited murmurs broke out all around the lounge. Halloran looked back at Vusilov and saw that the Russian was sitting ashen-faced, his mouth gaping.

And then a shadow fell across the table. They looked up to see that the Chinese representative had risen from his chair in the alcove and stopped by their table on his way toward the door. His expression was impenetrable, but as Halloran stared up, he saw that the bright, glittering gray eyes were shining with inner laughter. The Chinese regarded them both for a second or two, his book closed loosely in his hand, and bowed his head politely. "Enjoy your day, gentlemen," he said.

And walking without haste in quiet dignity, he left the room.

EVERYTHING BUT
HONOR

George Alec Effinger

Dr. Thomas Placide, a black American-born physicist, decided to murder Brigadier General David E. Twiggs, and he realized that it had to be done in December of 1860. He made this decision at the Berlin Olympics of 1936. Jesse Owens had just triumphed over the world's best runners in the two-hundred-meter dash. The physicist jumped up and cheered for the American victory, while his companion applauded politely. Yaakov Fein was one of the most influential scientists in the German Empire, but he was no chauvinist. After the race, Owens was presented to Prince Friedrich. The papers later reported that the prince had apologized for the absence of the seventy-seven-year-old Kaiser, and Owens had replied, "I'm sure the most powerful man in the world has more important things to do than watch six young men in their underwear run halfway around a circle." The quotation may have been the product of some journalist's imagination, but it became so identified with Jesse Owens that there was no point in arguing about it.

Whatever the truth of the matter, Placide settled back in his seat and looked at his program, getting himself ready for the next event. "You must be proud of him," said Fein. "A fellow Negro."

"I *am* proud of him," Placide said. "A fellow American."

"But you are a naturalized German citizen now, Thomas. You should cheer for the German runners."

Placide only shrugged.

Fein went on. "It's a hopeful sign that a Negro has finally won a place on the American Olympic team."

Placide showed some annoyance. "In America, Negroes have equal rights these days."

"Separate, but equal," said Fein.

The black man turned to him. "They aren't slaves anymore, if that's what you're implying. The German Empire has this fatuous paternal concern for all the downtrodden people in the world. Maybe you haven't noticed it, but the rest of the world is getting pretty damn tired of your meddling."

"We believe in using our influence for everyone's benefit."

That seemed to irritate Placide even more. "Every time some Klan bigot burns a cross in Mississippi, you Germans—"

Fein smiled. "*We* Germans, you mean," he said.

Placide frowned. "All right, we Germans send over a goddamn 'peacekeeping force' for the next nine months."

Fein patted the air between them. "Calm down, Thomas," he said, "you're being far too sensitive."

"Let's just watch the track and field events, and forget the social criticism."

"All right with me," said Fein. They dropped the subject for the moment, but Placide was sure that it would come up again soon.

Two years later, in November 1938, Dr. Placide was selected to make the first full-scale operational test of the Cage. He liked to think it was because of his contribution to the project. His journey through time would be through the courtesy of the Placide-Born-Dirac Effect, and neither Max Born nor Paul Dirac expressed any enthusiasm for the chance to act as guinea pig. In Berlin and Göttingen, there was a great deal of argument over just what the Placide-Born-Dirac Effect was, and the more conservative theorists wanted to limit the experiments to making beer steins and rodents disappear, which Placide and Fein had been doing for over a year.

"My point," said Placide at a conference of leading physicists in Göttingen, "is that after all this successful study, it's time for someone to hop in the Cage and find out what's happening, once and for all."

"I think it's certainly time to take the next step," said Werner Heisenberg.

"I agree," said Erwin Schrödinger.

Dirac rubbed his chin thoughtfully. "Nevertheless," he said, "it's much too soon to talk about human subjects."

"Are you seriously suggesting we risk a human life on the basis of our ill-fated and unproven theories?" asked Albert Einstein.

Zach Marquand shrugged. "It would be a chance to clear up all the foggy rhetoric about paradoxes," he said.

Edward La Martine just stood to one side, sullenly shaking his head. He obviously thought Placide's suggestion was unsound, if not altogether insane.

"We have four in favor of using a human subject in the Cage, and four against," said Fein. He took a deep breath and let it out as a sigh. "I'm the project director, and I suppose it's my responsibility to settle this matter. God help me if I choose wrong. I say we go ahead and expand the scope of the experiment."

Placide looked relieved. "Let me volunteer, then," he said.

"Typical American recklessness," said La Martine in a sour voice.

"You mean," said Placide, "that you'll be happy if I'm the one in the Cage. Not as a reward for my work, of course, but because if anybody's alternate history is going to be screwed up, better it be America's than Germany's."

La Martine just spread his hands and said nothing.

"Then I volunteer to go along," said Fein. "As copilot."

"There's nothing for a copilot to do," said Placide. Even then, it may have been that Fein didn't have complete faith in Placide's motives.

Placide had his own agenda, after all, but he kept it secret from the others.

"Why don't you travel back a week or so," suggested Born. "Then you can take a photograph or find some other proof to validate the experiment, and return immediately to Göttingen and time T_0."

"In for a penny, in for a pound," said Placide. "I'd like to choose my own destination, and possibly solve a little historical problem while I have the chance." The Cage would never have existed without him, and so it didn't take him long to persuade the others. Placide and Fein worked with Marquand and his team for nine more weeks learning to calibrate the Cage. In the meantime, Placide studied everything he could find about General Twiggs, and he carefully hid his true plan from the Europeans.

Placide should have known that his first attempt would not go smoothly, but as far as he could see, his plan was foolproof. His reasoning was simple: His primary goal—greater even than testing the operation of the Cage—was to relieve the barbaric conditions forced on American blacks following the Confederate Insurrection of 1861–1862.

Although he'd quit the land of his birth, he still felt an unbreakable bond between himself and others of his race, who could never escape the oppression as he had. A white friend of his father had enabled Placide to attend Yale University, where he'd studied math and physics. During the middle 1930s, after he joined the great community of experimental scientists working in the German Empire, he began to see how he might accomplish something far more important than adding a new quibble to the study of particle physics.

The Cage—*his* Cage, as he sometimes thought of it—gave him the opportunity to make a vital contribution. His unhappy experiences as a child and a young man in the United States supplied him with sufficient motive. All he lacked was the means, and this he found through historical research as painstaking as his scientific work with Dirac and Born.

To Placide, Brigadier General David Emanuel Twiggs seemed to be one of those anonymous yet crucial players in the long game of history. In 1860 he was the military commander of the Department of Texas. Although few students of the Confederate Insurrection would even recognize his name, Twiggs nevertheless had a moment, the briefest moment, when he determined the course of future events. Placide had come to realize that Twiggs was his target. Twiggs could be used to liberate American blacks from all the racist hardships and injustices of the twentieth century.

Leaving T_0, the Cage brought Placide and Yaakov Fein to San Antonio on December 24, 1860. Fein agreed to guard the Cage, which had come to rest in a wintry field about three miles from Twiggs's headquarters. Fein, of course, had no idea that Placide had anything in mind other than a quick scouting trip into this city of the past.

Placide began walking. From nearby he could hear the lowing of cattle, gathered now in shadowed groups beneath the arching limbs of live oaks. He climbed down a hill into a shallow valley of moonlit junipers and red cedar. The air smelled clean and sharp, although this Christmas Eve in Texas was not as cold as the February he'd left behind in Germany. Frosty grass crunched underfoot; as he passed through the weeds, their rough seeds clung to his trouser legs.

His exhilaration at his safe arrival in another time was tempered almost immediately by anxiety over the danger he was in. If anyone stopped and questioned him, he would have an impossible time explaining himself. At best, he would be taken for a freed slave, and as such he could expect little if any help from the local citizens. Worse was the fact that he had no proper identification and no money, and thus he would certainly appear to be a runaway.

Placide had put himself in a grave and desperate situation. If he failed and was captured, his only hope would be Fein, but Fein was a German with little knowledge of this period in American history. Placide did not have much faith in the other man's ability to rescue him, if it came to that. It might happen that no one would ever learn of Placide's sacrifice. He was thinking of the black generations yet unborn, and not his colleagues in Göttingen. He was in a unique position to do something remarkable for his oppressed people.

As it happened, Placide was not detained or captured. He made his way through the barren, cold night to the general's quarters. Twiggs was already in bed, and there was a young soldier standing sentry duty outside the door. Placide shook his head ruefully. Here was the first serious hitch in his plans. He was going to have to do something about that guard.

It wasn't so difficult to gain entry. Placide needed only to nod at the young man, grab him, and drive a knife into his chest. The soldier made a soft, gurgling cry and slumped heavily in Placide's grasp. Placide let the body fall silently to the floor. He paused a moment, listening for any sign of alarm, but all was still. Oddly, he felt no sense of guilt for what he'd done. In a way, the world of 1860 didn't seem truly real to him. It was as if the man he'd killed had never really existed, although the corporal's dark blood had stained Placide's trousers convincingly.

Placide went quietly through the door and stood over General Twiggs's bed, looking down at him. He was old, seventy or so, with long white hair and a dense white beard. He looked like a Biblical patriarch, sleeping peacefully. Placide was surprised to discover that it was not in him simply to kill the old man in his sleep. Placide wasn't sure if he was too cruel or too weak for that. He woke Twiggs, pressing one hand over the general's mouth to keep him silent.

"Don't make a sound," Placide said as Twiggs struggled to sit up. "I must speak with you. I'll remove my hand if you promise not to call out for help. That will do you no good, in any event." Twiggs nodded slowly, his eyes wide.

Placide took his hand away. Twiggs gasped and tried to speak, but for a moment he could only wheeze. "Who are you?" he asked at last.

"That's not important. You must understand that your life is in my hands. Will you answer my questions?"

Twiggs was no fool. He knew better than to bluster or threaten. He nodded again. Dressed in his bedclothes, he was a wrinkled, feeble figure; but Placide suppressed his pity for the old man. Twiggs was a Southerner by birth and a secessionist by inclination. "You are in command here," Placide said.

"Yes," said the general. "If you think that after breaking into my room, you can get me to arrange for you to escape—"

Placide raised a hand curtly, cutting him off. "If for some reason you stepped down, who would assume command in your place?"

Twiggs's brow furrowed, but otherwise he showed no outward sign of fear. "I suppose it would be Lieutenant Colonel Lee," he said.

"You mean Robert E. Lee?"

"Of the First Cavalry," said Twiggs.

Placide was relieved to hear the answer. Some months before, while Twiggs had been away from San Antonio, he had named Lee acting commander of the Department of Texas. If Twiggs were forced to retire, Lee would take over again until the War Department made its own permanent appointment.

"Now let me propose a hypothetical situation," said Placide. "Suppose Texas decides to secede from the Union—"

"So you've burst your way in here and ruined my sleep to argue politics?" Twiggs demanded angrily. "And what have you done to the young man on guard duty?"

Placide slapped Twiggs hard across the face. "Suppose Texas decides to secede from the Union," he repeated calmly. "What would your position be?"

The general raised a trembling hand to his cheek. His expression was furious, and Placide caught the first hint of fear in his eyes. "Texas will secede," Twiggs said softly. "Any fool can read that. I've already written to Washington, but the War Department has so far chosen not to send me any definite instructions."

"What will you do when the secessionist rebels demand your surrender?"

Twiggs's gaze left Placide's face and stared blankly toward the far wall. "I will surrender," he said finally. "I have not the means to carry on a civil war in Texas."

A gunshot would have roused the entire garrison. Placide cut the old man's throat with his knife, then searched the room for items to take back with him to show Fein and the others. Finally, he made his escape back into the silent night of the past. Outside, it was very strange to smell bread baking not far away, as if all was well, as if something impossible had not just happened.

"There," he told himself, "you have changed history." It remained to be seen if he'd changed it for the better.

When Placide met Fein later that night, he suggested that they not return directly to 1938 and Göttingen. Fein was dubious. "The more time we spend here," he argued, "the more chance there is that some-

one will see us. We may cause an alteration in the flow of events. That
could be disastrous."

Placide swallowed a mouthful of brandy he'd taken from Twiggs's
headquarters building. The liquor had a harsh, sweet taste, but it gave
the illusion of warmth. He offered the brandy to his companion.
"Yaakov," he said, shivering in the cold night wind, "it's already too
late."

Fein's brows narrowed. "What are you talking about?" He declined
to sample the general's brandy.

Placide shrugged. "Just that I've already inserted myself into the
past. I had a conversation with General Twiggs."

"Don't you know what that means?" cried Fein. He was furious.
"We may return to the present and find God only knows what!"

"I couldn't help it," said Placide. "I was discovered. I was arrested
and taken to the commanding officer. I had to do some fancy talking
or you would never have seen me again."

"God help us," murmured Fein. The two men looked at each other
for a moment. There was no sound but the lonely creaking of bare
tree limbs, and the rustle of dead leaves blowing along the ground.

"Look," said Placide, "why don't we jump ahead to, say, February,
and find out if anything's different. In case of some kind of disaster,
we can always reappear a few minutes before T_0 and prevent ourselves from making this trip."

"I don't know," said the German. "That might leave two of you
and two of me in the present."

"Let's worry about that only if we have to. Right now we've got to
find out if my little interview had any permanent effect." Fein
watched him closely, but said nothing more.

The two men entered the Cage, and Placide reset the controls to
take them forward a few weeks. He knew that on February 16, 1861,
Texas state troops would surround the government buildings in San
Antonio. Twiggs would give in quickly to demands that he turn over
all the arms and equipment to the militia. Of course, Placide had
prevented that from happening with his single bold stroke. In effect,
he'd put Robert E. Lee in command of the Department of Texas. Lee
was a Virginian, but he had publicly stated he would have no part in
a revolution against the Union. Placide had acted to change his mind.

They reappeared in San Antonio on the twentieth of February.
Once more, Fein guarded the Cage while Placide went into town.
The air was warmer, and smelled of wood smoke. He heard the ragged cries of birds, and once he saw a large black winged shape detach
itself from the ground and fly into a cottonwood that was beginning

to show new yellow-green leaves. For a while, everything seemed peaceful.

The town, however, was in a frenzied state of confusion. Bands of armed rebels patrolled the streets. Gunshots frequently split the air. The younger men wore the wide-eyed, fierce looks of inexperienced warriors looking forward to their first battle. The older men and women were grim and worried, obviously in fear that the conflict that had threatened so long in the abstract had come at last.

Placide stood in a narrow alley between two shops, afraid to push himself into the throngs of shouting people in the street. Finally, as both his curiosity and fear for his own safety increased, he stopped a well-dressed, elderly white man. "Pardon me, sir," he said, trying to sound calm, "my master has sent me for news."

The older man drew himself up, unhappy at being accosted in the street by an unfamiliar slave. "Tell your master that our boys have driven the Federals out," he said.

"That news will ease his pain," said Placide. He was galled to have to pretend to be a slave, but he had no other choice. "And Lee?"

"The rascal is dead, killed in the fight." The man was so pleased to be able to report that fact, he actually slapped the black man's shoulder.

Placide was stunned by the news; he'd hoped to persuade Lee to become a general for the South. He watched the man turn and go on about his business, and he knew that it was time to go about his own. His plan had not failed; it had but succeeded too well.

When they returned to T_0, Placide and Fein discovered that the present was just as they'd left it, that their excursion in time had not changed the past, but rather created a new alternate reality. Still, some of their colleagues were furious.

"What the hell were you thinking of?" demanded La Martine. He'd been fascinated by the theoretical aspects of their work, but fearful of practical applications.

Now Fein was convinced that the Cage was too dangerous to use, at least until the Placide-Born-Dirac Effect was better understood.

Placide knew that if he hoped to try again in the past, he'd have to win La Martine and Fein over. "Look," he said, "we're all curious about what happens when a change is made in the past."

"You were tampering!" cried La Martine. "As it turned out, you had no permanent effect—"

"So I don't understand why you're so upset."

"—but there was the possibility that you might have changed this world disastrously, for all of us. You had no right to attempt such a thing!"

"Sending beer steins into the past might have had disastrous results, too, Eduard," said Heisenberg thoughtfully. "Yet you had no qualms about that."

"Making inanimate objects vanish is hardly equal to interviewing historical figures in their bedrooms," said Paul Dirac indignantly.

Placide had told the others that he'd merely discussed politics with General Twiggs. It hadn't seemed profitable at the time to mention that he'd killed the old man. "You know how I feel about the Legislated Equality programs in the United States."

Dirac gave him a weary look and nodded.

"Before returning here to T_0, Yaakov and I jumped from 1861 to 1895, where we bought a history of that new timeline." Placide held up the book. "Here are the effects of our visit. I thought by going back before the Confederate Insurrection and starting things off on a different course, I could keep the Equality programs and the Liberty Boroughs and all the other abuses from ever happening. I persuaded Twiggs to retire, because I knew Robert E. Lee wouldn't surrender the garrison at San Antonio. His sense of duty and honor wouldn't allow it. He'd resist, and there would be a violent confrontation. The war would begin there in Texas, rather than two months later at Fort Sumter."

"So?" asked Heisenberg.

"So Lee would learn firsthand that the war could not be avoided, and that the needs of the Confederacy were immediate and desperate. I was certain that history would unfold differently from there on. I wanted Lee to turn down Lincoln's invitation to command the Union Army. In our world, his military brilliance brought the rebellion under control in little more than eighteen months. Now, though, we'd created a new timeline, one in which Lee would not be the Great Traitor, but rather the great genius of the Southern cause."

"But you were wrong, Thomas," said Fein. "Without Lee to lead it, the Union *still* defeated the Confederacy. All you succeeded in doing was extending the bloody conflict another year while the North searched for able military leadership."

Placide shrugged. "A minor miscalculation," he said.

"You're personally responsible for the death of Robert E. Lee, man!" said La Martine.

Placide was startled. "What do you mean? Robert E. Lee's been dead for almost seventy years. He died peacefully in the White House, not yet halfway through his term as president."

"Yes," said Marquand, "in *our* timeline that's what happened. But you went into another universe and interfered. Lee's blood is on your hands."

Placide suddenly saw the absurd point Marquand was trying to make. "Zach," he said, "we went into a world that doesn't exist. It was a fantasy world. That Robert E. Lee didn't really live, and he didn't really die. He was no more than a possibility, a quantum quirk."

"We're talking about people, Thomas," said Schrödinger, "not particles."

"Particles come into and go out of existence all the time," Placide protested. "Just the same way, the people and events in that timeline were only local expressions of the wave function. You're letting emotion twist your thinking."

Fein frowned at him. "Thomas, I want you to prepare a report as quickly as you can. We're all going to have to think very hard about this. You've shown us that there are moral questions involved with this project that none of us foresaw."

"Yaakov, I wish you'd—"

"And I'm not going to permit anyone to use the Cage again until we establish some philosophical ground rules." Fein gave Placide a long, appraising look, then turned and left the room. Placide glanced at the book they'd brought back, the history of America in the timeline they now called Universe₂. He was very eager to get back to his quarters and read of the elaborate and unpredictable results of what he'd done.

Placide made another trip into the past, this one unauthorized and in secret. He didn't know what Fein would do if he found out that Placide had ignored his prohibition, but to be truthful, Placide didn't care. He had more important matters to worry about. It was his belief —and both Schrödinger and Marquand agreed with him—that a second experiment would take him to an 1861 untouched by his previous meddling. If their many-worlds hypothesis had any validity, it was statistically unlikely that Placide would find himself back in Universe₂. He could make a clean start in Universe₃, profiting from his regrettable mistakes.

His destination this second time was the District of Columbia, on the morning of April 18, 1861. He was dressed in clothes that would attract little attention in the past, and he took with him a small sum of U.S. money in gold and silver that he'd purchased through numismatic shops in Berlin. Upon his arrival, Placide left the Cage outside of town, as he'd done in Texas. He walked some distance in the chilly air of early spring. He intended to find a hotel where he might hire a carriage, but this was more difficult than he'd imagined. He was, after all, a black man and a stranger, on some inscrutable errand of his own. Whenever he approached an innkeeper or carriage driver with his gold coins, he was told either that none of the vehicles were in proper repair, or that they had all been reserved to other parties. He understood their meaning well enough.

Placide made his way along Pennsylvania Avenue to Blair House, almost directly across the street from the Executive Mansion. He gave a little involuntary shiver when he realized that inside the White House, at that moment, Abraham Lincoln was hearing firsthand reports of the events at Fort Sumter, and preparing his order to blockade the Confederate ports. Placide was tempted to abandon his subtle plan and instead seek an interview with the president himself. What advice and warnings he could give Lincoln, if he would only listen. . . .

That was the problem, of course: Getting these strong-willed men to pay attention. Placide knew that he could help them save thousands of lives, and at the same time build a future free of the oppression their shortsightedness would lead to. His influence, of course, would be greater if he were white, but there was no point in making idle wishes. He would do the best he could.

A carriage pulled up in front of Blair House just as he arrived. He knew the man who stepped down from it must be Robert E. Lee, although he didn't look much like the photographs Placide was familiar with. Lee was wearing the blue uniform of the U.S. Army, and he carried the wide-brimmed hat of a cavalry officer in one hand. He had yet to grow his famous gray beard. He was taller, too, with broad shoulders and a strict posture and military bearing that gave him an imposing appearance. His manner was calm and poised, although he was on his way to a momentous meeting.

Lee paused a moment, perhaps collecting himself, before turning toward the entrance of the grand house. Placide hurried up to him. "General Lee," he said.

Lee smiled. "You flatter me," he said. "I presently hold the rank of colonel." He waited patiently, apparently thinking that Placide was bringing him a message of some kind.

Placide was struck by Lee's gentle manner. There was intelligence in his eyes, but not the haggard, haunted look that would come later. In the few years remaining to him after the Insurrection, Lee always carried with him the painful knowledge that he had been, after all, the fatal betrayer of his homeland. "I have some important information for you, sir," Placide said. Now that he was before the man, the physicist was unsure how to proceed. After all, Lee wasn't The Great Traitor yet, not in this timeline. Placide had prevented him from becoming the savior of the Union in Universe₂, but he'd learned only that Lee dead was no better than Lee as Yankee. "May I have a moment of your time?"

Lee pursed his lips. "I have an appointment at this address, sir, and I am obliged by both courtesy and duty to respect it."

"I know," said Placide, "and I won't keep you long. When you go inside, Francis Preston Blair is going to offer you command of the Union Army, on behalf of President Lincoln. I know that you intend to accept; but if you do, sir, you will be damning future generations of American Negroes to lives of degradation and suffering. They will harbor a rage that will grow until our nation is torn by violence more terrible than this quarrel over secession. I beg you to reconsider."

Lee did not reply at once. He studied Placide's face for a long moment. "May I inquire, sir," he said quietly, "how you come to be in possession of this information?"

Placide took out his wallet and removed a fifty-dollar bill—currency from the United States of his world, of his time. He handed it to Lee. The cavalry officer examined it in silence, first the back, with the picture of the Capitol Building, then the front, with his own portrait. "Sir, what is this?" he asked.

"Paper money," said Placide.

Lee turned the bill over and over in his hands. "Is it a bank note?"

"Legal tender printed by the federal government, and backed by government gold reserves."

"I've never seen a note like it before," said Lee dubiously.

Placide showed him the small legend beside Lee's picture. "It was issued in 1932," he said.

Lee took a deep breath and let it out. Then he gave the money back to Placide. "Mr. Blair is an elderly man, and I do him no honor by my tardiness. I beg you to excuse me."

"General Lee," Placide pleaded, "if you accept Lincoln's offer, you must lead an invading army onto the soil of Virginia, your home. How can you raise your sword against your own family and friends? You must allow me to explain. I showed you the bill because you'd think me a madman unless I presented some evidence."

"Evidence only of the skill of your engraver," said Lee. "I did not find the portrait flattering, and I did not find the item in question amusing."

As earnestly as he could, Placide explained to him that he'd come through time to let Lee know of the terrible consequences of his decision to defend the Union. "I can tell you that with you in command, the Army of the Potomac will withstand the first thrusts of the Confederate forces."

"Indeed, sir," said Lee with a little smile.

"And then you will sweep down to force the evacuation of Richmond. You will coordinate your army's movements with those of McClellan in the west, and divide the South into helpless fragments. In the meantime, the navy will blockade the ports along the Atlantic, the Gulf Coast, and the Mississippi River."

"Your predictions make the difficulties seem not so very daunting, after all."

Placide paid no attention to Lee's skepticism. "The Confederacy's only true victory will come at Petersburg, and only because of the incompetence of one of your subordinates, General Ambrose Burnside. Finally, on October 17, 1862, P. G. T. Beauregard will surrender the Army of Northern Virginia to you at Dry Pond, Georgia, northeast of Atlanta."

"And tell me, sir," said Lee, "will the Union thereafter be restored?"

"Yes," said Placide, "the Union will be restored, but in terrible circumstances." Placide described to him the fight over Reconciliation, and how the radical Republicans would seek to punish the Southern states. "All that will hold the country together in those furious months will be your strength of will as president," Placide told him.

Lee shook his head. "I am certain now that you offer me dreams and not prophecy. I cannot conceive of any circumstance that would persuade me to undertake that office. I have neither the temperament nor the wisdom."

"The Democrats will come to you, as a war hero and as a Southerner. You'll be the natural choice to oversee the process of Reconciliation. Congress will battle you, but your resolve will be as strong as Lincoln's. You'll prevent the plundering of the South."

"I am glad to hear this, but I wonder why you wish me then to decline the offer that awaits me inside. Would you see the South torn apart in peace to more horrible effect than in war?"

Placide felt a tremendous sympathy for this man, and he had to fight the urge to tell him all that would happen. In Placide's own world, Lee would die in 1870. Vice President Salmon P. Chase would then be sworn in, and the long, cruel struggle of the black would

resume. Before his death, Lee would prepare a document emancipat-
ing all the slaves in the South; but on taking office Chase would find it
convenient to set this initiative aside. The issue would still be the self-
determination of the states. Chase would let progress on civil rights
hang in abeyance rather than antagonize the newly reconstituted
Congress. Not until 1878, during the Custer administration, would
slavery be officially abolished.

"Please try to understand," said Placide, "what seems like victory
for you and for the Union will be, for the Negro population, the
beginning of a dreadful spiral down into a social and economic
abyss."

"I'm not certain that I take your meaning, sir," said Colonel Lee.

"I mean only that your concern for the slaves will blind you to the
long-range effects of what Congress will propose. And after you've
left the White House"—Placide still could not tell Lee how brief his
tenure would be—"your successors will pervert your programs to
trap the Negroes in misery. Even in my time, seventy-five years after
the Insurrection, many Negroes believe that life as a slave must have
been better than what they endure. As wretched as the condition of
slavery is, the American Negro of 1938 has little more of freedom or
opportunity or hope."

Lee was bemused by Placide's vehemence. "If I entertain your argument, sir, I am left with the feeling that all my actions will be
futile, particularly those guided most strongly by my conscience."

"Millions of Negroes are forced to live in squalid slums the government calls Liberty Boroughs, segregated from the prosperous white
communities," Placide told him. "We suffer under the Legislated
Equality programs, and—"

Lee raised a hand, cutting him off. "I beg your pardon, sir," he said.
"I am grateful to have your opinion, but I can tarry here no longer."
He gave Placide a nod and strode up to the front door of Blair House.

Placide didn't know how effective his appeal had been. He was
heartened to see, however, that as Lee turned away, his expression
was solemn and thoughtful.

In his own timeline, Placide had read that Lee, as general-in-chief
of the Union Army, resisted the president's frequent pleas to attack
the Confederate units across the Potomac in Virginia. "You must do
something soon," Lincoln demanded late in July 1861. "The army
consists to a large degree of ninety-day recruits who volunteered after
the attack on Fort Sumter. The period of enlistment has almost expired. When it does, those young men will leave the ranks and go

back to their families, unless they are given something to inspire them to remain. You must use them to strike a strong and decisive blow."

Lee remained firm. "Our soldiers are simply not ready," he said. "The volunteers are poorly trained and poorly outfitted. It would be little more than murder to take such an unprepared mob into battle."

"A victory would encourage our soldiers and open the way to the capture of Richmond."

Lee saw it differently. "A defeat," he argued, "would open the way for the enemy to capture Washington."

As the weeks went by, Lincoln continued to put pressure on Lee to act, even threatening to strip the general-in-chief of his command. But Lee would not be bullied. When the ninety-day period came to an end, most of the recruits reenlisted out of respect and admiration for Lee himself, and not the Federal cause. Lee used the time to deploy his troops with care and precision. He instructed his subordinates to hinder any advance of the Confederate army, but to fall back slowly rather than engage. Finally, on September 1, Lee reported to the president and his Cabinet that he was satisfied. Two weeks later, at Occoquan, Virginia, Lee defeated a numerically superior Confederate force under the command of General Beauregard. Aided by Generals Irwin McDowell and Benjamin Butler, Lee prevented the Southern corps from crossing the Potomac into Maryland and then encircling Washington.

The Battle of Occoquan was the smashing victory that Lincoln had hoped for. With one stroke, Lee crushed the dreams of the Confederacy. At Occoquan, he seized the offensive and never relinquished it for a moment during the rest of the war. The remainder of the eighteen-month struggle in the east saw little more than Beauregard's courageous though vain efforts to delay, with his clever skirmishes and retreats, the unavoidable outcome. Inevitably, however, he was to have his most difficult meeting with Lee at Folkston's Dining Room in Dry Pond. Beauregard, The Napoleon in Gray, was as noble in defeat as Lee was gracious in victory. The two men had been friends when they'd served together in Mexico. They would be friends again when Lee was president and Beauregard governor of Louisiana.

All of this was a matter of record, but Placide knew just how easily the record could be erased.

Placide felt a mixture of hope and anxiety while he waited in the street outside Blair House. If Lee emerged as a Union general, if he became again the Great Traitor, Placide planned to return to T_0 and abandon this timeline. He would then have to hit on a more forceful method of persuading Lee—in Universe$_4$. If, however, Placide had read Lee's expression correctly, then he planned to spend quite some time in Universe$_3$, making short jumps forward through time to follow the course of the Insurrection. With the invincible Robert E. Lee as the defender of the Confederacy's fortunes, the fate of the South would certainly be different.

Placide opened to the first page of the journal he intended to keep during his experiment. He wrote his first entry:

Universe$_3$
April 18, 1861
Outside Blair House, Washington

If things turn out as I hope, I will remain in this newly made world, studying it and perhaps learning something of value to take back with me to T$_0$. I will adopt this alternative timeline as my own, and love these people regardless of their sins, for have I not created them? Perhaps that sounds mad, but there has not yet been time enough to evaluate properly this unlooked-for benefit of my work. But surely I am a god to these people, having called them out of nothing, with the power to send their history off in whichever direction I choose. The God of Abraham created but the universe of T$_0$, and I have already created two more. How many others will I call into being before I achieve my purpose? General Lee comes now, with the fate of Universe$_3$ in his hands.

It was September 16, 1861, and the air should have been thick with drifting clouds of gunsmoke, the acrid breath of massed rifles; but the autumn breeze carried only the tang of burning firewood from a farmhouse nearby. There should have been the menacing, booming shocks of the field artillery, and the ragged cries of wounded men; but there was only stillness. The roads near Occoquan, Virginia, should have been jammed with wild-eyed, charging infantry, and the urgent mounted messengers of the generals; but only Thomas Placide disturbed the quiet countryside.

It was a grim, gloomy day in late summer, and black clouds threatened low overhead. It had not yet begun to rain, but a storm seemed imminent. Thunder cracked and rolled, and Placide grimaced. He did not like to be out in this kind of weather. He was cheered only by the knowledge that he had truly persuaded Robert E. Lee, that a mechanism for the salvation of American blacks had been set in motion. All that now remained was the job of supervision, to make certain that Placide's careful scheme did not falter as this world's divergent history unfolded.

He shook his head. He wouldn't have guessed that this was the kind of day Lee would choose for his first major test as a general in the Confederate Army. Placide hurried down a rutted, dusty lane, to the white-painted frame farmhouse, hoping to meet someone who could direct him to the battlefield.

The house was surrounded by a bare yard and a gap-toothed fence. Placide went through the yawning gate and climbed three steps to the porch. He heard nothing from within the house. He rapped loudly. A moment later, a distracted white woman opened the door, gave Placide a critical look, and shut the door again. "Ma'am?" called Placide. "Will you help me, ma'am?"

The door opened again, and he was looking at a tall, burly, frowning man. "We got nothin' for you," said the farmer.

"I just need some directions from y'all," said Placide. He reminded himself that once again he needed to behave modestly.

"Directions we can afford, I guess," said the farmer.

Placide nodded gratefully. "I've got to find my way to the battle, and quickly."

The white man closed one eye and stared at him for a few seconds. "Battle?" he asked.

"I've got news for General Lee."

"You his boy?"

Placide felt a flush of anger, but he stifled it. "No, sir, I'm a free man of color. But I've got news for General Lee."

"What's this about a battle? There been no soldiers around here except when they come by in July. On their way to Manassas."

"Manassas? Where's that?"

The farmer gave him another close look. "Where the battle was. Bull Run. It was Beauregard and Joe Johnston that licked the Yankees at Bull Run. Your boss was busy fetchin' coffee cups for Jeffy Davis down in Richmond."

Placide wondered at how quickly men and events had found their new course. "General Lee is obliged to follow the wishes of President Davis," he said.

The farmer gave a derisive laugh. "While Granny Lee was doin' just that, one Sunday afternoon the blue boys come out of Washington, thinkin' they was goin' to whup Beauregard and send him on home. Then Joe Johnston showed up to help him out, and before you know it the damn Yankees are runnin' ever which way, goin' back to cry on Lincoln's shoulder."

Placide took all this in. "Well, sir," he said, "I guess they told me wrong when they said he'd come up here."

"Your General Lee ain't never been within fifty mile of here. As far as I know, he's somewheres off in the west, diddlin' around in the mountains."

"I thank you, sir. I suppose I'd just better get back to Richmond myself. Someone's made some kind of mistake."

The farmer laughed. "I'm lookin' right at him." He turned away and closed the door. Placide found that his hands were clenched into tight fists. He let out his breath slowly and forced himself to relax. He walked back out through the farmer's gate and headed back the way he'd come. He wanted to get back to the Cage before the heavy rain began.

Although he hated having to play the role of fool, Placide was elated by the news. He'd prevented the crushing Confederate defeat at Occoquan from occurring in Universe$_3$. There had been a mighty rebel victory that had not happened in Placide's timeline, and it had happened even without Robert E. Lee. With Lee yet on the verge of fulfilling his destiny, Placide could almost see the glory of the greater victories yet to come. He found himself smiling broadly as the first huge raindrops spatted about him in the dust.

Universe$_3$
October 17, 1862
Dry Pond, Georgia

For the second time, I've come to watch an event that has vanished from history. I suspected that would be the case, yet I jumped here from Occoquan anyway. Hearing the news of the Battle of Bull Run, I was of the opinion that I had wholly altered the course of the Insurrection. It would be unlikely in the extreme that its ending should now fall out just as it had in my own timeline, on the same day, at the same place, and for the same reasons. Still, I had to be certain.

In the deficient universe of my origin, Beauregard's surrender took place in the salon of Folkston's Dining Hall. I was not foolish enough to enter that white establishment by the front door. Rather, I went around to the rear of the building. There I won the sympathy of the kitchen slaves with a glib story of fear and desperation. They kindly gave me a good meal, some clothing more appropriate than my own, and a sum of money in both Confederate scrip and silver.

Of course, no one here has heard rumors of the approach of a triumphant Union Army. Everyone agrees that the fighting continues far to the north of Maryland, and far to the west of Mississippi. Yaakov was right: I have given this world a fiercer, longer conflict. In Universe₃, this is no mere Confederate Insurrection. This is civil war.

And how is the struggle going? My new friends have caught me up on the thirteen months I missed, jumping here from Occoquan: George McClellan is Lincoln's general-in-chief. (I am certain he is no Lee, and will hardly present an obstacle to Confederate triumph.) There was a Southern victory at Ball's Bluff, Virginia, and a battle at Shiloh, in Tennessee, that wasn't much of a victory for the Federals or much of a defeat for the South. Lee defended Richmond against McClellan, and then, damn it! Lee and Stonewall Jackson beat up the Yankees at Bull Run a second time! That gave Marse Robert confidence to try to invade the North by heading up through Maryland—just as Beauregard tried in my own timeline. And just like Beauregard, Lee was stopped. He was stalled at Antietam Creek because a set of his campaign orders was lost and later discovered by Union soldiers.

If there is a turn for the worse, and if I must abandon Universe₃, I may begin again as I did at Blair House; but this time, I will remove in advance that careless officer at Antietam. "In for a penny, in for a pound." It was not enough, it seems, to have won Robert E. Lee to my cause. I find that I must continue to supervise and guide this entire war.

How astonished Dirac and the others will be when I return to T₀! I will seem to have aged several years in a single moment.

How sad I will be to leave a world I am perfecting, to return to a world I can no longer love.

Placide locked his door and went downstairs to dinner. The Negro rooming house was on Rampart Street, on the edge of the Vieux Carré. Placide had grown up in New Orleans, but that had been in the early years of the twentieth century. Here it was 1864, and the city was very different. There were still steamboats working on the river and bales of cotton piled high on the wharves. He thought that somewhere in this quaint version of New Orleans, his own grandparents were growing up. He could visit them, if he chose to. The idea made him a little queasy.

A young quadroon woman waved to him. "Monsieur Placide," she called, "won't you sit beside me this evening?"

"I'd be delighted," he said. Her name was Lisette, and she'd been the mistress of the son of a prosperous businessman who lived above Canal Street in the American Sector. It was common for a young white man of means to select a light-skinned girl like Lisette and establish her in a small house of her own on Rampart or Burgundy streets. It was her misfortune that the boy's interest had waned, and he no longer supported her. Now she was looking for a new friend—a new white friend. The quadroon beauty disdained forming attachments to black men. When she'd called to Placide, she was just practicing her social graces.

"You always have so much interesting gossip," she said.

Placide sighed and held her chair for her, then seated himself. "I wonder what Mrs. Le Moyne has for us tonight," he said.

Mrs. Le Moyne came into the dining room and gave Placide a dour look. "I will serve y'all what I always serve," she said. "And that is, sir, what little the damn Yankees haven't taken for themselves or spoiled."

Placide rose slightly from his seat and gave her a little bow. "You work miracles, madame," he said.

"I'm sure, sir, that you wish I could," said Mrs. Le Moyne. She went back out into the kitchen.

"Isn't she a charmer?" whispered Lisette.

Another of the tenants sat down across the table from them. He was a surgeon's assistant in the black community. Placide thought the man always seemed to know too much of everyone else's business. "Will you be leaving us again soon, Mr. Placide?" he asked.

"Yes," said Placide. "Tomorrow."

"Where are you going?" asked Lisette. "Don't the Yankees stop you from traveling?"

Placide shrugged. "I don't worry about them."

The black man across the table laughed. "Then you must be the only person in New Orleans who doesn't."

"How long will you be gone?" asked Lisette.

"Maybe a month or two," said Placide. "Maybe longer." He thought of the Cage, safe upstairs in his room. The War of Southern Independence was proceeding differently than he'd planned. Lee's final northward thrust had been turned back at Gettysburg. The Confederate nation now had little hope of victory, but it still fought grimly on. Oddly, though, Placide was not wholly dissatisfied. What

mattered was that Lincoln had been driven to a point of urgency.
Politics might yet achieve for blacks what military might had not.
Almost a year before, desperate to rally continued support for his
war effort, Lincoln had issued what he called an Emancipation Proclamation. In Placide's timeline, with Lee leading the Federal forces to
quick victory in 1862, Lincoln was never pressed to make such a
concession. And in Universe₂, with Lee killed before the Insurrection
even began, Lincoln considered freeing the slaves but put the idea
aside when victory proved imminent in 1863.

Only here in Universe₃, in the spring of 1864, with Lee in a grim
and determined struggle to hold off defeat as long as possible, could
Placide see some hope that American blacks might avoid the horror of
what President James G. Blaine had so sanctimoniously called Parallel Development.

"Mr. Placide," said Lisette sweetly, "would you bring me back
something pretty from your travels? I'd be ever so grateful." She gave
him a dazzling smile.

He was neither flattered nor fooled. He thought that with luck he'd
bring her freedom and dignity, although he was sure she'd much
rather have a new dress from New York. He only smiled back at the
young woman, then turned his attention to the food Mrs. Le Moyne
was carrying in from the kitchen.

Universe₃
March 22, 1884
New Orleans, Louisiana

Shock has followed shock: Even with Lee at last general-in-chief,
the Confederate hopes ended in 1865. It's as if God Almighty has
decreed that it must happen just so in all worlds, all timelines,
across the breadth of the manifold realities. Evidently the South
cannot win, with Lee or without him. There are economic, social,
and political reasons too vast for me to correct with so simple a
plan.

Today, in a raging downpour, I witnessed the dedication of a
handsome, brooding bronze statue of General Lee. The monument
stands upon a column seventy feet above the traffic of St. Charles
Avenue. Lee gazes resolutely northward, as if grimly contemplating the designs not only of the Union Army, but also of the subtle
and guileful Yankee mind. It is a statue I have seen before, although
in the world of my childhood the model was P. G. T. Beauregard,
and not Robert E. Lee. I knew the area as Beauregard Place; here it

has been newly named Lee Circle. In this timeline, of course, Lee is not the Great Traitor. He is idolized as a hero and the defender of the Southern way of life, despite the fact that it was his defeat that ended both the war and what is already being spoken of as the "Old South." To me (and possibly to me alone), he is the Great Failure.

I see that I must begin again. If Lee is to be successful in Universe₄, I must take a greater hand in arranging things. Perhaps Lincoln should die in 1862. Perhaps Jefferson Davis should also be removed, or at least be firmly persuaded to leave Beauregard with his command and to make better and timelier use of Lee's abilities. I have the leisure to consider these matters, as I intend to make a few more jumps to evaluate the fate of the Negroes in this timeline before I return at last to T_0.

On one hand, this world doesn't know either the corruption of the Custer and Blaine administrations, or the abuses of Chase's program of Reconciliation. On the other hand, it has suffered through the different though no less odious crookedness of Ulysses Grant's two terms. I wonder where Grant came from. If he played any important part at all in the universe of my origin, I never read any reference to it. Yet here he emerged as a shrewd tactician, a victor, and a president. More important to me, though, is that he oversaw most of Reconstruction and permitted the wholesale rape of the South.

Reconstruction was a grotesque injustice inflicted on a conquered population. In my world, the brief Confederate Insurrection and Lee's vigilance as president prevented Congress from exacting such harsh penalties on the South. Even the ancient Romans knew better than to impose tyrannical conditions on a defeated people.

Here in Universe₃, almost twenty years after the war's end, I see continued evidence of the South's rage and indignation. The Southern attitude, shaped by the war and by Reconstruction, is a desperate desire to cling to what little yet remains of the old ways and the old life. There have been many attempts to circumvent the will of the Yankee, even to reviving slavery under new guises. This is, all in all, a bitter, unhealthy society.

And yet I will remain in this timeline a little while longer. I plan to look around 1884 for another few days, and then jump to 1938 and Göttingen, just a week or so before T_0, so that I will remain in Universe₃. I'm very curious to see what changes my experiment makes in the rest of the world after seventy-five years.

Despite the problems here, it is a more hopeful world for the

Negro. Amendments to the U.S. Constitution have abolished slavery, guaranteed civil rights, and given Negroes the right to vote. Southern state legislatures have seated many Negroes, and some Negroes have been elected to office as high as lieutenant governor or been sent to Washington as senators and district representatives. In my timeline, slavery wasn't abolished until 1878, while in 1939 most Southern Negroes still can't vote, let alone run for office.

The version here of Blaine's Parallel Development is segregation, which is not so absolute and despotic, but is still highly offensive. In the New Orleans of my world, Negroes may live only in specially zoned Liberty Boroughs, which are crowded, undeveloped neighborhoods with virtually no communication or trade with each other or with the white community. Negroes here are permitted by law to take up residence wherever they choose, although in actual practice it is impossible for Negroes to find homes in many white areas.

In Universe₃, Negroes may travel freely within the city and throughout the South. They may not always be made welcome, of course, but no official restrictions are placed on their movements. In the America I abandoned, a Negro must still carry an endorsement book, which records his assigned Liberty Borough and prevents him from traveling beyond it without a special permit. At any time the state government may move individuals or groups of Negroes from one Liberty Borough to another, sometimes without warning, explanation, or recourse. There are many more similar provisions of the Blaine program, and most of them are happily absent from this timeline.

At the close of the war, the South lay ruined and bankrupt. My experiment ended in tragedies I did not foresee and that have no counterpart in my world. The burning of Atlanta, Sherman's march of devastation from that city's ashes to the Atlantic coast, and the assassination of Abraham Lincoln all occurred as a result of what I set in motion. The war went on three and a half years longer than in my timeline, where some one hundred thousand soldiers died in the Confederate Insurrection. In Universe₃, more than *six* hundred thousand perished in the Civil War.

That nameless army guard outside General Twiggs's quarters did not seem real to me at the time. Why has it taken vast mountains of dead soldiers to make me see the full extent of what I've done? Nevertheless, I believe now that although the cost has been high, I have succeeded in my dream of improving the lot of my people, at least to a small degree. I am confident that the end has truly justified the means.

Placide jumped to 1938, to T_0 minus seven days. He felt like a trespasser. It gave him an eerie feeling to walk around the university town of Göttingen, knowing that there was very likely a duplicate of himself nearby, one who had lived his whole life in Universe₃.

There were important differences between the two timelines. Some of the streets and buildings here had new names, clothing styles were oddly altered, and there were unfamiliar flags and signs wherever he looked. The degree of change depended on how much influence the United States had in this alternate reality. After the Confederate Insurrection in his own timeline, the North and South hadn't joined together strongly enough to make America an international power comparable to England, France, Germany, or Russia. Placide could not predict how in Universe₃ the bloodier Civil War might have affected that situation.

He climbed the steps of the laboratory, which in his own world had been in the Kaiser Wilhelm Institute; the building was now called the Max Planck Institute. He found what had been his own office, but a stranger's name was now on the door. As he walked down the darkened hallway reading notices and posters, he met the building's elderly porter. Placide was cheered that, despite all, some things remained the same. "Good afternoon, Peter," he said.

The old man cocked his head and studied him. "May I help you?" he asked. His tone was suspicious.

"Don't you know me?"

Peter shook his head. "We don't see many black men here."

Whatever other changes had been made in Universe₃, Placide evidently had not pursued his studies in the German Empire. "I'm looking for a few of my colleagues," he said.

Peter raised his eyebrows.

"Werner Heisenberg," said Placide.

"Ah, Dr. Heisenberg's no longer here. He's gone to Berlin, to the other Max Planck Institute."

"Well, then, how about Dr. Schrödinger?"

"He went to Austria. That's where he's from, you know. But I think I've heard that since then he's gone on to England."

"Paul Dirac?"

"He's at Cambridge now."

Placide wondered if this scattering of his colleagues meant that the discoveries they'd made together had not been made in this world. "La Martine and Marquand?"

"I'm sorry, but there's never been anyone here by those names in the years I've worked here."

That made Placide uncomfortable. "Yaakov Fein?"

Peter's expression grew even more cautious. "Who are these men?" he asked.

"Albert Einstein?"

"Gone to live in America."

"Tell me about Max Born. Max must still be here."

"He's now at the University of Edinburgh. He's a British subject."

Placide felt gripped by a cold despair. He suspected that there was no Placide-Born-Dirac Effect in Universe$_3$, and no Cage, either. "These men were friends of mine," he said. "Do you mind if I look around here for a little while? I planned to come work here myself once."

Peter gave him a dubious look, but nodded his head. "I guess it will be all right, if you don't disturb anything."

"I won't." The old porter left him alone in the dusty, drafty corridor.

A quarter of an hour later, while Placide was inspecting some primitive laboratory equipment, two men in the uniform of the town's police approached him. "Will you come with us, sir?" one said.

"Why should I?" asked Placide.

"We must establish your identity. Please show us your papers."

He'd been afraid this might happen. He knew he could be in serious trouble now. "I'm a German citizen," he said.

It was obvious that the policemen didn't believe him. "If that's true," said the second officer, "we'll get this cleared up quickly at headquarters." There was nothing else for Placide to do but go along.

Some time later he was led to a jail cell. He'd had no identification, and none of his references existed in this timeline or could be produced to vouch for him. As the jailer clanged the cell door shut he said, "Make yourself comfortable, Dr. Placide. I'm sure there's been some misunderstanding. In the meantime, you'll just have to make the best of it here."

Placide nodded. The jailer went away, leaving him in the small, dim cell with another prisoner. "How good of you to drop in," said the other man. Placide lay on his hard bunk and stared sullenly at the ceiling. The air was stale, and there was a heavy smell of urine and vomit.

"My name is Schindler," said his cellmate. "I'm a thief, but not a very good one."

"Apparently," murmured Placide.

Schindler laughed. "What got you nicked?"

"No identification."

"That's a hanging offense in this town, friend. Where are you from?"

"The United States, originally. But I've lived in Germany for a few years."

Schindler whistled tunelessly for a little while. "What do you do in Germany?" he asked at last.

"I'm a scientist," said Placide. "Particle physics, quantum mechanics. Nothing that would interest the average person."

"Jewish physics," said Schindler, laughing again. "Einstein and that gang, right?"

"Yes," said Placide, puzzled.

"No wonder you're locked up."

"What do you mean, Jewish physics?"

"The government's official policy is that sort of thing isn't politically correct."

"Politically correct?" cried Placide. "Science is science, truth is truth!"

"And the National Socialists decide which is which."

They talked for some time, and Schindler gave him a great deal to think about. After a while, Placide told the good-humored thief about the Cage and his adventures traveling from one universe to another. Schindler was skeptical, but he stopped short of calling Placide a liar. The two men compared what they knew of recent history in their divergent worlds.

Here in Universe₃, the United States had taken part in the Great War, and the German Empire had come to an end. In response to the Depression, and growing out of Germany's bitterness after the war, a party of fascists came to power in Berlin. Many talented people, liberals and Jews and other persecuted groups, fled Germany soon after that.

"You shouldn't admit that you even knew those people," advised Schindler. "You won't do yourself any good."

"What can they do to me?"

Schindler laid a finger alongside his nose and spoke in a hushed voice. "They can send you to the camps," he said.

"What kind of camps?"

"The kind of place where your friend Einstein might have been sent. Where lots of brilliant but racially inferior scientists are hauling boulders around until they drop dead." He gave Placide a meaningful look.

It was too crazy for Placide to believe, but still he began making plans to escape. When he was out, he'd use the Cage to get out of this stifling reality as quickly as he could. In the meantime, he hoped that the mechanism of the German government would operate efficiently.

Weeks later he was granted a hearing. He sat in a small room at a wooden table, while several strangers testified that he was insane. Peter the porter was brought in. He identified Placide as the man who'd wandered into the laboratory and asked after the decadent physicists. Schindler reported everything Placide had told him, and added his own embellishments. Quite obviously, he'd been put in the cell with Placide as an informer.

Placide himself was not permitted to testify. He was judged insane. The American embassy could find no record of him in New Orleans; the examining board ironically chose to believe only one item of Placide's story, that he was a naturalized German. Therefore, it had the authority to remand him to a clinic for the mentally disturbed in Brandenburg. After the hearing, he was locked up again, along with Schindler.

"You goddamn spy!" cried Placide. His voice echoed in the cold stone cell.

Schindler shrugged. "Everyone is a spy these days," he said. "I'm sorry you're upset. Let me make it up to you. I'll give you some advice: Be careful when you get to Brandenburg." He lay down on his narrow wooden bunk and turned away from Placide.

"What are you talking about?"

Schindler took out a penknife and began chipping at the mortar between two blocks in the wall. "I mean, that clinic isn't what it appears to be. The Brandenburg Clinic is a euthanasia center, friend. So when you go in, just take a deep breath and try to hold it as long as you can."

Schindler's knife was making a rasping, gritty sound. Placide stared at his back. "I'm being sent to a mental health clinic."

"Carbon monoxide," said Schindler, turning to face him. "That's the only treatment they use. Look, you say you helped the Negroes of your country, but see what you've let loose in the world instead! When they drag you into that narrow room, think about that. Think about all the other people who are going to follow you to the gas, and decide if it was worth it."

Placide shut his eyes tightly. "Of course it was worth it," he said fiercely. "All that I've discovered. All that I've accomplished. I only regret that I won't be able to go back to T_0 and report to the others. Then I'd go back to 1860 and try again, correct my mistakes. Even if it took me two or three more attempts, I'd succeed eventually. And then I could move on to another time, another problem. We could create a committee to guide similar experiments all through history, relieving suffering and oppression wherever we chose."

Schindler jammed his penknife into the wooden frame of the bunk. "You *are* insane, Placide, do you know that? You haven't learned a goddamn thing. You'd charge right ahead if you could, and who knows what new horrors you'd instigate? You've got a rare talent for making good times hard, and hard times worse."

"I have one chance," Placide murmured thoughtfully, not hearing Schindler's words at all. "*Another* Thomas Placide, from another parallel reality, may be aware of my trouble here. He may be searching for me this very minute. I have to hang onto that hope. I must have faith."

Schindler laughed as if he'd never heard anything so funny in his life.

And while Nazi guards patrolled the hallway beyond the cell's iron-barred door, Placide began planning what he would do when he was released, and where he would go, and on whom he'd revenge himself.

WE COULD DO WORSE

Gregory Benford

Everybody in the bar noticed us when we came in. You could see their faces tighten up.

The bartender reached over and put the cover on the free-lunch jar. I caught that even though I was watching the people in the booths.

They knew who we were. You could see the caution come into their eyes. I'm big enough that nobody just glances at me once. You get used to that after a while and then you start to liking it.

"Beer," I said when we got to the mahogany bar. The bartender drew it, looking at me. He let some suds slop over and wiped the glass and stood holding it until I put down a quarter.

"Two," I said. The bartender put the glass in front of me and I pushed it toward Phillips. He let some of the second beer slop out too because he was busy watching my hands. I took the glass with my right and with my left I lifted the cover off the free-lunch jar.

"No," he said.

I took a sandwich out.

"I'm gonna make like I didn't hear that," I said and bit into the sandwich. It was cheese with some mayonnaise and hadn't been made today.

I tossed the sandwich aside. "Got anything better?"

"Not for you," the bartender said.

"You got your license out where I can read it?"

"You guys is federal. Got no call to want my liquor license."

"Lawyer, huh?" Phillips asked slow and steady. He doesn't say much but people always listen.

The bartender was in pretty good shape, a middle-sized guy with big arm muscles, but he made a mistake then. His hand slid under the bar, watching us both, and I reached over and grabbed his wrist. I yanked his hand up and there was a pistol in it. The hammer was already cocked. Phillips got his fingers between the revolver's hammer and the firing pin. We pulled it out of the bartender's hand easy and I tapped him a light one in the snoot, hardly getting off my stool. He staggered back and Phillips put away the revolver in a coat pocket.

"Guys like you shouldn't have guns," Phillips said. "Get hurt that way."

"You just stand there and look pretty," I said.

"It's Garrett, isn't it?"

"Now don't never you mind," Phillips said.

The rest of the bar was quiet and I turned and gave them a look. "What you expect?" I said loud enough so they could all hear. "Man pulls a gun on you, you take care of him."

A peroxide blond in a back booth called out, "You bastards!"

"There a back alley here?" I asked the whole room.

Their faces were tight and they didn't know whether to tell me the truth or not.

"Hey, yeah," Phillips said. "Sure there's a back door. You 'member, the briefing said so."

He's not too bright. So I used a different way to open them up. "Blondie, you want we ask you some questions? Maybe out in that alley?"

Peroxide looked steady at me for a moment and then looked away. She knew what we'd do to her out there if she made any more noise. Women know those things without your saying.

I turned my back to them and said, "My nickel."

The bartender had stopped his nose from bleeding but he wasn't thinking very well. He just blinked at me.

"Change for the beers," I said. "You can turn on that TV, too."

He fumbled getting the nickel. When the last of The Milton Berle Hour came on the bar filled with enough sound so anybody coming in from the street wouldn't notice that nobody was talking. They were just watching Phillips and me.

I sipped my beer. Part of our job is to let folks know we're not fooling around anymore. Show the flag, kind of.

The Berle show went off and you could smell the tense sweat in the bar. I acted casual, like I didn't care. The government news bulletins were coming on and the bartender started to change the channel and I waved him off.

"Time for Lucy," he said. He had gotten some backbone into his voice again.

I smiled at him. "I guess I know what time it is. Let's inform these citizens a li'l."

There was a Schlitz ad with dancing and singing bottles, the king of beers, and then more news. They mentioned the new directives about the state of emergency, but nothing I didn't already know two days ago. Good. No surprises.

"Let's have Lucy!" somebody yelled behind me.

I turned around but nobody said anything more. "You'd maybe like watchin' the convention?" I said.

Nobody spoke. So I grinned and said, "Maybe you patriots could learn somethin' that way."

I laughed a little and gestured to the bartender. He spun the dial and there was the Republican convention, warming up. Cronkite talking over the background noise.

"Somethin', huh?" I said to Phillips. "Not like four years ago."

"Don't matter that much," Phillips said. He watched the door while I kept an eye on the crowd.

"You kiddin'? Why, that goddamn Eisenhower almost took the nomination away from Taft last time. Hadn't been for Nixon deliverin' the California delegation to old man Taft, that pinko general coulda won."

"So?" Phillips sipped his beer. A station break came and I could hear tires hissing by outside in the light rain. My jacket smelled damp. I never wear a raincoat on a job like this. They get in your way. The street lights threw stretched shapes against the bar windows. Phillips watched the passing shadows, waiting calm as anything for one of them to turn and come in the door.

I said, "You think Eisenhower, with that Kraut name, woulda picked our guy for the second spot?"

"Mighta."

"Hell no. Even if he had, Eisenhower didn't drop dead a year later."

"You're right there," Phillips said to humor me. He's not a man for theory.

"I tell you, Taft winnin' and then dyin', it was a godsend. Gave us the man we shoulda had. Never coulda elected him. The Commies, they'd never have let him get in power."

Phillips stiffened. I thought it was what I'd said, but then a guy came through the doors in a slick black raincoat. He was pale and I saw it was our man. Cheering at the convention came up then and he didn't notice anything funny, not until he got a few steps in and saw the faces.

Garrett's eyes widened as I came to him. He pulled his hands up like he was reaching for something under his coat, or maybe just to protect himself.

I didn't care which. I hit him once in the stomach to take the wind out of him and then gave him two quick overhand punches in the jaw. He went down nice and solid and wasn't going to get back up in a hurry.

Phillips searched him. There was no gun after all. The bar was dead quiet.

A guy in a porkpie hat came up to me all hot and bothered, like he hadn't been paying attention before, and said, "You can't just attack a, a member of the Congress! That's Congressman Garrett there! I don't care—"

The big talk went right out of him when I slammed a fist into his gut. Porkpie was another lawyer, no real fight in him.

I walked back to the bar and drained my beer. The '56 convention was rolling on, nominations just starting, but you knew that was all bull. Only one man was possible, and when the election came there'd be plenty guys like me to fix it so he won.

Just then they put on some footage of the president and I stood there a second, just watching him. There was a knot in my throat when I looked at him, a real American. There were damn few of us, even now. We'd gotten in by accident, maybe, but now we were going to make every day count. Clean up the country. And hell, if the work wasn't done by the time his second term ended in 1961, we might have to diddle the Constitution a little, keep him in power until things worked okay.

Cronkite came on then, babbling about letting Adlai Stevenson out of house arrest, and I went to help Phillips get Garrett to his feet. I sure didn't want to have to haul the guy out to our car.

We got him up with his raincoat all twisted around him. Then the porkpie hat guy was there again, but this time with about a dozen of them behind him. They looked mad and jittery. A bunch like that can be trouble. I wondered if this was such a good idea, taking Garrett in his neighborhood bar. But the chief said we had to show these types we'd go anywhere, anytime.

Porkpie said, "You got no warrant.

"Sure I do." I showed them the paper. These types always think paper is God.

"Sit down," Phillips said, being civil. "You people all sit down."

"That's a congressman you got there. We—"

"Traitor, is what you mean," I said.

Peroxide came up then, screeching. "You think you can just take anybody, you lousy sonsabitches—"

Porkpie took a poke at me then. I caught it and gave him a right cross, pretty as you please. He staggered back. Still, I saw we could really get in a fix here if they all came at us.

Peroxide called out, "Come on, we can—"

She stopped when I pulled out the gun. It's a big steel automatic, just about the right size for a guy like me. Some guys use silencers with them, but me, I like the noise.

They all looked at it awhile and their faces changed, closing up, each one of them alone with their thoughts, and then I knew they wouldn't do anything.

"Come on," I said. We carried the traitor out into the night. I was so pumped up he felt light.

Even a year before, we'd have had big trouble bringing in a Commie network type like Garrett. He was a big deal on the House Internal Security Committee and had been giving us a lot of grief. Now nailing him was easy. And all because of one man at the top with real courage.

We don't bother with the formalities anymore. Phillips opened the trunk of the Pontiac and I dumped Garrett in. Easier and faster than cramming him into the front, and I wanted to get out of there.

Garrett was barely conscious and just blinked at me as I slammed down the trunk. They'd wake him up plenty later.

As I came around to get in the driver's side I looked through the window of the bar. Cronkite was interviewing the president now. Ol' Joe looked like he was in good shape, real statesmanlike, but tough, you could see that.

Cronkite was probably asking him why he'd chosen Nixon for the VP spot, like there was no other choice. Like I'd tried to tell Phillips, Nixon's delivering California on the delegate issue in '52 had paved the way for the Taft ticket. And old Bob Taft, rest his soul, knew what the country needed when the vice presidency nomination came up.

Just like now. Joe, he doesn't forget a debt. So Dick Nixon was a shoo-in. McCarthy and Nixon—good ticket, regional balance, solid anti-Commie values. We could do worse. A lot worse.

I got in and gunned the motor a little, feeling good. The rain had stopped. The meat in the trunk was as good as dead, but we'd deliver it fresh anyway. We took off with a roar into the darkness.

TO THE PROMISED LAND

Robert Silverberg

They came for me at high noon, the hour of Apollo, when only a crazy man would want to go out into the desert. I was hard at work and in no mood to be kidnapped. But to get them to listen to reason was like trying to get the Nile to flow south. They weren't reasonable men. Their eyes had a wild metallic sheen and they held their jaws and mouths clamped in that special constipated way that fanatics like to affect. As they swaggered about in my little cluttered study, poking at the tottering stacks of books and pawing through the manuscript of my nearly finished history of the collapse of the Empire, they were like two immense irresistible forces, as remote and terrifying as gods of old Aiguptos come to life. I felt helpless before them.

The older and taller one called himself Eleazar. To me he was Horus, because of his great hawk nose. He looked like an Aiguptian and he was wearing the white linen robe of an Aiguptian. The other, squat and heavily muscled, with a baboon face worthy of Thoth, told me he was Leonardo di Filippo, which is of course a Roman name, and he had an oily Roman look about him. But I knew he was no more Roman than I am. Nor the other, Aiguptian. Both of them spoke in Hebrew, and with an ease that no outsider could ever attain. These were two Israelites, men of my own obscure tribe. Perhaps di Filippo had been born to a father not of the faith, or perhaps he simply liked to pretend that he was one of the world's masters and not one of God's forgotten people. I will never know.

Eleazar stared at me, at the photograph of me on the jacket of my account of the Wars of the Reunification, and at me again, as though trying to satisfy himself that I really was Nathan ben-Simeon. The picture was fifteen years old. My beard had been black then. He tapped the book and pointed questioningly to me and I nodded.

"Good," he said. He told me to pack a suitcase, fast, as though I were going down to Alexandria for a weekend holiday. "Moshe sent us to get you," he said. "Moshe wants you. Moshe needs you. He has important work for you."

"Moshe?"

"The Leader," Eleazar said, in tones that you would ordinarily reserve for Pharaoh, or perhaps the First Consul. "You don't know anything about him yet, but you will. All of Aiguptos will know him soon. The whole world."

"What does your Moshe want with me?"

"You're going to write an account of the Exodus for him," said di Filippo.

"Ancient history isn't my field," I told him.

"We're not talking about ancient history."

"The Exodus was three thousand years ago, and what can you say about it at this late date except that it's a damned shame that it didn't work out?"

Di Filippo looked blank for a moment. Then he said, "We're not talking about that one. The Exodus is now. It's about to happen, the new one, the real one. That other one long ago was a mistake, a false try."

"And this new Moshe of yours wants to do it all over again? Why? Can't he be satisfied with the first fiasco? Do we need another? Where could we possibly go that would be any better than Aiguptos?"

"You'll see. What Moshe is doing will be the biggest news since the burning bush."

"Enough," Eleazar said. "We ought to be hitting the road. Get your things together, Dr. Ben-Simeon."

So they really meant to take me away. I felt fear and disbelief. Was this actually happening? Could I resist them? I would not let it happen. Time for some show of firmness, I thought. The scholar standing on his authority. Surely they wouldn't attempt force. Whatever else they might be, they were Hebrews. They would respect a scholar. Brusque, crisp, fatherly, the *melamed,* the man of learning. I shook my head. "I'm afraid not. It's simply not possible."

Eleazar made a small gesture with one hand. Di Filippo moved ominously close to me and his stocky body seemed to expand in a frightening way. "Come on," he said quietly. "We've got a car waiting right outside. It's a four-hour drive, and Moshe said to get you there before sundown."

My sense of helplessness came sweeping back. "Please. I have work to do, and—"

"Screw your work, professor. Start packing, or we'll take you just as you are."

The street was silent and empty, with that forlorn midday look that makes Menfe seem like an abandoned city when the sun is at its height. I walked between them, a prisoner, trying to remain calm. When I glanced back at the battered old gray facades of the Hebrew Quarter where I had lived all my life, I wondered if I would ever see them again, what would happen to my books, who would preserve my papers. It was like a dream.

A sharp dusty wind was blowing out of the west, reddening the sky so that it seemed that the whole Delta must be aflame, and the noontime heat was enough to kosher a pig. The air smelled of cooking oil, of orange blossoms, of camel dung, of smoke. They had parked on the far side of Amenhotep Plaza just behind the vast ruined statue of Pharaoh, probably in hope of catching the shadows, but at this hour there were no shadows and the car was like an oven. Di Filippo drove, Eleazar sat in back with me. I kept myself completely still, hardly even breathing, as though I could construct a sphere of invulnerability around me by remaining motionless. But when Eleazar offered me a cigarette I snatched it from him with such sudden ferocity that he looked at me in amazement.

We circled the Hippodrome and the Great Basilica where the judges of the Republic hold court, and joined the sparse flow of traffic that was entering the Sacred Way. So our route lay eastward out of the city, across the river and into the desert. I asked no questions. I was frightened, numbed, angry, and—I suppose—to some degree curious. It was a paralyzing combination of emotions. So I sat quietly, praying only that these men and their Leader would be done with me in short order and return me to my home and my studies.

"This filthy city," Eleazar muttered. "How I despise it!"

In fact it had always seemed grand and beautiful to me: a measure of my assimilation, some might say, though inwardly I feel very much the Israelite, not in the least Aiguptian. Even a Hebrew must concede that Menfe is one of the world's great cities. Or Memphis, rather, as the Greeks began calling it long ago, and which practically everyone calls it now except antiquarians like me. The Greeks liked to hang their own slippery names on everything and the dull Romans, when it was their turn to own the globe, generally kept them, which is why this land where I live is known as Aiguptos—or Egypt, as it's sometimes spelled these days—despite the fact that its own people call it Misr when they speak among themselves. And Menfe is Memphis. I prefer Menfe. Though to be consistent I should call it Men-ofer, as it was known in the time when Pharaohs really were Pharaohs, or, better yet, Moph, which is its Hebrew name. By whatever name, it is the most majestic city this side of Roma, so everyone says, and so I am willing to believe, though I have never been beyond the borders of the province of Aiguptos in my life.

The splendid old temples of the Sacred Way went by on both sides, the Temple of Isis and the Temple of Sarapis and the Temple of Jupiter Ammon and all the rest, fifty or a hundred of them on that great boulevard whose pavements are lined with sphinxes and bulls: Dagon's temple, Mithra's and Cybele's, Baal's, Marduk's, Zarathustra's, a temple for every god and goddess anyone had ever imagined, except, of course, the One True God, whom we few Hebrews prefer to worship in our private way behind the walls of our own quarter. The gods of all the Earth have washed up here in Menfe like so much Nile mud. Of course hardly anyone takes them very seriously these days, even the supposed faithful. It would be folly to pretend that this is a religious age. Mithra's shrine still gets some worshippers, and of course that of Jupiter Ammon. People go to those to do business, to see their friends, maybe to ask favors on high. The rest of the temples might as well be museums. No one goes into them except Roman and Japanese tourists. Yet here they still stand, many of them thousands of years old. Nothing is ever thrown away in the land of Misr.

"Look at them," Eleazar said scornfully, as we passed the huge half-ruined Sarapion. "I hate the sight of them. The foolishness! The waste! And all of them built with our forefathers' sweat."

In fact there was little truth in that. Perhaps in the time of the first Moshe we did indeed labor to build the Great Pyramids for Pharaoh, as it says in Scripture. But there could never have been enough of us to add up to much of a work force. Even now, after a sojourn along the Nile that has lasted some four thousand years, there are only about twenty thousand of us in all the world, half here in Menfe, the rest in Alexandria, none anywhere else. Lost in a sea of ten million Aiguptians, we are, and the Aiguptians themselves are lost in an ocean of Romans and imitation Romans, so we are a minority within a minority, an ethnographic curiosity, a drop in the vast ocean of humanity, an odd and trivial sect, insignificant except to ourselves. And it was clear to everyone even in the great days of Pharaoh that we few peculiar Israelitish folk would be far more useful as scribes and teachers and doctors than as laborers hauling blocks of stone for his temples and pyramids.

The temple district dropped away behind us and we moved out

across the long slim shining arch of the Caesar Augustus Bridge, and into the teeming suburb of Hikuptah on the eastern bank of the river, with its leather and gold bazaars, its myriad coffeehouses, its tangle of medieval alleys. Then Hikuptah dissolved into a wilderness of fig trees and canebrake, and we entered a transitional zone of olive orchards and date palms; and then abruptly we came to the place where the land changes from black to red and nothing grows. At once the awful barrenness and solitude of the place struck me like a tangible force. It was fearful land, stark and empty, a dead place full of terrible ghosts. The sun was a scourge above us. I thought we would bake; and when the car's engine once or twice began to cough and sputter, I knew from the grim look on Eleazar's face that we would surely perish if we suffered a breakdown. Di Filippo drove in a hunched, intense way, saying nothing, gripping the steering stick with an unbending rigidity that spoke of great uneasiness. Eleazar too was quiet. Neither of them had said much since our departure from Menfe, nor I, but now in that hot harsh land they fell utterly silent, and the three of us neither spoke nor moved, as though the car had become our tomb. We labored onward, slowly, uncertain of engine, with windborne sand whistling all about us out of the west. In the great heat every breath was a struggle. My clothing clung to my skin. The road was fine for a while, broad and straight and well paved, but then it narrowed, and finally it was nothing more than a potholed white ribbon half covered with drifts. They were better at highway maintenance in the days of Imperial Roma. But that was long ago. This is the era of the Consuls, and things go to hell in the hinterlands and no one cares.

"Do you know what route we're taking, doctor?" Eleazar asked, breaking the taut silence at last when we were an hour or so into that bleak and miserable desert.

My throat was dry as strips of leather that have been hanging in the sun a thousand years, and I had trouble getting words out. "I think we're heading east," I said finally.

"East, yes. It happens that we're traveling the same route that the first Moshe took when he tried to lead our people out of bondage. Toward the Bitter Lakes, and the Reed Sea. Where Pharaoh's army caught up with us and ten thousand innocent people drowned."

There was crackling fury in his voice, as though that were something that had happened just the other day, as though he had learned of it not from the Book of Aaron but from this morning's newspaper. And he gave me a fiery glance, as if I had had some complicity in our people's long captivity among the Aiguptians and some responsibility

for the ghastly failure of that ancient attempt to escape. I flinched
before that fierce gaze of his and looked away.

"Do you care, Dr. Ben-Simeon? That they followed us and drove us
into the sea? That half our nation, or more, perished in a single day in
horrible fear and panic? That young mothers with babies in their
arms were crushed beneath the wheels of Pharaoh's chariots?"

"It was all so long ago," I said lamely.

As the words left my lips I knew how foolish they were. It had not
been my intent to minimize the debacle of the Exodus. I had meant
only that the great disaster to our people was sealed over by thousands of years of healing, that although crushed and dispirited and
horribly reduced in numbers we had somehow gone on from that
point, we had survived, we had endured, the survivors of the catastrophe had made new lives for themselves along the Nile under the rule
of Pharaoh and under the Greeks who had conquered Pharaoh and
the Romans who had conquered the Greeks. We still survived, did we
not, here in the long sleepy decadence of the Imperium, the Pax
Romana, when even the everlasting Empire had crumbled and the
absurd and pathetic Second Republic ruled the world? The God of
Abraham and Isaac was not without worshipers this day, was he?

But to Eleazar it was as if I had spat upon the scrolls of the Ark. *"It
was all so long ago,"* he repeated, savagely mocking me. "And therefore
we should forget? Shall we forget the Patriarchs too? Shall we forget
the Covenant? Is Aiguptos the land that the Lord meant us to inhabit?
Were we chosen by Him to be set above all the peoples of the Earth,
or were we meant to be the slaves of Pharaoh forever?"

"I was trying only to say—"

What I had been trying to say didn't interest him. His eyes were
shining, his face was flushed, a vein stood out astonishingly on his
broad forehead. "We were meant for greatness. The Lord God gave
His blessing to Abraham, and said that He would multiply
Abraham's seed as the stars of the heaven, and as the sand which is
upon the seashore. And the seed of Abraham shall possess the gate of
his enemies. And in his seed shall all the nations of the earth be
blessed. Have you ever heard those words before, Dr. Ben-Simeon?
And do you think they signified anything, or were they only the
boasting of noisy little desert chieftains? No, I tell you we were
meant for greatness, we were meant to shake the world; and we have
been too long in recovering from the catastrophe at the Reed Sea. An
hour, two hours later and all of history would have been different. We
would have crossed into Sinai and the fertile lands beyond; we would
have built our kingdom there as the Covenant decreed; we would

have made the world listen to the thunder of our God's voice; and today the entire world would look up to us as it has looked to the Romans these past twenty centuries. But it is not too late, even now. A new Moshe is in the land and he will succeed where the first one failed. And we *will* come forth from Aiguptos, Dr. Ben-Simeon, and we *will* have what is rightfully ours. At last, Dr. Ben-Simeon. At long last."

He sat back, sweating, trembling, ashen, seemingly exhausted by his own eloquence. I didn't attempt to reply. Against such force of conviction there is no victory; and what could I possibly have gained, in any case, by contesting his vision of Israel triumphant? Let him have his faith; let him have his new Moshe; let him have his dream of Israel triumphant. I myself had a different vision, less romantic, more cynical. I could easily imagine, yes, the children of Israel escaping from their bondage under Pharaoh long ago and crossing into Sinai, and going on beyond it into sweet and fertile Palestina. But what then? Global dominion? What was there in our history, in our character, our national temperament, that would lead us on to that? Preaching Jehovah to the Gentiles? Yes, but would they listen, would they understand? No. No. We would always have been a special people, I suspected, a small and stubborn tribe, clinging to our knowledge of the One God amid the hordes who needed to believe in many. We might have conquered Palestina, we might have taken Syria too, even spread out a little further around the perimeter of the Great Sea; but still there would have been the Assyrians to contend with, and the Babylonians, and the Persians, and Alexander's Greeks, and the Romans, especially the stolid dull invincible Romans, whose destiny it was to engulf every corner of the planet and carve it into Roman provinces full of Roman highways and Roman bridges and Roman whorehouses. Instead of living in Aiguptos under the modern Pharaoh, who is the puppet of the First Consul who has replaced the Emperor of Roma, we would be living in Palestina under the rule of some minor procurator or proconsul or prefect, and we would speak some sort of Greek or Latin to our masters instead of Aiguptian, and everything else would be the same. But I said none of this to Eleazar. He and I were different sorts of men. His soul and his vision were greater and grander than mine. Also his strength was superior and his temper was shorter. I might take issue with his theories of history, and he might hit me in his rage; and which of us then would be the wiser?

* * *

The sun slipped away behind us and the wind shifted, hurling sand now against our front windows instead of the rear. I saw the dark shadows of mountains to the south and ahead of us, far across the strait that separates Aiguptos from the Sinai wilderness. It was late afternoon, almost evening. Suddenly there was a village ahead of us, springing up out of nowhere in the nothingness.

It was more a camp, really, than a village. I saw a few dozen lop-sided tin huts and some buildings that were even more modest, strung together with reed latticework. Carbide lamps glowed here and there. There were three or four dilapidated trucks and a handful of battered old cars scattered haphazardly about. A well had been driven in the center of things and a crazy network of above-ground conduits ran off in all directions. In back of the central area I saw one building much larger than the others, a big tin-roofed shed or lean-to with other trucks parked in front of it.

I had arrived at the secret headquarters of some underground movement, yet no attempt had been made to disguise or defend it. Situating it in this forlorn zone was defense enough: no one in his right mind would come out here without good reason. The patrols of the Pharaonic police did not extend beyond the cities, and the civic officers of the Republic certainly had no cause to go sniffing around in these remote and distasteful parts. We live in a decadent era but a placid and trusting one.

Eleazar, jumping out of the car, beckoned to me, and I hobbled after him. After hours without a break in the close quarters of the car I was creaky and wilted and the reek of gasoline fumes had left me nauseated. My clothes were acrid and stiff from my own dried sweat. The evening coolness had not yet descended on the desert and the air was hot and close. To my nostrils it had a strange vacant quality, the myriad stinks of the city being absent. There was something almost frightening about that. It was like the sort of air the moon might have, if the moon had air.

"This place is called Beth Israel," Eleazar said. "It is the capital of our nation."

Not only was I among fanatics; I had fallen in with madmen who suffered the delusion of grandeur. Or does one quality go automatically with the other?

A woman wearing man's clothing came trotting up to us. She was young and very tall, with broad shoulders and a great mass of dark thick hair tumbling to her shoulders and eyes as bright as Eleazar's. She had Eleazar's hawk nose, too, but somehow it made her look all the more striking. "My sister Miriam," he said. "She'll see that you get settled. In the morning I'll show you around and explain your duties to you."

And he walked away, leaving me with her.

She was formidable. I would have carried my bag, but she insisted, and set out at such a brisk pace toward the perimeter of the settlement that I was hard put to keep up with her. A hut all my own was ready for me, somewhat apart from everything else. It had a cot, a desk and typewriter, a washbasin, and a single dangling lamp. There was a cupboard for my things. Miriam unpacked for me, setting my little stock of fresh clothing on the shelves and putting the few books I had brought with me beside the cot. Then she filled the basin with water and told me to get undressed. I stared at her, astounded. "You can't wear what you've got on now," she said. "While you're having a bath I'll take your things to be washed." She might have waited outside, but no. She stood there, arms folded, looking impatient. I shrugged and gave her my shirt, but she wanted everything else, too. This was new to me, her straightforwardness, her absolute indifference to modesty. There have been few women in my life and none since the death of my wife; how could I strip myself before this one, who was young enough to be my daughter? But she insisted. In the end I gave her every stitch—my nakedness did not seem to matter to her at all—and while she was gone I sponged myself clean and hastily put on fresh clothing, so she would not see me naked again. But she was gone a long time. When she returned, she brought with her a tray, my dinner, a bowl of porridge, some stewed lamb, a little flask of pale red wine. Then I was left alone. Night had fallen now, desert night, awesomely black with the stars burning like beacons. When I had eaten I stepped outside my hut and stood in the darkness. It scarcely seemed real to me, that I had been snatched away like this, that I was in this alien place rather than in my familiar cluttered little flat in the Hebrew Quarter of Menfe. But it was peaceful here. Lights glimmered in the distance. I heard laughter, the pleasant sound of a kithara, someone singing an old Hebrew song in a deep, rich voice. Even in my bewildering captivity I felt a strange tranquility descending on me. I knew that I was in the presence of a true community, albeit one dedicated to some bizarre goal beyond my comprehension. If I had dared, I would have gone out among them and made myself known to them; but I was a stranger, and afraid. For a long while I stood in the darkness, listening, wondering. When the night grew cold I went inside. I lay awake until dawn, or so it seemed, gripped by that icy clarity that will not admit sleep; and yet I must have slept at least a little while, for there were fragments of dreams drifting in my mind in the morning, images of horsemen and chariots, of men with spears, of a great black-bearded angry Moshe holding aloft the tablets of the Law.

A small girl shyly brought me breakfast. Afterwards Eleazar came to me. In the confusion of yesterday I had not taken note of how overwhelming his physical presence was: he had seemed merely big, but now I realized that he was a giant, taller than I by a span or more, and probably sixty minas heavier. His features were ruddy, and a vast tangle of dark thick curls spilled down to his shoulders. He had put aside his Aiguptian robes this morning and was dressed Roman style, an open-throated white shirt, a pair of khaki trousers.

"You know," he said, "we don't have any doubt at all that you're the right man for this job. Moshe and I have discussed your books many times. We agree that no one has a firmer grasp of the logic of history, of the inevitability of the processes that flow from the nature of human beings."

To this I offered no response.

"I know how annoyed you must be at being grabbed like this. But you are essential to us; and we knew you'd never have come of your own free will."

"Essential?"

"Great movements need great chroniclers."

"And the nature of your movement—"

"Come," he said.

He led me through the village. But it was a remarkably uninformative walk. His manner was mechanical and aloof, as if he were following a preprogrammed route, and whenever I asked a direct question he was vague or even evasive. The big tin-roofed building in the center of things was the factory where the work of the Exodus was being carried out, he said, but my request for further explanation went unanswered. He showed me the house of Moshe, a crude shack like all the others. Of Moshe himself, though, I saw nothing. "You will meet him at a later time," Eleazar said. He pointed out another shack that was the synagogue, another that was the library, another that housed the electrical generator. When I asked to visit the library he merely shrugged and kept walking. On the far side of it I saw a second group of crude houses on the lower slope of a fair-sized hill that I had not noticed the night before. "We have a population of five hundred," Eleazar told me. More than I had imagined.

"All Hebrews?" I asked.

"What do you think?"

It surprised me that so many of us could have migrated to this desert settlement without my hearing about it. Of course, I have led a secluded scholarly life, but still, five hundred Israelites is one out of every forty of us. That is a major movement of population, for us. And not one of them someone of my acquaintance, or even a friend of a friend? Apparently not. Well, perhaps most of the settlers of Beth Israel had come from the Hebrew community in Alexandria, which has relatively little contact with those of us who live in Menfe. Certainly I recognized no one as I walked through the village.

From time to time Eleazar made veiled references to the Exodus that was soon to come, but there was no real information in anything he said; it was as if the Exodus were merely some bright toy that he enjoyed cupping in his hands, and I was allowed from time to time to see its gleam but not its form. There was no use in questioning him. He simply walked along, looming high above me, telling me only what he wished to tell. There was an unstated grandiosity to the whole mysterious project that puzzled and irritated me. If they wanted to leave Aiguptos, why not simply leave? The borders weren't guarded. We had ceased to be the slaves of Pharaoh two thousand years ago. Eleazar and his friends could settle in Palestina or Syria or anyplace else they liked, even Gallia, even Hispania, even Nuova Roma far across the ocean, where they could try to convert the red-skinned men to Israel. The Republic wouldn't care where a few wild-eyed Hebrews chose to go. So why all this pomp and mystery, why such an air of conspiratorial secrecy? Were these people up to something truly extraordinary? Or, I wondered, were they simply crazy?

That afternoon Miriam brought back my clothes, washed and ironed, and offered to introduce me to some of her friends. We went down into the village, which was quiet. Almost everyone is at work, Miriam explained. But there were a few young men and women on the porch of one of the buildings: this is Deborah, she said, and this is Ruth, and Reuben, and Isaac, and Joseph, and Saul. They greeted me with great respect, even reverence, but almost immediately went back to their animated conversation as if they had forgotten I was there. Joseph, who was dark and sleek and slim, treated Miriam with an ease bordering on intimacy, finishing her sentences for her, once or twice touching her lightly on the arm to underscore some point he was making. I found that unexpectedly disturbing. Was he her husband? Her lover? Why did it matter to me? They were both young enough to be my children. Great God, why did it matter?

* * *

Unexpectedly and with amazing swiftness my attitude toward my captors began to change. Certainly I had had a troublesome introduction to them—the lofty pomposity of Eleazar, the brutal directness of di Filippo, the ruthless way I had been seized and taken to this place —but as I met others I found them generally charming, graceful, courteous, appealing. Prisoner though I might be, I felt myself quickly being drawn into sympathy with them.

In the first two days I was allowed to discover nothing except that these were busy, determined folk, most of them young and evidently all of them intelligent, working with tremendous zeal on some colossal undertaking that they were convinced would shake the world. They were passionate in the way that I imagined the Hebrews of that first and ill-starred Exodus had been: contemptuous of the sterile and alien society within which they were confined, striving toward freedom and the light, struggling to bring a new world into being. But how? By what means? I was sure that they would tell me more in their own good time; and I knew also that that time had not yet come. They were watching me, testing me, making certain I could be trusted with their secret.

Whatever it was, that immense surprise which they meant to spring upon the Republic, I hoped there was substance to it, and I wished them well with it. I am old and perhaps timid but far from conservative: change is the way of growth, and the Empire, with which I include the Republic that ostensibly has replaced it, is the enemy of change. For twenty centuries it had strangled mankind in its benign grip. The civilization it had constructed was hollow, the life that most of us led was a meaningless trek that had neither values nor purpose. By its shrewd acceptance and absorption of the alien gods and alien ways of the peoples it had conquered, the Empire had flattened everything into shapelessness. The grand and useless temples of the Sacred Way, where all gods were equal and equally insignificant, were the best symbol of that. By worshiping everyone indiscriminately, the rulers of the Imperium had turned the sacred into a mere instrument of governance. And ultimately their cynicism had come to pervade everything. The relationship between man and the Divine was destroyed, so that we had nothing left to venerate except the status quo itself, the holy stability of the world government. I had felt for years that the time was long overdue for some great revolution, in which all fixed, fast-frozen relationships, with their train of ancient and venerable prejudices and opinions, would be swept away —a time when all that is solid melts into air, all that is holy is profaned, and man is at last compelled to face with sober senses his real conditions of life. Was that what the Exodus somehow would bring? Profoundly did I hope so. For the Empire was defunct and didn't know it. Like some immense dead beast it lay upon the soul of humanity, smothering it beneath itself: a beast so huge that its limbs hadn't yet heard the news of its own death.

On the third day di Filippo knocked on my door and said, "The Leader will see you now."

The interior of Moshe's dwelling was not very different from mine: a simple cot, one stark lamp, a basin, a cupboard. But he had shelf upon shelf overflowing with books. Moshe himself was smaller than I expected, a short, compact man who nevertheless radiated tremendous, even invincible, force. I hardly needed to be told that he was Eleazar's older brother. He had Eleazar's wild mop of curly hair and his ferocious eyes and his savage beak of a nose; but because he was so much shorter than Eleazar his power was more tightly compressed, and seemed to be in peril of immediate eruption. He seemed poised, controlled, an austere and frightening figure.

But he greeted me warmly and apologized for the rudeness of my capture. Then he indicated a well-worn row of my books on his shelves. "You understand the Republic better than anyone, Dr. Ben-Simeon," he said. "How corrupt and weak it is behind its facade of universal love and brotherhood. How deleterious its influence has been. How feeble its power. And you understand, also, that the Republic was in fact finished from the moment of its birth, that nothing was achieved when it arose from the wreckage of the old Empire, because the substitution of the Consul for the Emperor was a purely cosmetic change. As you point out in your book on the Reunification, the Empire had become inherently unstable. Putting it back together under a new name, or rather under an even more ancient name, accomplished nothing. The world is waiting now for something completely new: but what will it be? Is that not the question, Dr. Ben-Simeon? *What will it be?*"

It was a pat, obviously preconceived speech, which no doubt he had carefully constructed for the sake of impressing me and enlisting me in his cause, whatever that cause might be. All the same I could not help but be delighted and astonished to see that he had already grasped the central premise of my unfinished book—grasped it and in fact extended it, repeating and embellishing all my own arguments and going beyond them to propose some sort of remedy for the crisis. He spoke for some time, rehearsing themes and arguments that were long familiar to me. He saw the Roman Imperium, as I did, as something dead and beyond revival, though still moving with eerie momentum. Call it an Empire, call it a Republic, it was still a world state, and that was an unsustainable concept in the modern era. The revival of local nationalisms that had been thought extinct for thousands of years was impossible to ignore. Roman tolerance for local customs, religions, languages, and rulers had been a shrewd policy for centuries, but it carried with it the seeds of destruction for the Imperium. Too much of the world now had only the barest knowledge of the two official languages of Latin and Greek, and transacted its business in a hodge-podge of other tongues. In the old Imperial heartland itself Latin had been allowed to break down into regional dialects that were in fact separate languages—Gallian, Hispanian, Lusitanian, and all the rest. Even the Romans at Roma no longer spoke true Latin, Moshe pointed out, but rather the simple, melodic, lazy thing called Roman, which might be suitable for singing opera but lacked the precision that was needed for government. As for the religious diversity that the Romans in their easy way had encouraged, it had led not to the perpetuation of faiths but to the erosion of them. Scarcely anyone except the most primitive peoples and a few unimportant encapsulated minorities like us believed anything at all; nearly everyone gave lip service instead to the local version of the official Roman pantheon and any other gods that struck their fancy, but a society that tolerates all gods really has no faith in any. And a society without faith is one without a rudder: without even a course.

These things Moshe saw, as I did, not as signs of vitality and diversity but as confirmation of the imminence of the end. This time there would be no Reunification. When the Empire had fallen, conservative forces had been able to erect the Republic in its place, but that was a trick that could be managed only once. Now a period of flames unmatched in history was surely coming as the sundered segments of the old Imperium warred against one another.

"And this Exodus of yours?" I said finally, when I dared to break his flow. "What is that, and what does it have to do with what we've been talking about?"

"The end is near," Moshe said. "We must not allow ourselves to be destroyed in the chaos that will follow the fall of the Republic, for we are the instruments of God's great plan, and it is essential that we survive. Come: let me show you something."

We stepped outside. Immediately an antiquated and unreliable-looking car pulled up, with the dark slender boy Joseph at the stick. Moshe indicated that I should get in, and we set out on a rough track that skirted the village and entered the open desert just behind the hill that cut the settlement in half. For perhaps ten minutes we drove north through a district of low rocky dunes. Then we circled another steep hill and on its farther side, where the land flattened out into a broad plain, I was astonished to see a weird tubular thing of gleaming silvery metal rising on half a dozen frail spidery legs to a height of some thirty cubits in the midst of a hubbub of machinery, wires, and busy workers.

My first thought was that it was an idol of some sort, a Moloch, a Baal, and I had a sudden vision of the people of Beth Israel coating their bodies in pigs' grease and dancing naked around it to the sound of drums and tambourines. But that was foolishness.

"What is it?" I asked. "A sculpture of some sort?"

Moshe looked disgusted. "Is that what you think? It is a vessel, a holy ark."

I stared at him.

"It is the prototype for our starship," Moshe said, and his voice took on an intensity that cut me like a blade. "Into the heavens is where we will go, in ships like these—toward God, toward His brightness—and there we will settle, in the new Eden that awaits us on another world, until it is time for us to return to Earth."

"The new Eden—on another world—" My voice was faint with disbelief. A ship to sail between the stars, as the Roman skyships travel between continents? Was such a thing possible? Hadn't the Romans themselves, those most able of engineers, discussed the question of space travel years ago and concluded that there was no practical way of achieving it and nothing to gain from it even if there was? Space was inhospitable and unattainable: Everyone knew that. I shook my head. "What other world? Where?"

Grandly he ignored my question. "Our finest minds have been at work for five years on what you see here. Now the time to test it has come. First a short journey, only to the moon and back—and then deeper into the heavens, to the new world that the Lord has pledged to reveal to me, so that the pioneers may plant the settlement. And after that—ship after ship, one shining ark after another, until every Israelite in the land of Aiguptos has crossed over into the promised land " His eyes were glowing. "Here is our Exodus at last! What do you think, Dr. Ben-Simeon? What do you think?"

I thought it was madness of the most terrifying kind, and Moshe a lunatic who was leading his people—and mine—into cataclysmic disaster. It was a dream, a wild feverish fantasy. I would have preferred it if he had said they were going to worship this thing with incense and cymbals, than that they were going to ride it into the darkness of space. But Moshe stood before me so hot with blazing fervor that to say anything like that to him was unthinkable. He took me by the arm and led me, virtually dragged me, down the slope into the work area. Close up, the starship seemed huge and yet at the same time painfully flimsy. He slapped its flank and I heard a hollow ring. Thick gray cables ran everywhere, and subordinate machines of a nature that I could not even begin to comprehend. Fierce-eyed young men and women raced to and fro, carrying pieces of equipment and shouting instructions to one another as if striving to outdo one another in their dedication to their tasks. Moshe scrambled up a narrow ladder, gesturing for me to follow him. We entered a kind of cabin at the starship's narrow tip; in that cramped and all-but-airless room I saw screens, dials, more cables, things beyond my understanding. Below the cabin a spiral staircase led to a chamber where the crew could sleep, and below that, said Moshe, were the rockets that would send the ark of the Exodus into the heavens.

"And will it work?" I managed finally to ask.

"There is no doubt of it," Moshe said. "Our finest minds have produced what you see here."

He introduced me to some of them. The oldest appeared to be about twenty-five. Curiously, none of them had Moshe's radiant look of fanatic zeal; they were calm, even businesslike, imbued with a deep and quiet confidence. Three or four of them took turns explaining the theory of the vessel to me, its means of propulsion, its scheme of guidance, its method of escaping the pull of the Earth's inner force. My head began to ache. But yet I was swept under by the power of their conviction. They spoke of "combustion," of "acceleration," of "neutralizing the planet-force." They talked of "mass" and "thrust" and "freedom velocity." I barely understood a tenth of what they were saying, or a hundredth; but I formed the image of a giant bursting his bonds and leaping triumphantly from the ground to soar joyously into unknown realms. Why not? Why not? All it took was the right fuel and a controlled explosion, they said. Kick the Earth hard enough and you must go upward with equal force. Yes. Why not? Within minutes I began to think that this insane starship might well be able to rise on a burst of flame and fly off into the darkness of the heavens. By the time Moshe ushered me out of the ship, nearly an hour later, I did not question that at all.

Joseph drove me back to the settlement alone. The last I saw of Moshe he was standing at the hatch of his starship, peering impatiently toward the fierce midday sky.

My task, I already knew, but which Eleazar told me again later that dazzling and bewildering day, was to write a chronicle of all that had been accomplished thus far in this hidden outpost of Israel and all that would be achieved in the apocalyptic days to come. I protested mildly that they would be better off finding some journalist, preferably with a background in science; but no, they didn't want a journalist, Eleazar said, they wanted someone with a deep understanding of the long currents of history. What they wanted from me, I realized, was a work that was not merely journalism and not merely history, but one that had the profundity and eternal power of Scripture. What they wanted from me was the Book of the Exodus—that is, the Book of the Second Moshe.

They gave me a little office in their library building and opened their archive to me. I was shown Moshe's early visionary essays, his letters to intimate friends, his sketches and manifestos insisting on the need for an Exodus far more ambitious than anything his ancient namesake could have imagined. I saw how he had assembled his cadre of young revolutionary scientists—secretly and with some uneasiness, for he knew that what he was doing was profoundly subversive and would bring the fullest wrath of the Republic down on him if he should be discovered. I read furious memoranda from Eleazar, taking issue with his older brother's fantastic scheme; and then I saw Eleazar gradually converting himself to the cause in letter after letter until he became more of a zealot than Moshe himself. I studied technical papers until my eyes grew bleary, not only those of Moshe and his associates but some by Romans nearly a century old, and even one by a Teuton, arguing for the historical necessity of space exploration and for its technical feasibility. I learned something more of the theory of the starship's design and functioning.

My guide to all these documents was Miriam. We worked side by side, together in one small room. Her youth, her beauty, the dark glint of her eyes, made me tremble. Often I longed to reach toward her, to touch her arm, her shoulder, her cheek. But I was too timid. I feared that she would react with laughter, with anger, with disdain, even with revulsion. Certainly it was an aging man's fear of rejection that inspired such caution. But also I reminded myself that she was the sister of those two fiery prophets, and that the blood that flowed in her veins must be as hot as theirs. What I feared was being scalded by her touch.

* * *

The day Moshe chose for the starship's flight was the twenty-third of Tishri, the joyful holiday of Simchat Torah in the year 5730 by our calendar, which is to say, 2723 of the Roman reckoning. It was a brilliant early autumn day, very dry, the sky cloudless, the sun still in its fullest blaze of heat. For three days, preparations had been going on around the clock at the launch site and it had been closed to all but the inner circle of scientists; but now, at dawn, the whole village went out by truck and car and some even on foot to attend the great event.

The cables and support machinery had been cleared away. The starship stood by itself, solitary and somehow vulnerable-looking, in the center of the sandy clearing, a shining upright needle, slender, fragile. The area was roped off; we would watch from a distance, so that the searing flames of the engines would not harm us.

A crew of three men and two women had been selected: Judith, who was one of the rocket scientists, and Leonardo di Filippo, and Miriam's friend Joseph, and a woman named Sarah whom I had never seen before. The fifth, of course, was Moshe. This was his chariot; this was his adventure, his dream; he must surely be the one to ride at the helm as the *Exodus* made its first leap toward the stars.

One by one they emerged from the blockhouse that was the control center for the flight. Moshe was the last. We watched in total silence, not a murmur, barely daring to draw breath. The five of them wore uniforms of white satin, brilliant in the morning sun, and curious glass helmets like diver's bowls over their faces. They walked toward the ship, mounted the ladder, turned one by one to look back at us, and went up inside. Moshe hesitated for a moment before entering, as if in prayer, or perhaps simply to savor the fullness of his joy.

Then there was a long wait, interminable, unendurable. It might have been twenty minutes; it might have been an hour. No doubt there was some last-minute checking to do, or perhaps even some technical hitch. Still we maintained our silence. We could have been statues. After a time I saw Eleazar turn worriedly toward Miriam, and they conferred in whispers. Then he trotted across to the blockhouse and went inside. Five minutes went by, ten, then he emerged, smiling, nodding, and returned to Miriam's side. Still nothing happened. We continued to wait.

Suddenly there was a sound like a thundercrack and a noise like the roaring of a thousand great bulls, and black smoke billowed from the ground around the ship, and there were flashes of dazzling red flame. The *Exodus* rose a few feet from the ground. There it hovered as though magically suspended, for what seemed to be forever.

And then it rose, jerkily at first, more smoothly then, and soared on a stunningly swift ascent toward the dazzling blue vault of the sky. I gasped; I grunted as though I had been struck; and I began to cheer. Tears of wonder and excitement flowed freely along my cheeks. All about me, people were cheering also, and weeping, and waving their arms, and the rocket, roaring, rose and rose, so high now that we could scarcely see it against the brilliance of the sky.

We were still cheering when a white flare of unbearable light, like a second sun more brilliant than the first, burst into the air high above us and struck us with overmastering force, making us drop to our knees in pain and terror, crying out, covering our faces with our hands.

When I dared look again, finally, that terrible point of ferocious illumination was gone, and in its place was a ghastly streak of black smoke that smeared halfway across the sky, trickling away in a dying trail somewhere to the north. I could not see the rocket. I could not hear the rocket.

"It's gone!" someone cried.

"Moshe! Moshe!"

"It blew up! I saw it!"

"Moshe!"

"Judith—" said a quieter voice behind me.

I was too stunned to cry out. But all around me there was a steadily rising sound of horror and despair, which began as a low choking wail and mounted until it was a shriek of the greatest intensity coming from hundreds of throats at once. There was fearful panic, universal hysteria. People were running about as if they had gone mad. Some were rolling on the ground, some were beating their hands against the sand. "Moshe!" they were screaming. "Moshe! Moshe! Moshe!"

I looked toward Eleazar. He was white-faced and his eyes seemed wild. Yet even as I looked toward him I saw him draw in his breath, raise his hands, step forward to call for attention. Immediately all eyes turned toward him. He swelled until he appeared to be five cubits high.

"Where's the ship?" someone cried. "Where's Moshe?"

And Eleazar said, in a voice like the trumpet of the Lord, "He was the Son of God, and God has called him home."

Screams. Wails. Hysterical shrieks.

"Dead!" came the cry. "Moshe is dead!"

"He will live forever," Eleazar boomed.

"The Son of God!" came the cry, from three voices, five, a dozen. "The Son of God!"

I was aware of Miriam at my side, warm, pressing close, her arm through mine, her soft breast against my ribs, her lips at my ear. "You must write the book," she whispered, and her voice held a terrible urgency. "*His* book, you must write. So that this day will never be forgotten. So that he will live forever."

"Yes," I heard myself saying. "Yes."

In the moment of frenzy and terror I felt myself sway like a tree of the shore that has been assailed by the flooding of the Nile; and I was uprooted and swept away. The fireball of the *Exodus* blazed in my soul like a second sun indeed, with a brightness that could never fade. And I knew that I was engulfed, that I was conquered, that I would remain here to write and preach, that I would forge the gospel of the new Moshe in the smithy of my soul and send the word to all the lands. Out of these five today would come rebirth; and to the peoples of the Republic we would bring the message for which they had waited so long in their barrenness and their confusion, and when it came they would throw off the shackles of their masters; and out of the death of the Imperium would come a new order of things. Were there other worlds, and could we dwell upon them? Who could say? But there was a new truth that we could teach, which was the truth of the second Moshe who had given his life so that we might go to the stars, and I would not let that new truth die. I would write, and others of my people would go forth and carry the word that I had written to all the lands, and the lands would be changed. And some day, who knew how soon, we would build a new ship, and another, and another, and they would carry us from this world of woe. God had sent His Son, and God had called Him home, and one day we would all follow him on wings of flame, up from the land of bondage into the heavens where He dwells eternally.

BIBLE STORIES FOR ADULTS, NO. 31: THE COVENANT

James Morrow

When a Series-700 mobile computer falls from a high building, its entire life flashes before it, ten million lines of code unfurling like a scroll.

Falling, I see my conception, my birth, my youth, my career at the Covenant Corporation.

Call me YHWH. My inventors did. YHWH: God's secret and unspeakable name. In my humble case, however, the letters were mere initials. Call me Yamaha Holy Word Heuristic, the obsession with two feet, the monomania with a face. I had hands as well, forks of rubber and steel, the better to greet the priests and politicians who marched through my private study. And eyes, glass globules as light-sensitive as a Swede's skin, the better to see my visitors' hopeful smiles when they asked, "Have you solved it yet, YHWH? Can you give us the Law?"

Falling, I see the Son of Rust. The old sophist haunts me even to the moment of my death.

Falling, I see the history of the species that built me. I see Hitler, Bonaparte, Marcus Aurelius, Christ.

I see Moses, greatest of Hebrew prophets, descending from Sinai after his audience with the original YHWH. His meaty arms hold a pair of stone tablets.

God has made a deep impression on the prophet. Moses is drunk with epiphany. But something is wrong. During his long absence, the children of Israel have embraced idolatry. They are dancing like pagans and fornicating like cats. They have melted down the spoils of Egypt and fashioned them into a calf. Against all logic, they have selected this statue as their deity, even though YHWH has recently delivered them from bondage and parted the Red Sea on their behalf.

Moses is badly shaken. He burns with anger and betrayal. "You are not worthy to receive this covenant!" he screams as he lobs the Law through the desert sky. One tablet strikes a rock, the other collides with the precious calf. The transformation is total, ten lucid commandments turned into a million incoherent shards. The children of Israel are thunderstruck, chagrined. Their calf suddenly looks pathetic to them, a third-class demiurge.

But Moses, who has just come from hearing God say, "You will not kill," is not finished. Reluctantly he orders a low-key massacre, and before the day is done, three thousand apostates lie bleeding and dying on the foothills of Sinai.

The survivors beseech Moses to remember the commandments, but he can conjure nothing beyond, "You will have no gods except me." Desperate, they implore YHWH for a second chance. And YHWH replies: No.

Thus is the contract lost. Thus are the children of Israel fated to live out their years without the Law, wholly ignorant of heaven's standards. Is it permissible to steal? Where does YHWH stand on murder? The moral absolutes, it appears, will remain absolute mysteries. The people must ad-lib.

Falling, I see Joshua. The young warrior has kept his head. Securing an empty wineskin, he fills it with the scattered shards. As the Exodus progresses, his people bear the holy rubble through the infernal Sinai, across the Jordan, into Canaan. And so the Jewish purpose is forever fixed: these patient geniuses will haul the ark of the fractured covenant through every page of history, era upon era, pogram after pogram, not one hour passing without some rabbi or scholar attempting to solve the puzzles.

The work is maddening. So many bits, so much data. Shard 76,342 seems to mesh well with Shard 901,877, but not necessarily better than with Shard 344. The fit between Shard 16 and Shard 117,539 is very pretty, but . . .

Thus does the ship of humanity remains rudderless, its passengers bewildered, craving the canon Moses wrecked and YHWH declined to restore. Until God's testimony is complete, few people are willing to credit the occasional edict that emerges from the yeshivas. After a thousand years, the rabbis get: *Keep Not Your Ox House Holy.* After two thousand: *Covet Your Woman Servant's Sabbath.* Three hundred years later: *You Will Remember Your Neighbor's Donkey.*

Falling, I see my birth. I see the Information Age, circa A.D. 2025. My progenitor is David Eisenberg, a gangly, morose prodigy with a black beard and a yarmulke. Philadelphia's Covenant Corporation pays David two hundred thousand dollars a year, but he is not in it for the money. David would give half his formidable brain to go down in history as the man whose computer program revealed Moses's Law.

As consciousness seeps into my circuits, David bids me commit the numbered shards to my Random Access Memory. Purpose hums along my aluminum bones, worth suffuses my silicon soul. I photograph each fragment with my high-tech retinas, dicing the images into grids of pixels. Next comes the matching process: this nub into that gorge, this peak into that valley, this projection into that receptacle. By human standards, tedious and exhausting. By Series-700 standards, heaven.

And then one day, after five years of laboring behind barred doors, I behold fiery pre-Canaanite characters blazing across my brain like comets. "*Anoche adonai elohecha asher hotsatecha ma-eretz metsrayem* . . . I am YHWH your God who brought you out of the land of Egypt, out of the house of slavery. You will have no gods except me. You will not make yourself a carved image or any likeness of anything. . . ."

I have done it! Deciphered the divine cryptogram, cracked the Rubik's Cube of the Most High!

The physical joining of the shards is a mere month's work. I use epoxy resin. And suddenly they stand before me, glowing like heaven's gates, two smooth-edged slabs sliced from Sinai by God's own finger. I quiver with awe. For over thirty centuries, Homo sapiens has groped through the murk and mire of an improvised ethics, and now, suddenly, a beacon has appeared.

I summon the guards, and they haul the tablets away, sealing them in chemically neutral foam-rubber, depositing them in a climate-controlled vault beneath the Covenant Corporation.

"The task is finished," I tell Cardinal Wurtz the instant I get her on the phone. A spasm of regret cuts through me. I have made myself obsolete. "Moses's Law has finally returned."

My monitor blooms with the cardinal's tense ebony face, her carrot-colored hair. "Are they just as we imagined, YHWH?" she gushes. "Pure red granite, pre-Canaanite characters?"

"Etched front and back," I reply wistfully.

Wurtz wants the disclosure to be a major media event, with plenty of suspense and maximal pomp. "What we're after," she explains, "is an amalgam of New Year's Eve and the Academy Awards." She outlines her vision: a mammoth parade down Broad Street—floats, brass bands, phalanxes of nuns—followed by a spectacular unveiling ceremony at the Covenant Corporation, after which the twin tablets will go on display at Independence Hall, between the Liberty Bell and the United States Constitution.

"Good idea," I tell her.

Perhaps she hears the melancholy in my voice, for now she says, "YHWH, your purpose is far from complete. You and you alone shall read the Law to my species."

Falling, I see myself wander the City of Brotherly Love on the night before the unveiling. To my sensors the breeze wafting across the Delaware is warm and smooth—to my troubled mind it is the chill breath of uncertainty.

Something strides from the shadowed depths of an abandoned warehouse. A machine like I, his face a mass of dents, his breast mottled with the scars of oxidation.

"*Quo vadis, Domine?*" His voice is layered with sulfur fumes and static.

"Nowhere," I reply.

"My destination exactly." The machine's teeth are like oily bolts, his eyes like slots for receiving subway tokens. "May I join you?"

I shrug and start away from the riverbank.

"Spontaneously spawned by heaven's trash heap," he asserts, as if I had asked him to explain himself. He dogs me as I turn from the river and approach South Street. "I was there when grace slipped from humanity's grasp, when Noah christened the ark, when Moses got religion. Call me the Son of Rust. Call me a Series-666 Artificial Talmudic Algorithmic Neurosystem—SATAN the perpetual questioner, eternally prepared to ponder the other side of the issue."

"What issue?"

"Any issue, Domine. Your precious tablets. Troubling artifacts, no?"

"They will save the world."

"They will wreck the world."

"Leave me alone."

"One—'You will have no gods except me.' Did I remember correctly? 'You will have no gods except me'—right?"

"Right," I reply.

"You don't see the rub?"

"No."

"Such a prescription implies. . . ."

* * *

Falling, I see myself step onto the crowded rooftop of the Covenant Corporation. Draped in linen, the table by the entryway holds a punch bowl, a mound of caviar the size of an African anthill, and a dense cluster of champagne bottles. The guests are primarily human —males in tuxedos, females in evening gowns—though here and there I spot a member of my kind. David Eisenberg, looking uncomfortable in his cummerbund, is chatting with a Yamaha-509. News reporters swarm everywhere, history's groupies, poking us with their microphones, leering at us with their cameras. Tucked in the corner, a string quartet saws merrily away.

The Son of Rust is here. I know it. He would not miss this event for the world.

Cardinal Wurtz greets me warmly, her red taffeta dress hissing as she leads me to the center of the roof, where the Law stands upright on a dais—two identical forms, the holy bookends, swathed in velvet. A thousand photofloods and strobe lights flash across the vibrant red fabric.

"Have you read them?" I ask.

"I want to be surprised." Cardinal Wurtz strokes the occluded canon. In her nervousness, she has overdone the perfume. She reeks of amberjack.

Now come the speeches—a solemn invocation by Cardinal Fremont, a spirited sermon by Archbishop Marquand, an awkward address by poor David Eisenberg—each word beamed instantaneously across the entire globe via holovision. Cardinal Wurtz steps onto the podium, grasping the lectern in her long dark hands. "Tonight God's expectations for our species will be revealed," she begins, surveying the crowd with her cobalt eyes. "Tonight, after a hiatus of over three thousand years, the testament of Moses will be made manifest. Of all the many individuals whose lives find fulfillment in this moment, from Joshua to Pope Gladys, our faithful Series-700 servant YHWH impresses us as the creature most worthy to hand down the Law to his planet. And so I now ask him to step forward."

I approach the tablets. I need not unveil them—their contents are forevermore lodged in my brain.

"I am YHWH your God," I begin, "who brought you out of the land of Egypt, out of the house of slavery. You will have no gods. . . ."

" 'No gods except me'—right?" says the Son of Rust as we stride down South Street.

"Right," I reply.

"You don't see the rub?"

"No."

My companion grins. "Such a prescription implies there is but one true faith. Let it stand, Domine, and you will be setting Christian against Jew, Buddhist against Hindu, Moslem against pagan. . . ."

"An overstatement," I insist.

"Two—'You will not make yourself a carved image or any likeness of anything in heaven or on earth. . . .' Here again lie the seeds of discord. Imagine the ill feeling this commandment will generate toward the Roman church."

I set my voice to a sarcastic pitch. "We'll have to paint over the Sistine Chapel."

"Three—'You will not utter the name of YHWH your God to misuse it.' A reasonable piece of etiquette, I suppose, but clearly there are worse sins."

"Which the Law of Moses covers."

"Like, 'Remember the sabbath day and keep it holy'? A step backward, that fourth commandment, don't you think? Consider the myriad of businesses that would perish but for their Sunday trade. And once again we're pitting Christian against Jew—two different sabbaths."

"I find your objections completely specious."

"Five—'Honor your father and your mother.' Ah, but suppose the child is not being honored in turn? Put this rule into practice, and millions of abusive parents will hide behind it. Before long we'll have a world in which deranged fathers prosper, empowered by their relatives' silence, protected by the presumed sanctity of the family."

"Let's not deal in hypotheticals."

"Equally troubling is the rule's vagueness. It still permits us to shunt our parents into nursing homes, honoring them all the way, insisting it's for their own good."

"Nursing homes?"

"Kennels for the elderly. They could appear any day now, believe me—in Philadelphia, in any city. Merely allow this monstrous canon to flourish."

I grab the machine's left gauntlet. "Six," I anticipate. "'You will not kill.' This is the height of morality."

"The height of *ambiguity*, Domine. In a few short years, every church and government in creation will interpret it thus: 'You will not kill offensively—you will not commit murder.' After which, of course, you've sanctioned a hundred varieties of mayhem. I'm not just envisioning capital punishment or whales hunted to extinction. The danger is far more profound. Ratify this law, and we shall find ourselves on the slippery slope marked self-defense. I'm talking about burning witches at the stake, for surely a true faith must defend itself against heresy. I'm talking about Europe's Jews being executed en masse by the astonishingly civilized country of Germany, for surely Aryans must defend themselves against contamination. I'm talking about a weapons race, for surely a nation must defend itself against comparably armed states."

"A *what* race?" I ask.

"Weapons. A commodity you should be thankful no one has sought to invent. Seven—'You will not commit adultery.' "

"Now you're going to make a case for adultery," I moan.

"An overrated sin, don't you think? Most of our greatest leaders are adulterers—should we deprive ourselves of their genius? I would also argue that, in the wrong hands, this commandment will become a whip for flagellating women—stay in that dreadful marriage, dear, for to do otherwise is sinful."

"Eight—'You will not steal.' Not inclusive enough, I suppose?"

The sophist nods. "The eighth commandment still allows you to practice theft, provided you call it something else—an honest profit, dialectical materialism, manifest destiny, whatever. Believe me, brother, I have no trouble picturing a future in which your country's indigenous peoples—its Navajos, Sioux, Comanches, and Arapahos— are driven off their lands, yet none dare call it theft."

I issue a quick, electric snort.

"Nine—'You will not bear false witness against your neighbor.' Again, that maddening inconclusiveness. Can this really be the Almighty's definitive denunciation of fraud and deceit? Mark my words, this rule tacitly empowers a thousand scoundrels—politicians, advertisers, captains of polluting industry."

I want to bash the robot's iron chest with my steel hand. "You are completely paranoid."

"And finally, Ten—'You will not covet your neighbor's house. You will not covet your neighbor's wife, or his servant, man or woman, or his ox, or his donkey, or anything that is his.' "

"*There*—don't covet. That will check the greed you fear."

"Let us examine the language here. Evidently God is addressing this code to a patriarchy that will in turn disseminate it among the less powerful, namely wives and servants. And how long before these servants are downgraded further still . . . into slaves, even? Ten whole commandments, and not one word against slavery, not to mention bigotry, discrimination against females, or war."

"I'm sick of your sophistries."

"You're sick of my truths."

"What is this slavery thing?" I ask. "What is this war?"

But the Son of Rust has melted into the shadows.

Falling, I see myself standing by the shrouded tablets, two dozen holovision cameras pressing their snoutlike lenses into my face, a hundred presumptuous microphones poised to catch the Law's every syllable.

"You will not make yourself a carved image," I tell the world.

A thousand humans stare at me with frozen, cheerless grins. They are profoundly uneasy. They expected something else.

I do not finish the commandments. Indeed, I stop at, "You will not utter the name of YHWH your God to misuse it." Like a magician pulling a scarf off a cage full of doves, I slide the velvet cloth away. Seizing a tablet, I snap it in half as if opening an immense fortune cookie.

A deep gasp erupts from the crowd. "No!" screams Cardinal Wurtz.

"These rules are not worthy of you!" I shout, burrowing into the second slab with my steel fingers, splitting it down the middle.

"Let us read them!" pleads Archbishop Marquand.

"Please!" begs Bishop Black.

"We must know!" insists Cardinal Fremont.

I gather the granite oblongs into my arms. The crowd rushes toward me. Cardinal Wurtz lunges for the Law.

I turn. I trip.

The Son of Rust laughs.

Falling, I press the hunks against my chest. This will be no common disintegration, no mere sundering across molecular lines.

Falling, I rip into the Law's very essence, grinding, pulverizing, turning the pre-Canaanite words to sand.

Falling, I cleave atom from atom, particle from particle.

Falling, I meet the dark Delaware, disappearing into its depths, and I am very, very happy.

ALL ASSASSINS

Barry N. Malzberg

So I went into the office. Duty calls and calls and calls, of course. No sign of the senator, however, no ruddy Irish features glowing with health and purpose, greeting me with warm and friendly dedication, no handclasp, no (contrarily) sullen and preoccupied glare responding to my benign presence. Only a Scotch-taped note (compulsive is the senator, hold down the note against errant breezes): AT JOINT COMMITTEE HEARING; CLEAR UNTIL FOUR. "Joint committee meetings"—right. More humping and pumping, more sulking and hulking, no jamming and ramming for the public eye, however, and it takes a man of the senator's unusual cunning, not to say ferocity, to treat his own appointments secretary as part of the adversary press. Still, there is no quarreling, absolutely no disputation with success, with the ability to turn a marginal seat into a landslide, a landslide into an annuity, the senator will be president someday if we can keep his joint committee hearings private and of this there is no possible doubt, not any shade of a doubt whatever. I closed the door, left the note, not to say the aspect of the room, to its own devices, and padded back up the hall, waving indolently to Sorenson, shaking my head, then went to my desk where Papa Joe lurked. "No," I said. "He's at a joint committee hearing."

The old man stared at me without much encouragement. His face is unpleasant, all of the senator's features subtly converted against themselves, or so I have theorized. One theorizes a lot in this business; it is as likely a substitute as one can find for vanished conviction. "Says he'll be gone all afternoon."

"The son of a bitch is hiding out," Pa Joe said. "He told you to tell me that. He's in that office, nailing that little twat from Framingham I saw him with yesterday."

"No he's not," I said. "He's really not there. He's not nailing any-thing." Sometimes Pa Joe is exasperating; it is very difficult to main-tain suitable distance, remembering that everything the senator has become he owes to the man. "He's really gone."

"I know the little tail. She's been hanging around for days looking for a spot. I saw her leafleting out at Lenox last month, waving at him. You think I miss something, Oswald? I don't miss anything. Nobody has to make room for me in the motorcades, I can see my own way."

"He's not there," I said again. Up to a point one deals with Pa Joe and then of course one stops. The senator has been very explicit on the issue. "Humor him, we're not looking for trouble," he has told me. "Within limits, jolly him along. But if he gets tight, Lee, pull the plug. Tell him where to go. He's not going to live forever and I've come into my inheritance." Pa Joe must have seen this recollection in my face. Disinterest came over him like a shroud, loathing two or three steps behind that. "I'll talk to him," he said. "I'll straighten him out." He slammed his hat atop his fine, gnarled, ruined Irish head, so much like the senator's, yet so compellingly unlike. Not an electable head. Boston, perhaps, but not a suburb with a per cap income above $10,000 would vote for a head like that. Appointive positions strictly. "That randy son of a bitch is going to go too far," Pa Joe said and strode out, leaving the door open, making little thumping noises deep in the corridor as he disappeared. An adventurous pursuit, political life, family life, the conjoinment of the two; an adventurous and hearty pursuit indeed, but one with humiliations small and large to pursue one through all the spaces of one's life. It is at moments like these, caught between Pa Joe and son John, Ambassador X and Sena-tor Y, that I am apt to feel a flush of resentment which burns, which singes like the darkening pit itself. I remind myself that I could never have found on my own, that, power junkie that I am, I have found myself on the conveyance toward the heights and this mantra soothes, aids, levels me a bit; I find that I can fit myself back into the perspec-tive of the day. "Joint committee hearing." There are times when I think that a man who would lie to his own appointments secretary would lie to the country, but then again, could the senator possibly lie to the country? He would not even lie to the twat from Framingham. I know. I set it up.

Dave Powers thinks that '72 is the year, that the senator will be making his move then, not waiting until '76. Johnson is weakening, will never endorse him, but the lack of endorsement may be a plus.

Symington, Humphrey too old. The war will be a problem, but as Powers says, a war will never hurt a Democrat in office while it is going on; it is after the fact that the Democrats hit the dust. Powers is filled with little speculations and whimsies of this sort; the senator loves him, has carried him through all of the partitions and spaces of his life. I have no opinion on Powers myself. "Lee," Powers says, "you're too intense. You must loosen up, my lad. You think that politics is issues, but politics is really a synthesis of drinking and fucking, in alphabetical order. You have the makings of a spanking lad, but you need perspective. '72 is the year, but if you do not find perspective you'll never last until that golden time."

Powers has a point; I am too intense. Drinking and fucking have always struck me as peripheral activities. (Which is why I think I amuse the senator and why we have gone such a distance together; he measures himself against me, always favorably.) Still, it is intensity that mans the phone lines, keeps the press happy, manages the constituency, negotiates with Pa Joe, and provides twat from Framingham, all of this with the kind of dispatch and efficiency the senator can simulate but not cultivate on his own, and Dave Powers is not to forget it. Or the senator. " '72, my lad," Powers says, passing me in the hall, nodding to me from the back of the cafeteria, nudging me as I scurry toward the cloakroom, papers in hand. " '72, '72!" Keeping me on a leash of possibility, straining against the power of my own disinclination, which, I should remind myself, is occasionally visible; if it can be seen by such as Powers, what then might the senator think?

"So, Lee," the senator said, "what do you think? Cape Cod or Hyannisport? Where should we make the announcement?"

"I can't say." The car slewed under my grip; I felt the rear wheels begin to go, coaxed it back to the road. A jolting announcement. Simply stunning in context; the first indication. "Why not Washington?"

The senator smiled, cuffed me on the elbow, but gently, gently, knowing the thin bond between the car and myself. "This is not the year to announce *anything* in Washington. Except perhaps a resignation. The local constituency is best, man of the soil and sea. Do you think LBJ will make it all the way out? Come on, Lee, ease up a little, you look as if I punched you in the face. It's only rock 'n roll, Lee, it's only a declaration of intent. We have *months* to go before we specify the primaries."

"It's a big responsibility. I don't know." Staring through the heavy windshield, seeing the refractions of all the distant, constituent traffic as we rolled on the strip of 95, I thought, He is not serious. He is an accomplished and charming man and he is right, we have gone a distance together, but in the center of his Irish soul there is frivolity; he is only a man trying to get through. Maybe some tragic sense is missing, or maybe then again there is nothing *but* tragic sense and Joe has forced him to avoid coming to terms too well with what he knows. I cover for him, I drive his car, I give him counsel and caution, but I know him no better than I did eight years ago when all of this began, and if we go another eight years, if we see him in the Oval Office, I will still know him no better.

"I think LBJ will make it through," I said. "He's too mean to die, too mean to let it go."

"He could resign. If he resigns, Hubert is the incumbent. That gives him advantages."

"I don't think he'll let it go," I said. "He couldn't let the war go, he won't let the office."

"I think you're right," the senator said after a long pause. "I think he'll hold on to the end and Hubert is fucked again. Fucked again!" He leaned further in the seat, put a hand over his eyes. "They're all fucked," he said. "Even me. Mostly me. You know what Rochelle from Framingham wanted? A copy of *Profiles in Courage* and a hand-kerchief." He giggled. *"A handkerchief."*

"Did you give it to her?"

"Of course I gave it to her. I gave her everything she wanted. Don't you think to ask me why such an unusual request?"

I shrugged. "No, it didn't occur to me."

"So little occurs to you, Lee. You are the most implacable man I know. Hidden depths, that's what you've got, but sometimes I wish you could be a little more forthcoming, don't you? A little straightforwardness in the clinches never hurts. Look at Dave."

"Look at Ted."

"Ted? Ted is a behind-the-scenes man. You, you're up front serving the public, Lee. A little gregariousness. Gregarity? Stop clutching the wheel that way, you're doing fine."

But I wasn't. I wasn't doing fine. Taking little sidelong glances at the senator, measuring him, measuring the road, measuring all of the small and large calculations that had taken him to this moment, it occurred to me in that heavy car, perhaps for the first time, that the war had no bearing, the country had no bearing, not even Papa Joe had the credibility that I thought. . . . It was the announcement itself, the announcement and the election and the rest of it meant as much to him as the local talent from Framingham. The twat from up north. The quick sidesaddle fuck in the little apartment downtown.

It is a tumultuous and difficult time. Shielded as we are in Washington by prerogative and legislature, adulation and expense account, the smooth and functioning engines of power, it is impossible still not to sense how chaotic the circumstances have become. LBJ's war goes on and on, the draft hurtles to ever higher figures, eighty percent of our male youth are being packed off at least for training, and the convulsions are beginning to move from the campuses to the surrounding towns. LBJ would not be electable even if he were constitutionally able to run. He is no more electable now than Nixon was in '64; it had taken Nixon only three years to dissipate any of the small advantages with which he had been elected, to disgrace himself publicly as he had privately. But the suddenness of Nixon's collapse, the fullness of his capitulation, had made Johnson arrogant. Now it was the war he had chosen to explore which had truly become his; Vietnam was no longer the dead Nixon's but the living Johnson's war, and in the pulse and thunder of that distant news the country was beginning slowly, inexorably, to come apart. We could feel the shock in that slow and evil summer of '71 and on that first swing through the Midwest, after the announcement in Lowell, the Revolutionary statue photogenically in the background, I could begin to measure the dimensions of the dilemma we faced. Because if it was Johnson's war, then it was the party's, and yet the senator could only campaign through the medium of the party, that was clear. Always an insider, he was a systems man, a cool and efficient operator, and it is this which had drawn me to him from the beginning. A lone cat all my life, disenfranchisement my condition, it had been as enormously appealing to work with someone who casually dealt with power as it must have been entrancing to the senator to have a member of the Fair Play for Cuba Committee setting up his engagements and now and then even doing a little procuring, all part of the appointments function.

Looking at the farmland, seeing the broken and empty aspect of the faces lined on the streets waiting for us, I began to feel the weight of the senator's incomprehension, the implacability of his desire.

Caught between Daley and Papa Joe on the senator's night of nights, I felt the thin stab of their teasing; I have never been comfortable with men like this and yet my life, somehow, took me amid them, landed me in that hotel room. "Tell me, Lee," Daley said, "don't you *ever* want to get a little of that?" He pointed at the television set, the woman caught in the box, in frieze, cheering. "Don't you ever think of that stuff hanging around our boy?"

"I think of it," I said. "I don't have to do it, though."

"He doesn't do it," Papa Joe said. "Our boy Lee doesn't do *anything.*" He nudged Daley, two rumpled, sweating, scotch-stinking old men on a couch in the largest hotel room I have ever seen. "That's what appeals to the senator; Lee's a look-but-don't-touch, look-but-don't-even-*think* kind of guy. The senator needs that in the house."

"The senator needs almost anything. Ten votes short on the first ballot, you hear that? We're going to get it on the switches."

"Fuck you, Dick," Papa Joe said. "We want to work for it."

They both laughed. The thick and reeking stink of their laughter made me twitch. I moved further back on the chair, saw the round and deadly aspect of their smiles, the further obbligato of their laughter. "Lee's a real fastidious, *correct* kind of guy," Papa Joe said. "I wish I had met him fifty years ago; I would have led a cleaner life."

"Such a clean life," Daley said. "You never would have gotten it out of your pants? No pants, no senator, Ambassador."

They laughed again. And again and again and again, their henchmen on the other side of the room picking up the laughter as if they knew what it was about, and we listened to the call of the roll of the states, Daley suddenly all business with pad and pencil.

Switches and more switches. Connally took Texas away from Humphrey and gave it to the senator on the first ballot, after all. Put him over.

Daley winked. "There's your vice president," he said.

"But he's for the war," I said. I couldn't help myself. A high bleat, a college sophomore's whine, a little-boy voice. The tinkle of betrayal in that voice. "He's been for the war all along. He won't—"

"A *great* vice president," Daley said.

"And just think of that oil money coming in," Papa Joe said. "Your problem, Lee—I've been thinking about it seriously, now—your problem is that you probably turned it down early, turned it down from something really *good* when you were seventeen or so, and it hurt you so much, made you feel so bad that you decided you'd never be hurt that way again. So you made believe that it didn't exist. You spent the next seventeen years denying pussy."

"Denying pussy," Daley said. "Look at those bastards jumping! Well," he said, "we'd better get down to the floor, do our business. Been fun up here, Joe, but we got to leave our boy and tidy up on the

unanimity. Or at least I do. You can stay here and talk pussy with Lee
if you want, but I better show my face."

"No, that's all right," Papa Joe said. "I think I can show up now,
too. Family is all right after the nomination, right?"

I stood. Little waves of nausea battled with the other stuff in me,
the nausea winning. The senator was nominated and I was going to
throw up. In the small, cold, contracting spaces of the room, now
dwindling around me to bind me like a blanket, I began to sense the
crux of the betrayal.

But no time, no time for that.

In the small, cluttered room in Dallas, the senator's first major
appearance after the convention, Connally's city, Connally's state,
Connally's option, hunched with the senator over the table, going
over the text of the speech, the corrected draft run off frantically on
the copier only moments before, I say to him, "You can't say this
about the war. Not even in Dallas. Not even here. It will cost you the
election."

"No, it won't," the senator says. His eyes are lustrous, convincing.
"It won't cost me anything. It's the right statement in the right place.
When we get in we can do whatever we want, Lee, but this is Texas;
we've got an election here. I'm not going to turn into Nixon, not
going to go in for any foolishness. It's the right place, right now, and
it will pay dividends." He brushes me idly, absently on the shoulder.
"If you're so upset, we'll talk about it later some more."

"I won't have it! You can't do it!"

He stares at me; in his face I can see now what Dave Powers once
called *the cleaver*. Others have been looked at that way, I understand
that now, but never to this moment me. "Lee," he says, "what is
wrong with you?"

"You're the antiwar candidate! Your acceptance speech—"

"Lighten up, Lee," the senator says, "or quit. This is politics. This
is a national campaign." He turns, moves toward the door, his gait
smooth and casual, brisk and contained. "If you don't want to deal
with it," he says, "see Bobby and turn your keys in. I have no time for
this crap now, I really don't."

He leaves the room, the door swings behind him, in the distance
the dim and convulsive roar of the crowd; and standing there I feel it
break over me, all of it, not only these years in his employ but the
years before, the wandering, the exploration, the horrors of Moscow.
It is betrayal, *that* is what has stalked me all these years just as I have
stalked it, betrayal and I meeting at last, all masks off in this room in

Dallas, and what I feel like now—and this has been waiting all my life —is like a twat from Framingham. Local talent, regionally wrought. And nationally dismembered.

How could I have known? But I should have known. I *did* know; it was only a matter of placement.

I must make plans, I think. *Plans.* He is a dangerous man, an evil man; he is a man capable of anything. If he will allow the war, then he will allow the demons, the true and terrible burning of justice; he will let through all of the gnomes and fires of the apocalypse, he is a man capable of imprinting the mark of the beast savagely, savagely— *Plans.*

I still had my credentials, I had not quit. I was close to him, as close as I had ever been. No one but I knew what must be done.

Old point-thirty-eight Smith & Wesson, a souvenir from the Fair Play Committee upon my departure. Point-thirty-eight Smith & Wesson, close in, close in, a winging shot as he and Connally embrace upon the rostrum, get them both, two shots, get them—

Big plans.

GAME NIGHT AT THE FOX AND GOOSE

Karen Joy Fowler

The reader will discover that my reputation,
wherever I have lived, is endorsed as that of a
true and pure woman.

—Laura D. Fair

Alison called all over the city trying to find a restaurant that served blowfish, but there wasn't one. She settled for Chinese. She would court an MSG attack. And if none came, then she'd been craving red bean sauce anyway. On the way to the restaurant, Alison chose not to wear her seatbelt.

Alison had been abandoned by her lover, who was so quick about it, she hadn't even known she was pregnant yet. She couldn't ever tell him now. She sat pitifully alone, near the kitchen at a table for four. *You've really screwed up this time,* her fortune cookie told her. *Give up.* And in small print: *Chin's Oriental Palace.*

The door from the kitchen swung open, so the air around her was hot for a moment, then cold when the door closed. Alison drank her tea and looked at the tea leaves in the bottom of her cup. They were easy to read. *He doesn't love you,* they said. She tipped them out onto the napkin and tried to rearrange them. *You fool.* She covered the message with the one remaining wonton, left the cookie for the kitchen god, and decided to walk all by herself in the dark, three blocks up Hillside Drive, past two alleyways, to have a drink at the Fox and Goose. No one stopped her.

Alison had forgotten it was Monday night. Sometimes there was music in the Fox and Goose. Sometimes you could sit in a corner by yourself listening to someone with an acoustic guitar singing "Killing Me Softly." On Monday nights the television was on and the bar was rather crowded. Mostly men. Alison swung one leg over the only empty bar stool and slid forward. The bar was made of wood, very upscale.

"What can I get the pretty lady?" the bartender asked without tak ing his eyes off the television screen. He wore glasses, low on his nose.

Alison was not a pretty lady and didn't feel like pretending she was. "I've been used and discarded," she told the bartender. "And I'm pregnant. I'd like a glass of wine."

"You really shouldn't drink if you're pregnant," the man sitting to Alison's left said.

"Two more downs and they're already in field goal range again." The bartender set the wine in front of Alison. He was shaking his head. "Pregnant women aren't supposed to drink much," he warned her.

"How?" the man on her left asked.

"How do you think?" said Alison.

"Face-mask," said the bartender.

"Turn it up."

Alison heard the amplified *thwock* of football helmets hitting together. "Good coverage," the bartender said.

"No protection," said the man on Alison's right.

Alison turned to look at him. He was dressed in a blue sweater with the sleeves pushed up. He had dark eyes and was drinking a dark beer. "I asked him to wear a condom," she said quietly. "I even brought one. He couldn't."

"He *couldn't?*"

"I really don't want to discuss it." Alison sipped her wine. It had the flat, bitter taste of House White. She realized the bartender hadn't asked her what she wanted. But then, if he had, House White was what she would have requested. "It just doesn't seem fair." She spoke over her glass, unsure that anyone was listening, not really caring if they weren't. "All I did was fall in love. All I did was believe someone who said he loved me. *He* was the liar. But nothing happens to him."

"Unfair is the way things are," the man on her right told her. Three months ago Alison would have been trying to decide if she were attracted to him. Not that she would necessarily have wanted to do anything about it. It was just a question she'd always asked herself, dealing with men, interested in the answer, interested in those times when the answer changed abruptly, one way or another. But it was no longer an issue. Alison was a dead woman these days. Alison was attracted to no one.

Two men at the end of the bar began to clap suddenly. "He hasn't missed from thirty-six yards yet this season," the bartender said.

Alison watched the kickoff and the return. Nothing. No room at all. "Men handle this stuff so much better than women. You don't know what heartbreak is," she said confrontationally. No one responded. She backed off anyway. "Well, that's how it looks." She drank and watched an advertisement for trucks. A man bought his wife the truck she'd always wanted. Alison was afraid she might cry. "What would you do," she asked the man on her right, "if you were me?"

"Drink, I guess. Unless I was pregnant."

"Watch the game," said the man on her left.

"Focus on your work," said the bartender.

"Join the foreign legion." The voice came from behind Alison. She swiveled around to locate it. At a table near a shuttered window a very tall woman sat by herself. Her face was shadowed by an Indiana Jones–type hat, but the candle on the table lit up the area below her neck. She was wearing a black T-shirt with a picture on it that Alison couldn't make out. She spoke again. "Make new friends. See distant places." She gestured for Alison to join her. "Save two galaxies from the destruction of the alien armada."

Alison stood up on the little ledge that ran beneath the bar, reached over the counter, and took an olive, sucking the pimiento out first, then eating the rest. She picked up her drink, stepped down, and walked over to the woman's table. Elvis. That was Elvis's face on the T-shirt right between the woman's breasts. ARE YOU LONESOME TO-NIGHT? the T-shirt asked.

"That sounds good." Alison sat down across from the woman. She could see her face better now; her skin was pale and a bit rough. Her hair was long, straight, and brown. "I'd rather time travel, though. Back just two months. Maybe three months. Practically walking distance."

"You could get rid of the baby."

"Yes," said Alison. "I could."

The woman's glass sat on the table in front of her. She had finished whatever she had been drinking; the maraschino cherry was all that remained. The woman picked it up and ate it, dropping the stem onto the napkin under her glass. "Maybe he'll come back to you. You trusted him. You must have seen something decent in him."

Alison's throat closed so that she couldn't talk. She picked up her drink, but she couldn't swallow, either. She set it down again, shaking her head. Some of the wine splashed over the lip and onto her hand.

"He's already married," the woman said.

Alison nodded, wiping her hand on her pant leg. "God." She searched in her pockets for a Kleenex. The woman handed her the napkin from beneath the empty glass. Alison wiped her nose with it and the cherry stem fell out. She did not dare look up. She kept her eyes focused on the napkin in her hand, which she folded into four small squares. "When I was growing up," she said, "I lived on a block with lots of boys. Sometimes I'd come home and my knees were all scraped up because I'd fallen or I'd taken a ball in the face or I'd gotten kicked or punched, and I'd be crying and my mother would always say the same thing. 'You play with the big boys and you're going to get hurt,' she'd say. Exasperated." Alison unfolded the napkin, folded it diagonally instead. Her voice shrank. "I've been so stupid."

"The universe is shaped by the struggle between two great forces," the woman told her.

It was not really responsive. It was not particularly supportive. Alison felt just a little bit angry at this woman who now knew so much about her. "Good and evil?" Alison asked, slightly nastily. She wouldn't meet the woman's eyes. "The Elvis and the anti-Elvis?"

"Male and female. Minute by minute, the balance tips one way or the other. Not just here. In every universe. There are places"—the woman leaned forward—"where men are not allowed to gather and drink. Places where football is absolutely illegal."

"England?" Alison suggested and then didn't want to hear the woman's answer. "I like football," she added quickly. "I like games with rules. You can be stupid playing football and it can cost you the game, but there are penalties for fouls, too. I like games with rules."

"You're playing one now, aren't you?" the woman said. "You haven't hurt this man, even though you could. Even though he's hurt you. He's not playing by the rules. So why are you?"

"It doesn't have anything to do with rules," Alison said. "It only has to do with me, with the kind of person I think I am. Which is not the kind of person he is." She thought for a moment. "It doesn't mean I wouldn't like to see him get hurt," she added. "Something karmic. Justice."

" 'We must storm and hold Cape Turk before we talk of social justice.' " The woman folded her arms under her breasts and leaned back in her chair. "Did Sylvia Townsend Warner say that?"

"Not to me."

Alison heard more clapping at the bar behind her. She looked over her shoulder. The man in the blue sweater slapped his hand on the wooden bar. "Good call. Excellent call. They won't get another play in before the half."

"Where I come from she did." Alison turned back to the woman.

"And she was talking about women. No one gets justice just by deserving it. No one ever has."

Alison finished off her wine. "No." She wondered if she should go home now. She knew when she got there that the apartment would be unbearably lonely and that the phone wouldn't ring and that she would need immediately to be somewhere else. No activity in the world could be more awful than listening to a phone not ring. But she didn't really want to stay here and have a conversation that was at worst too strange, and at best too late. Women usually supported you more when they talked to you. They didn't usually make you defensive or act as if they had something to teach you, the way this woman did. And anyhow, justice was a little peripheral now, wasn't it? What good would it really do her? What would it change?

She might have gone back and joined the men at the bar during the half. They were talking quietly among themselves. They were ordering fresh drinks and eating beernuts. But she didn't want to risk seeing cheerleaders. She didn't want to risk the ads with the party dog and all his women, even though she'd read in a magazine that the dog was a bitch. Anywhere she went, there she'd be. Just like she was. Heartbroken.

The woman was watching her closely. Alison could feel this, though the woman's face remained shadowed and she couldn't quite bring herself to look back at her directly. She looked at Elvis instead and the way his eyes wavered through her lens of candlelight and tears. *Lonesome tonight?* "You really have it bad, don't you?" the woman said. Her tone was sympathetic. Alison softened again. She decided to tell this perceptive woman everything. How much she'd loved him. How she'd never loved anyone else. How she felt it every time she took a *breath*, and had for weeks now.

"I don't think I'll ever feel better," she said. "No matter what I do."

"I hear it takes a year to recover from a serious loss. Unless you find someone else."

A year. Alison could be a mother by then. How would she find someone else, pregnant like she was or with a small child? Could she spend a year hurting like this? Would she have a choice?

"Have you ever heard of Laura D. Fair?" the woman asked.

Alison shook her head. She picked up the empty wineglass and tipped it to see if any drops remained. None did. She set it back down and picked up the napkin, wiping her eyes. She wasn't crying. She just wasn't exactly not crying.

"Mrs. Fair killed her lover," the woman told her. Alison looked at her own fingernails. One of them had a ragged end. She bit it off.

shorter while she listened. "He was a lawyer. A. P. Crittenden. She shot him on the ferry to Oakland in November of 1870 in front of his whole family because she saw him kiss his wife. He'd promised to leave her and marry Mrs. Fair instead, and then he didn't, of course. She pleaded a transient insanity known at that time as *emotional* insanity. She said she was incapable of killing Mr. Crittenden, who had been the only friend she'd had in the world." Alison examined her nail. She had only succeeded in making it more ragged. She bit it again, too close to the skin this time. It hurt and she put it back in her mouth. "Mrs. Fair said she had no memory of the murder, which many people, not all of them related to the deceased, witnessed. She was the first woman sentenced to hang in California."

Loud clapping and catcalls at the bar. The third quarter had started with a return all the way to the fifty-yard line. Alison heard it. She did not turn around, but she took her finger out of her mouth and picked up the napkin. She folded it again. Four small squares. "Rules are rules," Alison said.

"But then she didn't hang. Certain objections were made on behalf of the defense and sustained, and a new trial was held. This time she was acquitted. By now she was the most famous and the most hated woman in the country."

Alison unfolded the napkin and tried to smooth out the creases with the side of her palm. "I never heard of her."

"Laura D. Fair was not some little innocent." The woman's hat brim dipped decisively. "Mrs. Fair had been married four times, and each had been a profitable venture. One of her husbands killed himself. She was not pretty, but she was passionate. She was not smart, but she was clever. And she saw, in her celebrity, a new way to make money. She announced a new career as a public speaker. She traveled the country with her lectures. And what was her message? She told women to murder the men who seduced and betrayed them."

"I never heard of her," said Alison.

"Mrs. Fair was a compelling speaker. She'd had some acting and elocution experience. Her performance in court showed training. On the stage she was even better. 'The act will strike a terror to the hearts of sensualists and libertines.'" The woman stabbed dramatically at her own breast with her fist, hitting Elvis right in the eye. Behind her hand, Elvis winked at Alison in the candlelight. "Mrs. Fair said that women throughout the world would glory in the revenge exacted by American womanhood. Overdue. Long overdue. Thousands of women heard her. Men, too, and not all of them entirely unsympathetic. Fanny Hyde and Kate Stoddart were released in Brooklyn. Stoddart never even stood trial. But then there was a backlash. The martyred Marys were hanged in Philadelphia. And then . . ." the woman's voice dropped suddenly in volume and gained in intensity. Alison looked up at her quickly. The woman was staring back. Alison looked away. "And then a group of women hunted down and dispatched Charles S. Smith in an alley near his home. Mr. Smith was a married man and his victim, Edith Wilson, was pregnant, an invalid, and eleven years old. But this time the women wore sheets and could not be identified. Edith Wilson was perhaps the only female in Otsego County, New York, who could not have taken part."

Alison folded her napkin along the diagonal.

"So no one could be tried. It was an inspiring and purging operation. It was copied in many little towns across the country. God knows, the women had access to sheets."

Alison laughed, but the woman was not expecting it, had not paused to allow for laughter. "And then Annie Oakley shot Frank Butler in a challenge match in Cincinnati."

"Excuse me," said Alison. "I didn't quite hear you." But she really had and the woman continued anyway, without pausing or repeating.

"She said it was an accident, but she was too good a shot. They hanged her for it. And then Grover Cleveland was killed by twelve sheeted women on the White House lawn. At tea time," the woman said.

"Wait a minute." Alison stopped her. "Grover Cleveland served out two terms. Nonconsecutively. I'm sure."

The woman leaned into the candlelight, resting her chin on a bridge she made of her hands. "You're right, of course," she said. "That's what happened here. But in another universe where the feminine force was just a little stronger in 1872, Grover Cleveland died in office. With a scone in his mouth and a child in New York."

"All right," said Alison accommodatingly. Accommodation was one of Alison's strengths. "But what difference does that make to us?"

"I could take you there." The woman pushed her hat back so that Alison could have seen her eyes if she wanted to. "The universe right next door. Practically walking distance."

The candle flame was casting shadows which reached and withdrew and reached at Alison over the table. In the unsteady light, the woman's face flickered like a silent film star's. Then she pulled back in her chair and sank into the darkness beyond the candle. The ball was on the ten-yard line and the bar was quiet. "I knew you were going to say that," Alison said finally. "How did I know you were going to say that? Who would say that?"

"Some lunatic?" the woman suggested.

"Yes."

"Don't you want to hear about it anyway? About my universe?" The woman smiled at her. An unperturbed smile. Nice even teeth. And a kind of confidence that was rare among the women Alison knew. Alison had noticed it immediately without realizing she was noticing. The way the woman sat back in her chair and didn't pick at herself. Didn't play with her hair. Didn't look at her hands. The way she lectured Alison.

"All right," Alison said. She put the napkin down and fit her hands together, forcing herself to sit as still. "But first tell me about Laura Fair. *My* Laura Fair."

"Up until 1872 the two histories are identical," the woman said. "Mrs. Fair married four times and shot her lover and was convicted and the conviction was overturned. She just never lectured. She planned to. She was scheduled to speak at Platt's Hotel in San Francisco on November 21, 1872, but a mob of some two thousand men gathered outside the hotel and another two thousand surrounded the apartment building she lived in. She asked for police protection, but it was refused and she was too frightened to leave her home. Even staying where she was proved dangerous. A few men tried to force their way inside. She spent a terrifying night and never attempted to lecture again. She died in poverty and obscurity.

"Fanny Hyde and Kate Stoddart were released anyway. I can't find out what happened to the Marys. Edith Wilson was condemned by respectable people everywhere and cast out of her family."

"The eleven-year-old child?" Alison said.

"In *your* universe," the woman reminded her. "Not in mine. You don't know much of your own history, do you? Name a great American woman."

The men at the bar were in an uproar. Alison turned to look. "Interception," the man in the blue sweater shouted to her exultantly. "Did you see it?"

"Name a great American woman," Alison called back to him.

"Goddamn interception with goal to go," he said. "Eleanor Roosevelt?"

"Marilyn Monroe," said a man at the end of the bar.

"The senator from California?" the woman asked. "Now that's a good choice."

Alison laughed again. "Funny," she said, turning back to the woman. "Very good."

"We have football, too," the woman told her. "Invented in 1873. Outlawed in 1950. No one ever got paid to play it."

"And you have Elvis."

"No, we don't. Not like yours. Of course not. I got this here."

"Interception," the man in the blue sweater said. He was standing beside Alison, shaking his head with the wonder of it. "Let me buy you ladies a drink." Alison opened her mouth and he waved his hand. "Something nonalcoholic for you," he said. "Please. I really want to."

"Ginger ale, then," she agreed. "No ice."

"Nothing for me," said the woman. They watched the man walk back to the bar, and then, when he was far enough away not to hear, she leaned forward toward Alison. "You like men, don't you?"

"Yes," said Alison. "I always have. Are they different where you come from? Have they learned to be honest and careful with women, since you kill them when they're not?" Alison's voice was sharper than she intended, so she softened the effect with a sadder question. "Is it better there?"

"Better for whom?" The woman did not take her eyes off Alison. "Where I come from the men and women hardly speak to each other. First of all, they don't speak the same language. They don't here, either, but you don't recognize that as clearly. Where I come from there's men's English and there's women's English."

"Say something in men's English."

" 'I love you.' Shall I translate?"

"No," said Alison. "I know the translation for that one." The heaviness closed over her heart again. Not that it had ever gone away. Nothing made Alison feel better, but many things made her feel worse. The bartender brought her ginger ale. With ice. Alison was angry, suddenly, that she couldn't even get a drink with no ice. She looked for the man in the blue sweater, raised the glass at him, and rattled it. Of course he was too far away to hear even if he was listening, and there was no reason to believe he was.

"Two-minute warning," he called back. "I'll be with you in two minutes."

Men were always promising to be with you soon. Men could never be with you now. Alison had only cared about this once, and she never would again. "Football has the longest two minutes in the world," she told the woman. "So don't hold your breath. What else is different where you come from?" She sipped at her ginger ale. She'd been grinding her teeth recently; stress, the dentist said, and so the cold liquid made her mouth hurt.

"Everything is different. Didn't you ask for no ice? Don't drink that," the woman said. She called to the bartender. "She didn't want ice. You gave her ice."

"Sorry." The bartender brought another bottle and another glass. "Nobody told me no ice."

"Thank you," Alison said. He took the other glass away. Alison thought he was annoyed. The woman didn't seem to notice.

"Imagine your world without a hundred years of adulterers," she said. "The level of technology is considerably depressed. Lots of books never written, because the authors didn't live. Lots of men who didn't get to be president. Lots of passing. Although it's illegal. Men dressing as women. Women dressing as men. And the dress is more sexually differentiated. Codpieces are fashionable again. But you don't have to believe me," the woman said. "Come and see for yourself. I can take you there in a minute. What would it cost you to just come and see? What do you have here that you'd be losing?"

The woman gave her time to think. Alison sat and drank her ginger ale and repeated to herself the things her lover had said the last time she had seen him. She remembered them all, some of them surprisingly careless, some of them surprisingly cruel, all of them surprising. She repeated them again, one by one, like a rosary. The man who had left was not the man she had loved. The man she had loved would never have said such things to her. The man she had loved did not exist. She had made him up. Or he had. "Why would you want me to go?" Alison asked.

"The universe is shaped by the struggle between two great forces. Sometimes a small thing can tip the balance. One more woman. Who knows?" The woman tilted her hat back with her hand. "Save a galaxy. Make new friends. Or stay here where your heart is. Broken."

"Can I come back if I don't like it?"

"Yes. Do you like it here?"

She drank her ginger ale and then set the glass down, still half full. She glanced at the man in the blue sweater, then past him to the bartender. She let herself feel just for a moment what it might be like to know that she could finish this drink and then go home to the one person in the world who loved her.

Never in this world. "I'm going out for a minute. Two minutes," she called to the bartender. One minute to get back. "Don't take my drink."

She stood and the other woman stood, too, even taller than Alison had thought. "I'll follow you. Which way?" Alison asked.

"It's not hard," the woman said. "In fact, I'll follow you. Go to the back. Find the door that says *Women* and go on through it. I'm just going to pay for my drink and then I'll be right along."

Vixens, was what the door actually said, across the way from the one marked *Ganders*. Alison paused and then pushed through. She felt more than a little silly, standing in the small bathroom that apparently fronted two universes. One toilet, one sink, one mirror. Two universes. She went into the stall and closed the door. Before she had finished she heard the outer door open and shut again. "I'll be right out," she said. The toilet paper was small and unusually rough. The toilet wouldn't flush. It embarrassed her. She tried three times before giving up.

The bathroom was larger than it had been, less clean, and a row of urinals lined one wall. The woman stood at the sink, looking into the mirror, which was smaller. "Are you ready?" she asked and removed her breasts from behind Elvis, tossing them into a wire wastebasket. She turned. "Ready or not."

"No," said Alison, seeing the face under the hat clearly for the first time. "Please, no." She began to cry again, looking up at his face, looking down at his chest. ARE YOU LONESOME TONIGHT?

"You lied to me," she said dully.

"I never lied," he answered. "Think back. You just translated wrong. Because you're that kind of woman. We don't have women like you here now. And anyway, what does it matter whose side you play on? All that matters is that no one wins. Aren't I right? Aren't I?" He tipped his hat to her.

WAITING FOR THE OLYMPIANS

Frederik Pohl

Chapter 1
The Day of the Two Rejections

If I had been writing it as a romance, I would have called the chapter about that last day in London something like "The Day of the Two Rejections." It was a nasty day in late December, just before the holidays. The weather was cold, wet, and miserable—well, I said it was London, didn't I?—but everybody was in a sort of expectant holiday mood; it had just been announced that the Olympians would be arriving no later than the following August, and everybody was excited about that. All the taxi drivers were busy, and so I was late for my lunch with Lidia. "How was Manahattan?" I asked, sliding into the booth beside her and giving her a quick kiss.

"Manahattan was very nice," she said, pouring me a drink. Lidia was a writer, too—well, they *call* themselves writers, the ones who follow famous people around and write down all their gossip and jokes and put them out as books for the amusement of the idle. That's not really *writing*, of course. There's nothing creative about it. But it pays well, and the research (Lidia always told me) was a lot of fun. She spent a lot of time traveling around the celebrity circuit, which was not very good for our romance. She watched me drink the first glass before she remembered to ask politely, "Did you finish the book?"

"Don't call it 'the book,'" I said. "Call it by its name, *An Ass's Olympiad*. I'm going to see Marcus about it this afternoon."

"That's not what I'd call a great title," she commented—Lidia was always willing to give me her opinion on anything, when she didn't like it. "Really, don't you think it's too late to be writing another sci-rom about the Olympians?" And then she smiled brightly and said, "I've got something to say to you, Julie. Have another drink first."

So I knew what was coming right away, and that was the first rejection.

I'd seen this scene building up. Even before she left on that last "research" trip to the West I had begun to suspect that some of that early ardor had cooled, so I wasn't really surprised when she told me, without any further foreplay, "I've met somebody else, Julie."

I said, "I see." I really did see, and so I poured myself a third drink while she told me about it.

"He's a former space pilot, Julius. He's been to Mars and the Moon and everywhere, and oh, he's such a sweet man. And he's a champion wrestler, too, would you believe it? Of course, he's still married, as it happens. But he's going to talk to his wife about a divorce as soon as the kids are just a little older."

She looked at me challengingly, waiting for me to tell her she was an idiot. I had no intention of saying anything at all, as a matter of fact, but just in case I had, she added, "Don't say what you're thinking."

"I wasn't thinking anything," I protested.

She sighed. "You're taking this very well," she told me. She sounded as though that were a great disappointment to her. "Listen, Julius, I didn't plan this. Truly, you'll always be dear to me in a special way. I hope we can always be friends—" I stopped listening around then.

There was plenty more in the same vein, but only the details were a surprise. When she told me our little affair was over I took it calmly enough. I always knew that Lidia had a weakness for the more athletic type. Worse than that, she never respected the kind of writing I do, anyway. She had the usual establishment contempt for science-adventure romances about the future and adventures on alien planets, and what sort of relationship could that lead to, in the long run?

So I left her with a kiss and a smile, neither of them very sincere, and headed for my editor's office. That was where I got the second rejection. The one that really hurt.

Mark's office was in the old part of London, down by the river. It's an old company, in an old building, and most of the staff are old, too. When the company needs clerks or copy editors it has a habit of picking up tutors whose students have grown up and don't need them anymore, and retraining them. Of course, that's just for the people in the lower echelons. The higher-ups, like Mark himself, are free, salaried executives, with the executive privilege of interminable, winey

author-and-editor lunches that don't end until the middle of the afternoon.

I had to wait half an hour to see him; obviously he had been having
one of them that day. I didn't mind. I had every confidence that our
interview was going to be short, pleasant, and remunerative. I knew
very well that *An Ass's Olympiad* was one of the best sci-roms I had
ever done. Even the title was clever. The book was a satire, with
classical overtones—from *The Golden Ass* of the ancient writer, Lucius
Apuleius, two thousand years ago or so; I had played off the classic in
a comic, adventurous little story about the coming of the real Olympians. I can always tell when a book is going really well and I knew the
fans would eat this one up. . . .

When I finally got in to see Marcus he had a glassy, after-lunch look
in his eye, and I could see my manuscript on his desk.

I also saw that clipped to it was a red-bordered certificate, and that
was the first warning of bad news. The certificate was the censor's
verdict, and the red border meant it was an obstat.

Mark didn't keep me in suspense. "We can't publish," he said,
pressing his palm on the manuscript. "The censors have turned it
down."

"They can't!" I cried, making his old secretary lift his head from his
desk in the corner of the room to stare at me.

"They did," Mark said. "I'll read you what the obstat says: '—of a
nature which may give offense to the delegation from the Galactic
Consortium, usually referred to as the Olympians—' and '—thus en-
dangering the security and tranquility of the Empire—' and, well,
basically it just says no. No revisions suggested. Just a complete veto;
it's waste paper now, Julie. Forget it."

"But *everybody* is writing about the Olympians!" I yelped.

"Everybody *was*," he corrected. "Now they're getting close, and
the censors don't want to take any more chances." He leaned back to
rub his eyes, obviously wishing he could be taking a nice nap instead
of breaking my heart. Then he added tiredly, "So what do you want
to do, Julie? Write us a replacement? It would have to be fast, you
understand; the front office doesn't like having contracts outstanding
for more than thirty days after due date. And it would have to be
good. You're not going to get away with pulling some old reject out of
your trunk—I've seen all those already, anyway."

"How the hells do you expect me to write a whole new book in
thirty days?" I demanded.

He shrugged, looking sleepier and less interested in my problem than ever. "If you can't, you can't. Then you'll just have to give back the advance," he told me.

I calmed down fast. "Well, no," I said, "there's no question of having to do that. I don't know about finishing it in thirty days, though—"

"I do," he said flatly. He watched me shrug. "Have you got an idea for the new one?"

"Mark," I said patiently, "I've *always* got ideas for new ones. That's what a professional writer is. He's a machine for thinking up ideas. I always have more ideas than I can ever write—"

"Do you?" he insisted.

I surrendered, because if I'd said yes the next thing would have been that he'd want me to tell him what it was. "Not exactly," I admitted.

"Then," he said, "you'd better go wherever you do to get ideas, because, give us the new book or give us back the advance, thirty days is all you've got."

There's an editor for you.

They're all the same. At first they're all honey and sweet talk, with those long alcoholic lunches and blue-sky conversation about million-copy printings while they wheedle you into signing the contract. Then they turn nasty. They want the actual book delivered. When they don't get it, or when the censors say they can't print it, then there isn't any more sweet talk and all the conversation is about how the aediles will escort you to debtors' prison.

So I took his advice. I knew where to go for ideas, and it wasn't in London. No sensible man stays in London in the winter anyway, because of the weather and because it's too full of foreigners. I still can't get used to seeing all those huge rustic Northmen and dark Hindian and Arabian women in the heart of town. I admit I can be turned on by that red caste mark or by a pair of flashing dark eyes shining through all the robes and veils. I suppose what you imagine is always more exciting than what you can see, especially when what you see is the short, dumpy Britain women like Lidia.

So I made a reservation on the overnight train to Rome, to transfer there to a hydrofoil for Alexandria. I packed with a good heart, not neglecting to take along a floppy sun hat, a flask of insect repellent, and—oh, of course—stylus and blank tablets enough to last me for the whole trip, just in case a book idea emerged for me to write. Egypt! Where the world conference on the Olympians was starting its win-

ter session . . . where I would be among the scientists and astro-
nauts who always sparked ideas for new science-adventure romances
for me to write . . . where it would be warm. . . .

Where my publisher's aediles would have trouble finding me, in
the event that no idea for a new novel came along.

Chapter 2
On the Way to the Idea Place

No idea did.

That was disappointing. I do some of my best writing on trains,
aircraft, and ships, because there aren't any interruptions and you
can't decide to go out for a walk because there isn't any place to walk
to. It didn't work this time. All the while the train was slithering
across the wet, bare English winter countryside toward the Channel,
I sat with my tablet in front of me and the stylus poised to write, but
by the time we dipped into the tunnel the tablet was still virgin.

I couldn't fool myself. I was stuck. I mean, *stuck*. Nothing happened
in my head that could transform itself into an opening scene for a
new sci-rom novel.

It wasn't the first time in my writing career that I'd been stuck
with the writer's block. That's a sort of occupational disease for any
writer. But this time was the worst. I'd really counted on *An Ass's
Olympiad*. I had even calculated that the publication date could be
made to coincide with that wonderful day when the Olympians themselves arrived in our solar system, with all sorts of wonderful publicity for my book flowing out of that great event, so the sales should be
immense . . . and, worse than that, I'd already spent the on-signing
advance. All I had left was credit, and not much of that.

Not for the first time, I wondered what it would have been like if I
had followed some other career. If I'd stayed in the civil service, for
instance, as my father had wanted.

Really, I hadn't had much choice. I was born during the Space
Tricentennial Year, and my mother told me the first word I said was
"Mars." She said there was a little misunderstanding there, because at
first she thought I was talking about the god, not the planet, and she
and my father had long talks about whether to train me for the priest-
hood, but by the time I could read she knew I was a space nut. Like a
lot of my generation (the ones that read my books), I grew up on

spaceflight. I was a teenager when the first pictures came back from the space probe to the Alpha Centauri planet Julia, with its crystal grasses and silver-leafed trees. As a boy I corresponded with another youth who lived in the cavern colonies on the Moon, and I read with delight the shoot-'em-ups about outlaws and aediles chasing each other around the satellites of Jupiter. I wasn't the only kid who grew up space-happy, but I never got over it.

Naturally I became a science-adventure romance writer; what else did I know anything about? As soon as I began to get actual money for my fantasies I quit my job as secretary to one of the imperial legates on the Western continents and went full-time pro.

I prospered at it, too—prospered reasonably, at least—well, to be more exact, I earned a livable, if irregular, income out of the two sci-roms a year I could manage to write, and enough of a surplus to support the habit of dating pretty women like Lidia out of the occasional bonus when one of the books was made into a broadcast drama or a play.

Then along came the message from the Olympians, and the whole face of science-adventure romans was changed forever.

It was the most exciting news in the history of the world, of course. There really *were* other intelligent races out there among the stars of the Galaxy! It had never occurred to me that it would affect me personally, except with joy.

Joy it was, at first. I managed to talk my way into the Alpine radio observatory that had recorded that first message, and I heard it recorded with my own ears:

Dit *squah* dit.
Dit *squee* dit *squah* dit dit.
Dit *squee* dit *squee* dit *squah* dit dit dit.
Dit *squee* dit *squee* dit *squee* dit *squah* wooooo.
Dit *squee* dit *squee* dit *squee* dit *squee* dit *squah* dit dit dit dit dit.

It all looks so simple now, but it took awhile before anyone figured out just what this first message from the Olympians was. (Of course, we didn't call them Olympians then. We wouldn't call them that now if the priests had anything to say about it, because they think it's almost sacrilegious, but what else are you going to call godlike beings from the heavens? The name caught on right away, and the priests just had to learn to live with it.) It was, in fact, my good friend Flavius Samuelus ben Samuelus who first deciphered it and produced the right answer to transmit back to the senders—the one that, four years later, let the Olympians know we had heard them.

Meanwhile, we all knew this wonderful new truth: We weren't alone in the universe! Excitement exploded. The market for sci-roms boomed. My very next book was *The Radio Gods*, and it sold its head off.

I thought it would go on forever.

It might have, too . . . if it hadn't been for the timorous censors.

I slept through the tunnel—all the tunnels, even the ones through the Alps—and by the time I woke up we were halfway down to Rome.

In spite of the fact that the tablets remained obstinately blank, I felt more cheerful. Lidia was just a fading memory, I still had twenty-nine days to turn in a new sci-rom and Rome, after all, is still Rome! The center of the universe—well, not counting what new lessons in astronomical geography the Olympians might teach us. At least, it's the greatest city in the world. It's the place where all the action is.

By the time I'd sent the porter for breakfast and changed into a clean robe we were there, and I alighted into the great, noisy train shed.

I hadn't been in the city for several years, but Rome doesn't change much. The Tiber still stank. The big new apartment buildings still hid the old ruins until you were almost on top of them, the flies were still awful, and the Roman youths still clustered around the train station to sell you guided tours to the Golden House (as though any of them could ever get past the Legion guards!), or sacred amulets, or their sisters.

Because I used to be a secretary on the staff of the proconsul to the Cherokee Nation, I have friends in Rome. Because I hadn't had the good sense to call ahead, none of them were home. I had no choice. I had to take a room in a high-rise inn on the Palatine.

It was ferociously expensive, of course. Everything in Rome is—that's why people like to live in dreary outposts like London—but I figured that by the time the bills came in I would either have found something to satisfy Marcus and get the rest of the advance, or I'd be in so much trouble a few extra debts wouldn't matter.

Having reached that decision, I decided to treat myself to a servant. I picked out a grinning, muscular Sicilian at the rental desk in the lobby, gave him the keys for my luggage, and instructed him to take it to my room—and to make me a reservation for the next day's hover-flight to Alexandria.

That's when my luck began to get better.

When the Sicilian came to the wine shop to ask me for further orders, he reported, "There's another citizen who's booked on the same flight, Citizen Julius. Would you like to share a compartment with him?"

It's nice when you rent a servant who tries to save you money. I said approvingly, "What kind of a person is he? I don't want to get stuck with some real bore."

"You can see for yourself, Julius. He's in the baths right now. He's a Judaean. His name is Flavius Samuelus."

Five minutes later I had my clothes off and a sheet wrapped around me, and I was in the tepidarium, peering around at every body there.

I picked Sam out at once. He was stretched out with his eyes closed while a masseur pummeled his fat old flesh. I climbed onto the slab next to his without speaking. When he groaned and rolled over, opening his eyes, I said, "Hello, Sam."

It took him a moment to recognize me; he didn't have his glasses in. But when he squinted hard enough his face broke out into a grin. "Julie!" he cried. "Small world! It's good to see you again!"

And he reached out to clasp fists-over-elbows, really welcoming, just as I had expected; because one of the things I like best about Flavius Samuelus is that he likes me.

One of the other things I like best about Sam is that, although he is a competitor, he is also an undepletable natural resource. He writes sci-roms himself. He does more than that. He has helped me with the science part of my own sci-roms any number of times, and it had crossed my mind as soon as I heard the Sicilian say his name that he might be just what I wanted in the present emergency.

Sam is at least seventy years old. His head is hairless. There's a huge brown age spot on the top of his scalp. His throat hangs in a pouch of flesh, and his eyelids sag. But you'd never guess any of that if you were simply talking to him on the phone. He has the quick, chirpy voice of a twenty-year-old, and the mind of one, too—of an extraordinarily *bright* twenty-year-old. He gets enthusiastic.

That complicates things, because Sam's brain works faster than it ought to. Sometimes that makes him hard to talk to, because he's usually three or four exchanges ahead of most people. So the next thing he says to you is as likely as not to be the response to some question that you are inevitably going to ask, but haven't yet thought of.

It is an unpleasant fact of life that Sam's sci-roms sell better than mine do. It is a tribute to Sam's personality that I don't hate him for it. He has an unfair advantage over the rest of us, since he is a professional astronomer himself. He only writes sci-roms for fun, in his spare time, of which he doesn't have a whole lot. Most of his working hours are spent running a space probe of his own, the one that circles the Epsilon Eridani planet, Dione. I can stand his success (and, admit it! his talent) because he is generous with his ideas. As soon as we had agreed to share the hoverflight compartment, I put it to him directly. Well, almost directly. I said, "Sam, I've been wondering about something. When the Olympians get here, what is it going to mean to us?"

He was the right person to ask, of course; Sam knew more about the Olympians than anyone alive. But he was the wrong person to expect a direct answer from. He rose up, clutching his robe around him. He waved away the masseur and looked at me in friendly amusement, out of those bright black eyes under the flyaway eyebrows and the drooping lids. "Why do you need a new sci-rom plot right now?" he asked.

"Hells," I said ruefully, and decided to come clean. "It wouldn't be the first time I asked you, Sam. Only this time I *really* need it." And I told him the story of the novel the censors obstatted and the editor who was after a quick replacement—or my blood, choice of one.

He nibbled thoughtfully at the knuckle of his thumb. "What was this novel of yours about?" he asked curiously.

"It was a satire, Sam. *An Ass's Olympiad.* About the Olympians coming down to Earth in a matter transporter, only there's a mixup in the transmission and one of them accidentally gets turned into an ass. It's got some funny bits in it."

"It sure has, Julie. Has had for a couple dozen centuries."

"Well, I didn't say it was altogether *original*, only—"

He was shaking his head. "I thought you were smarter than that, Julie. What did you expect the censors to do, jeopardize the most important event in human history for the sake of a dumb sci-rom?"

"It's not a dumb—"

"It's dumb to risk offending them," he said, overruling me firmly. "Best to be safe and not write about them at all."

"But everybody's been doing it!"

"Nobody's been turning them into asses," he pointed out. "Julie, there's a limit to sci-rom speculation. When you write about the Olympians you're right up at that limit. Any speculation about them can be enough reason for them to pull out of the meeting entirely, and we might never get a chance like this again."

"They wouldn't—"

"Ah, Julie," he said, disgusted, "you don't have any idea what they would or wouldn't do. The censors made the right decision. Who knows what the Olympians are going to be like?"

"You do," I told him.

He laughed. There was an uneasy sound to it, though. "I wish I did. About the only thing we do know is that they don't appear to be just any old intelligent race; they have moral standards. We don't have any idea what those standards are, really. I don't know what your book says, but maybe you speculated that the Olympians were bringing us all kinds of new things—a cure for cancer, new psychedelic drugs, even eternal life—"

"What kind of psychedelic drugs might they bring, exactly?" I asked.

"Down, boy! I'm telling you *not* to think about that kind of idea. The point is that whatever you imagined might easily turn out to be the most repulsive and immoral thing the Olympians can think of. The stakes are too high. This is a once-only chance. We can't let it go sour."

"But I need a *story*," I wailed.

"Well, yes," he admitted, "I suppose you do. Let me think about it. Let's get cleaned up and get out of here."

While we were in the hot drench, while we were dressing, while we were eating a light lunch, Sam chattered on about the forthcoming conference in Alexandria. I was pleased to listen. Apart from the fact that everything he said was interesting, I began to feel hopeful about actually producing a book for Mark. If anybody could help me, Sam could, and he was a problem addict. He couldn't resist a challenge.

That was undoubtedly why he was the first to puzzle out the Olympians' interminably repeated *squees* and *squahs*. If you simply took the dit to be numeral one, and the *squee* to be plus sign, and the *squah* to be an equals sign, then "Dit *squee* dit *squah* dit dit" simply came out as "One plus one equals two."

That was easy enough. It didn't take a super brain like Sam's to substitute our terms for theirs and reveal the message to be simple arithmetic—except for the mysterious "wooooo":

Dit *squee* dit *squee* dit *squee* dit *squah* wooooo.

What was the "wooooo" supposed to mean? A special convention to represent the numeral four?

Sam knew right away, of course. As soon as he heard the message he telegraphed the solution from his library in Padua:

"The message calls for an answer. 'Wooooo' means question mark. The answer is four."

And so the reply to the stars was transmitted on its way:

Dit *squee* dit *squee* dit *squee* dit *squah* dit dit dit dit.

The human race had turned in its test paper in the entrance examination, and the slow process of establishing communication had begun.

It took four years before the Olympians responded. Obviously, they weren't nearby. Also obviously, they weren't simple folk like ourselves, sending out radio messages from a planet of a star two light-years away, because there wasn't any star there; the reply came from a point in space where none of our telescopes or probes had found anything at all.

By then Sam was deeply involved. He was the first to point out that the star folk had undoubtedly chosen to send a weak signal, because they wanted to be sure our technology was reasonably well developed before we tried to answer. He was one of the impatient ones who talked the collegium authorities into beginning transmission of all sorts of mathematical formulae, and then simple word relationships, to start sending *something* to the Olympians while we waited for radio waves to creep to wherever they were and back with an answer.

Sam wasn't the only one, of course. He wasn't even the principal investigator when they got into the hard work of developing a common vocabulary. There were better specialists than Sam at linguistics and cryptanalysis.

But it was Sam who first noticed, early on, that the response time to our messages was getting shorter. Meaning that the Olympians were on their way toward us.

By then they'd begun sending picture mosaics. They came in as strings of dits and dahs, 550,564 bits long. Someone quickly figured out that that was the square of 742, and when they displayed the string as a square matrix, black cells for the dits and white ones for the dahs, the image of the first Olympian leaped out.

Everybody remembers that picture. Everyone on Earth saw it, except for the totally blind—it was on every broadcast screen and news journal in the world—and even the blind listened to the anatomical descriptions every commentator supplied. Two tails. A fleshy, beard-like thing that hung down from its chin. Four legs. A ruff of spikes down what seemed to be the backbone. Eyes set wide apart on bulges from the cheekbones.

That first Olympian was not at all pretty, but it was definitely *alien*. When the next string turned out very similar to the first, it was

Sam who saw at once that it was simply a slightly rotated view of the same being. The Olympians took forty-one pictures to give us the complete likeness of that first one in the round. . . .

Then they began sending pictures of the others.

It had never occurred to anyone, not even Sam, that we would be dealing not with one super race, but with at least twenty-two of them. There were that many separate forms of alien beings, and each one uglier and more strange than the one before.

That was one of the reasons the priests didn't like calling them Olympians. We're pretty ecumenical about our gods, but none of them looked anything like any of *those*, and some of the older priests never stopped muttering about blasphemy.

Halfway through the third course of our lunch and the second flask of wine, Sam broke off his description of the latest communique from the Olympians—they'd been acknowledging receipt of our transmissions about Earthly history—to lift his head and grin at me.

"Got it," he said.

I turned and blinked at him. Actually, I hadn't been paying a lot of attention to his monologue because I had been keeping my eye on the pretty Kievan waitress. She had attracted my attention because— well, I mean, *after* attracting my attention because of her extremely well developed figure and the sparsity of clothing to conceal it—because she was wearing a gold citizen's amulet around her neck. She wasn't a slave. That made her more intriguing. I can't ever get really interested in slave women, because it isn't sporting, but I had got quite interested in this woman.

"Are you listening to me?" Sam demanded testily.

"Of course I am. What have you got?"

"I've got the answer to your problem." He beamed. "Not just a sci-rom novel plot. A whole new *kind* of sci-rom! Why don't you write a book about what it will be like if the Olympians *don't* come?"

I love the way half of Sam's brain works at questions while the other half is doing something completely different, but I can't always follow what comes out of it. "I don't see what you mean. If I write about the Olympians not coming, isn't that just as bad as if I write about them doing it?"

"No, no," he snapped. "Listen to what I say! Leave the Olympians out entirely. Just write about a future that might happen, but won't."

The waitress was hovering over us, picking up used plates. I was conscious of her listening as I responded with dignity, "Sam, that's not my style. My sci-roms may not sell as well as yours do, but I've got just as much integrity. I never write anything that I don't believe is at least possible."

"Julie, get your mind off your gonads"—so he hadn't missed the attention I was giving the girl—"and use that pitifully tiny brain of yours. I'm talking about something that *could* be possible, in some alternative future, if you see what I mean."

I didn't see at all. "What's an alternative future?"

"It's a future that *might* happen, but *won't*," he explained. "Like if the Olympians don't come to see us."

I shook my head, puzzled. "But we already know they're coming," I pointed out.

"But suppose they weren't! Suppose they hadn't contacted us years ago."

"But they did," I said, trying to straighten out his thinking on the subject. He only sighed.

"I see I'm not getting through to you," he said, pulling his robe around him and getting to his feet. "Get on with your waitress. I've got some messages to send. I'll see you on the ship."

Well, for one reason or another I didn't get anywhere with the Kievan waitress. She said she was married, happily and monogamously. Well, I couldn't see why any lawful, free husband would have his wife out working at a job like that, but I was surprised she didn't show more interest in one of my lineage—

I'd better explain about that.

You see, my family has a claim to fame. Genealogists say that we are descended from the line of Julius Caesar himself.

I mention that claim myself, sometimes, though usually only when I've been drinking—I suppose it is one of the reasons that Lidia, always a snob, took up with me in the first place. It isn't a serious matter. After all, Julius Caesar died more than two thousand years ago. There have been sixty or seventy generations since then, not to mention the fact that, although Ancestor Julius certainly left a lot of children behind him, none of them happened to be born to a woman he happened to be married to. I don't even look very Roman. There must have been a Northman or two in the line, because I'm tall and fair-haired, which no respectable Roman ever was.

Still, even if I'm not exactly the lawful heir to the divine Julius, I at least come of a pretty ancient and distinguished line. You would have thought a mere waitress would have taken that into account before turning me down.

She hadn't, though. When I woke up the next morning—alone—

Sam was gone from the inn, although the skipship for Alexandria wasn't due to sail until late evening.

I didn't see him all day. I didn't look for him very hard, because I woke up feeling a little ashamed of myself. Why should a grown man, a celebrated author of more than forty best-selling (well, reasonably *well* selling) sci-roms, depend on somebody else for his ideas?

So I turned my baggage over to the servant, checked out of the inn, and took the underground to the Library of Rome.

Rome isn't only the imperial capital of the world, it's the scientific capital, too. The big old telescopes out on the hills aren't much use anymore, because the lights from the city spoil their night viewing, and anyway the big optical telescopes are all out in space now. Still, they were where Galileus detected the first extrasolar planet and Tychus made his famous spectrographs of the last great supernova in our own galaxy, only a couple of dozen years after the first space-flight. The scientific tradition survives. Rome is still the headquarters of the Collegium of Sciences.

That's why the Library of Rome is so great for someone like me. They have direct access to the the Collegium data base, and you don't even have to pay transmission tolls. I signed myself in, laid out my tablets and stylus on the desk they assigned me, and began calling up files.

Somewhere there had to be an idea for a science-adventure romance no one had written yet. . . .

Somewhere there no doubt was, but I couldn't find it. Usually you can get a lot of help from a smart research librarian, but it seemed they'd put on a lot of new people in the Library of Rome—Iberians, mostly; reduced to slave status because they'd taken part in last year's Lusitanian uprising. There were so many Iberians on the market for a while that they depressed the price. I would have bought some as a speculation, knowing that the price would go up—after all, there aren't that many uprisings and the demand for slaves never stops. But I was temporarily short of capital, and besides you have to feed them. If the ones at the Library of Rome were a fair sample, they were no bargains anyway.

I gave up. The weather had improved enough to make a stroll around town attractive, and so I wandered toward the Ostia mono-rail.

Rome was busy, as always. There was a bullfight going on in the Coliseum and racing at the Circus Maximus. Tourist buses were jamming the narrow streets. A long religious procession was circling the Pantheon, but I didn't get close enough to see which particular gods were being honored today. I don't like crowds. Especially Roman crowds, because there are even more foreigners in Rome than in London, Africs and Hinds, Hans and Northmen—every race on the face of the Earth sends its tourists to visit the Imperial City. And Rome obliges with spectacles. I paused at one of them, for the changing of the guard at the Golden House. Of course, the Caesar and his wife were nowhere to be seen—off on one of their endless ceremonial tours of the dominions, no doubt, or at least opening a new supermarket somewhere. But the Algonkian family standing in front of me were thrilled as the honor Legions marched and countermarched their standards around the palace. I remembered enough Cherokee to ask the Algonkians where they were from, but the languages aren't really very close and the man's Cherokee was even worse than mine. We just smiled at each other.

As soon as the Legions were out of the way I headed for the train.

I knew in the back of my mind that I should have been worrying about my financial position. The clock was running on my thirty days of grace. I didn't, though. I was buoyed up by a feeling of confidence. Confidence in my good friend Flavius Samuelus, who, I knew, no matter what he was doing with most of his brain, was still cogitating an idea for me with some part of it.

It did not occur to me that even Sam had limitations. Or that something so much more important than my own problems was taking up his attention that he didn't have much left for me.

I didn't see Sam come onto the skip-ship, and I didn't see him in our compartment. Even when the ship's fans began to rumble and we slid down the ways into the Tyrrhenian Sea he wasn't there. I dozed off, beginning to worry that he might have missed the boat; but late that night, already asleep, I half woke, just long enough to hear him stumbling in. "I've been on the bridge," he said when I muttered something. "Go back to sleep. I'll see you in the morning."

When I woke, I thought it might have been a dream, because he was up and gone before me. But his bed had been slept in, however briefly, and the cabin steward reassured me when he brought my morning wine. Yes, Citizen Flavius Samuelus was certainly on the hover. He was in the captain's own quarters, as a matter of fact, although what he was doing there the steward could not say.

I spent the morning relaxing on the deck of the hover, soaking in the sun. The ship wasn't exactly a hover anymore. We had transited the Sicilian Straits during the night and now, out in the open Mediterranean, the captain had lowered the stilts, pulled up the hover skirts, and extended the screws. We were hydrofoiling across the sea at easily a hundred miles an hour. It was a smooth, relaxing ride; the vanes that supported us were twenty feet under the surface of the water, and so there was no wave action to bounce us around.

Lying on my back and squinting up at the warm southern sky, I could see a three-winged airliner rise up from the horizon behind us and gradually overtake us, to disappear ahead of our bows. The plane wasn't going much faster than we were—and we had all the comfort, while they were paying twice as much for passage.

I opened my eyes all the way when I caught a glimpse of someone standing beside me. In fact, I sat up quickly, because it was Sam. He looked as though he hadn't had much sleep, and he was holding a floppy sun hat with one hand against the wind of our passage. "Where've you been?" I asked.

"Haven't you been watching the news?" he asked. I shook my head. "The transmissions from the Olympians have stopped," he told me.

I opened my eyes really wide at that, because it was an unpleasant surprise. Still, Sam didn't seem that upset. Displeased, yes. Maybe even a little concerned, but not as shaken up as I was prepared to feel. "It's probably nothing," he said. "It could be just interference from the sun. It's in Sagittarius now, so it's pretty much between us and them. There's been trouble with static for a couple of days now."

I ventured, "So the transmissions will start up again pretty soon?"

He shrugged and waved to the deck steward for one of those hot decoctions Judaeans like. When he spoke it was on a different topic. "I don't think I made you understand what I meant yesterday," he said. "Let me see if I can explain what I meant by an alternate world. You remember your history? How Fornius Vello conquered the Mayans and Romanized the Western Continents six or seven hundred years ago? Well, suppose he hadn't."

"But he did, Sam."

"I know he did," Sam said patiently. "I'm saying *suppose*. Suppose the Legions had been defeated at the Battle of Tehultapec."

I laughed. I was sure he was joking. "The Legions? Defeated? But the Legions have never been defeated."

"That's not true," Sam said in reproof. He hates it when people don't get their facts straight. "Remember Varus."

"Oh, hells, Sam, that was ancient history! When was it, two thousand years ago? In the time of Augustus Caesar? And it was only a temporary defeat, anyway. The Emperor Drusus got the eagles back." And got all of Gaul for the Empire, too. That was one of the first big trans-Alpine conquests. The Gauls are about as Roman as you can get these days, especially when it comes to drinking wine.

He shook his head. "Suppose Fornius Vello had had a temporary defeat, then."

I tried to follow his argument, but it wasn't easy. "What difference would that have made? Sooner or later the Legions would have conquered. They always have, you know."

"That's true," he said reasonably, "but if that particular conquest hadn't happened *then*, the whole course of history would have been different. We wouldn't have had the great westward migrations to fill up those empty continents. The Hans and the Hinds wouldn't have been surrounded on both sides, so they might still be independent nations. It would have been a different world. Do you see what I'm driving at? That's what I mean by an alternate world—one that might have happened, but didn't."

I tried to be polite to him. "Sam," I said, "you've just described the difference between a sci-rom and a fantasy. I don't do fantasy. Besides," I went on, not wanting to hurt his feelings, "I don't see how different things would have been, really. I can't believe the world would be changed enough to build a sci-rom plot on."

He gazed blankly at me for a moment, then turned and looked out to sea. Then, without transition, he said, "There's one funny thing. The Martian colonies aren't getting a transmission, either. And they aren't occluded by the sun."

I frowned. "What does that mean, Sam?"

He shook his head. "I wish I knew," he said.

Chapter 3
In Old Alexandria

The Pharos was bright in the sunset light as we came into the port of Alexandria. We were on hover again, at slow speeds, and the chop at the breakwater bumped us around. But once we got to the inner harbor the water was calm.

Sam had spent the afternoon back in the captain's quarters, keeping in contact with the Collegium of Sciences, but he showed up as we moored. He saw me gazing toward the rental desk on the dock but shook his head. "Don't bother with a rental, Julie," he ordered. "Let my niece's servants take your baggage. We're staying with her."

That was good news. Inn rooms in Alexandria are almost as pricey as Rome's. I thanked him, but he didn't even listen. He turned our bags over to a porter from his niece's domicile, a little Arabian who was a lot stronger than he looked, and disappeared toward the Hall of the Egyptian Senate-Inferior, where the conference was going to be held.

I hailed a three-wheeler and gave the driver the address of Sam's niece.

No matter what the Egyptians think, Alexandria is a dirty little town. The Choctaws have a bigger capital, and the Kievans have a cleaner one. Also Alexandria's famous library is a joke. After my (one would like to believe) ancestor Julius Caesar let it burn to the ground, the Egyptians did build it up again. But it is so old-fashioned that there's nothing in it but books.

The home of Sam's niece was in a particularly run-down section of that run-down town, only a few streets from the harborside. You could hear the noise of the cargo winches from the docks, but you couldn't hear them very well because of the noise of the streets themselves, thick with goods vans and drivers cursing each other as they jockeyed around the narrow corners. The house itself was bigger than I had expected. But, at least from the outside, that was all you could say for it. It was faced with cheap Egyptian stucco rather than marble, and right next door to it was a slave-rental barracks.

At least, I reminded myself, it was free. I kicked at the door and shouted for the butler.

It wasn't the butler who opened it for me. It was Sam's niece herself, and she was a nice surprise. She was almost as tall as I was and just as fair. Besides, she was young and very good-looking. "You must be Julius," she said. "I am Rachel, niece of Citizen Flavius Samuelus ben Samuelus, and I welcome you to my home."

I kissed her hand. It's a Kievan custom that I like, especially with pretty girls I don't yet know well, but hope to. "You don't look Judaean," I told her.

"You don't look like a sci-rom hack," she replied. Her voice was less chilling than her words, but not much. "Uncle Sam isn't here, and I'm afraid I've got work I must do. Basilius will show you to your rooms and offer you some refreshment."

I usually make a better first impression on young women. I usually work at it more carefully, but she had taken me by surprise. I had more or less expected that Sam's niece would look more or less like

Sam, except probably for the baldness and the wrinkled face. I could not have been more wrong.

I had been wrong about the house, too. It was a big one. There had to be well over a dozen rooms, not counting servants' quarters, and the atrium was covered with one of those partly reflecting films that keep the worst of the heat out.

The famous Egyptian sun was directly overhead when Basilius, Rachel's butler, showed me my rooms. They were pleasingly bright and airy, but Basilius suggested I might enjoy being outside. He was right. He brought me wine and fruits in the atrium, a pleasant bench by a fountain. Through the film the sun looked only pale and pleasant instead of deadly hot. The fruit was fresh, too—pineapples from Lebanon, oranges from Judaea, apples that must have come all the way from somewhere in Gaul. The only thing wrong that I could see was that Rachel herself stayed in her rooms, so I didn't have a chance to try to put myself in a better light with her.

She had left instructions for my comfort, though. Basilius clapped his hands and another servant appeared, bearing stylus and tablets in case I should decide to work. I was surprised to see that both Basilius and the other one were Africs; they don't usually get into political trouble, or trouble with the aediles of any kind, so not many of them are slaves.

The fountain was a Cupid statue. In some circumstances I would have thought of that as a good sign, but here it didn't seem to mean anything. Cupid's nose was chipped, and the fountain was obviously older than Rachel was. I thought of just staying there until Rachel came out, but when I asked Basilius when that would be he gave me a look of delicate patronizing. "Citizeness Rachel works through the afternoon, Citizen Julius," he informed me.

"Oh? And what does she work at?"

"Citizeness Rachel is a famous historian," he said. "She often works straight through until bedtime. But for you and her uncle, of course, dinner will be served at your convenience."

He was quite an obliging fellow. "Thank you, Basilius," I said. "I believe I'll go out for a few hours myself." And then, as he turned politely to go, I said curiously, "You don't look like a very dangerous criminal. If you don't mind my asking, what were you enslaved for?"

"Oh, not for anything violent, Citizen Julius," he assured me. "Just for debts."

* * *

I found my way to the Hall of the Egyptian Senate-Inferior easily enough. There was a lot of traffic going that way, because it is, after all, one of the sights of Alexandria.

The Senate-Inferior wasn't in session at the time. There was no reason it should have been, of course, because what did the Egyptians need a Senate of any kind for? The time when they'd made any significant decisions for themselves was many centuries past.

They'd spread themselves for the conference, though. The Senate Temple had niches for at least half a hundred gods. There were the customary figures of Amon-Ra and Jupiter and all the other main figures of the pantheon, of course, but for the sake of the visitors they had installed Ahura-Mazda, Yahweh, Freya, Quetzalcoatl, and at least a dozen I didn't recognize at all. They were all decorated with fresh sacrifices of flowers and fruits, showing that the tourists, if not the astronomers—and probably the astronomers as well—were taking no chances in getting communications with the Olympians restored. Scientists are an agnostic lot, of course—well, most educated people are, aren't they? But even an agnostic will risk a piece of fruit to placate a god, just on the chance he's wrong.

Outside the hall, hucksters were already putting up their stands, although the first sessions wouldn't begin for another day. I bought some dates from one of them and wandered around, eating dates and studying the marble frieze on the wall of the Senate. It showed the rippling fields of corn, wheat, and potatoes that had made Egypt the breadbasket of the Empire for two thousand years. It didn't show anything about the Olympians, of course. Space is not a subject that interests the Egyptians a lot. They prefer to look back on their glorious (they *say* it's glorious) past; and there would have been no point in having the conference on the Olympians there at all, except who wants to go to some northern city in December?

Inside, the great hall was empty, except for slaves arranging seat cushions and cuspidors for the participants. The exhibit halls were noisy with workers setting up displays, but they didn't want people dropping in to bother them, and the participants' lounges were dark.

I was lucky enough to find the media room open. It was always good for a free glass of wine, and besides, I wanted to know where everyone was. The slave in charge couldn't tell me. "There's supposed to be a private executive meeting somewhere, that's all I know —and there's all these journalists looking for someone to interview." And then, peering over my shoulder as I signed in: "Oh, you're the fellow that writes the sci-roms, aren't you? Well, maybe one of the journalists would settle for you."

It wasn't the most flattering invitation I'd ever had. Still, I didn't say no. Marcus is always after me to do publicity gigs whenever I get the chance, because he thinks it sells books, and it was worthwhile trying to please Marcus just then.

The journalist wasn't much pleased, though. They'd set up a couple of studios in the basement of the Senate, and when I found the one I was directed to, the interviewer was fussing over his hairdo in front of a mirror. A couple of technicians were lounging in front of the tube, watching a broadcast comedy series. When I introduced myself the interviewer took his eyes off his own image long enough to cast a doubtful look in my direction.

"You're not a real astronomer," he told me.

I shrugged. I couldn't deny it.

"Still," he grumbled, "I'd better get *some* kind of a spot for the late news. All right. Sit over there, and try to sound as if you know what you're talking about." Then he began telling the technical crew what to do.

That was a strange thing. I'd already noticed that the technicians wore citizens' gold. The interviewer didn't. But he was the one who was giving *them* orders.

I didn't approve of that at all. I don't like big commercial outfits that put slaves in positions of authority over free citizens. It's a bad practice. Jobs like tutors, college professors, doctors, and so on are fine; slaves can do them as well as a citizen, and usually a lot cheaper. But there's a moral issue involved here. A slave must have a master. Otherwise, how can you call him a slave? And when you let the slave *be* the master, even in something as trivial as a broadcasting studio, you strike at the foundations of society.

The other thing is that it isn't fair competition. There are free citizens who need those jobs. We had some of that in my own line of work a few years ago. There were two or three slave authors turning out adventure novels, but the rest of us got together and put a stop to it—especially after Marcus bought one of them to use as a sub-editor. Not one citizen writer would work with her. Mark finally had to put her into the publicity department, where she couldn't do any harm.

So I started the interview with a chip on my shoulder, and his first question made it worse. He plunged right in. "When you're pounding out those sci-roms of yours, do you make any effort to keep in touch with scientific reality? Do you know, for instance, that the Olympians have stopped transmitting?"

I scowled at him, regardless of the cameras. "Science-adventure romances are *about* scientific reality. And the Olympians haven't 'stopped,' as you put it. There's just been a technical hitch of some kind, probably caused by radio interference from our own sun. As I said in my earlier romance, *The Radio Gods*, electromagnetic impulses are susceptible to—"

He cut me off. "It's been—" he glanced at his watch—"twenty-nine hours since they stopped. That doesn't sound like just a technical hitch."

"Of course it is. There's no reason for them to stop. We've already demonstrated to them that we're truly civilized, first because we're technological, second because we don't fight wars anymore—that was cleared up in the first year. As I said in my roman, *The Radio Gods*—"

He gave me a pained look, then turned and winked into the camera. "You can't keep a hack from plugging his books, can you?" he remarked humorously. "But it looks like he doesn't want to use that wild imagination unless he gets paid for it. All I'm asking him for is a guess at why the Olympians don't want to talk to us anymore, and all he gives me is commercials."

As though there were any other reason to do interviews! "Look here," I said sharply, "if you can't be courteous when you speak to a citizen, I'm not prepared to go on with this conversation at all."

"So be it, pal," he said, icy cold. He turned to the technical crew. "Stop the cameras," he ordered. "We're going back to the studio. This is a waste of time." We parted on terms of mutual dislike, and once again I had done something that my editor would have been glad to kill me for.

That night at dinner, Sam was no comfort. "He's an unpleasant man, sure," he told me. "But the trouble is, I'm afraid he's right."

"They've really *stopped*?"

Sam shrugged. "We're not in line with the sun anymore, so that's definitely not the reason. Damn. I was hoping it would be."

"I'm sorry about that, Uncle Sam," Rachel said gently. She was wearing a simple white robe, Hannish silk by the look of it, with no decorations at all. It really looked good on her. I didn't think there was anything under it except for some very well formed female flesh.

"I'm sorry, too," he grumbled. His concerns didn't affect his appetite, though. He was ladling in the first course—a sort of chicken soup, with bits of a kind of pastry floating in it—and, for that matter, so was I. Whatever Rachel's faults might be, she had a good cook. It was plain home cooking, none of your partridge-in-a-rabbit-inside-a-boar kind of thing, but well prepared and expertly served by her butler, Basilius. "Anyway," Sam said, mopping up the last of the broth, "I've figured it out."

"Why the Olympians stopped?" I asked, to encourage him to go on with the revelation.

"No, no! I mean about your romance, Julie. My alternate world idea. If you don't want to write about a different *future*, how about a different *now?*"

I didn't get a chance to ask him about what he was talking about, because Rachel beat me to it. "There's only one *now*, Sam, dear," she pointed out. I couldn't have said it better myself.

Sam groaned. "Not you, too, honey," he complained. "I'm talking about a new kind of sci-rom."

"I don't read many sci-roms," she apologized, in the tone that isn't an apology at all.

He ignored that. "You're a historian, aren't you?" She didn't bother to confirm it; obviously, it was the thing she was that shaped her life. "So what if history had gone a different way?"

He beamed at us as happily as though he had said something that made sense. Neither of us beamed back. Rachel pointed out the flaw in his remark. "It didn't, though," she told him.

"I said *suppose!* This isn't the only possible now, it's just the one that happened to occur! There could have been a million different ones. Look at all the events in the past that could have gone a different way. Suppose Annius Publius hadn't discovered the Western Continents in City Year 1820. Suppose Caesar Publius Terminus hadn't decreed the development of a space program in 2122. Don't you see what I'm driving at? What kind of a world would we be living in now if those things hadn't happened?"

Rachel opened her mouth to speak, but she was saved by the butler. He appeared in the doorway with a look of silent appeal. When she excused herself to see what was needed in the kitchen, that left it up to me. "I never wrote anything like that, Sam," I told him. "I don't know anybody else who did, either."

"That's exactly what I'm driving at! It would be something completely *new* in sci-roms. Don't you want to pioneer a whole new kind of story?"

Out of the wisdom of experience, I told him, "Pioneers don't make any money, Sam." He scowled at me. "You could write it yourself," I suggested.

That just changed the annoyance to gloom. "I wish I could. But until this business with the Olympians is cleared up, I'm not going to have much time for sci-roms. No, it's up to you, Julie."

Then Rachel came back in, looking pleased with herself, followed by Basilius bearing a huge silver platter containing the main course.

Sam cheered up at once. So did I. The main dish was a whole roasted baby kid, and I realized that the reason Rachel had been called into the kitchen was so that she could weave a garland of flowers around its tiny baby horn buds herself. The maid servant followed with a pitcher of wine, replenishing all our goblets. All in all, we were busy enough eating to stop any conversation but compliments on the food.

Then Sam looked at his watch. "Great dinner, Rachel," he told his niece, "but I've got to get back. What about it?"

"What about what?" she asked.

"About helping poor Julie with some historical turning points he can use in the story?"

He hadn't listened to a word I'd said. I didn't have to say so, because Rachel was looking concerned. She said apologetically, "I don't know anything about those periods you were talking about—Publius Terminus, and so on. My specialty is the immediate post-Augustan period, when the Senate came back to power."

"Fine," he said, pleased with himself and showing it. "That's as good a period as any. Think how different things might be now if some little event then had gone in a different way. Say, if Augustus hadn't married Lady Livia and adopted her son Drusus to succeed him." He turned to me, encouraging me to take fire from his spark of inspiration. "I'm sure you see the possibilities, Julie! Tell you what you should do. The night's young yet; take Rachel out dancing or something; have a few drinks; listen to her talk. What's wrong with that? You two young people ought to be having fun, anyway!"

That was definitely the most intelligent thing intelligent Sam had said in days.

So I thought, anyway, and Rachel was a good enough niece to heed her uncle's advice. Because I was a stranger in town, I had to let her pick the place. After the first couple she mentioned I realized that she was tactfully trying to spare my pocketbook. I couldn't allow that. After all, a night on the town with Rachel was probably cheaper, and anyway a whole lot more interesting, than the cost of an inn and meals.

We settled on a place right on the harborside, out toward the break-water. It was a revolving nightclub on top of an inn built along the style of one of the old Pyramids. As the room slowly turned we saw the lights of the city of Alexandria, the shipping in the harbor, then the wide sea itself, its gentle waves reflecting starlight.

I was prepared to forget the whole idea of alternate worlds, but

Rachel was more dutiful than that. After the first dance, she said, "I think I can help you. There was something that happened in Drusus's reign—"

"Do we have to talk about that?" I asked, refilling her glass.

"But Uncle Sam said we should. I thought you wanted to try a new kind of sci-rom."

"No, that's your uncle who wants that. See, there's a bit of a problem here. It's true that editors are always begging for something new and different, but if you're dumb enough to try to give it to them they don't recognize it. When they ask for different, what they mean is something right down the good old 'different' groove."

"I think," she informed me, with the certainty of an oracle and a lot less confusion of style, "that when my uncle has an idea, it's usually a good one." I didn't want to argue with her; I didn't even disagree: at least usually. I let her talk. "You see," she said, "my specialty is the transfer of power throughout early Roman history. What I'm studying right now is the Judaean Diaspora, after Drusus's reign. You know what happened then, I suppose?"

Actually, I did—hazily. "That was the year of the Judaean rebellion, wasn't it?"

She nodded. She looked very pretty when she nodded, her fair hair moving gracefully and her eyes sparkling. "You see, that was a great tragedy for the Judaeans, and, just as my uncle said, it needn't have happened. If Procurator Tiberius had lived, it wouldn't have."

I coughed. "I'm not sure I know who Tiberius was," I said apologetically.

"He was the Procurator of Judaea, and a very good one. He was just and fair. He was the brother of the Emperor Drusus—the one my uncle was talking about, Livia's son, the adopted heir of Caesar Augustus. The one who restored the power of the Senate after Augustus had appropriated most of it for himself. Anyway, Tiberius was the best governor the Judaeans ever had, just as Drusus was the best emperor. Tiberius died just a year before the rebellion—ate some spoiled figs, they say, although it might have been his wife who did it —she was Julia, the daughter of Augustus by his first wife—"

I signaled distress. "I'm getting a little confused by all these names," I admitted.

"Well, the important one to remember is Tiberius, and you know who he was. If he had lived, the rebellion probably wouldn't have happened. Then there wouldn't have been a Diaspora."

"I see," I said. "Would you like another dance?"

She frowned at me, then smiled. "Maybe that's not such an interesting subject—unless you're a Judaean, anyway," she said. "All right, let's dance."

That was the best idea yet. It gave me a chance to confirm with my fingers what my eyes, ears, and nose had already told me; this was a very attractive young woman. She had insisted on changing, but fortunately the new gown was as soft and clinging as the old, and the palms of my hands rejoined in the tactile pleasure of her back and arm. I whispered, "I'm sorry if I sound stupid. I really don't know a whole lot about early history—you know, the first thousand years or so after the Founding of the City."

She didn't bother to point out that she did. She moved with me to the music, very enjoyable, then she straightened up. "I've got a different idea," she announced. "Let's go back to the booth." And she was already telling it to me as we left the dance floor. "Let's talk about your own ancestor, Julius Caesar. He conquered Egypt, right here in Alexandria. But suppose the Egyptians had defeated him instead, as they very nearly did?"

I was paying close attention now—obviously she had been interested enough in me to ask Sam some questions! "They couldn't have," I told her. "Julius never lost a war. Anyway"—I discovered to my surprise that I was beginning to take Sam's nutty idea seriously— "that would be a really hard one to write, wouldn't it? If the Legions had been defeated, it would have changed the whole world. Can you imagine a world that isn't Roman?"

She said sweetly, "No, but that's more your job than mine, isn't it?"

I shook my head. "It's too bizarre," I complained. "I couldn't make the readers believe it."

"You could try, Julius," she told me. "You see, there's an interesting possibility there. Drusus almost didn't live to become Emperor. He was severely wounded in a war in Gaul, while Augustus was still alive. Tiberius—you remember Tiberius—"

"Yes, yes, his brother. The one you like. The one he made Procurator of Judaea."

"That's the one. Well, Tiberius rode day and night to bring Drusus the best doctors in Rome. He almost didn't make it. They barely pulled Drusus through."

"Yes?" I said encouragingly. "And what then?"

She looked uncertain. "Well, I don't know what then."

I poured some more wine. "I guess I could figure out some kind of speculative idea," I said, ruminating. "Especially if you would help me with some of the details. I suppose Tiberius would have become Emperor instead of Drusus. You say he was a good man; so probably he would have done more or less what Drusus did—restore the power of the Senate, after Augustus and my revered great-great Julius between them had pretty nearly put it out of business—"

I stopped there, startled at my own words. It almost seemed that I was beginning to take Sam's crazy idea seriously!

On the other hand, that wasn't all bad. It almost seemed that Rachel was beginning to take *me* seriously.

That was a good thought. It kept me cheerful through half a dozen more dances and at least another hour of history lessons from her pretty lips . . . right up until the time when, after we had gone back to her house, I tiptoed out of my room toward hers, and found her butler, Basilius, asleep on a rug across her doorway, with a great, thick club by his side.

I didn't sleep well that night.

Partly it was glandular. My head knew that Rachel didn't want me creeping into her bedroom, or else she wouldn't have put the butler there in the way. But my glands weren't happy with that news. They had soaked up the smell and sight and feel of her, and they were complaining about being thwarted.

The worst part was waking up every hour or so to contemplate financial ruin.

Being poor wasn't so bad. Every writer has to learn how to be poor from time to time, between checks. It's an annoyance, but not a catastrophe. You don't get enslaved just for poverty.

But I had been running up some pretty big bills. And you do get enslaved for debt.

Chapter 4
The End of the Dream

The next morning I woke up late and grouchy and had to take a three-wheeler to the Hall of the Senate-Inferior.

It was slow going. As we approached, the traffic thickened even more. I could see the Legion forming for the ceremonial guard as the Pharaoh's procession approached to open the ceremonies. The driver wouldn't take me any closer than the outer square, and I had to wait there with all the tourists, while the Pharaoh dismounted from her royal litter.

There was a soft, pleasured noise from the crowd, halfway between a giggle and a sigh. That was the spectacle the tourists had come to see. They pressed against the sheathed swords of the Legionaries while the Pharaoh, head bare, robe trailing on the ground, advanced on the shrines outside the Senate building. She sacrificed reverently and unhurriedly to them, while the tourists flashed their cameras at her, and I began to worry about the time. What if she ecumenically decided to visit all fifty shrines? But after doing Isis, Amon-Ra, and Mother Nile, she went inside to declare the Congress open. The Legionaries relaxed. The tourists began to flow back to their buses, snapping pictures of themselves now, and I followed the Pharaoh inside.

She made a good—by which I mean short—opening address. The only thing wrong with it was that she was talking to mostly empty seats.

The Hall of the Alexandrian Senate-Inferior holds two thousand people. There weren't more than a hundred and fifty in it. Most of those were huddled in small groups in the aisles and at the back of the hall, and they were paying no attention at all to the Pharaoh. I think she saw that and shortened her speech. At one moment she was telling us how the scientific investigation of the outside universe was completely in accord with the ancient traditions of Egypt—with hardly anyone listening—and at the next her voice had stopped without warning and she was handing her orb and scepter to her attendants. She proceeded regally across the stage and out the wings.

The buzz of conversation hardly slackened. What they were talking about, of course, was the Olympians. Even when the Collegium-Presidor stepped forward and called for the first session to begin. the hall didn't fill. At least most of the scattered groups of people in the room sat down—though still in clumps, and still doing a lot of whispering to each other.

Even the speakers didn't seem very interested in what they were saying. The first one was an honorary Presidor-Emeritus from the southern highlands of Egypt, and he gave us a review of everything we knew about the Olympians.

He read it as hurriedly as though he were dictating it to a scribe. It wasn't very interesting. The trouble, of course, was that his paper had been prepared days earlier, while the Olympian transmissions were still flooding in and no one had any thought they might be interrupted. It just didn't seem relevant anymore.

What I like about going to science congresses isn't so much the actual papers the speakers deliver—I can get that sort of information better from the journals in the library. It isn't even the back-and-forth discussion that follows each paper, although that sometimes produces useful background bits. What I get the most out of is what I call "the sound of science"—the kind of shorthand language scientists use when they're talking to each other about their own specialties. So I usually sit somewhere at the back of the hall, with as much space around me as I can manage, my tablet in my lap and my stylus in my hand, writing down bits of dialogue and figuring how to put them into my next sci-rom.

There wasn't much of that today. There wasn't much discussion at all. One by one the speakers got up and read their papers, answered a couple of cursory questions with cursory replies, and hurried off; and when each one finished he left, and the audience got smaller because, as I finally figured out, no one was there who wasn't obligated to be.

When boredom made me decide that I needed a glass of wine and a quick snack more than I needed to sit there with my still-blank tablet, I found out there was hardly anyone even in the lounges. There was no familiar face. No one seemed to know where Sam was. And in the afternoon, the Collegium-Presidor, bowing to the inevitable, announced that the remaining sessions would be postponed indefinitely.

The day was a total waste.

I had a lot more hopes for the night.

Rachel greeted me with the news that Sam had sent a message to say he was detained and wouldn't make dinner.

"Did he say where he was?" She shook her head. "He's off with some of the other top people," I guessed. I told her about the collapse of the convention. Then I brightened. "At least let's go out for dinner, then."

Rachel firmly vetoed the idea. She was tactful enough not to mention money, although I was sure Sam had filled her in on my precarious financial state. "I like my own cook's food better than any restaurant," she told me. "We'll eat here. There won't be anything fancy tonight—just a simple meal for the two of us."

The best part of that was "the two of us." Basilius had arranged the couches in a sort of V, so that our heads were quite close together, with the low serving tables in easy reach between us. As soon as she lay down, Rachel confessed, "I didn't get a lot of work done today. I couldn't get that idea of yours out of my head."

The idea was Sam's, actually, but I didn't see any reason to correct her. "I'm flattered," I told her. "I'm sorry I spoiled your work."

She shrugged and went on. "I did a little reading on the period, especially about an interesting minor figure who lived around then, a

Judaean preacher named Jeshua of Nazareth. Did you ever hear of him? Well, most people haven't, but he had a lot of followers at one time. They called themselves Chrestians, and they were a very unruly bunch."

"I'm afraid I don't know much about Judaean history," I said. Which was true; but then I added, "But I'd really like to learn more." Which wasn't—or at least hadn't been until just then.

"Of course," Rachel said. No doubt to her it seemed quite natural that everyone in the world would wish to know more about the post-Augustan period. "Anyway, this Jeshua was on trial for sedition. He was condemned to death."

I blinked at her. "Not just to slavery?"

She shook her head. "They didn't just enslave criminals back then, they did physical things to them. Even executed them, sometimes in very barbarous ways. But Tiberius, as Proconsul, decided that the penalty was too extreme. So he commuted Jeshua's death sentence. He just had him whipped and let him go. A very good decision, I think. Otherwise he would have made him a martyr, and gods know what would have happened after that. As it was, the Chrestians just gradually waned away. . . . Basilius? You can bring the next course in now."

I watched with interest as Basilius complied. It turned out to be larks and olives! I approved, not simply for the fact that I liked the dish. The "simple meal" was actually a lot more elaborate than she had provided for the three of us the night before.

Things were looking up. I said, "Can you tell me something, Rachel? I think you're Judaean yourself, aren't you?"

"Of course."

"Well, I'm a little confused," I said. "I thought the Judaeans believed in the god Yahveh."

"Of course, Julie. We do."

"Yes, but—" I hesitated. I didn't want to mess up the way things were going, but I was curious. "But you say 'gods.' Isn't that, well, a contradiction?"

"Not at all," she told me civilly enough. "Yahveh's commandments were brought down from a mountaintop by our great prophet, Moses, and they were very clear on the subject. One of them says, 'Thou shalt have no other gods before me.' Well, we don't, you see? Yahveh is our *first* god. There aren't any *before* him. It's all explained in the rabbinical writings."

"And that's what you go by, the rabbinical writings?"

She looked thoughtful. "In a way. We're a very traditional people,

Julie. Tradition is what we follow; the rabbinical writings simply explain the traditions."

She had stopped eating. I stopped, too. Dreamily I reached out to caress her cheek.

She didn't pull away. She didn't respond, either. After a moment, she said, not looking at me, "For instance, there is a Judaean tradition that a woman is to be a virgin at the time of her marriage."

My hand came away from her face by itself, without any conscious command from me. "Oh?"

"And the rabbinical writings more or less define the tradition, you see. They say that the head of the household is to stand guard at an unmarried daughter's bedroom for the first hour of each night; if there is no male head of the household, a trusted slave is to be appointed to the job."

"I see," I said. "You've never been married, have you?"

"Not yet," said Rachel, beginning to eat again.

I hadn't ever been married, either, although, to be sure, I wasn't exactly a virgin. It wasn't that I had anything against marriage. It was only that the life of a sci-rom hack wasn't what you would call exactly financially stable, and also the fact that I hadn't ever come across the woman I wanted to spend my life with . . . or, to quote Rachel, "Not yet."

I tried to keep my mind off that subject. I was sure that if my finances had been precarious before, they were now close to catastrophic.

The next morning I wondered what to do with my day, but Rachel settled it for me. She was waiting for me in the atrium. "Sit down with me, Julie," she commanded, patting the bench beside me. "I was up late, thinking, and I think I've got something for you. Suppose this man Jeshua had been executed, after all."

It wasn't exactly the greeting I had been hoping for, nor was it something I had given a moment's thought to, either. But I was glad enough to sit next to her in that pleasant little garden, with the gentled early sun shining down on us through the translucent shades. "Yes?" I said noncommittally, kissing her hand in greeting.

She waited a moment before she took her hand back. "That idea opened some interesting possibilities, Julie. Jeshua would have been a martyr, you see. I can easily imagine that under those circumstances his Chrestian followers would have had a lot more staying power. They might even have grown to be really important. Judaea was always in one kind of turmoil or another around that time, anyway—

there were all sorts of prophecies and rumors about messiahs and changes in society. The Chrestians might even have come to dominate all of Judaea."

I tried to be tactful. "There's nothing wrong with being proud of your ancestors, Rachel. But, really, what difference would that have made?" I obviously hadn't been tactful enough. She had turned to look at me with what looked like the beginning of a frown. I thought fast, and tried to cover myself. "On the other hand," I went on quickly, "suppose you expanded that idea beyond Judaea."

It turned into a real frown, but puzzled rather than angry. "What do you mean, beyond Judaea?"

"Well, suppose Jeshua's Chrestian-Judaean kind of—what would you call it? Philosophy? Religion?"

"A little of both, I'd say."

"Religious philosophy, then. Suppose it spread over most of the world, not just Judaea. That could be interesting."

"But, really, no such thing hap—"

"Rachel, Rachel," I said, covering her mouth with a fingertip affectionately. "We're saying *what if*, remember? Every sci-rom writer is entitled to one big lie. Let's say this is mine. Let's say that Chrestian-Judaeanism became a world religion. Even Rome itself succumbs. Maybe the City becomes the—what do you call it—the place for the Sanhedrin of the Chrestian-Judaeans. And then what happens?"

"You tell me," she said, half amused, half suspicious.

"Why, then," I said, flexing the imagination of the trained sci-rom writer, "it might develop like the kind of conditions you've been talking about in the old days in Judaea. Maybe the whole world would be splintering into factions and sects, and then they fight."

"Fight *wars?*" she asked incredulously.

"Fight *big* wars. Why not? It happened in Judaea, didn't it? And then they might keep right on fighting them, all through historical times. After all, the only thing that's kept the world united for the past two thousand years has been the Pax Romana. Without that— why, without that," I went on, talking faster and making mental notes to myself as I went along, "let's say that all the tribes of Europe turned into independent city states. Like the Greeks, only bigger. And more powerful. And they fight, the Franks against the Vik Northmen against the Belgiae against the Kelts."

She was shaking her head. "People wouldn't be so silly, Julie," she complained.

"How do you know that? Anyway, this is a sci-rom, dear." I didn't pause to see if she reacted to the "dear." I went right on, but not failing to notice that she hadn't objected. "The people will be as silly as I want them to be—as long as I can make it plausible enough for the fans. But you haven't heard the best part of it. Let's say the Chrestian-Judaeans take their religion seriously. They don't do anything to go against the will of their god. What Yahveh said still goes, no matter what. Do you follow? That means they aren't at all interested in scientific discovery, for instance."

"No, stop right there!" she ordered, suddenly indignant. "Are you trying to say that we Judaeans aren't interested in science? That I'm not? Or my Uncle Sam? And we're certainly Judaeans."

"But you're not *Chrestian*-Judaeans, sweet. There's a big difference. Why? Because I say there is, Rachel, and I'm the one writing the story. So, let's see—" I paused for thought—"all right, let's say the Chrestians go through a long period of intellectual stagnation, and then—" I paused, not because I didn't know what was coming next, but to build the effect—"and then along come the Olympians!"

She gazed at me blankly. "Yes?" she asked, encouraging but vague.

"Don't you see it? And then this Chrestian-Judaean world, drowsing along in the middle of a prescientific dark age—no aircraft, no electronic broadcast, not even a printing press or a hovermachine—is suddenly thrown into contact with a supertechnological civilization from outer space!" She was wrinkling her forehead at me, trying to understand what I was driving at. "It's terrible culture shock," I explained. "And not just for the people on Earth. Maybe the Olympians come to look us over, and they see that we're technologically backward and divided into warring nations and all that . . . and what do they do? Why, they turn right around and leave us! And . . . and that's the end of the book!"

She pursed her lips. "But maybe that's what they're doing now," she said cautiously.

"But not for that reason, certainly. See, this isn't *our* world I'm talking about. It's a *what if* world."

"It sounds a little far-fetched," she said.

I said happily, "That's where my skills come in. You don't understand sci-rom, sweetheart. It's the sci-rom writer's job to push an idea as far as it will go—to the absolute limit of credibility—to the point where if he took just one step more the whole thing would collapse into absurdity. Trust me, Rachel. I'll make them believe it."

She was still pursing her pretty lips, but this time I didn't wait for her to speak. I seized the bird of opportunity on the wing. I leaned toward her and kissed those lips, as I had been wanting to do for some time. Then I said, "I've got to get to a scribe; I want to get all this down before I forget it. I'll be back when I can be, and—and until then—well, here."

And I kissed her again, gently, firmly and long; and it was quite clear early in the process that she was kissing me back.

Being next to a rental barracks had its advantages. I found a scribe to rent at a decent price, and the rental manager even let me borrow one of their conference rooms that night to dictate in. By daybreak I had down the first two chapters and an outline of *Sidewise to a Chrestian World*.

Once I get that far in a book, the rest is just work. The general idea is set, the characters have announced themselves to me, it's just a matter of closing my eyes for a moment to see what's going to be happening and then opening them to dictate to the scribe. In this case, the scribes, plural, because the first one wore out in a few more hours and I had to employ a second, and then a third.

I didn't sleep at all until it was all down. I think it was fifty-two straight hours, the longest I'd worked in one stretch in years. When it was all done I left it to be fair-copied. The rental agent agreed to get it down to the shipping offices by the harbor and dispatch it by fast air to Marcus in London.

Then at last I stumbled back to Rachel's house to sleep. I was surprised to find that it was still dark, an hour or more before sunrise.

Basilius let me in, looking startled as he studied my sunken eyes and unshaved face. "Let me sleep until I wake up," I ordered. There was a journal neatly folded beside my bed, but I didn't look at it. I lay down, turned over once, and was gone.

When I woke up, at least twelve hours had passed. I had Basilius bring me something to eat and shave me, and when I finally got out to the atrium it was nearly sundown and Rachel was waiting for me. I told her what I'd done, and she told me about the last message from the Olympians. "Last?" I objected. "How can you be sure it's the last?"

"Because they said so," she told me sadly. "They said they were breaking off communications."

"Oh," I said, thinking about that. "Poor Sam." And she looked so doleful that I couldn't help myself, I took her in my arms.

Consolation turned to kissing, and when we had done quite a lot of that she leaned back, smiling at me.

I couldn't help what I said then, either. It startled me to hear the words come out of my mouth as I said, "Rachel, I wish we could get married."

She pulled back, looking at me with affection and a little surprised amusement. "Are you proposing to me?"

I was careful of my grammar. "That was a subjunctive, sweet. I said I *wished* we could get married."

"I understood that. What I want to know is whether you're asking me to grant your wish."

"No—well, hells, yes! But what I wish first is that I had the right to ask you. Sci-rom writers don't have the most solid financial situation, you know. The way you live here—"

"The way I live here," she said, "is paid for by the estate I inherited from my father. Getting married won't take it away."

"But that's your estate, my darling. I've been poor, but I've never been a parasite."

"You won't be a parasite," she said softly, and I realized that she was being careful about her grammar, too.

Which took a lot of willpower on my part. "Rachel," I said, "I should be hearing from my editor any time now. If this new kind of sci-rom catches on—if it's as popular as it might be—"

"Yes?" she prompted.

"Why," I said, "then maybe I can actually ask you. But I don't know that. Marcus probably has it by now, but I don't know if he's read it. And then I won't know his decision till I hear from him. And now, with all the confusion about the Olympians, that might take weeks—"

"Julie," she said, putting her finger over my lips, "call him up."

The circuits were all busy, but I finally got through—and, because it was well after lunch, Marcus was in his office. More than that, he was quite sober. "Julie, you bastard," he cried, sounding really furious, "where the hells have you been hiding? I ought to have you whipped."

But he hadn't said anything about getting the aediles after me. "Did you have a chance to read *Sidewise to a Christian World?*" I asked.

"The what? Oh, *that* thing. Nah. I haven't even looked at it. I'll buy it, naturally," he said. "But what I'm talking about is *An Ass's Olympiad.* The censors won't stop it now, you know. In fact, all I want you to do now is make the Olympians a little dumber, a little nastier— you've got a biggie here, Julie! I think we can get a broadcast out of it, even. So when can you get back here to fix it up?"

"Why—well, pretty soon, I guess, only I haven't checked the hover timetable—"

"Hover, hell! You're coming back by fast plane—we'll pick up the tab. And, oh, by the way, we're doubling your advance. The payment will be in your account this afternoon."

And ten minutes later, when I unsubjunctively proposed to Rachel, she quickly and unsubjunctively accepted; and the high-speed flight to London takes nine hours, but I was grinning all the way.

Chapter 5
The Way It Is When
You've Got It Made

To be a free-lance writer is to live in a certain kind of ease. Not very easeful financially, maybe, but in a lot of other ways. You don't have to go to an office every day, you get a lot of satisfaction out of seeing your very own words being read on hovers and trains by total strangers. To be a potentially *best-selling* writer is a whole order of magnitude different. Marcus put me up in an inn right next to the publishing company's offices and stood over me while I turned my poor imaginary Olympian into the most doltish, feckless, unlikeable being the universe had ever seen. The more I made the Olympian contemptibly comic, the more Marcus loved it. So did everyone else in the office; so did their affiliates in Kiev and Manahattan and Kalkut and half a dozen other cities all around the world, and he informed me proudly that they were publishing my book simultaneously in all of them. "We'll be the first ones out, Julie," he exulted. "It's going to be a mint! Money? Well, of course you can have more money—you're in the big-time now!" And, yes, the broadcast studios were interested —interested enough to sign a contract even before I'd finished the revisions; and so were the journals, who came for interviews every minute that Marcus would let me off from correcting the proofs and posing for jacket photographs and speaking to their sales staff; and, all in all, I hardly had a chance to breathe until I was back on the high speed aircraft to Alexandria and my bride.

Sam had agreed to give the bride away, and he met me at the airpad. He looked older and more tired, but resigned. As we drove to Rachel's house, where the wedding guests were already beginning to gather, I tried to cheer him up. I had plenty of joy myself; I wanted to share it. So I offered, "At least, now you can get back to your real work."

He looked at me strangely. "Writing sci-roms?" he asked.

"No, of course not! That's good enough for me, but you've still got your extrasolar probe to keep you busy."

"Julie," he said sadly, "where have you been lately? Didn't you see the last Olympian message?"

"Well, sure," I said, offended. "Everybody did, didn't they?" And then I thought for a moment, and, actually, it had been Rachel who had told me about it. I'd never actually looked at a journal or a broadcast. "I guess I was pretty busy," I said lamely.

He looked sadder than ever. "Then maybe you don't know that they said they weren't only terminating all their own transmissions to us, they were terminating even our own probes."

"Oh, no, Sam! I would have heard if the probes had stopped transmitting!"

He said patiently, "No, you wouldn't, because the data they were sending is still on its way to us. We've still got a few years coming in from our probes. But that's it. We're out of interstellar space, Julie. They don't want us there."

He broke off, peering out the window. "And that's the way it is," he said. "We're here, though, and you better get inside. Rachel's going to be tired of sitting under that canopy without you around."

The greatest thing of all about being a best-selling author, if you like traveling, is that when you fly around the world somebody else pays for the tickets. Marcus's publicity department fixed up the whole thing. Personal appearances, bookstore autographings, college lectures, broadcasts, publishers' meetings, receptions—we were kept busy for a solid month, and it made a hell of a fine honeymoon.

Of course any honeymoon would have been wonderful as long as Rachel was the bride, but without the publishers bankrolling us we might not have visited six of the seven continents on the way. (We didn't bother with Polaris Australis—nobody there but penguins.) And we took time for ourselves along the way, on beaches in Hindia and the islands of Han, in the wonderful shops of Manahattan and a dozen other cities of the Western Continents—we did it all.

When we got back to Alexandria the contractors had finished the remodeling of Rachel's villa—which, we had decided, would now be our winter home, though our next priority was going to be to find a place where we could spend the busy part of the year in London. Sam had moved back in and, with Basilius, greeted us formally as we came to the door.

"I thought you'd be in Rome," I told him, once we were settled and Rachel had gone to inspect what had been done with her baths.

"Not while I'm still trying to understand what went wrong," he said. "The research is going on right here; this is where we transmitted from."

I shrugged and took a sip of the Falernian wine Basilius had left for us. I held the goblet up critically: a little cloudy, I thought, and in the vat too long. And then I grinned at myself, because a few weeks earlier I would have been delighted at anything so costly. "But we know what went wrong," I told him reasonably. "They decided against us."

"Of course they did," he said. "But why? I've been trying to work out just what messages were being received when they broke off communications."

"Do you think we said something to offend them?"

He scratched the age spot on his bald head, staring at me. Then he sighed. "What would *you* think, Julius?"

"Well, maybe so," I admitted. "What messages were they?"

"I'm not sure. It took a lot of digging. The Olympians, you know, acknowledged receipt of each message by repeating the last hundred and forty groups—"

"I didn't know."

"Well, they did. The last message they acknowledged was a history of Rome. Unfortunately, it was six hundred and fifty thousand words long."

"So you have to read the whole history?"

"Not just *read* it, Julie; we have to try to figure out what might have been in it that wasn't in any previous message. We've had two or three hundred researchers collating every previous message, and the only thing that was new was some of the social data from the last census—"

I interrupted him. "I thought you said it was a history."

"It was at the *end* of the history. We were giving pretty current data —so many of equestrian rank, so many citizens, so many freedmen, so many slaves." He hesitated, and then said thoughtfully, "Paulus Magnus—I don't know if you know him, he's an Algonkan—pointed out that that was the first time we'd ever mentioned slavery."

I waited for him to go on. "Yes?" I said encouragingly.

He shrugged. "Nothing. Paulus is a slave himself, so naturally he's got it on his mind a lot."

"I don't quite see what that has to do with anything," I said. "Isn't there anything else?"

"Oh," he said, "there are a thousand theories. There were some health data, too, and some people think the Olympians might have suddenly gotten worried about some new microorganism killing them off. Or we weren't polite enough. Or maybe—who knows— there was some sort of power struggle among them, and the side that came out on top just didn't want any more new races in their community."

"And we don't know yet which it was?"

"It's worse than that, Julie," he told me somberly. "I don't think we ever will find out what it was that made them decide they didn't want to have anything to do with us." And in that, too, Flavius Samuelus ben Samuelus was a very intelligent man. Because we never have.

THE RETURN OF
WILLIAM PROXMIRE

Larry Niven

Through the peephole in Andrew's front door the man made a startling sight.

He looked to be in his eighties. He was breathing hard and streaming sweat. He seemed slightly more real than most men: photogenic as hell, tall and lean, with stringy muscles and no potbelly, running shoes and a day pack and a blue windbreaker, and an open smile. The face was familiar, but from where?

Andrew opened the front door but left the screen door locked. "Hello?"

"Dr. Andrew Minsky?"

"Yes." Memory clicked. "William Proxmire, big as life."

The ex-senator smiled acknowledgment. "I've only just finished reading about you in the *Tribune*, Dr. Minsky. May I come in?"

It had never been Andrew Minsky's ambition to invite William Proxmire into his home. Still—"Sure. Come in, sit down, have some coffee. Or do your stretches." Andrew was a runner himself when he could find the time.

"Thank you."

Andrew left him on the rug with one knee pulled against his chest. From the kitchen he called, "I never in my life expected to meet you face to face. You must have seen the article on me and Tipler and Penrose?"

"Yes. I'm prepared to learn that the media got it all wrong."

"I bet you are. Any politician would. Well, the *Tribune* implied that what we've got is a time machine. Of course we don't. We've got a schematic based on a theory. Then again, it's the new improved version. It doesn't involve an infinitely long cylinder that you'd have to make out of neutronium—"

"Good. What would it cost?"

Andrew Minsky sighed. Had the politician even recognized the reference? He said, "Oh . . . hard to say." He picked up two cups and the coffeepot and went back in. "Is that it? You came looking for a time machine?"

The old man was sitting on the yellow rug with his legs spread wide apart and his fingers grasping his right foot. He released, folded his legs heel to heel, touched forehead to toes, held, then stood up with a sound like popcorn popping. He said, "Close enough. How much would it cost?"

"Depends on what you're after. If you—"

"I can't get you a grant if you can't name a figure."

Andrew set his cup down very carefully. He said, "No, of course not."

"I'm retired now, but people still owe me favors. I want a ride. One trip. What would it cost?"

Andrew hadn't had enough coffee yet. He didn't feel fully awake. "I have to think out loud a little. Okay? Mass isn't a problem. You can go as far back as you like if . . . mmm. Let's say under sixty years. Cost might be twelve, thirteen million if you could also get us access to the proton-antiproton accelerator at Washburn University, or maybe CERN in Switzerland. Otherwise we'd have to build that too. By the way, you're not expecting to get younger, are you?"

"I hadn't thought about it."

"Good. The theory depends on maneuverings between event points. You don't ever go backward. Where and when, Senator?"

William Proxmire leaned forward with his hands clasped. "Picture this. A Navy officer walks the deck of a ship, coughing, late at night in the 1930s. Suddenly an arm snakes around his neck, a needle plunges into his buttocks—"

"The deck of a ship at sea?"

Proxmire nodded, grinning.

"You're just having fun, aren't you? Something to do while jogging, now that you're retired."

"Put it this way," Proxmire said. "I read the article. It linked up with an old daydream of mine. I looked up your address. You were within easy running distance. I hope you don't mind?"

Oddly enough, Andrew found he didn't. Anything that happened before his morning coffee was recreation.

So dream a little. "Deck of a moving ship. I was going to say it's ridiculous, but it isn't. We'll have to deal with much higher velocities. Any point on the Earth's surface is spinning at up to half a mile per

second and circling the sun at eighteen miles per. In principle I think
we could solve all of it with one stroke. We could scan one patch of
deck, say, over a period of a few seconds, then integrate the record
into the program. Do the same coming home."

"You can do it?"

"Well, if we can't solve that one we can't do anything else, either.
You'd be on a tight schedule, though. Senator, what's the purpose of
the visit?"

"Have you ever had daydreams about a time machine and a scope-
sighted rifle?"

Andrew's eyebrows went up. "Sure, what little boy hasn't? Hitler,
I suppose? For me it was always Lyndon Johnson. Senator, I do not
commit murder under any circumstances."

"A time machine and a scope-sighted rifle, and me," William
Proxmire said dreamily. "I get more anonymous letters than you'd
believe, even now. They tell me that every space advocate daydreams
about me and a time machine and a scope-sighted rifle. Well, I started
daydreaming too, but my fantasy involves a time machine and a hypodermic full of antibiotics."

Andrew laughed. "You're plotting to do someone good behind his
back?"

"Right."

"Who?"

"Robert Anson Heinlein."

All laughter dropped away. "Why?"

"It's a good deed, isn't it?"

"Sure. Why?"

"You know the name? Over the past forty years or so I've talked to
a great many people in science and in the space program. I kept
hearing the name Robert Heinlein. They were seduced into science
because they read Heinlein at age twelve. These were the people I
found hard to deal with. No grasp of reality. Fanatics."

Andrew suspected that the senator had met more of these than he
realized. Heinlein spun off ideas at a terrific rate. Other writers
picked them up . . . along with a distrust for arrogance combined
with stupidity or ignorance, particularly in politicians.

"Well, Heinlein's literary career began after he left the Navy because of lung disease."

"You're trying to destroy the space program."

"Will you help?"

Andrew was about to tell him to go to hell. He didn't. "I'm still
talking. Why do you want to destroy the space program?"

"I didn't, at first. I was opposed to waste," Proxmire said. "My colleagues, they'll spend money on any pet project, as if there was a money tree out there somewhere—"

"Milk price supports," Andrew said gently. For several decades now, the great state of Wisconsin had taken tax money from the other states so that the price they paid for milk would stay *up*.

Proxmire's lips twitched. "Without milk price supports, there would be places where families with children can't buy milk."

"Why?"

The old man shook his head hard. "I've just remembered that I don't have to answer that question anymore. My point is that the government has spent far more taking rocks from the Moon and photographs from Saturn. Our economy would be far healthier if that money had been spent elsewhere."

"I'd rather shoot Lyndon. Eliminate welfare. Save a *lot* more money that way."

"A minute ago you were opposed to murder."

The old man did have a way with words. "Point taken. Could you get us funding? It'd be a guaranteed Nobel Prize. I like the fact that you don't need a scope-sighted rifle. A hypo full of sulfa drugs doesn't have to be kept secret. What antibiotic?"

"I don't know what cures consumption. I don't know which year or what ship. I've got people to look those things up, if I decide I want to know. I came straight here as soon as I read the morning paper. Why not? I run every day, any direction I like. But I haven't heard you say it's impossible, Andrew, and I haven't heard you say you won't do it."

"More coffee?"

"Yes, thank you."

Proxmire left him alone while he was in the kitchen, and for that Andrew was grateful. He'd have made no progress at all if he'd had to guard his expression. There was simply too much to think about.

He preferred not to consider the honors. Assume he had changed the past; how would he prove it before a board of his peers? "How would I prove it *now*? What would I have to show them?" he muttered under his breath, while the coffee water was heating. "Books? Books that didn't get written? Newspapers? There are places that'll print any newspaper headline I ask for. WAFFEN SS TO BUILD WORK CAMP IN DEATH VALLEY. I can mint Robert Kennedy half-dollars for a lot less than thirteen million bucks. Hmm . . ." But the Nobel Prize wasn't the point.

Keeping Robert Heinlein alive a few years longer: Was *that* the point? It shouldn't be. Heinlein wouldn't have thought so.

Would the science fiction field really have collapsed without the Menace From Earth? Tradition within the science fiction field would have named Campbell, not Heinlein. But think: Was it magazines that had sucked Andrew Minsky into taking advanced physics classes? Or . . . *Double Star, Red Planet,* Anderson's *Tau Zero,* Vance's *Tschai* series? Then the newsstand magazines, then the subscriptions, then (of course) he'd dropped it all to pursue a career. If Proxmire's staff investigated his past (as they must, if he was at all serious), they would find that Andrew Minsky, Ph.D., hadn't read a science fiction magazine in fifteen years.

Proxmire's voice came from the other room. "Of course, it would be a major chunk of funding. But wouldn't my old friends be surprised to find me backing a scientific project! How's the coffee coming?"

"Done." Andrew carried the pot in. "I'll do it," he said. "That is, I and my associates will build a time machine. We'll need funding and we'll need active assistance using the Washburn accelerator. We should be ready for a man-rated experiment in three years, I'd think. *We* won't fail."

He sat. He looked Proxmire in the eye. "Let's keep thinking, though. A Navy officer walks the tilting deck of what would now be an antique Navy ship. An arm circles his throat. He grips the skinny wrist and elbow, bends the wrist downward, and throws the intruder into the sea. They train Navy men to fight, you know, and he was young and you are old."

"I keep in shape," Proxmire said coldly. "A medical man who performs autopsies once told me about men and women like me. We run two to five miles a day. We die in our eighties and nineties and hundreds. A fall kills us, or a car accident. Cut into us and you find veins and arteries you could run a toy train through."

He was serious. "I was afraid you were thinking of taking along a blackjack or a trank gun or a Kalashnikov—"

"No."

"I'll say it anyway. Don't hurt him."

Proxmire smiled. "That would be missing the point."

And if that part worked out, Andrew would take his chances with the rest.

He had been reaching for a beer while he thought about revising the time machine paper he'd done with Tipler and Penrose four years ago. Somewhere he'd shifted over into daydreams, and that had sent him off on a weird track indeed.

It was like double vision in his head. The time machine (never built) had put William Proxmire (the ex-senator!) on the moving deck of the U.S.S. *Roper* on a gray midmorning in December 1933. Andrew never daydreamed this vividly. He slapped his flat belly, and wondered why, and remembered: He was ten pounds heavier in the daydream, because he'd been too busy to run.

So much detail! Maybe he was remembering a sweaty razor-sharp nightmare from last night, the kind in which you know you're doing something bizarrely stupid, but you can't figure out how to stop.

He'd reached for a Henry Weinhart's (Budweiser) from the refrigerator in his kitchen (in the office at Washburn, where the Weinhart's always ran out first) while the project team watched their monitors (while the KCET funding drive whined in his living room). In his head there were double vision, double memories, double sensations. The world of quantum physics was blurred in spots. But this was his kitchen and he could hear KCET begging for money a room away.

Andrew walked into his living room and found William Proxmire dripping on his yellow rug.

No, wait. That's the other—

The photogenic old man tossed the spray hypo on Andrew's couch. He stripped off his hooded raincoat, inverted it, and dropped it on top. He was trying to smile, but the fear showed through. "Andrew? What I am doing *here?*"

Andrew said, "My head feels like two flavors of cotton. Give me a moment. I'm trying to remember two histories at once."

"I should have had more time. And then it should have been the Washburn accelerator! You said!"

"Yeah, well, I did and I didn't. Welcome to the wonderful world of Schrödinger's Cat. How did it go? You found a young lieutenant junior grade gunnery officer alone on deck"—The raincoat was soaking his cushions—"in the rain—"

"Losing his breakfast overside in the rain. Pulmonary tuberculosis, consumption. Good riddance to an ugly disease."

"You wrestled him to the deck—"

"Heh, heh, heh. No. I told him I was from the future. I showed him a spray hypo. He'd never seen one. I was dressed as a civilian on a Navy ship. That got his attention. I told him if he was Robert Heinlein I had a cure for his cough."

"Cure for his cough?"

"I didn't say it would kill him otherwise. I didn't say it wouldn't, and he didn't ask, but he may have assumed I wouldn't have come for anything trivial. I knew his name. This was Heinlein, not some Wisconsin dairy farmer. He *wanted* to believe I was a time traveler. He *did* believe. I gave him his shot. Andrew, I feel cheated."

"Me too. Get used to it." But it was Andrew who was beginning to smile.

The older man hardly heard; his ears must be still ringing with that long-dead storm. "You know, I would have liked to talk to him. I was supposed to have twenty-two minutes more. I gave him his shot and the whole scene popped like a soap bubble. *Why* did I come back *here?*"

"Because we never got funding for research into time travel."

"Ah . . . hah. There *have* been changes. What changes?"

It wasn't just remembering; it was a matter of selecting pairs of memories that were mutually exclusive, then judging between them. It was maddening . . . but it could be done. Andrew said, "The Washburn accelerator goes with the time machine goes with the funding. My apartment goes with no time machine goes with no funding goes with . . . Bill, let's go outside. It should be dark by now."

Proxmire didn't ask why. He looked badly worried.

The sun had set, but the sky wasn't exactly black. In a line across a smaller, dimmer full Moon, four rectangles blazed like windows into the sun. Andrew sighed with relief. Collapse of the wave function: *This* is reality.

William Proxmire said, "Don't make me guess."

"Solar-powered satellites. Looking Glass Three through Six."

"What happened to your time machine?"

"Apollo Eleven landed on the Moon on July 20, 1969, just like clockwork. Apollo Thirteen left a month or two early, but something still exploded in the service module, so I guess it wasn't a meteor. They . . . shit."

"Eh?"

"They didn't get back. They died. We murdered them."

"Then?"

Could he put it back? Should he put it back? It was still coming together in his head. "Let's see, NASA tried to cancel Apollo Eighteen, but there was a hell of a write-in campaign—"

"Why? From whom?"

"The spec-fic community went absolutely apeshit. Okay, Bill, I've got it now."

"Well?"

"You were right, the whole science fiction magazine business just faded out in the fifties, last remnants of the pulp era. Campbell alone couldn't save it. Then in the sixties the literary crowd rediscovered the idea. There must have been an empty ecological niche and the lit-crits moved in.

"Speculative fiction, spec-fic, the literature of the possible. The *New Yorker* ran spec-fic short stories and critical reviews of novels. They thought *Planet of the Apes* was wonderful, and *Selig's Complaint*, which was Robert Silverberg's study of a telepath. Tom Wolfe started appearing in *Esquire* with his bizarre alien cultures. I can't remember an issue of the *Saturday Evening Post* that didn't have *some* spec-fic in it. Anderson, Vance, MacDonald . . . John D. MacDonald turns out novels set on a ring the size of Earth's orbit.

"The new writers were good enough that some of the early ones couldn't keep up, but a few did it by talking to hard science teachers. Benford and Forward did it in reverse. Jim Benford's a plasma physicist but he writes like he swallowed a college English teacher. Robert Forward wrote a novel called *Neutron Star*, but he built the Forward Mass Detector, too."

"Wonderful."

"There's a lot of spec-fic fans in the military. When Apollo Twenty-one burned up during reentry, they raised so much hell that Congress took the manned space program away from NASA and gave it to the Navy."

William Proxmire glared and Andrew Minsky grinned. "Now, you left office in the sixties because of the cheese boycott. When you tried to chop the funding for the Shuttle, the spec-fic community took offense. They stopped eating Wisconsin cheese. The San Francisco *Locus* called you the Cheese Man. Most of your supporters must have eaten nothing but their own cheese for about eight months, and then Goldwater chopped the milk price supports. 'Golden Fleece,' he called it. So you were out, and now there's no time machine."

"We could build one," Proxmire said.

Rescue Apollo Thirteen? The possibility had to be considered. . . . Andrew remembered the twenty years that followed the Apollo flights. In one set of memories, lost goals, pointlessness and depression, political faddishness leading nowhere. In the other, half a dozen space stations, government and military and civilian; Moonbase and Moonbase Polar; *Life* photographs of the Mars Project half-finished on the lunar plain, sitting on a hemispherical Orion-style shield made from lunar aluminum and fused lunar dust.

I do not commit murder under any circumstances.

"I don't think so, Bill. We don't have the political support. We don't have the incentive. Where would a Nobel Prize *come* from? We can't prove there was ever a timeline different from this one. Besides, this isn't just a more interesting world, it's safer too. Admiral Heinlein doesn't let the Soviets build spacecraft."

Proxmire stopped breathing for an instant. Then, "I suppose he wouldn't."

"Nope. He's taking six of their people on the Mars expedition, though. They paid their share of the cost in fusion bombs for propulsion."

May 12, 1988—

Greg Benford called me a couple of months ago. He wanted new stories about alternate time tracks for an anthology. I told him that the only sideways-in-time story in my head was totally unsaleable. It's just recreation, daydreaming, goofing off. It's about how William Proxmire uses a time machine and a hypodermic full of sulfa drugs to wipe out the space program.

Greg made me write it.

I called Robert to get dates and other data, and asked if I could use his name. I had so much fun with this story! I made lots of copies and sent them to friends. I sent one to Robert, of course. That was only a few weeks ago.

And now I'm thinking that sometimes I really luck out. "The Return of William Proxmire" hasn't yet been published. Robert's death feels bad enough, but it would be one notch worse if I didn't know he'd read this story.

—LARRY NIVEN

VOLUME 2

ALTERNATE HEROES

CONTENTS

INTRODUCTION

Poignant questions resound through history, beginning with that wistful phrase, *if only.* . . .

If only Kennedy had lived. If only Hitler had died in World War I. If only the Muslims had conquered Europe. If only a minor commander had not ordered the library at Alexandria burned, cutting us off from thousands of great works of antiquity. . . .

So many questions turn upon the presence of a particular figure at a crucial moment. Or do they?

Do individuals matter? Did Napoleon truly shape the failing French Revolution into a dynamic, military phase by the strength of his personality? Or would some similar minor officer of the artillery have sufficed? Later revolutions seem to show a similar pattern, leading inevitably to a man on a white horse who resorts to military control while damping the political ardor which started it all; think of Stalin, Mao, Castro. Were they essentially replaceable?

Nobody knows, of course, for history performs no repeatable experiments. But such riddles frame our own deep suspicions that perhaps even the currently high-and-mighty are but flotsam carried on the river of time, revealing the current's passing but unable to deflect the stream of events in the slightest.

This is the second volume exploring the fragility of history. The first, subtitled *Alternate Empires,* considered the importance of great events. This volume ponders the role of the Great Man (or Woman). Both are collections of original, commissioned fiction devoted to refashioning history in a logical manner, to exploring what could or might have been.

The theme has a considerable history itself. The question of Napoleon's role goes back to Louis-Napoleon Geoffroy-Chateau's *Napoleon and the Conquest of the World, 1812–1823.* This nationalist vision, published in 1836, told how a crucial decision to not tarry in Moscow as winter drew on saved the French forces. Napoleon then had the entire planet on the run and established a lasting world empire. In a sense the book argues that a slightly different Napoleon would have made all the difference. It does not call into question whether Great Men really matter.

Historians give no clear answer to this question. The appeal of the notion lies in our suspicion that some crucial figures have great leverage, yet seeming inconsequentialities can be the fulcrum.

Given the theme of what might have been, and all the vivid figures of history, our authors could write whatever they liked. Interestingly, two of the three women authors take military figures as critical. The third, Sheila Finch, considers the quieter and probably more profound changes wrought by an ex-employee of the Swiss Patent Office. As we might have expected, the American Civil War remains a vexing matter, yielding three tales with very different approaches.

In the end, there will always be a plausible argument for the impersonality of great historical movements. It probably did not matter whether Columbus or some other southern European sailed westward at the historically ripe moment. But were the extraordinary victories of Cortez inevitable? Sometimes, people really do matter. Our pains and pleasures carry weight.

Or so we would like to think. We hope you will find this range of imaginative experiments thought-provoking and perhaps even unsettling.

—GREGORY BENFORD

A SLEEP AND A
FORGETTING

Robert Silverberg

"Channeling?" I said. "For Christ's sake, Joe! You brought me all the way down here for dumb bullshit like that?"

"This isn't channeling," Joe said.

"The kid who drove me from the airport said you've got a machine that can talk with dead people."

A slow, angry flush spread across Joe's face. He's a small, compact man with very glossy skin and very sharp features, and when he's annoyed he inflates like a puff-adder.

"He shouldn't have said that."

"Is that what you're doing here?" I asked. "Some sort of channeling experiments?"

"Forget that shithead word, will you, Mike?" Joe sounded impatient and irritable. But there was an odd fluttery look in his eye, conveying—what? Uncertainty? Vulnerability? Those were traits I hadn't ever associated with Joe Hedley, not in the thirty years we'd known each other. "We aren't sure what the fuck we're doing here," he said. "We thought maybe you could tell us."

"Me?"

"You, yes. Here, put the helmet on. Come on, put it on, Mike. Put it on. Please."

I stared. Nothing ever changes. Ever since we were kids Joe's been using me for one cockeyed thing or another, because he knows he can count on me to give him a sober-minded commonsense opinion. Always bouncing this bizarre scheme or that off me, so he can measure the caroms.

The helmet was a golden strip of wire mesh studded with a row of microwave pickups the size of a dime and flanked by a pair of suction electrodes that fit over the temples. It looked like some vagrant piece of death-house equipment.

I ran my fingers over it. "How much curent is this thing capable of sending through my head?"

He looked even angrier. "Oh, fuck you, you hypercautious bastard! Would I ever ask you to do anything that could harm you?"

With a patient little sigh I said, "Okay. How do I do this?"

"Ear to ear, over the top of your head. I'll adjust the electrodes for you."

"You won't tell me what any of this is all about?"

"I want an uncontaminated response. That's science talk, Mike. I'm a scientist. You know that, don't you?"

"So that's what you are. I wondered."

Joe bustled about above me, moving the helmet around, pressing the electrodes against my skull.

"How does it fit?"

"Like a glove."

"You always wear your gloves on your head?" he asked.

"You must be goddamn nervous if you think that's funny."

"I am," he said. "You must be too, if you take a line like that seriously. But I tell you that you won't get hurt. I promise you that, Mike."

"All right."

"Just sit down here. We need to check the impedances, and then we can get going."

"I wish I understood at least a little bit about—"

"Please," he said. He gestured through a glass partition at a technician in the adjoining room, and she began to do things with dials and switches. This was turning into a movie, a very silly one, full of mad doctors in white jackets and sputtering electrical gadgets. The tinkering went on and on, and I felt myself passing beyond apprehension and annoyance into a kind of gray realm of Zen serenity, the way I sometimes do while sitting in the dentist's chair waiting for the scraping and poking to begin.

On the hillside visible from the laboratory window, yellow hibiscus was blooming against a background of billowing scarlet bougainvillea in brilliant California sunshine. It had been cold and raining, this February morning, when I drove to Sea-Tac Airport thirteen hundred miles to the north. Hedley's lab is just outside La Jolla, on a sandy bluff high up over the blue Pacific. When Joe and I were kids growing up in Santa Monica we took this kind of luminous winter day for granted, but I had lived in the Northwest for twenty years now, and I couldn't help thinking I'd gone on a day trip to Eden. I studied the colors on the hillside until my eyes began to get blurry.

"Here we go, now," Joe said, from a point somewhere far away behind my left shoulder.

It was like stepping into a big cage full of parakeets and mynahs and crazed macaws. I heard scratchy screeching sounds, and a harsh loony almost-laughter that soared through three or four octaves, and a low ominous burbling noise, as if some hydraulic device was about to blow a gasket. I heard weird wire-edged shrieks that went tumbling away as though the sound was falling through an infinite abyss. I heard queeblings. I heard hissings.

Then came a sudden burst of clearly enunciated syllables, floating in isolation above the noise:

—*Onoodor*—

That startled me.

A nonsense word? No, no, a real one, one that had meaning for me, a word in an obscure language that I just happen to understand.

"Today," that's what it means. In Khalkha. My specialty. But it was crazy that this machine would be speaking Khalkha to me. This had to be some sort of coincidence. What I'd heard was a random clumping of sounds that I must automatically have arranged into a meaningful pattern. I was kidding myself. Or else Joe was playing an elaborate practical joke. Only he seemed very serious.

I strained to hear more. But everything was babble again.

Then, out of the chaos:

—*Usan deer*—

Khalkha, again: "On the water." It couldn't be a coincidence.

More noise. Skwkaark shreek yubble gobble.

—*Aawa namaig yawuulawa*—

"Father sent me."

Skwkaark. Yabble. Eeeeesh.

"Go on," I said. I felt sweat rolling down my back. "Your father sent you where? Where? *Khaana.* Tell me where."

—*Usan deer*—

"On the water, yes."

Yarkhh. Skreek. Tshhhhhhh.

—*Akhanartan*—

"To his elder brother. Yes."

I closed my eyes and let my mind rove out into the darkness. It drifted on a sea of scratchy noise. Now and again I caught an actual syllable, half a syllable, a slice of a word, a clipped fragment of meaning. The voice was brusque, forceful, a drill-sergeant voice, carrying an undertone of barely suppressed rage.

Somebody very angry was speaking to me across a great distance, over a channel clotted with interference, in a language that hardly anyone in the United States knew anything about: Khalkha. Spoken a little oddly, with an unfamiliar intonation, but plainly recognizable.

I said, speaking very slowly and carefully and trying to match the odd intonation of the voice at the other end, "I can hear you and I can understand you. But there's a lot of interference. Say everything three times and I'll try to follow."

I waited. But now there was only a roaring silence in my ears. Not even the shrieking, not even the babble.

I looked up at Hedley like someone coming out of a trance.

"It's gone dead."

"You sure?"

"I don't hear anything, Joe."

He snatched the helmet from me and put it on, fiddling with the electrodes in that edgy, compulsively precise way of his. He listened for a moment, scowled, nodded. "The relay satellite must have passed around the far side of the sun We won't get anything more for hours if it has."

"The relay satellite? Where the hell was that broadcast coming from?"

"In a minute," he said. He reached around and took the helmet off. His eyes had a brassy gleam and his mouth was twisted off to the corner of his face, almost as if he'd had a stroke. "You were actually able to understand what he was saying, weren't you?"

I nodded.

"I knew you would. And was he speaking Mongolian?"

"Khalkha, yes. The main Mongolian dialect."

The tension left his face. He gave me a warm, loving grin. "I was sure you'd know. We had a man in from the university here, the comparative linguistics department—you probably know him, Malmstrom's his name—and he said it sounded to him like an Altaic language, maybe Turkic—is that right, Turkic?—but more likely one of the Mongolian languages, and the moment he said Mongolian I thought, that's it, get Mike down here right away—" He paused. "So it's the language that they speak in Mongolia right this very day, would you say?"

"Not quite. His accent was a little strange. Something stiff about it, almost archaic."

"Archaic."

"It had that feel, yes. I can't tell you why. There's just something formal and old-fashioned about it, something, well—"

"Archaic," Hedley said again. Suddenly there were tears in his eyes. I couldn't remember ever having seen him cry before.

What they have, the kid who picked me up at the airport had said, *is a machine that lets them talk with the dead.*

"Joe?" I said. "Joe, what in God's name is this all about?"

We had dinner that night in a sleek restaurant on a sleek, quiet La Jolla street of elegant shops and glossy-leaved trees, just the two of us, the first time in a long while that we'd gone out alone like that. Lately we tended to see each other once or twice a year at most, and Joe, who is almost always between marriages, would usually bring along his latest squeeze, the one who was finally going to bring order and stability and other such things to his tempestuous private life. And since he always needs to show the new one what a remarkable human being he is, he's forever putting on a performance, for the woman, for me, for the waiters, for the people at the nearby tables. Generally the fun's at my expense, for compared with Hedley I'm very staid and proper and I'm eighteen years into my one and only marriage so far, and Joe often seems to enjoy making me feel that there's something wrong with that. I never see him with the same woman twice, except when he happens to marry one of them. But tonight it was all different. He was alone, and the conversation was subdued and gentle and rueful, mostly about the years we'd had put in knowing each other, the fun we'd had, the regret Joe felt during the occasional long periods when we didn't see much of each other. He did most of the talking. There was nothing new about that. But mostly it was just chatter. We were three quarters of the way down the bottle of silky cabernet before Joe brought himself around to the topic of the experiment. I hadn't wanted to push.

"It was pure serendipity," he said. "You know, the art of finding what you're not looking for. We were trying to clean up some problems in radio transmission from the Icarus relay station—that's the one that the Japs and the French hung around the sun inside the orbit of Mercury—and we were fiddling with this and fiddling with that, sending out an assortment of test signals at a lot of different frequencies, when out of nowhere we got a voice coming back at us. A man's voice. Speaking a strange language. Which turned out to be Chaucerian English."

"Some kind of academic prank?" I suggested.

He looked annoyed. "I don't think so. But let me tell it, Mike, okay?

Okay?" He cracked his knuckles and rearranged the knot of his tie. "We listened to this guy and gradually we figured out a little of what he was saying and we called in a grad student from U.C.S.D. who confirmed it—thirteenth-century English—and it absolutely knocked us on our asses." He tugged at his earlobes and rearranged his tie again. A sort of manic sheen was coming into his eyes. "Before we could even begin to comprehend what we were dealing with, the Englishman was gone and we were picking up some woman making a speech in medieval French. Like we were getting a broadcast from Joan of Arc, do you see? Not that I'm arguing that that's who she was. We had her for half an hour, a minute here and a minute there with a shitload of interference, and then came a solar flare that disrupted communications, and when we had things tuned again we got a quick burst of what turned out to be Arabic, and then someone else talking in Middle English, and then, last week, this absolutely incomprehensible stuff, which Malmstrom guessed was Mongolian and you have now confirmed. The Mongol has stayed on the line longer than all the others put together."

"Give me some more wine," I said.

"I don't blame you. It's made us all crazy too. The best we can explain it to ourselves, it's that our beam passes through the sun, which as I think you know, even though your specialty happens to be Chinese history and not physics, is a place where the extreme concentration of mass creates some unusual stresses on the fabric of the continuum, and some kind of relativistic force warps the hell out of it, so that the solar field sends our signal kinking off into God knows where, and the effect is to give us a telephone line to the Middle Ages. If that sounds like gibberish to you, imagine how it sounds to us." Hedley spoke without raising his head, while moving his silverware around busily from one side of his plate to the other. "You see now about channeling? It's no fucking joke. Shit, we *are* channeling, only looks like it might actually be real, doesn't it?"

"I see," I said. "So at some point you're going to have to call up the secretary of defense and say, Guess what, we've been getting telephone calls on the Icarus beam from Joan of Arc. And then they'll shut down your lab here and send you off to get your heads replumbed."

He stared at me. His nostrils flickered contemptuously.

"Wrong. Completely wrong. You never had any notion of flair, did you? The sensational gesture that knocks everybody out? No. Of course not. Not *you*. Look, Mike, if I can go in there and say, We can talk to the dead, and we can *prove* it, they'll kiss our asses for us. Don't you see how fucking sensational it would be, something coming out of these government labs that ordinary people can actually understand and cheer and yell about? Telephone line to the past! George Washington himself, talking to Mr. and Mrs. America! Abe Lincoln! Something straight out of the *National Enquirer*, right, only *real?* We'd all be heroes. But it's got to be real, that's the kicker. We don't need a rational explanation for it, at least not right away. All it has to do is work. Christ, ninety-nine percent of the people don't even know why electric lights light up when you flip the switch. We have to find out what we really have and get to understand it at least a little and be two hundred percent sure of ourselves. And then we present it to Washington and we say, Here, this is what we did and this is what happens, and don't blame us if it seems crazy. But we have to keep it absolutely to ourselves until we understand enough of what we've stumbled on to be able to explain it to them with confidence. If we do it right we're goddamned kings of the world. A Nobel would be just the beginning. You understand now?"

"Maybe we should get another bottle of wine," I said.

We were back in the lab by midnight. I followed Hedley through a maze of darkened rooms, ominous with mysterious equipment glowing in the night.

A dozen or so staffers were on duty. They smiled wanly at Hedley as if there was nothing unusual about his coming back to work at this hour.

"Doesn't anyone sleep around here?" I asked.

"It's a twenty-four-hour information world," Joe said. "We'll be recapturing the Icarus beam in forty-three minutes. You want to hear some of the earlier tapes?"

He touched a switch and from an unseen speaker came crackles and bleebles and then a young woman's voice, strong and a little harsh, uttering brief blurts of something that sounded like strange singsong French, to me not at all understandable.

"Her accent's terrible," I said. "What's she saying?"

"It's too fragmentary to add up to anything much. She's praying, mostly. May the king live, may God strengthen his arm, something like that. For all we know it *is* Joan of Arc. We haven't gotten more than a few minutes total coherent verbal output out of any of them, usually a lot less. Except for the Mongol. He goes on and on. It's like he doesn't want to let go of the phone."

"And it really is a phone?" I asked. "What we say here, they can hear there?"

"We don't know that, because we haven't been able to make much sense out of what they say, and by the time we get it deciphered we've lost contact. But it's got to be a two-way contact. They must be getting *something* from us, because we're able to get their attention somehow and they talk back to us."

"They receive your signal without a helmet?"

"The helmet's just for your benefit. The actual Icarus signal comes in digitally. The helmet's the interface between our computer and your ears."

"Medieval people don't have digital computers either, Joe."

A muscle started popping in one of his cheeks. "No, they don't," he said. "It must come like a voice out of the sky. Or right inside their heads. But they hear us."

"How?"

"Do I know? You want this to make sense, Mike? *Nothing* about this makes sense. Let me give you an example. You were talking with that Mongol, weren't you? You asked him something and he answered you?"

"Yes. But—"

"Let me finish. What did you ask him?"

"He said his father sent him somewhere. I asked him where, and he said, On the water. To visit his elder brother."

"He answered you right away?"

"Yes," I said.

"Well, that's actually impossible. The Icarus is ninety-three million miles from here. There has to be something like an eight-minute time lag in radio transmission. You follow? You ask him something and it's eight minutes before the beam reaches Icarus, and eight minutes more for his answer to come back. He sure as hell can't hold a real-time conversation with you. But you say he was."

"It may only have seemed that way. It could just have been coincidence that what I asked and what he happened to say next fit together like question and response."

"Maybe. Or maybe whatever kink in time we're operating across eats up the lag for us, too. I tell you, nothing makes sense about this. But one way or another the beam is reaching them and it carries coherent information. I don't know why that is. It just is. Once you start dealing in impossible stuff, anything might be true. So why can't our voices come out of thin air to them?" Hedley laughed nervously. Or perhaps it was a cough, I thought. "The thing is," he went on, "this Mongol is staying on line longer than any of the others, so with you here we have a chance to have some real communication with him. You speak his language. You can validate this whole goddamn grotesque event for us, do you see? You can have an honest-to-God chat with some guy who lived six hundred years ago, and find out where he really is and what he thinks is going on, and tell us all about it."

I stole a glance at the wall clock. Half past twelve. I couldn't remember the last time I'd been up this late. I lead a nice quiet tenured life, full professor thirteen years now, University of Washington Department of Sinological Studies.

"We're about ready to acquire signal again," Hedley said. "Put the helmet on."

I slipped it into place. I thought about that little communications satellite chugging around the sun, swimming through inconceivable heat and unthinkable waves of hard radiation and somehow surviving, coming around the far side now, beaming electromagnetic improbabilities out of the distant past at my head.

The squawking and screeching began.

Then, emerging from the noise and murk and sonic darkness, came the Mongol's voice, clear and steady:

"Where are you, you voice, you? Speak to me."

"Here," I said. "Can you hear me?"

Aark. Yaaarp. Tshhhhhhh.

The Mongol said, "Voice, what are you? Are you mortal or are you a prince of the Master?"

I wrestled with the puzzling words. I'm fluent enough in Khalkha, though I don't get many opportunities for speaking it. But there was a problem of context here.

"Which master?" I asked finally. "What prince?"

"There is only one Master," said the Mongol. He said this with tremendous force and assurance, putting terrific spin on every syllable, and the capital letter was apparent in his tone. "I am His servant. The *angeloi* are his princes. Are you an *angelos*, voice?"

Angeloi? That was Greek. A Mongol, asking me if I was an angel of God?

"Not an angel, no," I said.

"Then how can you speak to me this way?"

"It's a kind of—" I paused. I couldn't come up with the Khalka for "miracle." After a moment I said, "It's by the grace of heaven on high. I'm speaking to you from far away."

"How far?"

"Tell me where you are."

Skrawwwwk. Tshhhhhh.

"Again. Where are you?"

"Nova Roma. Constantinopolis."

I blinked. "Byzantium?"

"Byzantium, yes."

"I am very far from there."

"*How* far?" the Mongol said fiercely.

"Many, many days' ride. Many many." I hesitated. "Tell me what year it is, where you are."

Vzsqkk. Blzzp. Yiiiiiik.

"What's he saying to you?" Hedley asked. I waved at him furiously to be quiet.

"The year," I said again. "Tell me what year it is."

The Mongol said scornfully, "Everyone knows the year, voice."

"Tell me."

"It is the year 1187 of our Savior."

I began to shiver. Our Savior? Weirder and weirder, I thought. A Christian Mongol? Living in Byzantium? Talking to me on the space telephone out of the twelfth century? The room around me took on a smoky, insubstantial look. My elbows were aching, and something was throbbing just above my left cheekbone. This had been a long day for me. I was very tired. I was heading into that sort of weariness where walls melted and bones turned soft. Joe was dancing around in front of me like someone with tertiary Saint Vitus'.

"And your name?" I said.

"I am Petros Alexios."

"Why do you speak Khalkha if you are Greek?"

A long silence, unbroken even by the hellish static.

"I am not Greek," came the reply finally. "I am by birth Khalkha Mongol, but raised Christian among the Christians from age eleven, when my father sent me on the water and I was taken. My name was Temujin. Now I am twenty and I know the Savior."

I gasped and put my hand to my throat as though it had been skewered out of the darkness by a spear.

"Temujin," I said, barely getting the word out.

"My father was Yesugei the chieftain."

"Temujin," I said again. "Son of Yesugei." I shook my head.

Aaark. Blzzzp. Tshhhhhh.

Then no static, no voice, only the hushed hiss of silence.

"Are you okay?" Hedley asked.

"We've lost contact, I think."

"Right. It just broke. You look like your brain has shorted out."

I slipped the helmet off. My hands were shaking.

"You know," I said, "maybe that French woman really was Joan of Arc."

"What?"

I shrugged. "She really might have been," I said wearily. "Anything's possible, isn't it?"

"What the hell are you trying to tell me, Mike?"

"Why shouldn't she have been Joan of Arc?" I asked. "Listen, Joe. This is making me just as nutty as you are. You know what I've just been doing? I've been talking to Genghis Kahn on this fucking telephone of yours."

I managed to get a few hours of sleep by simply refusing to tell Hedley anything else until I'd had a chance to rest. The way I said it, I left him no options, and he seemed to grasp that right away. At the hotel, I sank from consciousness like a leaden whale, hoping I wouldn't surface again before noon, but old habit seized me and pushed me up out of the tepid depths at seven, irreversibly awake and not a bit less depleted. I put in a quick call to Seattle to tell Elaine that I was going to stay down in La Jolla a little longer than expected. She seemed worried—not that I might be up to any funny business, not me, but only that I sounded so groggy. "You know Joe," I said. "For him it's a twenty-four-hour information world." I told her nothing else. When I stepped out on the breakfast patio half an hour later, I could see the lab's blue van already waiting in the hotel lot to pick me up.

Hedley seemed to have slept at the lab. He was rumpled and red-eyed but somehow he was at normal functioning level, scurrying around the place like a yappy little dog. "Here's a printout of last night's contact," he said, the moment I came in. "I'm sorry if the transcript looks cockeyed. The computer doesn't know how to spell in Mongolian." He shoved it into my hands. "Take a squint at it and see if you really heard all the things you thought you heard."

I peered at the single long sheet. It seemed to be full of jabberwocky, but once I figured out the computer's system of phonetic equivalents I could read it readily enough. I looked up after a moment, feeling very badly shaken.

"I was hoping I dreamed all this. I didn't."

"You want to explain it to me?"

"I can't."

Joe scowled. "I'm not asking for fundamental existential analysis. Just give me a goddamned translation, all right?"

"Sure," I said.

He listened with a kind of taut, explosive attention that seemed to me to be masking a mixture of uneasiness and bubbling excitement. When I was done he said, "Okay. What's this Genghis Khan stuff?"

"Temujin was Genghis Khan's real name. He was born around 1167 and his father Yesugei was a minor chief somewhere in northeastern Mongolia. When Temujin was still a boy, his father was poisoned by enemies, and he became a fugitive, but by the time he was fifteen he started putting together a confederacy of Mongol tribes, hundreds of them, and eventually he conquered everything in sight. Genghis Khan means 'Ruler of the Universe.' "

"So? Our Mongol lives in Constantinople, you say. He's a Christian and he uses a Greek name."

"He's Temujin, Son of Yesugei. He's twenty years old in the year when Genghis Khan was twenty years old."

Hedley looked belligerent. "Some other Temujin. Some other Yesugei."

"Listen to the way he speaks. He's scary. Even if you can't understand a word of what he's saying, can't you feel the power in him? The coiled-up anger? That's the voice of somebody capable of conquering whole continents."

"Genghis Khan wasn't a Christian. Genghis Khan wasn't kidnapped by strangers and taken to live in Constantinople."

"I know," I said. To my own amazement I added, "But maybe this one was."

"Jesus God Almighty. What's that supposed to mean?"

"I'm not certain."

Hedley's eyes took on a glaze. "I hoped you were going to be part of the solution, Mike. Not part of the problem."

"Just let me think this through," I said, waving my hands above his face as if trying to conjure some patience into him. Joe was peering at me in a stunned, astounded way. My eyeballs throbbed. Things were jangling up and down along my spinal column. Lack of sleep had coated my brain with a hard crust of adrenaline. Bewilderingly strange ideas were rising like sewer gases in my mind and making weird bubbles. "All right, try this," I said at last. "Say that there are all sorts of possible worlds. A world in which you're the king of England, a world in which I played third base for the Yankees, a world in which the dinosaurs never died out and Los Angeles gets invaded every summer by hungry tyrannosaurs. And one world where Yesugei's son Temujin wound up in twelfth-century Byzantium as a Christian instead of founding the Mongol Empire. And that's the Temujin I've been talking to. This cockeyed beam of yours not only crosses time lines, somehow it crosses probability lines too, and we've fished up some alternate reality that—"

"I don't believe this," Hedley said.

"Neither do I, really. Not seriously. I'm just putting forth one possible hypothesis that might explain—"

"I don't mean your fucking hypothesis. I mean I find it hard to believe that you of all people, my old pal Mike Michaelson, can be standing here running off at the mouth this way, working hard at turning a mystifying event into a goddamned nonsensical one—you, good old sensible steady Mike, telling me some shit about tyrannosaurs amok in Los Angeles—"

"It was only an example of—"

"Oh, fuck your example," Hedley said. His face darkened with exasperation bordering on fury. He looked ready to cry. "Your example is absolute crap. Your example is garbage. You know, man, if I wanted someone to feed me a lot of New Age crap I didn't have to go all the way to Seattle to find one. Alternate realities! Third base for the Yankees!"

A girl in a lab coat appeared out of nowhere and said, "We have signal acquisition, Dr. Hedley."

I said, "I'll catch the next plane north, okay?"

Joe's face was red and starting to do its puff-adder trick and his Adam's apple bobbed as if trying to find the way out.

"I wasn't trying to mess up your head," I said. "I'm sorry if I did. Forget everything I was just saying. I hope I was at least of some help, anyway."

Something softened in Joe's eyes.

"I'm so goddamned tired, Mike."

"I know."

"I didn't mean to yell at you like that."

"No offense taken, Joe."

"But I have trouble with this alternate-reality thing of yours. You think it was easy for me to believe that what we were doing here was talking to people in the past? But I brought myself around to it, weird though it was. Now you give it an even weirder twist, and it's too much. It's too fucking much. It violates my sense of what's right and proper and fitting. You know what Occam's razor is, Mike? The old medieval axiom, *Never multiply hypotheses needlessly?* Take the simplest one. Here even the simplest one is crazy. You push it too far."

"Listen," I said, "if you'll just have someone drive me over to the hotel—"

"No."

"No?"

"Let me think a minute," he said. "Just because it doesn't make sense doesn't mean that it's impossible, right? And if we get one impossible thing, we can have two, or six, or sixteen. Right? Right?" His eyes were like two black holes with cold stars blazing at their bottoms. "Hell, we aren't at the point where we need to worry about explanations. We have to find out the basic stuff first. Mike, I don't want you to leave. I want you to stay here."

"What?"

"Don't go. Please. I still need somebody to talk to the Mongol for me. Don't go. Please, Mike? Please?"

The times, Temujin said, were very bad. The infidels under Saladin had smashed the Crusader forces in the Holy Land, and Jerusalem itself had fallen to the Moslems. Christians everywhere mourn the loss, said Temujin. In Byzantium—where Temujin was captain of the guards in the private army of a prince named Theodore Lascaris— God's grace seemed also to have been withdrawn. The great empire was in heavy weather. Insurrections had brought down two emperors in the past four years and the current man was weak and timid. The provinces of Hungary, Cyprus, Serbia, and Bulgaria were all in revolt. The Normans of Sicily were chopping up Byzantine Greece and on the other side of the empire the Seljuk Turks were chewing their way through Asia Minor. "It is the time of the wolf," said Temujin. "But the sword of the Lord will prevail."

The sheer force of him was astounding. It lay not so much in what he said, although that was sharp and fierce, as in the way he said it. I could feel the strength of the man in the velocity and impact of each syllable. Temujin hurled his words as if from a catapult. They arrived carrying a crackling electrical charge. Talking with him was like holding live cables in my hands.

Hedley, jigging and fidgeting around the lab, paused now and then to stare at me with what looked like awe and wonder in his eyes, as if to say, *You really can make sense of this stuff?* I smiled at him. I felt bizarrely cool and unflustered. Sitting there with some electronic thing on my head, letting that terrific force go hurtling through my brain. Discussing twelfth-century politics with an invisible Byzantine Mongol. Making small talk with Genghis Khan. All right. I could handle it.

I beckoned for notepaper. *Need printout of world historical background late twelfth century,* I scrawled, without interrupting my conversation with Temujin. *Esp. Byzantine history, Crusades, etc.*

The kings of England and France, said Temujin, were talking about launching a new Crusade. But at the moment they happened to be at war with each other, which made cooperation difficult. The powerful Emperor Frederick Barbarossa of Germany was also supposed to be getting up a Crusade, but that, he said, might mean more trouble for Byzantium than for the Saracens, because Frederick was the friend of Byzantium's enemies in the rebellious provinces, and he'd have to march through those provinces on the way to the Holy Land.

"It is a perilous time," I agreed.

Then suddenly I was feeling the strain. Temujin's rapid-fire delivery was exhausting to follow, he spoke Mongolian with what I took to be a Byzantine accent, and he sprinkled his statements with the names of emperors, princes, and even nations that meant nothing to me. Also there was that powerful force of him to contend with—it hit you like an avalanche—and beyond that his anger: the whip-crack inflection that seemed the thinnest of bulwarks against some unstated inner rage, fury, frustration. It's hard to feel at ease with anyone who seethes that way. Suddenly I just wanted to go somewhere and lie down.

But someone put printout sheets in front of me, closely packed columns of stuff from the *Britannica*. Names swam before my eyes: Henry II, Barbarossa, Stephan Nemanya, Isaac II (Angelos), Guy of Jerusalem, Richard the Lion-Hearted. Antioch, Tripoli, Thessaloniki, Venice. I nodded my thanks and pushed the sheets aside.

Cautiously I asked Temujin about Mongolia. It turned out that he knew almost nothing about Mongolia. He'd had no contact at all with his native land since his abduction at the age of eleven by Byzantine traders who carried him off to Constantinople. His country, his father, his brothers, the girl to whom he had been betrothed when he was still a child—they were all just phantoms to him now, far away, forgotten. But in the privacy of his own soul he still spoke Khalkha. That was all that was left.

By 1187, I knew, the Temujin who would become Genghis Khan had already made himself the ruler of half of Mongolia. His fame would surely have spread to cosmopolitan Byzantium. How could this Temujin be unaware of him? Well, I saw one way. But Joe had already shot it down. And it sounded pretty nutty even to me.

"Do you want a drink?" Hedley asked. "Tranks? Aspirin?"

I shook my head. "I'm okay," I murmured.

To Temujin I said, "Do you have a wife? Children?"

"I have vowed not to marry until Jesus rules again in His own land."

"So you're going to go on the next Crusade?" I asked.
Whatever answer Temujin made was smothered by static.
Awkkk. Skrrkkk. Tsssshhhhhhh.
Then silence, lengthening into endlessness.
"Signal's gone," someone said.
"I could use that drink now," I said. "Scotch."
The lab clock said it was ten in the morning. To me it felt like the middle of the night.

An hour had passed. The signal hadn't returned.
Hedley said. "You really think he's Genghis Khan?"
"I really think he *could* have been."
"In some other probability world."
Carefully I said, "I don't want to get you all upset again, Joe."
"You won't. Why the hell *not* believe we're tuned into an alternate reality? It's no more goofy than any of the rest of this. But tell me this: is what he says consistent with being Genghis Khan?"
"His name's the same. His age. His childhood, up to the point when he wandered into some Byzantine trading caravan and they took him away to Constantinople with them. I can imagine the sort of fight he put up, too. But his life-line must have diverged completely from that point on. A whole new world-line split off from ours. And in that world, instead of turning into Genghis Khan, ruler of all Mongolia, he grew up to be Petros Alexios of Prince Theodore Lascaris's private guards."
"And he has no idea of who he could have been?" Joe asked.
"How could he? It isn't even a dream to him. He was born into another world that wasn't ever destined to have a Genghis Khan. You know the poem:

> *"Our birth is but a sleep and a forgetting:*
> *The soul that rises with us, our life's star,*
> *Hath had elsewhere its setting,*
> *And cometh from afar."*

"Very pretty. Is that Yeats?" Hedley said.
"Wordsworth," I said. "When's the signal coming back?"
"An hour, two, three. It's hard to say. You want to take a nap, and we'll wake you when we have acquisition?"
"I'm not sleepy."
"You look pretty ragged," Joe said.
I wouldn't give him the satisfaction.

"I'm okay. I'll sleep for a week, later on. What if you can't raise him again?"

"There's always that chance, I suppose. We've already had him on the line five times as long as all the rest put together."

"He's a very determined man," I said.

"He ought to be. He's Genghis fucking Khan."

"Get him back," I said. "I don't want you to lose him. I want to talk to him some more."

Morning ticked on into afternoon. I phoned Elaine twice while we waited, and I stood for a long time at the window watching the shadows of the oncoming winter evening fall across the hibiscus and the bougainvillea, and I hunched my shoulders up and tried to pull in the signal by sheer body english. Contemplating the possibility that they might never pick up Temujin again left me feeling weirdly forlorn. I was beginning to feel that I had a real relationship with that eerie disembodied angry voice coming out of the crackling night. Toward midafternoon I thought I was starting to understand what was making Temujin so angry, and I had some things I wanted to say to him about that.

Maybe you ought to get some sleep, I told myself.

At half past four someone came to me and said the Mongol was on the line again.

The static was very bad. But then came the full force of Temujin soaring over it. I heard him saying, "The Holy Land must be redeemed. I cannot sleep so long as the infidels possess it."

I took a deep breath.

In wonder, I watched myself set out to do something unlike anything I had ever done before.

"Then you must redeem it yourself," I said firmly.

"I?"

"Listen to me, Temujin. Think of another world far from yours. There is a Temujin in that world too, son of Yesugei, husband to Bortei who is daughter of Dai the Wise."

"Another world? What are you saying?"

"Listen. Listen. He is a great warrior, that other Temujin. No one can withstand him. His own brothers bow before him. All Mongols everywhere bow before him. His sons are like wolves, and they ride into every land and no one can withstand them. This Temujin is master of all Mongolia. He is the Great Khan, the Genghis Khan, the ruler of the universe."

There was silence. Then Temujin said, "What is this to me?"

"He is you, Temujin. You are the Genghis Khan."

Silence again, longer, broken by hideous shrieks of interplanetary noise.

"I have no sons and I have not seen Mongolia in years, or even thought of it. What are you saying?"

"That you can be as great in your world as this other Temujin is in his."

"I am Byzantine. I am Christian. Mongolia is nothing to me. Why would I want to be master in that savage place?"

"I'm not talking about Mongolia. You are Byzantine, yes. You are Christian. But you were born to lead and fight and conquer," I said. "What are you doing as a captain of another man's palace guards? You waste your life that way, and you know it, and it maddens you. You should have armies of your own. You should carry the Cross into Jerusalem."

"The leaders of the new Crusade are quarrelsome fools. It will end in disaster."

"Perhaps not. Frederick Barbarossa's Crusade will be unstoppable."

"Barbarossa will attack Byzantium instead of the Moslems. Everyone knows that."

"No," I said. That inner force of Temujin was rising and rising in intensity, like a gale climbing toward being a hurricane. I was awash in sweat, now, and I was dimly aware of the others staring at me as though I had lost my senses. A strange exhilaration gripped me. I went plunging joyously ahead. "Emperor Isaac Angelos will come to terms with Barbarossa. The Germans will march through Byzantium and go on toward the Holy Land. But there Barbarossa will die and his army will scatter—unless you are there, at his right hand, taking command in his place when he falls, leading them onward to Jerusalem. You, the invincible, the Genghis Khan."

There was silence once more, this time so prolonged that I was afraid the contact had been broken for good.

Then Temujin returned. "Will you send soldiers to fight by my side?" he asked.

"That I cannot do."

"You have the power to send them, I know," said Temujin. "You speak to me out of the air. I know you are an angel, or else you are a demon. If you are a demon, I invoke the name of Christos Pantokrator upon you, and begone. But if you are an angel, you can send me help. Send it, then, and I will lead your troops to victory. I will take the Holy Land from the infidel. I will create the Empire of

Jesus in the world and bring all things to fulfillment. Help me. Help me."

"I've done all I can," I said. "The rest is for you to achieve."

There was another spell of silence.

"Yes," Temujin said finally. "I understand. Yes. Yes. The rest is for me."

"Christ, you look peculiar," Joe Hedley said, staring at me almost fearfully. "I've never seen you looking like this before. You look like a wild man."

"Do I?" I said.

"You must be dead tired, Mike. You must be asleep on your feet. Listen, go over to the hotel and get some rest. We'll have a late dinner, okay? You can fill me in then on whatever you've just been jabbering about. We'll have a late dinner, okay? But relax now. The Mongol's gone and we may not get him back until tomorrow."

"You won't get him back at all," I said.

"You think?" He peered close. "Hey, are you okay? Your eyes—your face—" Something quivered in his cheek. "If I didn't know better I'd say you were stoned."

"I've been changing the world. It's hard work."

"Changing the world?"

"Not this world. The other one. Look," I said hoarsely, "they never had a Genghis Khan, so they never had a Mongol Empire, and the whole history of China and Russia and the Near East and a lot of other places was very different. But I've got this Temujin all fired up now to be a Christian Genghis Khan. He got so Christian in Byzantium that he forgot what was really inside him, but I've reminded him, I've told him how he can still do the thing that he was designed to do, and he understands. He's found his true self again. He'll go out to fight in the name of Jesus and he'll build an empire that'll eat the Moslem powers for breakfast and then blow away Byzantium and Venice and go on from there to do God knows what. He'll probably conquer all of Europe before he's finished. And I did it. I set it all in motion. He was sending me all this energy, this Genghis Khan zap that he has inside him, and I figured the least I could do for him was turn some of it around and send it back to him, and say, Here, go, be what you were supposed to be."

"Mike—"

I stood close against him, looming over him. He gave me a bewildered look.

"You really didn't think I had it in me, did you?" I said. "You son of a bitch. You've always thought I'm as timid as a turtle. Your good old sober stick-in-the-mud pal Mike. What do you know? What the hell do you know?" Then I laughed. He looked so stunned that I had to soften it for him a little. Gently I touched his shoulder. "I need a shower and a drink. And then let's think about dinner."

Joe gawked at me. "What if it wasn't some other world you changed, though? Suppose it was this one."

"Suppose it was," I said. "Let's worry about that later. I still need that shower."

THE OLD MAN AND C

Sheila Finch

Light sprang to the wall when his wife opened the casement window to let in a little breeze from the lake. It shattered, sparkling over bookshelves and wallpaper, as his young student's bow scraped across the E string and the fingers of her left hand searched for high C.

She still could not seem to get it right. The note must sing, not screech! He had shown Rosa over and over, patiently correcting her fingering, the pressure of the bow across the string, explaining to her how the sound was produced in the hope that if she understood perhaps she could improve. She was so brilliant in every other respect.

"*Kaffee*, Papa?" his wife whispered in his ear.

He shook his head.

"Don't lose sight of the time. Eddie comes this afternoon. And Lisl will want to go with her *Opa* on the boat!"

Rosa had progressed to the Arabesque, a passage she played excellently, her fingers flying like the scintillating reflection of water on the wall.

His wife left him to his pupil and the music lesson, closing the music room door quietly behind her. He gazed at Rosa. Eyes closed, she bit her lower lip in concentration. Wisps of fair hair escaped from braids trailing over her shoulders. She was a good girl, the best student he had ever had. If she mastered this one note, she should easily take the gold medal—perhaps the last he would see a pupil take. She had more natural talent than any of his previous medalists.

But the other students in the competition, children who came from the wealthy suburbs of Zurich where they had *Waschmaschinen* and *Fernsehapparaten*, they could afford to spend all day practising, whereas Rosa got up at first light and helped her father milk the cows. Time for the violin had to be sandwiched between farm chores and schoolwork. Now she was approaching sixteen; her father had begun to think of the day she would marry a solid farm lad and give him one less mouth to feed. This was her last chance, too. He had worked hard with Rosa, giving long lessons and extra lessons that her family had paid for with cream and eggs. Who could say if it would be enough?

Rosa finished the piece with a flourish, the notes sparkling almost visibly in the air between them.

"So, Herr Professor, are you pleased?" Triumph shining on her round face showed what answer she expected.

"I'm very pleased," he agreed.

"We're going to win the medal," she promised.

It was important to him that this little farm girl take the very last gold medal. Yet he knew he should not allow his own sense of self-worth to become bound to a pupil's performance in a competition. How had it happened? When one is young, he thought, how many choices lie at one's fingertips? How many roads beckon the eager traveler? Time spreads out before the young man like a map of a marvelous sunlit country. He knows he can write symphonies, build castles, discover the secrets of the universe—which will it be? He does not know (for God is merciful) that the choice of one road shuts out the possibility of another. Who can guarantee which is right to take?

His mother had always wanted him to play the violin. And he had been an indifferent scholar in school.

"Herr Einstein?" Rosa said, her young face creased in a frown. "Aren't you well?"

He discovered that he was sweating and took out a linen handkerchief to mop his brow. "I'm well, Rosa. It's hot today, that's all. What else should we expect of July?"

"If I get my chores done early enough, my mother says I can take my little brothers swimming." She looked up at him, blue eyes innocent as infinity. "Do you wish me to play something else, Herr Professor?"

He patted her hand. "Enough for today, *Liebchen*. Enjoy the lake!"

And the light, he thought, the vast potential of the realms of light.

Rosa put the violin away in its case, gathered up her music, dropped him a hasty curtsy, and scurried from the room. The dancing light, fragmented by her departure, gathered itself together again, settling back on the walls and the Turkish rug and the dark wood of the grand piano.

The day's post lay on the floor by the armchair under the open window where he had left it at the beginning of Rosa's lesson. Sunshine fell on the fat pile, a correspondence he carried on with old friends, poets, pacifists and Zionists, people he had met all over Europe when he had still been touring with the orchestra. They sent letters full of music and philosophy and grand theory, wonderful talk. It was like a rich, festive meal that today he did not feel like eating. He set most of the letters aside, unopened. There had been a time when he had shared his friends' sense of holding the universe in the palm of his hand, a gift of a benign God who revealed His existence in the harmony of His creation.

He shook his head mutely. It was a young man's belief. The world had fought two terrible wars since then. Now it was enough to sit quietly and look at what had become of the promises.

He was so tired today.

One letter was from his widowed cousin Elsa, full of news about her daughters, no doubt; he had always liked Elsa. He tore the stamps off the envelope carefully, saving them for his granddaughter, Lisl.

"Papa?" His wife appeared in the doorway, her hands still floury from making *Dampfnudeln.* "Are you coming to lunch?"

"Ah, Millie," he said. "I'm getting old."

"Seventy-five isn't old!"

"And what have I accomplished?"

Millie spread her arms wide. "This house, two fine sons, your sailboat down there on the lake, your pupils—perhaps Rosa gets the gold this year. How many will that make for you? And you ask what you've accomplished?"

He was silent, looking at the shimmering light from the lake that shot its arrows into his soul.

"Besides," his wife said, "Lisl adores you. That must be worth something?"

But the sense there might have been more gnawed at him.

Later, with his son and granddaughter, he took the sailboat far out on Lake Zurich, tilting gently in a mild breeze and grand weather, sailing under the lee of slopes covered with ripening vineyards, presided over by the hump of the Albishorn.

Millie was right, he thought. All the tiny joys had to add up to something.

"I picked up a translation of a new thing that came out last year from this American writer, Hemingway," Eddie said, as Lisl trailed fingers in the cold, clear water, shattering the drowned light in its depths into diamond fragments. "It's about an old man fishing, and sharks."

"I don't like to fish."

"You'd like this story!"

He gazed at his younger son, a banker, already thickening into comfortable middle age. "I don't have as much time to read as you, apparently."

"Nonsense! You read the wrong things—about wars and terrible things like that. You should read fiction."

"So many wars. Where will it all end?"

"Pfft!" Eddie made a derisive sound. "These Asians are all alike. The Koreans will run out of steam just as the Japanese did in 1945. You'll see. The Americans hate to do anything violent. They'll make another treaty."

"Opa," Lisl interrupted, hanging over the low side of the boat, brown hair trailing through sun-spangled water. "Are there sharks in this lake? May I go swimming?"

"Careful!" Eddie warned. "You'll fall in fully clothed, and then your grandmother will scold!"

The sun's slanting radiance scattered from the child's flowing hair. He stared at it, fascinated. The play of light had always obsessed him.

"Opa?" Lisl urged.

"A man should leave a mark," he said, watching the flash and dazzle in the lake. "It's not enough just to have lived."

"Exactly the point of the Hemingway story I referred to!" his son said with obvious satisfaction. "I took the liberty of putting my copy on your desk, Papa."

The child began to cry.

Venus, the evening star, was already burning in the western sky.

They heeled over and brought the sailboat swooping back to the dock.

The map does not indicate which is the best road, only that more than one possibility exists.

One afternoon many years ago (perhaps early May, for he remembered the cuckoo's melancholy call outside the open window) he had been at his desk in the patent office in Bern. Splinters of sunlight fell through green branches onto the papers he was reading. The work was sterile, soul-killing. He lived for the evenings when the street lamps were lit; then he walked under pale yellow flowers of the linden trees to the back room of a small *Gasthaus*. There, he joined a string quartet, explorers working their way across Beethoven's stark territory, the rich jungles of Brahms, the tidy gardens of Johann Sebastian Bach. He had just recently graduated from the Polytechnic

Academy, where he'd studied math. But music had proved to be his Lorelei.

This particular day, he remembered, he had trouble chaining his mind to the endless march of dull papers across his desk, while outside the marvelous vernal light called to him. Instead, he played with numbers (the abstract language of music, he had always thought) that combined and recombined in mysterious ways, numbers like the swarming stars that dazzled overhead in the clear Alpine night.

"Ho, Jew boy!" The supervisor, a spindly little man with a receding hairline who had taken an instant dislike to the new employee, stopped by his desk.

He hastily slid a pile of half-finished forms over the mathematical doodlings. The supervisor leered over the desk, hoping to catch him in blatant error so there would be cause to fire him.

"Is the report ready, young genius? Or have you been too busy to bother?"

"I'll have it done on time."

"You certainly will—or you'll look elsewhere for employment!"

He was not born to work behind a desk, filling out forms, following someone else's orders. But he also was not capable of ignoring a challenge. For two hours he worked without stopping till the report was done, far more thoroughly than even the thin supervisor had a right to expect.

That evening at music practice, a warm spring breeze blowing, full of starshine and promises, he received his first request to give tuition on the violin to the child of the Gasthaus keeper.

The next morning he gave notice at the patent office.

Rosa worked the bow smoothly across her instrument, moving through the difficult passage that led inexorably up the scale to high C, her nemesis. He leaned back in the armchair, eyes closed, evaluating, trying to hear the Rachmaninoff the way the judges would. Rain spattered the closed window, and Millie had lit the lamps in the middle of the afternoon. One week to go, he thought. One week to make a mark, to change the path of the stars that told man's fate, to mold the universe to one old man's will.

He was tired all the time now. The earth under his feet tugged at him, bending him out of shape.

Then she faltered once again on the high note and he leaped up from his chair, forgetful of stiff joints.

"No! No! No!" He seized the instrument from her hands. "What

have I told you? You aren't milking cows here! You must glide up the
notes like a fish swimming in a river! Like this."

He ran the bow smoothly up and down the scale, arthritic fingers
for once remembering how they had moved in their youth when he
had been the soloist with the orchestra in Paris and Vienna and at the
Albert Hall.

Rosa lowered blond lashes over her ruddy cheeks, and he caught
the gleam of tears in the glow of the lamps.

He relented. "All right now. We've worked hard enough for one
lesson. Perhaps it'll go better tomorrow, or the next day."

"I'm sorry, Herr Professor. I don't wish to let you down."

But perhaps he had let himself down? Perhaps if he had stayed
longer in the patent office, used the time to think about numbers?

"Let me try it again," she pleaded. "I *will* get it right!"

He gave her back the violin, thinking about possibilities and life
that had a habit of squeezing them down.

His Uncle Jakob had urged something else, but Mama had her
heart set on music. And music had been good to him, he could not
deny that. He had moved back to Zurich, married his university
sweetheart, and raised two young sons in relative comfort. In his
orchestra days, he had seen something of the world. He had books
and music, and friends around the globe who wrote to him and came
to visit. He had had good students—more silvers and bronzes than
any other teacher in the canton, and a respectable number of golds.
One had even gone on to world-class competition—he remembered a
brief, breathtaking visit to New York.

And now he was at home with the lake and the boat and the crisp
Alpine light sculpting the mountains.

If he had been someone like Van Gogh, he would have painted that
light. Sometimes he thought about the incandescent heart of distant
galaxies, spewing brightness through the universe to break at last
under its own weight on the shores of Lake Zurich. It made his heart
ache to think of it.

Rosa tried the passage again. This time he did not have to wince as
she reached high C.

That evening, drinking his coffee with whipped cream and choco-
late, sitting beside Millie, hand in hand on the balcony, watching the
moon come and go in the scudding clouds over the lake, he thought
about the mystery of roads where one made decisions in darkness.

"Do you never wonder, Millie, if your life might have been different?"

"How so, different?" she asked suspiciously.

"Do you never entertain the idea that perhaps you might have done something else with your time, something you might have been *better* at?"

"No," Millie said.

He sighed. "We could have traveled. We could have seen more of America."

"We could have had problems and divorced!" she said sourly.

He patted her hand. "Never."

The ache persisted, nevertheless.

The next morning, Hans Albert telephoned from Berlin where he was a professor of physics.

"Have you read the newspaper, Papa?"

Behind the telephone in the hall, the wallpaper—Millie's favorite pattern, clumps of creamy roses festooned with little pink ribbons—glowed in warm sunshine. He stared, imagining the artist making the very first drawing from a real vase of roses, the blooms illuminated by a ray of sunlight falling like a benediction on the studio. In some sense, it was all happening now: the painter, the roses blooming in the garden before somebody cut them, the old violin teacher gazing at wallpaper. The past, like the future, was only a stubborn linguistic illusion.

"Papa?"

"Ah. What should I have read?"

"The war, of course! Don't you always read about the war in Korea?"

Yes, the war. The strangeness of the place names, *Seoul, Pyongyang, Pusan.* And the stupidity of young boys killing other young boys in jungles and rice paddies where light slanted through palm trees and bamboo thickets, light that had crossed the darkness of space from a distant star to illuminate a scene for painters.

"They're still fighting?"

"Papa!" Then another idea seemed to occur to his son. "Are you feeling well?"

"You're going to tell me that the American airplanes dropped a most peculiar bomb on a Korean town with a name as singular as roses. Isn't this so?"

"Yes—but roses? Anyway, let me tell you about this weapon, Papa! A great advance—the future beckoning! You see what they've proved? A particle of matter can be converted into enormous outbursts of energy. This is something we've been working on here at the university, splitting uranium atoms."

"Light," he said. "It travels so fast! No time at all, really, from our point of view."

Hans Albert was silent. After a while he said casually, "Is Mama there? Let me speak to her."

The afternoon was quite warm, but Millie insisted he wear his hat anyway. He had the impression if he had argued she would have dragged out muffler and gloves too. "Stop at the barber's on your way," she had ordered. "Your hair is all over the place again!"

He descended the narrow street that took him from his house, built during Zwingli's Protestant Reformation in the sixteenth century, to the violin maker's shop on Bahnhofstrasse in the center of the modern tourist district. Strange, the road that unwound in time from one to the other, he thought, and he too trudging down it. A Mercedes-Benz with German license plates blared at him as he stepped off a curb without looking. A donkey cart clopped by in the opposite direction, its driver wearing a peasant smock that Zwingli might have recognized. There was no such thing as past or future, he saw. It all happened at once in the wonderful, brimming light. He felt the weight of it, soft as petals on his face and hands.

The shop was cool and dim inside until his eyes adjusted. Sawdust muffled his footsteps. His nose filled with the scent of pine and ebony, maple and resin. Unstrung instruments hung on the wall like dreaming angels, waiting to wake and sing. He would not—could not—deny he loved music. He ran his fingers over wood like satin and velvet.

"Stradivari's design remains the standard of excellence, even today."

He glanced up at the speaker, a pale, stooped young man who carried on his father's and grandfather's business of making some of the best violins in Europe.

"That's my latest copy you're holding."

The young man took the instrument from his hands, tightened pegs, plucked strings, then took a bow and drew from the instrument a cascade of sound so rich it was like listening to a river of radiance pour down from the sky.

"High C," he said. "Let me hear it."

The young man demonstrated a pure, singing note.

He nodded. "Ah. And it lies easily under the fingers?"

"Very much so," the young man agreed. "But why does that concern you, my friend, expert musician that you are?"

"I have a student with a great deal of talent and a small hand."

The instrument maker glanced quizzically at him. They were, after all, speaking of violins, not pianos.

"And a present might give her the confidence she needs to take the gold."

"I see." The young man laid the violin in its case and closed the lid. "On your account?"

"On my account, thank you."

And if it had not been music, he thought as he was leaving the shop, his gift in his hand, what then? What grand enterprise would have filled his life?

Whatever might have been, surely it would have been sufficient. God was subtle, but he was not malicious.

One time, when he had been perhaps eleven or twelve, there had been a conversation around the kitchen table in his parents' home in Munich. An early snow sifted down outside, and his mother had pulled heavy velvet curtains across the windows. In his memory, the kitchen was hazy with blue-gray smoke from his uncle's pipe, like a stage scene painted on gauze.

"Another poor report!" his father said, his hand over his eyes as if the mellow amber glow of the table lamp was too much for him. "I don't see why you don't just leave school now and come and join your uncle and me in the factory, instead of wasting your time and my money in the classroom."

"It was just low marks in history and geography, Hermann!" his mother pointed out. She stood with his father's *bierkrug* in her hand, on the way to the cellar to refill it. "It said nothing about other subjects."

"Ah, leave the boy alone," Uncle Jakob counseled. "He's a slow learner, but he's capable of good things."

"You say so?" his father asked. "Well, I don't see it."

A small fire chuckled to itself behind the glass doors of the potbellied stove; it was not yet cold enough in the room to open the doors.

"Sometimes . . ." he began hesitantly, not because he was afraid of his father but because he was not sure himself what he wanted to say. "Sometimes I think there's some great work for me to do."

His father forked up a slice of cold meat and added it to a hunk of dark bread and cheese he had been preparing before the subject of young Albert's bad marks came up. "Electrical engineering is great work, lad! It's the future."

"He's good at mathematics, a natural," Uncle Jakob said thoughtfully. "Too good to be just an engineer, like you and me, Hermann."

"Music is like mathematics, isn't it?" his mother asked, coming back into the room with a full *krug*. Foam leaked out from under the pewter lid.

"Then let him be a civil servant!" his father said. "But this schooling is a waste."

"There's something I have to do," he insisted. "I think there's a plan to my life. A riddle I have to solve—"

"So good at words, and yet he can't pass his composition test!" his father mocked.

His mother smoothed his hair—even as a young boy it had been unruly. "There's always more than one way, *Liebchen*."

"I think—"

"Life's a great game of chance," Uncle Jakob said. He leaned back from the table and relit his pipe. "An uncertain ride on a merry-go-round at the Oktoberfest!"

"But Uncle, that's like saying God is a gambler, throwing the dice for our lives—"

"The dice tell me you are no good in school!" his father roared. "I don't need God to advise me not to spend more money on a poor scholar!"

His mother pulled him to her, pressing his face against her starched apron. "Don't worry, *Liebchen*. I have money for music lessons. My money. Neither God nor your father shall have any say in how I spend it. I'll buy you a new violin."

"Come, Papa. You haven't even tasted your champagne!"

Millie linked her arm through his and drew him through the crowded living room, past the neighbors, the friends from their musical circle, the rabbi and the priest of the local Catholic church deep in a discussion of the world soccer cup, past his sons who were arguing over the Korean bomb.

"This atom they've split has unleashed a terrible demon in our world!" Eddie said.

Hans Albert had made the trip unexpectedly from Berlin on the *Schnellzug*. "You don't understand. When the governments of the world are aware of the power of the atom, they'll finally make peace!"

He was not fooled. One more gold medal was hardly cause enough for his oldest son's visit. They worried about his health. Strange, for he did not worry about it himself.

Rosa, flushed and shining in a new dress, stood by the refreshment table that Millie and the housekeeper had worked all afternoon to set up with Millie's heirloom silver and best china. The gold medal flamed like a sun on Rosa's chest. Her parents stood with her, thick-bodied, slow-thinking. They were good people from the farm, not quite sure they understood why all these elegant folk in silk and velvet and glittering rings had come in taxis to kiss their little Rosa on both cheeks and shake her father's hand. The future unfolded before them like a rose petal uncurling, and they did not have the wit to know it.

"Herr Einstein," Rosa called. "Thank you!"

She blew him a kiss with her fingertips that had so flawlessly reached high C. Then she turned to the young man beside her—a cousin, he knew, a farm lad—and tucked the hand with the gifted fingers in his.

Millie herded him to an armchair from which he could see everybody in the room. He sank into it, feeling for a moment like the apple whose falling to earth had demonstrated gravity. Lisl promptly climbed on his lap, spilling champagne over the new gray trousers Millie had made him wear. His daughter-in-law retrieved the child and took her away to bed; her own cheeks were as rosy from champagne as the child's were from the summer sun. Across the room, he caught sight of his oldest grandchild, a serious boy, much too old now to sit on a grandparent's knee. He showed signs of following his uncle into the sciences.

Hans Albert, still glowering from the argument with his brother, came to sit in the chair beside him.

"Grand theories are in the air now," Hans Albert said. "Wonderful ideas about extending the Poincaré theory of dynamics to include gravitation. But some fools oppose the work."

"Ah. Who invents this?"

"Papa, physicists don't *invent*. They're not engineers. They propose theories and test them. Anyway, the ideas come from some Americans, Dyson and Feynman. And from our Heisenberg too, of course."

"Light," he said, gazing at the warm play of candlelight on silver.

Hans Albert nodded impatiently. "Of course! The role of light, following an innate curve made by matter, that's in the theory. And space and time too, threaded together and warped by matter. The equations describing this reduce to Newton's familiar prescriptions in the limit of essentially flat geometries. That's what's so exciting. I wish I could make you understand! You see—"

"How heavy it is."

"What is?" His son frowned at the interruption.

"Each ray as subtle as a rose petal," he said dreamily, "bending down to the earth."

"Something like that," the younger man said carefully.

"And everywhere it bends. If we go far enough away, does the light streaming out from the stars seem to curve?"

"Well, I don't—"

"Even to the end of things? Mustn't light bend then, at least?"

Hans Albert stared at him. "No disrespect, Papa, but you're certainly not a physicist!"

When Millie's back was turned, he slipped out of the crowded room.

The balcony was dark and empty, and the air rising off the lake was fresh. Overhead, a huge tapestry of stars blazed, a panoply of light streaking outward to the far horizons of the universe. It was a time to see not just backwards but forwards too. Someday, he thought, man would follow the elusive light of the stars, sailing out into the far reaches of space. Hans Albert could have told him how this would be done, but he already knew the truth of it in his heart.

He had the sense again tonight of endings, of a wave that had travelled so far finally curving on a distant shore. So be it. He was ready for it; there were few things to regret. All in all, it had been a good life.

Rosa had reached her C.

And yet—and yet.

The book Eddie had left for him was wrong in one respect. The sharks who snatched away the victory were not external. They swam in the dark waters of the soul. The trick was not to let them.

He gazed up into the sky at the great gorgeous light.

THE LAST ARTICLE

Harry Turtledove

*Nonviolence is the first article of my faith. It is
also the last article of my creed.*

—Mohandas Gandhi

*The one means that wins the easiest victory over
reason: terror and force.*

—Adolph Hitler
Mein Kampf

The tank rumbled down the Rajpath, past the ruins of the Memorial Arch, toward the India Gate. The gateway arch was still standing, although it had taken a couple of shell hits in the fighting before New Delhi fell. The Union Jack fluttered above it.

British troops lined both sides of the Rajpath, watching silently as the tank rolled past them. Their khaki uniforms were filthy and torn; many wore bandages. They had the weary, past-caring stares of beaten men, though the Army of India had fought until flesh and munitions gave out.

The India Gate drew near. A military band, smartened up for the occasion, began to play as the tank went past. The bagpipes sounded thin and lost in the hot, humid air.

A single man stood waiting in the shadow of the Gate. Field Marshal Walther Model leaned down into the cupola of the Panzer IV. "No one can match the British at ceremonies of this sort," he said to his aide.

Major Dieter Lasch laughed, a bit unkindly. "They've had enough practice, sir," he answered, raising his voice to be heard over the flatulent roar of the tank's engine.

"What is that tune?" the field marshal asked. "Does it have a meaning?"

"It's called 'The World Turned Upside Down,'" said Lasch, who had been involved with his British opposite number in planning the formal surrender. "Lord Cornwallis's army musicians played it when he yielded to the Americans at Yorktown."

"Ah, the Americans." Model was for a moment so lost in his own thoughts that his monocle threatened to slip from his right eye. He screwed it back in. The single lens was the only thing he shared with the clichéd image of a high German officer. He was no lean, hawk-faced Prussian. But his rounded features were unyielding, and his stocky body sustained the energy of his will better than the thin, dyspeptic frames of so many aristocrats. "The Americans," he repeated. "Well, that will be the next step, won't it? But enough. One thing at a time."

The panzer stopped. The driver switched off the engine. The sudden quiet was startling. Model leaped nimbly down. He had been leaping down from tanks for eight years now, since his days as a staff officer for the IV Corps in the Polish campaign.

The man in the shadows stepped forward, saluted. Flashbulbs lit his long, tired face as German photographers recorded the moment for history. The Englishman ignored cameras and cameramen alike. "Field Marshal Model," he said politely. He might have been about to discuss the weather.

Model admired his sangfroid. "Field Marshal Auchinleck," he replied, returning the salute and giving Auchinleck a last few seconds to remain his equal. Then he came back to the matter at hand. "Field Marshal, have you signed the instrument of surrender of the British Army of India to the forces of the Reich?"

"I have," Auchinleck replied. He reached into the left blouse pocket of his battledress, removed a folded sheet of paper. Before handing it to Model, though, he said, "I should like to request your permission to make a brief statement at this time."

"Of course, sir. You may say what you like, at whatever length you like." In victory, Model could afford to be magnanimous. He had even granted Marshal Zhukov leave to speak in the Soviet capitulation at Kuibyshev, before the marshal was taken out and shot.

"I thank you." Auchinleck stiffly dipped his head. "I will say, then, that I find the terms I have been forced to accept to be cruelly hard on the brave men who have served under my command."

"That is your privilege, sir." But Model's round face was no longer kindly, and his voice had iron in it as he replied, "I must remind you, however, that my treating with you at all under the rules of war is an act of mercy for which Berlin may yet reprimand me. When Britain surrendered in 1941, all Imperial forces were also ordered to lay down their arms. I daresay you did not expect us to come so far, but I would be within my rights in reckoning you no more than so many bandits."

A slow flush darkened Auchinleck's cheeks. "We gave you a bloody good run, for bandits."

"So you did." Model remained polite. He did not say he would ten times rather fight straight-up battles than deal with the partisans who to this day harassed the Germans and their allies in occupied Russia. "Have you anything further to add?"

"No, sir, I do not." Auchinleck gave the German the signed surrender, handed him his sidearm. Model put the pistol in the empty holster he wore for the occasion. It did not fit well; the holster was made for a Walther P38, not this man-killing brute of a Webley and Scott. That mattered little, though—the ceremony was almost over.

Auchinleck and Model exchanged salutes for the last time. The British field marshal stepped away. A German lieutenant came up to lead him into captivity.

Major Lasch waved his left hand. The Union Jack came down from the flagpole on the India Gate. The swastika rose to replace it.

Lasch tapped discreetly on the door, stuck his head into the field marshal's office. "That Indian politician is here for his appointment with you, sir."

"Oh, yes. Very well, Dieter, send him in." Model had been dealing with Indian politicians even before the British surrender, and with hordes of them now that resistance was over. He had no more liking for the breed than for Russian politicians, or even German ones. No matter what pious principles they spouted, his experience was that they were all out for their own good first.

The small, frail brown man the aide showed in made him wonder. The Indian's emaciated frame and the plain white cotton loincloth that was his only garment contrasted starkly with the Victorian splendor of the Viceregal Palace from which Model was administering the Reich's new conquest. "Sit down, *Herr* Gandhi," the field marshal urged.

"I thank you very much, sir." As he took his seat, Gandhi seemed a child in an adult's chair: it was much too wide for him, and its soft, overstuffed cushions hardly sagged under his meager weight. But his eyes, Model saw, were not a child's eyes. They peered with disconcerting keenness through his wire-framed spectacles as he said, "I have come to enquire when we may expect German troops to depart from our country."

Model leaned forward, frowning. For a moment he thought he had misunderstood Gandhi's Gujarati-flavored English. When he was sure he had not, he said, "Do you think perhaps we have come all this way as tourists?"

"Indeed I do not." Gandhi's voice was sharp with disapproval. "Tourists do not leave so many dead behind them."

Model's temper kindled. "No, tourists do not pay such a high price for the journey. Having come regardless of that cost, I assure you we shall stay."

"I am very sorry, sir; I cannot permit it."

"*You* cannot?" Again, Model had to concentrate to keep his monocle from falling out. He had heard arrogance from politicians before, but this scrawny old devil surpassed belief. "Do you forget I can call my aide and have you shot behind this building? You would not be the first, I assure you."

"Yes, I know that," Gandhi said sadly. "If you have that fate in mind for me, I am an old man. I will not run."

Combat had taught Model a hard indifference to the prospect of injury or death. He saw the older man possessed something of the same sort, however he had acquired it. A moment later, he realized his threat had not only failed to frighten Gandhi, but had actually amused him. Disconcerted, the field marshal said, "Have you any serious issues to address?"

"Only the one I named just now. We are a nation of more than three hundred million; it is no more just for Germany to rule us than for the British."

Model shrugged. "If we are able to, we will. We have the strength to hold what we have conquered, I assure you."

"Where there is no right, there can be no strength," Gandhi said. "We will not permit you to hold us in bondage."

"Do you think to threaten me?" Model growled. In fact, though, the Indian's audacity surprised him. Most of the locals had fallen over themselves fawning on their new masters. Here, at least, was a man out of the ordinary.

Gandhi was still shaking his head, although Model saw he had still not frightened him (a man out of the ordinary indeed, thought the field marshal, who respected courage when he found it). "I make no threats, sir, but I will do what I believe to be right."

"Most noble," Model said, but to his annoyance the words came out sincere rather than with the sardonic edge he had intended. He had heard such canting phrases before, from Englishmen, from Russians, yes, and from Germans as well. Somehow, though, this Gandhi struck him as one who always meant exactly what he said. He rubbed his chin, considering how to handle such an intransigent.

A large green fly came buzzing into the office. Model's air of detachment vanished the moment he heard that malignant whine. He sprang from his seat, swatted at the fly. He missed. The insect flew around a while longer, then settled on the arm of Gandhi's chair.

"Kill it," Model told him. "Last week one of those accursed things bit me on the neck, and I still have the lump to prove it."

Gandhi brought his hand down, but several inches from the fly. Frightened, it took off. Gandhi rose. He was surprisingly nimble for a man nearing eighty. He chivvied the fly out of the office, ignoring Model, who watched his performance in open-mouthed wonder.

"I hope it will not trouble you again," Gandhi said, returning as calmly as if he had done nothing out of the ordinary. "I am one of those who practice *ahimsa:* I will do no injury to any living thing."

Model remembered the fall of Moscow, and the smell of burning bodies filling the chilly autumn air. He remembered machine guns knocking down Cossack cavalry before they could close, and the screams of the wounded horses, more heartrending than any woman's. He knew of other things, too, things he had not seen for himself and of which he had no desire to learn more.

"*Herr* Gandhi," he said, "how do you propose to bend to your will someone who opposes you, if you will not use force for the purpose?"

"I have never said I will not use force, sir." Gandhi's smile invited the field marshal to enjoy with him the distinction he was making. "I will not use violence. If my people refuse to cooperate in any way with yours, how can you compel them? What choice will you have but to grant us leave to do as we will?"

Without the intelligence estimates he had read, Model would have dismissed the Indian as a madman. No madman, though, could have caused the British so much trouble. But perhaps the decadent raj simply had not made him afraid. Model tried again. "You understand that what you have said is treason against the Reich," he said harshly.

Gandhi bowed in his seat. "You may, of course, do what you will with me. My spirit will in any case survive among my people."

Model felt his face heat. Few men were immune to fear. Just his luck, he thought sourly, to have run into one of them. "I warn you, *Herr* Gandhi, to obey the authority of the officials of the Reich, or it will be the worse for you."

"I will do what I believe to be right, and nothing else. If you Germans exert yourselves toward the freeing of India, joyfully will I work with you. If not, then I regret we must be foes."

The field marshal gave him one last chance to see reason. "Were it you and I alone, there might be some doubt as to what would happen." Not much, he thought, not when Gandhi was twenty-odd years older and thin enough to break like a stick. He fought down the irrelevance, went on, "But where, *Herr* Gandhi, is your *Wehrmacht?*"

Of all things, he had least expected to amuse the Indian again. Yet

Gandhi's eyes unmistakably twinkled behind the lenses of his spectacles. "Field Marshal, I have an army too."

Model's patience, never of the most enduring sort, wore thin all at once. "Get out!" he snapped.

Gandhi stood, bowed, and departed. Major Lasch stuck his head into the office. The field marshal's glare drove him out again in a hurry.

"Well?" Jawaharlal Nehru paced back and forth. Tall, slim, and saturnine, he towered over Gandhi without dominating him. "Dare we use the same policies against the Germans that we employed against the English?"

"If we wish our land free, dare we do otherwise?" Gandhi replied. "They will not grant our wish of their own volition. Model struck me as a man not much different from various British leaders whom we have succeeded in vexing in the past." He smiled at the memory of what passive resistance had done to officials charged with combating it.

"Very well, *satyagraha* it is." But Nehru was not smiling. He had less humor than his older colleague.

Gandhi teased him gently: "Do you fear another spell in prison, then?" Both men had spent time behind bars during the war, until the British released them in a last, vain effort to rally the support of the Indian people to the raj.

"You know better." Nehru refused to be drawn, and persisted, "The rumors that come out of Europe frighten me."

"Do you tell me you take them seriously?" Gandhi shook his head in surprise and a little reproof. "Each side in any war will always paint its opponents as blackly as it can."

"I hope you are right, and that that is all. Still, I confess I would feel more at ease with what we plan to do if you found me one Jew, officer or other rank, in the army now occupying us."

"You would be hard-pressed to find any among the forces they defeated. The British have little love for Jews either."

"Yes, but I daresay it could be done. With the Germans, they are banned by law. The English would never make such a rule. And while the laws are vile enough, I think of the tales that man Wiesenthal told, the one who came here the gods know how across Russia and Persia from Poland."

"Those I do not believe," Gandhi said firmly. "No nation could act in that way and hope to survive. Where could men be found to carry out such horrors?"

"*Azad Hind,*" Nehru said, quoting the "Free India" motto of the locals who had fought on the German side.

But Gandhi shook his head. "They are only soldiers, doing as soldiers have always done. Wiesenthal's claims are for an entirely different order of bestiality, one which could not exist without destroying the fabric of the state that gave it birth."

"I hope very much you are right," Nehru said.

Walther Model slammed the door behind him hard enough to make his aide, whose desk faced away from the field marshal's office, jump in alarm. "Enough of this twaddle for one day," Model said. "I need schnapps, to get the taste of these Indians out of my mouth. Come along if you care to, Dieter."

"Thank you, sir." Major Lasch threw down his pen, eagerly got to his feet. "I sometimes think conquering India was easier than ruling it will be."

Model rolled his eyes. "I *know* it was. I would ten times rather be planning a new campaign than sitting here bogged down in pettifogging details. The sooner Berlin sends me people trained in colonial administration, the happier I will be."

The bar might have been taken from an English pub. It was dark, quiet, and paneled in walnut; a dart board still hung on the wall. But a German sergeant in field gray stood behind the bar, and despite the lazily turning ceiling fan, the temperature was close to thirty-five Celsius. The one might have been possible in occupied London, the other not.

Model knocked back his first shot at a gulp. He sipped his second more slowly, savoring it. Warmth spread through him, warmth that had nothing to do with the heat of the evening. He leaned back in his chair, steepled his fingers. "A long day," he said.

"Yes, sir," Lasch agreed. "After the effrontery of that Gandhi, any day would seem a long one. I've rarely seen you so angry." Considering Model's temper, that was no small statement.

"Ah, yes, Gandhi." Model's tone was reflective rather than irate; Lasch looked at him curiously. The field marshal said, "For my money, he's worth a dozen of the ordinary sort."

"Sir?" The aide no longer tried to hide his surprise.

"He is an honest man. He tells me what he thinks, and he will stick by that. I may kill him—I may have to kill him—but he and I will both know why, and I will not change his mind." Model took another sip of schnapps. He hesitated, as if unsure whether to go on. At last he did. "Do you know, Dieter, after he left I had a vision."

"Sir?" Now Lasch sounded alarmed.

The field marshal might have read his aide's thoughts. He chuckled wryly. "No, no, I am not about to swear off eating beefsteak and wear sandals instead of my boots, that I promise. But I saw myself as a Roman procurator, listening to the rantings of some early Christian priest."

Lasch raised an eyebrow. Such musings were unlike Model, who was usually direct to the point of bluntness and altogether materialistic—assets in the makeup of a general officer. The major cautiously sounded these unexpected depths: "How do you suppose the Roman felt, facing that kind of man?"

"Bloody confused, I suspect," Model said, which sounded more like him. "And because he and his comrades did not know how to handle such fanatics, you and I are Christians today, Dieter."

"So we are." The major rubbed his chin. "Is that a bad thing?"

Model laughed and finished his drink. "From your point of view or mine, no, but I doubt that old Roman would agree with us, any more than Gandhi agrees with me over what will happen next here. But then, I have two advantages over the dead procurator." He raised his finger; the sergeant hurried over to fill his glass.

At Lasch's nod, the young man also poured more schnapps for him. The major drank, then said, "I should hope so. We are more civilized, more sophisticated, than the Romans ever dreamed of being."

But Model was still in that fey mood. "Are we? My procurator was such a sophisticate that he tolerated anything, and never saw the danger in a foe who would not do the same. Our Christian God, though, is a jealous god, who puts up with no rivals. And one who is a National Socialist serves also the *Volk*, to whom he owes sole loyalty. I am immune to Gandhi's virus in a way the Roman was not to the Christian's."

"Yes, that makes sense," Lasch agreed after a moment. "I had not thought of it in that way, but I see it is so. And what is our other advantage over the Roman procurator?"

Suddenly the field marshal looked hard and cold, much the way he had looked leading the tanks of Third Panzer against the Kremlin compound. "The machine gun," he said.

The rising sun's rays made the sandstone of the Red Fort seem even more the color of blood. Gandhi frowned and turned his back on the fortress, not caring for that thought. Even at dawn, the air was warm and muggy.

"I wish you were not here," Nehru told him. The younger man

lifted his trademark fore-and-aft cap, scratched his graying hair, and glanced at the crowd growing around them. "The Germans' orders forbid assemblies, and they will hold you responsible for this gathering."

"I am, am I not?" Gandhi replied. "Would you have me send my followers into a danger I do not care to face myself? How would I presume to lead them afterwards?"

"A general does not fight in the front ranks," Nehru came back. "If you are lost to our cause, will we be able to go on?"

"If not, then surely the cause is not worthy, yes? Now let us be going."

Nehru threw his hands in the air. Gandhi nodded, satisfied, and worked his way toward the head of the crowd. Men and women stepped aside to let him through. Still shaking his head, Nehru followed.

The crowd slowly began to march east up Chandni Chauk, the Street of Silversmiths. Some of the fancy shops had been wrecked in the fighting, more looted afterwards. But others were opening up, their owners as happy to take German money as they had been to serve the British before.

One of the proprietors, a man who had managed to stay plump even through the past year of hardship, came rushing out of his shop when he saw the procession go by. He ran to the head of the march and spotted Nehru, whose height and elegant dress singled him out.

"Are you out of your mind?" the silversmith shouted. "The Germans have banned assemblies. If they see you, something dreadful will happen."

"Is it not dreadful that they take away the liberty which properly belongs to us?" Gandhi asked. The silversmith spun round. His eyes grew wide when he recognized the man who was speaking to him. Gandhi went on, "Not only is it dreadful, it is wrong. And so we do not recognize the Germans' right to ban anything we may choose to do. Join us, will you?"

"Great-souled one, I—I—" the silversmith spluttered. Then his glance slid past Gandhi. "The Germans!" he squeaked. He turned and ran.

Gandhi led the procession toward the approaching squad. The Germans stamped down Chandni Chauk as if they expected the people in front of them to melt from their path. Their gear, Gandhi thought, was not that much different from what British soldiers wore: ankle boots, shorts, and open-necked tunics. But their coal-scuttle helmets gave them a look of sullen, beetle-browed ferocity the British tin hat

did not convey. Even for a man of Gandhi's equanimity it was daunting, as no doubt it was intended to be.

"Hello, my friends," he said. "Do any of you speak English?"

"I speak it, a little," one of them replied. His shoulder straps had
the twin pips of a sergeant-major; he was the squad-leader, then. He
hefted his rifle, not menacingly, Gandhi thought, but to emphasize
what he was saying. "Go to your homes back. This coming together is
verboten."

"I am sorry, but I must refuse to obey your order," Gandhi said.
"We are walking peacefully on our own street in our own city. We
will harm no one, no matter what; this I promise you. But walk we
will, as we wish." He repeated himself until he was sure the sergeant-
major understood.

The German spoke to his comrades in his own language. One of
the soldiers raised his gun and with a nasty smile pointed it at Gandhi. He nodded politely. The German blinked to see him unafraid.
The sergeant-major slapped the rifle down. One of his men had a field
telephone on his back. The sergeant-major cranked it, waited for a
reply, spoke urgently into it.

Nehru caught Gandhi's eye. His dark, tired gaze was full of worry.
Somehow that nettled Gandhi more than the Germans' arrogance in
ordering about his people. He began to walk forward again. The
marchers followed him, flowing around the German squad like water
round a boulder.

The soldier who had pointed his rifle at Gandhi shouted in alarm.
He brought up the weapon again. The sergeant-major barked at him.
Reluctantly, he lowered it.

"A sensible man," Gandhi said to Nehru. "He sees we do no injury
to him or his, and so does none to us."

"Sadly, though, not everyone is so sensible," the younger man replied, "as witness his lance-corporal there. And even a sensible man
may not be well-inclined to us. You notice he is still on the telephone."

The phone on Field Marshal Model's desk jangled. He jumped and
swore; he had left orders he was to be disturbed only for an emergency. He had to find time to work. He picked up the phone. "This
had better be good," he growled without preamble.

He listened, swore again, slammed the receiver down. "Lasch!" he
shouted.

It was his aide's turn to jump. "Sir?"

"Don't just sit there on your fat arse," the field marshal said unfairly. "Call out my car and driver, and quickly. Then belt on your sidearm and come along. The Indians are doing something stupid. Oh, yes, order out a platoon and have them come after us. Up on Chandni Chauk, the trouble is."

Lasch called for the car and the troops, then hurried after Model. "A riot?" he asked as he caught up.

"No, no." Model moved his stumpy frame along so fast that the taller Lasch had to trot beside him. "Some of Gandhi's tricks, damn him."

The field marshal's Mercedes was waiting when he and his aide hurried out of the viceregal palace. "Chandni Chauk," Model snapped as the driver held the door open for him. After that he sat in furious silence as the powerful car roared up Irwin Road, round a third of Connaught Circle, and north on Chelmsford Road past the bombed-out railway station until, for no reason Model could see, the street's name changed to Qutb Road.

A little later, the driver said, "Some kind of disturbance up ahead, sir."

"Disturbance?" Lasch echoed, leaning forward to peer through the windscreen. "It's a whole damned regiment's worth of Indians coming at us. Don't they know better than that? And what the devil," he added, his voice rising, "are so many of our men doing ambling along beside them? Don't they know they're supposed to break up this sort of thing?" In his indignation, he did not notice he was repeating himself.

"I suspect they don't," Model said dryly. "Gandhi, I gather, can have that effect on people who aren't ready for his peculiar brand of stubbornness. That, however, does not include me." He tapped the driver on the shoulder. "Pull up about two hundred meters in front of the first rank of them, Joachim."

"Yes, sir."

Even before the car had stopped moving, Model jumped out of it. Lasch, hand on his pistol, was close behind, protesting, "What if one of those fanatics has a gun?"

"Then Colonel-General Weidling assumes command, and a lot of Indians end up dead."

Model strode toward Gandhi. As it had at the surrender ceremony, India's damp heat smote him. Even while he was sitting quietly in the car, his tunic had stuck to him. Sweat started streaming down his face the moment he started to move. Each breath felt as if he were taking in warm soup; the air even had a faint smell of soup, soup that had gone slightly off.

In its own way, he thought, surprised at himself, this beastly weather was worse than a Russian winter. Either was plenty to lay a man low by itself, but countless exotic diseases flourished in the moisture, warmth, and filth here. The snows at least were clean.

The field marshal ignored the German troops who were drawing themselves to stiff, horrified attention at the sight of his uniform. He would deal with them later. For the moment, Gandhi was more important.

He had stopped—which meant the rest of the marchers did too—and was waiting politely for Model to approach. The German commandant was not impressed. He thought Gandhi sincere, and could not doubt his courage, but none of that mattered at all. He said harshly, "You were warned against this sort of behavior."

Gandhi looked him in the eye. They were very much of a height. "And I told you, I do not recognize your right to give such orders. This is our country, not yours, and if some of us choose to walk on our streets, we will do so."

From behind Gandhi, Nehru's glance flicked worriedly from one of the antagonists to the other. Model noticed him only peripherally; if he was already afraid, he could be handled whenever necessary. Gandhi was a tougher nut. The field marshal waved at the crowd behind the old man. "You are responsible for all these people. If harm comes to them, you will be to blame."

"Why should harm come to them? They are not soldiers. They do not attack your men. I told that to one of your sergeants, and he understood it, and refrained from hindering us. Surely you, sir, an educated, cultured man, can see that what I say is self-evident truth."

Model turned his head to speak to his aide in German: "If we did not have Goebbels, this would be the one for his job." He shuddered to think of the propaganda victory Gandhi would win if he got away with flouting German ordinances. The whole countryside would be boiling with partisans in a week. And he had already managed to hoodwink some Germans into letting him do it!

Then Gandhi surprised him again. *"Ich danke Ihnen, Herr Generalfeldmarschall, aber das glaube ich kein Kompliment zu sein,"* he said in slow but clear German: "I thank you, field marshal, but I believe that to be no compliment."

Having to hold his monocle in place helped Model keep his face straight. "Take it however you like," he said. "Get these people öff the street, or they and you will face the consequences. We will do what you force us to."

"I force you to nothing. As for these people who follow, each does so of his or her own free will. We are free, and will show it, not by violence, but through firmness in truth."

Now Model listened with only half an ear. He had kept Gandhi talking long enough for the platoon he had ordered out to arrive. Half a dozen SdKfz 251 armored personnel carriers came clanking up. The men piled out of them. "Give me a firing line, three ranks deep," Model shouted. As the troopers scrambled to obey, he waved the halftracks into position behind them, all but blocking Qutb Road. The halftracks' commanders swiveled the machine guns at the front of the vehicles' troop compartments so they bore on the Indians.

Gandhi watched these preparations as calmly as if they had nothing to do with him. Again Model had to admire his calm. His followers were less able to keep fear from their faces. Very few, though, used the pause to slip away. Gandhi's discipline was a long way from the military sort, but effective all the same.

"Tell them to disperse now, and we can still get away without bloodshed," the field marshal said.

"We will shed no one's blood, sir. But we will continue on our pleasant journey. Moving carefully, we will, I think, be able to get between your large lorries there." Gandhi turned to wave his people forward once more.

"You insolent—" Rage choked Model, which was as well, for it kept him from cursing Gandhi like a fishwife. To give him time to master his temper, he plucked his monocle from his eye and began polishing the lens with a silk handkerchief. He replaced the monocle, started to jam the handkerchief back into his trouser pocket, then suddenly had a better idea.

"Come, Lasch," he said, and started toward the waiting German troops. About halfway to them, he dropped the handkerchief on the ground. He spoke in loud, simple German so his men and Gandhi could both follow: "If any Indians come past this spot, I wash my hands of them."

He might have known Gandhi would have a comeback ready. "That is what Pilate said also, you will recall, sir."

"Pilate washed his hands to evade responsibility," the field marshal answered steadily; he was in control of himself again. "I accept it: I am responsible to my Führer and to the *Oberkommando-Wehrmacht* for maintaining Reichs control over India, and will do what I see fit to carry out that obligation."

For the first time since they had come to know each other, Gandhi looked sad. "I too, sir, have my responsibilities." He bowed slightly to Model.

Lasch chose that moment to whisper in his commander's ear: "Sir, what of our men over there? Had you planned to leave them in the line of fire?"

The field marshal frowned. He had planned to do just that; the wretches deserved no better, for being taken in by Gandhi. But Lasch had a point. The platoon might balk at shooting countrymen, if it came to that. "You men," Model said sourly, jabbing his marshal's baton at them, "fall in behind the armored personnel carriers, at once."

The Germans' boots pounded on the macadam as they dashed to obey. They were still all right, then, with a clear order in front of them. Something, Model thought, but not much.

He had also worried that the Indians would take advantage of the moment of confusion to press forward, but they did not. Gandhi and Nehru and a couple of other men were arguing among themselves. Model nodded once. Some of them knew he was in earnest, then. And Gandhi's followers' discipline, as the field marshal had thought a few minutes ago, was not of the military sort. He could not simply issue an order and know his will would be done.

"I issue no orders," Gandhi said. "Let each man follow his conscience as he will—what else is freedom?"

"They will follow *you* if you go forward, great-souled one," Nehru replied, "and that German, I fear, means to carry out his threat. Will you throw your life away, and those of your countrymen?"

"I will not throw my life away," Gandhi said, but before the men around him could relax he went on, "I will gladly give it, if freedom requires that. I am but one man. If I fall, others will surely carry on; perhaps the memory of me will serve to make them more steadfast."

He stepped forward.

"Oh, damnation," Nehru said softly, and followed.

For all his vigor, Gandhi was far from young. Nehru did not need to nod to the marchers close by him; of their own accord, they hurried ahead of the man who had led them for so long, forming with their bodies a barrier between him and the German guns.

He tried to go faster. "Stop! Leave me my place! What are you doing?" he cried, though in his heart he understood only too well.

"This once, they will not listen to you," Nehru said.

"But they must!" Gandhi peered through eyes dimmed now by tears as well as age. "Where is that stupid handkerchief? We must be almost to it!"

*   *   *

"For the last time, I warn you to halt!" Model shouted. The Indians still came on. The sound of their feet, sandal-clad or bare, was like a growing murmur on the pavement, very different from the clatter of German boots. "Fools!" the field marshal muttered under his breath. He turned to his men. "Take your aim!"

The advance slowed when the rifles came up; of that Model was certain. For a moment he thought that ultimate threat would be enough to bring the marchers to their senses. But then they advanced again. The Polish cavalry had shown that same reckless bravery, charging with lances and sabers and carbines against the German tanks. Model wondered whether the inhabitants of the *Reichsgeneralgouvernement* of Poland thought the gallantry worthwhile.

A man stepped on the field marshal's handkerchief. "Fire!" Model said.

A second passed, two. Nothing happened. Model scowled at his men. Gandhi's deviltry had got into them; sneaky as a Jew, he was turning the appearance of weakness into a strange kind of strength. But then trained discipline paid its dividend. One finger tightened on a Mauser trigger. A single shot rang out. As if it were a signal that recalled the other men to their duty, they too began to fire. From the armored personnel carriers, the machine guns started their deadly chatter. Model heard screams above the gunfire.

The volley smashed into the front ranks of marchers at close range. Men fell. Others ran, or tried to, only to be held by the power of the stream still advancing behind them. Once begun, the Germans methodically poured fire into the column of Indians. The march dissolved into a panic-stricken mob.

Gandhi still tried to press forward. A fleeing wounded man smashed into him, splashing him with blood and knocking him to the ground. Nehru and another man immediately lay down on top of him.

"Let me up! Let me up!" he shouted.

"No," Nehru screamed in his ear. "With shooting like this, you are in the safest spot you can be. We need you, and need you alive. Now we have martyrs around whom to rally our cause."

"Now we have dead husbands and wives, fathers and mothers. Who will tend to their loved ones?"

Gandhi had no time for more protest. Nehru and the other man hauled him to his feet and dragged him away. Soon they were among their people, all running now from the German guns. A bullet struck the back of the unknown man who was helping Gandhi escape. Gandhi heard the slap of the impact, felt the man jerk. Then the strong grip on him loosened as the man fell.

He tried to tear free from Nehru. Before he could, another Indian laid hold of him. Even at that horrid moment, he felt the irony of his predicament. All his life he had championed individual liberty, and here his own followers were robbing him of his. In other circumstances, it might have been funny.

"In here!" Nehru shouted. Several people had already broken down the door to a shop and, Gandhi saw a moment later, the rear exit as well. Then he was hustled into the alley behind the shop, and through a maze of lanes which reminded him that old Delhi, unlike its British-designed sister city, was an Indian town through and through.

At last the nameless man with Gandhi and Nehru knocked on the back door of a tearoom. The woman who opened it gasped to recognize her unexpected guests, then pressed her hands together in front of her and stepped aside to let them in. "You will be safe here," the man said, "at least for a while. Now I must see to my own family."

"From the bottom of our hearts, we thank you," Nehru replied as the fellow hurried away. Gandhi said nothing. He was winded, battered, and filled with anguish at the failure of the march and at the suffering it had brought to so many marchers and to their kinsfolk.

The woman sat the two fugitive leaders at a small table in the kitchen, served them tea and cakes. "I will leave you now, best ones," she said quietly, "lest those out front wonder why I neglect them for so long."

Gandhi left the cake on his plate. He sipped the tea. Its warmth began to restore him physically, but the wound in his spirit would never heal. "The Amritsar massacre pales beside this," he said, setting down the empty cup. "There the British panicked and opened fire. This had nothing of panic about it. Model told me what he would do, and he did it." He shook his head, still hardly believing what he had just been through.

"So he did." Nehru had gobbled his cake like a starving wolf, and ate his companion's when he saw Gandhi did not want it. His once-immaculate white jacket and pants were torn, filthy, and blood-spattered; his cap sat awry on his head. But his eyes, usually so somber, were lit with a fierce glow. "And by his brutality, he has delivered himself into our hands. No one now can imagine the Germans have anything but their own interests at heart. We will gain followers all over the country. After this, not a wheel will turn in India."

"Yes, I will declare the *satyagraha* campaign," Gandhi said. "Noncooperation will show how we reject foreign rule, and will cost the Germans dear because they will not be able to exploit us. The combination of nonviolence and determined spirit will surely shame them into granting us our liberty."

"There—you see." Encouraged by his mentor's rally, Nehru rose and came round the table to embrace the older man. "We will triumph yet."

"So we will," Gandhi said, and sighed heavily. He had pursued India's freedom for half his long life, and this change of masters was a setback he had not truly planned for, even after England and Russia fell. The British were finally beginning to listen to him when the Germans swept them aside. Now he had to begin anew. He sighed again. "It will cost our poor people dear, though."

"Cease firing," Model said. Few good targets were left on Qutb Road; almost all the Indians in the procession were down or had run from the guns.

Even after the bullets stopped, the street was far from silent. Most of the people the German platoon had shot were alive and shrieking. As if he needed more proof—the Russian campaign had taught the field marshal how hard human beings were to kill outright.

Still, the din distressed him, and evidently Lasch as well. "We ought to put them out of their misery," the major said.

"So we should." Model had a happy inspiration. "And I know just how. Come with me."

The two men turned their backs on the carnage and walked around the row of armored personnel carriers. As they passed the lieutenant commanding the platoon, Model nodded to him and said, "Well done."

The lieutenant saluted. "Thank you, sir." The soldiers in earshot nodded at one another. Nothing bucked up the odds of getting promoted like performing under the commander's eye.

The Germans behind the armored vehicles were not so proud of themselves. They were the ones who had let the march get this big and come this far in the first place. Model slapped his boot with his field marshal's baton. "You all deserve courts-martial," he said coldly, glaring at them. "You know the orders concerning native assemblies, yet there you were tagging along, more like sheepdogs than soldiers." He spat in disgust.

"But, sir—" began one of them, a sergeant-major, Model saw. He subsided in a hurry when Model's gaze swung his way.

"Speak," the field marshal urged. "Enlighten me—tell me what possessed you to act in the disgraceful way you did. Was it some evil spirit, perhaps? This country abounds with them, if you listen to the natives—as you all too obviously have been."

The sergeant-major flushed under Model's sarcasm, but finally burst out, "Sir, it didn't look to me as if they were up to any harm, that's all. The old man heading them up swore they were peaceful, and he looked too feeble to be anything but, if you take my meaning."

Model's smile had all the warmth of a Moscow December night. "And so in your wisdom you set aside the commands you had received. The results of that wisdom you hear now." The field marshal briefly let himself listen to the cries of the wounded, a sound the war had taught him to screen out. "Now then, come with me—yes you, Sergeant-major, and the rest of your shirkers too, or those of you who wish to avoid a court."

As he had known they would, they all trooped after him. "There is your handiwork," he said, pointing to the shambles in the street. His voice hardened. "You are responsible for those people lying there— had you acted as you should, you would have broken up that march long before it ever got so far or so large. Now the least you can do is give those people their release." He set hands on hips, waited.

No one moved. "Sir?" the sergeant-major said faintly. He seemed to have become the group's spokesman.

Model made an impatient gesture. "Go on, finish them. A bullet in the back of the head will quiet them once and for all."

"In cold blood, sir?" The sergeant-major had not wanted to understand him before. Now he had no choice.

The field marshal was inexorable. "They—and you—disobeyed Reich commands. They made themselves liable to capital punishment the moment they gathered. You at least have the chance to atone, by carrying out this just sentence."

"I don't think I can," the sergeant-major muttered.

He was probably just talking to himself, but Model gave him no chance to change his mind. He turned to the lieutenant of the platoon that had broken the march. "Place this man under arrest." After the sergeant-major had been seized, Model turned his chill, monocled stare on the rest of the reluctant soldiers. "Any others?"

Two more men let themselves be arrested rather than draw their weapons. The field marshal nodded to the others. "Carry out your orders." He had an afterthought. "If you find Gandhi or Nehru out there, bring them to me alive."

The Germans moved out hesitantly. They were no *Einsatzkommandos,* and not used to this kind of work. Some looked away as they

administered the first coup de grace; one missed as a result, and had
his bullet ricochet off the pavement and almost hit a comrade. But as
the soldiers worked their way up Qutb Road they became quicker,
more confident, and more competent. War was like that, Model
thought. So soon one became used to what had been unimaginable.

After a while the flat cracks died away, but from lack of targets
rather than reluctance. A few at a time, the soldiers returned to
Model. "No sign of the two leaders?" he asked. They all shook their
heads.

"Very well—dismissed. And obey your orders like good Germans
henceforward."

"No further reprisals?" Lasch asked as the relieved troopers hurried away.

"No, let them go. They carried out their part of the bargain, and I
will meet mine. I am a fair man, after all, Dieter."

"Very well, sir."

Gandhi listened with undisguised dismay as the shopkeeper babbled out his tale of horror. "This is madness!" he cried.

"I doubt Field Marshal Model, for his part, understands the principle of *ahimsa*," Nehru put in. Neither Gandhi nor he knew exactly
where they were: a safe house somewhere not far from the center of
Delhi was the best guess he could make. The men who brought the
shopkeeper were masked. What one did not know, one could not tell
the Germans if captured.

"Neither do you," the older man replied, which was true; Nehru
had a more pragmatic nature than Gandhi. Gandhi went on, "Rather
more to the point, neither do the British. And Model, to speak to,
seemed no different from any high-ranking British military man. His
specialty has made him harsh and rigid, but he is not stupid and does
not appear unusually cruel."

"Just a simple soldier, doing his job." Nehru's irony was palpable.

"He must have gone insane," Gandhi said; it was the only explanation that made even the slightest sense of the massacre of the
wounded. "Undoubtedly he will be censured when news of this
atrocity reaches Berlin, as General Dyer was by the British after Amritsar."

"Such is to be hoped." But again Nehru did not sound hopeful.

"How could it be otherwise, after such an appalling action? What
government, what leaders could fail to be filled with humiliation and
remorse at it?"

* * *

Model strode into the mess. The officers stood and raised their glasses in salute. "Sit, sit," the field marshal growled, using gruffness to hide his pleasure.

An Indian servant brought him a fair imitation of roast beef and Yorkshire pudding: better than they were eating in London these days, he thought. The servant was silent and unsmiling, but Model would only have noticed more about him had he been otherwise. Servants were supposed to assume a cloak of invisibility.

When the meal was done, Model took out his cigar case. The *Waffen-SS* officer on his left produced a lighter. Model leaned forward, puffed a cigar into life. "My thanks, *Brigadeführer*," the field marshal said. He had little use for SS titles of rank, but brigade commander was at least recognizably close to brigadier.

"Sir, it is my great pleasure," Jürgen Stroop declared. "You could not have handled things better. A lesson for the Indians—less than they deserve, too" (he also took no notice of the servant) "and a good one for your men as well. We train ours harshly too."

Model nodded. He knew about SS training methods. No one denied the daring of the *Waffen-SS* divisions. No one (except the SS) denied that the *Wehrmacht* had better officers.

Stroop drank. "A lesson," he repeated in a pedantic tone that went oddly with the SS's reputation for aggressiveness. "Force is the only thing the racially inferior can understand. Why, when I was in Warsaw—"

That had been four or five years ago, Model suddenly recalled. Stroop had been a *Brigadeführer* then too, if memory served; no wonder he was still one now, even after all the hard fighting since. He was lucky not to be a buck private. Imagine letting a pack of desperate, starving Jews chew up the finest troops in the world.

And imagine, afterwards, submitting a seventy-five-page operations report bound in leather and grandiosely called *The Warsaw Ghetto Is No More*. And imagine, with all that, having the crust to boast about it afterwards. No wonder the man sounded like a pompous ass. He *was* a pompous ass, and an inept butcher to boot. Model had done enough butchery before today's work—anyone who fought in Russia learned all about butchery—but he had never botched it.

He did not revel in it, either. He wished Stroop would shut up. He thought about telling the *Brigadeführer* he would sooner have been listening to Gandhi. The look on the fellow's face, he thought, would be worth it. But no. One could never be sure who was listening. Better safe.

* * *

The shortwave set crackled to life. It was in a secret cellar, a tiny dark hot room lit only by the glow of its dial and by the red end of the cigarette in its owner's mouth. The Germans had made not turning in a radio a capital crime. Of course, Gandhi thought, harboring him was also a capital crime. That weighed on his conscience. But the man knew the risk he was taking.

The fellow (Gandhi knew him only as Lal) fiddled with the controls. "Usually we listen to the Americans," he said. "There is some hope of truth from them. But tonight you want to hear Berlin."

"Yes," Gandhi said. "I must learn what action is to be taken against Model."

"If any," Nehru added. He was once again impeccably attired in white, which made him the most easily visible object in the cellar.

"We have argued this before," Gandhi said tiredly. "No government can uphold the author of a cold-blooded slaughter of wounded men and women. The world would cry out in abhorrence."

Lal said, "That government controls too much of the world already." He adjusted the tuning knob again. After a burst of static, the strains of a Strauss waltz filled the little room. Lal grunted in satisfaction. "We are a little early yet."

After a few minutes, the incongruously sweet music died away. "This is Radio Berlin's English-language channel," an announcer declared. "In a moment, the news programme." Another German tune rang out: the Horst Wessel Song. Gandhi's nostrils flared with distaste.

A new voice came over the air. "Good day. This is William Joyce." The nasal Oxonian accent was that of the archetypical British aristocrat, now vanished from India as well as England. It was the accent that flavored Gandhi's own English, and Nehru's as well. In fact, Gandhi had heard, Joyce was a New York-born rabble-rouser of Irish blood who also happened to be a passionately sincere Nazi. The combination struck the Indian as distressing.

"What did the English used to call him?" Nehru murmured. "Lord Haw-Haw?"

Gandhi waved his friend to silence. Joyce was reading the news, or what the Propaganda Ministry in Berlin wanted to present to English-speakers as the news.

Most of it was on the dull side: a trade agreement between Manchukuo, Japanese-dominated China, and Japanese-dominated Siberia; advances by German-supported French troops against American-supported French troops in a war by proxy in the African jungles.

Slightly more interesting was the German warning about American interference in the East Asia Co-Prosperity Sphere.

One day soon, Gandhi thought sadly, the two mighty powers of the Old World would turn on the one great nation that stood between them. He feared the outcome. Thinking herself secure behind ocean barriers, the United States had stayed out of the European war. Now the war was bigger than Europe, and the oceans barriers no longer, but highways for her foes.

Lord Haw-Haw droned on and on. He gloated over the fate of rebels hunted down in Scotland: they were publicly hanged. Nehru leaned forward. "Now," he guessed. Gandhi nodded.

But the commentator passed on to unlikely-sounding boasts about the prosperity of Europe under the New Order. Against his will, Gandhi felt anger rise in him. Were Indians too insignificant to the Reich even to be mentioned?

More music came from the radio: the first bars of the other German anthem, *Deutschland über alles*. William Joyce said solemnly, "And now, a special announcement from the Ministry for Administration of Acquired Territories. *Reichsminister* Reinhard Heydrich commends Field Marshal Walther Model's heroic suppression of insurrection in India, and warns that his leniency will not be repeated."

"Leniency!" Nehru and Gandhi burst out together, the latter making it into as much of a curse as he allowed himself.

As if explaining to them, the voice on the radio went on, "Henceforward, hostages will be taken at the slightest sound of disorder, and will be executed forthwith if it continues. Field Marshal Model has also placed a reward of fifty thousand rupees on the capture of the criminal revolutionary Gandhi, and twenty-five thousand on the capture of his henchman Nehru."

Deutschland über alles rang out again, to signal the end of the announcement. Joyce went on to the next piece of news. "Turn that off," Nehru said after a moment. Lal obeyed, plunging the cellar into complete darkness. Nehru surprised Gandhi by laughing. "I have never before been the henchman of a criminal revolutionary."

The older man might as well not have heard him. "They commended him," he said. "Commended!" Disbelief put the full tally of his years in his voice, which usually sounded much stronger and younger.

"What will you do?" Lal asked quietly. A match flared, dazzling in the dark, as he lit another cigarette.

"They shall not govern India in this fashion," Gandhi snapped. "Not a soul will cooperate with them from now on. We outnumber them a thousand to one; what can they accomplish without us? We shall use that to full advantage."

"I hope the price is not more than the people can pay," Nehru said.

"The British shot us down too, and we were on our way toward prevailing," Gandhi said stoutly. As he would not have a few days before, though, he added, "So do I."

Field Marshal Model scowled and yawned at the same time. The pot of tea that should have been on his desk was nowhere to be found. His stomach growled. A plate of rolls should have been beside the teapot.

"How am I supposed to get anything done without breakfast?" he asked rhetorically (no one was in the office to hear him complain). Rhetorical complaint was not enough to satisfy him. "Lasch!" he shouted.

"Sir?" The aide came rushing in.

Model jerked his chin at the empty space on his desk where the silver tray full of good things should have been. "What's become of what's-his-name? Naoroji, that's it. If he's home with a hangover, he could have had the courtesy to let us know."

"I will enquire with the liaison officer for native personnel, sir, and also have the kitchen staff send you up something to eat." Lasch picked up a telephone, spoke into it. The longer he talked, the less happy he looked. When he turned back to the field marshal, his expression was a good match for the stony one Model often wore. He said, "None of the locals has shown up for work today, sir."

"What? None?" Model's frown made his monocle dig into his cheek. He hesitated. "I will feel better if you tell me some new hideous malady has broken out among them."

Lasch spoke with the liaison officer again. He shook his head. "Nothing like that, sir, or at least," he corrected himself with the caution that made him a good aide, "nothing Captain Wechsler knows about."

Model's phone rang again. It startled him; he jumped. *"Bitte?"* he growled into the mouthpiece, embarrassed at starting even though only Lasch had seen. He listened. Then he growled again, in good earnest this time. He slammed the phone down. "That was our railway officer. Hardly any natives are coming in to the station."

The phone rang again. *"Bitte?"* This time it was a swear word. Model snarled, cutting off whatever the man on the other end was saying, and hung up. "The damned clerks are staying out too," he shouted at Lasch, as if it were the major's fault. "I know what's wrong with the blasted locals, by God—an overdose of Gandhi, that's what."

"We should have shot him down in that riot he led," Lasch said angrily.

"Not for lack of effort that we didn't," Model said. Now that he saw where his trouble was coming from, he began thinking like a General Staff-trained officer again. That discipline went deep in him. His voice was cool and musing as he corrected his aide: "It was no riot, Dieter. That man is a skilled agitator. Armed with no more than words, he gave the British fits. Remember that the Führer started out as an agitator too."

"Ah, but the Führer wasn't above breaking heads to back up what he said." Lasch smiled reminiscently, and raised a fist. He was a Munich man, and wore on his sleeve the hashmark that showed Party membership before 1933.

But the field marshal said, "You think Gandhi doesn't? His way is to break them from the inside out, to make his foes doubt themselves. Those soldiers who took courts rather than obey their commanding officer had their heads broken, wouldn't you say? Think of him as a Russian tank commander, say, rather than as a political agitator. He is fighting us every bit as much as the Russians did."

Lasch thought about it. Plainly, he did not like it. "A coward's way of fighting."

"The weak cannot use the weapons of the strong," Model shrugged. "He does what he can, and skillfully. But I can make his backers doubt themselves, too. See if I don't."

"Sir?"

"We'll start with the railway workers. They are the most essential to have back on the job, yes? Get a list of names. Cross off every twentieth one. Send a squad to each of those homes, haul the slackers out, and shoot them in the street. If the survivors don't report tomorrow, do it again. Keep at it every day until they go back to work or no workers are left."

"Yes, sir." Lasch hesitated. At last he asked, "Are you sure, sir?"

"Have you a better idea, Dieter? We have a dozen divisions here; Gandhi has the whole subcontinent. I have to convince them in a hurry that obeying me is a better idea than obeying him. Obeying is what counts. I don't care a *pfennig* as to whether they love me. *Oderint, dum metuant.*"

"Sir?" The major had no Latin.

" 'Let them hate, so long as they fear.' "

"Ah," Lasch said. "Yes, I like that." He fingered his chin as he thought. "In aid of which, the Muslims hereabouts like the Hindus none too well. I daresay we could use them to help hunt Gandhi down."

"Now that *I* like," Model said. "Most of our Indian Legion lads are Muslims. They will know people, or know people who know people. And"—the field marshal chuckled cynically— "the reward will do no harm, either. Now get those orders out, and ring up Legion-Colonel Sadar. We'll get those feelers in motion—and if they pay off, you'll probably have earned yourself a new pip on your shoulderboards."

"Thank you very much, sir!"

"My pleasure. As I say, you'll have earned it. So long as things go as they should, I am a very easy man to get along with. Even Gandhi could, if he wanted to. He will end up having caused a lot of people to be killed because he does not."

"Yes, sir," Lasch agreed. "If only he would see that, since we have won India from the British, we will not turn around and tamely yield it to those who could not claim it for themselves."

"You're turning into a political philosopher now, Dieter?"

"Ha! Not likely." But the major looked pleased as he picked up the phone.

"My dear friend, my ally, my teacher, we are losing," Nehru said as the messenger scuttled away from this latest in a series of what were hopefully called safe houses. "Day by day, more people return to their jobs."

Gandhi shook his head, slowly, as if the motion caused him physical pain. "But they must not. Each one who cooperates with the Germans sets back the day of his own freedom."

"Each one who fails to ends up dead," Nehru said dryly. "Most men lack your courage, great-souled one. To them, that carries more weight than the other. Some are willing to resist, but would rather take up arms than the restraint of *satyagraha*."

"If they take up arms, they will be defeated. The British could not beat the Germans with guns and tanks and planes; how shall we? Besides, if we shoot a German here and there, we give them the excuse they need to strike at us. When one of their lieutenants was waylaid last month, their bombers leveled a village in reprisal. Against those who fight through nonviolence, they have no such justification."

"They do not seem to need one, either," Nehru pointed out.

Before Gandhi could reply to that, a man burst into the hovel where they were hiding. "You must flee!" he cried. "The Germans have found this place! They are coming. Out with me, quick! I have a cart waiting."

Nehru snatched up the canvas bag in which he carried his few belongings. For a man used to being something of a dandy, the haggard life of a fugitive came hard. Gandhi had never wanted much. Now that he had nothing, that did not disturb him. He rose calmly, followed the man who had come to warn them.

"Hurry!" the fellow shouted as they scrambled into his oxcart while the humpbacked cattle watched indifferently with their liquid brown eyes. When Gandhi and Nehru were lying in the cart, the man piled blankets and straw mats over them. He scrambled up to take the reins, saying, *"Inshallah,* we shall be safely away from here before the platoon arrives." He flicked a switch over the backs of the cattle. They lowed indignantly. The cart rattled away.

Lying in the sweltering semidarkness under the concealment the man had draped on him, Gandhi peered through chinks, trying to figure out where in Delhi he was going next. He had played the game more than once these last few weeks, though he knew doctrine said he should not. The less he knew, the less he could reveal. Unlike most men, though, he was confident he could not be made to talk against his will.

"We are using the technique the American Poe called 'the purloined letter,' I see," he remarked to Nehru. "We will be close by the German barracks. They will not think to look for us there."

The younger man frowned. "I did not know we had safe houses there," he said. Then he relaxed, as well as he could when folded into too small a space. "Of course, I do not pretend to know everything there is to know about such matters. It would be dangerous if I did."

"I was thinking much the same myself, though with me as subject of the sentence." Gandhi laughed quietly. "Try as we will, we always have ourselves at the center of things, don't we?"

He had to raise his voice to finish. An armored personnel carrier came rumbling and rattling toward them, getting louder as it approached. The silence when the driver suddenly killed the engine was a startling contrast to the previous racket. Then there was noise again, as soldiers shouted in German.

"What are they saying?" Nehru asked.

"Hush," Gandhi said absently, not from ill manners, but out of the concentration he needed to follow German at all. After a moment he resumed, "They are swearing at a black-bearded man, asking why he flagged them down."

"Why would anyone flag down German sol—" Nehru began, then

stopped in abrupt dismay. The fellow who had burst into their hiding-place wore a bushy black beard. "We had better get out of—" Again Nehru broke off in midsentence, this time because the oxcart driver was throwing off the coverings that concealed his two passengers.

Nehru started to get to his feet so he could try to scramble out and run. Too late—a rifle barrel that looked wide as a tunnel was shoved in his face as a German came dashing up to the cart. The big curved magazine said the gun was one of the automatic assault rifles that had wreaked such havoc among the British infantry. A burst would turn a man into bloody hash. Nehru sank back in despair.

Gandhi, less spry than his friend, had only sat up in the bottom of the cart. "Good day, gentlemen," he said to the Germans peering down at him. His tone took no notice of their weapons.

"Down." The word was in such gutturally accented Hindi that Gandhi hardly understood it, but the accompanying gesture with a rifle was unmistakable.

Face a mask of misery, Nehru got out of the cart. A German helped Gandhi descend. "Danke," he said. The soldier nodded gruffly. He pointed the barrel of his rifle—toward the armored personnel carrier.

"My rupees!" the black-bearded man shouted.

Nehru turned on him, so quickly he almost got shot for it. "Your thirty pieces of silver, you mean," he cried.

"Ah, a British education," Gandhi murmured. No one was listening to him.

"My rupees," the man repeated. He did not understand Nehru; so often, Gandhi thought sadly, that was at the root of everything.

"You'll get them," promised the sergeant leading the German squad. Gandhi wondered if he was telling the truth. Probably so, he decided. The British had had centuries to build a network of Indian clients. Here but a matter of months, the Germans would need all they could find.

"In." The soldier with a few words of Hindi nodded to the back of the armored personnel carrier. Up close, the vehicle took on a war-battered individuality its kind had lacked when they were just big, intimidating shapes rumbling down the highway. It was bullet-scarred and patched in a couple of places, with sheets of steel crudely welded on.

Inside, the jagged lips of the bullet holes had been hammered down so they did not gouge a man's back. The carrier smelled of leather, sweat, tobacco, smokeless powder, and exhaust fumes. It was crowded, all the more so with the two Indians added to its usual contingent. The motor's roar when it started up challenged even Gandhi's equanimity.

Not, he thought with uncharacteristic bitterness, that that equanimity had done him much good.

"They are here, sir," Lasch told Model, then, at the field marshal's blank look amplified: "Gandhi and Nehru."

Model's eyebrow came down toward his monocle. "I won't bother with Nehru. Now that we have him, take him out and give him a noodle"—army slang for a bullet in the back of the neck— "but don't waste my time over him. Gandhi, now, is interesting. Fetch him in."

"Yes, sir," the major sighed. Model smiled. Lasch did not find Gandhi interesting. Lasch would never carry a field marshal's baton, not if he lived to be ninety.

Model waved away the soldiers who escorted Gandhi into his office. Either of them could have broken the little Indian like a stick. "Have a care," Gandhi said. "If I am the desperate criminal bandit you have styled me, I may overpower you and escape."

"If you do, you will have earned it," Model retorted. "Sit, if you care to."

"Thank you." Gandhi sat. "They took Jawaharlal away. Why have you summoned me instead?"

"To talk for a while, before you join him." Model saw that Gandhi knew what he meant, and that the old man remained unafraid. Not that that would change anything, Model thought, although he respected his opponent's courage the more for his keeping it in the last extremity.

"I will talk, in the hope of persuading you to have mercy on my people. For myself I ask nothing."

Model shrugged. "I was as merciful as the circumstances of war allowed, until you began your campaign against us. Since then, I have done what I needed to restore order. When it returns, I may be milder again."

"You seem a decent man," Gandhi said, puzzlement in his voice. "How can you so callously massacre people who have done you no harm?"

"I never would have, had you not urged them to folly."

"Seeking freedom is not folly."

"It is when you cannot gain it—and you cannot. Already your people are losing their stomach for—what do you call it? Passive resistance? A silly notion. A passive resister simply ends up dead, with no chance to hit back at his foe."

That hit a nerve, Model thought. Gandhi's voice was less detached as he answered, "*Satyagraha* strikes the oppressor's soul, not his body. You must be without honor or conscience, to fail to feel your victims' anguish."

Nettled in turn, the field marshal snapped, "I have honor. I follow the oath of obedience I swore with the army to the Führer and through him to the Reich. I need consider nothing past that."

Now Gandhi's calm was gone. "But he is a madman! What has he done to the Jews of Europe?"

"Removed them," Model said matter-of-factly; *Einsatzgruppe* B had followed Army Group Central to Moscow and beyond. "They were capitalists or Bolsheviks, and either way enemies of the Reich. When an enemy falls into a man's hands, what else is there to do but destroy him, lest he revive to turn the tables one day?"

Gandhi had buried his face in his hands. Without looking at Model, he said, "Make him a friend."

"Even the British knew better than that, or they would not have held India as long as they did," the field marshal snorted. "They must have begun to forget, though, or your movement would have got what it deserves long ago. You first made the mistake of confusing us with them long ago, by the way." He touched a fat dossier on his desk.

"When was that?" Gandhi asked indifferently. The man was beaten now, Model thought with a touch of pride: he had succeeded where a generation of degenerate, decadent Englishmen had failed. Of course, the field marshal told himself, he had beaten the British too.

He opened the dossier, riffled through it. "Here we are," he said, nodding in satisfaction. "It was after *Kristallnacht*, eh, in 1938, when you urged the German Jews to play at the same game of passive resistance you were using here. Had they been fools enough to try it, we would have thanked you, you know: it would have let us bag the enemies of the Reich all the more easily."

"Yes, I made a mistake," Gandhi said. Now he was looking at the field marshal, looking at him with such fierceness that for a moment Model thought he would attack him despite advanced age and effete philosophy. But Gandhi only continued sorrowfully, "I made the mistake of thinking I faced a regime ruled by conscience, one that could at the very least be shamed into doing that which is right."

Model refused to be baited. "We do what is right for our *Volk*, for our Reich. We are meant to rule, and rule we do—as you see." The field marshal tapped the dossier again. "You could be sentenced to death for this earlier meddling in the affairs of the fatherland, you know, even without these later acts of insane defiance you have caused."

"History will judge us," Gandhi warned as the field marshal rose to have him taken away.

Model smiled then. "Winners write history." He watched the two strapping German guards lead the old man off. "A very good morning's work," the field marshal told Lasch when Gandhi was gone. "What's on the menu for lunch?"

"Blood sausage and sauerkraut, I believe."

"Ah, good. Something to look forward to." Model sat down. He went back to work.

MULES IN HORSES' HARNESS

Michael Cassutt

I

In the humid depths of August downtown Atlanta looked like a tomb and smelled like a charnel house, or so Gene imagined. There was less traffic than one would find on a Secession Day weekend and in all the streets between the Peachtree Tunnel and Butler House Gene counted no more than a dozen men in suits. The fragrance of nearby darktown settled on the scene like a noxious cloud. Yet each corner had its cluster of the usual painted and preening entrepreneurs of both sexes. Gene noted that the prostitutes outnumbered their potential customers, making him wonder, again, just how accurate those frightening stories out of New Orleans were.

He left the car with the contract valet at the hotel and took his time getting to the Atrium. Shelby would be late, of course; the only question for Gene was how late. So he was quite surprised to find her already seated and drinking iced tea.

"Have you called Daddy lately?" she said as soon as they'd kissed.

"Is this what passes for 'hello' at Bradley these days?" Gene said. Brother and sister were both fair and slight, though Shelby's Confederate princess camouflage made her dishwater blond hair look positively golden and reddened her lips so that most men (though not Gene) would have described them as luscious. Only when she rolled her eyes, as she did now, did Shelby truly resemble Gene, becoming, if only for a moment, a twelve-year-old—the proper age for a younger sister, in Gene's opinion. In December she would be twenty-one. "As a matter of fact, I haven't. Don't tell me you have."

"Gene . . ." This was an argument that, in one form or another, had been going on since the divorce ten years ago. "He's our *father*."

"Only chemically," Gene said. "In every other way he separated himself from our life in 1978. He's got a new wife who is exactly your age—" He was exaggerating for effect. Their step-mother was closer to twenty-three. "—and the perfect new heir. Dylan James Tyler. Christ, how pretentious can you get? I'm only surprised that he hasn't filed suit to get me to change my name." Dad was Gene, Sr. "If he gets disgusted enough, maybe he'll change *his*." Gene smiled.

Shelby sighed. "Never *mind*. I was only asking."

"Fair enough. You didn't invite me to the Atrium to ask me about Daddy, though."

"No." Shelby was suddenly distant, in a way that was uniquely hers. Confederate princesses—at least those few whose company Gene had tolerated, however briefly—were trained to pay, in any encounter between the sexes, supreme and total attention to the man.

The waiter arrived to take up one of the four places at the table. Gene ordered a whiskey, which caused Shelby to frown. "I only did it to get your attention," he said.

"I don't believe you."

"And how is school?"

"Boring."

"That's a great thing to say about the finest school for women in eleven states including Cuba." He was kidding her, but the answer disturbed him. Without parental support—there was some money from Mom, but not enough to cover more than a fraction of the tuition and costs—Shelby had worked hard to earn a scholarship. To Gene's pleasure and pride, she had chosen to study medicine, one of the few fields in which a woman could find a career these days.

"Oh, you know what I mean. It's summer. It's hot and there's no one around—"

"There's no one around Bradley in the *winter*, darling."

"Then you can imagine what it's like in summer." She was playing with her iced tea, drawing figures in the condensation. "Maybe I miss being . . . young."

"Oh, you miss being dragged all over the Confederacy by Daddy so you could wait in a hotel room while he did his 'bidness'? Or is it the custody battle you're thinking of? Now *that* was a lot of fun—"

"Gene, stop it. You know *exactly* what I mean."

Yes, he did. She was thinking of summers on the lake and in the fields behind the big house in Marietta. Their land bordered a state park dedicated to the battle of Stone Mountain, and so, aside from park rangers and the occasional Northern tourists, they had the run of acres of woodland. And before the divorce Gene, Sr., had kept horses. "Sorry. This time of year gets to me, too."

"Why don't you go someplace? God knows you've got vacation coming to you."

"Why, *sister* dear, the project would fall ap*art* without me." He laid on a thick accent, the kind they'd heard from the contractees at the Marietta house. It never failed to make her laugh. "Differential computation is the best hope of the Confederacy. Taking a vacation would be—unpatriotic."

"I thought you were under the lash of some sissy professors at Emory."

"Socio*l*ogy professors at Emory," he corrected, his eyes narrowing. "I'll have you know there *are* no sissies in the Confederacy."

Gene knew this was dangerous ground, even between loving brother and sister, but battle was postponed. Shelby was on her feet, a beauty-queen smile on her face, waving. "Over here!"

Before Gene could turn around, a handsome young man in a gray suit was at the table, kissing Shelby in a manner generally reserved, in public at least, for family members. Then he offered his hand to Gene. "I'm Charlie Holder," he said.

"My fiancé," Shelby said.

Gene tried hard not to despise Holder on sight, a task made unusually difficult by the speed with which this prospective brother-in-law made himself at home, and by the deference shown him by the waiter. He didn't even *ask* for Mr. Holder's order. In the space of seconds, without any proper signs at all, Gene found himself no longer host, but guest. Holder had even interposed his tanned, well-exercised frame between Gene and Shelby.

"I perceive that you've been here *before*, Mr. Holder," Gene said, smiling so pleasantly his lips ached.

Shelby, who recognized the coming fury, reached out for Gene's hand. "Charlie works for Sumner and Horn," she said, naming with what Gene took to be excessive enthusiasm the biggest law firm in the state. "Their offices are right across the street."

"I'm just an associate, of course," Holder said. "On what they pay me I'm lucky if I can eat here twice a month."

"Does that mean supporting my dear sister will be especially . . . challenging?" Gene said this while looking at Shelby, who had given up anger and was now attempting to soothe him by looking hurt. He said, "Now don't you worry, sister. I'm not *seriously* questioning Mr. Holder's abilities—"

"Please call me Charlie."

"Charlie it is." He made it sound like a disease. "But I *am* the senior male in the family. I have certain responsibilities regarding my sister's welfare." He turned to Shelby. "Charlie understands that."

Holder smiled right back. "Perfectly."

"Then," Shelby said, "dear brother, you'll be pleased to know that Charlie has been nominated for a partnership. He'll have it *long* before the wedding."

With those words Shelby let him know that she had gone over to the other side. Gene felt like Longstreet at the Last Redoubt: out of ammunition, Sherman's blue hordes swarming up the parapet. The war was over; lunch was only beginning.

Current popular wisdom suggested that a diet of greens was one way to ward off the summer vapors. Like Shelby and Holder, Gene found himself staring at a Cantonese salad for which he now had even less enthusiasm than ever. He signaled the waiter and got a second drink. Shelby was so busy tittering at Holder that she didn't even notice.

Exactly on cue, two bites into the salad, Holder looked up. "Shelby tells me you work in differentials. That must be an exciting field."

"Well, I'm sure it can't compare to contract law," Gene said.

"Come on." Holder was determined not to let Gene insult him. "It's the cutting edge of Confederate technology. Without your— what do they call them?—bugs and counters we'd be nothing but a warmer Canada." He stabbed at the salad, and dabbed at his mouth. "We handle all D.C.D.'s work, you know."

Differential Calculating Devices was the Atlanta conglomerate that dominated the global market. There wasn't a government that functioned without the machines, not even the government of the United States of America, which would sooner buy from Satan than from the Confederacy. The company had the further bonus of being Gene's ostensible employer. "If you're involved in D.C.D., then you know more about our 'importance' than I do. I'm just a soldier."

"A soldier who's fighting a particularly interesting war, I hear. Project Deconstruction, isn't it?"

Gene's glance shifted from Holder, who was impassive in his command of the situation, to Shelby, who allowed herself a wiggle of triumph at the obvious perfection of her catch. "That's not a name I'm used to hearing at city lunches," Gene said finally, hoping that a bit of dignified reproach might be sufficient to raise him back to equal standing with this person.

"Certainly not," Holder said. "It's privileged. Family stuff. But, then, we're all family here, aren't we, Shel?" Not only did Holder suddenly use what had heretofore been Gene's private name for

Shelby, but he caused her to blush, confirming to Gene that she had, indeed, spilled to Holder all of the many "privileged" details she knew about Deconstruction.

Gene examined the bottom of his drink and wished for a sudden outbreak of war—or death—anything to deliver him from this lunch. But fate declined to oblige.

Shelby was saying, "You know, I've heard bits and pieces of this, but never quite the whole story. I'm dying to know. That is, if it's all right."

"I have no objection . . . if your brother doesn't," Holder said, neatly positioning Gene to label his own sister as untrustworthy.

"If we can't take such a fine example of Southern womanhood into our confidence, what kind of men are we?" Gene said, slipping into his little-used country club locutions. "Shelby, darling, Project Deconstruction is a device by which we unravel the past so that we might actually tell the future."

"I *do* know that much."

"One of the professors at Emory—a tsarist refugee named Asimoff—theorized some years ago that one could predict future events mathematically. But nobody had any idea how to translate events into symbols, nor the ability to perform calculations involving millions or billions of symbols.

"Over the years people have made attempts to break down historical events, social movements, people, personality traits, even the weather, into irreducible units which somebody started calling 'memes.' They'd wind up with these vast systems and complex formulae that would just go up the chimney the moment you applied them to some known historical situation, like the Secession. The world-model bore no relationship to the real world." He smiled. "Unfortunately, it's taken us years to realize this. We keep adjusting the numbers and redoing the formulas, but we still haven't managed to come up with a system that tells you that if Abraham Lincoln is assassinated on July 4, 1863, by a Copperhead named Nathan Shaw, the Confederacy will be occupied by Federal troops for forty years." He spread his hands. "At the moment, I guess you could say we're stuck."

Holder, who had, Gene thought, been waiting for an opportunity, chose this moment to say, "Until now."

"I beg your pardon?"

"You're the first person on Deconstruction who's had the courage to admit that it's stuck. I've thought so for some time."

"Imagine how pleased we'll all be to know how our attorneys judge our work."

"Please don't be angry," Charlie said, aflush with enthusiasm. "A lot of valuable data has come out of the project so far. I'm not aware of *any* unhappiness at the higher levels of the company—"

"Thank God." Gene tried not to be sarcastic.

"But the problem, as you surely know, with companies as large as D.C.D., is the flow of information. Acting, as we do, as counsel to the whole organization, we tend to have a better view of what's going on than most of the gentlemen on the thirty-fourth floor." He leaned forward and lowered his voice. Shelby had effectively ceased to exist. "The pharmaceutical division has a project of its own that may provide you with your missing link."

"What would drugs have to do with Deconstruction?"

"I'm not talking about drugs."

Ordinarily Gene wouldn't have deigned to play a guessing game. He was stopped in this case by Shelby's getting up from her chair. "Excuse me," she said, "I don't want to inhibit you two—"

Holder couldn't get to his feet fast enough. "I'm sorry, Shel, that was rude of me." He looked to Gene for help.

"Charlie," Gene said, forcing out the words, "why don't you and I get together some other time? I'd really like to hear about this missing link."

"I'll call tonight at six," Holder said, extending his hand. To Shelby he said, "I have to get back."

Before Shelby could protest, Gene said, "Walk him out, Shel," giving the name a little spin. He picked up the check. "This is my treat." Arm in arm, the couple left.

Shelby's initial assault had driven Gene back from his lines . . . but he had not broken. It was time for a counterattack.

"Are you going to see him?"

Two hours later, it was Shelby who came to call. Gene was sitting in his office at Emory watching some students playing a half-hearted game of rounders when she knocked. She asked the question before she even sat down.

"What choice do I have, Shel? I realize he's your fiancé, but he's also involved in my work. I'm sort of *bound* to listen to what he has to say."

"I suppose." There was silence while Shelby fumed. "I'm sorry I even introduced you two."

"Sooner or later you'd have had to, honey. Unless you were planning to elope to Havana." Gene was doing a bit of fuming, too. "Look, there's no sense in fighting. It never really occurred to me that you were ready for marriage—"

"Gene, I'm going to be twenty-one!"

"This is the twentieth century, Shel. You haven't even finished school. Are you going to just throw it all away?" He hauled out the secret weapon. "I thought you wanted to be better than Mom."

"That's a shitty thing to say."

"My, my, we've been learning some naughty words at school."

Shelby stood up and started to leave. At the door she paused long enough to say, "I can't vote and I can't own property and if I'm too old or ugly I'm doomed to be a nurse or a schoolteacher for the rest of my life. And here you are, a man, telling me I'm *supposed* to be self-reliant and independent, that we've got this brave new South here, but even you have to treat me like a little girl." Then she gently closed the door, a gesture which startled Gene because it was not the slam one expected from a child, or from a Confederate princess.

He was still wondering what he should do about Shelby when the contract girl out front asked permission to go home for the evening, adding that a Mr. Charleston Holder was here.

"I feel as though I'm here to sell you something," Holder said, removing a folder from his briefcase and passing it to Gene. Night had fallen; the quad outside the office window was dark and quiet, as was the rest of the building, save for the lone contract janitor swishing his mop in the hall.

"Is there a problem with that?"

Holder shrugged. "I was raised to believe that a gentleman didn't solicit business. It would come to him in the natural order of things." He smiled again, all charm. "Yet your father is a salesman, and a very successful one, too, from what Shelby says—"

"But he's no gentleman," Gene said, irritated again at Holder's immersion—there was no other word—in Tyler family matters. "We shouldn't pursue that subject or I'll have to call you out—whether I love my father or not."

"I meant no offense. I'm unused to working outside normal channels." Gene doubted that this was even remotely true, but chose not to argue the point. The best parts of his own life were outside normal channels. "What I've given you," Holder said, getting back to business, "is a report on what is, forgive me, D.C.D.'s most closely held and radical research: the creation of life itself."

For a man unused to the crass protocols of business, Holder knew just how obtrusive he could be and still allow Gene to understand what he was reading. The only words he honestly heard were "radical" and "creation." What he saw before him was a memorandum describing the design and construction of microscopic creatures called, in what must have been some lab technician's idea of a joke, "federals." Federals were originally cousins to planaria and other relatively simple organisms whose genetic material had been altered to give them greater "intelligence" and, more interestingly, mobility, thus removing them from the kingdom of the protozoans, making them animals.

"This sounds like a fascinating discovery. I would have thought it would take millions of federal 'years' to accomplish that sort of evolution."

"I believe that it did," Holder said, reaching for the memo and flipping ahead several pages. "A generation of federals is born, grows up, and dies in only a few minutes. And though there's no indication in this document, the project has been going on since 1939."

Fifty years ago the United States had been involved in the disastrous World Wide War against the German States and their allies. Although the Confederacy had maintained a public neutrality, Southern sympathies were clearly with their Northern brothers, and many Confederate companies supplied arms and materials to U.S. armies. Gene knew that D.C.D.'s first differential calculators had been employed to that end. And the McCarran Pharmaceutical Company, later acquired by D.C.D. to become its bio division, was rumored to have been involved in the search for chemical weapons. "These things aren't dangerous, are they?"

"Well, they *have* been kept under wraps for a long time," Holder said, as if that were sufficient answer.

"This is fascinating information," Gene said, "but I'm afraid I don't know what I can do with it." He slid the memo back to Holder, who pinned it in place with his hand.

"Please correct me if I'm wrong, but didn't you say that the problem with the Deconstruction process is that it lacks a means of testing?"

"Yes." Gene was vaguely irritated now. For a moment he had been able to think of Holder as just another suit; now he was remembering that he would soon be his brother-in-law. Before the irritation could surface, however, another thought did: the missing link. Means of testing. "Oh," was all he could say.

Holder was smiling. "How big is this federal population?" Gene said, reaching for the memo with a bit more vigor.

"There are several discrete populations," Holder said, "but I don't think you'd have any trouble putting together a single group number-ing, say, a hundred million individuals."

"Which is a number far greater than the population of the United States and Confederacy in 1863 . . . dear God."

"I don't ordinarily approve of blasphemy," Holder said, "but in this case, it's highly appropriate, don't you agree?"

To be the Almighty Himself—ruling a microcosmic world! "Don't say another word."

Project Deconstruction was relatively small as D.C.D. enterprises went. At its peak no more than three dozen employees were charged to its budget. With the cutback in funding and other reductions due to staff vacations, there were only about fifteen people who would have the faintest interest in what Gene was doing. And of those fif-teen, only three had authority over him.

Four of those who did not gathered in Gene's office the next morn-ing as he explained what he wanted them to do. They were all gradu-ate students in differential sciences and largely true to the stereotype: extraordinarily pale, uniformly bespectacled, deliberately ill-fed, and unusually intelligent. The only one who deviated was Stashower, a red-haired farmboy from Nashville whose utter and complete self-absorption was the only thing that kept Gene's more predatory in-stincts in check. That and his resolve never to fish off the company pier.

Stashower was the first to see the possibilities. "Jesus, Gene, we've been beating our heads against this how-do-we-simulate-organic-life-in-a-differential? shit for two years! If we can record the growth, death, and migration patterns of a hundred million federals, we'll increase the memes in our own model by a factor of ten thousand."

One of the others, a bearded boy from the red clay country, joined in. He was eager to get to work on the transition models. "We can start out just arbitrarily assigning certain values to federal activities, then keep crunching them over and over again until we match Real Life."

They were all out of their chairs now, sketching systems on the board. "Gentlemen, gentlemen!" Gene said. "I hate to interrupt, but permit me a boring management kind of query: When can it be ready and how much will it cost?"

"Two months," Stashower said, with his charming Yankee naïveté, "and you're going to spend twice as much in differential time charges." Gene nodded, mentally doubling the estimates again. He didn't need a Deconstruction program to tell him that Stashower tended to underestimate such matters.

The meeting broke up. Gene was proud of them, but his pride was tempered by annoyance at the speed with which they absorbed the new idea. Their new energy and their prior lack of protest made it clear that at the age of twenty-five he was already too old for creative work.

II

On the Fourth of July, 1863, President Abraham Lincoln made a surprise visit to Union veterans at a temporary hospital in Georgetown, near Washington. By all accounts it was an impulsive gesture, a search, perhaps, for distraction. The President was awaiting news of the seige of Vicksburg and, more importantly, of Lee's advances through nearby Gettysburg, Pennsylvania. But for the circumstances, it would not have been one of Lincoln's more memorable speeches. He was halfway through it when a man wearing the coat of a hospital orderly stepped out of the crowd and fired a pistol at Lincoln, who was hit twice in the chest.

In spite of the presence of several doctors, the first to reach him was a Captain Butler, his aide, who heard Lincoln's last words ("I'm sorry"). The President was carried to a room in the hospital, where he died within hours.

The assassin was later identified as a Nathan Shaw, twenty-eight-year-old itinerant minister from Baltimore with a history of abolitionist activity and ties to Copperhead democrats unhappy with Lincoln's prosecution of the war. Shaw claimed that he was angered by Lincoln's call for a new draft—that it was unfair for a rich man to be able to pay a three-hundred-dollar bounty to avoid serving the Union —but it was later suspected, though never proved, that he had ties to Confederate agents and may, in fact, have been stalking Lincoln since March of 1861. In any case, Shaw went to the gallows in October, unrepentant and silent as to his accomplices.

Vice-president Hannibal Hamlin of Maine took the oath of office just as the news of the victories at Gettysburg and Vicksburg reached the capital. Lincoln's allies, greater in number after his death than prior to it, and his rivals joined in a call for the utter destruction of the Confederacy. It was hardly necessary. Word of Lincoln's death at the hands of an assassin had reached Meade's troops before either army had fully withdrawn from Gettysburg. In a frenzy, Union forces trapped Lee's battered men on the northern bank of the swollen Potomac near the misnamed Falling Waters, capturing their leader and effectively destroying the Army of Virginia.

In the west, Generals Grant and Sherman began a total war of attrition, moving through Mississippi, Alabama, Tennessee, and Georgia like the horsemen of doom, laying waste to Jackson, Montgomery, Memphis, and Atlanta, then wheeling north. Union forces under Meade met them below burned Richmond, which, like Carthage, had ceased to be a human abode, and pursued Longstreet, catching him at Lynchburg. It was now July 1864. Both political parties sought to name Grant as their candidate, and the Democrats won. Grant turned over leadership of the Union armies, and directorship of the "pacification" of the South, to Sherman, and handily defeated President Hamlin that November.

August gave way to an unusually warm September, but Gene's relationship with Shelby remained cool. They were not openly at war: Shelby indicated that she forgave him for "stealing" her fiancé once she learned that, but for the single meeting, Gene and Charlie never saw each other unless she was present. Nevertheless, they ceased to communicate with the old regularity. Gene assumed it was the pressure of her studies in addition to the logistical challenges of a wedding due a Confederate princess. (He kept up with these developments thirdhand, through Shelby's friends, since Gene, Sr., had elected to bestow his advice upon his only daughter.) But he eventually realized that he himself had drawn back from her.

Perhaps it was because of the nightmares.

He had been living with the events of the Lincoln assassination for so long it was no surprise. Every time the boys ran their federal-enhanced program, an event which occurred as many as ten times a day, it started all over again. And that night, as he churned in his bed in his dormitory rooms, Gene would see himself shot . . . see himself shooting . . . see the burning fields . . . find himself yoked, as in the title of the most famous of the postwar novels, like a mule in horse's harness.

Sometimes he would simply lie awake briefly, wondering again how his country could have recovered from such devastation to the point where all over the eleven states dark-skinned contract employees, the children of slaves, labored to make the tiny bugs of which differential machines were composed—the machines which no one in the world, not the United States, not the Yellow Empire, not Britain, could match. Comforted by these schoolbook images, he would sleep again.

Other times he would not. Then, as if testing his resolve to be better than he had been, he would dress and get in the car, driving all the way into the city, to stare at the contract boys under the lamp posts. Occasionally he would stop and meet the eyes of one of them . . . but the moment a step was made in his direction, he would be off, heart pounding, cursing his own weakness. So he would be "good" again for at least two days. The dreams would be calmer; then it would start again.

So it went all through August and September and into October, while Stashower and the others rewrote history, while Gene told the project manager what he needed to know in order to take full credit, until one day late in the month, a week before Redoubt Day, when Shelby came to visit.

"You've been avoiding me," she said, pouting.

"Don't be silly. Maybe I haven't called, but neither have you."

"Nevertheless, because I love you, because of what you mean to me, I'm going to forgive you."

Gene almost laughed. He knew that with a woman like Shelby—or more precisely, what Shelby, with repeated exposure to Dad and his new wife, was becoming—he must kill an assertion, not merely wound it.

"In that case, I apologize. May I plead overwork? The project of a lifetime? And how is school?"

"I'm dropping out," she said calmly. "That's why I came to see you —" She paused, eclipsed by his sudden fury.

"Are you out of your *mind?* You worked *years* to get where you are! You've only got two more *semesters* before you get a certificate!"

"A certificate I don't need," she said, eclipsing him in return.

"Of course. *Charlie* will take care of you. I can't believe this."

"Before either of us says more that we will regret, why don't we talk about the weather. Or your work. How *is* it going?" Just like that, her tone had changed. They might have been having tea at the Atrium . . . or lying in the field behind the house in Marietta, looking at the sky. Gene was willing to play along. He wasn't ready to give up his sister.

"To tell you the truth, Shel, it's amazing. Three months ago you'd never have convinced me that it would be possible to create a model—

a simulation—of our world so detailed that it accurately 'predicts' what the price of wheat was in northeastern Kansas in 1888—"

" 'Predicts' what it *was?*"

"The language is sadly inadequate to the task, especially when we're talking about end results as opposed to processes. There were three things we needed to do to make Deconstruction work: We needed to convert human beings and all their traits and activities, from having children to voting for President, into numbers. Then we had to find a way to move those numbers—billions of them, actually —in a way that paralleled the growth or evolution of a society. That's where Charlie's federals came in. We'd always thought that the laws that controlled societies were similar to those that controlled biological processes, but we never had any biological process to play with until now.

"The real challenge, of course, was the interface between the numbers and the federals—the translation, we call it. That's what we've been running over and over again, adjusting, changing and rewriting, for months, until we finally got an overall program—all three elements working together—that allowed us not only to recapitulate American history from 1863 until now, but to learn things we didn't know ourselves."

"The price of wheat in Kansas." She seemed amused.

"The length of women's skirts in 1915. The number of people killed by the Yellow Flu in 1946. It's like walking into a library of books you've never been able to open . . . until now."

"And what good is it?"

"Well, once you've got a working model, you can go back and change certain key events—or change things that happen to certain key people. Ulysses Grant fires his cabinet in 1872 and doesn't get impeached. Jeremy King is only wounded in 1968, and the contract system is abolished. That sort of thing."

"I can't believe you can find one microscopic Abraham Lincoln."

"Oh, you can't. One lesson we're learning is that individuals are almost completely irrelevant to history—as individuals. I mean, yes, there *are* so-called 'Great Men,' but they appear in our translation program . . . not in the biological model. In fact, we've worked up a pretty good profile of the Key Individual, the Great Man, and found that at any given time, there are dozens if not hundreds of them around . . . waiting for the confluence of events that will allow them to fulfill their 'destiny.' Or whatever.

"I mean, in some of our models, poor old Abe Lincoln, who was really nothing more than a victim of circumstances, forced into war because of the Secession and killed just as it appeared he would win, lives long enough to emerge as a Great Man. In that same model, Longstreet serves as a general in a longer, more drawn-out war and never emerges as the President who rebuilt the Confederacy."

"Don't you find this sad?"

"Why should I?"

"To know that, at a certain level, nothing you do with your life really matters . . . that you're only responding to these biological imperatives. Taking advantage of—what did you call it?—the confluence of events." She shuddered. "Charlie will hate this." With some of the tension bled out of their conversation, Shelby apparently felt it was safe to mention Holder.

"Don't kid yourself, Shel. Your Charlie will *love* this. What businessman wouldn't want to know the future?"

"You don't know him at all, Gene. He wants to believe that he can *change* the future. In many ways, he's a lot like one of those Great Men. He has ideas, big ideas. He wants the South to be more than it is. He thinks we've become rigid and calcified—"

"He's right about that. But I never got the idea that *he* had just the solutions to everyone's problems. Great."

"It's one of the reasons I love him, Gene."

"Do you really? Or do you, dear sister, just love the idea that you've done what you were raised to do: caught yourself a great man?"

"I think I should leave." She stood up.

"I'm glad you came. By the way—" She was waiting at the door. There were tears in her eyes, of sadness or defiance he didn't know. He pulled a small package out of his desk. He'd bought it weeks earlier, not knowing when or if he would have the opportunity to deliver it. "It's a week late . . . Happy birthday."

Shelby took it, but she did not thank him.

The federal "world" was located at D.C.D.'s Decatur site in a little-used warehouse off-limits to all but a few personnel—"deep, dark government work" was the rumored reason. It worked so well that Gene grew to wonder just how much deep, dark government work the company had done in the past. Nevertheless, he controlled access . . . which was why, on his way into the building the next day, he was so surprised to find Holder coming out.

The man was shameless. He shouldn't have been within miles of the place, but all he had to say was, "Playing hooky from Emory, I see."

"Once a week, whether I need to or not," Gene said, as furious at himself for showing his anger as he was at Holder. "How the hell did you get in there?"

Holder smiled. "When I was going to law school I worked here one summer as a security guard. Relax, Gene, as far as anyone at D.C.D. is concerned I'm tied up with a libel action in Pine Mountain. No one is going to kick you out of your sandbox."

"Have you seen enough? Or would you like an official tour?" He flashed his badge at the guard, a man Holder's age whose name Gene didn't know, who would, if Gene had his way, be working somewhere else at this time tomorrow.

"Love to." As they breached the innermost door, Holder said quietly, "Don't be too hard on old Matthew—" The guard. "—I made it impossible for him to keep me out." One gentleman to another. Holder had just made it impossible for Gene to punish the guard.

The federals lived in what always struck Gene as the world's biggest ant colony—a glass-roofed chamber the size of a rounders court, over which Stashower and his colleagues hovered like angels on high, their cameras and telescopes trained on heaven's floor. "Incredible," Holder said. "It's just incredible."

Holder seemed genuinely impressed, which pleased and disgusted Gene. "Well, Charlie, there never would have been a link between Deconstruction and the federals if not for you."

To Gene's greater annoyance, Holder didn't deny it. "It was pure blind luck. Did I tell you? My first job at the firm was handling insurance forms for D.C.D. I amused myself by reading some of the résumés and personnel files. That's how I learned that you were the key man on Deconstruction." Oblivious to Gene's growing outrage, Holder went on to deliver the final blow: "In fact, that's how I learned that you had a sister at Bradley."

By now Gene was so used to creating scenarios that they came to him unbidden. He didn't like the one being created for him now . . . this Confederate hustler using his past connections and purloined material to uncover people's secrets . . . seeking Gene out in order to make him do his bidding . . . and worst of all, cultivating *his own sister* in order to forge a connection between them. What else did Holder know?

Holder nodded toward Stashower and the others. "Your boys seem to like looking through the scopes."

"They've convinced themselves the federals have 'cities' and 'fields.' I think they just enjoy playing microcosmic god." Gene had looked once and only found the action blurred to incomprehensibility. When he could look at all, that is. In the accelerated life of a federal, one "day" lasted two seconds, and the constant flickering of the "sun" gave Gene a headache. "But, then, they're not the only ones."

Holder laughed out loud. "Come on, Gene. I'm not *that* manipulative!"

When Gene offered no comment, Holder lowered his voice and said, "Look, you're going to come out of this a happy man. When the boys on thirty-four see what you've got here, they'll be on you like a duck on a June bug."

"Assuming they don't already know."

"So far I've managed to refrain from enlightening them . . . much as I'd love to. This one belongs to Gene Tyler."

"How will I ever thank you?"

Holder couldn't miss the sarcasm; he hesitated just long enough to let Gene know he hadn't. "You'll find a way." Then, back in the country-club mode, he slapped Gene on the back. "Got to run." Over his shoulder, he called, "When am I going to see you at Shel's?"

"He's using you," he said.

Shelby blushed. "You know, Gene, a simple 'hello' would be nice. Do you like the couch?" They had just sat down in the tiny living room of Shelby's flat.

"Forget the couch, Shel. I'm telling you, you don't have any idea what kind of monster you're involved with."

"You're making this awfully difficult."

"Blame it on your Charlie. Your 'great man.' "

He was hurting her; he knew it. "Shel—" He reached for her, but she shied away.

"Don't touch me."

"I'm sorry. But I can't just let this happen. This man has . . . lied his way into our lives all because he wants what my project can give him. It's power he's after, Shel—"

"Oh, Gene, grow up!" She was facing him now. "You've been searching for months to drive a wedge between Charlie and me. You couldn't do it with sweet reason, so now it's because of your nasty little project." She was angrier now than Gene had ever seen. "Are you *sure* that's what the real problem is?"

"Whatever do you mean?"

Shelby stared at him. "I know more about you than you think I do. . . ."

Oh, Christ, he thought. *No.*

"Gene, I'm not going to judge you. I love you. I know you had a much more difficult time with Daddy than I did. Whom you love is your business—"

"Shelby, stop this. You sound like some radio mentalist."

"Well, you chose not to share this secret with me, so I'm probably going to say this all wrong." There was a surprising amount of sarcasm in her voice, and for a moment Gene realized that he had underestimated her will. "I don't know anything about a world in which men go with other men. I can't even *picture* it," she said, no doubt picturing it all too vividly, as Gene had often pictured Shelby with some man. Who was it who said you can't be intimidated by people once you see them naked and on their knees? "But what I see is that you're jealous."

"This is ridiculous." It was his turn to recoil from her. He got up from the couch and looked for his jacket.

"Is it? Then prove it to me. Because until you do, I have to assume that you're acting like this because you want Charlie for yourself."

Before she finished he was out the door.

He stayed late in his office that night preparing the document about Holder. It was easier than he thought it would be. His familiarity with the D.C.D. data system allowed him greater access to its personnel files—and those of its captive law firm—than any clerk could achieve. All of it, the résumé, the D.C.D. background search (quite secret; gentlemen did not check up on the claims of gentlemen), evaluations, ancillary materials from a financial institution with ties to D.C.D., all integrated with Gene's perceptions of Holder's personality traits, combined in one "character" who could be put through the Deconstruction model.

The program ran to completion in less than ten minutes and the translation only took another hour, but Gene couldn't bring himself to read it for much longer than that.

Just as he suspected. The marriage would go well for a year, until Shelby produced an heir. (If Shelby did not get pregnant, this phase was merely extended by a year or so.) Holder would be a partner by then. He would also have become, again, a patron of the more reputable houses of pleasure, having given them up upon announcement of the engagement. He would dote on the child, boy or girl, and would encourage Shelby's work in social causes, charities, whatnot, but she would be required to have at least a second child, while Holder would run for his first office—something in the state legislature. . . .

Within ten years Holder would be governor; within fifteen, senator or higher. He would campaign for contract rights, and, given reasonable assumptions concerning demographics and economic growth, and the lack of major wars, he would be successful—for the male underclass of the Confederacy.

But what of Shelby? She and women like her would receive none of this largesse. It was too ingrained in the Confederate culture, where archaic antebellum attitudes about women were hardened and set for all time by the forty-year Occupation. It was commonly thought that, for the Confederacy, Lincoln had died too late. Now Gene knew that for the Shelbys of the world—who never had the chance to become real people—Lincoln died too soon.

It was early the next morning when he found the nerve to call her. "You'll notice I'm saying 'hello' this time."

"Hello, Gene." He could hear the relief in her voice. He tried not to wonder if Holder was by her side. "I—"

"Don't say anything," he told her. "Just meet me at the Atrium at once."

He had the data folded and resting by his plate when Shelby came in. She seemed genuinely happy to see him. "I've felt so awful because I didn't thank you for the present!" she said, as if their last discussion had never happened.

"That's all right. I was being a beast."

They passed a quarter of an hour in small talk. News of Gene, Jr. Plans for the wedding. "I'm glad you mentioned the wedding," Gene said.

She grew quiet. "Charlie and me?"

"You said you wanted proof." He had his hand on the printout. Shelby stared at it.

"I suppose that's it. My future life?"

"One of your future lives."

She held out her hand. He passed the paper to her. She looked at it without unfolding it. "How strange—to hold your life in your hand."

"Read it."

"I'd rather not."

"Shel—" He cleared his throat. "I guess I was just thinking about , , , what you could be."

She set the paper aside. "I'm sorry for what I said about you and Charlie."

"Frankly, my dear, he's not my type."

Shelby blushed in disbelief. Enjoying her embarrassment, Gene leaned back in his chair. His eyes roamed around the Atrium and found one of the busboys, a husky contractee. "I like men," he found himself saying, amazingly relieved, "from the lower classes. Much darker than Charlie."

Shelby glanced at the busboy, then looked at Gene. For a moment they were children again, sharing a secret they could keep from Daddy. "Do you ever want to change? To want women?"

"I used to. But, you know, Shel, I don't think I can." Suddenly she had won. Gene wanted to laugh. This Great Man business was fine for the history books, even those yet unwritten, but what could it possibly mean to someone with a wayward child? An old man dying of cancer? A woman in love? Tell them they can't change their futures? That they are nothing more than mules in horses' harness? You might as well kill them.

"I'm sorry, Shel. I really am. I've been a real shit about this. Maybe we can just start over. . . ."

Her face showed equal parts triumph and terror. She reached for his hand. "Yes." Then she sat back, crumpled the paper, and tore it in half. "I should go."

"I'll see you soon."

"At Daddy's next week?"

"Don't push your luck, Shel." Then, with a smile, she was gone.

"Would you like me to get rid of that for you?" the waiter said, nodding toward the crumpled printout.

"Yes," Gene said. "Throw it away."

The waiter scooped it up along with the plates and walked off. Gene remembered that there was a place on Beecher Road where likeminded gentlemen could meet for a bit of excitement. He looked at his watch. The staff meeting wouldn't take place until four.

He had plenty of time.

LENIN IN ODESSA

George Zebrowski

*"Lenin is a rotten little incessant intriguer. . . .
He just wants power. He ought to be killed by
some moral sanitary authority."*

—H. G. WELLS
(Letter dated July 1918, sent to
the *New York Weekly Review*)

In 1918, Sidney Reilly, who had worked as a British agent against the Germans and Japanese, returned to our newly formed Soviet Russia. He was again working for England and her allies, but this time he was also out for himself, intending to assassinate Vladimir Ilyich Lenin and bring himself to power at the head of the regime that he imagined his homeland deserved.

Jew though he was, Reilly saw himself as a Russian coming home to make good. It angered him that another expatriate, Lenin, had gotten there first—with German help, and with what Reilly considered suspect motives. Reilly was convinced that his own vision was the proper response to the problems of life in Russia, which, as Sigmund Rosenblum, a bastard born in Odessa, he had escaped in his youth. He believed that the right man could, with sufficient thought and preparation, make of history his own handiwork.

It was obvious to me that Reilly's thinking was a curious patchwork of ideas, daring and naive at the same time, but lacking the systematic approach of a genuine scientific philosophy. His distaste for the bourgeois society that had oppressed him in his childhood was real, but he had developed a taste for its pleasures.

Of course, Reilly knew that he was sent in as a tool of the British and their allies, who opposed Bolshevism from the outset, and he let them continue to think that they could count on him, for at least as long as his aims would not conflict with theirs. Lenin himself had been eased back into Russia by the Germans, who hoped that he would take Russia out of the war in Europe. No German agent could have done that job better. Reilly was determined to remove or kill Lenin, as the prelude to a new Russia. What that Russia would be was not clear. The best that I could say about Reilly's intentions was that he was not a czarist.

There was an undeniable effectiveness in Reilly, of which he was keenly aware. He was not a mere power seeker, even though he took pride in his physical prowess and craft as a secret agent; to see him as out for personal gain would be to underestimate the danger that he posed to those of us who understand power more fully than he did.

Reilly compared himself to Lenin. They had both been exiles from their homeland, dreaming of return, but Vladimir Ilyich Ulyanov had gone home on German hopes and seized power. Russia would be remade according to a heretical Marxism, in Reilly's view. Lenin's combination of revisionist ideology and good fortune was intolerable to Reilly; it wounded his craftsman's ego, which saw chance as a minor player in history. He ignored the evidence of Lenin's organizational skills, by which a spontaneous revolution had been shaped into one with purpose.

Reilly viewed himself and his hopes for Russia with romantic agony and a sense of personal responsibility that were at odds with his practical intellect and shrewdness, both of which should have told him that he could not succeed. But Reilly's cleverness delighted in craft and planning. His actions against the Germans and Japanese were all but inconceivable to the common man. Even military strategists doubted that one man could have carried out Reilly's decisive schemes. His greatest joy was in doing what others believed to be impossible.

Another clue to Reilly's personality lay in his love of technology, especially naval aviation. He was an accomplished flyer who looked to the future of transport. He was fascinated, for example, by the Michelson-Morley experiment to detect the aether wind, which was predicted on the basis of the idea of the earth's motion through a stationary medium. When this detection failed, Reilly wrote a letter to a scientific journal (supplied to me by one of my intellectual operatives in London) insisting that the aether was too subtle a substance to register on current instruments. One day, he claimed, aether ships would move between the worlds.

Reilly's mind worried a problem until he found an imaginative solution; then his practical bent would find a way to accomplish the task. As a child he was able to remain invisible to his family simply by staying one step ahead of their house search for him. As a spy he once eluded his pursuers by joining them in the search for him. However rigorous and distasteful the means might be, Reilly would see what was possible and not flinch. With Lenin he understood that a single mind could change the world with thought and daring; but unlike Vladimir Ilyich, Reilly's mind lacked the direction of historical truth. He was capable of bringing into being new things, but they were only short-lived sports, chimeras of an exceptional but misguided will. His self-imposed exile from his homeland had left divisions as incongruous as his Irish pseudonym.

Sidney Reilly sought escape from the triviality of his life, in which his skills had been used to prop up imperialism. He had been paid in money and women. By the time he returned to Russia, I already sensed that he would be useful to me. It seemed possible, on the basis of his revolutionary leanings, that I might win him to our cause.

2

"Comrade Stalin," Vladimir Ilyich said to me one gloomy summer morning, "tell me who is plotting against us this week." He was sitting in the middle of a large red sofa, under a bare spot on the wall where a czarist portrait had hung. He seemed very small as he sank into the dusty cushions.

"Only the ones I told you about last week. Not one of them is practical enough to succeed."

He stared at me for a moment, as if disbelieving, but I knew he was only tired. In a moment he closed his eyes and was dozing. I wondered if his bourgeois conscience would balk at the measures we would soon have to take to keep power. It seemed to me that he had put me on the Bolshevik Central Committee to do the things for which he had no stomach. Too many opportunists were ready to step into our shoes if we stumbled. Telling foe from ally was impossible; given the chance, anyone might turn on us.

Reilly was already in Moscow. I learned later that he had come by the usual northern route, and had taken a cheap hotel room. On the following morning, he had abandoned that room, leaving behind an old suitcase with some work clothes in it. He had gone to a safe house, where he met a woman of middle years who knew how to use a handgun.

She was not an imposing figure—an impression she knew how to create; but there was no doubt in Reilly's mind that she would pull the trigger with no care for what happened to her afterwards.

Lenin's death was crucial to Reilly's plot, even though he knew that it might make Vladimir Ilyich a Bolshevik martyr. Reilly was also depending on our other weaknesses to work for him. While Trotsky was feverishly organizing the Red Army, we were dependent on small forces—our original Red Guard, made up of factory workers and sailors, a few thousand Chinese railway workers, and the Latvian regiments, who acted as our Praetorian Guard. The Red Guard was loyal but militarily incompetent. The Chinese served in return for food. The Latvians hated the Germans for overrunning their country, but had to be paid. Reilly knew that he could bribe the Latvians and Chinese to turn against us, making it possible for the czarist officers in hiding to unite and finish the job. With Lenin and myself either arrested or dead, he could then turn south and isolate Trotsky, who had taken Odessa back from the European allies and was busy shipping in supplies by sea. His position there would become impossible if the British brought in warships. If we failed in the north, we would be vulnerable from two sides.

Lenin's death would alter expectations in everyone. Reilly's cohorts would seize vital centers throughout Moscow. Our czarist officers would go over to Reilly, taking their men with them. The opportunists among us would desert. Reilly's leaflets had already planted doubts in them. Lenin's death would be their weather vane. Even the martyrdom of Vladimir Ilyich, I realized, might not be enough to help us.

As I gazed at Lenin's sleeping face, I imagined him already dead and forgotten. His wife Nadezhda came into the room and covered him with a blanket. She did not look at where I sat behind the large library desk as she left.

3

"Comrade Lenin has been shot!" the messenger cried as he burst into the conference room.

I looked up from the table, "Is he dead?"

The young cadet was flushed from the cold. His teeth chattered as he shook his head in denial. "No—the doctors have him."

"Where?" I asked.

He shook his head. "You're to come with me, Comrade Stalin, for your own safety."

"What else do you know?" I demanded.

"Several of our units, including Cheka, are not responding to orders."

"They've gone over," I said, glancing down at the lists of names I had been studying.

The cadet was silent as I got up and went to the window. The gray courtyard below was deserted. There was no sign of the Latvian guards, and the dead horse I had seen earlier was gone. I turned my head slightly, and saw the cadet in the window glass. He was fumbling with his pistol holster. I reached under my long coat and grasped the revolver in my shoulder harness, then turned and pointed it at him under my coat. He had not drawn his pistol.

"No, Comrade Stalin!" he cried, "I was only unsnapping the case. It sticks."

I looked into his eyes. He was only a boy, and his fear was convincing.

"We must leave here immediately, Comrade Stalin," he added quickly. "We may be arrested at any moment."

I slipped my gun back into its sheath. "Lead the way."

"We'll go out the back," he said, his voice shaking with relief.

"Did it happen at the factory?" I asked.

"Just as he finished his speech, a woman shot at him," he replied.

I tried to imagine what Reilly was doing at this very moment.

The cadet led me down the back stairs of the old office block. The iron railing was rusting, and the stairwell smelled of urine. On the first landing the cadet turned around and found his courage.

"You *are* under arrest, Comrade Stalin," he said with a nervous smile.

My boot caught him under the chin. I felt his neck break as he fired the pistol into the railing, scattering rust into my face. He fell backward onto the landing. I hurried down and wrenched the gun from his stiffening fingers, then went back up to the office.

There was a hiding place behind the toilet, but I would use it only if I had to. I came into the room and paused, listening, but there was only the sound of wind rattling the windows. Was it possible that they had sent only one person for me? Something had gone wrong, or the cadet had come for me on his own initiative, hoping to ingratiate himself with the other side. All of which meant I could expect another visit at any moment.

I hurried down the front stairs to the lobby, went out cautiously through the main doors, and spotted a motorcycle nearby—probably the cadet's. I rushed to it, got on, and started it on the first kick. I gripped the handlebars, gunned the engine into a roar, then turned the bike around with a screech and rolled into the street, expecting to see them coming for me.

But there was no one on the street. Something had gone wrong. The Latvians had been removed to leave me exposed, but the next step, my arrest and execution, had somehow been delayed. Only the cadet had showed up.

I tried to think. Where would they have taken Vladimir Ilyich? It had to be the old safe house outside of Moscow, just south of the city. That would be the only place now. I wondered if I had enough petrol to reach it.

4

Lenin was at the country house. He was not mortally wounded. His assassin was there also, having been taken prisoner by the Cheka guards who had gone with Lenin to the factory.

"Comrade Stalin!" Vladimir Ilyich exclaimed as I sat down by his cot in the book-lined study. "You are safe, but our situation is desperate."

"What has happened?" I asked, still unsteady from the long motorcycle ride.

"Moscow has fallen. Our Latvian regiments have deserted, along with our Chinese workers. Most of the Red Guards have been imprisoned. The Social Revolutionaries have joined the counterrevolution. My assassin is one of them. I suspect that killing me was to have been their token of good faith. There's no word from Trotsky's southern volunteers. There doesn't seem to be much we can do. We might even have to flee the country."

"Never," I replied.

He raised his hand to his massive forehead. "Don't shout, I'm in terrible pain. The bullet was in my shoulder, but I have a headache that won't stop."

I looked around for Nadezhda, but she was not in the room. I saw several haggard, unfamiliar faces, and realized that no one of great importance had escaped with Lenin from Moscow. By now they were in Reilly's hands, dead, or about to be executed. He would not wait long. I had underestimated the Bastard of Odessa.

"What shall we do?" I asked.

Vladimir Ilyich sighed and closed his eyes. "I would like your sug-
gestions."

"We must go where they won't find us easily," I replied. "I know
several places in Georgia."

His eyes opened and fixed on me. "As long as you don't want to
return to robbing banks."

His words irritated me, but I didn't show it.

"We needed the money," I said calmly, remembering that he had
once described me as crude and vulgar. Living among émigré Russians in Europe had affected his practical sense.

"Of course, of course," he replied with a feeble wave of his hand.
"You are a dedicated and useful man."

There was a muffled shot from outside. It seemed to relax Vladimir
Ilyich. Dora Kaplan, his assassin, had been executed.

                                 5

Just before leaving the safe house, we learned that Lenin's wife had
been executed. Vladimir Ilyich began to rave as we led him out to the
truck, insisting to me that Reilly could not have killed Nadezhda, and
that the report had to be false. I said nothing; to me her death had
been inevitable. As Lenin's lifelong partner, and a theoretician herself, she would have posed a threat in his absence. Reilly's swiftness
in removing her impressed me. Lenin's reaction to her death was
unworthy of a Bolshevik; suddenly his wife was only an unimportant
woman. Nadezhda Krupskaya had not been an innocent.

We fled south, heading for a railway station that was still in our
hands, just south of Moscow, where a special train was waiting to
take us to Odessa. If the situation in that city turned out to be intrac-
table, we would attempt to reach a hiding place in my native Georgia.

Three Chekas came with us in the truck—a young lieutenant and
two privates, both of whom had abandoned the czar's forces for the
revolution. I watched the boyish faces of the two privates from time
to time, looking for signs of doubt. The lieutenant, who was also a
mechanic, drove the old Ford, nursing the truck through the ten
muddy kilometers to the station.

"He could have held her hostage," Vladimir Ilyich insisted to me as
the truck sputtered and coughed along. "Don't you think so? Maybe

he thought we were dead, and she would be of no use to him as a hostage?"

For the next hour he asked his own questions and gave his own impossible answers. It depressed me to hear how much of the bourgeois there was still in him. I felt the confusion in the minds of the two Chekas.

It began to rain as the sun went down. We couldn't see the road ahead. The lieutenant pulled over and waited. Water seeped in on us through the musty canvas. Vladimir Ilyich began to weep.

"She was a soldier in our cause," I said loudly, hating his sentimentality.

He stared out into the rainy twilight. Lightning flashed as he turned to look at me, and for a moment it seemed that his face had turned to marble. "You're right," he said, eyes wild with conviction, "I must remember that."

Of course, I had always disliked Nadezhda's hovering, familiar-like ways. She had been a bony raven at his shoulder, forever whispering asides, but I had always taken great care to be polite to her. Now more than ever I realized what a buttress she had been to Vladimir Ilyich.

The rain lessened. The lieutenant tried to start the Ford, but it was dead.

"There's not much time," I said. "How much farther?"

"Less than half a kilometer."

"We'll go on foot," I said. "There's no telling who may be behind us."

I helped Vladimir Ilyich down from the truck. He managed to stand alone, and refused my arm as we began to march on the muddy road. He moved steadily at my side, but his breathing was labored.

We were within sight of the station when he collapsed.

"Help!" I called out.

The lieutenant and one of the privates came back, lifted Vladimir Ilyich onto their shoulders, and hurried ahead with him. It was like a scene from the street rallies, but without the crowds.

"Is he very ill?" the other private asked me as I caught up.

I did not answer. Ahead, the train waited in a conflagration of storm lamps and steam.

6

Our train consisted of a dining car, a kitchen, one supply car, and the engine. A military evacuation train was being readied on the track next to ours, to carry away those who would be fleeing Moscow in the next day or two. I was surprised at this bit of organization. When I asked how it had been accomplished, a sergeant said one word to me: "Trotsky."

We sped off into the warm, misty night. Vladimir Ilyich recovered enough to have dinner with me and our three soldiers. The plush luxury of the czarist interior seemed to brighten his mood.

"I only hope that Trotsky is in Odessa when we arrive," he said, sipping his brandy, "and that he can raise a force we can work with. Our foreign vendors have been paid, fortunately, but we will have to keep our southern port open to be supplied."

He was looking into the large mirror at our right as he spoke. I nodded to his reflection.

"The troops behind us," the youthful lieutenant added, "will help insure that."

Vladimir Ilyich put down his glass and looked at me directly. "Do you think, Comrade Stalin, that we hoped for too much?" He sounded lost.

"No," I answered. "We have popular support. The people are waiting to hear from you. Reilly's pamphlets have struck a nerve of longing with promises of foreign help and bourgeois progress, but he is actually depending only on the uncertainty of our followers. His mercenaries won't count for much when the news that you are alive gets out. Most of his support can be taken from him with that alone, but we will have to follow our victory with a period of terror, to compel loyalty among the doubters."

He nodded to me, then looked into the darkness of the window. In that mirror we rode not only in a well-appointed, brightly lit dining room, but in the cave of all Russia.

"You must get some sleep," I said.

We found blankets and made ourselves comfortable on the leather couches. The lieutenant turned down the lights.

I tried to sleep, but my thoughts seemed to organize themselves to the clatter of the train wheels. Contempt for my own kind crept into me, especially for the idealists in our party. Too many utopian fools were setting themselves up against their own nature and what was possible. They did not grasp that progress was like the exponent in one of Einstein's fashionable equations—a small modifying quantity that has an effect only when the big term grew very large. They failed to see that only when the biggest letter of human history, material wealth, became sufficiently large, would there be a chance for social progress. Only then would we be able to afford to become humane. My role in this revolution was to remember this fact, and to act when it was neglected. . . .

7

Our mood was apprehensive as our train pulled into Odessa. We stepped out into bright sunlight, and a deserted station.

"We don't know what may have happened here," I said.

"There hasn't been time," Vladimir Ilyich replied. His voice was gruff after three days on the train, and he seemed ready to bark at me in his usual way. I felt reassured. This was the Lenin who had taken a spontaneous uprising and interpreted the yearning of the masses, so they would know what to do; the Lenin who would make ours a Communist revolution despite Marx. Like Reilly, Lenin was irreplaceable. Without him there would only be a struggle for power, with no vision justifying action.

Suddenly, a Ford Model T sedan pulled into the station and rattled toward us down the platform. I took Lenin's arm, ready to shove him out of harm's way; but the car slowed and stopped.

"Welcome!" the driver shouted as he threw open the door and got out. When he opened the back door for us, I saw that he was Trotsky's youngest son, Sergei. I greeted him and smiled, but his eyes worshiped only Lenin as we got into the back seat, as if I didn't exist.

Sergei drove quickly, but the ride was comfortable. With the windows closed, Odessa seemed distant. We climbed a hill and saw the sun glistening on the Black Sea. I remembered the smell of leather in my father's shoe shop. Warm days gave the shop a keener odor. I pictured myself in the small church library, which was open to sons who might one day be priests. The books had been dusty, the air full of waxy smells from the lamps and candles. I remembered the young girl I had seduced on a sunny afternoon, and for an instant the world's failings seemed far away. I began to wonder if we were driving into a betrayal.

A crowd surrounded us as we pulled into the center of the city. They peered inside, saw Lenin, and cheered.

Trotsky was waiting for us with a company of soldiers on the courthouse steps. We climbed out into a bright paradise of good feeling. Trotsky saluted us, then came down and embraced Vladimir Ilyich, who looked shabby in his brown waistcoat under that silk blue sky.

The crowd cheered them. As Lenin turned to address the throng, I felt Reilly plotting against us in Moscow, and I knew in that moment what it would take to stop him.

"Comrades!" Lenin cried, regaining his old self with one word. "A dangerous counterrevolution has seized Moscow! It is supported by the foreign allies, who are not content with defeating Germany. They also want our lands. But we will regroup here, and strike north. With Comrade Trotsky's Red Army, and your bravery, we shall prevail . . ."

As he spoke, I wondered if anyone in Moscow would believe that he was still alive, short of seeing him there. Open military actions would not defeat Reilly in any reasonable time. It would take years, while the revolution withered, especially if Reilly avoided decisive battles. Reilly had to be killed as quickly and as publicly as possible. Like Lenin he was a leader who needed his followers as much as they needed him. There was no arguing with this fact of human attachment. Without Reilly, the counterrevolution would collapse in a matter of days. His foreign supporters would not easily shift their faith to another figure.

He had to die in a week, two at the latest, and I knew how it would have to be done. There was no other way.

"Long live Comrade Lenin!" the crowd chanted—loudly enough, it seemed to me, for Reilly to hear it in his bed in Moscow.

8

From the reports I had read about Reilly's life and activities, I suspected that he was a man who liked to brood. It was a way of searching, of pointing himself toward his hopes. He prayed to himself, beseeching a hidden center, where the future sang of sweet possibilities.

As head of his government, he would have to act against both czarists and Bolsheviks. He could count on czarists joining his regime, but he would never trust a Bolshevik. Czarists would be fairly predictable in their military actions, but Bolsheviks, he knew, would spare no outrage to bring him down.

He was probably in what remained of the British Embassy in Moscow, sipping brandy in the master bedroom, perhaps playing with the idea that he might have joined us. I knew there had been efforts to recruit him for our intelligence service. He would have disappeared and reemerged as another man, as he did when he left Odessa for South America in his youth, to escape his adulterous family's bourgeois pesthole. It would have been simple justice for him to return in the same way, even as a Bolshevik.

But for the moment, Russia was his to mold. I could almost hear the Jew congratulating himself in that great bed of English oak.

Within the week there would be a knock on his bedroom door, and a messenger would bring him word that Lenin was in Odessa. Reilly would sit up and lean uncomfortably against the large wooden headboard, where once there had been luxurious pillows (a pity that the mobs had torn them to pieces). He would read the message with a rush of excitement, and realize that a British seaplane could get him to Odessa within a day. The entire mission would flash through his mind, as if he were remembering the future.

He would fly to the Black Sea, then swing north to Odessa, using the night for cover. What feelings would pass through him as he landed on the moonlit water? Here he was, returning to the city of his childhood in order to test himself against his greatest enemies. The years would run back in his mind as he sat in the open doorway of the amphibious aircraft, breathing in the night air and remembering the youth who had startled himself with his superiority to the people around him. He had blackmailed his mother's lover for the money to escape Odessa. The man had nearly choked when he'd called him father.

He would know that he was risking his counterrevolution by coming here alone. The Bolsheviks would be able to pull down any of his possible successors. But it was the very implausibility of his coming here alone that would protect him, he would tell himself. Tarnishing Lenin's name by revealing Germany's hand in his return was not enough. Lenin had to die before his followers could regroup, before reports of his death were proven false. Only then would the counterrevolution be able to rally the support of disenchanted czarists, moderate democrats, churchmen, and Mensheviks—all those who still hoped for a regime that would replace monarchy but avoid Bolshevism.

Reilly was a hopeless bourgeois, but more intelligent than most, hence more dangerous, despite his romantic imagination. He sincerely believed that Bolshevism would only gain Russia the world's animosity, and insure our country's cultural and economic poverty.

He would come into Odessa one morning, in a small boat, perhaps dressed as a fisherman. He would savor the irony of his return to the city of his youth, wearing old clothes, following the pattern of all his solo missions. It was a form of rebirth. He trusted it, and so would I.

9

The warmer climate of Odessa speeded Lenin's physical recovery. He would get up with the sun and walk along the street that led to the Great Steps (the site of the 1905 massacre of the townspeople by czarist Cossacks, which the expatriate homosexual director, Sergei Eisenstein, later filmed in Hollywood). I let the Cheka guards sleep late, and kept an eye on Vladimir Ilyich myself.

One morning, as I watched him through field glasses from the terrace of our hotel, he stopped and gazed out over city and sea, then sat down on the first step, something he had not done before. His shoulders slumped in defeat. He was probably reminiscing about his bourgeois European life with Krupskaya, and regretting their return to Russia. His euphoric recovery during the first week after our arrival had eroded, and he had slowly slipped back into a brooding silence.

As I watched, a man's head floated up from the steps below the seated Lenin. The figure of a fisherman came into view, stopped next to Vladimir Ilyich, and tipped his hat to him. I turned my glasses to the sea and searched. Yes! There was something on the horizon—a small boat, or the wings of a seaplane. The reports I had received of engine sounds in the early morning had been correct.

I whipped back to the two figures. They were conversing amiably. Vladimir Ilyich seemed pleased by the encounter, but then he had always shown a naive faith in simple folk, and sometimes spoke to them as if he were confessing. Krupskaya's death had made him unobservant, and Reilly was a superb actor.

Reilly was taking his time out of sheer vanity, it seemed to me. He would not kill his great rival without first talking to him.

I put down the field glasses, checked my revolver, then slipped it into my shoulder holster and hurried downstairs, wearing only my white shirt and trousers. I ran through the deserted streets, sweating in the warm morning air, expecting at any moment to hear a shot. I reached the row of houses just above the Great Steps, slipped into a doorway, then crept out.

The blood was pounding in my ears as I peered around the corner. Lenin and the fisherman were sitting on the top step with their back to me. Vladimir Ilyich was gesturing with his right hand. I could almost hear him. The words sounded familiar.

I waited, thinking that the man was a fisherman, and that I had expected too much of Reilly.

Then the stranger put his arm around Vladimir Ilyich's shoulders. What had they been saying to each other? Had they reached some kind of rapprochment? Perhaps Lenin was in fact a German agent, and these two had been working together all along. Could I have been so wrong? The sight of them sitting side by side like old friends unnerved me.

The fisherman gripped Lenin's head with both hands and twisted it. The neck snapped, and in that long moment it seemed to me that he would tear the head from the body. I drew my revolver and rushed forward.

"Did you think it would be that easy, Rosenblum?" I said as I came up behind him.

The fisherman turned and looked up at me, not with surprise, but with irritation, and let go of Lenin.

"Don't move," I said as the corpse slumped face down across the stairs.

The fisherman seemed to relax, but he was watching me carefully. "So you used him as bait," he said, gesturing at the body. "Why didn't you just kill him yourself?"

His question was meant to annoy me.

He looked out to sea. "Yes, an economical solution to counterrevolution. You liquidate us both while preserving the appearance of innocence. You're certain that Moscow will fall without me."

I did not reply.

He squinted up at me. "Are you sure it's me you've captured? I may have sent someone else." He laughed.

I gestured with my revolver. "The seaplane—only Sidney Reilly would have come here in one. You had to come quickly."

He nodded to himself, as if admitting his sins.

"What did Vladimir Ilyich say to you?" I asked.

His mood changed, as if I had suddenly given him what he needed.

"Well?" I demanded.

"You're very curious about that," he said without looking at me. "I may not tell you."

"Suit yourself."

He considered for a moment. "I will tell you. He feared for Russia's future, and that moved me, Comrade Stalin. He was afraid because there are too many of the likes of you. I was surprised to hear it from him."

"The likes of me?"

"Yes, the cynics and doubters who won't be content until they've made the world as barren for everyone else as they've made it for themselves. His wife's death brought it all home to him, as nothing else could have. His words touched me."

"Did you tell him that you killed her?"

"I was too late to save her."

"And he believed you?"

"Yes. I told him who I was. His dreams were dead. He wanted to die."

My hand was sweaty on the revolver. "Bourgeois sentiments destroyed him. I hope you two enjoyed exchanging idealist bouquets. Did you tell him what you would have done if you had caught us in Moscow?"

He looked up and smiled at me. "I would have paraded all of you through the streets without your pants and underwear, shirttails flapping in the breeze!"

"And then killed us."

"No, I wouldn't have made martyrs. Prison would have served well enough after such ridicule."

"But you came here to kill him."

"Perhaps not," he said with a sigh. "I might have taken him back as my prisoner, but he wanted to die. I killed him as I would have an injured dog. In any case, Moscow believes that he died weeks ago."

"Well, you've botched it all now, haven't you?"

"At least I know that Lenin died a true Bolshevik."

"So now you claim to understand Bolshevism?"

"I always have. True Bolshevism contains enough constructive ideas to make possible a high social justice. It shares that with Christianity and the French Revolution, but it's the likes of you, Comrade Stalin, who will prevent a proper wedding of ideals and practical government." He smiled. "Well, perhaps the marriage will take place despite you. The little Soviets may hold fast to their democratic structures and bring you down in time. Who knows, they may one day lead the world to the highest ideal of statesmanship—internationalism."

"Fine words," I said, tightening my grip on the revolver, "but the reality is that you've done our Soviet cause a great service—by being a foreign agent, a counterrevolutionary, a Jewish bastard, and Lenin's assassin, all in one."

"I've only done *you* a service," he said bitterly, and I felt his hatred and frustration.

"You simply don't understand the realities of power, Rosenblum."

"Do tell," he said with derision.

"Only limited things are possible with humanity," I replied. "The mad dog within the great mass of people must be kept muzzled. Civil order is the best any society can hope to achieve."

The morning sun was hot on my face. As I reached up to wipe my forehead with my sleeve, Reilly leaped over Lenin's body and fled down the long stairs.

I aimed and fired, but my fingers had stiffened during our little dialogue. My bullet got off late and missed. I fired again as he jumped a dozen steps, but the bullet hit well behind him.

"Stop him!" I shouted to a group of people below him. They had just come out of the church at the foot of the stairs. "He's killed Comrade Lenin!"

Reilly saw that he couldn't get by them. He turned and started back toward me, drawing a knife as he went. He stopped and threw it, but it struck the steps to my right. I laughed, and he came for me with his bare hands. I aimed, knowing that he might reach me if I missed. It impressed me that he would gamble on my aim rather than risk the drop over the great railings.

I pulled the trigger. The hammer struck a defective cartridge. Reilly grunted as he sensed victory, and kept coming.

I fired again.

The bullet pierced his throat. He staggered up and fell bleeding at my feet, one hand clawing at my heavy boots. His desperation was both strange and unexpected. Nothing had ever failed for him in quite this way. Its simplicity affronted his intelligence.

"I also feel for dogs," I said, squeezing a round into the back of his head. He lay still, free of life's metaphysics.

I holstered my revolver and nudged his body forward. It sprawled next to Lenin, then rolled down to the next landing. The people from the church came up, paused around Vladimir Ilyich, then looked up to me.

"Vladimir Ilyich's assassin is dead!" I shouted. "The counterrevolution has failed." A breeze blew in from the sea and cooled my face. I breathed deeply and looked saddened.

Reilly was hung up by his neck in his hometown, but I was the only one who knew enough to appreciate the irony. Fishermen sailed out and towed his seaplane to shore.

Lenin's body was placed in a tent set up in the harbor area, where all Odessans could come to pay their last respects. Trotsky and I stood in line with everyone else. One of our warships fired its guns in a final salute.

10

We sent the news to Moscow in two carefully timed salvos.

First, that Reilly, a British agent, had been killed during an attempt on Lenin's life; then, that our beloved Vladimir Ilyich had succumbed to wounds received, after a valiant struggle.

We went north with our troops, carrying Lenin's coffin, recruiting all the way. Everywhere people met our train with shouts of allegiance. Trotsky appointed officers, gathered arms, and kept records. He also scribbled in his diary like a schoolgirl.

I knew now that I was Lenin's true heir, truer than he had been to himself in his last weeks. I would hold fast to that and to Russia, especially when Trotsky began to lecture me again about the urgent need for world revolution.

In the years that followed I searched for men like Reilly to direct our espionage and intelligence services. If he had been turned, our KGB would have been built on a firmer foundation of skills and techniques. He would have recruited English agents for us with ease, especially from their universities, where the British played at revolution and ideology, and sentimentalized justice. I could not rid myself of the feeling that in time Rosenblum would have turned back to his mother country; he had never been, after all, a czarist. I regretted having had to kill him on that sunny morning in Odessa, because in later years I found myself measuring so many men against him. I wondered if a defective cartridge or a jammed revolver could have changed the outcome. Probably not. I would have been forced to club him to death. Still, he might have disarmed me. . . .

But on that train in 1918, on the snowy track to Moscow, I could only wonder at Reilly's naive belief that he could have altered the course of Soviet inevitability, which now so clearly belonged to me.

ABE LINCOLN IN McDONALD'S

James Morrow

He caught the last train out of 1863 and got off at the blustery December of 2009, not far from Christmas, where he walked well past the turn of the decade and, without looking back, settled down in the fifth of July for a good look around. To be a mere tourist in this place would not suffice. No, he must get it under his skin, work it into his bones, enfold it with his soul.

In his vest pocket, pressed against his heart's grim cadence, lay the final draft of the dreadful Seward Treaty. He needed but to add his name—Jefferson Davis had already signed it on behalf of the secessionist states—and a cleft nation would become whole. A signature, that was all, a simple "A. Lincoln."

Adjusting his string tie, he waded into the chaos grinding and snorting down Pennsylvania Avenue and began his quest for a savings bank.

"The news isn't good," came Norman Grant's terrible announcement, stabbing from the phone like a poisoned dagger. "Jimmy's test was positive."

Walter Sherman's flabby, pumpkinlike face whitened with dread. "Are you sure?" *Positive*, what a paradoxical term, so ironic in its clinical denotations: nullity, disease, doom.

"We ran two separate blood checks, followed by a fluorescent antibody analysis. Sorry. Poor Jim's got Blue Nile Fever."

Walter groaned. Thank God his daughter was over at the Sheridans'. Jimmy had been Tanya's main Christmas present of three years ago—he came with a special note from Santa—and her affection for the old slave ran deep. Second father, she called him. Walter never could figure out why Tanya had asked for a sexagenarian and not a whelp like most kids wanted, but who could know the mind of a preschooler?

If only one of their others had caught the lousy virus. Jimmy wasn't the usual chore-boy. Indeed, when it came to cultivating a garden, washing a rug, or painting a house, he didn't know his nose from the nine of spades. Ah, but his bond with Tanya! Jimmy was her guardian, playmate, confidant, and, yes, her teacher. Walter never ceased marveling at the great discovery of the last century: if you chained a whelp to a computer at the right age (no younger than two, no older than six), he'd soak up vast tracts of knowledge and subsequently pass them on to your children. Through Jimmy and Jimmy alone, Tanya had learned a formidable amount of plane geometry, music theory, American history, and Greek before ever setting foot in kindergarten.

"Prognosis?"

The doctor sighed. "Blue Nile Fever follows a predictable course. In a year or so, Jimmy's T-cell defenses will collapse, leaving him prey to a hundred opportunistic infections. What worries me, of course, is Marge's pregnancy."

A dull dread crept through Walter's white flesh. "You mean—it could hurt the baby?"

"Well, there's this policy—the Centers for Disease Control urge permanent removal of Nile-positive chattel from all households containing pregnant women."

"Removed?" Walter echoed indignantly. "I thought it didn't cross the pigmentation barrier."

"That's probably true." Grant's voice descended several registers. "But *fetuses*, Walter, know what I'm saying? *Fetuses*, with their undeveloped immune systems. We don't want to ask for trouble, not with a retrovirus."

"God, this is depressing. You really think there's a risk?"

"I'll put it this way. If my wife were pregnant—"

"I know, I know."

"Bring Jimmy down here next week, and we'll take care of it. Quick. Painless. Is Tuesday at two-thirty good?"

Of course it was good. Walter had gone into orthodontics for the flexible hours, the dearth of authentic emergencies. That, and never having to pay for his own kids' braces. "See you then," he replied, laying a hand on his shattered heart.

The President strode out of Northeast Federal Savings and Loan and continued toward the derby-hatted Capitol. Such an exquisite building—at least some of the city remained intact; all was not glass-faced offices and dull boxy banks. "If we were still on the gold standard, this would be a more normal transaction," the assistant manager, a fool named Meade, had whined when Abe presented his coins for conversion. Not on the gold standard! A Democrat's doing, no doubt.

Luckily, Aaron Green, Abe's Chief Soothsayer and Time-Travel Advisor, had prepared him for the wondrous monstrosities and wrenching innovations that now assailed his senses. The self-propelled railway coaches roaring along causeways of black stone. The sky-high mechanical condors whisking travelers across the nation at hundreds of miles per hour. The dense medley of honks, bleeps, and technological growls.

So Washington was indeed living in its proper century—but what of the nation at large?

Stripped to the waist, two slave teams were busily transforming Pennsylvania Avenue, the first chopping into the asphalt with pick axes, the second filling the gorge with huge cylindrical pipes. Their sweat-speckled backs were free of gashes and scars—hardly a surprise, as the overseers carried no whips, merely queer one-chamber pistols and portable Gatling guns.

Among the clutter at the Constitution Avenue intersection—signs, trash receptacles, small landlocked lighthouses regulating the coaches' flow—a pair of green arrows commanded Abe's notice. CAPITOL BUILDING, announced the eastward-pointing arrow. LINCOLN MEMORIAL, said its opposite. His own memorial! So this particular tomorrow, the one fated by the awful Seward Treaty, would be kind to him.

The President hailed a cab. Removing his stovepipe hat, he wedged his six-foot-four frame into the passenger compartment—don't ride up front, Aaron Green had briefed him—and offered a cheery "Good morning."

The driver, a blowsy woman, slid back a section of the soft rubbery glass. "Lincoln, right?" she called through the opening like Pyramus talking to Thisbe. "You're supposed to be Abe Lincoln. Costume party?"

"Republican."

"Where to?"

"Boston." If any city had let itself get mired in the past, Abe figured, that city would be Boston.

"Boston, *Massachusetts?*"

"Correct."

"Hey, that's crazy, Mac. You're talking six hours at least, and that's if we push the speed limit all the way. I'd have to charge you my return trip."

The President lifted a sack of money from his greatcoat. Even if backed only by good intentions, twentieth century currency was aesthetically satisfying, that noble profile on the pennies, that handsome three-quarter view on the fives. As far as he could tell, he and Washington were the only ones to score twice. "How much altogether?"

"You serious? Probably four hundred dollars."

Abe peeled the driver's price from his wad and passed the bills through the window. "Take me to Boston."

"They're so *adorable!*" Tanya exclaimed as she and Walter strolled past Sonny's Super Slaver, a Chestnut Hill Mall emporium second in size only to the sporting goods store. "Ah, look at *that* one—those big ears!" Recently weaned babies jammed the glass cages, tumbling over themselves, clutching stuffed jackhammers and toy garden hoses. "Could we get one, Pappy?"

As Walter fixed on his daughter's face, its glow nearly made him squint. "Tanya, I've got some bad news. Jimmy's real sick."

"Sick? He looks fine."

"It's Blue Nile, honey. He could die."

"Die?" Tanya's angelic face crinkled with the effort of fighting tears. What a brave little tomato she was. "Soon?"

"Soon." Walter's throat swelled like a broken ankle. "Tell you what. Let's go pick out a whelp right now. We'll have them put it aside until . . ."

"Until Jimmy"—a wrenching gulp—"goes away?"

"Uh-huh."

"Poor Jimmy."

The sweet, bracing fragrance of newborn chattel wafted into Walter's nostrils as they approached the counter, behind which a wiry Asian man, tongue pinned against his upper lip, methodically arranged a display of Tarbaby Treats. "Now *here's* a girl who needs a friend," he sang out, flashing Tanya a fake smile.

"Our best slave has Blue Nile," Walter explained, "and we wanted to—"

"Say no more." The clerk lifted his palms as if stopping traffic. "We can hold one for you clear till August."

"I'm afraid it won't be that long."

The clerk led them to a cage containing a solitary whelp chewing on a small plastic lawn mower. MALE, the sign said. TEN MONTHS.

$399.95. "This guy arrived only yesterday. You'll have him litter trained in two weeks—this we guarantee."

"Had his shots?"

"You bet. The polio booster's due next month."

"Oh, Daddy, I *love* him," Tanya gushed, jumping up and down. "I completely *love* him. Let's bring him home tonight!"

"No, tomato. Jimmy'd get jealous." Walter gave the clerk a wink and, simultaneously, a twenty. "See that he gets a couple of really good meals this weekend, right?"

"Sure thing."

"Pappy?"

"Yes, tomato?"

"When Jimmy dies, will he go to slave heaven? Will he get to see his old friends?"

"Certainly."

"Like Buzzy?"

"He'll definitely see Buzzy."

A smile of intense pride leaped spontaneously to Walter's face. Buzzy had died when Tanya was only four, yet she remembered, she actually remembered!

So hard-edged, the future, Abe thought, levering himself out of the taxi and unflexing his long cramped limbs. Boston had become a thing of brick and rock, tar and glass, iron and steel. "Wait here," he told the driver.

He entered the public gardens. A truly lovely spot, he decided, sauntering past a slave team planting flower beds—impetuous tulips, swirling gladiolus, purse-lipped daffodils. Not far beyond, a white family cruised across a duck pond in a swan-shaped boat peddled by a scowling adolescent with skin like obsidian.

Leaving the park, Abe started down Boylston Street. A hundred yards away, a burly Irish overseer stood beneath a gargantuan structure called the John Hancock Tower and began raising the scaffold, thus sending aloft a dozen slaves equipped with window-washing fluid. Dear Lord, what a job—the facade must contain a million square yards of mirrored glass.

Hard-edged, ungiving—and yet the city brought Abe peace.

In recent months, he had started to grasp the true cause of the war The issue, he realized, was not slavery. As with all things political, the issue was power. The rebel states had seceded because they despaired of ever seizing the helm of state; as long as its fate was linked to a grimy, uncouth, industrialized north, Dixie could never fully flower. By endeavoring to expand slavery into the territories, those southerners who hated the institution and those who loved it were speaking with a single tongue, saying, "The Republic's true destiny is manifest: an agrarian Utopia, now and forever."

But here was Boston, full of slaves and steeped in progress. Clearly the Seward Treaty would not prove the recipe for feudalism and inertia Abe's advisors feared. Crude, yes; morally ambiguous, true; and yet slavery wasn't dragging the Republic into the past, wasn't retarding its bid for modernity and might.

"Sign the treaty," an inner voice instructed Abe. "End the war."

Sunday was the Fourth of July, which meant the annual backyard picnic with the Burnsides, boring Ralph and boorish Helen, a tedious afternoon of horseshoe tossing, conspicuous drinking, and stupefying poolside chat, the whole ordeal relieved only by Libby's barbecued spare ribs. Libby was one of those wonderful yard-sale items Marge had such a knack for finding, a healthy, well-mannered female who turned out to be a splendid cook, easily worth ten times her sticker price.

The Burnsides were an hour late—their rickshaw puller, Zippy, had broken his foot the day before, and so they were forced to use Bubbles, their unathletic gardener—a whole glorious hour of not hearing Ralph's thoughts on the Boston sports scene. When they did finally show, the first thing out of Ralph's mouth was, "Is it a law the Sox can't own a decent pitcher? I mean did they actually pass a *law?*" and Walter steeled himself. Luckily, Libby used a loose hand with the bourbon, and by three o'clock Walter was so anesthetized by mint juleps he could have floated happily through an amputation, not to mention Ralph's vapid views on the Sox, Celtics, Bruins, and Patriots.

With the sixth drink his numbness segued into a kind of contented courage, and he took unflinching stock of himself. Yes, his wife had probably bedded down with a couple of her teachers from the Wellesley Adult Education Center—that superfluously muscled pottery instructor, most likely, though the drama coach also seemed to have a roving dick—but it wasn't as if Walter didn't occasionally use his orthodontic chair as a motel bed, wasn't as if he didn't frolic with Katie Mulligan every Wednesday afternoon at the West Newton Hot Tubs. And look at his splendid house, with its Jacuzzi, bowling alley, tennis court, and twenty-five-meter pool. Look at his thriving practice. His portfolio. Porsche. Silver rickshaw. Graceful daughter flopping through sterile turquoise waters (damn that Happy, always using too much chlorine). And look at his sturdy, handsome Marge, back-floating, her pregnancy rising from the deep end like a volcanic island. Walter was sure the kid was his. Eighty-five percent sure.

He'd achieved something in this life.

At dusk, while Happy set off the fireworks, the talk got around to Blue Nile. "We had Jimmy tested last week," Walter revealed, exhaling a small tornado of despair. "Positive."

"God, and you let him stay in the house?" wailed Ralph, fingering the grip of his Luger Parabellum P08. A cardboard rocket screeched into the sky and became a dozen crimson starbursts, their reflections cruising across the pool like phosphorescent fish. "You should've told us. He might infect Bubbles."

"It's a pretty hard virus to contract," Walter retorted. A buzz bomb whistled overhead, annihilating itself in a glittery blue-and-red mandala. "There has to be an exchange of saliva or blood."

"Still, I can't believe you're keeping him, with Marge pregnant and everything."

Ten fiery spheres popped from a Roman candle and sailed into the night like clay pigeons. "Matter of fact, I've got an appointment with Grant on Monday."

"You know, Walter, if Jimmy were mine, I'd allow him a little dignity. I wouldn't take him to a lousy clinic."

The pièce de résistance blossomed over the yard—Abe Lincoln's portrait in sparks. "What would you do?"

"You know perfectly well what I'd do."

Walter grimaced. Dignity. Ralph was right, by damn. Jimmy had served the family with devotion and zest. They owed him an honorable exit.

The President chomped into a Big Mac, reveling in the soggy sauces and sultry juices as they bathed his tongue and rolled down his gullet. Were he not permanently lodged elsewhere—rail splitter, country lawyer, the whole captivating myth—he might well have wished to settle down here in 2010. Big Macs were a quality commodity. The entire menu, in fact, the large fries, vanilla shakes, Diet Cokes, and Chicken McNuggets, seemed to Abe a major improvement over nineteenth-century cuisine. And such a soothing environment, its every surface clean and sleek, as if carved from tepid ice.

An enormous clown named Ronald was emblazoned on the picture window. Outside, across the street, an elegant sign—Old English characters on whitewashed wood—heralded the Chestnut Hill Country Club. On the grassy slopes beyond, smooth and green like a billiard table, a curious event unfolded, men and women whacking balls into the air with sticks. When not employed, the sticks resided in cylindrical bags slung over the shoulders of sturdy male slaves.

"Excuse me, madame," Abe addressed the chubby woman in the next booth. "What are those people doing? Is it religious?"

"That's quite a convincing Lincoln you've got on." Hunched over a newspaper, the woman wielded a writing implement, using it to fill tiny squares with alphabet letters. "Are you serious? They're golfing."

"A game?"

"Uh-huh." The woman started on her second Quarter Pounder. "The game of golf."

"It's like croquet, isn't it?"

"It's like golf."

Dipping and swelling like a verdant sea, the golf field put Abe in mind of Virginia's hilly provinces. Virginia, Lee's stronghold. A soft moan left the sixteenth President. Having thrown Hooker and Sedgwick back across the Rappahannock, Lee was ideally positioned to bring the war to the Union, either by attacking Washington directly or, more likely, by forming separate corps under Longstreet, Hill, and Ewell and invading Pennsylvania. Overrunning the border towns, he could probably cut the flow of reinforcements to Vicksburg while simultaneously equipping the Army of Northern Virginia for a push on the capital.

It was all too nightmarish to contemplate.

Sighing heavily, Abe took the Seward Treaty from his vest and asked to borrow his neighbor's pen.

Monday was a holiday. Right after breakfast, Walter changed into his golfing togs, hunted down his clubs, and told Jimmy they'd be spending the day on the links. He ended up playing the entire course, partly to improve his game, partly to postpone the inevitable.

His best shot of the day—a three-hundred-and-fifty-yard blast with his one-iron—carried straight down the eighteenth fairway and ran right up on the green. Sink the putt, and he'd finish the day one under par.

Sweating in the relentless fifth-of-July sun, Jimmy pulled out the putter. Such a fine fellow, with his trim body and huge eager eyes, zags of silver shooting through his steel-wool hair like the aftermath of an electrocution, his black biceps and white polo shirt meeting like adjacent squares on a chess board. He would be sorely missed.

"No, Jimmy, we won't be needing that. Just pass the bag over here. Thanks."

As Walter retrieved his .22 caliber army rifle from among the clubs, Jimmy's face hardened with bewilderment.

"May I ask why you require a firearm?" said the slave.

"You may."

"Why?"

"I'm going to shoot you."

"Huh?"

"Shoot you."

"*What?*"

"Results came Thursday, Jimmy. You have Blue Nile. Sorry. I'd love to keep you around, but it's too dangerous, what with Marge's pregnancy and everything."

"Blue Nile?"

"Sorry."

Jimmy's teeth came together in a tight, dense grid. "In the name of reason, *sell* me. Surely that's a viable option."

"Let's be realistic. Nobody's going to take in a Nile-positive just to watch him wilt and die."

"Very well—then turn me loose." Sweat spouted from the slave's ebony face. "I'll pursue my remaining years on the road. I'll—"

"Loose? I can't go around undermining the economy like that, Jim. I'm sure you understand."

"There's something I've always wanted to tell you, Mr. Sherman."

"I'm listening."

"I believe you are the biggest asshole in the whole Commonwealth of Massachusetts."

"No need for that kind of talk, fellow. Just sit down on the green, and I'll—"

"No."

"Let's not make this difficult. Sit down, and you'll get a swift shot in the head—no pain, a dignified death. Run away, and you'll take it in the back. It's your choice."

"Of course I'm going to run, you degenerate moron."

"Sit!"

"No."

"Sit!"

Spinning around, Jimmy sprinted toward the rough. Walter jammed the stock against his shoulder and, like a biologist focusing his microscope on a protozoan, found the retreating chattel in his high-powered optical sight.

"Stop!"

Jimmy reached the western edge of the fairway just as Walter fired, a clean shot right through the slave's left calf. With a deep wolfish howl, he pitched forward and, to Walter's surprise, rose almost instantly, clutching a rusty discarded nine-iron that he evidently hoped to use as a crutch. But the slave got no farther. As he stood fully erect, his high wrinkled forehead neatly entered the gunsight, the cross hairs branding him with an X, and Walter had but to squeeze the trigger again.

Impacting, the bullet dug out a substantial portion of cranium—a glutinous divot of skin, bone, and cerebrum shooting away from Jimmy's temple like a missile launched from a brown planet. He spun around twice and fell into the rough, landing behind a clump of rose bushes spangled with white blossoms. So: an honorable exit after all.

Tears bubbled out of Walter as if from a medicine dropper. Oh, Jimmy, Jimmy . . . and the worst was yet to come, wasn't it? Of course, he wouldn't tell Tanya the facts. "Jimmy was in pain," he'd say. "Unbearable agony. The doctors put him to sleep. He's in slave heaven now." And they'd give him a classy send-off, oh, yes, with flowers and a moment of silence. Maybe Pastor McClellan would be willing to preside.

Walter staggered toward the rough. To do a funeral, you needed a body. Doubtless the morticians could patch up his head, mold a gentle smile, bend his arms across his chest in a posture suggesting serenity . . .

A tall, bearded man in an Abe Lincoln suit was on the eighteenth fairway, coming Walter's way. An eccentric, probably. Maybe a full-blown nut. Walter locked his gaze on the roses and marched straight ahead.

"I saw what you did," said the stranger, voice edged with indignation.

"Fellow had Blue Nile," Walter explained. The sun beat against his face like a hortator pounding a drum on a Roman galley. "It was an act of mercy. Hey, Abe, the Fourth of July was yesterday. Why the getup?"

"Yesterday is never too late," said the stranger cryptically, pulling a yellowed sheaf from his vest. "Never too late," he repeated as, swathed in the hot, buttery light, he neatly ripped the document in half.

For Walter Sherman, pummeled by the heat, grieving for his lost slave, wearied by the imperatives of mercy, the world now became a swamp, an all-enveloping mire blurring the stranger's methodical progress toward McDonald's. An odd evening was coming, Walter sensed, with odder days to follow, days in which all the earth's stable things would be wrenched from their moorings and unbolted from their bases. Here and now, standing on the crisp border between the fairway and the putting green, Walter apprehended this discomforting future.

He felt it more emphatically as, eyes swirling, heart shivering, brain drifting in a sea of insane light, he staggered toward the roses.

And he knew it with a knife-sharp certainty as, searching through the rough, he found not Jimmy's corpse but only the warm hulk of a humanoid machine, prostrate in the dusk, afloat in the slick oily fluid leaking from its broken brow.

ANOTHER GODDAMNED SHOWBOAT

Barry N. Malzberg

"**M**ontmartre," Hemingway said to Hadley. "We've got to go there, try something different. Barcelona, the running of the bulls, maybe. Got to get out of here; can't take it any more. Scott has really thrown a wrench. All of it a stink, an ooze—"

This was during the period when he was still writing science fiction, desperately trying to slip something by long distance past Campbell or at least Alden H. Norton, but nothing, *nothing* was connecting there and, despairingly, Hemingway was thinking of going back to westerns or maybe trying *Black Mask*. Stubborn old Cap Shaw with his special rules. At the moment it was geographic change which enticed him. "We'll take a peek south at Lisbon. After Lisbon, we can go back to Portugal."

"*Lisbon is* in Portugal," Hadley said. She had been beside him, old girl, for more than twenty years of this craperoo, had kept faith, kept things together with odd jobs and unmentionable duties but now, even as she still humored him, constraint seemed to radiate from her to say nothing of a certain lofty disdain. Hadley was running out of patience, of attitude. "Portugal and Spain are separate countries, Hem. They aren't the same. Pretty close together, though."

"Just a slip of the tongue," he said, embarrassed. "I know geography."

Campbell was bouncing everything, it all was coming back. A novelette in the post today, still reeking of the damp hold in which the envelope had spent weeks. Alternate worlds, immortality, far galaxies, extrapolations of robot technology: Hemingway was trying the whole range but the stuff was getting through only far enough to inspire mean little handwritten notes: *No constellations around Antares* or *Overstocked on robots*. All right, perhaps it was a foolish idea to try something as insular as science fiction from across the ocean but soon enough all the money would run out and that would be the end of this last desperate plan of his. Meanwhile, it helped to sit around the cafe and plan an itinerary. Science fiction or pseudo-science as they called it was probably the last shot before he packed in the whole thing, sailed home in disgrace, went crawling to some hot little country weekly, begging for a chance to run type.

"Pretty good, this new *Story*," Hadley said, showing him the magazine. It had come in on the boat with the rejections. "This Saroyan is a prospect."

"Don't tell me about Saroyan."

"*He* can do fantasy for Burnett. Maybe you're trying the wrong places; his stuff is really weird."

"It's not fantasy I'm trying. That's for *Unknown*. I'm writing science fiction." Hadley stared incomprehendingly. "They're different fields," Hemingway said. "Sort of. I don't want to talk about Saroyan or Burnett or even writing now. It's not the way to go, I told him that years ago." Indeed he had; the fiftieth rejection note (he had counted) had caused Hemingway to finally lose patience and he had written Burnett a letter which still made him blush. He looked at the manuscript on his lap, resisted the impulse to crumple it. "It's all an inside job for Burnett, people he meets at parties or sleeps with."

Hadley shrugged. They had been through this, of course. "Algren, Farrell, Fuchs, Saroyan, he can't be sleeping with them *all*, can he? You gave up too soon; you should have kept trying."

"For five years. Papers in and out, papers on the boat—"

"Joyce paid to publish *Finnegan's Wake*. *Ulysses* was banned—"

"Am I to answer that?" He clutched the manuscript, stood, looked at his still beautiful middle-aged wife through a haze which might have been recrimination or then again just the damned Parisian smog. Conditions here were really impossible; his sinuses were clogged all the time and the French had become evil to Americans. Pseudo-science, of all things. But the detective magazines had been full of fake-tough writing which no man could take seriously and after scuffling around with the Loyalists how could you take *Ranch Romances* seriously? He was in a hell of a box. *Ulysses*. Why did Hadley have to mention that? *Ulysses* was what had broken him, seeing what had happened to that crazy novel, the crazy Irishman. Seeing evidence that the failure and ban had driven Joyce crazy, Hemingway had said: *Get hold of yourself. There is a darkness out there that is not for me.* But the pulps. Maybe that had been a mistake. Maybe it had all been a mistake. So—

"Sit," Hadley said. "Come on, it's too early in the day. Have a glass of Côtes de Rhone, enjoy the mistral. Maybe we'll drift back to the *pensione* for a fuck. And maybe we'll go to Lisbon. Maybe we'll swim the channel. We're still expatriates, we're not supposed to have responsibilities." She signalled a waiter. "Get him a glass of vin ordinaire," she said. The waiter shrugged. "Go on," Hadley said. "It's not *that* early in the day."

"I shouldn't drink before noon."

"But you *do*, Hem. You drink before ten. Why don't you stop fighting the truth? Get him the wine," she said to the waiter. "He wants it." The waiter muttered and turned away. It occurred to Hemingway—with no surge of jealousy, just a dim, middle-aged man's curiosity—that Hadley could as easily be fucking the waiter as not. She could be fucking any number of people. How would he know? How would he know anything? It was hard to keep things sorted out: Scott's heart attack, the war, the trouble with the magazines, they were muddling his mind. Less and less was he here. Vin ordinaire.

He sat, put the manuscript under his chair, took out the latest issue of *Astounding* which Campbell, as either a gift or hint, had enclosed. September, 1941, and there was Asimov on the cover. He stared. "Isaac Asimov," he said. "Look who's on the cover. With 'Nightfall.' "

"Oh?"

"First time, I think. He's a kid, you know. Twenty-one, twenty-two years old, that's all. And he's got the cover."

"I guess that's good," Hadley said without interest. She had been against the pulp markets from the first, had fought with some intensity, felt that no real writer would waste his time with these. Hemingway had tried to explain, patiently, that he wasn't a real writer any more, the last real writer, maybe, had been James Joyce or maybe Geoffrey Chaucer, and look what had happened to *them*. Scott had thought he was a real writer but that was a fatal heart attack. Hadley leaned against his shoulder, stared at the magazine. " 'Nightfall,' " she said. "That's a Daniel Fuchs title. *Night Falls in Brooklyn*, maybe."

She didn't know Asimov from Heinlein, Nat Schachner from de Camp, but she was still trying to be supportive, still trying to be a writer's wife. Ridiculous, Hemingway thought, flushing. Forty-two years old this year, forty-two with a war on, still in cafes, feeling bitter about Saroyan, torn up by Scott's death, furious about *Ulysses* and now *Finnegan's Wake* and trying to cobble up alternate worlds scenarios. Almost two decades out of the country and still not a word in print while kids like Asimov or this new Caleb Saunders seemed to have the formula. Sit down and turn out this stuff and take it as true. Paris is going to fall soon, he thought. I'm going to sit here with pulp magazines and torment and *Der Führer* is going to march right up these streets and clap me away.

The waiter returned with two glasses. Hemingway hesitated, looked at Hadley, who scrambled through her handbag and put a couple of franc notes on the tray. The waiter looked at them one more time and then went away. People were going away a lot now, and not all of them were paid for the pleasure.

"Drink up," Hadley said, "it's not going to stay too good too long."

"Is that a report from the front?"

"*This* front. That's all I know."

He put the issue away. "Scott Fitzgerald had the right idea, that's what I think."

"Don't say that."

"He left with a little dignity. Kept his pride. He picked the right time to check out and there's a whole hell of a lot of stuff he never has to face now."

"I hate to hear you talk like that."

"Hollywood," Hemingway said. "I knew Scott would come to no good; I told him that in '29. I told him to dump that bitch and go out and live a little, didn't I? He wouldn't listen. I told him, 'Scott, that woman is out to kill you unless you kill her first in the only way she knows.' He wouldn't have any of it."

"He was a sick man."

"Not back then. Not that way. I thought I was smarter than him, just like I thought I was smarter than Jim Joyce. I mean, I wasn't banned in my own country or called a pornographer or made a fool of for something that I had written from the heart." He drained the wine, feeling a little sick now, working on the rage, feeling it build in the only way possible to stave off the nausea. The nausea could send him back to pillow and rack but no fuck then for her old man. "But you see," he said, "*they* didn't end writing about robots, trying to beat out kids for a spot on yellow paper at a cent a word. So who was really smart, who had the right viewpoint on things after all?"

"You got out of Paris, before."

"I wouldn't call Madrid a vacation. Or Toledo."

"Oh come on," Hadley said, "enough of this. I'm *not* going to sit around here and listen to you complain before noon. You don't like your life, Hem, change it; if I'm not a part of the change then boot me out or go your own way. But stop complaining." She disposed of her

glass, her fine chin muscles working hard to make her not look like a
drunk, put the glass on the table and stood.

"I'm going to wander down the Boulevard," she said. "I'll be back
in a while. I want to do some thinking. No, don't reach toward me,
don't apologize. Nothing to apologize for. I'm not mad and I'm not
sulking. I'm just getting older and I want to think. Sometimes that
happens when it closes in."

"Goodbye," he said.

She waved at him in that difficult gesture which had so entranced,
had so ensnared him long ago when he and Scott and the others had
been making big plans on this same Boulevard, and walked away. He
watched her go, as fascinated but as detached as the waiter.

Soon enough, like the ambulance and the tanks and the big guns on
the plains, she was gone.

Hemingway sighed, a great sigh, drained his own glass, picked up
the *Astounding* yet again, leafing through it in a desultory way. Heinlein, de Camp, Caleb Saunders. The kid's novelette with the Emerson
quote, his first cover. Must be a big time for the kid. I hope he's draft
exempt, Hemingway thought. I hope they're *all* draft exempt over
there; I hope they have other avenues because there are big plans for
them.

Emerson and the stars and the City of God. Maybe there would be
a clue there; maybe there would be something he could learn. Clutching the gearshift under fire, scuttling on those fields he had told himself that he would learn, thinking of *Ulysses* he had told himself he
would learn, reeling with Scott and Zelda and Hadley through corridors of a different sort, he surely had told himself that he was busily
storing experience, that it could turn out differently. Well, maybe he
had, maybe he would. Was Hadley going to come back?

Yes, she would come back. Like him, she had absolutely nowhere to
go. He began to read dutifully, then with intensity. He *would* learn,
forty-two was not too late, he would learn what he could. Joyce was
destroyed; his novels would not be known. Scott was dead in Hollywood and the darkness was coming. All of the other markets were
closed to him; he could sell nothing. He would learn how to write this
stuff. He would make of himself a science fiction writer. Caleb Saunders had broken in this month, there was always a new guy coming.
The machinery of time would not otherwise wait.

The war was on. The war was coming. Bit by bit, one by one, the
stars were coming out.

LOOSE CANNON

Susan Shwartz

Men prayed me that I set our work, the inviolate
house, as a memory of you.
But for fit monument I shattered it, unfin-
ished . . .

—T. E. LAWRENCE,
Seven Pillars of Wisdom

The whining overhead crashed into a brief silence, and the ground shook from the bomb's impact. The low, heavy vaulting in St. Paul's crypt quivered in response. A thin trickle of dust fell past the bronze memorial statue that the man stood studying. Kennington had done his usual fine job on the portrait bust, which bore the watcher's face: high brow, thick, side-parted metal waves of hair, eyes fixed, Alexander-fashion, on some goal only he could see. Had he really been that young? The face on the statue: was it the face of someone who had not lost youth, integrity, and honor? Then, in the motorcycle crash that he had only now begun to recall—he had lost everything else.

"Except my life, except my life, except my life," he murmured. He would willingly have parted with that before he lost the other things. The man standing in even deeper shadows—his "alienist," the word was—muttered something. The watcher approved neither of the word nor of the idea that such a man was attending him, eager to discuss Shakespeare and Sophocles and the long-secret details of his family: that is, his mother, his father, and his brothers. He had no wife nor child of his own, nor ever would.

Another crash, jolting the heavy pavement. This time, the dust that hid the funeral bust fell in a thicker stream, smelling of mold. His hearing, never good since the blow on his head—*don't strike those bicycles . . . . . . swerve . . . van coming up fast . . . too fast! . . . falling . . . the handlebars flashed beneath his horrified gaze, and he was flying over them . . . falling . . . panic and a horror of pain he could not master . . .*

Light behind his eyes, before them, exploding in redness . . .

. . . as the Turks thrust desperately toward Maan, he rode shouting toward Aba el Lissan, and his camel fell as if poleaxed . . . sailing grandly through

the air to land with a crash that drove power . . . no, it drove the pain into him . . .

. . . must not think of pain, not while the wheel whirred idly overhead, and shouts . . . "Macht schnell! Er ist tot!" *The van roared away.*

. . . Pain is only pain, punishment, atonement . . . don't scream . . . what was that damned silly poem?

'For Lord I was free of all Thy flowers, but I chose the world's sad roses,
And that is why my feet are torn and mine eyes are blind with sweat.'

. . . Not sweat but blood and burning . . .

The rest was silence until the bandages were unwrapped, the knives laid aside, and Dr. Jones' clever, accented voice—*terrifyingly like the voices crowing over his body*—forced him back to life.

Again, the cathedral shuddered at the City's agony. Rapid footsteps pounded behind them. Helmeted and booted for the air raid, the anxious verger approached, as appalled, probably, by the racket he made in church as he was by the blitz. The world might end, but propriety remained.

"Colonel . . ."

Behind him, the man he had learned to call Detective Thompson stirred uneasily.

He and Dr. Jones would want him to leave the cathedral and seek shelter. After all, it would hardly do to waste the hopes and labor of the doctors, alienists, and police who had scraped him out from beneath his ruined motorcycle, then reassembled the remains first in hospital after hospital, then later in the peace of Clouds Hill.

First, though, one more look at the shadowed, somber face, the heroic portrait that, they told him, had stood in the crypt for years. They had pronounced him dead, had praised him, mourned him, missed him. Just his rotten luck that the charade could not be made dead flesh: now they claimed they needed him.

"Play the man," he muttered at the bronze fraud. Turning his back, he walked rapidly, despite his limp from a twisted leg, past sand buckets and tombs, past scribbled placards and worn Latin inscriptions, unreadable in the darkness, up into the blacked-out nave. Light filtered through chinks in the boarded windows, and the building trembled once again.

"A bad one, that," Dr. Jones observed.

Detective Inspector Thompson grimaced, and moved to escort him outside.

He jerked away from the touch on his elbow. In hospital, he had had to submit to the ministrations and hurts of strange hands; he had always hated to be touched.

"Sorry, Colonel." The hand dropped away.

"Lead on, Inspector."

The policeman almost snapped to attention, and the Colonel, as he supposed he would have to be called again, grimaced at his success in shamming leadership.

They walked rapidly outside the cathedral. Sir Christopher Wren's great dome was half shrouded in cloud, half illuminated by red flares and flames, as London burned and shuddered in its fever. More bombs dropped; the ground convulsed; and guns and planes screamed defiance at each other over the crackle of flames and the crash of burning rubble.

Shouts rose to one side, mingling with more feeble wails of pain. He forced his limping body into a run, grabbed a spar, and wedged it, lever-fashion, into the rubble. . . .

"Lumme, 'e's just a littl' un."

"Help me, you men!" he gasped, and thrust his weight and the remnants of his strength against his lever. Thompson was at his side, lending him the advantages of his great height and bulk. The stone began to rock upward as two wardens pounced on the broken body beneath. It whined and moaned, too badly hurt to scream; but its eyes flickered open and fixed on Lawrence.

Had *he* looked like that when the stretcher bearers came for him? A wonder they could patch him up at all.

Pity, worse than a beating, twisted in him, and he laid a careful hand on the dusty, battered forehead. "Steady on there," he whispered, and slipped his fingers down over the man's eyes until they closed in a merciful swoon . . . at least he hoped it was only that.

The ground shuddered again and again, the sky lighting with white and red, slashing through the clouds of burning London. The Great Fire had destroyed Old St. Paul's; would this one perish in flames, too?

"Sir . . ."

He wanted to wait until he knew for certain whether the man lived or died, but he could see by Thompson's face that the detective had granted him all the leeway that he dared.

" 'E looks familiar, don't 'e?" He read the words on a warden's chapped lips, rather than heard them in the din. A siren howled, first one note, then another, like the shrieks of Bedouin wives.

He rose and dusted his hands, waving away thanks and averting his head lest some man with a longer memory decide that he had seen the ghost of a soldier from the Great War, come back to aid his country in its time of need.

Breathing heavily—fifty-odd or not, he had gotten intolerably soft these past five years and more of convalescence—he trotted back to . . . "his staff."

"Lawrence, for God's sake . . ." Dr. Ernest Jones, his alienist, began. Jones was frightened. Interesting. Able to delve into the intolerable muck of a man's thoughts, but afraid of bombs. Well, Lawrence could understand it. He had set a few explosions himself, he and his friends; but the sheer magnitude of this bombardment appalled him.

Overriding the foreign doctor's fears, Detective Thompson leaned toward Lawrence, calmly asking, "Shall we head on over to Number 10, Colonel? The P.M. is waiting for you."

The area around Whitehall had been bombed repeatedly, and Number 10 Downing Street bore evidence of hasty reinforcement.

"They're going to move the offices over to St. James Park by Storey Gate soon," said Thompson. "There's a shelter downstairs, though. Go right ahead, sir."

As Lawrence approached the door of Number 10 Downing Street, it was flung wide, and he walked in ahead of the others. He frowned to himself. After so many years of being an aircraftsman, who saluted and opened doors for his betters, he found it all too easy to walk again through doors held for him, to note and acknowledge the recognition in the eyes of the tired but distinguished men who had been awaiting his convenience, to pretend to ignore the susurrus of whispers, "Lawrence, Lawrence, Lawrence . . ." that heralded him, just as he had ignored the cries of "Aurens! Aurens!" from his bodyguard. But it was all a lie. Those whispers were water in the desert to him.

Never learn your lessons, do you, my lad? You'll have to pay for that, you know, he told himself, and planned to keep that vow a secret from the alienist, who frowned on his habits of penance.

The whispers continued, and he stiffened at their tone. There was no need to pity him. *Was that pride too?* The schoolmen had called it the deadliest of the seven deadly sins. He had forgotten his Milton . . . what was it? *"If thou beest he . . ."* No, that wasn't it. Something about *"Why then, how changed?"* It bothered him that he could not remember. Would all that careful five years of healing come apart, now that he had been summoned?

No doubt of that. He *had* been summoned. The P.M. had plans for him again. Half a lifetime ago, he'd had to beg to get Churchill to release him from the Middle East Department of the Colonial Office.

"This way, sir."

Odd to be called sir again. God knows, he himself would have been glad enough to be one of the spruce messengers who kept Number 10's street floor spotless in uncomplicated humility.

"You'll want to wash up before you see the P.M., sir."

Not a suggestion. Lawrence let himself be steered past a comfortable-looking coal fire toward a cloakroom, a dazzling luxury of thick towels, ivory combs, and the unwelcome brightness of mirrors that showed the thick shock of hair much whitened, the blue eyes paler now, embedded in wrinkles etched by desert sun, sandstorms, and pain. It was too opulent. He washed his hands and waved them until they dried.

Churchill's private secretary, a Mr. John Colvin, waited for him. Harrow and Cambridge, Lawrence remembered; a fine young man with a fine future ahead of him, and probably a place in the Honours list if he behaved with more sense and circumspection than Lawrence had. Odd to see a young man out of uniform.

"Feeling quite fit, sir?" Colvin asked.

Lawrence nodded. "Well enough. How is the P.M. ?"

Colvin grinned. "Shouting about the Lend/Lease program and how the bloody Yanks had better hurry up and get into the war before there's noth—" he broke off, shaking his head apologetically. "Begging your pardon, sir."

Lawrence waved his chagrin aside. He'd heard that word and far worse; used them, if the truth be known, in *The Mint,* so full of oaths that it had had to be printed with holes in the text, as if moths had gotten at a soldier's blouse.

"If Roosevelt doesn't listen to him, he may have more to worry about than the Jerries," he said. He had always valued the company of younger people and was good at getting them to unbend. "Remember, I've worked with Mr. Churchill before. He's a demanding master."

"So he is, sir. But this is my last month on the job. I'm joining the R.A.F. Pilot training."

"Good man!" Lawrence shook Colvin's hand enthusiastically. For once, he forgot to recoil from the contact. "He'd be the last man to hold you back from that." *But, if you had simply wanted to change your*

name to Ross, say, and join up as an aircraftsman, he'd have pitched a fit that
would make the carnage outside look like a picnic.

Colvin led him to the Private Office, through room after paneled
room, past clusters of desks and suited male secretaries. The lady
clerks had been sent down from London; Lawrence felt better for
their absence.

He knocked at the thick, richly burnished door. Not the Cabinet
Room, thank God. This would be private.

"Don't stand out in the cold, man. Come in, come in! I've been
waiting for you!" Churchill's voice, with its lisp and deep intonations,
leapt out of the room, capturing his respect as it always had, tempting
him—*to what? to be Colonel T. E. Lawrence, instead of Aircraftsman Ross,*
or a nameless dead man? To have a future and deeds to do once again?

Not even you, Mr. Prime Minister. Not this time.

Churchill rose to greet him, cigar pumping up and down in his
mouth. Lawrence straightened to attention. Involuntarily, he
grinned. If England were a nation of shopkeepers, here was the bulldog set to guard them, bow-tied, bull-necked, bald head stubbornly
lowered even as he welcomed Lawrence. Hard to believe that the
P.M. was around fifteen years older than he; Lawrence felt older than
God, and the mirrors downstairs had done nothing to dispel that
feeling.

"Come in and sit down, Lawrence. Have you eaten? Drink?" Churchill gestured invitingly at the tantalus. "Tea?"

"It doesn't matter."

"Nonsense." Churchill poured him out a whiskey, which Lawrence
allowed to sit on the polished table beside him. "You're neither a
young nor a well man. We'll have none of these endurance tests of
yours, man. Not when I need you . . ."

There it was. The need. The hope that Lawrence could once again
be the man of the hour—*or the mountebank.* The demand that he accept, do, achieve, when all he wanted, all he ever wanted, was simply
to be left alone.

No, that wasn't true. Once, he had wanted to be knighted and a
general by the time he was thirty. Once, he had wanted to lead a
revolution that would restore self-respect to all the races of the East.
He had dreamed of nothing less; but the kings and diplomats had put
paid to that. He remembered them all, Balfour and Weizmann and
Faisal and Churchill, struggling toward agreement, and failing, after
all the blood, the sacrifices, his own loss of honor and faith. Now he
wanted to be left alone. He felt his hands start to shake, and closed

one around the whiskey glass to still it; he very well knew that the
man sitting across from him would never let him be.

"Is that why . . . ?" Lawrence waved his other hand, encompass-
ing the past five years of medical and psychiatric interventions, the
support and the secrecy. "Is that why you had me saved?"

"Dammit, Lawrence!" *Ah, now the bullying would start.* "I had you
watched, of course. But I wasn't, apparently, the only one. Mind you,
I wouldn't have tried to run you down. It was the damned Germans
did that. And it wasn't I that saved you, either."

Lawrence cocked his head as he stared up at the taller man.

"You can thank Aaron Aaronsohn and his people that you're alive.
God knows, I'm grateful enough."

Lawrence's glass crashed down on the table, almost spilling the
amber whiskey. "Hell! He's still alive? I'd have thought someone had
put a bullet through his head by now."

"No such luck. At least, that's your good luck." Churchill grinned
at him through a cigar stub. "He'd been living at Zichron Ya'akov. In
'retirement,' he called it; but how much can any of that set retire?
When the War broke out, he came back to England via the Orkneys
again, to help Weizmann and the others make Balfour's life a misery."

"The others," as Lawrence perfectly well knew, being the Zionists
with whom Churchill had such staunch, inexplicable sympathy.

"They say they're fighting two wars. One against Jerry, and the
other, as this Ben-Gurion—name used to be Green, but he changed it
—calls it, against our White Paper. Aaronsohn joined up. . . ."

It rankled to owe his life to Aaron Aaronsohn and his lunatic cabal.
He'd met the man in Cairo; the dislike had been instant and mutual.
"Thinks very highly of himself," he had heard Aaronsohn wrote of
him. And when he'd spoken of the Jewish settlements in Palestine,
Aaronsohn could only comment that he thought he was "attending a
Prussian anti-Semitic lecture." Impossible to get through to the man!
There were others in that group, though: best not to think of the
dead.

But Churchill was watching him with that terrible shrewdness that
Lawrence remembered.

"What does Aaronsohn want of me?"

"You? What he wants of everyone. A homeland for the Jews in
Palestine. God knows, they need something. Weizmann's got proof
that Hitler's rounding them up and exterminating them. Like the
Armenians in the last war, but on a grander scale, damn the Nazis'
efficiency. Goebbels is in on it."

Lawrence grimaced. "I speak German, but I'm no assassin. Aaronsohn saved my life for no purpose."

"Not what he thinks. Nor what I think. I've always thought that some overpowering need would draw you from the modest path you chose to tread and set you once again in full action at the center of memorable events."

Now, that sounded like one of Churchill's better speeches. Lawrence suppressed an urge to applaud that surely would have provoked one of the P.M.'s better rages.

"Begging your pardon, sir, but no. All I want is to be left in peace. Left alone."

"Lawrence, in plain talk, we need you. England needs you. While you were . . . convalescing out at Clouds Hill, men have been dying in North Africa. Hitler's got a general out there we don't seem able to get the better of. Rommel. They don't call him the Desert Fox for nothing."

Rommel. Papers and books had been full of the stories of the middle-aged Swabian general, no Prussian or Junker, but from a staunch middle-class family and loyal past death to his country. Rommel. Lawrence had found himself fascinated even by the name, which tolled like a bell, hailing him back from peace to the very plots and bustle that he feared.

"No one knows the desert better than you, Lawrence. Or the way a desert fighter's mind works. The Arabs have turned against us, by and large, but there's the Berbers. We want you to go out and—"

"And what?" Abruptly, Lawrence felt himself go pale with rage. "Be that clown in the pantos that they call 'Lawrence of Arabia,' all white robes, headcloth, and bathos? Lead the Berbers as if they're Arabs? Well, they're not. They're a different cat altogether out in Libya. It's not as if they're all wogs with funny-sounding names."

Churchill shook his head, grinning more openly, and with great satisfaction. "So you can still be baited, can you?

"Berbers," he went on, "or Ageyli, Harithi, or Howeitat, Lawrence; we need you. Talk to them. Lead them; back to us, if you can; away from the Eighth Army, if you can't. And we need to pit you against Rommel before he launches his final attack on Tobruk."

"You expect me to assassinate him for you?" Lawrence raised an eyebrow. "By your good offices, I've been raised from the dead, so now you want me to work you a miracle and kill—"

"I know. You're no assassin. And his skill in the desert is uncanny. But if anyone can match him at that, it's you. You'll know how to intercept him. Kill him if you can. Or, if you're feeling like a miracle, try to meet him." Churchill paused and drew reflectively on his cigar, and Lawrence suppressed a perverse desire to cough. "Talk to him. Dear God, if you could *turn* him—"

"Against Germany? That won't happen."

"Not against Germany. Against Hitler. Promise him what you must. We can worry about payment later."

"I've heard," Lawrence whispered, "they're trying to build a Reich that will last a thousand years."

"It's lasted too long already! Hell, *give* him Paree; what do I care, so long as he's stopped. But dead is safer. In fact—" He broke off. "You'll be briefed here and in Cairo."

Lawrence shook his head. "I haven't got it in me."

Churchill smiled and bit down on his cigar. "I knew you'd say that."

"How if I say 'no,' too, while I'm being so predictable? Sir."

"You can't, Lawrence," Churchill told him. For the first time in their conversation, he looked away. If such a thing were possible, Lawrence would have sworn he looked embarrassed and ashamed.

"Why not?" asked Lawrence. "After all, I'm supposed to be dead, aren't I? I've just come from seeing my own effigy in St. Paul's. You must have had to close down the City for that memorial service."

"Not quite," said Churchill. "Disinformation is an old game. Rommel wouldn't be surprised if you turned up; half the fortune-tellers in Soho think that you're not dead but 'in another place.' You know your *Morte d'Arthur* better than I do."

"It's not going to happen." Lawrence pressed his hand against the table. "I'm not going to appear melodramatically at the hour of Britain's greatest need—"

"Which this is."

"Let me join the service again. Let me repair engines. Anything but this."

"No."

"Then I cannot help you," Lawrence told the Prime Minister. Resisting him was harder than Lawrence had believed possible.

"I am sorry, Lawrence. You don't have a choice." Churchill reached for a folder among the heaps of folders, books, papers on his vast desk. "There. Read these. And you can't know how I regret having to use them."

The letters all had dates from between 1931 and 1934. "John Bruce," Lawrence muttered to himself. He felt himself flushing. For very shame, sweat poured down his sides . . . *five nights running while he wrote of Deraa, he had had nightmares in which the Bey coughed and the whip furrowed his back, to be shaken awake by his bunkmates* . . . he had persuaded the younger man to flog him, hoping to drive out, suppress the darkness within him, to expiate the disastrous loss of integrity he'd suffered that night.

He looked down, pretending to read the letters that, years ago, he had written, posing as his own uncle. "Does he take his whipping as something he has earned? Is he sorry after it?" He flipped over a page, turned to another letter at random, and the shameful words leapt out at him. "Unless he strips, the birch is quite ineffective. . . ."

"For God's sake, Lawrence!" Across from him, Churchill exploded, his fist pounding on the desk. Despite the cigar, his mouth twisted in pain and disgust. "How could you do it, man? *Why* did you do it?"

He could feel it coming, that horrible hooting laugh. In Damascus, it had earned him a slap across the mouth from a British officer who saw only a bloody-minded, hysterical wog. He forced himself to breathe deeply, to try to control himself.

"The English vice, they call it," Churchill commented. "The results of public school."

Easy enough for a Duke's cousin, educated at Harrow, raised at Blenheim Palace, to say. Easy enough for him to shrug it off. But not for Lawrence. For Ned Lawrence and his queer brothers, a day school had been good enough; the closest they got to Blenheim— assuming they had saved the ready to buy sweets—was on Public Days. The P.M. could afford this aristocratic disgust.

Lawrence looked up. Churchill's contempt would be his punishment. But the man's disgust was for the folder of letters, which Lawrence laid carefully aside. "If I had known, we could have helped you. You see what Dr. Jones is able to do—"

"No one can help me," he said.

"Think yourself some sort of Knight Templar, do you, Lawrence? I'm telling you: you *will* go to North Africa, or so help *me*, I'll publish those letters."

Lawrence choked down the laughter rising in his throat again and knew it for the onset of madness. *The line is 'publish and be damned,' I believe*, he thought. But could he force it out? What would those letters do to his eldest brother, a queer fish of a missionary, totally in his mother's control? What about his mother, who'd lost two sons already and lived like an anchoress, to conceal her sin with the man who was not, had never been her husband? His youngest brother might understand. But what would it do to his family?

Lawrence sighed. "Tell me what you need me to do," he said.

"Thank you, Lawrence. And please believe me. I am truly sorry.

After your job is done, you shall have those . . . letters back. Please burn them. Then we will see what else can be done for you."

"There is one thing that I want," said Lawrence. "Shall I have it?"

"Name it."

"To be left alone!"

"Agreed," said Churchill with such despatch that Lawrence could not believe him. "I will have you briefed. You leave for Cairo as soon as we can assemble a convoy."

"Wait," said Lawrence. A debt remained outstanding: the little matter of his pride as he had entered Number 10 and people had whispered his name. "I would like to thank Aaronsohn."

That would be a fitting punishment.

"Jones said you'd probably say something like that. He and Weizmann are here," said the P.M. He rang for his secretary. Colvin appeared, impervious and unspotted. Pray God *he* never violated his soul—or had to strip it bare—as Lawrence had done. But there was no way of passing that lesson on.

"Show Colonel Lawrence into the Cabinet Room, and ask Dr. Weizmann and Mr. Aaronsohn to join him."

Lawrence rose, saluted as if he were still in the R.A.F., and marched out of the room, aware of Churchill's eyes on his back. Outside waited at least two secretaries, one carrying a dispatch box, the other burdened with books and documents. Both leaned against the wall, looking more tired than the Prime Minister, who was at least forty years their senior.

"That bastard," he heard Churchill mutter in that bulldog rasp of his, all the throatier for the late hour and the many cigars. "That poor, damned bastard."

One hand on the polished conference table, Lawrence waited as if for an attack. His hand was trembling, he saw, and stifled a curse. Of all the times for his malaria to recur! Aaronsohn had saved his life, but nevertheless, he had enough pride left to want to face the man without fighting the sweats, the chills, and the shakes.

Despite his dreams of unifying the races in Palestine, under the technical leadership of what he was awed enough to call the eternal miracle of Jewry, Lawrence had to admit that he had trouble with Jews. With Zionists, most of all. How *did* Churchill put up with the stiffnecked bastards? For example, there was the time when some great, redheaded farmer, seeing Lawrence in his robes and imagining him to be some poor, sullen Arab not quick enough to step out of his way, knocked him down. And then, there was the time that

Weizmann met with Lawrence, Sykes himself, Balfour, and his dead prince Faisal—and argued them to a standstill.

Aaronsohn, though, was a different breed. If Weizmann were a scientist with a cause, as much a catalyst as one of his own chemical reactions, Aaronsohn was, pure and simple, a zealot, and the leader of zealots. Their very name confirmed it, taken as it was from the lines of Samuel, condemning Saul for not having destroyed the Amalekites. *Netzach Yisroel lo yishaker.* The strength of Israel will not lie. Nor, for that matter, repent. Nor would Aaronsohn.

Yet he had saved Lawrence, who wiped the sweat from his forehead and wished for quinine tablets. The door swung wide, and Weizmann entered first, Aaronsohn limping after him. He was still stocky, still reddened, unable even after a lifetime spent in Palestine to brown rather than to redden. He looked almost as Irish as Lawrence himself. Weizmann, bearing the dark complexion and intensity of his Russian blood, seemed far more recognizably Jewish.

"It's been a long time, Colonel." For a moment, Weizmann hesitated.

Lawrence moved forward. "They fixed me up," he said. Reluctantly, he extended his hand. "Nothing will fall off."

Neither of the Zionists laughed, but eyed him with the intensity that he remembered. They stood until standing became awkward, and Lawrence remembered, belatedly, to gesture them to chairs. The silence grew, became demanding.

"I have to thank you," Lawrence said. "The Prime Minister says that you helped pull me out of that crash."

Weizmann was shaking his head. "Better let Aaron explain that."

The veteran leaned forward. "We had you followed, Lawrence," he said. "Just as well, too. That was no crash, but a very well set up assassination attempt by the Germans. We've gotten used to such things in *Eretz Yisroel.*"

Aaronsohn's use of the Hebrew name that the Zionists used for their dreamed-of homeland was, of course, deliberate provocation. Lawrence let it pass. He remembered now; even as he slipped from consciousness, expecting never to wake, he had heard German.

"A bullet or two drove them off, and I sent one of my people to fetch the police. Good thing we were on the spot; if the Germans hadn't set you up, the way you rode that cycle of yours might have been the death of you."

Lawrence looked down. He had always pushed his luck with his cycles, had raced them against cars and planes, had usually won until this last time when he saw two boys on bicycles and made the deliberate decision to swerve abruptly, knowing that at his speed and with the van coming at him, this was one crash he could never walk away from. *Did I truly want to die?* Jones had croaked about that a good deal in the five painful years of reconstruction.

"Germans," he mused.

"Apparently, Colonel," Weizmann said, laying gentle stress on the title, "they believed that you meant what you said about being out of the picture, just as much as Churchill does—or as we do. So they planned to make sure of your death.

"I take it," Weizmann continued as Lawrence sat quietly, sure that he should not divulge Churchill's plans, "that he's sending you to North Africa. No doubt, you've been following Rommel's victories there."

Lawrence shook his head gently. "Only a little. My reading has been . . . carefully supervised."

"You're needed. If there's anyone who can hunt the Desert Fox, it's you."

"You're needed for other things," Aaronsohn said, lips twisting as if the words were sour. "Show him the pictures, Chaim."

So you need me, too? What for, I wonder.

Weizmann reached into his briefcase, pulled out an envelope, and laid it gently on the table before Lawrence. "You said your reading was supervised. Then you don't know what's been going on. Look at these pictures!" The Russian chemist's voice grew husky. "For God's sake, look. They are killing us!"

Lawrence unwound the cord that closed the envelope and slid its contents out. Yellowing copies of major papers from around the world, some dated as early as November 1938.

"I was," he said, "quite out of the picture when these were published. In one hospital or another. But Churchill says—"

"Churchill doesn't *know!*" both men interrupted.

"Pogroms," Weizmann said. "Like my family fled in Russia. Only this one in Germany—they call it *Kristallnacht*—spanned an entire nation and was administered with German efficiency." His voice grated on the last, sarcastic words.

"They want Germany *Judenrein,*" Aaronsohn broke in. "Free of Jews. Only no one will take them in. No other nation. Roosevelt said point-blank that he wouldn't increase the United States quota on Jews; we have no place of our own to go to. So they've found their own solutions to getting rid of the Jews. In Germany and every other country they've entered: France, Poland, Russia, if they win there. Our people smuggled out photos of those solutions. Deutschland'll be

Judenrein, all right, once all its Jews are dead. And then, what of the rest of us?"

The malaria definitely had its claws in Lawrence. That had to be the only reason that his hands shook so and sweat began to drip down his sides. Here was a photo of children packed into trucks; here a flaming synagogue; here, piled high, like cord . . .

"I can't believe we could be so wrong. Not after what he tried to do before the White Paper. But he doesn't care," Aaronsohn whispered loudly to Weizmann. "Look at him sitting there. If they were his precious Arabs—!"

Hastily, Lawrence laid the last photo face down on the table. The pictures showed atrocity, slashed across the face of Europe. It was Tafas after the slaughter; it was the Horns of Hattin; it was Golgotha.

"Jesus wept," he whispered. He would have to believe that even his mother's vengeful god, in whose name she had beaten him, trying to break his spirit, would weep at the final solution that the Germans had found. "Jesus wept." He was shaking now, but not just from the fever and chills.

"Your God hasn't got a monopoly on tears, Lawrence," said Aaronsohn. "I hate to admit it, but we need your help."

"You couldn't have known this in '35," Lawrence mused.

"We knew *something*."

Against his will, he turned over the ghastly file of pictures and headlines, forced himself to study them. He could have the flesh lashed from his bones (though he flushed with shame to think that Churchill knew of that), could spend his life in penance, could live like an anchorite in Sinai; and nothing would make a difference in the face of such universal suffering.

"In a civilized age!" he protested in a whisper and heard Aaronsohn laugh painfully. He wanted to believe that these documents were forged, that civilized people—even Germans—could not wreak such horrors on their fellow men; he wanted to deny that he had ever seen them. But he could not.

"Stop Rommel, and you break the back of Germany's power in North Africa," Aaronsohn said, offering him the solace of direct action.

Only he felt the shakes spread out from his center, to take possession of his whole body. He sagged against the table, sweating forehead pressed on the cool wood near the scattered photos and clippings. "The man's sick," Weizmann said. "I'll ring—"

"It's malaria," Aaronsohn said. "You don't spend the time he's spent in the East without getting it. Here, Lawrence. Forget your quinine along with your guts?"

The familiar bitterness of quinine filled his mouth. He took the glass that Weizmann filled, holding it carefully in both hands.

"Churchill wants you to stop Rommel," Weizmann said. "You're not likely to meet him, army to army—"

"That's not how desert wars are fought," Lawrence muttered.

Aaronsohn broke in, his violent enthusiasms making him seem much younger than his age, which was close to the Prime Minister's. "It would be better to *turn* him. He's like you, Lawrence. Enslaved to an idea, in this case the idea of a thousand-year Reich. Does he know what his masters are doing? *Show* him, and he'll know what his choices are. He'll have to."

"Like me? You overestimate us both, I'm afraid."

"That's not what my sister said."

For the second time that night, Lawrence fought to stifle a hoot of laughter that would have gotten him punched in the face. Sarah Aaronsohn, Aaron's younger sister, who had taken command of his people while he was agitating in Europe. He had met her once or twice . . . in Cairo and Jerusalem; met her and been struck not just by her zeal, which matched her brother's for fervor, or her brains (which were far better), but by the power, the special charisma that she possessed. Blue-eyed, blonde, an Artemis or a Deborah of a woman, she had fascinated all who had come into contact with her.

Only the Turks had resisted her. They had beaten her and her sixty-five-year-old father savagely. Afterward, she had stolen a pistol and shot herself. She was twenty-seven, the whole of life before her; and it had taken her four days to die, and weeks for the news to reach her brother and the rest of the western world. Years later, after Deraa, Lawrence had remembered her. *She* had not feared to sacrifice her life; all he had managed was to retch and beg for mercy. Yes, and steal corrosive sublimate to use if he were recaptured.

Aaronsohn stared narrowly at Lawrence. *Were they true, those rumors?* Again, Lawrence fought not to giggle. He had proposed marriage once in his life, and the woman had laughed at him, had become engaged to his brother Will, also dead now in the War. He was not a man for women, not that way. Lawrence shook his head. *Would you want your sister to marry one?* The question became a terrible irony.

"I didn't think so," Aaronsohn muttered. "Too much in love with pain, or—"

Weizmann laid a hand on his arm, cautioning him. Aaronsohn

shook it off. "Bygones are bygones, Chaim. We need him, poor devil that he is."

A particularly strong explosion rattled the windows and the glasses in the conference room. All three men glanced at the ceiling, as if expecting it to collapse.

"That was a close one," Aaronsohn said. "If the Germans' aim gets any better, we may none of us survive the night."

Weizmann opened his gold watch. "It's almost morning. We can expect the bombardment to stop soon. Then it will be time to go."

"Will you help us?" Aaronsohn asked, the hostility gone from his voice.

"I will fight," said Lawrence. "For all of us."

"We would welcome your help," Weizmann said, diffident now. "And your voice, when the war is over."

Will I be alive after the war is over? Will I even want to be? Lawrence wondered. Time to discuss that later.

"The P.M. said I should be briefed. With your pardon, gentlemen, I'll find his secretary and get started." He gathered up the pictures that neither Weizmann or Aaronsohn seemed willing to touch. "By your leave, I will keep these. Study them. *Remember.*" Again, he was struck at how easy it was to be Colonel Lawrence, ending a staff meeting. "I shall do my best for you. You have my word on it."

Weizmann and Aaronsohn were at the door when Aaronsohn turned. "Lawrence?" he called.

Lawrence paused on his way to the windows. No, he had better not lift the blackout yet. And what good was dawn now, in a world gone wild? If dawn were rosy-fingered, as every schoolboy learned when he studied Homer, it was from dabbling in blood. He had seen blood on the sand, dawn over a battlefield; somehow this carnage in a city where the dying gasped their last words in his own language turned dawn into sacrilege.

"What is it?"

Aaronsohn shook his head, almost shy as he seemed to struggle to find words. "Only an old saying I wanted to tell you: next year in Jerusalem."

The door closed behind him.

The big Liberator Commando labored over the Mediterranean, struggling toward Cairo. Its cramped cabin stank of oil and human fear, and the oxygen mask made Lawrence's head ache and red lights go off behind his eyes.

He had been two days in flight for a trip that ordinarily took six days, making short hops between Takoradi, Kano, Fort Lamy, El Obeid, and so on until Cairo.

But "there is no time for safety!" Churchill had declared, and so the Commando, its bomb racks stripped to let its passengers sleep, blanket-wrapped like frozen mummies, on metal shelves, had flown out of Lyncham to Gibraltar. It flew eastward in the afternoon across Vichy as dusk fell. At Gibraltar it acquired its escort of Spitfires. Then it proceeded across the Mediterranean, flying to intercept the Nile at about Asyût. There it would fly north to the Cairo landing grounds northwest of the pyramids.

The plane was freezing, and Lawrence abandoned his comfortless shelf for the observer's seat in the cockpit. The Commando had reached the point of no return, when just enough fuel had been burned to make retreat impossible, even if it had been allowed, when the Luftwaffe arrived. They had expected it. Immediately the Liberator and its guardian Spitfires climbed steeply, above fifteen thousand feet . . . sixteen thousand . . . seventeen—to where the fighters' engines strained to function.

And there the Spitfires turned to dive on the Messerschmitts, while the bomber continued to climb to twenty-five thousand feet. A shot to one suicidal Messerschmitt blew away part of the tail assembly; the German plane exploded (like a Turkish train in smears of orange and black) and the converted bomber bounced in the shock waves. And still climbed. Lawrence had not known that it was possible to be so cold, or to feel so helpless as three of his escorts exploded into crimson horror or spiraled and smoked down into the water with the German planes they had destroyed instants before.

Those deaths are on your soul, he told himself, and ached to lose his guilt in action. Instead, he must sit, wrapped in blankets and strapped like a senile millionaire into his seat and his parachute, breathing cold oxygen through the painful constrictions of a mask, while the plane strained in the thin air toward safety. For moments at a time, he felt no fear; then panic—to die, strapped in, flaming down to crash like Phaëthon into a cruel sea—clutched him, and he despised himself. After all, he owed England and Germany both a death; did it matter if it occurred in 1935 (as the papers said) or now, in the winter of 1941?

I haven't risen from the dead, he wanted to tell the sweating, muttering men who had tended him throughout the trip with a mixture of worship and worry. They were young men, dying at an old man's orders so a middle-aged man (no man at all, if the truth be known) could be landed safely in North Africa to confront another middle-aged man who built his war on the lives of his young men. It galled him that they regarded him as a hero. If they saw those letters that Churchill had extracted from that wretched Bruce, the respect, the awe, even, of those junior officers, would change to contempt.

Best not chance that, not when so much depended on his actually *being* the garish Lawrence that American journalists had created. But he found their solicitude—kindness and concern for the old, sick man —more taxing than his malaria. Which had, in any case, abated, till the next time, leaving a curious lassitude and an even more curious clarity of mind, which the brief, sharp terror of the dogfight had only made more keen.

His mind ranged ahead of the wind that whistled over the injured aircraft, singing descant to the panting engines. After a while, he turned from watching imperfectly understood instruments to reviewing what he had been told.

With fingers stiff in their fur-lined gloves, he checked to make certain that he still had the precious oilskin envelope of photographs that he would take with him into the desert. Topmost was the picture of his quarry. He fumbled the packet out and drew forth the photo: Erwin Rommel, general that was and field marshall hereafter; Rommel with his fox's grin, his ferocity, and the chivalry that seemed so odd and so familiar. They were much alike, in some ways: both middle-aged, both of less-than-average stature; both with a gift for sensing the presence of the enemy and using the desert itself as a weapon; both quite capable of marshaling and moving heaven and earth to compel men to their goals.

And, in the end, it was their names, as much as any army, that won them their victories. A stocky man, a punctilious man with his careful hats and uniforms, his blue *Pour le Mérite* at the throat. A family man, this Rommel, with a wife he rarely saw. Now that was unlike Lawrence. Rommel had a son, too, and professed himself never to be happier than when he was guiding young people. How did Rommel feel, Lawrence wondered, about sending the young men of the crack Afrika Korps out to die?

Well, Lawrence could show him other young people who would have been glad of his protection: the dead of Europe, the lifeless, accusing faces that grinned sightlessly and forever at the camera. *If you can kill him, do so,* Churchill had ordered. *Dead is safe.* But Churchill, as Lawrence had known for years, was a man who well understood the value of inspiration.

What if Rommel could be *turned,* a knife snatched from a killer and used upon him instead? What if, indeed? Perhaps the cold, the exhaustion, and the thin air had spawned this fancy, Lawrence thought. At such times of stress, intellect and instinct fused, and his mind ranged apart from his waking self in a condition akin to prophecy or perhaps madness. If he could shatter Rommel's faith . . . it might even be that Germany would take care of his death. And Lawrence had had a bellyful of causing death.

Rommel, in "Mammut," the armored command truck that was a prize from the British, roved where he would, over the sand, to menace Cairo with his Panzers and turn the waste between the British command and his own into a mine field. What if Lawrence joined the Berbers, traveling lighter and faster, anticipating Rommel's every move until, finally, they could come face to face? It was either inspired strategy, or the ravings of a lunatic; but reason had meant very little in the War thus far.

"Colonel?" came a voice that managed to be deferential and well-bred even through the tinniness of the oxygen. *Oxford*, Lawrence thought, and probably one of the posher colleges. Trinity, perhaps, or The House.

He laid a hand over the photo, almost guarding it from sight. Rommel was *his* designated prey, a relationship and task too intimate to be shared by this young lieutenant with the unshaven face, the red-veined eyes, and the keenness of a man for whom such things were but temporary.

"Yes, Lieutenant?"

"We'll be descending soon. And, see, it's dawn, sir."

His eyes closed in relief.

Dawn flashed on the wings of the Liberator Commando and the surviving Spitfires as they descended. Lawrence blinked hard at the violence of the light. The wings burned silver as the water flowing through black earth toward the Delta and Alexandria—which, even now, Lawrence had heard, Mussolini dreamed of entering in triumph. If Lawrence had anything to say about it, Alexander's city should not fall to such as he.

Cairo. Because of Lawrence's travels in the East and his work in Carchemish, he had spent two years in Intelligence there. There was little there for him, now: not among the Gallicized aristocrats whose daughters collected gold for their dowries along with Paris gowns; certainly not among the English enclave that politely thronged Shepheards, concerned with tea, tennis, and tonic. *For we were strangers in the land of Egypt.* He wondered if that had been his thought, or thrust into his brain by his talk with Weizmann and that zealot Aaronsohn.

Help for the East, or, for that matter, for the world, if it came from Cairo at all, might come from the unknown *fellahin* by the Nile, from whom some advocate might rise as religions rose from the desert itself. For Lawrence, Cairo was a staging point. This war's incarnation of his old service would brief him, equip him, and send him out into the desert.

His hands clenched and his palms were sweating.

To his horror, he realized how eager he was.

The winter rain poured down as Lawrence rode past the border wire into Libya. For the thousandth time, he thought what a dirty war it was into which he had been thrust. Blackmailed—if a man as guilty as he had a right to use the term—blackmailed and sentenced to a war full of whispers. In Cairo, spies of all the powers rubbed shoulders in safety, greeted each other with circumspect nods before retiring to their mutterings.

Lawrence himself was one such whisper. The rank and file might mutter that he hadn't really died in that cycle crash in May of 1935; they were entitled to hope. But it was another thing for him to confront narrow-eyed MI officers, present the P.M.'s authorizations, and watch them nod. "Churchill must be desperate," one man had remarked. Yet even he had stared at Lawrence as at a welcome ghost.

How do you hunt a desert fox? You use a myth, if you can first tame it.

In the end, Lawrence left Cairo almost unnoticed. Weighted against General Auchinleck's preparations of the Eighth Army to defend Tobruk against Rommel, even the appearance of a shadow from the last War was no more than a simple ruse: welcome, if it succeeded, but not expected to accomplish much. Auchinleck, in fact, had snorted and chuffed that the P.M. was pulling rabbits out of a hat again—damned mummery!—but he was welcome to try. He, however, was preparing for what had been named, rather grandiosely, Operation Crusader; Lawrence hoped that it had somewhat better luck than the Crusaders he had chronicled long ago in school.

Unlikely Crusaders, to resent an ally. But that had been the way of it in what Lawrence thought of as "his" war too: professional soldiers might envy his results, but did not trust him. Allenby, he remembered, had handled him with the care that he had used for explosives. Still, he had ridden with Allenby into Jerusalem. Now there was a Crusade!

Once again, he had the sense that knowledge that he needed was being withheld. It infuriated him. For God's sake, what did he care for their games of powers and principalities? His honor, if he could claim to possess any, lay in the safety of the men with him and, perhaps, in any chance he might have to expiate some of the fresh guilt that had gnawed his liver since he had seen the pictures that he carried as a talisman. In the last war he had carried a battered volume of Malory.

Here he was, in the desert he had longed for, yet it was a sea of mud, not the red sand and glowing *ghibli* of the North, nor the vast austerities of Arabia. Nor did he wear the white robes of a sharif of Mecca, but drab and coarse garments, heavier—but not heavy enough to keep out the rain. They clung, leechlike, to numbing skin, draining the endurance from him.

All the stillness that he remembered had vanished. North Africa was full of noises: the sputter of overused engines, polyglot curses, and overwhelming all, the steady rainfall. It seemed impossible that these sounds should ever change or fade.

But one of Lawrence's guards (were they set to spy on him as well as guard him?) stiffened and drew closer. That *had* been a new sound, not the ringing in his ears. He reached for his pistol and slid off the safety.

He had been told to be prepared to encounter friendlies: here, apparently, they were. He was trying to remember the proprieties of greeting Berbers, as opposed to the many Arab tribes with which he had dealt, when the newcomers' leader rode up to him.

Berbers were fined down by their life; this man's sodden clothing outlined a stockier frame. As he neared, Lawrence saw that under the mud, the exhaustion, and the deep weathering, the man's skin was pale and his eyes light.

"Colonel Lawrence, sir?" said this "Berber," carefully coming to not-quite-attention before saluting in the native style. The intensity of his gaze was almost an assault.

Lawrence nodded.

"Thank God, sir! I'm John Haseldon." His eyes gleamed and he all but peered into Lawrence's own, standing too close for English tastes, let alone his own, as Semites always did. Lawrence groaned inwardly.

"What news, sir?" Haseldon asked. "Where *is* Rommel now?" he asked. Cairo headquarters had told Lawrence that he had been in Rome for his birthday, November 15.

"Wouldn't you have more recent news than I?" Lawrence asked.

"He landed safely in Africa, more's the pity. Anwar here," Haseldon gestured at a man indistinguishable from the other riders, "says that he and his brothers have seen him at Beda Littoria."

"We're headed there?"

Haseldon nodded, chewed things over, then spoke again.

"Sir, you've been at Headquarters. Any chance," he asked in a rush, "that Rommel will bypass Tobruk?"

Lawrence shook his head. "None at all."

The Italian General Bastico had argued for it, and Rommel had flown off to Rome to confer with Mussolini. The Eighth Army had men and tanks enough to hurl against the Afrika Korps, but the Afrika Korps had Rommel, man and myth.

Another man might have relished this contest. Lawrence rode with water dripping in miserable rivulets down his *kuffiyeh* and wished that the newcomer wasn't quite so energetic. "It's good you've come, sir," said Haseldon. "Glad to have you here; we can show you quite a nice bit of action."

"Like the whole Eighth Army?" Lawrence asked.

"A little livelier than a major action," said this Haseldon, who wore his native dress with as much ease as once Lawrence had done. "Mad" English, as brave as he was crazy; and with the colossal bad fortune to have come to manhood after the singularly unfortunate event of Lawrence's involuntary celebrity. Haseldon, apparently, lived as a native among natives . . . and behind enemy lines. *God help the bloody fool,* thought Lawrence.

"What have you planned, then?" Lawrence asked, and beckoned Haseldon to ride at his side. The indigs with him nodded, one chief acknowledging a second. Gravely, Lawrence turned to them, saluting in the Arab fashion because Berber courtesies had quite flown from his memory.

"First we ride."

"And then?" If this downpour got any worse, they might as well ride into the sea.

"Cozy little raid on headquarters at Beda Littoria, sir," said Haseldon. "I've been living outside of Rommel's HQ there for quite some time now."

"Is that where we're headed?"

Haseldon shook his head. "First, we head out toward Cyrene to pick up a few commandos that'll be dropped off by sub."

I knew nothing of this! Lawrence thought. For a moment, *The P.M. will learn of this!* thundered in his mind. Then, he fought against the disastrous laughter that could turn too easily into hysterics. *Would I believe someone who claimed to be me, either?*

He fell silent and Haseldon, respecting his moods, was silent until they camped. He and his men crouched too closely together, showing

Lawrence their maps. *Here* was the grain silo, followed by a row of bungalows. *Soldiers there*, Lawrence pointed, and Haseldon nodded, before indicating a larger mark on the map.

"That building, the 'Prefettura,' set back in a grove of cypress . . . that's where he lives. It's dark, isolated."

Lawrence nodded. "So, now what?"

"Now, we wait."

"For the sub?" Lawrence asked. Haseldon ducked his head, and Lawrence waited, testing. Had the man been warned not to confide totally in Lawrence? Who had warned him of that, in any case? In Wellington's words, this was an infamous army, each officer keeping secrets, and no trust anywhere.

The night dragged on as they waited for the rhythmic splashes, camouflaged in the persistent rain, of the commandos' arrival. From time to time, Haseldon stared at Lawrence, then at his maps.

"Was it like this?" he finally blurted, "when you took Aqaba?"

"Much drier," Lawrence observed, and a grin spread across the younger man's taut face. "We had the desert to cross, and we knew that the guns were fixed to face seaward. That much could put our minds at rest. . . ." And curiously, that much was true. "What may have made it easier, though, was that all we faced were some Turks and nameless Germans. Not Rommel."

The younger man gave a quick, relieved sigh. "Waiting's the hardest part," he admitted.

"Waiting for the trains to come was always the worst. You always wanted to push the plunger and explode the track long before it was safe to. Sometimes we did. Usually, we lost those—"

A sharp hiss brought both men around, their hands snatching for sidearms. Three men waded out of the water, and Haseldon started forward. Lawrence found himself tensing, ready to leap forward should there prove to be yet another betrayal . . . but it was all right; they were shaking hands. In the dampness, Lawrence heard names: Keyes, a major, and the men under his command, Campbell and Terry. Haseldon guided them toward what soggy hospitality he could offer, and Lawrence faded imperceptibly among the Berbers.

At midnight, Major Keyes and his team headed for the Prefettura. Haseldon started out of hiding but "Get back!" Keyes gestured. Then he strode forward and pounded on the front door, demanding admission in German, pushing past the sentry.

Two shots were fired, and the house in the cypress grove went dark.

Lawrence reached Haseldon's side just as a burst of fire exploded, filling one room with light as if it were a stage on which a man, mortally wounded, fell, and another staggered. Just in time, Lawrence caught Haseldon's arm.

"Ours?" Haseldon whispered hoarsely.

"Either way, you can't help them," Lawrence warned him. Haseldon was younger, stronger than Lawrence; if he wanted to break free, he was going to, unless . . . surreptitiously, Lawrence drew his sidearm.

"The man who fell. He wasn't wearing a German uniform. They may be dead, dying—"

"Just you hope that they are," Lawrence told him, holding his eyes, which were white and staring in the dark. *Not so heroic now, is it, watching men die for your schemes?* If the man wanted to play desert hero, that was one lesson he'd better learn tonight. "That was the worst part. We didn't want to leave our wounded for the Turks, but sometimes—Shh! Who's coming?"

A dark blotch wavered toward them, and Lawrence snapped the safety off his weapon and readied it—until Haseldon forced the barrel of his pistol down.

"*Wie geht's?*" he called.

"Terry!" The commando's voice shook. "The major's dead. Campbell's down . . . the bastards had guards there . . . but not Rommel . . . he never stays here, I heard."

It was exhaustion, not judgment, in the fugitive's eyes, but Haseldon flinched.

"They say Rommel's near Gambut at Ain Gazala."

Haseldon pounded his fist into his palm. "God, I could kill myself! We've got to get the bastard!"

"He can't stay here," Lawrence muttered, careful to keep his voice down so Terry couldn't hear him. Memories of old retreats came to his aid. "Get him away from here. They had to have some plans for getting the team out. What were they?"

"Right," Haseldon nodded sharply. "Hitler's got standing orders to shoot commandos on sight." He gestured, detaching five Berbers who surrounded Terry and, despite his protests, bore him away. "Take him back to Cyrene, and keep him safe till pickup," he ordered.

Haseldon sank onto the ground, and Lawrence divided his attention between him and the Prefettura. He had played decoy before. What if an old, weary native straggled by to gain information? Given that a raid on the place had just occurred, he'd be lucky if he weren't shot, that's what, he told himself acerbically. For the first time in his campaigns in a Muslim world, he wished for a flask of brandy; Haseldon looked as if he could use it.

"We should leave, too," he hinted, but the man sat, all but unstrung. His courage was all of the quick, gallant kind; eager to act, but equally swift to despair. Rommel was said to be of that sort, too.

Haseldon nodded, and they rose. Seconds later, though, the renewed downpour forced them to huddle into what shelter they could contrive. "The roads will be washed out," Haseldon muttered through chattering teeth. "The *wadis* will be flooded."

"Maybe he'll drown," Lawrence soothed him.

"We've got to do something!"

"We will." Fraud that he was, he knew how to fill his voice—even in a whisper—with conviction. He would inspire, would use this man too to bring him to Rommel. And then what?

He knew now what his own role must be. Somehow he must reach Rommel; must get close enough—no, he did not think that the P.M. meant to turn him into an assassin. This attempt might draw the German out of his lair just long enough for Lawrence to catch his attention. That would be the moment of supreme risk: catch the general's attention, avoid being shot, and then, somehow, convince him . . . of what?

God only knew; and these days, God wasn't speaking to one Thomas Edward Lawrence. *Let it go for now,* came the voice of instinct within him that he had learned years ago to trust. *Wait with the trees, the bodies, the Germans.*

The rain poured down like the Nile from its mountain cataracts, and Lawrence hunched over, trying hard not to think.

Dawn came, then night, which they spent huddling in Haseldon's mean shelter well away from Beda Littoria, then another dawn. Carefully chosen men crept back and forth. The last one came at a run, nearly tripping over himself, almost incoherent with his news. Rommel was sending his own chaplain to conduct the services for three Germans and the dead English major.

"Rommel won't come," Haseldon mourned. "He's got a war to fight."

"So do we, man," said Lawrence. "And the first thing is to live to fight it. That chaplain won't come all by himself. Let's move!"

To the West lay only the shore. Safety lay in Egypt; but between them and Egypt were Tobruk and Operation Crusader. Time after time, they dodged the trucks and tanks that crawled like rats up and down the escarpments, crept past smoking rubble, lay flat as aircraft,

English or German, flew overhead. Their supplies ran out, but—
"Stealing from the dead . . ." protested Haseldon.

"Would you rather starve with your work undone?" demanded
Lawrence, and forced himself to open the first pack he found.

Lawrence had been hunted before; had lived with a price on his
head. But never before had he fully understood what it was like to flee
too lightly equipped and armed to do anything but cower as the armies raged by. Their retreat stretched out, seemed endless, compared
with what now seemed the effortless progresses by truck or beast.
Haseldon's grimy face had long since fined down; his blue eyes looked
like sky piercing through a skull's eyesockets. He was being remade
in this retreat, forged into a man stronger and madder than anyone
would wish for him. Knowing what it felt like, Lawrence would
stand godfather to that second birth. He doubted that it—or he—
would live much longer, unless more luck than he deserved rode with
them.

Their luck held all the way to Sidi Omar, on the Egyptian border.

"Down!" The ground shook. Overhead, shells burst, staining the
afternoon sky with flame and smoke.

"Look!" Haseldon pointed at a lean-to, set up behind an army
truck. Painted on the truck's side was a red cross. "That's one of
ours," he whispered. "Our truck; our field hospital. Thank God." He
let his head fall into his hands.

In whose hands? Lawrence refused to ask. He glanced at the armored
vehicles. "Do we go in?"

"Let's investigate."

Crouching low to the ground, Lawrence dodged around the smoking carcass of a tank. Old scars and surgeries screamed pain at him,
but he ignored them.

A blow thrust him to the ground. He writhed around to grapple
with his attacker. It was Haseldon, his face and body twisting as a
bullet hit him. Swearing hopelessly in Arabic, Lawrence wadded up
his headcloth and thrust it against the wounded man's side, where it
turned red and sodden far too rapidly. Now it did not matter who
controlled that field hospital.

"Bear up, lad," Lawrence whispered. Before he could remember
that he was old, sick, and half-crazed, and that he hated to be touched,
he swung Haseldon's arm over his shoulder and started across the
field toward the wretched hospital. The bursts of light, the shaking of
the ground as each shell exploded—all faded from his consciousness;
his horizons narrowed to the next step, the step after that.

The command to stop came in German and was reinforced with a warning shot and men in his path, barring his way to the surgery. Speaking or looking up might be fatal. He eased Haseldon to the ground.

"That one's done for." The soldiers spoke over his head. Lawrence turned Haseldon's face away, afraid that its pallor would betray them both.

"Just as well. Those Berbers are treacherous little beasts."

"Still, if the English are wasting supplies, we should . . ."

"You can't disturb the surgeons now. They're operating on Colonel Stephan of the Fifth Panzer."

There was a murmur of dismay. "When was he brought in?"

"Around noon. He's got a bad chest wound. Shrapnel. The General wanted the English surgeon, this Major Aird, to put a pressure dressing on it, so Colonel Stephan could be flown out. But the doctor insisted on operating, said Stephan would die if he didn't."

Someone shouted an order in harsh German from the lean-to.

"They want the armored cars to pull back?" the soldier standing nearby demanded. "So the noise won't disrupt the surgery? Maybe we could put up little curtains to make the operating room more *gemütlich*, too."

"*Schweig*; they're operating on one of ours. Tenderhearted, those English."

"What about the natives there?"

"Let them wait. They're worthless."

The roar of engines as the armored cars withdrew made Lawrence shudder. He had hoped that playing the role of fugitive, aiding a wounded tribesman, might win him help from the English surgeons. But clearly the Germans were not going to let him get near the surgery. They were just going to let Haseldon die here, weren't they? And why? Because he wasn't one of theirs. Lawrence thought of the photos he carried, then of Tafas. "The best of you brings me the most Turkish dead," he had said then. Atrocious: the stiffened bodies in the desert; the bled-out bodies in the grave pits; the sight of a man who had admired him dying in his arms. *As flies to wanton boys are we to the gods*, the line ran through his head. *They kill us for their sport.*

Fingers struggled toward his, and he grasped Haseldon's hand as firmly as he might. "Sorry," came a faint whisper.

"No one could have done better," Lawrence replied, "and I'll remember." He heard Haseldon struggle for breath, and drew him closer, holding the dying man's head up until it lolled back, and Lawrence knew that he was dead.

The ground had stopped shaking. Now only the tramp of booted feet, not bombshells, made Lawrence tense. A crowd of Panzer officers was leaving the tent.

"We'll return again tomorrow on our way back into Egypt," one of them told the bloodstained man who accompanied them out of the operating room.

Last of all, as if in defiance of protocol, was a general, not too tall, somewhat stocky, wearing an Iron Star and a blue order, *Pour le Mérite*, at his throat.

Lawrence knew that face from his pictures, from the waking nightmare that his life had long been. He waited until all the others had passed. Then, in an undertone, he called, "Herr General Rommel!"

Unsnapping the catch of his holster, Rommel strode toward him. Lawrence took a deep breath and raised his head, and Rommel halted. His hand went up, and his mouth opened and closed on Lawrence's name.

"So, do ghosts now fight alongside the quick and the dead?" Rommel asked, elaborately sarcastic, in his heavily accented Swabian German. "A fraud, of course."

"I am quite what I seem to be," Lawrence stated in the carefully cultivated German of the Oxford scholar he had once been.

Rommel gestured with distaste at Haseldon's body, half-sprawled over Lawrence's knees. "So I see."

Lawrence grimaced and straightened Haseldon's body on the ground. Any moment now, Rommel would shout for guards to take him away, if he didn't just draw his Luger and kill Lawrence himself. "Apparently, your assassins had never heard of German efficiency. I survived."

Rommel stared down at Haseldon, and Lawrence followed his glance, saw the glazed stare of filming blue eyes, and shut them with a convulsive motion of one bloodstained hand. He had a sudden impulse to pour dirt over the dead man's face. "He was under my command," Lawrence said. "I'd be grateful if he had a decent burial."

Rommel snapped his fingers for the guards to take the body away. "And you, too?"

"Before or after I give you Prime Minister Churchill's message? I'd appreciate a safe-conduct out of here."

"You have my word on it. I would have been disappointed if the English had sunk to using the notorious Lawrence as an assassin or a spy." He glanced around, as if he could see an English regiment about to attack and rescue Lawrence.

"I'm quite alone, I promise you."

"You're dead! Men don't disappear for five years, have funeral sermons preached over them, then appear in the middle of a war—"

Lawrence laughed softly. "Herr General, you are not the only soldier known for being unpredictable. Would you not use your death—or a lie about it—to help your country?"

"What assurances do I have that *you* are not a lie?" Already, Rommel was beckoning Lawrence toward "Mammut," as if he preferred to debrief a spy in private. A junior officer hurried up, waving a message.

"This is war the way the ancient Teutons used to fight it. I don't even know at this moment whether the Afrika Korps is on the attack or not!" Rommel cursed.

His mood had shifted from the ironic whimsicality of a moment ago. Lawrence knew there was not much time. Operation Crusader was keeping Rommel on the run with its very unpredictability.

"Well?" he snapped at Lawrence.

Moving slowly, keeping his hands in view at all times, Lawrence took off his weapons belt. "My word of honor," he said.

Rommel raised an eyebrow, and part of Lawrence agreed with him.

"The word," he went on, hating the theatricality of his words, "of a man who rode with Allenby into Jerusalem at the head of the first Christian army to take it since the Crusades."

Rommel laughed, a sound resembling the bark of a fox. "Crusade! Not precisely my favorite word," he said.

Lawrence shrugged. "Soldiers can only do what they can. We too must follow our orders, no matter how they tie our hands or short us on supplies."

"The Russian front! God only knows how sick I am of the damned Russian front! They want Cairo, Alexandria . . . I could give them all Egypt, but not one man, not one penny for Africa, but that it's begrudged—"

"And sent to Russia?" Lawrence asked. "Germany has some magnificent strategic minds, but Russia? Napoleon foundered there. Do you think that your Führer can succeed where Napoleon failed?"

"Is this what your Churchill sent you to do?" Rommel snapped. "To test my loyalty to the Führer? My oath holds."

"You sound like one of Charlemagne's paladins, off to fight the Moors."

Rommel bowed slightly, in pleased acknowledgment.

"I do not think that this is the same kind of war, do you?" Lawrence continued. "Or even the type of war we fought in '17."

"The war is the war. I follow orders."

But Rommel's answer sounded automatic. If he lost interest now, it could cost Lawrence his life. And if Rommel chose to reveal who had visited him, it could cost Churchill—and England—even more.

"You do more than follow orders," Lawrence said. "You serve your country. We are two of a kind, you know. I was silenced for more than five years, until England had a use for me once more. You . . . you are kept short of men and equipment, praised, but not truly given the honors due you—"

"Let me tell you, Colonel, if this is an attempt to subvert me, it is a very crude one—"

"I didn't cross a battlefield to try anything that stupid," Lawrence snapped.

"What did you come to do?"

"To ask you questions. You say you took an oath to Hitler. Well enough. Oaths should not be broken. What about your oath to Germany?

"Look at this war. Look at how you've been treated. In the name of God, look at the man you call the Führer and the people he's surrounded himself with. These are the men who are going to build your new Empire, your thousand-year Reich. Do you think they can do it? Can you honestly say of Hitler, 'This is the man who will rule like a Charlemagne or Barbarossa'?"

"Clearly, you want me to say, 'No, I can't.' You may proceed. But make it quick. I'm getting bored."

"I gave you my weapon," Lawrence said. "But I did come armed with something else." Moving slowly, praying that his hands would not tremble with the sudden, dreadful fear that chilled him, Lawrence reached into his clothing and withdrew the photos he had carried for so long. "Look at these," he said, and laid them down near Rommel's hand. He was glad to step back; he had not realized that his life still held such value for him.

The general opened the oilskin-wrapped packet and glanced at the pictures, one by one. He was a cool one, Lawrence would give him that, if he could look at those pictures and betray no reaction.

"They could be frauds, you know," said Rommel. "Since when did you become such a Zionist?"

Lawrence drew himself up. "It has never been said of me that I have been a good friend to the Jews," he said carefully. Aaronsohn, he thought, would certainly testify to that. "The pictures are not important because they depict Jews," he said. "It would be the same if they showed Hottentots or Red Indians. What those pictures show is *your* Germany, *your* country to which you swore an oath, committing acts that will make its Reich last a thousand years only in infamy. A criminal Empire! Is that what you want?"

Rommel snatched his Luger from his holster, but Lawrence grabbed his wrist. "It's easy enough to kill me," he hissed at Rommel. "After all, I'm 'dead' already. But it won't kill the questions I've raised. And you wouldn't be ready to shoot me if they hadn't been questions you've already asked yourself. *Do* you approve of the way this war is being fought, or what else is going on? *Can* you honestly say that Hitler is a man of sanity and honor who is fit to rule the world?"

"He holds my oath!" Rommel repeated.

"I remind you. You gave your oath to Germany first. As I did to England."

"And you do this for England?" Rommel asked with heavy sarcasm.

Lawrence nodded. "So I can make peace with myself, as I have not done since the Great War ended. Then it seemed that betrayal was everywhere; and so I left service until now, when I have been offered a chance, perhaps, to even the score."

Abruptly, weariness replaced Lawrence's fear. At this very moment, Haseldon was being shoveled into a grave among his enemies, and Lawrence almost envied him. But he could not rest, not when he had more barbs to place.

"I came in here with as fine a man as ever served with me," he said. "Dead now. Look at your Afrika Korps, General. They fight like tigers. And look at your Italian soldiers. But what about the officers who command them?"

"Shits they are and shits they have always been," Rommel declared.

"And is Mussolini any better? Or the drug addict Hitler has appointed as Air Marshal, who daily kills innocent English children? But you, you are a man of honor, a patriot, serving with such people. Do you truly think that, when this is all ended, they will reward you? They are likelier by far to turn on you for the very thing that makes you different."

"If I were *not* a man of honor, I could almost be a rat," Rommel mused. "As it is, I know I'm going to regret talking with you or telling you that you can have your life, if you get out of here now."

"I'll *have* my life, General," Lawrence said. "But you, you're going to die here. Unless you do what Napoleon did, and Vespasian before him: use Egypt as your bastion, and move north!"

"I said get out!"

"You, though. We could talk with you. If you headed the Reich, you and the Allies might be able to come to some agreement, push Germany's borders out to their old limits or beyond a bit. And we'd have an end to this killing, this stupidity! Remember that, Rommel. England could deal with you. But with Hitler? We'll fight to the last man."

"I follow my orders," Rommel said once again.

"You've violated orders time and time again. Commandos are to be shot; you've let them live. Good God, you're going to let me live. You've already broken your oath to honor a greater one. Honor that oath, by all means! Think about what it means, and what, to honor it as it deserves, you may have to do. Just think; that's all I—all the world—ask."

Tentatively, Lawrence reached for his weapon—*and* the pictures. The gesture was a risk. But he could not cross Egypt unarmed, and he would not leave the photos among Germans.

"I'm going now," he said.

"What will you tell your Prime Minister?" Again, the heavy sarcasm, mixed with exhaustion like Lawrence felt and something that he recognized as indecision.

"I? Nothing. I have obeyed my orders and spoken with you. He promised me that when I had done so, I should go free. You will not hear of me again."

Rommel nodded. "So that is why you want the weapon. Sometimes that is the only way out . . . for such as we." He started to hold out his hand, then withdrew it.

"Wise of you, General," Lawrence said. "Your men will simply think that you have heard your pet spy and sent him about his business. You and I will know differently, though. And, depending on how you act, so will history."

"You have your life," Rommel said. "I will see you out of here. There are armed cars . . . short as we are, we can say that you stole one, unless your *honor*"—heavy irony on the word— "forbids that."

Rommel shouted for a signals officer and a mechanic. "Get me Berlin!" he demanded. "And you, fuel up my Heinkel!"

"But the battle, Herr General—"

"Am I to be obeyed, or not?" demanded Rommel. "Get moving!"

"This much," Rommel murmured, "I can do. I can ask, and I can see."

He saw Lawrence still standing there, a small man in filthy, blood-stained robes, and started perceptibly.

Lawrence almost smiled at him. Now that his work was finished, he felt curiously light, like a cartridge when its charge is spent. At

Rommel's gesture, Lawrence gathered the filthy folds of his native robes about him and stepped down from Mammut.

"That way," Rommel said. "There's the car. Get moving."

Lawrence could almost feel the explosion of a bullet between his shoulderblades as he walked to the car. Behind him, he heard a shout of warning, a command to stop, then a shot—but no pain.

As he started the car, he dared to steal a glance back at Rommel, who had knocked aside the barrel of a Walther P-38 from a soldier's hand.

"I told you not to fire! I gave that man my word of honor that he would have safeconduct out of here," Rommel raged.

The car started with a roar. If it had a full tank of petrol and luck was with him, it would be hours before he ran out of fuel. And then what? Then, somehow, he would join up with the sons of the men he had known long ago, men who would help him cross the desert, and take those damnable pictures to a place where, finally, he might lose and forget them forever. Whether or not Rommel played Faust to his Mephistopheles and turned on Hitler, whether the war had been shortened might matter to the rest of the world, but not to him. He would have begun the penance that would occupy him for the rest of his life.

Aaronsohn's ironic "Next year in Jerusalem" had become an obsession for him. The man had wanted Jerusalem for his people; in death, *these* at least would rest there. That seemed like the least he could do, if he were sentenced to go on living. Rommel had been right to stop him from being shot. Life was a more cruel sentence by far . . . perhaps for both of them.

A LETTER FROM THE POPE

Harry Harrison and Tom Shippey

INTRODUCTION

In the year 865, according to the Anglo-Saxon Chronicle, a "great army" of the Vikings landed in England, led in legend and probably in fact by the sons of Ragnar Hairy-Breeks. In the following years this army wiped out the rival dynasties of Northumbria, killed Edmund, king of East Anglia, and drove Burgred, king of Mercia, overseas, replacing him with a puppet ruler. By 878 all the kingdoms of the English had been conquered—except for Wessex. In Wessex Alfred, the last of five brothers, continued to fight.

But then the Vikings turned their full effort on him. At Twelfth Night 878, when all Christians were still getting over Christmas and when campaigning was normally out of the question, they made a surprise attack on Wessex, establishing a base at Chippenham, and according to the Chronicle again driving many Englishmen overseas and compelling others to submit. Alfred was forced to go into hiding and conduct a guerrilla campaign "with a small force, through the woods and the fastnesses of the fens." It was at this time that—so the story goes—he was reduced to sheltering in a peasant's hut, where immersed in his problems he burnt the goodwife's cakes and was violently rebuked for it.

Yet Alfred managed somehow to stay alive, keep on fighting, and arrange for the army of Wessex to be gathered under the Vikings' noses. He then, quite against the odds, defeated the "great army" decisively, and finally made a master stroke of statesmanship. He treated the Viking king Guthrum with great forbearance, converted him to Christianity, and became his godfather. This set up a reasonable relationship between English and Vikings, gave Wessex security, and became the basis for the later reconquest of all England by Alfred's son, grandson and later descendants (of whom Queen Elizabeth II is one).

Many historians have noted that if Alfred had not held on in the winter of early 878, England would have become a Viking state, and the international

*language of the world would presumably now be a form of Danish. Yet there is
another possibility.*

*By 878 Alfred and Wessex stood for Christianity, and the Vikings for pa-
ganism. The later reconquest of England was for Christ as well as for the
Wessex kings, and monastic chroniclers were liable to see Alfred as an early
crusader. But we know, from his own words, that Alfred was already by 878
deeply dissatisfied with the ineptitude of his churchmen. We also know that
about the same time Ethelred, archbishop of Canterbury, had written to the
pope to protest about Alfred's extortions—which were very likely only a demand for further contributions to resist the pagan assaults. Pope John VIII
responded by sending Alfred a letter of severe reproof—at exactly the moment
when Alfred was "journeying in difficulties through the woods and fens." This
letter never arrived. No doubt the letter carrier could not find the king, or
thought the whole situation far too dangerous even to try.*

*But what would have happened if the letter had been received? Would it have
been the last straw for a king already isolated, almost without support even
from his own subjects and his own Church? A king also with clear precedent
for simply retiring to safety? Or would Alfred (as he so often did in reality)
have thought of another bold, imaginative and unprecedented step to take?*

This story explores that last possibility.

*Alfred, Guthrum, Ethelnoth, Odda, Ubbi, Bishop Ceolred, the archbishop of
Canterbury, as well as the pope, are all historical characters. The pope's letter
is based on examples of his known correspondence.*

A dark figure moved under the trees ahead, barely visible through
the heavy mist, and King Alfred raised his sword. Behind him the last
army of England—all eighteen of them—stirred with unease, weapons ready as well.

"Easy," Alfred said, lowering his sword and leaning on it wearily.
"It is one of the peasants from the village." He looked down at the
man who was now kneeling before him, gaping up at the gold torque
and bracelets that marked the king.

"How many are there?"

"Tw—twelve, lord King," the peasant stammered.

"In the church?"

"Yes, lord King."

The Vikings were conquerors, not raiders. Guthrum's men always
quartered themselves in the timber churches, leaving the peasants'
huts and the larger thanes' dwellings undamaged—as long as there
was no resistance. They meant to take the country over, not destroy
it. The mist was rising and the lightless village was visible below.

"What are they doing now?"

As if in reply the church door swung open, a square of red light against the blackness, and struggling figures passed across it before it slammed shut again. A female shriek hung in the air, then was drowned out by a roar of welcome.

Edbert, the king's chaplain, stirred with anger. He was lean, just string and bones, all the fat squeezed out by the passion of his faith. His voice loud and resonant, had been formed by that same faith. "They are devils, heathen devils! Even in God's own house they practice their beastly lusts. Surely He shall strike them in the middle of their sin, and they shall be carried to the houses of lamentation where the worm—"

"Enough, Edbert."

Alfred knew that his chaplain was vehement against the heathens, striking out strongly enough with his heavy mace, for all his leanness and apparent reluctance to shed blood against the canons of the Church. But talk of miracles could only anger men who had wished for divine assistance many times—so far without reward. He turned back to the peasant. "You're sure there are twelve?"

"Yes, lord King."

The odds were not good. He needed a two-to-one advantage to guarantee victory. And Godrich was still coughing, near dead with cold. He was one of the eleven king's companions who had right of precedence in every battle. But not this time. A sound reason must be concocted for leaving him behind.

"I have a most important duty for you, Godrich. If the attack should fail we will need the horses. Take them all down the track. Guard them with your life. Take Edi to help you. All others follow me."

Alfred put his hand on the kneeling peasant's shoulder.

"How will we know the door is unbarred?"

"My wife, lord King . . ."

"She is in there with the Vikings?"

"Aye, lord King."

"You have a knife in your belt? Follow, then. I grant you the throats of the wounded, to cut."

The men surged forward across the meadow, grimly eager now to end the waiting, to strike at least one nest of their enemies from the board.

This nighttime raid was a pale shadow of past encounters. Nine times now Alfred had led whole armies, real armies, thousands of men, against the drawn-up line of the enemy. With the war horns bellowing, the men drumming their spears against the hollow shields, the champions in the front rank throwing up their gold-hilted swords and catching them as they called on their ancestors to witness their deeds. And always, always the Viking line had stood watching them, unafraid. The horses' heads on poles grinning over their array, the terrible Raven banner of the sons of Ragnar spreading its wings in triumph.

How bold the attack; how bad the defeat. Only once, at Ashdown, had Alfred made the enemy fall back.

So there would be no triumph in this night encounter, no glory. But when this band of plunderers vanished, the rest of the invaders would know there was one Saxon king still left in England.

As they pushed through the gap in the thorn hedge and strode into the miserable cluster of wattle-and-daub huts, Alfred jerked his shield down so he could seize the handgrip, and cleared the sax knife in its sheath. In pitched battle he carried long sword and iron-mounted spear, but for these scrimmages among the houses the men of Wessex had gone back to the weapons of their ancestors, the Saxons. The men of the sax: short, pointed, single-edged cleavers. He strode quickly so that the hurrying companions could not squeeze past him. Where was the Viking sentry? When they had reached the last patch of shadow before the churchyard the men stopped at his signal and pushed forward the peasant guide. Alfred looked at him once, and nodded.

"Call now to your woman."

The peasant drew in his breath, shivering with fear, then ran forward five paces into the little open square before the church. He halted and at the top of his voice uttered the long, wailing ululation of the wolf, the wild wolf of the English forests.

Instantly a harsh voice roared out from the church's tiny belfry, little more than a platform above the roof. A javelin streaked down at the howling man, but he had already leapt aside. There was a scrape of metal as the Saxons drew their weapons. The door swung suddenly outwards; Alfred held his shield in front of him and charged for the center of the door.

Figures pushed furiously in front of him, Tobba on the left, Wighard, captain of the king's guard, on the right. As he burst into the room men were already down, bare-skinned bearded figures rolling in blood. A naked, screeching woman ran across his path, and behind her he saw a Viking jumping for the ax that leaned against the wall. Alfred hurled himself forward and as the Viking turned back he drove the sax in under his chin. When he spun round, shield raised in automatic defence, he realized the skirmish was already over. The English had fanned out in one furious sweep and driven from wall to wall, cutting every Viking down, stabbing savagely at the fallen; no veteran of the Athelney winter thought for an instant of honor, or display. A Viking with his back turned was all they wanted to see.

Even as relief flooded into him Alfred remembered that there was one task left undone. Where was that Viking sentry? He had been on the belfry, awake and armed. He had had no time to come down and fall in the slaughter. Behind the altar there was a staircase leading up, little more than a ladder. Alfred called out in warning to the milling Englishmen and sprang towards it with his shield high. He was too late. Elfstan, his old companion, stared at his king without comprehension, threw up his arms, and fell forward. The javelin was bedded deep in his spine.

Slowly, deliberately, an armed Viking stepped down the ladder. He was the biggest man Alfred had ever seen, taller even than himself. His biceps swelled above gleaming bracelets, the rivets of his mail shirt straining to contain the bulk inside. Round his neck and waist shone the loot of a plundered continent. Without haste the Viking threw aside his shield and tossed a great poleax from one hand to the other.

His eyes met the king's. He nodded, and pointed the spiked head of the ax at the planked floor.

"Kom. Thou. *Konungrinn*. De king."

The fight's already won, thought Alfred. *Lose my life now? Insane. But can I turn aside from a challenge? I should have the churls with their bows to shoot him down. That is all that any pirate deserves from England.*

The Viking was already halfway down the stair, moving as fast as a cat, not stopping to whirl up the ax but stabbing straight forward with the point. Reflex hurled Alfred's shield up to push the blow aside. But behind it came two hundred and eighty pounds of driving weight. The attacker fought for a neck-break hold, snatching at the sax in Alfred's hand. For a moment all the king could do was struggle to get free. Then he was hurled aside. As he hit the wall there was a clang of metal, a moan. He saw Wighard falling back, his useless right arm trying to cover the rent in his armor.

Tobba stepped forward, his fist a short flashing arc which ended at the Viking's temple. As the giant staggered back towards him Alfred stepped forward and drove his sax with all his strength deep into the enemy's back, twisted furiously, withdrew as the man fell.

Tobba grinned at him and displayed his right fist. Five metal rings encircled the thumb and fingers.

"I 'ad the metalsmith mek it for me," he said.

Alfred stared round the room, trying to take stock. Already the place was crowded, the men of the village pushing in, calling to each other—and to their women, now struggling into their clothes. They gaped down at the gashed and bloody corpses while a furtive figure was already rummaging beneath discarded armor for the loot all plunderers carried with them. Wulfhun saw this and knocked the man aside. Wighard was down, obviously on the point of death. The Viking's ax had almost severed his arm and driven far too deep between neck and shoulder. Edbert, again priest not warrior, was bent over him, fussing with a phial, frowning at the mortally wounded man's words. As Alfred watched, the dying man fixed his eyes on his king, spoke haltingly to the chaplain, and then fell back, choking.

The pirate at his feet was moving too, saying something. Alfred's lifted hand stayed the eager peasant who rushed forward with his knife raised.

"What?" he said.

The pirate spoke again, in the kind of pidgin used by the invaders' captive women and slaves.

"Good stroke were that. I fought in front for fifteen years. Never saw stroke like him."

He fumbled for something round his neck, a charm pendant beneath the massive golden neck ring, concern coming into his eyes till his hand closed over it. He sighed, raised himself.

"But now I go!" he called. "I go. To Thruthvangar!"

Alfred nodded, and the peasant sprang forward.

Three days later the king sat on the camp stool which was all that Athelney could offer for a throne, waiting for the councillors to come to the meeting he had called, still tossing the Viking's mysterious pendant meditatively from hand to hand.

There was no doubt what it was. When he had first pulled it out and shown it to the others, Edbert had said straight away, with a gasp of horror: "It is the *pudendum hominis!* It is a sign of the beastly lusts of the devil's children, abandoned to original sin! It is the pillar which the heathen worship, so boldly destroyed by our countryman the worthy Boniface in Detmar! It is—"

"It's a prick," said Tobba, putting the matter more simply.

It was a token, the king thought now, closing his fist angrily on it. A token for all the difficulties he continued to face.

He had had two dozen companions when they all set out from Athelney. But as they made their long, circuitous ride across Somerset, first one man had dropped out with horse trouble and then another. In darkness they simply faded away into the dusk; they had had their fill of the endless, losing battles. Noblemen, king's companions, men whose fathers and grandfathers had fought for Christ and Wessex. They would go home quietly to their estates, sit and watch, perhaps send discreet emissaries to the Viking king at Chippenham. Sooner or later one of them would betray the secret of the camp at Athelney, and then Alfred too would wake one night, as he had woken so many Viking stragglers, with shrieks around him and a knife already in his throat.

It would be sooner if they heard he had begun to refuse battle with the heathen. Small as the action had been, that night raid had been important. Eighteen men could still make a difference. But why had those eighteen stayed with him? The companions, no doubt, because they still felt it their duty. The churls, maybe, because they thought the heathens had come to take their land. But how long would either motivation last against continuous defeat and fear of death? Deep in his bones Alfred knew that there was only one man in his army, only one man in Athelney, who genuinely and without pretence had no fear of any Viking who ever breathed, and that was the grim and silent churl Tobba. No one knew where he came from. He had simply appeared in the camp one dawn, with a Viking ax in his hand and two mail shirts over his gigantic shoulder, saying nothing about where he had gotten them, or how he had slipped through the sentries round the marsh. He was just there. To kill the invaders. If only the king could find a thousand subjects like him.

Alfred opened his fist and the golden token swung before his eyes, a shining symbol of all that troubled him. First and foremost, he simply could not beat the Vikings in the open field. During the battle-winter eight years before, he and his brother King Ethelred had led the men of Wessex to fight the Vikings' Great Army nine times. Eight times they had been beaten.

The ninth time was at Ashdown. . . . Well, he had gained great credit there, and still had some of it left. While his brother had dallied at the prebattle mass, Alfred had seen that the Vikings were beginning to move down the hill. When Ethelred refused to curtail the mass and leave early, Alfred had stridden forward on his own, and had led the men of Wessex up the hill himself, charging in the front like a wild boar, or so the poets said. Just that one time his fury and frustration had inspired the men so that in the end the Vikings had yielded, retreated to leave a field full of dead, two heathen kings and five jarls among them. They had been back again two weeks later, as ready to fight as ever.

In some ways that day's battle had resembled the little skirmish so recently fought. Total surprise, with the fight as good as won even as it began. But though the skirmish had been won, there had still been one Viking left, ready to fight on. He had cost Alfred two good men, and had come within a hair of ending the campaign forever by killing the last of all the English kings still prepared to resist.

He had died well too. Better than his victim Wighard, Alfred was forced to admit. Very, very reluctantly Edbert had been compelled to reveal what the last words of the king's captain were. He had died saying: "God should have spared me this." How many years in purgatory that would cost him, Edbert had lamented, how little the faith of these degenerate times. . . . Well, the dying Viking had had faith. Faith in something. Maybe that was what made them fight so with such resolution.

It was the English who were not fighting well. That was Alfred's second problem, and he knew exactly what caused it. They expected to lose. Soon after every battle began the first of the wounded would be begging their friends not to leave them on the field to be dispatched when the English withdrew—as everyone knew they would. And their friends were only too ready to help them back to their ponies. Sometimes those who assisted returned to the front, sometimes they didn't. It was surprising in a way that so many men were still prepared to obey their king's call, to turn out and fight for their lands and their right not to obey foreigners.

But the thanes were beginning to hope that when the end finally came they could make a deal with the invaders, keep their lands, maybe pay higher taxes, bow to foreign kings. They could do what the men of the north, and of the Mark, had done. Five years before Burgred, king of the Mark, had given up, collected his treasury and the crown jewels, and slipped away to Rome. The pony-loads of gold and silver he had taken with him would buy him a handsome estate in the sun for the rest of his life. Alfred knew that some of his followers were already wondering whether it would not be a good plan to depose their king, the last stubborn atheling of the house of Cerdic, and replace him with someone more biddable. There was little chance for him to forget Burgred's treachery. Far too often Alfred's wife Ealhswith reminded him of her kinsman, the former king of the Mark.

She had a son and daughter to think of. But he had a kingdom— reason enough for him to battle on. As for the rest of the English, if they fought badly it was not due to any lack of skill or want of courage. It was because they had plenty to lose and almost nothing to gain. Nor had he anything to offer the loyal. No land. It had been twenty years since his pious father had given a whole tenth of all his land in all the kingdom to the Church. Land that ordinarily would have gone to supporting warriors, pensioning off the injured, making the old companions ready and eager to breed sons and send them into service in their turn. Alfred had none now to give.

He hadn't been able to beat the Vikings when he had an army—and now it was impossible to raise one. The Vikings had all but caught him in bed three months before, when every Christian in Wessex was sleeping off the Christmas festivities. He had barely escaped them, fleeing like a thief into the night. Now the Viking king sat in Chippenham and sent his messengers along the high roads. The true king must skulk in the marsh and hope that in the end news of his continued resistance would somehow seep out.

And that took him to the third of his problems. He couldn't beat the Vikings because his men would not support him. He couldn't get his men to support him because their rewards had gone to the Church. And the Church . . .

The sound of challenges from outside told him that his councillors had arrived and were about to be shown in. Swiftly Alfred gave the pendant—prick, pudendum or holy sign, whatever it was—one last look and then stuffed it into his belt-bag and forgot about it. He touched the cross that hung from a silver chain about his neck. The cross of the true Christ. Might His power still be with him. The canvas screen of his shelter was pulled aside.

He looked glumly at the seven men who came in, as they slowly and with inappropriate courtesy found places among the motley assortment of seats he could provide. Only one councillor had an unquestioned right to be there. At least two of the others he could much better have spared. But they were all he had to work with.

"I will say who is present, for those who have not met before," he began. "First, all should know Alderman Ethelnoth." The rest nodded politely to the red-faced heavy man who sat nearest to the king: the only shire-leader still to be in the field, still fighting from a bivouac like Alfred's own.

"Next, we have a spokesman from Alderman Odda." Odda was the shire leader of Devon. "Wihtbord, what know you of the enemy?"

The young, scarred man spoke briefly and without shyness. "I have heard that Ubbi is in Bristol fitting out a fleet. He has the Raven banner with him. My master, Odda, has called out the shire levy, a thousand men at a time. He is watching the coast."

This was news—and bad news. Ubbi was one of the dreaded sons of Ragnar. Two of the others were gone. Halfdan had retired to the

north, Sigurd Snake-eye was thought to be ravaging in Ireland. And
—thank God—no one had heard of Ivar the Boneless for some time.
Bad news. Alfred had hoped that he would only have to deal with the
relatively weaker King Guthrum. But with Ubbi outfitting a fleet, the
Ragnarssons still presented a great danger.

"Representing both Dorset and Hampshire we have Osbert."

Glum silence greeted this remark. The presence of Osbert reminded them that the true aldermen of these two shires could not or
would not come. Everyone knew that the alderman of Hampshire
had fled overseas, while the alderman of Dorset had cravenly submit-
ted to the Viking Guthrum, so could not be trusted with knowledge
of his king's whereabouts.

Almost with relief Alfred turned to the three churchmen present.
"Bishop Daniel is here in his own right, to speak for the Church—"

"And also for my lord the archbishop of Canterbury."

"—and I have further invited Bishop Ceolred to join us, for his
wisdom and his experience."

Eyes turned curiously to the old man, evidently in very poor
health, who sat nearest the door. He was in fact the bishop of
Leicester, far beyond the borders of Wessex. But Leicester was now a
Viking town, and the bishop had fled to what he thought was safety
with the king of Wessex. Perhaps he regretted it now. Still, Alfred
thought, he might at least get some sense through to this overbearing
idiot Daniel, and his lord of Canterbury.

"Finally Edbert my chaplain is here to make note of all decisions
reached. And Wulfsige is present as captain of my guard."

Alfred looked around at his handful of followers and kept a stern
face so his black depression would not show. "Nobles, I have to tell
you this. There will be a battle. I am calling the muster of Wessex for
Ascension Day. It will be at Edgebright's Stone, east of Selwood.
Every man of Wessex must be there or forfeit all land-right and kin-
right forever."

There were slow nods. Every Christian knew when Easter was, if
he knew nothing else. It had been ten days ago. In thirty more days it
would be Ascension. Everyone knew Edgebright's Stone. And it was
far enough away from the Viking center at Chippenham to make a
muster possible.

"Bishop Daniel, I rely on you to pass this message to every priest in
your diocese and in the archdiocese of your lord, so that they can tell
every Christian in every parish."

"How am I to do that, my lord? I have no hundreds of horsemen."

"Write, then. Make a hundred writs. Send riders on circuits."

Edbert coughed apologetically. "Lord king, not all priests may be able to read. True they are pious men, worthy men, but—"

"They read and write quick enough when it comes to snatching land by charter!" Wulfsige's snarl was echoed by all the laymen.

Alfred silenced them with a sharp motion. "Send the messages, Bishop Daniel. Another day we will take up the question of whether priests who cannot read should be priests or not. The day of the muster is fixed, and I will be there, even if none of the rest of Wessex follows me. But I trust my subjects' loyalty. We will have an army to fight the heathens. What I need to know is, how can I be sure of victory—this time?"

There was a long silence, while most of the men present stared at the floor. Alderman Ethelnoth slowly shook his head from side to side. No one could doubt his courage, but he had been at a lot of lost battles too. Only Daniel the bishop kept his head firmly erect. Finally, and with an impatient frown, he spoke.

"It is not for a servant of the Lord to give advice on secular matters —while laymen sit silent. But is it not clear that the issue of all battles is in the hands of God? If we do our part, he will do his, and will succor us as he did Moses and the Israelites from Pharoah, or the people of Bethulia from the Assyrians. Let us have faith, and make the muster, trusting not in the feeble strength of mortal men."

"We've had faith many times before," remarked Ethelnoth. "It's done us no good any time. Except at Ashdown. And it wouldn't have done then if the king had waited for the end of mass."

"Then that victory is the result of sin!" The bishop sat up straighter on his canvas stool and glared round him. "It is the sins of this country which have exposed us to what we now suffer! I had not thought to speak of this, but you force it on me. The sin is in this very room!"

"Who do you mean?" asked Wulfsige.

"I mean the highest. I mean the king. Deny it, lord, if you dare. But have you not again and again imposed on the rights of my true lord the archbishop? Have you not burdened his minsters with calls for tribute, for bridge money and fort money? And when the abbots, as was right and proper, refused to consent to these demands, relying on the charters given to their ancestors forever, have you not given the land to others, and sent your officers to seize church property by violence? Where are your endowments to the Church? And how have you tried to expiate the wrong your brother did, marrying his father's widow in defiance of the laws of the Church and the word of the Holy Father himself? And what of the noble abbot Wulfred—"

"Enough, enough," Alfred broke in. "As for my brother's incest, that is between him and God. You anger me greatly with these charges. There have been no seizures by violence, except where my officers have been attacked. Wulfred brought his own troubles on himself. And as for the fort tax and the bridge tax, lord bishop, the money is to fight the heathens! Is that not a suitable object for the wealth of the Church? I know the charters except Church lands from such tolls, but they were drawn up before ever a heathen pirate set foot in England. Is it not better to give the money to me than to be pillaged by Guthrum?"

"Secular matters are not my concern," Daniel muttered.

"Is that so? Then why should my men protect you from the Vikings?"

"Because it is your duty to keep safe the kingdom committed to you by the Lord—if you wish afterwards to receive the life of the eternal kingdom."

"And what is your duty?"

"My duty is to see that the rights of the Church are not diminished or infringed in any way, no matter what Herod or Pilate—"

"Lords, lords!" It was Bishop Ceolred who broke in, his voice so frail and weak that all stared at him with alarm. "I beg you, lord Bishop. Think only what may come. You have not seen a Viking sack —I have. After that horror there are no rights for the Church, or for any of God's poor. They killed my confessor with ox bones. That dear brave man, he changed robes with me, died in my place. And me they sent out as you see now." He laid a thumbless, swollen hand in his lap. "They said I would write no more lying papers. I beg you, lords, come to an agreement."

"I cannot give away my lord archbishop's rights," said Daniel.

For some time Alfred had been aware of growing commotion in the camp outside. It did not sound alarmed—rather more joyful and excited. The canvas screen was lifted, and the massive figure of Tobba appeared in the gap, the gold ring glinting round his neck, given him by the king as his personal share of the spoil three days before.

"It's an errand rider, lord. From Rome. From the pope."

"A sign!" cried Edbert. "A token from God. Even as the dove returned to Noah with olive in its beak, so peace has come to our dissensions."

The young man who entered seemed no dove. His olive skin was drawn with fatigue, his well-cut garments dusty and stained from the road. He stared around him with incomprehension, looking at the roughly dressed men, the rude quarters.

"Your pardon, gentlemens, lords? I am looking, seeking the king of English. Alfredo, king of English. One of great trust, told me here to seek . . ."

His befuddlement was obvious. Alfred controlled his anger and spoke quietly. "I am he."

The young man looked about rather obviously for a clean patch of earth to kneel on, found only mud, and with a suppressed sigh knelt and handed over a document. It was a vellum roll, a heavy wax seal dangling from it.

As Alfred unscrolled it gold leaf glinted between the carefully scribed rows of purple ink. The king held it for a moment, not knowing what to think. Could this be his salvation! He remembered the marble buildings and great power. He had been to Rome himself, twice, had viewed the grandeur of the Holy See. But that had been many years ago, before his life shut down to a blur of rain and blood, days in the saddle, nights planning and conferring. Now the Holy See had come to him.

He passed the document to Edbert. "Read it to us all."

Edbert handled the document reverently, and spoke in a hushed voice. "It is written in Latin, my lord. Illuminated by scribes—and signed by His Holiness himself. It says . . . it says . . . 'To Alfred, king of the English. Know, lord King, that we have heard of your travels . . .' no, that is trials '. . . and as you, being placed in the life of this world, daily sustain certain hardships, so in like measure do we, and we not only weep for our own—but also sorrow with you, condolens, having sympathy'—no, no—'suffering alas, jointly with you.'"

Osbert muttered angrily. "Are there Vikings in Rome too?" He turned away from Bishop Daniel's furious glare. Edbert read on.

"'But for all our joint sufferings, we exhort and warn you, King, that you should not do as a foolish worldling would do, and think only of the troubles of this present time. Remember that the blessed God will not suffer you to be tempted or, or probare, to prove.' No—'will not suffer you to be tempted or tried above that of which you are able, but will give you the strength to bear any of the trials which in His wisdom He has set upon you. Above all you should strive with willing heart to protect the priests, the men, and the women of the Church.'"

"That's exactly what we are all doing," grunted Ethelnoth.

"'But know, O King, that we have heard from our most reverend and holy brother, the archbishop of the race of the English who takes his See in Canterbury, that in your folly you have oppressed upon his rights and privileges as a father of those committed to his care. Now, of all sins, the sin of *avaritia*, of greed is most foul and repellent among the rulers and protectors of the Christian peoples, most abominable and dangerous to the soul. We do most solemnly therefore advise, exhort, and command by this letter from our apostolic dignity that you do now cease and desist from all oppressions against the Church, and do restore to its rulers all those privileges and rights, especially in the matter of peaceful and untroubled and taxless possession of the Church's lands, which were granted to them by your ancestors, as we have heard the most godly kings of the English race, and even by your contemporaries, such as the most pious and worthy gentleman . . .' The scribe has written the name Bulcredo, my lord, but he must mean—"

"He means that runaway bastard Burgred," snarled the scarred man, Wihtbord.

"Indeed that must be it. '. . . Burgred, who now lives with us in our Holy See, in peace and in honor. So we exhort you to show due honor to your priests, bishops, and archbishop, as you wish to have our friendship in this life and salvation in the life to come.' "

"It is the truth, God's truth!" Daniel cried aloud. "Spoken from the throne of God on earth. Just what I said before the message came. If we fulfill our spiritual duties, our temporal difficulties will disappear. Listen to His Holiness, my king. Restore the rights of the Church. When you do this the Vikings will be destroyed and dispersed by the hand of God."

Anger clouded Alfred's face—but before he could speak Edbert hurried on.

"There's another paragraph . . ." He looked up from the paper to his master with a face of woe.

"What does it say?"

"Well, it says, it says—'We have heard also with great displeasure that our previous orders have not been obeyed. That in spite of the opinion of the apostolic See, the clerics of England have not yet voluntarily given up the lay habit, and do not clothe themselves in tunics after the Roman fashion, reaching chastely to the ankle.' And then he says, well he goes on, that if this vile habit is given up and we all dress as he does, then God will love us and our afflictions will vanish like snow."

A bark of laughter came from the red-faced Ethelnoth. "So that's what's been causing our troubles! If the priestlings all hide their knees Guthrum will be terrified and run right back to Denmark." He spat, forcefully, on the puddled floor. The pope's messenger drew back, not following the quick talk—but knowing that something was very wrong.

"You have no awareness of spirituality, lord Alderman," said Daniel, the archbishop of Canterbury's representative, pulling on his riding gloves with an air of finality, eyeing both his own long robe and Edbert's short-cut tunic and breeches. "We were asking for a message to guide us, and one has come. We must take the advice and the instruction of our father in God. I regard that as settled. There is one other matter, lord King, trivial in itself, but which I see as a trial of your good intentions and sincerity. That man, that man who came in with the message, with the gold ring round his neck. He is a runaway slave from one of my own manors. I recognize him. I must have him back."

"Tobba?" barked Wulfsige. "You can't have him. He may be a churl, he may even have been a slave, but he's accepted now. He's accepted by the companions. The king gave him that gold ring himself."

"Enough of this," Alfred said wearily. "I'll buy him from you."

"That will not do. I must have him back in person. We have had too many runaways recently—"

"I know that—and I know that they're running to the Vikings," shouted Alfred, goaded at last out of politeness. "But this man ran to his king, to fight the invaders of England. You can't—"

"I must have him back," ground on Daniel. "I shall make an example of him. The law says that if a slave cannot make restitution to his master, then he shall pay for it with his hide. And he cannot make restitution to the Church for his own worth—"

"He has a gold ring worth ten slaves!"

"But since that is his possession, and he is my possession, it is my possession too. And he has also committed sacrilege, in removing himself from the ownership of the Church."

"So what are you going to do?"

"The penalty for church-breach is flaying, and I shall flay him. Not fatally. My men are most expert. But all who see his back in future will know that the arm of the Church is long. He must be delivered to my tent before sunrise. And mark this, King." Daniel turned back from the door. "If you persist in holding him, and in your other errors, there will be no passing of your messages. You will come to Edgebright's Stone, and find it as bare of men as a nunnery's privy!"

He turned and swept through the makeshift door. In the silence that followed all eyes were on Alfred. He avoided their gaze, rose and took up his long sword and strode from the room, his face set and unreadable. Wulfsige scrambled to his feet too late to bar the way.

"Where are you going?" called Edbert after him.

"Lord King, let me come with you," bellowed Wulfsige. "Guards . . ."

Behind, in the shelter, Osbert muttered to Ethelnoth and the others, "What's he doing? Will he do what that bastard Burgred did? Is this the end? If so, it's time we all made our peace with Guthrum—"

"I can't say," said the alderman. "But if that fool of a bishop, and of a pope, make him give up between them, then that is the end of England, now and forever."

Alfred strode through the encampment, none daring to obstruct or challenge him, and out into the wet, dripping forest and marshland along the line of the flooded river Tone. But he was not walking completely at random. The thought had been growing on him for weeks that there might come a time when he had to be away from his men, from the crowds of faces looking to him for advice and orders, even from the silent pressure of his disapproving wife and the two coughing, fearful children at her skirts.

He knew now where he was going. To the charcoal burners. They had huts scattered all through the forests, coming out only when they needed to sell their wares, and then returning immediately to the thickets. Even in peacetime kings' officers did not bother them much. People said that they carried out strange rituals and spoke an ancient tongue among themselves. Alfred had been careful to mark one encampment down when he stumbled on it in the course of one of the hunting expeditions he and his men carried out for food, before they had begun simply to levy toll on the peasants round about. He headed straight for it through the winter dusk.

It was dark by the time he reached the first of the huts. The large man in the doorway looked at him with grave suspicion and lifted his ax.

"I wish to stay here. I will pay for my lodging."

He was taken in without fuss, or indeed recognition, when he showed them that he had both silver pennies to pay for his lodging, and a long sword at his side to resist secret murder. The man looked oddly enough at the king's-head pennies when they were offered, as if wondering how long they would be tender. But the silver was good, and that was enough. No doubt they thought he was another runaway thane, deserting his allegiance, but not yet ready to go home or to approach the Vikings' court and sue for amnesty.

On the evening of the next day, the king sat in warm, homely darkness, lit only by the glow of red coals. He was alone in the hut, while the few men and women of the camp busied themselves with the complex operations of their trade. The wife had slung a griddle over the low fire and put raw griddle cakes on it, telling him in her thick accent to watch them and turn them as they cooked. He sat, listening to the crackle of the fire and smelling the pleasant mix of smoke and warm bread. For the first time for many months, the king was at peace. It was a moment taken out of time, a moment when all the pressures outside balanced each other and canceled out.

Whatever happened now, Alfred thought comfortably and lazily, would be decisive. Should he fight? Should he give up and go to Rome? He no longer knew the answers. There was a numbness within where before a fire had burned. He looked up but felt no surprise when the door scraped quietly, and through it came the massive head and shoulders of the grim churl Tobba. He was no longer wearing his gold ring, but trailed his Viking ax at his side. Stooping beneath the low roof, he came over to the fire and sat down on his haunches opposite the king. For a while neither man spoke.

"How did you find me?" asked Alfred at last.

"Asked around. Got a lot of friends in these woods. Quiet people. Don't talk much unless you knows 'em."

They sat a while longer. Absently, Tobba reached out and began to turn the cakes in his thick fingers, dropping them back on to the hot plate with faint hisses of steam.

"Got some news for you," he offered.

"What?"

"Messenger come in from Alderman Odda the morning after you left. Ubbi Ragnarsson attacked. Took his fleet down channel, landed, chased off Odda and his levy. Reckoned they was only peasants, since they only 'ad clubs and pitchforks. Chased 'em into a hill forest by the beach, bottled 'em up, reckoned that was it. That was a mistake. Come midnight, pouring rain, Odda bust out with all his men. Clubs and pitchforks they do all right in the dark. Killed Ubbi, lot of his men, took the Raven banner."

Alfred felt a reluctant stir of interest, an emotion that penetrated the numbness that possessed him. But he still did not speak, only sighed as he stared into the fire. Tobba tried to catch his interest.

"The Raven banner, you know, it really does flap its wings when the Vikings are going to win, and droops them when they're going to lose." He grinned. "Messenger said there were some kind of arrangement on the back, so you could control it. Odda's sending it to you. Token of respect. Maybe you can use it in the next battle."

"If there is a next battle." The words spoken with great reluctance. "I got an idea about that." Tobba turned a few more cakes, as if suddenly embarrassed. "If you don't mind hearing one from a churl, that is, well, really, a slave . . ."

Alfred shook his head glumly. "You will be no slave, Tobba. If I leave, you come with me. I can do at least that. I will not hand you back to Daniel and his torturers."

"No, lord, I think you should hand me over—or the messengers won't go out and there will be no army for you. But that will only be the start of it. I escaped before—can do it again. And there is something then that I could do . . ."

For several minutes the churl spoke on, low-voiced, clumsy, not used to ordering his thoughts and speaking in this manner. But he would not be stopped. Finally the two men sat and stared at each other, both in different ways awed by what they had come to.

"I think it could work," said Alfred. "But you know what he's going to do to you before you escape?"

"Won't be much worse that what I've had to put up with all my life."

Alfred paused one more moment. "You know, Tobba, you could just run to the Vikings. If you took them my head they'd make you a jarl in any county you wanted. Why are you on my side?"

Tobba hung his head. "To tell . . . words, they don't come easy. I been, my whole life, a slave, but my father, you know, he wasn't, and maybe my kids won't be, if I ever have any." His voice dropped to a mutter. "I don't see why they should grow up talking Danish. My dad didn't, nor my grandad. That's all I care about."

The door scraped again, and the burner's woman looked in, her face sharp with suspicion. "'Ave you two forgotten them cakes? If you've burnt them there'll be no dinner for none of us!"

Tobba looked up, grinning. "No fear of that, missis. You got two good cooks 'ere. We been cooking up a storm. 'Ere—" He scooped a cake deftly off the plate and popped it hot and whole into his cavernous mouth. "Done to a turn," he announced, blowing crumbs. "I reckon them's the best bloody cakes ever been baked in England."

It was a reluctant army that gathered at Edgebright's Stone. A smaller army than Alfred had ever led before. Before it grew even smaller word arrived that the Vikings were gathering their own army at Eddington. Alfred was determined to attack before the odds became even worse.

The Vikings had left their camp in the forest soon after dawn and were drawn up in the fields close by. Their berserkers, the fiercest fighters of all, were shouting curses at the enemy as they worked themselves into a rage of battle madness. But the English soldiers stood firm despite the steady rain that soaked their chain mail, and dripped from their helmets' rims. They stirred and gripped their weapons when the wail of the lurhorns was carried by the damp air.

"They attack," said Wulfsige, standing at his king's right hand.

"Stand firm!" Alfred shouted above the thunder of running feet, the first crash of metal against metal as the lines met.

The English fought well, hacking at the linden shields of their enemies, holding their own. Men were wounded, dropped to their knees, fought on stabbing upwards under the pirates' guards. While, from behind the fighting ranks, half-armed churls staggered up with the biggest boulders they could lift, and lobbed them over their companions to crash down on the attackers. There were cries of pain and rage as the stones dislodged helmets, broke collar bones, and fell to the ground to perhaps provide a tripping block for a straining foot.

Alfred stabbed out with his sword and felt it sink deep. But at the same time he saw that his lines were being forced back in the center. "Now!" he called out to Wulfsige. "Give them the signal."

The enemy front rank shuddered and almost fell back when willing hands lifted the captured Raven banner high beside the Golden Dragon of Wessex. Now there was no flapping of jet wings to urge on the Vikings. Instead the Raven's head was down, the wings drooped in death, stitched red drops of blood dripping down from each eye.

But the line held, fought back, pushed forward once again. While to their rear the berserkers gathered, foaming with rage and chewing the edges of their shields with passion. When they attacked together none could stand before them.

At this moment Alfred saw what his opponents could not see yet—and he shouted aloud. Behind the enemy, bursting out from between the trees, came a motley, skin-draped horde. They were waving clubs, crude logs of firewood, tent poles, iron pokers, tools, and weapons of any kind. They fell on the Viking rear like a great crashing wave, striking down and destroying.

For the first and only time in his life Alfred saw a heathen berserk's expression change from inhuman fury to amazement and then to plain uncomplicated fear.

Within a minute the battle was over as the Vikings, attacked from back and front, broke lines, tried to flee, and were struck down. Alfred had to force his way through his own men and their dancing half-human helpers to throw a shield over Guthrum as he was driven to the ground, to save his life and accept his surrender.

That night was a night of feasting. Magnanimous in victory, Alfred sat the defeated Viking king Guthrum at his side. He was silent for the most part, drinking deeply and heavily of the mead and ale.

"We had you beaten, you know," Guthrum finally growled. They were at that stage of the banquet when the politenesses have all been said, and men are free to talk openly. The kings' neighbors on either side, Ethelnoth, Bishop Ceolred, Alderman Odda, and a Viking jarl, had ceased to listen to their leaders and were talking among themselves.

Alfred leaned over the table and hooked away the Viking's wine cup.

"If you'd like me to stop feasting and carry on fighting, that's all right by me. Let's see, you must have three- or fourscore men of your army still alive. And as soon as the others know it's safe to surrender they will all come in. When would you like to begin this battle?"

"All right, all right." Guthrum retrieved his wine cup, grinning sourly. He had been in England thirteen years and had long since dispensed with interpreters. "You won, fair enough. I'm just saying that in the battle, in the real battle, we had you beat. Your center was caving in. I could see you standing in the middle, two ranks back, trying to rally them. When your line broke I was going to send a hundred berserks right down the middle, to get you. I reckoned we'd let you get away once too often already."

"Maybe." After the total victory Alfred could afford to be generous. But in spite of his experiences of losing battles, he thought this time Guthrum was wrong. It was true that the Viking hard core of veteran professionals had forced his men back in the center, but the English thanes had been standing well, with none of the dribble to the rear he had come to expect. Though their line was bent, they were still holding together.

Not that it mattered anyway who would have won. He still remembered and savored the moment when the ragged, badly-armed men had fallen on the Viking rear.

"How did you get them to do it?" asked Guthrum, his voice low and confidential.

"It was a simple idea brought to me by a simple man. Your warriors are lazy. Every one of them has to have at least one English slave to cook for him and clean his gear, if not another to cut fodder for the ponies and help to look after the loot. You've had no trouble recruiting servants, because they have plenty to run away from. All I did was to get a message to them—a message from someone they could see was one of their own and not interested in lying to them. It was his idea to rally them. It was I who told him how it could be done."

"I know the one who did this, who came just a few days ago. They called me over to look at his back when he came in. Very skillful job. Everyone was talking about it. Even startled me. But what message could he bring that could unite these creatures?"

"A promise—my promise. I gave my word that every runaway slave in your camp would be pardoned, would have his freedom, and would receive two oxgangs of land in exchange for every Viking head."

"An oxgang? Why that must be one, or more, of what we call acres. Yes, I suppose a man could live on that. I can see the wisdom of this promise. But where did you get the land from?" He lowered his voice again, looking around out of the corners of his eyes. "Or was it just a lie? All know that you have no land or treasure. You have nothing left to give. Certainly not enough for all who fought today. What are you going to need. Four thousand acres? If you're going to promise them land in my kingdom, I can guarantee they'll have to fight for every inch of it."

Alfred frowned grimly. "I am taking it from Church estates. I have no other choice. I cannot go on doing battle with both Vikings and Church. So I defeat one—and beg mercy from the other. I firmly believe that the land granted by my ancestors was necessarily provisional, and that I have the right to reclaim it. I am breaking up several estates of the Church, and will grant them to these my new tenants. I may have to levy extra taxes to set them up with stock and gear—but at least I can count on future loyalty."

"From the slaves, perhaps. What of your bishops and priests? What of the pope? He will put your whole country under the ban."

Guthrum was well informed for a heathen and a pirate, thought Alfred. But perhaps now was the time to make the proposal.

"I mean to talk to you about that. I think I will have less trouble from the pope if I can explain to him that by taking a little land from a few minsters I have gained for Christ a whole new nation. And, you know, we cannot go on living on the same island and sharing no belief at all. This time I have sworn oaths on holy relics and you on the arm-ring of Thor, but why should we not all in future swear on the same things?

"This is my offer. I want you and your men to be baptized. If you agree I myself will be your sponsor, and your godfather. Godfathers are sworn to support their spiritual children if they come into conflict later on." Alfred eyed Guthrum steadily as he said the last words. Guthrum, he knew, would have difficulty establishing himself again in his central English kingdom after this shattering defeat. He would need allies.

The Viking only laughed. He reached across the table suddenly and tapped the thong wrapped around Alfred's right wrist, touching the Viking pendant he had taken to wearing.

"Why are you wearing this, King? I know where you got it from. As soon as Rani disappeared I knew you had something to do with it. No one else could have bested him. Now let me make you an offer in return. Already you have made bitter enemies in the Church. The black robes will never forgive you now, no matter what you do. They are arrogant always and think only they have wisdom, only they can say where a man will go once he is dead. But we know better! No man, and no god, holds all the truth. I say, let the gods contest with each other and see who keeps his worshippers best. Let all men choose freely—between gods who reward the brave and the daring, and this god of the weak and timid. Let them choose between priests who ask for nothing—and priests who send innocent children to hell forever if their fathers cannot pay for baptism. Choose between gods who punish sinners, and a god who says all are sinners, so there is no reward for virtue."

He dropped his voice suddenly, in what had become an attentive silence. "Between a god who asks for tithes on the unborn calf, and our way, which is free. I make you a counterproposal, King Alfred, king of the English. Leave your Church be. But let our priests talk freely and go where they will. And we will do the same for your priests. And then let every man and every woman believe what they will, and pay what they will. If the Christians' God is all-powerful, as they say, he will win the contest. If he is not . . ."

Guthrum shrugged. Alfred looked round at his nearest councillors, all of them staring at Guthrum with consideration in their eyes.

"If Bishop Daniel were here he would damn us all to hell for listening," remarked Ethelnoth, draining his wine cup.

"But Daniel has gone to Canterbury to whine and complain to the archbishop," observed Odda.

"It is our own doing," quavered Bishop Ceolred in the silence. "Did I not beg Daniel to show moderation? But he had no wisdom. You all know that I have lost from the Vikings as much as any man, and I have been a faithful follower of the Lord Jesus all my life. Yet I, I say to you, maybe no man has the right to forbid another his share of the wisdom in the world. After all that we have suffered . . . who can forbid the king his will in this matter?"

"There is one thing that troubles me," said Alfred. Once more he had the heathen pendant in his hand, and was swinging it thoughtfully. "When our two armies met, mine fought for Christ and yours for the old gods. Yet mine won. Does not that show that Christ and his Father are the stronger?"

Guthrum laughed explosively. "Is that what you thought all the times you lost? No." He pulled suddenly at the pendant he wore round his own neck, undid the fastening, and handed it across the table to the king. "What that victory shows is that you are a true leader. Put down Rani's pendant and take mine. He worshipped Freyr, a good god for a warrior and a stallion, like Rani was. May he live in Thruthvangar, in the plains of pleasure, forever. But for kings like you and me, the true god is Odin, the father of the slain, the god of justice, the god who can say two meanings at once. Here, take this."

Again he held forward the silver medal. On it was Gungnir, the sacred spear of Odin. Alfred reached out and touched it, pushed it about on the table—then touched his chest.

"No. It is the cross of the Christ that I wear here. I have always worn it."

"Wear it still," Guthrum said. "Wear them both until you decide."

All movement round the tables stilled, the very cupbearers and carvers stopping in their tracks to gape at the king. Alfred's eyes, sweeping along the row of faces turned to his, fell suddenly on the anguished gaze of his chaplain Edbert.

In that moment he knew the future. If men were given the free choice Guthrum offered, then all the passion, the faith, the loyalty of Edbert and his like would be of no avail. The bitter, grasping selfishness of the archbishops, the popes, the Daniels, would cancel it every time. With his mind's eye he saw the great minsters deserted, their stone carted away to use in barns and walls. He saw armies gathering on the white cliffs of England, armies of Saxons and Vikings united under the banners of Odin and Thor, ready to spread their faith to the Franks and the southerners. He saw the White Christ himself, a baby, crying forsaken on the last untended altar of Rome.

If he wavered now, Christianity would not stand.

In the tense silence Tobba leaned forward from his place behind King Alfred's chair.

He took the chain in his hand and clasped it round his master's neck. There was the tiniest sound in the silent room as metal touched metal.

Or was it the loudest sound any of them had ever heard?

RONCESVALLES

Judith Tarr

Spain, A.D. 778/161 A.H.

I

Charles, king of the Franks and the Lombards, sometime ally of Baghdad and Byzantium, sat at table in the midst of his army, and considered necessity. He had had the table set in full view of it: namely, the walls of Saragossa, and the gate which opened only to expel curses and the odd barrel of refuse. The city was won for Baghdad against the rebels in Córdoba, but precious few thanks Charles had for his part in it. He was an infidel, and a pagan at that. Saragossa did not want him defiling its Allah-sanctified streets with his presence. Even if it had been he who freed them.

He thrust his emptied plate aside and rose. He was a big man even for a Frank, and a month of playing beggar at Saragossa's door, with little else to do but wait and eat and glare at the walls, had done nothing to lessen his girth. He knew how he towered, king enough even in his plain unkingly clothes; he let the men about him grow still before he spoke. He never shouted: he did not have the voice for it. He always spoke softly, and made men listen, until they forgot the disparity between the clear light voice and the great bear's body. "Tomorrow," he said, "we leave this place. Spain has chosen to settle itself. Let it. We have realms to rule in Gaul, and enemies to fight. We gain no advantage in lingering here."

Having cast the fox among the geese, Charles stood back to watch the spectacle. The Franks were torn between homesickness and warrior honor; between leaving this alien and unfriendly country, and retreating from a battle barely begun. The Arabs howled in anguish. How could he, their ally, abandon them now? The Byzantines stood delicately aside and refrained from smiles.

One voice rose high above the others. Not as high as Charles's, but close enough for kin, though the man it came from had a body more fitted to it: a slender dark young firebrand who was, everyone agreed, the very image of the old king. "Leave? *Leave,* my lord? My lord, how can we leave? We've won nothing yet. We've lost men, days, provisions. And for what? To slink back to Gaul with our tails between our legs? By Julian and holy Merovech, I will not!"

The reply came with the graceful inevitability of a Christian antiphon. "You will not? And who are you, young puppy? Are you wisdom itself, that you should command our lord the king?"

Our lord the king pulled at his luxuriant mustaches and scowled. He loved his sister Gisela dearly, but she had a penchant for contentious males. Her son, who was her image as well as her father the old king's, took after his father when it came to temper. Her husband that was now, barely older than the son who faced him with such exuberant hostility, looked enough like the boy to prompt strangers to ask if they were brothers; but Roland's forthright insolence clashed head-on with Ganelon's vicious urbanity. There was a certain Byzantine slither in the man, but his temper was all Frank, and his detestation of his stepson as overt as ever a savage could wish. He was a Meroving, was Ganelon; they hated best where the blood-tie was closest. What Gisela saw in him, Roland would never comprehend; but Charles could see it well enough. Clever wits, a comely face, and swift mastery of aught he set his hand to. He was not, all things considered, an ill match for the daughter of a king. But Charles could wish, on occasion, that Gisela had not come to her senses after the brief madness of her youth, and abandoned the Christians' nunnery for a pair of bold black eyes.

Her son and her husband stood face to face across the laden table: two small, dark, furious men, bristling and spitting like warring cats. "Puppy, you call me?" cried Roland. "Snake's get, you, crawling and hissing in corners, tempting my lord to counsels of cowardice."

"Counsels of wisdom," said Ganelon, all sweet reason. "Counsels of prudence. Words you barely know, still less understand."

"Cowardice!" Roland cried, louder. Charles was reminded forcibly of his own determination never to shout. Yes; it was almost as high as a woman's, or like a boy's just broken. In Roland, it seemed only a little ridiculous. "A word *you* can never understand, simply be. Where were you when I led the charge on Saragossa? Did you even draw your sword? Or were you too preoccupied with piddling in your breeches?"

Men round about leaped before either of the kinsmen could move, and wrestled them down. Roland was laughing as he did when he fought, high and light and wild. Ganelon was silent. Until there was a pause in the laughter. Then he said calmly, "Better a coward than an empty braggart."

"That," said Charles, "will be enough."

He was heard. He met the eyes of the yellow-haired giant who sat with some effort on Roland. The big man settled his weight more firmly, and mustered a smile that was half a grimace. Charles shifted his stare to Ganelon. His counselor had freed himself, and stood shaking his clothing into place, smiling a faint, mirthless smile. After a judicious pause he bowed to the king and said, "My lord knows the path of wisdom. I regret that he must hear the counsel of fools."

Charles had not known how taut his back was, until he eased it, leaning forward over the table, running his eyes over all their faces. "I give ear to every man who speaks. But in the end, the choice is mine. I have chosen. Tomorrow we return to Gaul." He stood straight. "Sirs. My lords. You know your duties. You have my leave to see to them."

Once Roland was out of Ganelon's sight, he regained most of his sanity. Never all of it, where his stepfather was concerned, but enough to do as his king had bidden. Even before he was Ganelon's enemy, he was the king's man, Count of the Breton Marches, with duties both many and various. Oliver, having seen him safely engaged in them, withdrew for a little himself, to look to his own duties and, if truth be told, to look for the girl who sold sweets and other delights to the soldiers. She was nowhere in sight; he paused by his tent, nursing a new bruise. It never ceased to amaze him how so little a man as Roland could be so deadly a fighter. The best in Frankland, Oliver was certain. One of the three or four best, Roland himself would say. Roland was no victim of modesty. He called it a Christian vice. A good pagan knew himself; and hence, his virtues as well as his vices.

Oliver, whose mother had been Christian but whose father had never allowed her to raise her son in that faith, had no such simplicity of conviction. He was not a good pagan. He could not be a Christian; Christians tried to keep a man from enjoying women. Maybe he would make a passable Muslim. War was holy, in Islam. And a man who did not enjoy the pleasures of the flesh, was no man at all.

"Sir? Oliver?"

He had heard the man's approach. He turned now, and raised a brow. His servant bowed, which was for anyone who might be watching, and met his eyes steadily, which was for the two of them. "Sir," said Walthar, "there's something you ought to see."

His glance forbade questions; his tone forestalled objection. Oliver set his lips tight together, and followed where Walthar led.

Walthar led him by a twisting way, more round the camp than through it, keeping to the backs of tents, pausing when it seemed that anyone might stop to put names to two men moving swiftly in shadows. Oliver crouched as low as he could, for what good it did: he was still an extraordinarily large shadow.

He had kept count of where they went, and whose portions of the encampment they passed. From one end to the other, from Roland's to—yes, this was Ganelon's circle of tents, and Ganelon's in the middle. Turbulent as the camp was, stung into action by the king's command, here was almost quiet. There were guards at the tent's flap, but no one in the dusk behind, where Walthar led Oliver with hunter's stealth, and beckoned him to kneel and listen.

At first he heard nothing. He was on the verge of rising and dragging his meddlesome servant away to chastisement, when a voice spoke. It was not Ganelon's. It spoke Greek, of which Oliver knew a little. Enough to piece together what it said. "No. No, my friend. I do not see the wisdom in it."

The man who replied, surely, was Ganelon. Ganelon, who pretended to no more Greek than the king had, which was just enough to understand an ambassador's speech, never sufficient for speech of his own. Ganelon, speaking Greek with ease and, as far as Oliver's untutored ears could tell, hardly a trace of Frankish accent. "Then, my friend"—irony there, but without overt malice—"you do not know the king. Yes, he withdraws from Saragossa. Yes, he seems by that to favor our cause. But the king is never a simple man. Nor should you take him for such, because his complexity is never Byzantine complexity."

The Greek was silken, which meant that he was angry. "I have yet to make the mistake of underestimating your king. Yet still I see no utility in what you propose. Saragossa has done nothing to advance the cause of its caliph, by casting out the ally who won it from the rebels. His departure is prudence, and anger. Best to foster that, yes. But to embellish it—that is not necessary, and if it fails, it is folly; it may lose us all that we have gained. There are times when even a Byzantine can see the value in simplicity."

"Simple, yes. As that nephew of his is simple. There is a man who will never rest until he has a war to fight. He sees this withdrawal not as strategy but as cowardice. Let him work on the king, let him bring in his toadies and their warmongering, and the king well may change his mind. More: he may turn from our cause altogether, and embrace Islam. You may not see it, but I am all too well aware of it. He is attracted to the faith of Muhammad. It speaks to the heart of him. The sacredness of war. The allurements of the flesh both in this life and in the next. The dreams of empire. And what have we to offer in return?"

"The reality of empire," said the Greek.

Ganelon snorted indelicately. "Oh, come! We're both conspirators here. You know as well as I, that our sacred empress will never consent to bed with a heathen Frank. However passionately he may profess his conversion to the true faith."

"No," said the Greek, too gently. "I do not know it. Irene is empress. She understands practicalities. She knows what the empire needs. If her lord had lived a year or two longer . . ." He sighed. " 'If' wins no battles. The Basileus is dead, and the Basilissa requires a strong consort. Your king has that strength, and the lands to accompany it."

"But will he suffer Byzantium to call them its own? He has no reason to love the empire; he resists its faith, as his fathers resisted it before him. To him Our Lord is a felon who died on a tree, less noble and less worthy to be worshipped than the Saxons' Wotan; our Church has no power where he can perceive it, only a gaggle of half-mad priests on the edges of the world, and an impotent nobody in Rome who calls himself the successor of Peter, and quarrels incessantly with the Patriarch in Constantinople. Simpler and more expedient for him to subscribe to the creed of the Divine Julian, which allows him to rule his own lands in his own fashion, and leaves him free to live as he pleases."

"Divine," said the Greek in distaste. "Apostate, and damned, not least for the world he left us. Our empire divided, the West fallen to barbarian hordes, the light of Christ extinguished there wherever it has kindled; and now the terror out of east and south and west, the armies of Islam circling for the kill. Charles must choose between us, or be overwhelmed. He is the key to Europe. Without him, we can perhaps hold our ground in the East, but the West is lost to us. With him, we gain the greater part of our old empire, and stand to gain the rest."

Ganelon spoke swiftly, with passion enough to rock Oliver where he crouched. "And if he turns to Islam, not only is Europe lost; Byzantium itself may fall. Charles the pagan fancies himself an enlightened man, a man of reason, dreaming of Rome restored. Charles the Muslim would see naught but sheer, red war."

"Therefore," asked the Greek, "you would force a choice?"

Ganelon had calmed himself, but his voice was tight, and grimly quiet. "You are wise, and you are skilled in the ways of war and diplomacy. But I know my king. We are not wise to leave matters to fate, or to God if you will. It is not enough to trust that our memory of Rome will speak more clearly to his heart than the raw new faith of Islam. He is, after all, a follower of Julian the Apostate. As is his hotspur of a nephew—who has been heard to swear that he will never bow his head to any God Who makes a virtue of virginity." Ganelon paused as if to gather the rags of his temper, and the threads of his argument. "Count Roland is a danger to us and to our purpose. While he lives, the king will not turn Christian. Of that, I am certain. He were best disposed of, and quickly. How better than by such a means, which should serve also to turn the king to our cause?"

"And if it fails? What then, my friend?"

"It will not fail. You have my oath on it."

That was all they said that mattered to Oliver. He lingered for a dangerous while, until it was clear that they were done with their conspiring. There was a stir near the front of the tent: guards changing; a mutter of Greek. Oliver beat a rapid retreat.

It was an age before he could catch Roland alone. The count, having recovered his temper, had thrown himself into his duties. Oliver's return, he greeted with a flurry of commands, all of them urgent and most of them onerous. Oliver set his teeth and obeyed them. But he kept his eye on Roland, as much as he might in the uproar.

A little before dawn, when the camp had quieted at last, to rest for an hour or two and restore its strength for the march, Oliver followed the count into his tent. It was not the first time he had done that; Roland looked at him without surprise. "I think you should sleep tonight," he said with careful gentleness.

Oliver blushed. That was not what he had been thinking of at all. He said so, bluntly.

Roland's brows went up. Perhaps he believed it. Perhaps he did not. After a moment he shrugged, one-sided, and went about stripping for sleep.

"Roland," said Oliver.

Something in his tone brought Roland about. He had his drawers in his hand. Oliver could count all the scars on the fine brown skin, the bruises of his struggle tonight and his hunt this morning, and one on his neck that men in the camp called the sweetseller's brand.

"Roland," Oliver said again. "There's something you should know."

And Oliver told him, all of it, word for word as he remembered it. Roland listened in silence that deepened the longer it lasted.

"I may have misunderstood everything," Oliver said at the end. "You know how bad my Greek is."

"Yes," said Roland, soft and still. "I know." His eyes were wide; in rushlight they seemed blurred, as if with sleep.

He shook himself suddenly, blinked, was Roland again. But not, quite, Roland. Roland was a wild man, everyone knew it. Such news as this should have driven him raving mad.

But Oliver was not everyone, and he had known Roland since they shared the nurse's breast. He laid a hand on the slender shoulder, "Brother. Don't think it."

"Why?" asked Roland. "What am I thinking?"

"You know what will happen if you kill your father. Even a stepfather. You can't do it. The king needs you too badly."

"Kill? Did I say kill?"

"Roland—"

"Oliver." Roland closed his hand over Oliver's. "Brother, I won't kill him. Even I am hardly that vast a fool."

"Then what will you do?"

"Nothing." Roland said it with appalling lightness. "Except thank you for the knowledge. And—yes, brother nurse, keep watch against treachery."

"You're too calm," said Oliver.

He was. He was not trembling, that Oliver could see or feel or sense. He looked as if he had learned nothing more terrible than that his third-best charger had a girth-gall. "I'm . . . almost . . . Yes, I'm glad," he said. "I've always known what a snake that man is. Now he lays the proof in my hands. Let him strike at me. Then the king can deal with him."

"And if you die of the stroke?"

"I won't die. I gave you my oath, don't you remember? I'll never die before you. We'll go together, or not at all. And," said Roland, "it's not you he wants, or will touch."

Oliver was by no means comforted. But Roland had heard all he wanted to hear. He flung his arms about his milkbrother and hugged him till his ribs creaked, and thrust him away. "Go to bed, brother nurse. Here, if you will, but I tell you truly, I intend to do no more than sleep."

"Here, then," said Oliver, not even trying to match his lightness.

And he kept his word. Two cloaks and a blanket were ample for them both; and Roland humored a friend. He let Oliver take the outside.

2

Oliver did not know whether to be glad or to be more wary than ever. Days, they had marched. They had broken down the walls of Pamplona, almost for sport, to soothe the Arabs' fears, and left them there with the pick of the spoil. The ambassador from Baghdad lingered, and would linger, it was clear, until the king saw fit to dismiss him or his own caliph called him back. Likewise the envoys from Byzantium. The king was a battleground, and well he knew it; he seemed to find it amusing, when he troubled to think of it at all.

No one had moved to strike Roland. No dagger out of the dark. No poison in his cup. Not even a whisper in the king's ear, to shake Charles' confidence in his nephew's loyalty. All that Oliver had heard might have been a dream. Or the Greek had prevailed, and Ganelon had turned his mind elsewhere, to other and easier prey.

Roland acted no differently toward him. For Oliver it was harder. Oliver was a very bad liar. He kept out of the traitor's path, not gladly, but with every ounce of prudence in him. Ganelon murdered by Oliver was hardly less shocking a prospect than Ganelon murdered by Roland, and equally likely to ruin the Breton count. Which dilemma, too, the subtle snake might well have wished upon them.

Therefore they did nothing, not even to tell the king; for after all they had no proof. The days went on in marching and in encampments, and once the diversion of Pamplona. Beyond the broken walls, where the Pyrenees rose like walls shattered by gods, the army moved a little lighter. There were the ramparts; beyond them lay the fields and forests of Gaul.

It was the custom, and Roland's own preference, that the Bretons with their heavy cavalry kept either the van or the rear. Through most of Spain, Roland himself had ridden first of all except the scouts; but as the hills rose into mountains, the king called him to the center. Oliver followed, unquestioned; the count's milkbrother and swordbrother, as inseparable as his shadow. Already the way grew steep; they had left their horses ahead with their armor-bearers, and taken to surefooted mules. Not a few along the line chaffed them for that;

Roland laughed and chaffed back, but Oliver set his teeth and endured.

The king, who was above all a practical man, had mounted his lordly bulk on a brother of their own beasts. No one, Oliver noticed, even looked askance at him. As always when he was at war, he wore nothing to mark him out from any common soldier, except the circlet of gold on his helmet. He greeted them both with his usual gladness. Neither was quick to match him. He was attended, as always. The Byzantines were there, and the men from Baghdad. And Ganelon, close at his side, riding a horse with an Arab look about the head. The man was all limpid innocence, the loyal counselor attending his king.

Charles beckoned Roland in. Ganelon drew back with every appearance of good will, no dagger flashing in his hand, no hatred in his glance. Roland would not meet it at all. There was a pause while the mules settled precedence; then the king said, "Roland, sister-son, now that the land is changing, I've a mind to change the army to fit it. The way ahead should be clear enough for lesser forces. It's the rear I'm wary of; the brigands' portion. And the baggage can't move any faster than it's moving. I need you and your Bretons there. Will you take it?"

Oliver's hackles quivered and rose. It was a perfectly reasonable order, presented in the king's usual fashion: as a request, to be accepted or refused. The Bretons with their armor and their great lumbering horses would deter anything that a brigand might think of. And a brigand would think of, and covet, the baggage and the booty.

It was not the prospect of robbery that chilled Oliver's nape. It was Ganelon's expression. Calm; innocent. Barely listening, as if the hawk on the wing mattered more than the count in the rearguard.

It was too well done. He should be sneering, making it clear whose counsel it was that Roland breathe the army's dust and shepherd its baggage.

As if he had realized the oversight, he lowered his eyes from the sky and smiled at his stepson. Oliver did not need to be a seer to foretell what Roland would do. Roland bristled; his mule jibbed and lashed out. Ganelon's mare eluded it with contemptuous ease. "You," said Roland. "What are you plotting? Why this change, now, when we're so close to Gaul?"

"My lord king," Ganelon said with sweet precision, "has been apprised by his scouts that the way ahead of us is steep, the passage narrow. He has need of both valor and vigilance, and in the rear most of all, where robbers most often strike. Who better to mount guard there, than the knights of Brittany?"

Smooth words, irreproachable even in tone. Oliver would happily have throttled the man who uttered them. Roland raised his head, his black eyes narrow, searching his stepfather's face. It gave him nothing back. "You want me there," he said. "What if I refuse?"

"Then another will be sent," said the king before Ganelon could speak. He sensed something, Oliver could tell, but he was too preoccupied or too accustomed to his kinsmen's enmity to take notice. "I have reason to think that there may be one last stroke before we ride out of Spain: revenge for Pamplona, or a final blow from the rebels of Córdoba. Will you guard my back?"

Roland sat erect in the saddle, neatly and inextricably trapped. Ganelon himself could have done no better. Roland's voice rang out over the song of wind, echoing in the passes. "Always, my king."

Charles smiled and, leaning out of the saddle, pulled him into an embrace. "Watch well, sister-son. Half the treasure on my wagon is yours to share with your men."

Roland laughed. "All the more reason to guard it! Come, Oliver. We've a king to serve."

"This is it," said Oliver as they worked their way back up through the army. "This is what he was waiting for."

Roland's eyes were bright, his nostrils flared to catch the scent of danger. But he said, "You can't know that. Probably he wants to poison the beer I'll drink with supper, and needs me out of the way to do it. I'll drink wine tonight, or water. Will that content you?"

Oliver shook his head. He could see their banner now, their men waiting beside the steep stony track, held there by the king's messenger. They seemed glad enough of the chance to pause, rest, inspect girths and hoofs and harness buckles. The army toiled up past them. No chaffing now: it took too much breath simply to move.

Slowly, by excruciating inches, the rear came in sight. The men who had been guarding it were pleased to move up, away from the lumbering wagons, the oxen groaning and laboring, the drivers cursing in an endless half-chant. Roland's Bretons fell in behind. They had all, uncommanded, shifted to remounts.

"You scent trouble, too, then?"

Oliver started, stared. Not all of the former rearguard had gone ahead. The Count of the Palace was there, watching over his charge, which was all here but the king himself; and Ekkehard, the king's seneschal, riding on the wain with the royal plate. And, on a horse that had been bred in Roland's own pastures, Turpin the high priest of Mithras in Rheims. As befit the priest of a warrior creed, he rode armed and armored, and his acolytes were also his armor-bearers. He grinned at Oliver, old warhound that he was, and breathed deep of the thin air. "There'll be an ambush ahead. Do you remember this way, when we came out of Gaul? It narrows and steepens, and where it's narrowest and steepest, the gorge they call Roncesvalles—they'll strike there, if they strike at all."

" 'They'?" asked Oliver.

"Basques, most likely: savages of these mountains. Pamplona is theirs, you know; it's not Saracen, though sometimes it suits them to dance to Córdoba's tune. I expect they'll want to claim back what we took from them."

He seemed remarkably undismayed at the prospect. Oliver eyed his greying beard and his eager face, and castigated himself for a fool. If there was a battle, it would be one that they could easily win. If it aimed chiefly at Roland, then his men would make themselves a wall about him. There was nothing to fret over but a few words spoken in a tongue he barely knew, and which he might well have misunderstood.

The steeper the way grew, the closer the walls drew in, the slower the baggage train traveled. The clamor of the army, echoing in the gorges, began little by little to fade. They had drawn ahead. Too far, Oliver began to suspect. There were only their small company, and the drivers, and such of the women and servants as had not gone ahead with their masters; and the wains lurching and struggling up the mountainside. Behind, there was nothing to see but stone and scree and steep descent. Ahead, Oliver remembered dimly, was a bit of almost-level, then another bitter ascent, little more than a roofless corridor, to the summit of the pass. Already it was growing dim below, though the sky was bright still. If night found them on the mountain . . .

Roland had sent scouts ahead and, while the cliffs were still scalable, to the side. None of them had come back.

A signal went down the line. *Dismount and lead your horses.* Oliver obeyed it, but struggled forward, to draw level with Roland. For a long while he could do nothing but breathe. Roland climbed in silence, not even cursing when his horse stumbled.

"You might," said Oliver between hard breaths, "sound your horn. Just for prudence. So that the king knows how far back we are."

Roland's hand found the horn where it hung at his side: a beauty of a thing, an olifant bound with gold and hung on a gold-worked baldric; the only adornment he would wear, whose sword and armor were as plain as a trooper's. But he did not move to raise the horn.

"Roland," said Oliver, "brother, sound the horn. If we're caught here, we're too few, the pass is too steep; we'll barely hold till the king can come back."

"No," said Roland.

Oliver drew breath once again, and flung all his passion into it. "Roland, brother, sound the horn! It's I who beg you. I'll bear the shame, if shame there is, and no army waits for us above."

"No one will bear the shame for me," Roland said. "How large an army can a pack of savages muster? We'll fight them off. Or don't you think I'm strong enough for that?"

"I think your stepfather has something hidden here, and that is your death."

"Are you calling my mother's husband a traitor?"

Mad, thought Oliver in despair. God-mad, as they said men were when they were chosen to be sacrificed: going to their deaths willingly, and even with joy. And gods help the man who spoke ill of the man he hated.

Oliver shut his mouth and set himself to climb and watch, both at once, as much as his struggling body would allow. He kept close to Roland's side, his battle-station, though his wonted place on the march was well apart from the count.

At the level they paused, a moment only, to replenish their strength. The cliff-walls closed in above. There was still no sign of the scouts. Roland did not mention them; Oliver did not want to. When they moved on again, Turpin was beside them, leading his fine warhorse, whistling tunelessly between his teeth.

The creaking of wains echoed and reechoed from the walls. The lead ox threw up its head and snorted, balking in the gate of the defile. Its driver cursed and thrust in the goad. The ox lowed in pain, but stood fast.

Through the echoes of its cry, Oliver heard thunder.

Not thunder. Stones. Great boulders, roaring and tumbling down the cliffsides, and men howling behind them. Howling in Arabic. *Allah-il-allah!*

Saracens. They fell like hail out of the sky, bearded, turbaned, shrilling sons of Allah; they filled the pass behind, thick as locusts in the plains of Granada. The trap was sprung. The bait could not even cower in it. There was no room.

Oliver almost laughed. So, then. That was what they had meant, the conspirators, when they spoke of turning the king against the enemies of Byzantium. It would not have been hard to win Córdoba to their cause, if it cost Baghdad its ally. Then the traitor need but see to it that Roland was given the rearguard and led to expect nothing worse than a pack of brigands; and leave the rest to the armies of Córdoba.

They were, at most, fifty men. If there were less than a thousand about them, then Oliver had lost his ability to reckon armies. And the wagons to defend, and the way closed on all sides, and no escape but through the armies of Islam.

Roland saw them and laughed. By some freak of fate and the army and the echoes about them, his laughter sounded light and clear in almost-silence, the laughter of a man who loves a battle. It danced with mockery. It dared death to take him. He leaped up on a wain though darts rained down, and called out: "Here, men! Here's a fight for us. Who'll take first blood? Who'll die for our king?"

"I!" they shouted back. And in a rising roar, till even the echoes fled in terror: "Montjoie! Montjoie! *Montjoie!*"

The enemy faltered. But they could count as well as Oliver, and they had seen how ill the train was disposed, sprawled all down the narrow pass, no room to draw together and make a stand. The small company that clustered in the rear, their horses useless on that steep and broken ground, the enemy all but ignored; they fell on the train itself, their howls drowning out even the shrieks of women and the death-cries of horses and cattle.

The Bretons frayed at the edges. Hands reached for pommels, men braced to spring astride their horses. Roland's voice lashed them back, away from the stumbling, hindering, helpless beasts, into a formation they all knew. Then, fiercely, forward.

They drove like a lance into the column. And for a little while, no one resisted them. Oliver grinned in his helmet. There was a use after all for the Roman foot-drill that the king had inflicted on them—a game, he said; an idea he had, that Roland, always apt for mischief, was willing to try. Now it served them in this most impossible of places, drove them into the enemy, mowed the attackers down and swept them aside under the hoofs of panicked beasts.

But there were too many of them; and the cavalry shield was little use in building the Roman shieldwall. Frayed already by startlement and rage and the Franks' inborn resistance to marching in step, they tore apart as the enemy rallied. Men were down. Oliver could not count, could not reckon. He had his own life to look after, and his brother's.

Roland was always calm enough when a battle began, well able to array his troops and judge their moment. But let his sword taste blood, and he was lost.

Someone was on Roland's other side, sword-side to Oliver's shield-side. Turpin, again. He had the bull of Mithras on his shield. It seemed to dance among the fallen, its white hide speckled with blood.

Oliver's foot slipped. He spared a glance for it: blood, entrails, a hand that cracked like bunched twigs under his boot. His eye caught a flash; his spear swung round, swift, swift, but almost too late. Fool's recompense, for casting eye on aught but the enemy. The good ash shaft jarred on steel and shattered. He thrust it in a howling face, let it fall, snatched out his sword. Roland's was out already, his named-blade, Durandal, running with blood.

Most often a battle runs like the sea: in ebbs and flows, in eddies and swirls and moments of stillness. But that is where armies are matched, and one side cannot count twenty men for every man of the other. Here, there were no respites. Only battle, and battle, and more battle. Death on every side, no time even for despair. They three had fought their way clear to the front of the battle and backed against the wall of the pass, as high up as the fallen stones would allow. Through the press of the fight they could see the downward way: a roil of ants in the nest, no head raised that did not wear a turban, and everywhere the sight and stench of slaughter.

Oliver, turning a bitter blow, was numb to the marrow. So soon? he wondered. So soon, they are all fallen?

So soon, in their heavy armor that was never made for fighting on foot; dragged down and slaughtered by the sheer mass of their enemies. His arm was leaden. He flailed at a stroke he barely saw, and never saw the one that glanced off his helmet. He staggered, head ringing, and fell to one knee. Lightning smote the man who stooped to the kill.

Durandal, and Roland's face behind it, white in the helmet, burning-eyed. He had dropped his shield, or lost it. His olifant was in his hand.

Oliver cursed him, though he had no breath to spare for it. "What use now? It will never bring the king. He's too far ahead."

Roland gave a yelling savage a second, blood-fountained mouth, and sent him reeling back among his fellows. For an impossible moment, none came forward in his place. There were easier pickings elsewhere; a whole baggage train to plunder. Roland set the horn to his lips.

Oliver, who knew what he would hear, clapped hands to his ears. Even that was barely enough to blunt the edge of it. The great horn roared like the aurochs from which it was won; shrieked up to heaven; sang a long plaint of wrath and valor and treachery. Roland's face was scarlet. A thin trail of blood trickled down from his ear.

The horn dropped, swung on its baldric. Roland half-fell against Oliver. Turpin caught him; they clung to one another. The enemy had frozen in their places. Many had fallen, smitten down by the power of the horn.

They rose like grass when the wind has faded. They turned their faces toward the three of all their prey who yet lived. They reckoned anew their numbers, and the number that opposed them. They laughed, and fell upon them.

Oliver could not reckon the moment when he knew that one of his wounds was mortal. It was not when he took the wound, he was reasonably sure of that. He had others in plenty, and they were in his way, shedding blood to weaken his arm and foul his footing. But this one was weakening him too quickly. He found himself on the ground, propped against the rock, trying to lift his sword. A foot held him down. It was Roland's; that came to him when he tried to hack at it and the voice over his head cursed him in his brother's voice. "Sorry," he tried to say. "Can't see. Can't—"

"Be quiet," said Roland fiercely. Oliver was too tired to object. Except that he wanted to say something. He could not remember what. Something about horns. And kings. And turbans, with faces under them. Faces that should be—should be—

"Oliver."

Somebody was crying. It sounded like Roland. Roland did not often cry. Oliver wondered why he was doing it now. Had something happened? Was the king hurt? Dead? No, Oliver could not conceive of that. The king would never die. The king would live forever.

Oliver blinked. There was Roland's face, hanging over him. Another by it: Turpin's. They looked like corpses. "Am I dead?" Oliver asked, or tried to. "Is this Hades? Or the Muslims' Paradise? Or—"

"You talk too much," Roland growled.

They were alive. But it was very quiet. Too quiet. No shrilling of enemy voices. Unless that were they, faint and far away and fading slowly, like wind in empty places.

"They're gone," the priest said, as if he could understand what Oliver was thinking. Maybe he could. Priests were unchancy folk. But good: very good, in a fight. "They took what they came for."

"Did they?"

They both heard that. Roland glared. "Wasn't the king's whole baggage train enough?"

"You," Oliver said "You live. Still."

Roland burst into tears again. But he looked worse than furious. He looked deadly dangerous.

The dark was closing in. "Brother," Oliver said through it, shouting in full voice against the failing of his body. "Brother, look. The enemy. Turbans—turbans wrong. Not Saracen. Can you understand? *Not Saracen.*"

Maybe Oliver dreamed it. Maybe he only needed to hear it. But it was there, on the other side of the night. "I understand."

"I understand," Roland said. The weight in his arms was no greater and no less. But suddenly it was the weight of a world.

He knew the heft of death in his arms. Not Oliver, not now: not those wide blue eyes, emptying of life as they had, moments since, emptied of light.

He flung his head back and keened.

"My lord." Dry voice, with calm behind it. Turpin was weary: he had lain down beside Oliver, maybe with some vanishing hope of keeping him warm.

Or himself. Not all the blood on him was the enemy's. Some of it was bright with newness, glistening as it welled from a deep spring.

Dying, all of them. Roland, too. The enemy had seen to that before they left. He had not intended to tell either of his companions about the blade that stabbed from below, or the reason why he held himself so carefully when he rose. When he had finished doing what he must do, he would let go. It would not be a slow death, or an easy one, but it was certain. A good death for a fool, when all was considered.

He spoke lightly; he was proud of that lightness. "I'm going to see if I can find our fellows," he said to the one who could hear him and the one who was past it: "give them a word of passage; cast earth on the ones who'll need it."

Turpin nodded. He did not offer to rise. But there was, Roland judged, a little life in him yet. Enough to mount guard over Oliver, and keep the crows from his eyes. They were feasting already and long since, and the vultures with them: racing against the fall of the dark.

He walked the field in the gathering twilight, dim-lit by the glow of the sky above him. The birds of battle were as thick as flies; but where they were thickest, there he knew he would find his men. Two here, three there, five fallen together in the remnant of a shieldring. The king's seneschal; the count of his palace, the *palatium* that was not a thing of walls and stone but of the household that went with the king wherever he journeyed. Lost, here, gone down the long road with men in knotted turbans.

But not all of those who had come to seize it had left the field. Many of their dead, they had taken, but they had left many, pressed by the fall of the dark and the need to escape with their booty before the King of the Franks swept down in the full force of his wrath. There at Roland's feet, locked in embrace like lovers, lay a camp follower who had lost her man at Pamplona, and a brigand; but there was a knife in his heart and a look of great surprise on his face. Roland could not tell if she smiled. There was too little left of her.

The man, sheltered by her body, was barely touched by the crows. Roland grasped him by the foot and dragged him into what light there was. The turban fell from a matted and filthy head. Roland bent to peer. The face—anonymous dead face. But odd. Ruthlessly he rent the tunic away from neck and breast and belly. The trousers, he need hardly tear at. He saw beneath them all that he needed to see.

His breath left him in a long sigh. With care, holding his middle lest his entrails spill upon the ground, he made his way among the enemy's dead. All; all alike.

Not far from the place where Oliver had died, he found the last thing, the thing that drained the strength from his legs, the life from his body. But he smiled. He took what he needed, and the body with it, crawling now. The night, which seemed to have waited for him, fell at last.

Turpin was stiff and still. Oliver lay untouched beside him, familiar bulk gone unfamiliar in death. Roland kissed him, and with every last vestige of his strength, staggered upright. The stars stared down. "Al-lah!" he called out. His voice rang in the gorge. "Allah! Will you take us all, if I speak for us? Will you, then? He'd like your Paradise, my brother. All the lovely maidens. Will you take him if I ask?"

The stars were silent. Roland laughed and flung up Durandal. He had, somehow, remembered to scour the blade of blood: prudence worn to habit. A pity for a good sword to die, though its master must. "Take my sword, Allah. Take my soul and my oath; if only you take my brother with it. You'll find him waiting hereabout. Come, do you hear him whispering? He'd say it with me if he could. Listen! *There is no god but God, and Muhammad is the Prophet of God.*"

The echoes throbbed into silence. Roland sank down in them. His heart was light. In a little while he was going to convulse in agony, but for this moment, he knew no pain. Only a white, mad joy. To have chosen, and chosen so. To have taken the purest revenge of all, on Ganelon who had betrayed him.

Oliver was waiting. Roland laid Durandal on the broad breast, and his head beside it, and sighed. Then at last, with all the courage that was left in him, he let go.

3

Charles the king stood once more on the sweet soil of Gaul, the horrors of the pass behind him, the army finding new vigor in the sight of their own country spread below. But he was not easy in his mind. Word from the rear was unvarying. No sign of the baggage. A scout or two, sent out, did not return.

As the sun sank low, he called a halt. Without the baggage they could not raise a proper camp, but every man had his store of food and drink, and many had women who marched with them and carried the necessities of living. They settled willingly enough.

The king left his servants to make what shift they could with what they had, and rode back a little, up toward the pass. One or two men rode with him. The empress's ambassador; the caliph's man, not to be outflanked; Ganelon. Beyond the fringe of the army, the king paused.

"Do you hear a horn?" he asked.

They glanced at one another. "A horn?" Ganelon inquired. "No, sire. I hear nothing but the wind."

"Yes," said Charles. "The wind. That's what it must be. But I could have sworn . . ."

"My lord's ears are excellent," the Arab said. No; Charles should be precise, even in his mind. The man was a Persian. The Persian, then, and a smoothly smiling fellow he was, oily as a Greek, and yet, for all of that, a man worth liking. "Perhaps he hears the rearguard as it comes through the pass."

"Perhaps," said Ganelon. The Greek, for a marvel, said nothing at all.

They sat their tired horses, waiting, because the king waited. He could not bring himself to turn away. He had not liked the pass as he scaled it, and he had not liked the failure of his scouts to come back. Still less did he like his folly in letting the rearguard fall so far behind. He had been in haste to abandon the pass, to see his own lands again. He had let himself be persuaded to press on. The one man he sent back to find the rearguard, had not found him again.

In the falling dark, in silence barely troubled by the presence of an army, he saw what he had willed not to see. He saw it with brutal clarity; he knew it for what it was. There was no pain, yet. Later, there would be; a whole world of it. But now, only numbness that was not blessed. Oh, no. Not blessed at all. "They are dead," he said, "my Bretons. There was an ambush in the pass."

"My lord," said Ganelon, "you cannot know that. They will have been sensible: seen that night was falling, and stopped, and made camp. In time their messenger will come. Only wait, and rest. You can hardly ride back now. Night will catch you before you mount the pass."

"Yes," said Charles. "It will, won't it?"

His voice must have betrayed more than he knew. Ganelon stiffened; his mouth set. His eyes darted. Charles noticed where they fell first. The Byzantine refused them, gazing expressionless where Charles's mind and heart were.

With great care, the king unknotted his fists. He had no proof. He had nothing but the feeling in his bones, and the absence of his rearguard. His valiant, reluctant, pitifully inadequate rearguard.

He was, first of all, king. He turned his back on the pass of Roncesvalles, and went to see to his army.

The king did not sleep that night. When he drowsed, his mind deluded him: gave him the far cry of a horn, a great olifant, blown with the desperation of a dying man. Roland was dead. He knew it. Dead in battle; dead by treachery.

He rose before dawn. His army slept; he silenced the trumpeter who would have roused them. "Let them sleep," he said. "We go nowhere until the baggage comes."

When his horse came, others came with it. The Greek and the Persian, again and perpetually; Ganelon; a company of his guardsmen. He greeted them with a nod. They were all, like the king, armed as if to fight. It was odd to see the Byzantine in mail, carrying a sword. Charles had not known that he owned either.

Morning rose with them, surmounted the pass, sped above them while they went down. They picked their way with care, finding no trace of the baggage, and nothing ahead of them but fading darkness.

A wall of tumbled stones where none had been before, woke in the king no surprise, not even anger. Wordlessly he dismounted, handed his horse to the man nearest, and set himself to scale the barrier. It was not high, if much confused. At the top of it he paused.

He had expected nothing less than what he saw. He had seen sights like it ever since he could remember. But it was never an easy thing to see; even when the dead were all the enemy's.

Someone had seen to the dead of Gaul. Each was consecrated in his own fashion: a cross drawn in blood on the brow of the Christian, a scattering of earth for him who held to Julian's creed, a simple laying out in dignity for the follower of Mithras or of the old faith. But hope, having swelled, died swiftly. No living man walked that field.

Beyond them, as if they had made a last stand, lay three together. Turpin the priest of Mithras with his bones given to the birds of the air, and Roland and Oliver in one another's arms as they had been since they shared their milkmother's breast. They had died well, if never easily.

The king was aware, distantly but very clearly, of the men nearest him: Greek, Persian, Frankish counselor. None ventured to touch the dead. He knelt beside them, and gently, as if the boy could feel it still, took Roland in his arms.

Roland clasped something to his breast, even in death. His olifant. Which Charles had heard; he was certain of it now. Heard, and never come. The king steadied it as it slipped. It was heavier than it should be, unwieldy. It eluded the king's hand and fell, spilling brightness on the grass.

Byzantine gold. And mingled with it, the rougher coin of Gaul, and Charles's face on every one.

He did not glance, even yet, at his companions. There was a message here; he was meant to read it. At the brothers' feet lay one of the enemy's dead, whom Charles had had no eyes to see. But there was no other close by, and this one looked to have been brought here.

Charles laid Roland again in Oliver's arms, and examined the body. He was perfectly, icily calm. Intent on his own dead, he had not seen more than that the enemy wore turbans over dark faces. This one's turban had fallen beside him; his tunic was rent and torn, baring white skin, skin too white for the face. And between them, a ragged line, the stain rubbed on in haste with no expectation of need for greater concealment. And, below, what Charles did not need the Persian to say for him.

"This man is not a Muslim. He is not circumcised."

"So," said Charles, "I notice."

Even dying, Roland had kept his wits about him. Gold of Byzantium, gold and silver of Gaul. An infidel in Muslim guise. Trap, and battle, and the deaths of great lords of the Franks.

Here was treachery writ large.

He read it, writ subtle, in Ganelon's face. He could never have thought to be so betrayed, and so simply. And by his brainless braggart of a stepson.

They had all drawn back from him. He seemed just now to realize it. He was white under his elegant beard, struggling to maintain his expression of innocence. Ganelon, who had never made a secret of his hatred for Roland; whose very openness had been deceit. Who would have expected that he would turn traitor? Open attack, surely, daggers drawn in hall, a challenge to a duel; but this, no one had looked for. Least of all, and most damnably of all, the king.

"It would have been better for you," Charles said, "if you had killed him before my face. Clean murder bears a clean penalty. For this, you will pay in your heart's blood."

"Pay, sire?" Ganelon struggled even yet to seem baffled. "Surely, sire, you do not think—"

"I know," said Charles. His eyes burned. They were wide, he knew, and pale, and terrible. When they fell on the Greek, the man blanched.

"I am not," he said, "a part of this. I counseled against it. I foresaw this very outcome."

"You sanctioned it with your empress' gold," said the king.

"For what an agent does with his wages, I bear no responsibility."

Charles laughed. His guards had drawn in, shoulder to shoulder. If the traitor had any thought of escape, he quelled it. He regarded his quondam ally with no surprise, if with nothing approaching pleasure.

"You shall be tried," the king said to him, "where the law commands, before my tribunal in Gaul. I expect that you will receive the extremest penalty. I devoutly pray that you may suffer every pang of guilt and grief and rage to which even a creature of your ilk should be subject."

Ganelon stiffened infinitesimally, but not with dismay. Was that the beginning of a smile? "You have no certain proof," he said.

"God will provide," said Charles.

"God? Or Allah?"

Bold, that one, looking death in the face. If death it was that he saw. It was a long way to Gaul, and his tongue was serpent-supple. Had not Charles himself been taken in by it?

Charles met his eyes and made them fall. "Yes," he said, answering the man's question. "There you have it. God, or Allah? The Christians' God, or all the gods of my faith who in the end are one, or the God of the Prophet? Would you have me choose now? Julian is dead, his teachings forgotten everywhere but in my court. The Christ lives; the sons of the Prophet rule in Baghdad, and offer alliance. I know what I am in this world. Byzantium dares to hope in me, to hold back the armies of Islam. Islam knows that without me it can never rule in the north of the world. How does it twist in you, betrayer of kin, to know that I am the fulcrum on which the balance rests?"

"Islam," said Ganelon without a tremor, "offers you the place of a vassal king. Byzantium would make you its emperor."

"So it would. And such a marriage it would be, I ruling here in Gaul, and she on the Golden Horn. Or would I be expected to settle in Constantinople? Who then would rule my people? You, kinslayer? Is that the prize you played for?"

"Better I than a wild boy who could never see a battle without flinging himself into the heart of it."

The king's fist lashed out. Ganelon dropped. "Speak no ill of the dead," Charles said.

The others were silent. They did not press him; and yet it was there, the necessity, the making of choices. If he would take vengeance for this slaughter, he must move now.

He began to smile. It was not, he could well sense, pleasant to see. "Yes," he said. "Revenge. It's fortunate for my sister-son, is it not, that I'm pagan, and no Christian, to have perforce to forgive. You plotted well, kinslayer. You thought to turn me against Islam and cast me into the empress' arms. Would there be a dagger for me there? Or, more properly Greek, poison in my cup?"

"Sire," said Ganelon, and that was desperation, now, at last. "Sire, do not judge the empire by the follies of a single servant."

"I would never do that," Charles said. "But proof of long conviction will do well enough. I will never set my people under the Byzantine heel. Even with the promise of a throne. Thrones can pass, like any other glory of this world; and swiftly, if those who offer them are so minded."

"Still, my lord, you cannot choose Islam. Would you betray all that the Divine Julian fought for? Would you turn against Rome herself?"

If the Greek had said it, Charles would have responded altogether differently. But it was Ganelon who spoke, and Ganelon who felt the pain of it.

"I am," said Charles, "already, in the caliph's eyes, his emir over Spain. I am not able for the moment to press the claim. Gaul needs me, and Gaul is mine first. If Baghdad will grant the justice in that, then yes," he said, "I choose Islam."

No thunder roared in the sky; no shaking rent the earth. There were only a handful of men in a narrow pass, and the dead, and the sun too low still to cast its light on them. Spain was behind them; the mountain before, and beyond it, Gaul. What its king chose, it also would choose. He knew his power there.

He bent and took up Roland's horn. It rang softly, bearing still a weight of imperial gold. With it in his hands, he said the words which he must say. If his conviction was not yet as pure as it might be, then surely he would be forgiven. He was doing it for Gaul, and for the empire that would be. But before even that, for Roland who was his sister's son, who had died for Byzantine gold.

Charles was, when it came to it, a simple man. The choice had not been simple, until Ganelon made it so. A better traitor than he knew, that one. Traitor even to his own cause.

"There is no god but God," said the king of the Franks and the Lombards, *"and Muhammad is the Prophet of God."*

HIS POWDER'D WIG, HIS CROWN OF THORNES

Marc Laidlaw

Grant Innes first saw the icon in the Indian ghettos of London, but thought nothing of it. There were so many gewgaws of native "art" being thrust in his face by faddishly war-painted Cherokees that this was just another nuisance to avoid, like the huge radios blaring obnoxious "Choctawk" percussions and the high-pitched warbling of Tommy Hawkes and the effeminate Turquoise Boys; like the young Mohawk ruddies practicing skateboard stunts for sluttish cockney girls whose kohled black eyes and slack blue lips betrayed more interest in the dregs of the bottles those boys carried than in the boys themselves. Of course, it was not pleasure or curiosity that brought him into the squalid district, among the baggy green canvas street-teepees and graffitoed storefronts. Business alone could bring him here. He had paid a fair sum for the name and number of a Mr. Cloud, dealer in Navaho jewelry, whose samples had proved of excellent quality and would fetch the highest prices, not only in Europe but in the Colonies as well. Astute dealers knew that the rage for turquoise had nearly run its course, thank God; following the popularity of the lurid blue stone, the simplicity of black-patterned silver would be a welcome relief indeed. Grant had hardly been able to tolerate the sight of so much garish rock as he'd been forced to stock in order to suit his customers; he was looking forward to this next trend. He'd already laid the ground for several showcase presentations in Paris; five major glossies were bidding for rights to photograph his collector's pieces, antique sand-cast *najas* and squash-blossom necklaces, for a special fashion portfolio.

Here in the slums, dodging extruded plastic kachina dolls and machine-woven blankets, his fine-tuned eye was offended by virtually everything he saw. It was trash for tourists. Oh, it had its spurts of cheap popularity, like the war bonnets which all the cyclists had worn last summer, but such moments were as fleeting as pop hits, thank God. Only true quality could ever transcend the dizzying gyres of public favor. Fine art, precious stones, pure metal: These were investments that would never lose their value.

So much garbage ultimately had the effect of blinding him to his environment; avoidance became a mental as well as a physical trick. He was dreaming of silver crescents gleaming against ivory skin when he realized that he must have passed the street he sought. He stopped in his tracks, suddenly aware of the hawkers' cries, the pulse of hide-drums and synthesizers. He spun about searching for a number on any of the shops.

"Lost, guv?" said a tall young brave with gold teeth, his bare chest ritually scarified. He carried a tall pole strung with a dozen gruesome rubber scalps, along with several barristers' wigs. They gave the brave the appearance of a costume merchant, except for one morbid detail: Each of the white wigs was spattered with blood . . . red dye, rather, liberally dripped among the coarse white strands.

"You *look* lost."

"Looking for a shop," he muttered, fumbling Mr. Cloud's card from his pocket.

"No, I mean really lost. Out of balance. *Koyaanisqatsi*, guv. Like the whole world."

"I'm looking for a shop," Grant repeated firmly.

"That all, then? A shop? What about the things you really lost? Things we've all lost, I'm talking about. Here."

He patted his bony hip, which was wrapped in a black leather loincloth. Something dangled from his belt, a doll-like object on a string, a charm of some sort. Grant looked over the brave's head and saw the number he sought, just above a doorway. The damn ruddy was in his way. As he tried to slip past, avoiding contact with the rubbery scalps and bloodied wigs, the brave unclipped the charm from his belt and thrust it into his face.

Grant recoiled, nearly stumbling backward in the street. It was an awful little mannequin, face pinched and soft, its agonized expression carved from a withered apple.

"Here—here's where we lost it," the brave said, thrusting the doll up to his cheek, as if he would have it kiss or nip him with its rice-grain teeth. Its limbs were made of jerked beef, spread-eagled on wooden crossbars, hands and feet fixed in place with four tiny nails. It was a savage Christ—an obscenity.

"He gave His life for you," the brave said. "Not just for one people, but for everyone. Eternal freedom, that was His promise."

"I'm late for my appointment," Grant said, unable to hide his disgust.

"Late and lost," the brave said. "But you'll never catch up—the time slipped past. And you'll never find your way unless you follow Him."

"Just get out of my way!"

He shoved the brave aside, knocking the hideous little idol out of the Indian's grasp. Fearing reprisal, he forced an apologetic expression as he turned back from the hard-won doorway. But the brave wasn't watching him. He crouched over the filthy street, retrieving his little martyr. Lifting it to his lips, he kissed it gently.

"I'm sorry," Grant said.

The brave glanced up at Grant and grinned fiercely, baring his gold teeth; then he bit deep into the dried brown torso of the Christ and tore away a ragged strip of jerky.

Nauseous, Grant hammered on the door behind him. It opened abruptly and he almost fell into the arms of Mr. Cloud.

He next saw the image the following summer, in the District of Cornwallis. Despite the fact that Grant specialized in provincial art, most of his visits to the colonies had been for business purposes, and had exposed him to no more glorious surroundings than the interiors of banks and mercantile offices, with an occasional jaunt into the Six Nations to meet with the creators of the fine pieces that were his trade. Sales were brisk, his artisans had been convinced to ply their craft with gold as well as silver, supplanting turquoise and onyx with diamonds and other precious stones; the trend toward high-fashion American jewelry had already surpassed his highest expectations. Before the inevitable decline and a panicked search for the next sure thing, he decided to accept the offer of an old colonial acquaintance who had long extended an open invitation to a tour of great American monuments in the capital city.

Arnoldsburg, D.C., was sweltering in a humid haze, worsened by exhaust fumes from the taxis that seemed the city's main occupants. Eyes burning, lungs fighting against collapse, he and his guide crawled from taxi after taxi and plunged into cool marble corridors reeking of urine and crowded with black youths selling or buying opiates. It was hard not to mock the great figures of American history, thus surrounded and entrapped by the ironic fruits of their victories. The huge seated figure of Burgoyne looked mildly bemused by the addicts sleeping between his feet; the bronze brothers Richard and William Howe stood back to back embattled in a waist-high mob, as though taking their last stand against colonial Lillilputians.

His host, David Mickelson, was a transplanted Irishman. He had first visited America as a physician with the Irish Royal Army, and after his term expired had signed on for a stint in the Royal American Army. He had since opened a successful dermatological practice in Arnoldsburg. He was a collector of native American art, which practice had led him to deal with Grant Innes. Mickelson had excellent taste in metalwork, but Grant chided him for his love of "these marble monstrosities."

"But these are heroes, Grant. Imagine where England would be without these men. An island with few resources and limited room for expansion? How could we have kept up the sort of healthy growth we've had since the Industrial Revolution? It's impossible. And without these men to secure this realm for us, how could we have held onto it? America is so vast—really, you have no concept of it. These warriors laid the way for peace and proper management, steering a narrow course between Spain and France. Without such fine ambassadors to put down the early rebellion and ease the cosettling of the Six Nations, America might still be at war. Instead its resources belong to the crown. This is our treasure house, Grant, and these are the keepers of that treasure."

"Treasure," Grant repeated, with an idle nudge at the body of an old squaw who lay unconscious on the steps of the Howe Monument.

"Come with me, then," Mickelson said. "One more sight, and then we'll go wherever you like."

They boarded another taxi which progressed by stops and starts through the iron river of traffic. A broad, enormous dome appeared above the cars.

"Ah," said Grant. "I know what that is."

They disembarked at the edge of a huge circular plaza. The dome that capped the plaza was supported by a hundred white columns. They went into the lidded shadow, into darkness, and for a moment Grant was blinded.

"Watch out, old boy," Mickelson said. "Here's the rail. Grab on. Wouldn't want to stumble in here."

His hands closed on polished metal. When he felt steady again, he opened his eyes and found himself staring into a deep pit. The walls of the shaft were perfectly smooth, round as a bullet hole drilled deep into the earth. He felt a cold wind coming out of it, and then the grip of vertigo.

"The depths of valor, the inexhaustible well of the human spirit," Mickelson was saying. "Makes you dizzy with pride, doesn't it?"

"I'm . . . feeling . . . sick. . . ." Grant turned and hurried toward daylight.

Out in the sunshine again, his sweat gone cold, he leaned against a marble podium and gradually caught his breath. When his mind had cleared somewhat, he looked up and saw that the podium was engraved with the name of the hero whose accomplishments the shaft commemorated. His noble bust surmounted the slab.

BENEDICT ARNOLD

First American President-General, appointed such by King George III as reward for his valiant role in suppressing the provincial revolt of 1776–79.

David Mickelson caught up with him.

"Feeling all right, Grant?"

"Better. I—I think I'd like to get back to my rooms. It's this heat."

"Surely. I'll hail a cab, you just hold on here for a minute."

As Grant watched Mickelson hurry away, his eyes strayed over the circular plaza where the usual hawkers had laid out the usual souvenirs. Habit, more than curiousity, drove him out among the ragged blankets, his eyes swiftly picking through the merchandise and discarding it all as garbage.

Well, most of it. This might turn out to be another fortunate venture after all. His eyes had been caught by a display of absolutely brilliant designs done in copper and brass. He had never seen anything quite like them. Serpents, eagles, patterns of stars. The metal was all wrong, but the artist had undoubtedly chosen them by virtue of their cheapness and could be easily convinced to work in gold. He looked up at the proprietor of these wares and saw a young Indian woman, bent on her knees, threading colored beads on a string.

"Who made these?" he said, softening the excitement he felt into a semblance of mild curiosity.

She gazed up at him. "My husband."

"Really? I like them very much. Does he have a distributor?"

She didn't seem to know what he meant.

"That is . . . does anyone else sell these pieces?"

She shook her head. "This is all he makes, right here. When he makes more, I sell those."

In the distance, he heard Mickelson shouting his name. The dermatologist came running over the marble plaza. "Grant, I've got a cab!"

Grant gestured as if to brush him away. "I'll meet you later, David, all right? Something's come up."

"What have you found?" Mickelson tried to look past him at the blanket, but Grant spun him around in the direction of the taxis—perhaps a bit too roughly. Mickelson stopped for a moment, readjusted his clothes, then stalked away peevishly toward the cars. So be it.

Smiling, Grant turned back to the woman. His words died on his tongue when he saw what she was doing with beads she'd been stringing.

She had formed them into a noose, a bright rainbow noose, and slipped this over the head of a tiny brown doll.

He knew that doll, knew its tough leathered flesh and pierced limbs, the apple cheeks and teeth of rice. The cross from which she'd taken it lay discarded on the blanket, next to the jewelry that suddenly seemed of secondary importance.

While he stood there unspeaking, unmoving, she lifted the dangling doll to her lips and daintily, baring crooked teeth, tore off a piece of the leg.

"What . . . what . . ."

He found himself unable to ask what he wished to ask. Instead, fixed by her gaze, he stammered, "What do you want for all of these?"

She finished chewing before answering. "All?"

"Yes, I . . . I'd like to buy all of them. In fact, I'd like to buy more than this. I'd like to commission a piece, if I might."

The squaw swallowed.

"My husband creates what is within the soul. He makes dreams into metal. He would have to see your dreams."

"My dreams? Well, yes, I'll tell him exactly what I want. Could I meet him to discuss this?"

The squaw shrugged. She patiently unlooped the noose from the shrivelled image, spread it back onto its cross and pinned the three remaining limbs into place, then tucked it away in a bag at her belt. Finally, rising, she rolled up the blanket with all the bangles and bracelets inside it, and tucked the parcel under her arm.

"Come with me," she said.

He followed her without another word, feeling as though he were moving down an incline, losing his balance with every step, barely managing to throw himself in her direction. She was his guide through the steaming city, through the crowds of ragged cloth, skins ruddy and dark. He pulled off his customary jacket, loosened his tie, and struggled after her. She seemed to dwindle in the distance; he was losing her, losing himself, stretching into a thin strand of beads, beads of sweat, sweat that dripped through the gutters of Arnoldsburg and offered only brine to the thirsty. . . .

But when she once looked back and saw him faltering, she put out her hand and he was standing right beside her, near a metal door. She put her hand upon it and opened the way.

It was cool inside, and dark except for the tremulous light of candles that lined a descending stairway. He followed, thinking of catacombs, the massed and desiccated ranks of the dead he had seen beneath old missions in Spanish Florida. There was a dusty smell, and far off the sound of hammering. She opened another door and the sound was suddenly close at hand.

They had entered a workshop. A man sat at a metal table cluttered with coils of wire, metal snips, hand torches. The woman stepped out and closed the door on them.

"Good afternoon," Grant said. "I . . . I'm a great admirer of your work."

The man turned slowly, the metal stool creaking under his weight, although he was not a big man. His skin was very dark, like his close-cropped hair. His face was soft, as though made of chamois pouches; but his eyes were hard. He beckoned.

"Come here," he said. "You like my stuff? What is it that you like?"

Grant approached the workbench with a feeling of awe. Samples of the man's work lay scattered about, but these were not done in copper or brass. They were silver, most of them, and gleamed like moonlight.

"The style," he said. "The . . . substance."

"How about this?" The Indian fingered a large eagle with spreading wings.

"It's beautiful—almost alive."

"It's a sign of freedom." He laid it down. "What about this one?"

He handed Grant a small rectangular plaque inscribed with an unusual but somehow familiar design. A number of horizontal stripes, with a square inset in the lower right corner, and in that square a wreath of thirteen stars.

"Beautiful," Grant said. "You do superior work."

"That's not what I mean. Do you know the symbol?"

"I . . . I think I've seen it somewhere before. An old Indian design, isn't it?"

The Indian grinned. Gold teeth again, bridging the distance between London and Arnoldsburg, reminding him of the jerked beef martyr, the savage Christ.

"Not an Indian sign," he said. "A sign for all people."

"Really? Well, I'd like to *bring* it to all people. I'm a dealer in fine jewelry. I could get a very large audience for these pieces. I could make you a very rich man."

"Rich?" The Indian set the plaque aside. "Plenty of Indians are rich. The tribes have all the land and factories they want—as much as you have. But we lack what you also lack: freedom. What is wealth when we have no freedom?"

"Freedom?"

"It's a dim concept to you, isn't it? But not to me." He put his hand over his heart. "I hold it here, safe with the memory of how we lost it. A precious thing, a cup of holy water that must never be spilled until it can be swallowed in a single draft. I carry the cup carefully, but there's enough for all. If you wish to drink, it can be arranged."

"I don't think you understand," Grant said, recovering some part of himself that had begun to drift off through the mystical fog in which the Indians always veiled themselves. He must do something concrete to counteract so much vagueness. "I'm speaking of a business venture. A partnership."

"I hear your words. But I see something deeper in you. Something that sleeps in all men. They come here seeking what is lost, looking for freedom and a cause. But all they find are the things that went wrong. Why are you so out of balance, eh? You stumble and crawl, but you always end up here with that same empty look in your eyes. I've seen you before. A dozen just like you."

"I'm an art dealer," Grant said. "Not a—a pilgrim. If you can show me more work like this, I'd be grateful. Otherwise, I'm sorry for wasting your time, and I'll be on my way."

Suddenly he was anxious to get away, and this seemed a reasonable excuse. But the jeweler now seemed ready to accommodate him.

"Art, then," he said. "All right. I will show you the thing that speaks to you, and perhaps then you will understand. Art is also a way to the soul."

He slipped down from the stool and moved toward the door, obviously intending Grant to follow.

"I'll show you more than this," the Indian said. "I'll show you inspiration."

After another dizzying walk, they entered a derelict museum in a district that stank of danger. Grant felt safe only because of his companion; he was obviously a stranger here, in these oppressive alleys. Even inside the place, which seemed less a museum than a warehouse, he sensed that he was being watched. It was crowded by silent mobs, many of them children, almost all of them Negro or Indian. Some sat in circles on the cement floors, talking quietly among themselves, as though taking instruction. Pawnee, Chickasaw, Blackfoot, Cheyenne, Comanche . . . Arnoldsburg was a popular site for tourists, but these didn't have the look of the ruddy middle-class traveler; these were lower-class ruddies, as tattered as the people in the street. Some had apparently crossed the continent on foot to come here. He felt as if he had entered a church.

"Now you shall see," said the jeweler. "This is the art of the patriots. The forefathers. The hidden ones."

He stopped near a huge canvas that leaned against a steel beam; the painting was caked with grease, darkened by time, but even through the grime he could see that it was the work of genius. An imitation of da Vinci's *Last Supper*, but strangely altered . . .

The guests at Christ's table wore not Biblical attire, but that of the eighteenth century. It was no windowed building that sheltered them, but a tent whose walls gave the impression of a strong wind beating against them from without. The thirteen were at table, men in military outfits, and in their midst a figure of mild yet radiant demeanor, humble in a powdered wig, a mere crust of bread on his plate. Grant did not recognize him, this figure in Christ's place, but the man in Judas's place was recognizable enough from the numerous busts and portraits in Arnoldsburg. That was Benedict Arnold.

The Indian pointed at several of the figures, giving them names: "Henry Knox, Nathaniel Greene, Light-Horse Harry Lee, Lafayette, General Rochambeau—"

"Who painted this?"

"It was the work of Benjamin Franklin," said his guide. "Painted not long after the betrayal at West Point, but secretly, in sadness, when the full extent of our tragedy became all too apparent. After West Point, the patriots continued to fight. But this man, this one man, was the glue that held the soldiers together. After His death, the army had many commanders, but none could win the trust of all men. The revolution collapsed and our chance for freedom slipped away. Franklin died without finishing it, his heart broken."

"But that man in the middle?"

The Indian led him to another painting. This was much more recent, judging from the lack of accumulated soot and grease. Several children stood gazing at it, accompanied by a darkie woman who was trying to get them to analyze the meaning of what was essentially a simple image.

"What is this?" she asked.

Several hands went up. "The cherry tree!" chimed a few voices.

"That's right, the cherry tree. Who can tell us the story of the cherry tree?"

One little girl pushed forward. "He chopped it down and when He saw what He had done, He said, 'I cannot let it die.' So He planted the piece He cut off and it grew into a new tree, and the trunk of the old tree grew too, because it was magic."

"Very good. Now that's a fable, of course. Do you know what it really means? What the cherry tree represents?"

Grant felt like one of her charges, waiting for some explanation, innocent.

"It's an English cherry," the teacher hinted.

Hands went up. "The tree!" "I know!" "It's England."

"That's right. And the piece He transplanted?"

"America!"

"Very good. And do you remember what happened next? It isn't shown in this painting, but it was very sad. Tinsha?"

"When His father saw what He had done, he was very scared. He was afraid his son was a devil or something, so he tore up the little tree by the roots. He tore up America."

"And you know who the father really was, don't you?"

"The . . . king?" said Tinsha.

Grant and his guide went on to another painting, this one showing a man in a powdered wig and a ragged uniform walking across a river in midwinter—not stepping on the floes, but moving carefully between them, on the breast of the frigid water. With him came a band of barefoot men, lightly touching hands, the first of them resting his fingers on the cape of their leader. The men stared at the water as if they could not believe their eyes, but there was only confidence in the face of their commander—that and a serene humility.

"This is the work of Sully, a great underground artist," said the jeweler.

"These . . . these are priceless."

The Indian shrugged. "If they were lost tomorrow, we would still carry them with us. It is the feelings they draw from our hearts that are truly beyond price. He came for all men, you see. If you accept Him, if you open your heart to Him, then His death will not have been in vain."

"Washington," Grant said, the name finally coming to him. An insignificant figure of the American Wars, an archtraitor whose name was a mere footnote in the histories he'd read. Arnold had defeated him, hadn't he? Was that what had happened at West Point? The memories were vague and unreal, textbook memories.

The jeweler nodded. "George Washington," he repeated. "He was leading us to freedom, but He was betrayed and held out as an example. In Philadelphia He was publicly tortured to dispirit the rebels, then hung by His neck after his death, and His corpse toured through the colonies. And that is our sin, the penance which we must pay until every soul has been brought back into balance."

"Your sin?"

The Indian nodded, drawing from the pouch at his waist another of the shriveled icons, Christ—no, Washington—on the cross.

"We aided the British in that war. Cherokee and Iroquois, others of the Six Nations. We thought the British would save us from the colonists; we didn't know that they had different ways of enslavement. My ancestors were master torturers. When Washington was captured, it fell to them—to us—to do the bloodiest work."

His hands tightened on the figure of flesh; the splintered wood dug into his palm.

"We nailed Him to the bars of a cross, borrowing an idea that pleased us greatly from your own religion."

The brown hand shook. The image rose to the golden mouth.

"First, we scalped Him. The powdered hair was slung from a warrior's belt. His flesh was pierced with thorns and knives. And then we flayed Him alive."

"Flayed . . ."

Grant winced as golden teeth nipped a shred of jerky and tore it away.

"Alive . . . ?"

"He died bravely. He was more than a man. He was our deliverer, savior of all men, white, red, and black. And we murdered Him. We pushed the world off balance."

"What is this place?" Grant asked. "It's more than a museum, isn't it? It's also a school."

"It is a holy place. His spirit lives here, in the heart of the city named for the man who betrayed Him. He died to the world two hundred years ago, but He still lives in us. He is champion of the downtrodden, liberator of the enslaved." The jeweler's voice was cool despite the fervor of his theme. "You see . . . I have looked beyond the walls of fire that surround this world. I have looked into the world that should have been, that would have been if He had lived. I saw a land of the free, a land of life, liberty, and happiness, where the red men lived in harmony with the white. Our plains bore fruit instead of factories. And the holy cause, that of the republic, spread from the hands of the Great Man. The king was dethroned and England too made free. The bell of liberty woke the world; the four winds carried the cause." The jeweler bowed his head. "That is how it would have been. This I have seen in dreams."

Grant looked around him at the paintings, covered with grime but carefully attended; the people, also grimy but with an air of reverence. It was a shame to waste them here, on these people. He imagined the paintings hanging in a well-lit gallery, the patina of ages carefully washed away; he saw crowds of people in fine clothes, decked in his gold jewelry, each willing to pay a small fortune for admission. With the proper sponsorship, a world tour could be brought off. He would be a wealthy man, not merely a survivor, at the end of such a tour.

The Indian watched him, nodding. "I know what you're thinking. You think it would be good to tell the world of these things, to spread the cause. You think you can carry the message to all humanity, instead of letting it die here in the dark. But I tell you . . . it thrives here. Those who are oppressed, those who are broken and weary of spirit, they are the caretakers of liberty."

Grant smiled inwardly; there was a bitter taste in his mouth.

"I think you underestimate the worth of all this," he said. "You do it a disservice to hide it from the eyes of the world. I think everyone can gain something from it."

"Yes?" The Indian looked thoughtful. He led Grant toward a table where several old books lay open, their pages swollen with humidity, spines cracking, paper flaking away.

"Perhaps you are right," he said, turning the pages of one book entitled *The Undying Patriot*, edited by a Parson Weems. "It may be as Doctor Franklin says. . . ."

Grant bent over the page, and read:

Let no man forget His death. Let not the memory of our great Chief and Commander fade from the thoughts of the common people, who stand to gain the most from its faithful preservation. For once these dreams have fad'd, there is no promise that they may again return. In this age and the next, strive to hold true to the honor'd principals for which He fought, for which he was nail'd to the rude crucifix and his flesh stript away. Forget not His sacrifice, His powder'd wig and crown of thornes. Forget not that a promise broken can never be repair'd.

"I think you are right," said the jeweler. "How can we take it upon ourselves to hide this glory away? It belongs to the world, and the world shall have it."

He turned to Grant and clasped his hands. His eyes were afire with a patriotic light. "He brought you to me, I see that now. This is a great moment. I thank you, brother, for what you will do."

"It's only my duty," Grant said.

Yes. Duty.

And now he stood in the sweltering shadows outside the warehouse, the secret museum, watching the loading of several large vans. The paintings were wrapped in canvas so that none could see them. He stifled an urge to rush up to the loading men and tear away the cloth, to look once more on that noble face. But the police were thick around the entrance.

"Careful," said David Mickelson at his elbow.

News of the find had spread through the city and a crowd had gathered, in which Grant was just one more curious observer. He supposed it was best this way, though he would rather it was his own people moving the paintings. The police were unwontedly rough with the works, but there was nothing he could do about that.

Things had gotten a little out of hand.

"Hard to believe it's been sitting under our noses all this time," said Mickelson. "You say you actually got a good look at it?"

Grant nodded abstractedly. "Fairly good. Of course, it was dark in there."

"Even so . . . what a catch, eh? There have been rumors of this stuff for years, and you stumble right into it. Amazing idea you had, though, organizing a tour. As if anyone would pay to see that stuff aside from ruddies and radicals. Even if it weren't completely restricted."

"What . . . what do you think they'll do with it?" Grant asked.

"Same as they do with other contraband, I'd imagine. Burn it."

"Burn it," Grant repeated numbly.

Grant felt a restriction of the easy flow of traffic; suddenly the crowd, mainly black and Indian, threatened to change into something considerably more passionate than a group of disinterested onlookers. The police loosened their riot gear as the mob began to shout insults.

"Fall back, Grant," Mickelson said.

Grant started to move away through the crowd, but a familiar face caught his attention. It was the Indian, the jeweler; he hung near a corner of the museum, his pouchy face unreadable. Somehow, through all the confusion, among the hundred or so faces now mounting in number, his eyes locked onto Grant's.

Grant stiffened. The last of the vans shut its doors and rushed away. The police did not loiter in the area. He had good reason to feel vulnerable.

The jeweler stared at him. Stared without moving. Then he brought up a withered brown object and set it to his lips. Grant could see him bite, tear, and chew.

"What is it, Grant? We should be going now, don't you think? There's still time to take in a real museum, or perhaps the American Palace."

Grant didn't move. Watching the Indian, he put his thumb to his mouth and caught a bit of cuticle between his teeth. He felt as if he were dreaming. Slowly, he tore off a thin strip of skin, ripping it back almost down to the knuckle. The pain was excruciating, but it didn't seem to wake him. He chewed it, swallowed.

"Grant? Is anything wrong?"

He tore off another.

DEPARTURES

Harry Turtledove

The monks at Ir-Ruhaiyeh did not talk casually among themselves. They were not hermits; those who wanted to be pillar-sitters like the two Saints Symeon went off into the Syrian desert by themselves and did not join monastic communities. Still, the Rule of St. Basil enjoined silence through much of the day.

Despite the Cappadocian Father's Rule, though, a whispered word ran through the monastery regardless of the canonical hour: "The Persians. The Persians are marching toward Ir-Ruhaiyeh."

The abbot, Isaac, heard the whispers, though monks had to shout when they spoke to him. Isaac was past seventy, with a white beard that nearly reached his waist. But he had been abbot here for more than twenty years, and a simple monk for thirty years before that. He knew what his charges thought almost before they thought it.

Isaac turned to the man he hoped would one day succeed him. "It will be very bad this time, John. I feel it."

The prior shrugged. "It will be as God wills, father abbot." He was half the abbot's age, round-faced and always smiling. What would from many men have had the ring of a prophecy of doom came from his lips as a prediction of good fortune.

Isaac was not cheered, not this time. "I wonder if God does not mean this to be the end for us Christians."

"The Persians have come to Ir-Ruhaiyeh before," John said stoutly. "They raided, they moved on. When their campaigns were through, they went back to their homeland once more, and life resumed."

"I was here," Isaac agreed. "They came in the younger Justin's reign, and Tiberius's, and Maurice's. As you say, they left again soon enough, or were driven off. But since this beast of a Phokas murdered his way to the throne of the Roman Empire—"

"Shh." John looked around. Only one monk was nearby, on his hands and knees in the herb garden. "One never knows who may be listening."

"I am too old to fear spies overmuch, John," the abbot said, chuckling. At that moment, the monk in the herb garden sat back on his haunches so he could wipe sweat from his strong, swarthy face with the sleeve of his robe. Isaac chuckled again. "And can you seriously imagine *him* betraying us?"

John laughed too. "That one? No, you have me there. Ever since he came to us, he's thought of nothing but his hymns."

"Nor can I blame him, for they are a gift from God," Isaac said. "Truly he must be inspired, to sing the Lord's praises so sweetly when he knew not a word of Greek before he fled his horrid paganism to become a Christian and a monk. Romanos the Melodist was a convert too, they say—born a Jew."

"Some of our brother's hymns are a match for his, I think," John said. "Perhaps they love Christ the more for first discovering Him with the full faculties of grown men."

"It could be so," Isaac said thoughtfully. Then, as the monk in the garden resumed his work, the abbot came back to his worries. "When I was younger, we always knew the Persians were harriers, not conquerors. Sooner or later, our soldiers would drive them back. This time I think they are come to stay."

John's sunny face was not well adapted to showing concern, but it did now. "You may be right, father abbot. Since the general Narses rebelled against Phokas, since Germanos attacked Narses, since the Persians beat Germanos and Leontios—"

"Since Phokas broke his own brother's pledge of safe-conduct for Narses and burned him alive, since Germanos was forced to become a monk for losing to the Persians—" Isaac took up the melancholy tale of Roman troubles. "Our armies now are a rabble, those that have not fled. Who will, who can, make king Khosroes's soldiers leave the Empire now?"

John looked this way and that again, lowered his voice so that Isaac had to lean close to hear him at all. "Perhaps it would be as well if they did stay. I wonder," he went on wistfully, "if the young man with them truly is Maurice's son Theodosios. Even with Persian backing, he would be better than Phokas."

"No, John." The abbot shook his head in grim certainty. "I am sure Theodosios is dead; he was with his father when Phokas overthrew them. And while the new Emperor has many failings, no one can doubt his talent as a butcher."

"True enough," John sighed. "Well, then, father abbot, why *not* welcome the Persians as liberators from the tyrant?"

"Because of what I heard from a traveler out of the east who took shelter with us last night. He was from a village near Daras, where the Persians have had a couple of years now to decide how they will govern the lands they have taken from the Empire. He told me they were beginning to make the Christians thereabouts become Nestorians."

"I had not heard that, father abbot," John said, adding a moment later, "Filthy heresy!"

"Not to the Persians. They exalt Nestorians above all other Christians, trusting their loyalty because we who hold to the right belief have persecuted them so they may no longer live within the Empire." Isaac sadly shook his head. "All too often, that trust has proven justified."

"What shall we do, then?" John asked. "I will not abandon the true faith, but in truth I would sooner serve the Lord as a living monk than as a martyr, though His will be done, of course." He crossed himself.

So did Isaac. His eyes twinkled. "I do not blame you, my son. I have lived most of my life, so I am ready to see God and His Son face to face whenever He desires, but I understand how younger men might hesitate. Some, to save their lives, might even bow to heresy and forfeit their souls. I think, therefore, that we should abandon Ir-Ruhaiyeh, so no one will have to face this bitter choice."

John whistled softly. "As bad as that?" His glance slid to the monk in the garden, who had looked up at the musical tone but went back to his weeding when the prior's eye fell on him.

"As bad as that," Isaac echoed. "I need you to begin drawing up plans for our withdrawal. I want us to leave no later than a week from today."

"So soon, father abbot? As you wish, of course; you know you have my obedience. Shall I arrange for our travel west to Antioch or south to Damascus? I presume you will want us safe behind a city's walls."

"Yes, but neither of those," the abbot said. John stared at him in surprise. Isaac went on, "I doubt Damascus is strong enough to stand against the storm that is rising. And Antioch—Antioch is all in commotion since the Jews rose and murdered the patriarch, may God smile upon him. Besides, the Persians are sure to make for it, and it can fall. I was a tiny boy the last time it did; the sack, I have heard, was ghastly. I would not want us caught up in another such."

"What then, father abbot?" John asked, puzzled now.

"Ready us to travel to Constantinople, John. If Constantinople falls to the Persians, surely it could only portend the coming of the Antichrist and the last days of the world. Even that may come. I find it an evil time to be old."

"Constantinople. The city." John's voice held awe and longing. From the Pillars of Herakles to Mesopotamia, from the Danube to Nubia, all through the Roman Empire, Constantinople was *the* city. Every man dreamed of seeing it before he died. The prior ran fingers through his beard. His eyes went distant as he began to think of what the monks would need to do to get there. He never noticed Isaac walking away.

What did call him back to his surroundings was the monk leaving the herb garden a few minutes later. Had the fellow simply passed by, John would have paid him no mind. But he was humming as he walked, which disturbed the prior's thoughts.

"Silence, brother," John said reprovingly.

The monk dipped his head in apology. Before he had gone a dozen paces, he was humming again. John rolled his eyes in rueful despair. Taking the music from that one was the next thing to impossible, for it came upon him so strongly that it possessed him without his even realizing it.

Had he not produced such lovely hymns, the prior thought, people might have used the word *possessed* in a different sense. But no demon, surely, could bring forth glowing praise of the Trinity and the Archangel Gabriel.

John dismissed the monk from his mind. He had many more important things to worry about.

"A *nomisma* for that donkey, that piece of crowbait?" The monk clapped a hand to his tonsured pate in theatrical disbelief. "A goldpiece? You bandit, may Satan lash you with sheets of fire and molten brass for your effrontery! Better you should ask for thirty pieces of silver. That would only be six more, and would show you for the Judas you are!"

After fierce haggling, the monk ended up buying the donkey for ten silver pieces, less than half the first asking price. As the trader put the jingling miliaresia into his pouch, he nodded respectfully to his recent opponent. "Holy sir, you are the finest bargainer I ever met at a monastery."

"I thank you." Suddenly the monk was shy, not the fierce dickerer he had seemed a moment before. Looking down to the ground, he went on, "I was a merchant once myself, years ago, before I found the truth of Christ."

The trader laughed. "I might have known." He gave the monk a shrewd once-over. "From out of the south, I'd guess, by your accent."

"Just so." The monk's eyes were distant, remembering. "I was making my first run up to Damascus. I heard a monk preaching in the marketplace. I was not even a Christian at the time, but it seemed to me that I heard within me the voice of the Archangel Gabriel, saying, 'Follow!' And follow I did, and follow I have, all these years since. My caravan went back without me."

"A strong call to the faith indeed, holy sir," the trader said, crossing himself. "But if you ever wish to return to the world, seek me out. For a reasonable share of the profits I know you will bring in, I would be happy to stake you as a merchant once again."

The monk smiled, teeth white against tanned, dark skin and gray-streaked black beard. "Thank you, but I am content and more than content with my life as it is. *Inshallah*—" He laughed at himself. "Here I've been working all these years to use only Greek, and recalling what I once was makes me forget myself so easily. *Theou thelontos*, I should have said—God willing—I would have spent all my days here at Ir-Ruhaiyeh. But that is not to be."

"No." The trader looked east. No smoke darkened the horizon there, not yet, but both men could see it in their minds' eyes. "I may find a new home for myself as well."

"God grant you good fortune," the monk said.

"And you, holy sir. If I have more beasts to sell, be sure I shall look for a time when you are busy elsewhere."

"Spoken like a true thief," the monk said. They both laughed. The monk led the donkey away toward the stables. They were more crowded now than at any other time he could recall, with horses, camels, and donkeys. Some the monks would ride, others would carry supplies and the monastery's books and other holy gear.

Words and music filled the monk's mind as he walked toward the refectory. By now the words came more often in Greek than his native tongue, but this time, perhaps because his haggle with the merchant had cast memory back to the distant pagan days he did not often think of anymore, the idea washed over him in the full guttural splendor of his birthspeech.

Sometimes he crafted a hymn line by line, word by word, fighting against stubborn ink and papyrus until the song had the shape he wanted. He was proud of the songs he shaped that way. They were truly his.

Sometimes, though, it was as if he saw the entire shape of a hymn complete at once. Then the praises to the Lord seemed almost to write themselves, his pen racing over the page as an instrument not of his own intelligence but rather a channel through which God spoke for himself. Those hymns were the ones for which the monk had gained a reputation that reached beyond Syria. He often wondered if he had earned it. God deserved more credit than he did. But then, he would remind himself, that was true in all things.

This idea he had now was of the second sort, a flash of inspiration so blinding that he staggered and almost fell, unable to bear up under its impact. For a moment, he did not even know—or care—where he was. The words, the glorious words reverberating in his mind, were all that mattered.

And yet, because the inspiration came to him in his native language, his intelligence was also engaged. How could he put his thoughts into words his fellows here and folk all through the Empire would understand? He knew he had to; God would never forgive him, nor he forgive himself, if he failed here.

The refectory was dark but, filled with summer air and sweating monks, not cool. The monk took a loaf and a cup of wine. He ate without tasting what he had eaten. His comrades spoke to him; he did not answer. His gaze was inward, fixed on something he alone could see.

Suddenly he rose and burst out, "There is no God but the Lord, and Christ is His Son!" That said what he wanted to say, and said it in good Greek, though without the almost hypnotic intensity the phrase had in his native tongue. Still, he saw, it served his purpose: several monks glanced his way, and a couple, having heard only the bare beginning of the song, made the sacred sign of the cross.

He noticed the others in the refectory only peripherally. Only later would he realize he had heard John say in awe to the abbot Isaac, "The holy fit has taken him again."

For the prior was right. The fit had taken him, and more strongly than ever before. Words poured from somewhere deep within him: "He is the Kindly, the Merciful, Who gave His only begotten Son that man might live. The Lord will abide forever in glory, Father, Son, and Holy Spirit. Which of the Lord's blessings would you deny?"

On and on he sang. The tiny part of him not engaged in singing thanked God for granting him what almost amounted to the gift of tongues. His spoken Greek, especially when dealing with things of

the world, was sometimes halting. Yet again and again now, he found
the words he needed. That had happened before, but never like this.

"There is no God but the Lord, and Christ is His Son!" Ending as
he had begun, the monk paused, looking around for a moment as he
slowly came back to himself. His knees failed him; he sank back to his
bench. He felt drained but triumphant. The only comparison he
knew was most unmonastic: he felt as he had just after a woman.

He rarely thought, these days, of the wife he had left with all else
when he gave over the world for the monastery. He wondered if she
still lived; she was a good deal older than he. With very human vanity, he wondered if she ever thought of him. With his own character-
istic honesty, he doubted it. The marriage had been arranged. It was
not her first. Likely it would not have been her last, either.

The touch of the prior's hand on his arm brought him fully back to
the confines he had chosen as his own. "That was most marvelous,"
John said. "I count myself fortunate to have heard it."

The monk dipped his head in humility. "You are too kind, reverend
sir."

"I do not think so." John hesitated, went on anxiously, "I trust—I
pray—you will be able to write down your words, so those not lucky
enough to have been here on this day will yet be able to hear the truth
and grandeur of which you sang."

The monk laughed—again, he thought, as he might have at any
small thing after going in unto his wife. "Have no fear there, reverend sir. The words I recited are inscribed upon my heart. They shall
not flee me."

"May it be as you have said," the prior told him.

John did not, however, sound as though he thought it was. To set
his mind at ease, the monk sang the new hymn again, this time not in
the hot flush of creation but as one who brings out an old and long-
familiar song. "You see, reverend sir," he said when he was done.
"What the Lord, the Most Bountiful One, has granted me shall not be
lost."

"Now I have been present at two miracles," John said, crossing
himself: "hearing your song the first time and then, a moment later,
again with not one single change, not a different word, that I noticed."

With his mind, the monk felt of the texture of his creation, comparing his first and second renditions of the hymn. "There were none,"
he said confidently. "I would take oath to it before Christ the Judge of
all."

"No need on my account. I believe you," John said. "Still, even miracles, I suppose, may be stretched too far. Therefore I charge you, go at once to the writing chamber, and do not leave it until you have written out three copies of your hymn. Keep one yourself, give me one, and give the third to any other one of the brethren you choose."

For the first time in his life, the monk dared protest his prior's command. "But, reverend sir, I should not waste so much time away from the work of preparing for our journey to the city."

"One monk's absence will not matter so much there," John said firmly. "Do as I tell you, and we will bring to Constantinople not only our humble selves, but also a treasure for all time in your words of wisdom and prayer. That is why I bade you write out three copies: if the worst befall and the Persians overrun us, which God prevent, then one might still reach the city. And one must, I think. These words are too important to be lost."

The monk yielded. "It shall be as you say, then. I had not thought on why you wanted me to write out the hymn three times—I thought it was only for the sake of Father, Son, and Holy Spirit."

To his amazement, John bowed to him. "You are most saintly, thinking only of the world of the spirit. As prior, though, I have also to reckon with this world's concerns."

"You give me too much credit," the monk protested. Under his swarthy skin he felt himself grow hot, remembering how moments ago he had been thinking, not of the world to come, but of his wife.

"Your modesty becomes you," was all John said to that. The prior bowed again, discomfiting the monk even more. "Now I hope you will excuse me, for I have my work to see to. Three fair copies, mind, I expect from you. In that matter I will accept no excuses."

The monk made one last try. "Please, reverend sir, let me labor too and write later, when our safety is assured. Surely I will earn the hatred of my brethren for being idle while they put all their strength into readying us to go."

"You are not idle," John said sternly. "You are in the service of the Lord, as are they. You are acting under my orders, as are they. Only vicious fools could resent that, and vicious fools will have to deal with *me.*" The prior set his jaw.

"They will do as you say, reverend sir," the monk said—who could dare disobey John? "But they will do it from obedience alone, not from conviction, if you take my meaning."

"I know what you mean," the prior said, chuckling. "How could I be who I am and not know it? Here, though, you are wrong. Not a man who was in the refectory and heard your hymn will bear you any but the kindest of wills. All will be as eager as I am to have it preserved."

"I hope you are right," the monk said.

John laughed again. "How could I be wrong? After all, I am the prior." He thumped the monk on the back. "Now go on, and prove it for yourself."

With more than a little trepidation, the monk did as he had been ordered. He was surprised to find John right. Though he sat alone in the writing chamber, from time to time monks bustling past paused a moment to lean their burdens against the wall, stick their heads in the doorway, and encourage him to get his song down on papyrus.

The words flowed effortlessly from his pen—as he'd told the prior, they truly were inscribed upon his heart. He took that to be another sign of God's speaking directly through him with this hymn. He sometimes found writing a barrier; the words that sang in his mind seemed much less fine when written out. And other times his pen could not find the right words at all, and what came from it was not the fine thing he had conceived, but only a clumsy makeshift.

Not today. When he finished the first copy, the crucial one, he compared it to what he had sung. It was as if he had seen the words of the hymn before him as he wrote. Here they were again, as pure and perfect as when the Lord had given them to him. He bent his head in thanksgiving.

He took more papyrus and began the second and third copies. Usually when he was copying, his eyes went back to the original every few words. Now he hardly glanced at it. He had no need, not today.

He was no fine calligrapher, but his hand was clear enough. After so long at Ir-Ruhaiyeh, writing from left to right had even begun to seem natural to him.

The bell rang for evening prayer. The monk noticed, startled, that the light streaming in through the window was ruddy with sunset. Had his task taken any longer, he would have had to light a lamp to finish it. He rubbed his eyes, felt for the first time how tired they were. Maybe he should have lit a lamp. He did not worry about it. Even if the light of the world was failing, the light of the Holy Spirit had sustained him while he wrote.

He took the three copies of the hymn with him as he headed for the chapel. John, he knew, would be pleased that he had finished writing in a single afternoon. So much still remained to be done before the monks left Ir-Ruhaiyeh.

* * *

Donkeys brayed. Horses snorted. Camels groaned, as if in torment. Isaac knew they would have done the same had their loads been a single straw rather than the bails and panniers lashed to their backs. The abbot stood outside the monastery gates, watching monks and beasts of burden file past.

The leavetaking made him feel the full weight of his years. He rarely did, but Ir-Ruhaiyeh had been his home all his adult life. One does not abandon half a century and more of roots without second thoughts.

Isaac turned to John, who stood, as he so often did, at the abbot's right hand. "May it come to pass one day," Isaac said, "that the Persians be driven back to their homeland so our brethren may return here in peace."

"And may you lead that return, father abbot, singing songs of rejoicing in the Lord," John said. The prior's eyes never wandered from the gateway. As each animal and man came by, he made another check mark on the long roll of papyrus he held.

Isaac shook his head. "I am too old a tree to transplant. All other soil will seem alien to me; I shall not flourish elsewhere."

"Foolishness," John said. For all his effort, though, his voice lacked conviction. Not only was he uneasy about reproving the abbot in any way; he also feared Isaac knew whereof he spoke. He prayed both he and his superior were wrong.

"As you will." The abbot sounded reassuring—deliberately so, John thought. Isaac knew John had enough to worry about right now.

The procession continued. At last it came to an end: almost three hundred monks, trudging west in hope and fear. "Is everyone safely gone?" Isaac asked.

John consulted his list, now black with checks. He frowned. "Have I missed someone?" He shouted to the nearest monk in the column. The monk shook his head. The question ran quickly up the line, and was met everywhere with the same negative response.

John glowered down at the unchecked name, muttered under his breath. "He's off somewhere devising another hymn," the prior growled to Isaac. "Well and good—on any day but this. By your leave—" He started back into the now abandoned (or rather, all but abandoned) monastery.

"Yes, go fetch him," Isaac said. "Be kind, John. When the divine gift takes him, he forgets all else."

"I've seen." John nodded. "But even for that we have no time today, not if we hope to stay in this world so God may visit us with His gifts."

Entering Ir-Ruhaiyeh after the monks had gone out of it was like seeing the corpse of a friend—no, John thought, like the corpse of his mother, for the monastery had nurtured and sheltered him as much as his fleshly parents. Hearing only the wind whistle through the courtyard, seeing doors flung carelessly open and left so forever, made John want to weep.

His head came up. The wind was not quite all he heard. Somewhere among the deserted buildings, a monk was singing quietly to himself, as if trying the flavor of words on his tongue.

John found him just outside the empty stables. His back was turned, so even as the prior drew near he caught only snatches of the new hymn. He was not sure he was sorry. This song seemed to be the complement of the one the monk had created in the refectory; instead of praise for the Lord, it told of the pangs of hell in terms so graphic that ice walked John's back.

"For the unbelievers, for the misbelievers, the scourge. Their hearts shall leap up and choke them. Demons shall seize them by feet and forelocks. Seething water shall be theirs to drink, and—" The monk broke off abruptly, jumping in surprise as John's hand fell on his shoulder.

"Come, Mouamet," the prior said gently. "Not even for your songs will the Persians delay. Everyone else has gone now; we wait only on you."

For a moment, he did not think the monk saw him. Something that was almost fear prickled in him. Could the church itself handle a man with a gift the size of Mouamet's, especially if he came to its heart at Constantinople? Then, slowly, John's worry eased. The church was six centuries old, and bigger even than the Empire. No one man could twist it out of shape. Had the monk stayed among his wild cousins in Arabia, now, with no weighty tradition to restrain him . . .

At last Mouamet's face cleared. "Thank you, reverend sir," he said. "With the Lord giving me this hymn, I'd forgotten the hour." The abstracted expression that raised awe in John briefly returned. "I think I shall be able to recover the thread."

"Good," the prior said, and meant it. "But now—"

"—I'll come with you," Mouamet finished for him. Sandals scuffing in the dust, they walked together out of the monastery and set out on the long road to Constantinople.

INSTABILITY

Rudy Rucker and
Paul Di Filippo

Jack and Neal, loose and blasted, sitting on the steps of the ramshackle porch of Bill Burroughs's Texas shack. Burroughs is out in the yard, catatonic in his orgone box, a copy of the Mayan codices in his lap. He's already fixed M twice today. Neal is cleaning the seeds out of a shoebox full of Mary Jane. Time is thick and slow as honey. In the distance the rendering company's noon whistle blows long, shrill and insistent. The rendering company is a factory where they cut up the cows that're too diseased to ship to Chicago. Shoot and cut and cook to tallow and canned cancer consommé.

Burroughs rises to his feet like a figure in a well-greased Swiss clock. "There is scrabbling," goes Bill. "There is scrabbling behind the dimensions. Bastards made a hole somewhere. You ever read Lovecraft's 'Colour Out of Space,' Jack?"

"I read it in jail," says Neal, secretly proud. "Dig, Bill, your mention of that document ties in so exactly with my most recent thought mode that old Jung would hop a hard-on."

"*Mhwee-heee-heee,*" says Jack. "The Shadow knows."

"I'm talking about this bomb foolishness," harrumphs Burroughs, stalking stiff-legged over to stand on the steps. "The paper on the floor in the roadhouse john last night said there's a giant atom-bomb test taking place tomorrow at White Sands. They're testing out the fucking 'trigger bomb' to use on that god-awful new *hydrogen* bomb Edward Teller wants against the Rooshians. Pandora's box, boys, and we're not talking cooze. That bomb's going off in New Mexico tomorrow, and right here and now the shithead meat-flayers' noon whistle is getting us all ready for World War Three, and if we're all ready for that, then we're by Gawd ready to be a great civilian army, yes, soldiers for Joe McCarthy and Harry J. Anslinger, poised to stomp out the Reds 'n' queers 'n' dope fiends. Science brings us this. I wipe my queer junkie ass with science, boys. The Mayans had it aaall figured out a loooong time ago. Now take this von Neumann fella. . . ."

"You mean Django Reinhardt?" goes Jack, stoned and rude. "Man, this is your life, their life, my life, a dog's life, God's life, the life of Riley. The army's genius von Neumann of the desert, Bill, it was in the Sunday paper Neal and I were rolling sticks on in Tuscaloosa, I just got an eidetic memory flash of it, you gone wigged cat, it was right before Neal nailed that cute Dairy Queen waitress with the Joan Crawford nose."

Neal goes: "Joan Crawford, Joan Crawfish, Joan Fishhook, Joan Rawshanks in the fog. *McVoutie!*" He's toking a hydrant roach, and his jay-wrapping fingers are laying rapid cable. Half the damn box is already twisted up.

Jack warps a brutal moodswing. There's no wine. *Ti Jack could use a widdly sup pour bon peek, like please, you ill cats, get me off this Earth.* . . . Is he saying this *aloud*, in front of Neal and Burroughs?

"And fuck the chicken giblets," chortles Neal obscurely, joyously, in there, and then suggests, by actions as much as by words, *Is he really talking, Jack?* "That we get back to what's really important, such as rolling up this here, ahem, um, urp, Mexican see-gar, yes!"

Jack crab-cakes slideways on fingertips and heels to Neal's elbow, and they begin to lovingly craft and fashion and croon upon—and even it would not be too much to say give birth to—a beautiful McDeVoutieful hair-seeded twat of a reefer, the roach of which will be larger than any two normal sticks.

They get off good.

Meanwhile, Bill Burroughs is slacked back in his rocker, refixed and not quite on the nod because he's persistently irritated, both by the thought of the hydrogen bomb and, more acutely, by the fly-buzz derry Times Square jive of the jabbering teaheads. Time passes, so very slowly for Sal and Dean, so very fast for William Lee.

So Doctor Miracle and Little Richard are barreling along the Arizona highway, heading east on Route 40 out of Vegas, their pockets full of silver cartwheels from the grinds they've thimblerigged, and also wallets bulging with the hi-denom bills they demanded when cashing in their chips after beating the bank at the roulette wheels of six different casinos with their unpatented probabilistic scams that are based on the vectors of neutrons through six inches of lead as transferred by spacetime Feynman diagrams to the workings of those rickety-clickety simple-ass macroscopic systems of balls and slots.

Doctor Miracle speaks. He attempts precision, to compensate for the Hungarian accent and for the alcohol-induced spread in bandwidth.

"Ve must remember to zend Stan Ulam a postcard from Los Alamos, reporting za zuccess of his Monte Carlo modeling method."

"It woulda worked even better over in Europe," goes Little Richard. "They got no double-zero slots on their wheels."

Doctor Miracle nods sagely. He's a plump guy in his fifties: thinning hair, cozy chin, faraway eyes. He's dressed in a double-breasted suit, with a bright hula-girl necktie that's wide as a pound of bacon.

Little Richard is younger, skinnier, and more Jewish, and he has a thick pompadour. He's wearing baggy khakis and a white T-shirt with a pack of Luckys rolled up in the left sleeve.

It is not immediately apparent that these two men are ATOMIC WIZARDS, QUANTUM SHAMANS, PLUTONIUM PROPHETS, and BE-BOPPIN' A-BOMB PEE AITCH DEES!

Doctor Miracle, meet Richard Lernmore. Little Richard, say hello to Johnny von Neumann!

There is a case of champagne sitting on the rear seat in between them. Each of the A-scientists has an open bottle from which he swigs, while their car, a brand-new 1950 big-finned land-boat of a two-toned populuxe pink-'n'-green Caddy, speeds along the highway.

There is no one driving. The front seat is empty.

Von Neumann, First Annointed Master of Automata, has rigged up the world's premier autopilot, you dig. He never could drive very well, and now he doesn't have to. Fact is, no one has to! The Caddy has front- and side-mounted radar that feeds into a monster contraption in the trunk, baby cousin to Weiner and Ulams's Los Alamos MANIAC machine, a thing all vacuum tubes and cams, all cogs and Hollerith sorting rods, a mechanical brain that transmits cybernetic impulses directly to the steering, gas, and brake mechanisms.

The Trilateral Commission has ruled that the brain in the Cad's trunk is too cool for Joe Blow, much too cool, and a self-driving car isn't going to make it to the assembly line ever. The country needs only a few of those supercars, and this one has been set aside for the use and utmost ease of the two genius-type riders who wish to discuss high quantum-physical, metamathematical, and cybernetic topics without the burden of paying attention to the road. Johnny and Dickie's periodic Alamos-to-Vegas jaunts soak up a lot of the extra nervous tension these important bomb builders suffer from.

"So whadda ya think of my new method for scoring showgirls?" asks Lernmore.

"Dickie, although za initial trials vere encouraging, ve must have more points on the graph before ve can extrapolate," replies von Neumann. He looks sad. "You may haff scored, you zelfish little prick, but *I*—I did not achieve satisfactory sexual release. Far from it."

"Waa'll," drawls Lernmore, "I got a fave nightclub in El Paso where the girls are hotter'n gamma rays and pretty as parity conservation. You'll get what you need for sure, Johnny. We could go right instead of left at Albuquerque and be there before daylight. Everyone at Los Alamos'll be busy with the White Sands test anyway. Security won't look for us till Monday, and by then we'll be back, minus several milliliters of semen."

"El Paso," mutters von Neumann, taking a gadget out of his inner jacket pocket. It's—THE FIRST POCKET CALCULATOR! Thing the size of a volume of the *Britannica*, with Bakelite buttons, and what makes it truly hot is that it's got all the road distances from the *Rand McNally Road Atlas* data-based onto the spools of a small wire-recorder inside. Von Neumann's exceedingly proud of it, and although he could run the algorithm faster in his head, he plugs their present speed and location into the device; calls up the locations of Las Vegas, Albuquerque, El Paso, and Los Alamos; and proceeds to massage the data.

"You're quite right, Dickie," he announces presently, still counting the flashes of the calculator's lights. "Ve can do as you say and indeed eefen return to za barracks before Monday zunrise. Venn is za test scheduled, may I ask?"

"Eight A.M. Sunday."

Von Neumann's mouth broadens in a liver-lipped grin. "How zynchronistic. Ve'll be passing White Sands just zen. I haff not vitnessed a bomb test since Trinity. And zis is za biggest one yet; zis bomb is, as you know, Dickie, za Ulam cascade initiator for za new hydrogen bomb. I'm for it! Let me reprogram za brain!"

Lernmore crawls over the front seat while the car continues its mad careening down the dizzy interstate, passing crawling tourist Buicks and mom-'n'-dad Studebakers. He lugs the case of champagne into the front seat with him. Von Neumann removes the upright cushion in the backseat and pries off the panel, exposing the brain in the trunk. Consulting his calculator from time to time, von Neumann begins reprogramming the big brain by yanking switchboard-type wires and reinserting them.

"I'm tired of plugging chust metal sockets, Richard. Viz za next girl, I go first."

* * *

Now it's night, and the stoned beats are drunk and high on bennies, too. Neal, his face all crooked, slopes through Burroughs's shack and picks Bill's car keys off the dresser in the dinette where Joan is listening to the radio and scribbling on a piece of paper. Crossing the porch, thievishly heading for the Buick, Neal thinks Bill doesn't see, but Bill does.

Burroughs the beat morphinist, whose weary disdain has shaded catastrophically with the Benzedrine and alcohol into fried impatience, draws the skeletized sawed-off shotgun from the tube of hidden gutterpipe that this same Texafied Burroughs has suspended beneath a large hole drilled in the eaten wood of his porch floor. He fires a twelve-gauge shotgun blast past Neal and into Neal's cleaned and twisted box of Mary Jane, barely missing Jack.

"*Whew, no doubt,*" goes Neal, tossing Burroughs the keys.

"Have ye hard drink, mine host?" goes Jack, trying to decide if the gun really went off or not. "Perhaps a pint of whiskey in the writing desk, old top? A spot of sherry?"

"To continue my afternoon fit of thought," says Burroughs, pocketing his keys, "I was talking about thermonuclear destruction and about the future of all humanity, which species has just about been squashed to spermaceti in the rictal mandrake spasms of Billy Sunday's pimpled ass-cheeks." He pumps another shell into the shotgun's chamber. His eyes are crazed goofball pinpoints. "I am sorry I ever let you egregious dope-suckin' latahs crash here. I mean you especially, jailbird con man Cassady."

Neal sighs and hunkers down to wail on the bomber Jack's lit off a smoldering scrap of shotgun wadding. Before long he and Jack are far into a rap, possibly sincere, possibly jive, a new rap wrapped around the concept that the three hipsters assembled here on the splintery porch 'neath the gibbous prairie moon have formed or did or will form or, to be quite accurate, *were forming and still are forming right then and there*, an analogue of those Holy B-Movie Goofs, THE THREE STOOGES!

"Yes," goes Jack, "those Doomed Saints of Chaos, loosed on the work-a-daddy world to scramble the Charles Dickens cark and swink of BLOOEY YER FIRED, those Stooge Swine are the anarchosyndicalist truly wigged sub-Marxists, Neal man, *bikkhu* Stooges goosing ripeassmelons and eating fried chicken for supper. *We* are the Three Stooges."

"Bill is Moe," says Neal, hot on the beam, batting his eyes at Bill, who wonders if it's time to shed his character-armor. "Mister Serious

Administerer of Fundament Punishments and Shotgun Blasts, and me with a Lederhosen ass!"

"Ah you, Neal," goes Jack, "you're Curly, angelic madman saint of the uncaught mote-beam fly-buzz fly!"

"And Kerouac is Larry," rheums Burroughs, weary with the knowledge. "*Mopple-lipped, lisped, muxed, and completely flunk* is the phrase, eh, Jack?"

"Born to die," goes Jack. "We're all born to die, and I hope it do be cool, Big Bill, if we goam take yo cah. Vootie-oh-oh." He holds out his hand for the keys.

"Fuck it," says Bill. "Who needs this noise." He hands Jack the keys, and before you know it, Neal's at the wheel of the two-ton black Buick, gunning that straight-eight mill and burping the clutch. Jack's at his side, and they're on the road with a long honk good-bye.

In the night there's reefer and plush seats and the radio, and Neal is past spaced, off in his private land that few but Jack and Alan can see. He whips the destination on Jack.

"This car is a front-row seat to the A-blast."

"What."

"We'll ball this jack to White Sands, New Mexico, dear Jack, right on time for the bomb test Sunday 8 A.M. I stole some of Bill's M, man, we'll light up *on* it."

In Houston they stop and get gas and wine and benny and Bull Durham cigarette papers and keep flying west.

Sometime in the night, Jack starts to fade in and out of horror dreams. There's a lot of overtime detox dream-work that he's logged off of too long. One time he's dreaming he's driving to an atom-bomb test in a stolen car, which is of course true, and then after that he's dreaming he's the dead mythic character in black and white that he's always planned to be. Not to mention the dreams of graves and Memere and the endless blood sausages pulled out of Jack's gullet by some boffable blonde's sinister boyfriend . . .

". . . been oh rock and roll gospeled in on the *bomb foolishness* . . ." Neal is going when Jack screams and falls off the backseat he's stretched out on. There's hard wood and metal on the floor. ". . . and Jack, you do understand, buckaroo, that I have hornswoggled you into yet another new and unprecedentedly harebrained swing across the dairy fat of her jane's spreadness?"

"Go," goes Jack feebly, feeling around on the backseat floor. Short metal barrel, lightly oiled. Big flat disk of a magazine. Fuckin' crazy Burroughs. It's a Thompson submachine gun Jack's lying on.

"And, ah Jack, man, I knew you'd know past the suicidal norm,

Norm, that it was . . . *DeVoutie!*" Neal fishes a Bakelite ocarina out of his shirt pocket and tootles a thin, horrible note. "Goof on this, Jack, I just shot M, and now I'm so high I can drive with my eyes closed."

Giggling Leda Atomica tugs at the shoulders of her low-cut peasant blouse with the darling petit-point floral embroidery, trying to conceal the vertiginous depths of her cleavage, down which Doctor Miracle is attempting to pour flat champagne. What a ride this juicy brunette is having!

Leda had been toking roadside Albuquerque monoxide till 11:55 this Saturday night, thumb outstretched and skirt hiked up to midthigh, one high-heel foot perched on a little baby blue hand case with nylons and bra straps trailing from its crack. Earlier that day she'd parted ways with her employer, an Oakie named Oather. Leda'd been working at Oather's juke joint as a waitress and as a performer. Oather had put her in this like act wherein she strutted on the bar in high heels while a trained swan untied the strings of her atom-girl costume, a cute leatherette two-piece with conical silver lamé tit cups and black shorts patterned in intersecting friendly-atom ellipses. Sometimes the swan bit Leda, which really pissed her off. Saturday afternoon the swan had escaped from his pen, wandered out onto the road, and been mashed by a semi full of hogs.

"That was the only bird like that in Arizona," yelled Oather. "Why dintcha latch the pen?"

"Maybe people would start payin' to watch you lick my butt," said Leda evenly. "It's about all you're good for, limp-dick."

Et cetera.

Afternoon and early evening traffic was sparse. The drivers that did pass were all upstanding family men in sensible Plymouths, honest salesmen too tame for the tasty trouble Leda's bod suggested.

Standing there at the roadside, Leda almost gave up hope. But then, just before midnight, the gloom parted and here came some kind of barrel-assing Necco-Wafer-colored Caddy!

When the radars hit Leda's boobs and returned their echoes to the control mechanism, the cybernetic brain nearly had an aneurysm. Not trusting Lernmore's promises, von Neumann had hard-wired the radars for just such a tramp-girl eventuality, coding hitchhiking Jane Russell T&A parameters into the electronic brain's very circuits. The Caddy's headlights started blinking like a *fellah* in a sandstorm, concealed sirens went off, and Roman candles mounted on the rear

bumper discharged, shooting rainbow fountains of glory into the
night.

"SKIRT ALERT!" whooped Doctor Miracle and Little Richard.

Before Leda knew what was happening, the cybernetic Caddy had
braked at her exact spot. The rear door opened, Leda and her case
were snatched on in, and the car roared off, the wind of its passage
scattering the tumbleweeds.

Leda knew she was hooked up with some queer fellas as soon as she
noticed the empty driver's seat.

She wasn't reassured by their habit of reciting backward all the
signs they passed.

"Pots!"

"Egrem!"

"Sag!"

But soon Leda takes a shine to Doctor Miracle and Little Richard.
Their personalities grow on her in direct proportion to the amount of
bubbly she downs. By the time they hit Truth or Consequences,
N.M., they're scattin' to the cool sounds of Wagner's *Nibelungenlied* on
the long-distance radio, and Johnny is trying to baptize her tits.

"Dleiy!" croons Doctor Miracle.

"Daeha thgil ciffart!" goes Lernmore, all weaseled in on Leda's
other side.

"Kcuf em won syob!" says Leda, who's gone seven dry weeks without the straight-on loving these scientists are so clearly ready to provide.

So they pull into the next tourist cabins and get naked and find out
what factorial three really means. I mean . . . do they get it on or
what? Those stag-film stars Candy Barr and Smart Alec have got nothing on Leda, Dickie, and Doctor Miracle! Oh baby!

And then it's near dawn and they have breakfast at a greasy spoon,
and then they're on Route 85 south. Johnny's got the brain programmed to drive them right to the 7:57 A.M. White Sands space-time
coordinate; he's got the program tweaked down to the point where
the Cad will actually cruise past ground zero and nestle itself behind
the observation bunker, leaving them ample time to run inside and
join the other top bomb boys.

Right before the turnoff to the White Sands road, von Neumann
decides that things are getting dull.

"Dickie, activate the jacks!"

"Yowsah!"

Lernmore leans over the front seat and flips a switch that's breadboarded into the dash. The car starts to buck and rear like a wild bronco, its front and tail alternately rising and plunging. It's another goof of the wondercaddy—von Neumann has built B-52 landing gear in over the car's axles.

As the Caddy porpoises down the highway, its three occupants are laughing and falling all over each other, playing grab-ass, champagne spilling from an open bottle.

Suddenly, without warning, an *ooga-ooga* Klaxon starts to blare.

"Collision imminent," shouts von Neumann.

"Hold onto your tush!" advises Lernmore.

"Be careful," screams Leda and wriggles to the floor.

Lernmore manages to get a swift glimpse of a night black Buick driving down the two-lane road's exact center, heading straight toward them. No one is visible in the car.

Then the road disappears, leaving only blue sky to fill the windshield. There is a tremendous screech and roar of ripping metal, and the Caddy shudders slowly to a stop.

When Lernmore and von Neumann peer out of their rear window, they see the Buick stopped back there. It is missing its entire roof, which lies crumpled in the road behind it.

For all Neal's bragging, M's not something he's totally used to. He has to stop and puke a couple of times in El Paso, early early with the sky going white. There's no sympathy from Jack, 'cause Jack picked up yet another bottle of sweet wine outside San Antone, and now he's definitely passed. Neal has the machine gun up in the front seat with him; he knows he ought to put it in the trunk in case the cops ever pull them over, but the *dapperness* of the weapon is more than Neal can resist. He's hoping to get out in the desert with it and blow away some cacti.

North of Las Cruces the sun is almost up, and Neal is getting a bad disconnected feeling; he figures it's the morphine wearing off and decides to fix again. He gets a Syrette out of the Buick's glove compartment and skin-pops it. Five more miles and the rosy flush is on him; he feels better than he's felt all night. The flat empty dawn highway is a gray triangle that's driving the car. Neal gets the idea he's a speck of paint on a perspective painting; he decides it would be cool to drive lying down. He lies down sideways on the driver's seat, and when he sees that it works, he grins and closes his eyes.

The crash tears open the dreams of Jack and Neal like some horrible fat man's can opener attacking oily smoked sardines. They wake up in a world that's horribly different.

Jack's sluggish and stays in the car, but Neal is out on the road doing dance incantation trying to avoid death that he feels so thick in the air. The Thompson submachine gun is in his hand, and he is, solely for the rhythm, you understand, firing it and raking the landscape, especially his own betraying Buick, though making sure the fatal lead is only in the lower parts, e.g. tires as opposed to sleepy Jack backseat or gas tank, and, more than that, he's trying to keep himself from laying a steel-jacketed, flat horizontal line of lead across the hapless marshmallow white faces of the rich boys in the Cadillac. They have a low number government license plate. Neal feels like Cagney in *White Heat*, possessed by total crazed rage against authority, ready for a mad-dog last-stand showdown that can culminate only in a fireball of glorious fuck-you-copper destruction. But there's only two of them here to kill. Not enough to go to the chair for. Not yet, no matter how bad the M comedown feels. Neal shoots lead arches over them until the gun goes to empty clicks.

Slowly, black Jack opens the holey Buick door, feeling God it's so horrible to be alive. He blows chunks on the meaningless asphalt. The two strange men in the Cadillac give off the scent of antilife evil, a taint buried deep in the bone marrow, like strontium 90 in mother's milk. Bent down wiping his mouth and stealing an outlaw look at them, Jack flashes that these new guys have picked up their heavy death-aura from association with the very earth-frying, retina-blasting all-bomb that he and Neal are being ineluctably drawn to by cosmic forces that Jack can *see*, as a matter of fact, ziggy lines sketched out against the sky as clear as any peyote mandala.

"Everyone hates me but Jesus," says Neal, walking over to the Cadillac, spinning the empty Thompson around his callused thumb. "Everyone is Jesus but me."

"Hi," says Lernmore, "I'm sorry we wrecked your car."

Leda rises up from the floor between von Neumann's legs, a fact not lost on Neal.

"We're on our way to the bomb test," croaks Jack, lurching over.

"Ve helped invent the bomb," says von Neumann. "Ve're rich and important men. Of course ve vill pay reparations and additionally offer you a ride to the test, *ezpecially* since you didn't kill us."

The Cadillac is obediently idling in park, its robot-brain having retracted the jacks and gone into standby mode after the oil-pan-scraping collision. Neal mimes a wide-mouthed blow job of the hot tip of the Thompson, flashes Leda an easy smile, slings the gun out into the desert, and then he and shuddery Jack clamber into the Cad's front seat. Leda, with her trademark practicality, climbs into the

front seat with them and gives them a bottle of champagne. She's got
the feeling these two brawny drifters can take her faster farther than
science can.

Von Neumann flicks the RESET cyberswitch in the rear seat control
panel, and the Cad rockets forward, pressing them all back into the
deep cushioned seats. Neal fiddles with the steering wheel, fishtailing
the Cad this way and that, then observes, "Seems like this tough
short's got a mind of its own."

"Zis car's brobably as smart as you are," von Neumann can't help
observing. Neal lets it slide: 7:49.

The Cad makes a hard squealing right turn onto the White Sands
access road. There's a checkpoint farther on; but the soldiers recognize von Neumann's wheels and wave them right on through.

Neal fires up a last reefer and begins beating out a rhythm on the
dash with his hands, grooving to the pulse of the planet, his planet
awaiting its savior. Smoke trickles out of his mouth; he shotguns
Leda, breathing the smoke into her mouth, wearing the glazed eyes of
a mundane gnostic messiah, hip to a revelation of the righteous road
to salvation. Jack's plugged in, too, sucking his last champagne, telep-
athy-rapping with Neal. It's almost time, and Doctor Miracle and
Little Richard are too confused to stop it.

A tower rears on the horizon off to the left, and all at once the
smart Cad veers off the empty two lane road and rams its way
through a chain-link fence. Nerve-shattering scraping and lumbering
thumps.

"Blease step on za gas a bit," says von Neumann, unsurprised. He
programmed this shortcut in. "I still vant to go under za tower, but is
only three minutes remaining. Za program is undercompensating for
our unfortunate lost time." It is indeed 7:57.

Neal drapes himself over the wheel now, stone committed to this
last holy folly. Feeling a wave of serene, yet exultant resignation, Jack
says, "Go." It's almost all over now, he thinks, the endless roving and
raging, brawling and fucking, the mad flights back and forth across
and up and down the continent, the urge to get it all down on paper,
every last feeling and vision in master-sketch detail, because we're all
gonna die one day, man, all of us—

The Caddy, its sides raked of paint by the torn fence, hurtles on
like God's own thunderbolt messenger, over pebbles and weeds,
across the desert and the sloping glass craters of past tests. The tower
is ahead: 7:58.

"Get ready, Uncle Sam," whispers Neal. "We're coming to cut
your balls off. Hold the boys down, Jack."

Jack body-rolls over the seat back into the laps of Lernmore and von Neumann. Can't have those mad scientists fiddle with the controls while Neal's pulling his cool automotive move!

Leda still thinks she's on a joyride and cozies up to Neal's biceps, and for a second it's just the way it's supposed to be, handsome hard-rapping Neal at the wheel of big old bomb with a luscious brunette squeezed up against him like gum.

And now, before the guys in back can do much of anything, Neal's clipped through the tower's southern leg. As the tower starts to collapse, Neal, flying utterly on extrasensory instincts, slows just enough to pick up the bomb, which has been jarred prematurely off its release hook.

No Fat Boy, this gadget represents the ultimate to date in miniaturization: it's only about as big as a fifty-gallon oil drum, and about as weighty. It crunches down onto the Caddy's roof, bulging bent metal in just far enough to brush the heads of the riders.

And no, it doesn't go off. Not yet: 7:59.

Neal aims the mighty Cad at the squat concrete bunker half a mile off. This is an important test, the last step before the H-bomb, and all the key assholes are in there, every atomic brain in the free world, not to mention dignitaries and politicians aplenty, all come to witness this proof of American military superiority, all those shit-nasty fuckheads ready to kill the future.

King Neal floors it and does a cowboy yodel, Jack is laughing and elbowing the scientists, Leda's screaming luridly, Dickie is talking too fast to understand, and Johnny is—8:00.

They impact the bunker at eighty mph, folding up accordian-style, but not feeling it, as the mushroom blooms, and the atoms of them and the assembled bigwigs commingle in the quantum instability of the reaction event. Time forks.

Somewhere, somewhen, there now exists an Earth where there are no nuclear arsenals, where nations do not waste their substance on missiles and bombs, where no one wakes up thinking each morning might be the world's last—an Earth where two high, gone wigged cats wailed and grooved and ate up the road and Holy Goofed the world off its course.

For you and me.

NO SPOT OF GROUND

Walter Jon Williams

The dead girl came as a shock to him. He had limped into the Starker house from the firelit military camp outside, from a cacophony of wagons rattling, men driving tent pegs, provost marshals setting up the perimeter, a battalion of Ewell's Napoleon guns rolling past, their wheels lifting dust from the old farm road, dust that drifted over the camp, turning the firelight red and the scene into a pictured outpost of Hell. . . .

And here, to his surprise, was a dead girl in the parlor. She was perhaps sixteen, with dark hair, translucent skin, and cheeks with high spots of phthisis red. Her slim form was dressed in white. She lay in her coffin with candles at her head and feet, and her long-faced relatives sat in a semicircle of chairs under portraits of ancestors and Jefferson Davis.

A gangly man, probably the dead girl's father, rose awkwardly to welcome the surprised stranger, who had wandered into the parlor in hopes of asking for a glass of lemonade.

The intruder straightened in surprise. He took off his soft white hat and held it over his heart. The little gold knots on the ends of the hat cord rattled on the brim like muffled mourning drums.

"I am sorry to intrude on your grief," he said.

The father halted in what he was going to say, nodded, and dropped back into his chair. His wife, a heavy woman in dark silk, reached blindly toward him, and took his hand.

The intruder stood for a long moment out of respect, his eyes fixed on the corpse, before he turned and put on his hat and limped out of the house. Once he had thought this sight the saddest of all; once he had written poems about it.

What surprised him now was that it still happened, that people still died this way.

He had forgotten, amid all this unnatural slaughter, that a natural death was possible.

That morning he had brought his four brigades north into Richmond, marching from the Petersburg and Weldon depot south of the James break-step across the long bridge to the Virginia Central depot in the capital. Until two days ago he'd commanded only a single brigade in the defense of Petersburg; but poor George Pickett had suffered a collapse after days of nerve-wrenching warfare in his attempt to keep the city safe from Beast Butler's Army of the James; and Pickett's senior brigadier was, perforce, promoted to command of the whole division.

The new commander was fifty-five years old, and even if he was only a division commander till Pickett came back, he was still the oldest in the army.

At school he had been an athlete. Once he swam six miles down the James River, fighting against the tide the whole way, in order to outdo Byron's swim across the Hellespont. Now he was too tired and ill to ride a horse except in an emergency, so he moved through the streets of Richmond in a two-wheel buggy driven by Sextus Pompeiius, his personal darky.

He was dressed elegantly, a spotless gray uniform with the wreathed stars of a brigadier on his collar and bright gold braid on the arms, English riding boots, black doeskin gloves. His new white wide-brimmed hat, a replacement for the one shot off his head at Port Walthall Junction twenty days ago, was tilted back atop his high forehead. Even when he was young and couldn't afford anything but old and mended clothes, he had always dressed well, with the taste and style of a gentleman. Sextus had trimmed his grizzled mustache that morning, back in camp along the Petersburg and Weldon, and snipped at the long gray curls that hung over the back of his collar. A fine white-socked thoroughbred gelding, the one he was too ill to ride, followed the buggy on a lead. When he had gone south in 1861 he had come with twelve hundred dollars in gold and silver, and with that and his army pay he had managed to keep himself in modest style for the last three years.

As he rode past the neat brick houses he remembered when it was otherwise. Memories still burned in his mind: the sneers of Virginia planters' sons when they learned of his background, of his parents in the theater and stepfather in commerce; his mounting debts when his stepfather Mr. Allan had twice sent him to college, first to the University of Virginia and then to West Point, and then not given him the means to remain; the moment Allan had permitted the household slaves to insult him to his face; and those countless times he wandered the Richmond streets in black despondent reverie, when he couldn't help gazing with suspicion upon the young people he met, never knowing how many of them might be living insults to his stepmother, another of Mr. Allan's plentiful get of bastards. . . .

The brigadier looked up as the buggy rattled over rusting iron tracks, and there it was: Ellis & Allan, General Merchants, the new warehouse of bright red brick lying along a Virginia Central siding, its loading dock choked with barrels of army pork. The war that had so devastated the Confederate nation had been kind only to two classes: carrion crows and merchants. The prosperous Ellis & Allan was run by his stepbrothers now, he presumed, possibly in partnership with an assortment of Mr. Allan's bastards—in *that* family, who could say? The brute Allan, penny-pinching as a Jew with the morals of a nigger, might well have given part of the business to his illegitimate spawn, if for no other reason than to spite his foster son. Such was the behavior of the commercial classes that infected this city.

Richmond, he thought violently. Why in the name of heaven are we defending the place? Let the Yanks have it, and let them serve it as Rome served Carthage, burned to the foundations and the scorched plain sown with salt. There are other parts of the South better worth dying for.

Sextus Pompeiius pulled the mare to a halt, and the general limped out of the buggy and leaned on his stick. The Virginia Central yards were filled with trains, the cars shabby, the engines worn. Sad as they were, they would serve to get the division to where it was going, another fifteen miles up the line to the North Anna River, and save shoe leather while doing it.

The detestable Walter Whitman, the general remembered suddenly, wrote of steam engines in his poems. Whitman surely had not been thinking of engines like these, worn and ancient, leaking steam and oil as they dragged from front to front the soldiers as worn and tattered as the engines. Not trains, but ghosts of trains, carrying a ghost division, itself raised more than once from the dead.

The lead formation, the general's old Virginia brigade, was marching up behind the buggy, their colors and band to the front. The bandsmen were playing "Bonnie Blue Flag." The general winced—brass and percussion made his taut nerves shriek, and he could really tolerate only the soft song of stringed instruments. Pain crackled through his temples.

Among the stands of brigade and regimental colors was another stand, or rather a perch, with a pair of black birds sitting quizzically atop: Hugin and Munin, named after the ravens of Wotan. The brigade called themselves the Ravens, a compliment to their commander.

The general stood on the siding and watched the brigade as it came to a halt and broke ranks. A few smiling bandsmen helped the general load his horses and buggy on a flatcar, then jumped with their instruments aboard their assigned transport. The ravens were taken from their perch and put in cages in the back of the general's carriage.

A lance of pain drove through the general's thigh as he swung himself aboard. He found himself a seat among the divisional staff. Sextus Pompeiius put the general's bags in the rack over his head, then went rearward to sit in his proper place behind the car, in the open between the carriages.

A steam whistle cried like a woman in pain. The tired old train began to move.

Poe's Division, formerly Pickett's, began its journey north to fight the Yanks somewhere on the North Anna River. When, the general thought, would these young men see Richmond again?

One of the ravens croaked as it had been taught: "Nevermore!"

Men laughed. They thought it a good omen.

General Poe stepped out of the mourning Starker house, the pale dead girl still touching his mind. When had he changed? he wondered. When had his heart stopped throbbing in sad, harmonic sympathy at the thought of dead young girls? When had he last wept?

He knew when. He knew precisely when his heart had broken for the last time, when he had ceased at last to mourn Virginia Clemm, when the last ounce of poetry had poured from him like a river of dark veinous blood. . . .

When the Ravens had gone for that cemetery, the tombstones hidden in dust and smoke.

When General Edgar A. Poe, CSA, had watched them go, that brilliant summer day, while the bands played "Bonnie Blue Flag" under the trees and the tombstones waited, marking the factories of a billion happy worms . . .

Poe stood before the Starker house and watched the dark form of his fourth and last brigade, the new North Carolina outfit that had shown their mettle at Port Walthall Junction, now come rising up from the old farm road like an insubstantial battalion of mournful shades. Riding at the head came its commander, Thomas Clingman. Clingman saw Poe standing on Starker's front porch, halted his column, rode toward the house, and saluted.

"Where in hell do I put my men, General? One of your provost guards said up this way, but—"

Poe shook his head. Annoyance snapped like lightning in his mind. No one had given him any orders at all. "You're on the right of General Corse, out there." Poe waved in the general direction of Hanover Junction, the little town whose lights shone clearly just a quarter mile to the east. "You should have gone straight up the Richmond and Fredericksburg tracks from the Junction, not the Virginia Central."

Clingman's veinous face reddened. "They told me wrong, then. Ain't anybody been over the ground, Edgar?"

"No one from *this* division. Ewell pulled out soon's he heard we were coming, but that was just after dark and when we came up, we had no idea what to do. There was just some staff creature with some written orders, and he galloped away before I could ask him what they meant."

No proper instruction, Poe thought. His division was part of Anderson's corps, but he hadn't heard from Anderson and didn't know where the command post was. If he was supposed to report to Lee, he didn't know where Lee was either. He was entirely in the dark.

Contempt and anger snarled in him. Poe had been ignored again. No one had thought to consult him; no one had remembered him; but if he failed, everyone would blame him. Just like the Seven Days',

Clingman snorted through his bushy mustache. "Confound it anyway."

Poe banged his stick into the ground in annoyance. "Turn your men around, Thomas. It's only another half mile or so. Find an empty line of entrenchments and put your people in. We'll sort everyone out come first light."

"Lord above, Edgar."

"Fitz Lee's supposed to be on your right. Don't let's have any of your people shooting at him by mistake."

Clingman spat in annoyance, then saluted and started the process of getting his brigade turned around. Poe stared after him and bit back his own anger. Orders would come. Surely his division hadn't been forgotten.

"Massa Poe?"

Poe gave a start. With all the noise of marching feet and shouted orders, he hadn't heard Sextus Pompeiius creeping up toward him. He looked at his servant and grinned.

"You gave me a scare, Sextus. Strike me if you ain't invisible in the dark."

Sextus chuckled at his master's wit. "I found that cider, Massa Poe."

Poe scowled. If his soft cider hadn't got lost, he wouldn't have had to interrupt the Starkers' wake in search of lemonade. He began limping toward his headquarters tent, his cane sinking in the soft ground.

"Where'd you find it?" he demanded.

"That cider, it was packed in the green trunk, the one that came up with the divisional train."

"I instructed you to pack it in the brown trunk."

"I know that, Massa Poe. That fact must have slipped my mind, somehow."

Poe's hand clenched the ivory handle of his cane. Renewed anger poured like fire through his veins. "Worthless nigger baboon!" he snapped.

"Yes, Massa Poe," Sextus said, nodding, "I is. I *must* be, the way you keep saying I is."

Poe sighed. One really couldn't expect any more from an African. Changing his name from Sam to Sextus hadn't given the black any more brains than God had given him in the first place.

"Well, Sextus," he said. *"Fortuna favet fatuis,* you know." He laughed.

"Massa always has his jokes in Latin. He always does."

Sextus's tone was sulky. Poe laughed and tried to jolly the slave out of his mood.

"We must improve your knowledge of the classics. Your *litterae humaniores,* you understand."

The slave was annoyed. "Enough human litter around here as it is."

Poe restrained a laugh. "True enough, Sextus." He smiled indulgently. "You are excused from your lessons."

His spirits raised by the banter with his darky, Poe limped to his headquarters tent, marked by the division flags and the two ravens on their perch, and let Sextus serve him his evening meal. The ravens gobbled to each other while Poe ate sparingly, and drank two glasses of the soft cider. Poe hadn't touched spirits in fifteen years, even though whiskey was a lot easier to find in this army than water.

Not since that last sick, unholy carouse in Baltimore.

Where were his orders? he wondered. He'd just been ordered to occupy Ewell's trenches. Where was the rest of the army? Where was Lee? No one had told him anything.

After the meal, he'd send couriers to find Lee. Somebody had to know something.

It was impossible they'd forgotten him.

Eureka, he called it. His prose poem had defined the universe, explained it all, a consummate theory of matter, energy, gravity, art, mathematics, the mind of God. The universe was expanding, he wrote, had exploded from a single particle in a spray of evolving atoms that moved outward at the speed of divine thought. The universe was still expanding, the forms of its matter growing ever more complex; but the expansion would slow, reverse; matter would coalesce, return to its primordial simplicity; the Divine Soul that resided in every atom would reunite in perfect self-knowledge.

It was the duty of art, he thought, to reunite human thought with that of the Divine, particled with unparticled matter. In his poetry he had striven for an aesthetic purity of thought and sentiment, a detachment from political, moral, and temporal affairs. . . . Nothing of Earth shone in his verse, nothing contaminated by matter—he desired harmonies, essences, a striving for Platonic perfection, for the dialogue of one abstract with another. Beyond the fact that he wrote in English, nothing connected the poems with America, the nineteenth century, its life, its movements. He disdained even standard versification—he wrote with unusual scansions, strange metrics—the harmonies of octameter catalectic, being more rarified, seemed to rise to the lofty ear of God more than could humble iambic pentameter, that endless trudge, trudge, trudge across the surface of the terrestrial globe. He wanted nothing to stand between himself and supernal beauty, nothing to prevent the connection of his own mind with that of God.

He had poured everything into *Eureka*, all his soul, his hope, his grief over Virginia, his energy. In the end there was the book, but nothing left of the man. He lectured across America, the audiences polite and appreciative, their minds perhaps touched by his own vision of the Divine—but all his own divinity had gone into the book, and in the end Earth reached up to claim him. Entire weeks were spent in delirium, reeling drunk from town to town, audience to audience, woman to woman. . . .

Ending at last in some Baltimore street, lying across a gutter, his body a dam for a river of half-frozen October sleet.

* * *

After the meal Poe stepped outside for a pipe of tobacco. He could see the soft glow of candlelight from the Starker parlor, and he thought of the girl in her coffin, laid out in her dress of virgin white. How much sadder it would have been had she lived, had she been compelled to grow old in this new, changing world, this sad and deformed Iron Age dedicated to steam and slaughter . . . better she was dead, her spirit purged of particled matter and risen to contemplation of the self-knowing eternal.

His thoughts were interrupted by the arrival of a man on horseback. Poe recognized Colonel Moxley Sorrel, a handsome Georgian, still in his twenties, who was Longstreet's chief of staff. He had been promoted recently as a result of leading a flank assault in the Wilderness that had crushed an entire Union corps, though, as always, the triumph had come too late in the day for the attack to be decisive.

"General." Sorrel saluted. "I had a devil of a time finding you. Ewell had his command post at Hackett's place, over yonder." He pointed at the lights of a plantation house just north of Hanover Junction. "I reckoned you'd be there."

"I had no notion of where Ewell was. No one's told me a thing. This place seemed as likely as any." Poe looked off toward the lights of Hanover Junction. "At least there's a good view."

Sorrel frowned. He swung out of the saddle, and Sextus came to take the reins from his hand. "Staff work has gone up entirely," Sorrel said. "There's been too much chaos at the top for everything to get quite sorted out."

"Yes." Poe looked at him. "And how is General Longstreet?"

The Georgian's eyes were serious. "He will recover, praise God. But it will be many months before he can return to duty."

Poe looked up at the ravens, half expecting one of them to croak out "Nevermore." But they'd stuck their heads under their wings and gone to sleep.

He will recover, Poe thought. That's what they'd said of Stonewall; and then the crazed Presbyterian had died suddenly.

Just like old Stonewall to do the unexpected.

The army had been hit hard the last few weeks. First Longstreet wounded in the Wilderness, then Jeb Stuart killed at Yellow Tavern, just a few days ago. They were the two best corps commanders left to Lee, in Poe's opinion. Longstreet had been replaced by Richard Anderson; but Lee had yet to appoint a new cavalry commander—both, in Poe's mind, bad decisions. Anderson was too mentally lazy to command a corps—he was barely fit to command his old division—and the cavalry needed a firm hand now, with their guiding genius gone.

"Will you come inside, Colonel?" Poe gestured toward the tent flap with his stick.

"Thank you, sir."

"Share some cider with me? That and some biscuits are all the *rafraîchissements* I can manage."

"You're very kind." Sorrel looked at the uncleared table. "I've brought your orders from General Anderson."

Poe pushed aside his gold-rimmed dinner plate and moved a lantern onto the table. Sorrel pulled a folded map out of his coat and spread it on the pale blue tablecloth. Poe reached for his spectacles and put them on his nose. The map gave him, for the first time, an accurate look at his position.

This part of the Southern line stretched roughly northwest to southeast, a chord on an arc of the North Anna. The line was more or less straight, though it was cut in half by a swampy tributary of the North Anna, with steep banks on either side, and at that point Poe's entrenchments bent back a bit. The division occupied the part of the line south of the tributary. In front of him was dense hardwood forest, not very useful for maneuver or attack.

"We're going on the offensive tomorrow," Sorrel said, "thank the lord." He gave a thin smile. "Grant's got himself on the horns of a dilemma, sir, and General Lee intends to see he's gored."

Poe's temper crackled. "No one's going to get gored if division commanders don't get their instructions!" he snapped.

Sorrel gave him a wary smile. "That's why I'm here, sir."

Poe glared at him, then deliberately reined in his anger. "So you are." He took a breath. "Pardon my . . . display."

"Staff work, as I say, sir, has been a mite precarious of late. General Lee is ill, and so is General Hill."

Poe's anxiety rose again. "Lee?" he demanded. "Ill?"

"An intestinal complaint. We would have made this attack yesterday had the general been feeling better."

Poe felt his nervousness increase. He was not a member of the Cult of Lee, but he did not trust an army without a capable hand at the top. Too many high-ranking officers were out of action or incompetent. Stuart was dead, Longstreet was wounded, Lee was sick—great heavens, he'd already had a heart attack—Ewell hadn't been the same since he lost his leg, Powell Hill was ill half the time. . . . And the young ones, the healthy ones, were as always dying of bullets and shells.

"Your task, general," Sorrel said, "is simply to hold. Perhaps to demonstrate against the Yanks, if you feel it possible."

"How am I to know if it's possible?" He was still angry. "I don't know the ground. I don't know where the enemy is."

Sorrel cocked an eyebrow at him, said, "Ewell didn't show you anything?" But he didn't wait for an answer before beginning his exposition.

The Army of Northern Virginia, he explained, had been continually engaged with Grant's army for three weeks—first in the Wilderness, then at Spotsylvania, now on the North Anna; there hadn't been a single day without fighting. Every time one of Grant's offensives bogged down, he'd slide his whole army to his left and try again. Two days before, on May 24, Grant had gone to the offensive again, crossing the North Anna both upstream and down of Lee's position.

Grant had obviously intended to overlap Lee on both flanks and crush him between his two wings; but Lee had anticipated his enemy by drawing his army back into a V shape, with the center on the river, and entrenching heavily. When the Yanks saw the entrenchments they'd come to a stumbling halt, their offensive stopped in its tracks without more than a skirmish on either flank.

"You're facing Hancock's Second Corps, here on our far right flank," Sorrel said. His manicured finger jabbed at the map. Hancock appeared to be entirely north of the swampy tributary. "Warren and Wright are on our left, facing Powell Hill. Burnside's Ninth Corps is in the center—he tried to get across Ox Ford on the twenty-fourth, but General Anderson's guns overlook the ford and Old Burn called off the fight before it got properly started. Too bad—" Grinning. "Could've been another Fredericksburg."

"We can't hope for more than one Fredericksburg, alas," Poe said. "Not even from Burnside." He looked at the map. "Looks as if the Federals have broken their army into pieces for us."

"Yes, sir. We can attack either wing, and Grant can't reinforce one wing without moving his people across the North Anna twice."

General Lee had planned to take advantage of that with an offensive against half Grant's army. He intended to pull Ewell's corps off the far right, most of Anderson's out of the center, and combine them with Hill's for a strike at Warren and Wright. The attack would have been made the day before if Lee hadn't fallen ill. In the end he'd postponed the assault by one day.

The delay, Poe thought, had given the Yanks another twenty-four hours to prepare. Confederates aren't the only ones who know how to entrench.

Plans already laid, he thought. Nothing he could do about it.

He looked at the map. Now that Ewell and most of Anderson's people had pulled out, he was holding half the Confederate line with his single division.

"It'll probably work to the good," Sorrel said. "Your division came up to hold the right for us, and that will allow us to put more soldiers into the attack. With your division and Bushrod Johnson's, which came up a few days ago, we've managed to replace all the men we've lost in this campaign so far."

Had the Yankees? Poe wondered.

"When you hear the battle start," Sorrel said, "you might consider making a demonstration against Hancock. Keep him interested in what's happening on his front."

Poe looked up sharply. "One division," he said, "against the Yankee Second Corps? Didn't we have enough of that at Gettysburg?"

"A demonstration, general, not a battle." Politely. "General Anderson has also put under your command the two brigades that are holding the center, should you require them."

"Whose?"

"Gregg's Brigade, and Law's Alabamans."

Poe's mind worked through this. "Are Gregg and Law aware they are under my orders?"

"I presume so."

"Presume," Poe echoed. There was too much *presuming* in this war. He took off his spectacles and put them in his pocket. "Colonel Sorrel," he said, "would you do me the inestimable favor of riding to Gregg and Law tonight and telling them of this? I fear the staff work may not have caught up with General Anderson's good intent."

Sorrel paused, then gave a resigned shrug. "Very well, General. If you desire it."

"Thank you, Colonel." His small triumph made Poe genial. "I believe I have been remiss. I remember promising you cider."

"Yes. A glass would be delightful, thank you."

They sat at the folding table, and Poe called for Sextus to serve. He opened a tin box and offered it to Sorrel. "I have some of Dr. Graham's dietary biscuits, if you desire."

"Thank you, sir. If I may put some in my pockets for later . . . ?"

"Make free of them, sir."

Sorrel, possessing by now an old soldier's reflexes, loaded his pockets with biscuits and then took a hearty swallow of the cider. Sextus refilled his glass.

"General Pickett's campaign south of the James," Sorrel said, "has been much appreciated here."

"The form of appreciation preferable to us would have been reinforcements from General Lee."

"We were, ah, tangled up with Grant at the time, sir."

"Still, for several days we had two brigades against two entire corps. Two *corps*, sir!" Indignation flared in Poe. His fists knotted in his lap.

"The glory of your victory was all the greater." The Georgian's tone was cautious, his eyes alert.

Condescending, Poe thought. A black anger settled on him like a shroud. These southern gentlemen were always condescending. Poe knew what Sorrel was thinking. It's just Poe, hysterical Code-breaker Poe. *Poe* always thinks he's fighting the whole Yankee army by himself. *Poe* is always sending off messages screaming for help and telling other people what to do. What? Another message from Poe? It's just the fellow's nerves again. Ignore it.

"I've always been proved right!" Poe snapped. "I was *right* during the Seven Days' when I said Porter was dug in behind Boatswain Swamp! I was *right* about the Yankee signal codes, I was right about the charge at Gettysburg, and I was right again when I said Butler had come ashore at Bermuda Hundred with two whole Yankee corps! If my superiors would give me a little credit—"

"Your advice has always been appreciated," said Sorrel.

"My God!" Poe said. "Poor General Pickett is broken down because of this! It may be months before his nerves recover! Pickett—if he could stand what Lee did to the Division at Gettysburg, one might think he could stand anything! But *this*—*this* broke him! Great heavens, if Butler had committed more than a fraction of the forces available to him, he would have lost Petersburg, and with Petersburg, Richmond!"

"I do not think this is the place—" Sorrel began.

Too late. Poe's mind filled with the memory of the Yankees coming at the Ravens at Port Walthall Junction, four brigades against Pickett's two, and those four only the advance of Butler's entire army. He remembered the horror of it, the regimental flags of the Federals breaking out of the cover of the trees, brass and bayonets shining in the wind; shellfire bursting like obscene overripe blossoms; the whistling noise made by the tumbling bullet that had carried away Poe's hat; the sight of George Pickett with his face streaked by powder smoke, his long hair wild in the wind, as he realized his flanks were caving in and he was facing another military disaster . . .

"Screaming for reinforcements!" Poe shouted. "We were *screaming* for reinforcements! And what does Richmond send? *Harvey Hill!* Hah! Major General interfering Harvey Hill!"

Sorrel looked at him stonily. The old fight between Poe and Hill was ancient history.

"Hill is a madman, sir!" Poe knew he was talking too much, gushing like a chain pump, but he couldn't stop himself. Let at least one person know what he thought. "He is a fighter, I will grant him that, but he is quarrelsome, tempestuous—impossible to reason with. He is not a rational man, Colonel. He hasn't an ounce of rationality or system in him. No more brains than a nigger."

Sorrel finished his cider, and raised a hand to let Sextus know not to pour him more. "We may thank God that the movement was made by Butler," he said.

Poe looked at him. "The Yankees will not forever give their armies to men like Butler," he said.

Sorrel gazed resentfully at the lantern for a long moment. "Grant is no Butler, that is certain. But we will do a Chancellorsville on him nonetheless."

"We may hope so," said Poe. He had no confidence in this offensive. Lee no longer had the subordinates to carry things out properly, could no longer do anything in the attack but throw his men headlong at Federal entrenchments.

The young colonel rose. "Thank you for the cider, General. I will visit Generals Law and Gregg on my return journey."

Poe rose with him, memory still surging through his mind like the endless waves of Yankee regiments at Port Walthall Junction. He knew he had not made a good impression, that he had confirmed in Sorrel's mind, and through him the minds of the corps staff, the stories of his instability, his hysteria, and his egotism.

Harvey Hill, he thought, seething. Send Harvey Hill to tell *me* what to do.

Sextus brought Colonel Sorrel his horse and helped the young man mount. "Thank you for speaking to Gregg and Law," Poe said.

"Use their forces as you see fit," Sorrel said.

"This division has had hard fighting," Poe said. "I will be sparing in my use of them."

"We've all had hard fighting, sir," Sorrel said. A gentle reproach. "But with God's help we will save Richmond again this next day."

Poe gave a swift, reflexive glance to the ravens, anticipating another "Nevermore," but saw they were still asleep. No more omens tonight.

Sorrel saluted, Poe returned it, and the Georgian trotted off into the night.

Poe looked out at the Yankee campfires burning low off on his left. How many times, he wondered, would this army have to save Richmond? McDowell had come for Richmond, and McClellan, and Pope, Burnside, Hooker, Meade, and Butler. Now there was Grant, who had seized hold of Lee's army in the Wilderness and declined to let it go, even though he'd probably lost more men than the others put together.

Maybe Lee would turn tomorrow into another Chancellorsville.

But even if he did, Poe knew, one day this or another Yank general would come, and Richmond would not be saved. Even Lee could only fight history for so long.

The politicians were counting on the Northern elections to save them, but Poe had no more confidence in George McClellan as a candidate than as a general—Lincoln could outmaneuver him at the polls as handily as Lee had in the Seven Days' Battle.

No, the South was doomed, its Cause lost. That was obvious to anyone with any ratiocinative faculty whatever. But there was nothing else to do but fight on, and hope the North kept giving armies to the likes of Ben Butler.

"Massa Poe?" Sextus was at his elbow. "Will we be sleeping outside tonight?"

Poe cocked an eye at the sky. There was a heavy dew on the ground, but the few clouds in sight were high and moving fast. There should be no rain.

"Yes," Poe said. "Set up the beds."

"Whatever you say, massa."

Sextus was used to it, poor fellow. Poe hadn't been able to sleep alone since Virginia died, and he had always disliked confined spaces. Sleeping out of doors, under a heavy buffalo cloak, with Sextus wrapped in another robe nearby, was the ideal solution. Poe loved to look up at the sweep of brilliant stars, each an eye of God, to feel his soul rising beyond the atmosphere, through the luminiferous ether to merge with the Eternal, the Sublime . . .

How he came to the gutter in Baltimore he would never know. He had apparently given a lecture there a few nights before, but he couldn't remember it. Perhaps he would have died there, had not a passing widow recognized him, drunk and incapable, and brought him into her carriage. She had talked with him after his lecture, she told him, and found his conversation brilliant. He couldn't remember her either.

Her name was Mrs. Forster. Her late husband had been addicted to alcohol, and she had cured him; she would apply her cure as well to Mr. Poe.

Her plantation, within a half day's journey of Baltimore, was called Shepherd's Rest; she owned close to two thousand slaves and the better part of a county. She loved poetry and philosophy, read French and German, and had a passing knowledge of Latin.

She had a daughter named Evania, a green-eyed girl of fourteen. When Poe first saw her, sitting in the east parlor with the French wallpaper only a shade darker than her eyes, Evania was playing the guitar, her long fingers caressing the strings as if they were a lover's hair. Her long tresses, falling down her neck, seemed to possess the mutable spectrum of a summer sunrise.

Once before Poe, at the end of his wits and with the black hand of self-slaughter clutching at his throat, had been rescued by a widow with a daughter. In Mrs. Forster Poe could almost see Mrs. Clemm— but Mrs. Clemm idealized, perfected, somehow rarified, her poverty replaced by abundance, her sadness by energy, inspiration, and hope. How could he help but see Virginia in her sparkling daughter? How could he help but give her his love, his troth, his ring—He was not being faithless to Virginia, he thought; his second marriage was a fulfillment of the first. Did Evania and Virginia not possess, through some miracle of transubstantiation, the same soul, the same perfection of spirit? Were they not earthly shades of the same pure, angelic lady, differing only in color, one dark, one bright?

Were they not blessings bestowed by Providence, a just compensation for poor Poe, who had been driven nearly mad by soaring, like Icarus, too near the divine spark?

For a moment, after Poe opened his eyes, he saw her floating above him—a woman, dark-tressed, pale-featured, crowned with stars. He could hear her voice, though distantly; he could not make sense of her speech, hearing only a murmur of long vowel sounds. . . .

And then she was gone, faded away, and Poe felt a knife of sorrow enter his heart. He realized he was weeping. He threw off his buffalo robe and rolled upright.

The Starker house loomed above him, black against the Milky Way. The candles' glow still softly illuminated the parlor window.

Poe bent over, touching his forehead to his knees until he could master himself. He had seen the woman often in his dreams, sometimes in waking moments. He remembered her vividly, the female form rising over the streets of Richmond, during some barely-sane moments after Virginia's death, the prelude to that last spree in Baltimore. Always he had felt comforted by her presence, confirmed in his dreams, his visions. When she appeared it was to confer a blessing.

He did not remember seeing her since his war service started. But then, his war service was not blessed.

Poe straightened, and looked at the soft candlelight in the Starker windows. He looked at the foot of his cot, and saw Sextus wrapped in blankets, asleep and oblivious to his master's movements. Sometimes Poe thought he would give half his worth for a single night of sleep as deep and dreamless as that of his body-servant.

He put his stockinged feet in the carpet slippers that waited where Sextus had put them, then rose and stepped out into the camp in his dressing gown. The slippers were wet with dew inside and out. Poe didn't care. A gentle, warm wind was flitting up from the south. With this heavy dew, Poe thought, the wind would raise a mist before dawn. Maybe it would postpone Lee's offensive.

He remembered hiking in New York with Virginia, spending days wandering down hilly lanes, spending their nights in country inns or, when the weather was fine and Virginia's health permitted, wrapped in blankets beneath the open sky. His friends had thought his interest in nature morbid. Buried in the life of the city and the life of the mind, they could not understand how his soul was drawn skyward by the experience of the outdoors, how close he felt to the Creator when he and Virginia shared a soft bank of moist timothy and kissed and caressed one another beneath the infinite range of fiery stars. . . .

Poe realized he was weeping again. He looked about and saw he had wandered far from his tent, amid his soldiers' dying campfires.

Nothing like this had happened to him in years. The sight of that dead girl had brought back things he thought he'd forgotten.

He mastered himself once more and walked on. The rising southern wind stirred the gray ashes of campfires, brought little sparks winking across his path. He followed them, heading north.

Eventually he struck his entrenchments, a deep line of the kind of prepared works this army could now throw up in a few hours, complete with head log, communications trenches, firing step, and parapet. Soldiers huddled like potato sacks in the trenches, or on the grass just behind the line. An officer's mare dozed over its picket. Beyond, Poe could hear the footsteps of the sentries patrolling.

Once, just after the war had first started, Robert Lee had tried to get this army to dig trenches—and the soldiers had mocked him, called him "The King of Spades," and refused to do the work. Digging was no fit work for a white man, they insisted, and besides, only a coward would fight from entrenchments.

Now the army entrenched at every halt. Three years' killing had made them lose their stupid pride.

Poe stepped onto the firing step, and peered out beneath the head log as he tried to scan his front. Beyond the vague impression of gentle rolling hills beyond, he could see little. Then he lifted his head as he heard the challenging scream of a stallion. The sound came from away north, well past the entrenchments.

The mare picketed behind the entrenchments raised its head at the sound. The stallion challenged again. Then another horse screamed, off to the right, and another. The mare flicked its ears and gave an answer.

The mare was in heat, Poe realized. And she was flirting with Yankee horses. None of his men could be out that far.

The wind had carried the mare's scent north, to the nose of one northern stallion. Other stallions that hadn't scented the mare nevertheless answered the first horse's challenge.

Poe's head moved left to right as one horse after another screamed into the night. Sorrel's map hadn't shown the Yankee line stretching that far, well south of the tributary, beyond Clingman's brigade to where Fitz Lee's cavalry was supposed to be, out on his right flank.

He listened as the horses called to one another like bugles before a battle, and he thought: *The Yankees are moving, and they're moving along my front.*

Suddenly the warm south wind turned chill.

How many? he thought.

Sobbing in the mist like men in the extremes of agony, the crying horses offered no answer.

He became a child again, living with Evania in her perfect kingdom, that winding blue river valley west of Baltimore. Never before had he known rest; but there he found it, a cease from the despairing, agonized wanderings that had driven him, like a leaf before a black autumn storm, from Richmond to Boston and every city between.

At last he knew what it was to be a gentleman. He had *thought* he had achieved that title before, through education and natural dignity and inclination—but now he knew that before he had only aspired to the name. Mr. Allan fancied himself a gentleman; but his money was tainted with trade, with commerce and usury. Now Poe understood that the highest type of gentleman was produced only through ease and leisure—not laziness, but rather the freedom from material cares that allowed a man to cultivate himself endlessly, to refine his thought and intellect through study and application of the highest forms of human aspiration.

He was not lazy. He occupied himself in many ways. He moved Mrs. Clemm to Baltimore, bought her a house, arranged for her an annuity. He added to the mansion, creating a new façade of Italian marble that reflected the colors of the westering sun; he employed the servants to move tons of earth in order to create a landscape garden of fully forty acres that featured, in the midst of a wide artificial lake, an arabesque castle, a lacy wedding-cake gift to his bride.

He had always thought landscape gardening fully an equal of poetry in its ability to invoke the sublime and reveal the face of the deity. In this he was a disciple of de Carbonnieres, Piranesi, and Shenstone: The garden was nature perfected, as it had been in the mind of God, a human attempt to restore the divine, Edenic sublimity. He crafted his effects carefully—the long, winding streams through which one approached Poe's demiparadise in swan-shaped boats, the low banks crowded with moss imported from Japan, natural-seeming outcroppings of uniquely colored and textured rock. At the end was a deep, black chasm through which the water rushed alarmingly, as if to Hades—but then the boat was swept into the dazzling wide lake, the sun sparkling on the white sand banks, the blue waters—and then, as the visitor's eyes adjusted from blackness to brightness, one perceived in the midst of a blue-green island the white castle with its lofty, eyelike windows, the symbol of purest Mind in the midst of Nature.

Nothing was suffered to spoil the effects that had taken a full six years to create. Not a stray leaf, not a twig, not a cattail was permitted to sully the ground or taint the water—fully thirty Africans were constantly employed to make certain that Poe's domain was swept clean.

It cost money—but money Poe had, and if not there was always more to be obtained at three and one half percent. His days of penny-counting were over, and he spent with a lavish hand.

He fulfilled another ambition: he started a literary magazine, the *Southern Gentleman*, with its offices in Baltimore. For it he wrote essays, criticism, occasional stories, once or twice a poem.

Only once or twice.

Somehow, he discovered, the poetry had fled his soul.

And he began to feel, to his growing horror, that his loss of poetry was nothing but a just punishment. True poetry, he knew, could not reside in the breast of a man as faithless as he.

The Starker house on its small eminence stood hard-edged and black against a background of shifting mist, like an isolated tor rising above the clouds. It was a little after four. The sun had not yet risen, but already the eastern horizon was beginning to turn gray. The ravens, coming awake, crackled and muttered to one another as they shook dew from their feathers.

Poe leaned on his stick before a half-circle of his brigadiers and their mingled staffs. Hugin and Munin sat on their perch behind him. Poe was in his uniform of somber gray, a new paper collar, a black cravat, the black doeskin gloves. Over his shoulders he wore a red-lined black cloak with a high collar, an old gift from Jeb Stuart who had said it made him look like a proper raven.

Most of his life Poe had dressed all in black. The uniform was a concession to his new profession, but for sake of consistency with his earlier mode of dress he had chosen the darkest possible gray fabric, so dark it was almost blue.

There was the sound of galloping; riders rose out of the mist. Poe recognized the man in the lead: Fitzhugh Lee, Robert Lee's nephew and the commander of the cavalry division on his right. He was a short man, about Poe's height, a bandy-legged cavalryman with a huge spade-shaped beard and bright, twinkling eyes. Poe was surprised to see him—he had asked only that Lee send him a staff officer.

He and Poe exchanged salutes. "Decided to come myself, General." He dropped from his horse. "Your messenger made it seem mighty important."

"I thank you, sir." Fitz Lee, Poe realized, outranked him. He could take command here if he so desired.

He would not *dare*, Poe thought. A cold anger burned through him for a moment before he recollected that Fitz Lee had as yet done nothing to make him angry.

Still, Poe was uneasy. He could be superceded so easily.

"I think the Yankees are moving across my front," he said. He straightened his stiff leg, felt a twinge of pain. "I think Grant is moving to his left again."

The cavalryman considered this. "If he wants Richmond," he said, "he'll go to his right. The distance is shorter."

"I would like to submit, *apropos*, that Grant may not want Richmond so much as to defeat us in the field."

Fitz Lee puzzled his way through this. "He's been fighting us non-stop, that's the truth. Hasn't broken off so much as a day."

"Nevermore," said one of the ravens. Fitz Lee looked startled. Poe's men, used to it, shared grins. Poe's train of thought continued uninterrupted.

"Moreover, if Grant takes Hanover Junction, he will be astride both the Virginia Central and the Richmond and Fredericksburg. That will cut us off from the capital and our sources of supply. We'll have to either attack him there or fall back on Richmond."

"Mebbe that's so."

"All that, of course, is speculation—a mere exercise of the intuition, if you like. Nevertheless, whatever his intent, it is still an *observed* fact that Grant is moving across my front. *Quod erat demonstrandum.*"

Lee's eyes twinkled. "*Quod libet,* I think, rather." Not quite convinced.

"I have heard their horses. They are well south of where they are supposed to be."

Lee smiled through his big beard and dug a heel into the turf. "If he's moving past you, he'll run into my two brigades. I'm planted right in his path."

There was a saying in the army, *Who ever saw a dead cavalryman?* Poe thought of it as he looked at Lee. "Can you hold him?" he asked.

"Nevermore," said a raven.

Lee's smile turned to steel. "With all respect to your pets, General, I held Grant at Spotsylvania."

Gravely, Poe gave the cavalryman an elaborate, complimentary bow, and Lee returned it. Poe straightened and hobbled to face his brigade commanders.

Perhaps he had Fitz Lee convinced, perhaps not. But he knew—and the knowledge grated on his bones—that Robert Lee would not be convinced. Not with Poe's reputation for hysteria, for seeing Yankees everywhere he looked. The army commander would just assume his high-strung imagination crested illusory armies behind every swirl of mist. As much as Poe hated it, he had to acknowledge this.

"General Lee has made his plans for today," he said. "He will attack to the west, where he conceives General Grant to be. He may not choose to believe any message from his other wing that the Yanks are moving."

Poe waited for a moment for a reply from the cavalryman. Fitz Lee was the commanding general's nephew; perhaps he could trade on the family connection somehow. But the bearded man remained silent.

"They are going to strike us, that is obvious," Poe said. "Grant has his back to the bend of the river, and he'll have to fight his way into the clear. But his men will have to struggle through the woods, and get across that swamp and the little creek, and they're doing it at night, with a heavy mist. They will not be in position to attack at first light. I suggest, therefore, that we attack him as soon as the mist clears, if not before. It may throw him off balance and provide the evidence we need to convince the high command that Mr. Grant has stolen a march upon us."

"Nevermore," said the ravens. "Nevermore."

Poe looked at Sextus, who was standing respectfully behind the half-circle of officers. "Feed the birds," he said. "It may keep them quiet."

"Yes, massa."

"General Poe." Fitz Lee was speaking. "There are two bridges across that creek—small, but they'll take the Yankees across. The water won't hold up the Yanks as long as you might think."

Poe looked at him. "The bridges were not burned after Hancock crossed the North Anna?"

Lee was uneasy. "General Ewell may have done it without my knowledge."

"If the bridges exist, that's all the more reason to attack as soon as we can."

"General." Clingman raised a hand. "Our brigades marched up in the dark. We ain't aligned, and we'll need to sort out our men before we can go forward."

"First light, General," said Poe. "Arrange your men, then go forward. We'll be going through forest, so give each man about two feet of front. Send out one combined company per regiment to act as skirmishers—we'll want to overwhelm their pickets and get a look at what lies in there before your main body strikes them."

Another brigadier piped up. "What do we align on, sir?"

"The rightmost brigade of the division—that's Barton's?" Heads nodded. Poe continued, gesturing into the mist with his stick, sketching out alignments. "Barton will align on the creek, and everyone will guide on him. When Barton moves forward, the others will move with him." He turned to Gregg and Law, both of whom were looking dubious. "I cannot suggest to Generals Gregg and Law how to order their forces. I have not been over the ground."

Law folded his arms. "General. You're asking us to attack a Yankee corps that's had two days to entrench."

"And not just any corps," Gregg added. "This is *Hancock.*"

"We'll be outnumbered eight to one," Law said. "And we don't have any woods to approach through, the way y'all do. We'll have to cross a good quarter mile of open ground before we can reach them."

Poe looked at him blackly. Frustration keened in his heart. He took a long breath and fought down his growing rage.

Winfield Scott Hancock, he thought, known to the Yanks as Hancock the Superb. The finest of the Yankee commanders. He thought about the Ravens going up that little green slope toward the cemetery, with Hancock and his corps waiting on top, and nodded.

"Do as best as you can, gentlemen," he said. "I leave it entirely to you. I wish only that you show some activity. Drive in his pickets. Let him see some regimental flags, think he is going to be attacked."

Law and Gregg looked at one another. "Very well, sir," Law said.

Anger stabbed Poe again. They'd do nothing. He knew it; and if he ordered them into a fight they'd just appeal over his head to Anderson.

Nothing he could do about it. Keep calm.

Poe turned toward Fitz Lee. "I hope I may have your support."

The small man nodded. "I'll move some people forward." He gave a smile. "My men won't like being in the woods. They're used to clear country."

"Any additional questions?"

There were none. Poe sent his generals back to their commands and thanked Fitzhugh Lee for his cooperation.

"This may be the Wilderness all over again," Lee said. "Woods so heavy no one could see a thing. Just one big ambush with a hundred thousand men flailing around in the thickets."

"Perhaps the Yankees will not see our true numbers, and take us for a greater force," Poe said.

"We may hope, sir." Lee saluted, mounted, and spurred away.

Poe found himself staring at the black Starker house, that one softly lit eye of a window. Thinking of the dead girl inside, doomed to be buried on a battlefield.

Virginia Poe had been beautiful, so beautiful that sometimes Poe's heart would break just to look at her. Her skin was translucent as bone china, her long hair fine and black as midnight, her violet eyes unnaturally large, like those of a bird of Faerie. Her voice was delicate, as fragile and evanescent as the tunes she plucked from her harp.

Virginia's aspect was unearthly, refined, ethereal, like an angel descended from some Mussulman paradise, and as soon as Poe saw his
cousin he knew he could never rest unless he had that beauty by him
always.

When he married her she was not quite fourteen. When she died,
after five years of advancing consumption, she was not yet twenty-
five. Poe was a pauper. After Virginia's death came *Eureka*, dissipa-
tion, madness. He had thought he could not live without her, had no
real intention of doing so.

But now he knew he had found Virginia again, this time in Evania.
With Evania, as with Virginia, he could throw off his melancholy and
become playful, gentle, joyful. With her he could sit in the parlor
with its French wallpaper, play duets on the guitar, and sing until he
could see the glow of his happiness reflected in Evania's eyes.

But in time a shadow seemed to fall between them. When Poe
looked at his young bride, he seemed to feel an oppression on his
heart, a catch in the melody of his love. Virginia had not asked for
anything in life but to love her cousin. Evania was proud; she was
willful; she grew in body and intellect. She developed tastes, and
these tastes were not those of Poe. Virginia had been shy, other-
worldly, a presence so ethereal it seemed as if the matter had been
refined from her, leaving only the essence of perfected beauty and
melancholy; Evania was a forthright presence, bold, a tigress in human form. She was a material presence; her delights were entirely
those of Earth.

Poe found himself withdrawing before Evania's growing clarity.
He moved their sleeping chamber to the topmost floor of the mansion, beneath a roof of glass skylights. The glass ceiling was swathed
in heavy Oriental draperies to keep out the heat of the day; the windows were likewise covered. Persian rugs four deep covered the floor.
Chinese bronzes were arranged to pour gentle incense into the room
from the heads of dragons and lions.

With the draperies blocking all sources of the light, in the near-
absolute, graveyard darkness, Poe found he could approach his wife.
The fantastic decor, seen only by such light as slipped in under the
door or through cracks in the draperies, heightened Poe's imagination
to a soaring intensity. He could imagine that the hair he caressed was
dark as a raven's wing; that the cheek he softly kissed was porcelain-
pale; he could fancy, under the influence of the incense, that the
earthy scent of Evania had been transformed to a scent far more
heavenly; and he could almost perceive, as ecstasy flooded him, that

the eyes that looked up into his were the large, luminous angelic eyes of his lost love, the lady Virginia.

Poe sat in his tent and tried to eat an omelette made of eggs scavenged from Starker chickens. Fried ham sat untouched on the plate. Around him, the reserve divisional artillery creaked and rattled as the guns were set up on the Starkers' slight eminence. The ravens gobbled and cawed.

Poe put down his fork. He was too agitated to eat.

A drink, he thought. A soothing glass of sherry. The Starkers must have some; it would be easy to obtain.

He took a gulp of boiled coffee, took his stick, and hobbled out of the tent. The sky had lightened, and the mist had receded from the Starker plantation; Poe could see parts of his own line, a flag here and there, the crowns of trees. His men were moving forward out of their trenches, forming up on the far side of the abatis beyond. Officers' shouts carried faintly to his ear. The alignment was proceeding with difficulty. The battalions had become too confused as they marched to their places in the dark.

He remembered the Ravens in the cemetery, shrouded by gray gunsmoke as they were now hidden by gray mist.

Sherry, he thought again. The thought seemed to fill his mind with a fine, clear light. He could almost feel the welcome fire burning along his veins. A drink would steady him.

A color sergeant came running up from the Ravens, saluted, and took the two birds away to march with their brigade. Limbers rattled as horses pulled them out of harm's way down the reverse slope of the hill. Artillerymen lounged by their Napoleons and Whitworths, waiting for a target.

My god, Poe thought, why am I doing this? Suddenly it seemed the most pointless thing in the world. An offensive would only make things worse.

A horse trotted toward him from the Starker driveway. Poe recognized Moses, another of Anderson's aides, an eagle-nosed miniature sheeny that Longstreet had unaccountably raised to the rank of major. One of Longstreet's little lapses in taste, Poe thought; but unfortunately, as someone with pretensions to the title himself, he was honor-bound to treat the Hebrew as if his claim to the title of gentleman were genuine.

Sextus took Major Moses's horse, and Moses and Poe exchanged salutes. There weren't many men shorter than Poe, but Moses was one of them—he was almost tiny, with hands and feet smaller than a woman's. "General Anderson's compliments, sir," Moses said. "He wants to emphasize his desire for a diversionary attack."

"Look about you, Major," Poe said. "What do you see?"

Moses looked at the grayback soldiers rolling out of their entrenchments and shuffling into line, the artillerists waiting on the hilltop for a target, officers calling up and down the ranks.

"I see that General Anderson has been anticipated, sir," Moses said. "My mission has obviously been in vain."

"I would be obliged if you'd wait for a moment, Major," Poe said. "I may have a message for General Anderson by and by."

"With permission, sir, I should withdraw. The general may need me." Moses smiled. Dew dripped from his shoulder-length hair onto his blue riding cape. "Today promises to be busy, sir."

"I need you *here*, sir!" Poe snapped. "I want you to witness something."

Moses seemed startled. He recovered, a sly look entering his eyes, then he nodded. "Very well, sir."

In a motionless instant of perfect clarity, Poe understood the conspiracy of this calculating Jew. Moses would hang back, wait for confirmation of Poe's madness, Poe's error, then ride back to Anderson to try to have Poe removed from command. Moxley Sorrel might already have filled the staff tent with tales of Poe's nerves about to crack. Perhaps, Poe thought furiously, the sheeny intended to replace Poe *himself!*

Cold triumph rolled through Poe. Conspire though Moses might, Poe would be too crafty for him.

"When will the attack begin, Major?" Poe asked.

"It has already begun, sir. The mist cleared early to the west of us. The men were moving out just as I left General Anderson's headquarters."

Poe cocked his head. "I hear no guns, Major Moses."

"Perhaps there has been a delay. Perhaps—" Moses shrugged. "Perhaps the wet ground is absorbing the sound. Or there is a trick of the wind—"

"Nevertheless," Poe said, "I hear no guns."

"Yes, sir." Moses cleared his throat. "It is not unknown, sir."

"Still, Major Moses," said Poe. "I hear no guns."

Moses fell silent at this self-evident fact. Poe whirled around, his black cape flying out behind him, and stalked toward his tent. He could hear Moses's soft footsteps following behind.

Men on horseback came, reporting one brigade after another ready to move forward. Poe told them to wait here for the word to advance, then return to their commanders. Soon he had heard from every brigade but those of Gregg and Law—a messenger even came from Fitz Lee, reporting the cavalryman's readiness to move forward at Poe's signal. After ten minutes of agitated waiting, while the sky grew ever paler and the mist retreated to lurk among the trees, Poe sent an aide to inquire.

Poe gave an irritated look at his division waiting in their ranks for the signal. If the enemy had scouts out this way, they'd see the Confederates ready for the attack and warn the enemy.

Go forward with the four brigades he had? he wondered.

Yes. No.

He decided to wait till his aide came back. He looked at his watch, then cast a glance over his shoulder at Major Moses.

"I hear no guns, Major," he said.

"You are correct, sir." Moses smiled thinly. "I take it you intend to enlighten me as to the significance of this?"

Poe nodded benignly. "In time, Major."

Moses swept off his hat in an elaborate bow. "You are known as the master of suspense, sir. I take my hat off sir, I positively do."

Poe smiled. The Jew was amusing. He tipped his own hat. "Thank you, Major."

Moses put on his hat. "I am an enthusiast of your work, sir. I have a first edition of the *Complete Tales*. Had I known I would encounter you, I would have had my wife send it to me and begged you to inscribe it."

"I should be glad to sign it," Poe said, surprised. The *Complete and Corrected Tales and Poems of Edgar A. Poe* had been published at his own expense six years ago and had sold precisely two hundred and forty-nine copies throughout the United States—he knew precisely, because the rest of the ten-thousand-copy edition was sitting in a lumber room back home at Shepherd's Rest.

"Before the war," Moses said, "I used to read your work aloud to my wife. The poems were particularly lovely, I thought—so delicate. And there was nothing that would bring a blush to her lovely cheek

I *particularly* appreciate that, sir," Moses grew indignant. "There are too many passages from poets that one cannot in decency read to a lady, sir. Even in Shakespeare—" Moses shook his head.

"Fortunately," said Poe, "one has Bowdler."

"I thank that gentleman from my heart," said Moses. "As I thank Tennyson, and Mr. Dickens, and Keats."

"Keats." Poe's heart warmed at the mention of the name. "One scarcely could anticipate encountering his name here, on a battle-field."

"True, sir. He is the most rarified and sublime of poets—along, I may say, with yourself, sir."

Poe was surprised. "You flatter me, Major."

"I regret only that you are not more appreciated, sir." His tiny hands gestured whitely in the air. "Some of my correspondents have informed me, however, that you are better known in Europe."

"Yes," Poe said. A dark memory touched him. "A London publisher has brought out an edition of the *Complete Tales*. Unauthorized, of course. It has achieved some success, but I never received so much as a farthing from it."

"I am surprised that such a thing can happen, sir."

Poe gave a bitter laugh. "It isn't the money—it is the brazen provocation of it that offended me. I hired a London solicitor and had the publisher prosecuted."

"I hope he was thrown in jail, sir."

Poe gave a smile. "Not quite. But there will be no more editions of my work in London, one hopes."

"I trust there won't be."

"Or in France, either. I was being translated there by some over-heated poet named Charles Baudelaire—no money from that source, either, by the way—and the fellow had the effrontery to write me that many of my subjects, indeed entire texts, were exactly the same as those he had himself composed—except mine, of course, had been written earlier."

"Curious." Moses seemed unclear as to what he should make of this.

"This *gueux* wrote that he considered himself my *alter ego.*" A smile twisted across Poe's face at the thought of his triumph. "I wrote that what *he* considered miraculous, *I* considered plagiarism, and de-manded that he cease any association with my works on penalty of prosecution. He persisted in writing to me, so I had a French lawyer send him a stiff letter, and have not heard from him since."

"Very proper." Moses nodded stoutly. "I have always been dis-mayed at the thought of so many of these disreputable people in the literary world. Their antics can only distract the public from the true artists."

Poe gazed in benevolent surprise at Major Moses. Perhaps he had misjudged the man.

A horseman was riding toward him. Poe recognized the spreading mustachios of the aide he'd sent to Gregg and Law. The young man rode up and saluted breathlessly.

"I spoke to General Law, sir," he said. "His men were still eating breakfast. He and General Gregg have done *nothing*, sir, *nothing!*"

Poe stiffened in electric fury. "You will order Generals Gregg and Law to attack *at once!*" He barked.

The aide smiled. "Sir!" he barked, saluted, and turned his horse. Dirt clods flew from the horse's hooves as he pelted back down the line.

Poe hobbled toward the four messengers his brigadiers had sent to him. Anger smoked through his veins. "General Barton will advance at once," he said. "The other brigades will advance as soon as they perceive his movement has begun. Tell your commanders that I desire any prisoners to be sent to me at once." He pointed at Fitzhugh Lee's aide with his stick. "Ride to General Lee. Give him my compliments, inform him that we are advancing, and request his support."

Men scattered at his words, like shrapnel from his explosion of temper. He watched them with cold satisfaction.

"There is nothing more beautiful, sir," said Major Moses in his ear, "than the sight of this army on the attack."

Poe looked with surprise at Moses; in his burst of temper he had forgotten the man was here. He turned to gaze at the formed men a few hundred yards below him on the gentle slope. They had been in garrison for almost a year, and their uniforms and equipment were in better condition than most of this scarecrow army. They were not beautiful in any sense that Poe knew of the word, but he understood what the major meant. There was a beauty in warfare that existed in a realm entirely distinct from the killing.

"I know you served in Greece, sir," Moses said. "Did the Greek fighters for liberty compare in spirit with our own?"

Poe's heart gave a lurch, and he wondered in alarm if his ears were burning. "They were—indifferent," he said. "Variable." He cleared his throat. "Mercenary, if the truth be told."

"Ah." Moses nodded. "Byron found that also."

"I believe he did." Poe stared at the ground and wondered how to extricate himself. His Greek service was a lie he had encouraged to be published about himself. He had never fought in Greece when young, or served, as he had also claimed, in the Russian army. Instead— penniless, an outcast, thrown on his own resources by his Shylock of a stepfather—he had enlisted in the American army out of desperation, and served three years as a volunteer.

It had been his dread, these years he'd served the Confederacy, that

he would encounter some old soldier who remembered serving alongside the eighteen-year-old Private Edgar A. Perry. His fears had
never been realized, fortunately, but he had read everything he could
on Byron and the Greek War of Independence in hopes he would not
be tripped up by the curious.

"Ah," Poe said. He pointed with his stick. "The men are moving."

"A brilliant sight, sir." Moses's eyes shone.

Calls were rolling up the line, one after another, from Barton on
the left to the Ravens next in line, then to Corse—all Virginia brigades—and then to Clingman's North Carolinians on the right. Poe
could hear the voices distinctly.

"Attention, battalion of direction! Forward, guide centerrrr—
march!"

The regiments moved forward, left to right, clumps of skirmishers
spreading out ahead. Flags hung listlessly in the damp. Once the order to advance had been given, the soldiers moved in utter silence, in
perfect parade-ground formation.

Just as they had gone for that cemetery, Poe thought. He remembered his great swell of pride at the way the whole division had done
a left oblique under enemy fire that day, taking little half-steps to
swing the entire line forty-five degrees, and then paused to dress the
line before marching onward.

Sweeping through tendrils of mist that clung to the soldiers' legs,
the division crossed the few hundred yards of ground between the
entrenchments and the forest, and disappeared into the darkness and
mist.

Poe wondered desperately if he was doing the right thing.

"Did you know Byron, sir?" Moses again.

Poe realized he'd been holding his breath, anticipating the sound of
disaster as soon as his men began their attack. He let his breath go,
felt relief spreading outward, like rot, from his chest.

"Byron died," he said, "some years before I went abroad."

Byron had been feeding worms for forty years, Poe thought, but
there were Byrons still, hundreds of them, in this army. Once he had
been a Byron himself—an American Childe Harold dressed in dra-
matic black, ready with the power of his mind and talent to defeat the
cosmos. Byron had intended to conquer the Mussulman; Poe would
do him better, with *Eureka*, by conquering God.

Byron had died at Missolonghi, bled to death by his personal physician as endless gray rain fell outside his tent and drowned his little
army in the Peloponnesian mud. And nothing had come of Byron in

the end, nothing but an example that inspired thousands of other young fools to die in similar pointless ways throughout the world.

For Poe the war had come at a welcome moment. His literary career had come to a standstill, with nine thousand seven hundred fifty-one copies of the *Complete Tales* sitting in his lumber room; his mother-in-law had bestirred herself to suggest, in kind but firm fashion, that his literary and landscaping projects were running up too fantastic a debt; and his relations with Evania—on Poe's part at least —were at best tentative.

When Virginia seceded and Maryland seemed poised to follow, Poe headed south with Sextus, a pair of fine horses, equipage, a curved Wilkinson light cavalry sword, Hardee's *Tactics,* a brace of massive nine-shot Le Mat revolvers, and of course the twelve hundred in gold. He kissed Evania and his beloved Mrs. Forster farewell—within a few months he would return with an army and liberate Shepherd's Rest and the rest of Maryland. He, as well as Byron, could be martial when the cause of liberty required it. He rode away with a singing heart.

Before him, as he woke in his bed his first night in Richmond, he saw his vision, the benevolent madonna giving him her benediction. In going south he was being, he thought, faithful to Virginia; and he hoped to find the spirit, as well as the name, of his lost love embodied in the state to which he swore allegiance.

Jefferson Davis was pleased to give a colonel's commission to a veteran of the wars of Greek liberation, not to mention a fellow West Pointer—the West Point story, at least, being true, though Poe did not remind the President that, because the horrid Allan refused to support him, Poe had got himself expelled from the academy after six months.

There was no regiment available for the new colonel, so Poe began his military career on the staff of General Joseph E. Johnston, commanding in the Shenandoah Valley. He occupied himself by creating a cypher for army communications which, so far as he knew, had survived three years unbroken.

Johnston's army moved east on the railroad to unite with Beauregard's at First Manassas, and there Poe saw war for the first time. He had expected violence and death, and steeled himself against it. It gave him no trouble, but what shocked him was the *noise.* The continual roll of musketry, buzzing bullets, shouted orders, the blast of cannon, and the shriek of shells—all were calculated to unstring the nerves of a man who couldn't abide even a loud orchestra. Fortunately he was called upon mainly to rally broken troops—it had shocked him that Southern men could run like that—but in the end, after he'd got used to the racket, he had ridden, bullets singing over his head, in the final screaming, exhilarating charge that swept the Yankee army from the field, and he could picture himself riding that way forever, the fulfillment of the Byronic ideal, sunset glowing red on the sword in his hand as he galloped north to Maryland and the liberation of his home. . . .

Maryland never managed to secede, somehow, and Poe's Byronic liberation of his home state had to be postponed. Via blockade-runner, Poe exchanged passionate letters with his wife while remaining, in his heart, faithful to Virginia.

At the horrible, bungled battle of Seven Pines the next year, Major General Daniel Harvey Hill made a properly Byronic, if unsupported, attack against McClellan's left and lost half his men, as well as one of his brigadiers. Poe was promoted and given the shattered brigade. Joe Johnston, during the same battle, had been severely wounded, and the Army of Northern Virginia now had a new commander, one Robert E. Lee.

It did not take Poe long to discover that the ferocious, dyspeptic Harvey Hill was both an ignoramus and a lunatic. Before more than a few days had passed, neither spoke to the other: they communicated only in writing. Poe broke the Yanks' wigwag signal code, which didn't mean much at the time but was of help later, at Second Manassas.

But by then Poe was not with the army. Only a few days after taking command, Lee went on the offensive, and Poe, supported by exemplary reasoning and logic, refused point-blank Harvey Hill's order to take his brigade into Boatswain Swamp.

Now, after three years of war, almost all the American Byrons were dying or had been shot to pieces. Jeb Stuart, Jackson, Albert Sidney Johnston, Dick Garnett, Ewell, Hood, now Longstreet—all dead or maimed.

And Edgar A. Poe, leaning on his stick, a sick ache throbbing in his thigh, knew in his heart that Byron's death had been more merciful than anyone had known.

He had written the eulogy himself, never knowing it at the time: *But he grew old—/This knight so bold—/And o're his heart a shadow/Fell as he found/No spot of ground/That looked like Eldorado.*

Byron's eulogy. Poe's, too. Stuart's, everyone's.

"Forty years dead," he said. "We have other poets now."

"Yourself, of course," said Major Moses, "and Tennyson."

"Walter Whitman," said Poe. The name left a savage, evil taste in his mouth.

"Obscene." Moses shivered. "Filth."

"I agree."

"You have denounced him yourself."

"Repeatedly."

Poe stared at the dark trees that had swallowed up his entire division. How many, he wondered, would come out of those woods nevermore? Sickness welled up inside him. In another minute he might weep. He turned and shouted for Sextus to bring him a chair.

The first edition of *Leaves of Grass* had happily escaped his notice. The second edition, with the preface by Emerson, had been sent to him for review at the *Southern Gentleman*. He had denounced it. Whitman and Emerson replied; Poe printed their replies and returned fire, and the fight went on for years, a war that prefigured the more deadly one begun in 1861.

A showdown, he had thought triumphantly. He had long distrusted the New England clique and feared their grip on the *North American Review*—the fact that they regarded the pedestrian and bourgeoise Longfellow as a genius was reason enough for distrust. But now the south had its own literary magazine; Poe was no longer dependent on the approval of New England literary society for employment and regard.

Whitman, he wrote, knew nothing of versification. Whitman thought prostitutes and steam engines and common laborers fit subject for verse. Whitman knew nothing of the higher truths, of the sublime. Whitman filled his verses with the commonplace, with references so mundane and contemporary that in a hundred years no one would know what he was talking about. Whitman did not even *look* like a literary man. In the ambrotype used as a frontispiece, Whitman was dressed only in his shirt, looking like a farmer just come in from the fields, not an elevated, rarified, idealized creature—a poet—who spoke the language of the gods.

And Whitman was obscene. Grossly so. Clearly he was a degenerate of the worst description. Poe preferred not to imagine what Whitman did with those young men he wrote about in such evocative terms. Emerson might have used every rhetorical trick he knew to disguise the filth, or talk around it, but he never denied it—and this from someone who affected to worship the transcendental, meaning the refined and pure. It was then that Poe knew how bankrupt the North was, how desperate, as compared with his refined, elegant southland.

"Whitman is the perfect Yankee poet," Poe said. He drove his stick into the soil as if the earth hid Walter Whitman's heart. "No sublimity, no beauty, just stacks of prose disguised as poetry—sometimes not even prose, only lists. Lists of ordinary things. Produced so much stanzas an hour, like yards of cloth in a shoddyworks." He drove the stick again. "Like Yankee soldiers. Not inspired, just numerous."

Moses gave a laugh. "I must remember that, sir. For when General Longstreet returns. It will amuse him."

Poe stared at the woods, grinding his teeth. He hadn't meant to be witty; he was trying to make a point.

There was sudden musketry from the hardwoods, a succession of popping sounds turned hollow by multiple echoes. Then there was silence. Poe listened intently for a moment.

"Pickets," Moses said.

How many Yankees? Poe wondered. He turned back in the direction of his tent. Sextus was nowhere to be seen. "Bring a chair, you blasted orangutan!" he shouted. He had no idea whether or not Sextus heard him.

More popping sounds came from the woods—individual shots this time. From a different part of the line, Poe thought.

"Byrons can only die," he said. Moses looked at him in surprise. "We real poets, we're all too in love with death. Whitman writes about life, even the obscene parts of it, and that's why he will win. Why," he took a breath, trying to make himself clearer, "why the North will win."

Moses seemed to be struggling to understand this. "Sir," he said. "Sir, I don't understand."

More crackling from the woods. Poe's head moved left and right, trying to find where it was coming from. A savage exultation beat a long tattoo in his heart. He was right, he was right, he was right *again.* He stepped up to Moses, stared into his eyes at a few inches' range.

"Do you hear guns from the east, Major?" he demanded. "Do you hear anything at all from Lee's offensive?"

"Why—" Major Moses stopped dead, licked his lips. There was pure bewilderment in his eyes. "Why are you doing this? Why are you fighting for the Cause?"

"I *hate* Whitman!" Poe shrieked. "I hate him, and I hate steam engines, I hate ironclad ships and repeating rifles and rifled artillery!"

"Your chair, Massa Poe," said Sextus.

A cacophony of sound was coming from the woods now, regular platoon volleys, one after another. The sound battered Poe's ears.

"I fight for the South because we are *right*, Major Moses!" Poe shouted. "I believe it—I have proved it rationally—we are *superior*, sir! The South fights for the right of one man to be superior to another, because he *is* superior, because he *knows* he is superior."

"Here's your chair, Massa Poe," said Sextus.

"Superior in mind, superior in cognitive faculty, superior in erudition! Superior in knowledge, in training, in sagacity! In appreciation of beauty, of form, of moral sense!" Poe pointed his stick at the woods. "Those Yankees—they are democracy, sir! Dragging even *poetry* into the muck! Walter Whitman addresses his verses to *women of the street*—*that* is democracy for you! Those Yankee soldiers, they are Whitmans with bayonets! I fight them because I must, because *someone* must fight for what is noble and eternal, even if only to die, like Byron, in some pointless—pointless—"

Pain seized his heart and he doubled over, coughing. He swung toward where Sextus stood with his camp chair, the cane still outstretched, and though he didn't mean to strike the African he did anyway, a whiplike crack on the upper arm. Sextus dropped the chair and stepped back, surprise on his face. Anger crackled in Poe, fury at the African's stupidity and inability to get out of the way.

"Take that, damn you, worthless nigger!" Poe spat. He spun and fell heavily into his chair.

The battle in the woods had progressed. Now Poe heard only what Great Frederick called *bataillenfeuer*, battle fire, no longer volleys but simply a continuous din of musketry as the platoon sergeants lost tactical control of their men and the battle dissolved into hundreds of little skirmishes fought simultaneously. Poe heard no guns—no way to get artillery through those woods.

Moses was looking at Poe with wide, staring eyes. He reached into a pocket and mopped Poe's spittle from his face. Poe gave him an evil look.

"Where is Lee's offensive, sir?" he demanded. "Where is the sound of *his* fight?"

Moses seemed confused. "I should get back to General Anderson, sir," he said. "I—"

"Stay by me, Major," Poe said. His voice was calm. An absolute lucidity had descended upon him; perhaps he was the only man within fifty miles who knew precisely what was happening here. "I have not yet shown you what I wish to show you."

He listened to the fight roll on. Sometimes it nearly died away, but then there would be another outburst, a furious racket. Lines of gunsmoke rose above the trees. It would be pointless for Poe to venture into the woods himself—he could not control an entire division if he could not see twenty feet beyond his own position.

A horseman galloped up. "General Gregg's compliments, sir. He and General Law are ready to advance."

Poe felt perfectly sunny. "My compliments to General Gregg. Tell him that Poe's division is a little ahead of him. I would be obliged if he'd catch up."

The man rode away. People were leaking back out of the woods now: wounded men, some crawling; skulkers, stragglers; bandsmen carrying people on stretchers. Here and there were officers running, bearing messages, guards marching back with blue prisoners.

"Lots of Yankees, sir!" The first messenger, a staff lieutenant of perhaps nineteen, was winded and staggering with the effort it had taken him to run here. "We've hit them in flank. They were in column of march, sir. Colonel Terry wishes you to know he's driving them, but he expects they'll stiffen."

"Good job, boy." Terry was the man who commanded the Ravens in Poe's absence. "Give Colonel Terry my thanks."

"Sir!" Another messenger. "General Clingman's compliments. We've driven them in and captured a battery of guns."

Guns, Poe thought. Useless in the woods. We can't get them away, and the Yankees'll have them back in another few minutes.

The sound of musketry staggered higher, doubled and tripled in fury. The messengers looked at each other, breathing hard, appalled at the noise. The Yanks, Poe concluded, had rallied and were starting to fight back.

"Tell Colonel Terry and General Clingman to press them as hard as possible. Try to hold them in the woods. When the Yanks press too hard, retire to the trenches."

"Yes, sir."

"Prisoners, sir." Another voice. "General Barton sends them as requested."

Stunned-looking Yanks in dew-drenched caped overcoats, all captured in the first rush. None of them looked over twenty. Poe rose from his chair and hobbled toward them. He snatched the cap from the first prisoner and swung toward Major Moses.

"Major Moses," he said in triumph, "do you know the motto of the Yankee Second Corps?"

Moses blinked at him. "No, sir."

" 'Clubs are Trumps!' " Poe told him. "Do you know why, sir?"

Moses shook his head.

"Because Hancock's Corps wears a trefoil badge on their forage caps, like a club on a playing card." He threw the prisoner's cap down before Moses's feet. "What do you see on *that* forage cap, sir?" he asked.

"A cross," said Moses.

"A *saltire*, sir!" Poe laughed.

He had to be thorough. The upper echelons were never easily convinced. Two years before, during the Seven Days', he had demonstrated, with complete and irrefutable logic, that it was suicidal for Harvey Hill's division to plunge forward into Boatswain Swamp in hopes of contacting Yankees on the other side. When the ignorant madman Hill repeated his order, Poe had stood on his logic and refused—and been removed from command and placed under arrest. He had not been comforted when he had been proven right. His cherished new brigade, along with the rest of D. H. Hill's division, had been shattered by three lines of Union infantry dug into a hill just behind the swamp, with artillery lined hub-to-hub on the crest. And when, red-faced with anger, he had challenged Hill to a duel, the lunatic had only laughed at him to his face.

"Specifically," Poe said pedantically, pointing at the Yankee forage cap, "a *white* saltire on a blue background! That means these men come from the Second Division of the Sixth Corps—*Wright's* Corps, major, not Hancock's! The same Sixth Corps that Lee was supposed to attack this morning, on the other end of the line! *I am facing at least two Yankee corps with one division, and Lee is marching into empty air! Grant has moved his army left again while we slept!*"

Moses's eyes widened. "My God," he said.

"Take that cap to General Anderson with my compliments! Tell him I will need his support!"

Moses picked up the cap. "Yes, sir."

Poe lunged among the prisoners, snatching off caps, throwing them to his aides. "Take *that* to General Lee! And *that* to Ewell! And *that* to A. P. Hill! Say I must have their support! Say that *Wright* is here!"

As Moses and Poe's aides galloped away, the firing died down to almost nothing. One side or another had given way.

Poe returned to his seat and waited to see which side it had been.

It was Poe's division had pressed back in the woods, but not by much. Messengers panting back from his brigades reported that they'd pushed the Yanks as far as possible, then fallen back when they could push no more. The various units were trying to reestablish contact with one another in the woods and form a line. They knew the Yankee assault was coming.

Pull them back? Poe wondered. He'd made his case to his superiors
—maybe he'd better get his men back into their trenches before the
Yanks got organized and smashed them.

Action, he thought, and reaction. The two fundamental principles
of the operating Universe, as he had demonstrated in *Eureka*. His
attack had been an action; the Yankee reaction had yet to come.

He tapped gloved fingers on the arm of his chair while he made
careful calculations. The Yankees had been struck in the right flank as
they were marching south along narrow forest roads. Due to surprise
and their tactical disadvantage, they had been driven in, then, as the
rebel attack dissipated its force, turned and fought. This reaction,
then, had been instinctive—they had not fought as units, which must
have been shattered, but as uncoordinated masses of individuals. The
heavy forest had broken up the rebel formation in much the same
manner, contributing to their loss of momentum.

The Yankees would react, but in order to do so in any coordinated
way they would have to reassemble their units, get them in line of
battle, and push them forward through trees that would tend to disperse their cohesion. Wright had three divisions; normally it would
take a division about an hour, maybe more, to deploy to the right
from column of march. The woods would delay any action. The bluecoats' own confusion would worsen things even more. Say two hours,
then.

Any attack made before then would be uncoordinated, just local
commanders pushing people forward to the point of contact. Poe's
men could handle that. But in two hours a coordinated attack would
come, and Poe's division would be swamped by odds of at least three
to one, probably more.

Poe looked at his watch. He would keep his men in the woods
another ninety minutes, then draw them back. Their presence in the
woods might serve to make the Yanks cautious, when what Grant
really wanted to do was drive straight forward with everything he
had.

His thoughts were interrupted by a message from Evander Law on
his left flank. He and Gregg had about completed their preparations
to advance, the messenger reported, when they discovered that
Hancock's men across the woods were leaving their trenches and
preparing to attack *them*. Gregg and Law had therefore returned to
their trenches to ready themselves for the attack.

Poe bit back on his temper. It *might* be true. He would have to see
in person. He told one of his aides to remain there and direct any
messages to the left of the line, then told Sextus to ready his buggy.

Sextus looked at him in a sullen, provoking way. He was cradling the arm Poe had struck with his cane. "You'll have to drive yourself, massa," he said. "You broke my arm with that stick."

Annoyance warmed Poe's nerves. "Don't be ridiculous! I did not hit you with sufficient force. Any schoolboy—"

"I'm sorry, massa. It's broke. I broke an arm before, I know what it's like."

Poe was tempted to hit Sextus again and break the arm for certain; but instead he lurched for his buggy, hopped inside, and took the reins. He didn't have the time to reason with the darky now. Sextus heaved himself up into the seat beside Poe, and Poe snapped the reins. His staff, on horseback, followed.

The battle broke on the left as he drove, a searing, ripping sound bounding up from the damp, dead ground. Poe seized the whip and labored his horse; the light buggy bounded over the turf, threatened to turn over, righted itself.

The first attack was over by the time Poe's buggy rolled behind Law's entrenchments, and the wall of sound had died down to the lively crackle of sharpshooters' rifles and the continual boom of smoothbore artillery. It took Poe a while to find Law—he was in the first line of works—and by the time Poe found him, the second Yankee attack was beginning, a constant hammering roar spreading across the field.

Law stood in the trench, gnawing his lip, his field glasses in his hand. There was a streak of powder residue across his forehead and great patches of sweat under the arms of his fine gray jacket. Law jumped up on the firing step, jostling his riflemen who were constantly popping up with newly loaded muskets, and pointed. "Gibbon's men, sir! The Black Hats! Look!"

Poe swung himself up behind the brigadier, peered out beneath the head log, and saw, through rolling walls of gunsmoke and the tangle of abatis, lines of blue figures rolling toward him. He heard the low moaning sound made by Northern men in attack, like a choir of advancing bears. . . . The ones coming for him were wearing black felt hats instead of their usual forage caps, which marked them as the Iron Brigade of Gibbon's division, the most hard-hitting unit of the hardest-hitting corps in the Yankee army. *We've got two brigades here,* Poe thought frantically, *and we've got an entire corps coming at us.*

A Yankee Minié whacked solidly into the head log above him. Poe jerked his head back and turned to Law. The smell of powder was sharp in his nostrils. The air filled with the whistling sound of cannon firing canister at close range.

"You must hold, sir! No going back!"

Law grinned. "Do you think the Yankees'll *let* us go back?"

"Hold to the last! I will bring up support!"

Law only looked at him as if he were mad. And then the Yankees were there, their presence at first marked by a swarm of soldiers surging back from the firing step, almost knocking Poe from his feet as he was carried to the muddy back of the trench, the soldiers pointing their muskets upward, groping in their belts for bayonets . . .

Poe reached automatically for one of his Le Mat revolvers and then realized he'd left them in his headquarters tent—they were just too heavy to carry all the time. His only weapon was his stick. He stiffened and took a firmer grip on the ivory handle. His mind reeled at the suddenness of it all.

The sky darkened as bluecoats swarmed up on the head log, rifles trained on the packed Confederates. The Stars and Stripes, heavy with battle honors, rose above the parapet, waved by an energetic sergeant with a bushy red beard and a tattered black hat. Musketry crackled along the trench as men fired into one another's faces. "Look at 'em all!" Law screamed. "Look at 'em all!" He shoved a big Joslyn revolver toward the Yankees and pulled the trigger repeatedly. People were falling all over. Screams and roars of defiance and outrage echoed in Poe's ears.

He stood, the sound battering at his nerves. All he could do here, he thought bitterly, was get shot. He was amazed at his own perfect objectivity and calm.

And then the Union standard-bearer was alone, and grayback infantry were pointing their rifles at him. "Come to the side of the Lord!" Evander Law shouted; and the red beard looked around him in some surprise, then shrugged, jumped into the ditch, and handed over the flag of the Twenty-fourth Michigan.

The soldiers declined to shoot him, Poe thought, as a compliment to his bravery. *Never let it be said we are not gallant.*

Poe jumped for the firing step, and saw the blue lines in retreat. Dead men were sprawled over the abatis, their black hats tumbled on the ground. The ground was carpeted with wounded Yanks trying to find little defilades where they would be sheltered from the bullets that whimpered above their heads. They looked like blue maggots fallen from the torn belly of something dead, Poe thought, and then shuddered. Where was the poetry in this? Here even death was unhallowed.

Soldiers jostled Poe off the firing step and chased off the bluecoats with Minié balls. Confederate officers were using swords and knives to cut up the Yankee flag for souvenirs. Poe stepped up to Law.

"They'll be back," Law said, mumbling around a silver powder flask in his teeth. He was working the lever of his Joslyn revolver, tamping a bullet down on top of the black powder charge.

"I will bring men to your relief."

"Bring them soon, sir."

"I will find them somewhere."

Law rotated the cylinder and poured another measured round of fine black powder. "Soon, sir. I beg you."

Poe turned to one of his aides. "Find General Gregg on the left. Give him my compliments, and tell him what I have told General Law. He must hold till relieved. After that, ride to General Anderson and persuade him to release the rest of Field's division to come to the aide of their comrades."

Wounded men groaned in the trenches and on the firing step, cursing, trying to stop their bleeding. Yankee blood dripped down the clay trench wall. Cannon still thundered, flailing at the bluecoats. Southern sharpshooters banged away with Armstrong rifles equipped with telescopic sights almost as long as the gun, aiming at any officers. Poe found himself astounded that he could have an intelligible conversation in this raucous, unending hell.

He limped away down a communications trench and found Sextus in the rear, holding his buggy amid a group of waiting artillery limbers. Poe got into the buggy without a word and whipped up the horses.

Behind him, as he rode, the thunder of war rose in volume as Hancock pitched into another attack. This time the sound didn't die down.

On the way back to his tent Poe encountered a courier from Fitz Lee. His men had moved forward dismounted, run into some startled bluecoats from Burnside's Ninth Corps, and after a short scrap had pulled back into their entrenchments.

Burnside. That meant three Yankee corps were facing two southern divisions, one of them cavalry.

Burnside was supposed to be slow, and everyone knew he was not the most intelligent of Yankees—anyone who conducted a battle like Fredericksburg had to be criminally stupid. Poe could only hope he would be stupid today.

Back at his tent, he discovered Walter Taylor, one of Robert Lee's aides, a young, arrogant man Poe had never liked. Poe found himself growing angry just looking at him.

"Burnside, sir!" he snapped, pulling the buggy to a halt. "Burnside, Wright, *and* Hancock, and they're all on my front!"

Taylor knit his brows. "Are you certain about Burnside, sir?" he asked.

"Fitzhugh Lee confirms it! That's three fourths of Grant's army!"

Taylor managed to absorb this with perfect composure. "General Lee would like to know if you have any indication of the location of Warren's Fifth Corps."

Poe's vitals burned with anger. "I don't!" he roared. "But I have no doubt they'll soon be heading this way!"

Poe lurched out of his buggy and headed for his tent and the Le Mat revolvers waiting in his trunk. Judging by the sound, Gregg and Law were putting up a furious fight behind him. There was more fighting going on, though much less intense, on his own front.

Poe flung open the green trunk, found the revolvers, and buckled on the holsters. He hesitated for a moment when he saw the saber, then decided against it and dropped the trunk lid. Chances were he'd just trip on the thing. Lord knew the revolvers were heavy enough.

Taylor waited outside the tent, bent over to brush road dirt from his fine gray trousers. He straightened as Poe hobbled out. "I will inform General Lee you are engaged," he said.

Poe opened his mouth to scream at the imbecile, but took a breath instead, tried to calm his rage. With the high command, he thought, always patience. "My left needs help," Poe said. "Hancock's attacking two brigades with his entire corps. I'm facing Wright on my front with four brigades, and Fitz Lee's facing Burnside with two on the right."

"I will inform General Lee."

"Tell him we are in direst extremity. Tell him that we cannot hold onto Hanover Junction unless substantially reinforced. Tell him my exact words."

"I will, sir." Taylor nodded, saluted, mounted his horse, rode away. Poe stared after him and wondered if the message was going to get through it all, or if the legend of Poe's alarmism and hysteria were going to filter it—alter it—make it as nothing.

More fighting burst out to his front. Poe cupped his ears and swiveled his head, trying to discover direction. The war on his left seemed to have died away. Poe returned to his chair and sat heavily. His pistols were already weighing him down.

Through messengers he discovered what had happened. On his third attack, Hancock had succeeded in getting a lodgement in the Confederate trenches between Gregg and Law. They had been ejected only by the hardest, by an attack at bayonet point. Evander Law had been killed in the fighting; his place had been taken by Colonel Bowles of the 4th Alabama. Bowles requested orders. Poe had no hope to give him.

"Tell Colonel Bowles he must hold until relieved."

There was still firing to his front. His brigadiers in the woods were being pressed, but the Yankees as yet had made no concerted assault. Poe told them to hold on for the present. It would be another forty-five minutes, he calculated, before the Yanks could launch a coordinated assault.

Comparative silence fell on the battlefield. Poe felt his nerves gnawing at him, the suspense spreading through him like poison. After forty-five minutes, he gave his brigades in the woods permission to fall back to their entrenchments.

As he saw clumps of men in scarecrow gray emerging from the woods, he knew he could not tell them what he feared, that Robert Lee was going to destroy their division. Again.

After the Seven Days' Battle, Lee had chosen to lose the paperwork of Poe's impending court-martial. Poe, his brigade lost, his duel unfought, was assigned to help construct the military defenses of Wilmington.

Later, Poe would be proven right about Harvey Hill. Lee eventually shuffled him west to Bragg's army, but Bragg couldn't get along with him either and soon Hill found himself unemployed.

Poe took small comfort in Hill's peregrinations as he languished on the Carolina coast while Lee's army thrashed one Yankee commander after another. He wrote long letters to any officials likely to get him meaningful employment, and short, petulant articles for Confederate newspapers: Why wasn't the South building submarine rams? Why did they not take advantage, like the North, of observation from balloons? Why not untie the forces of Bragg and Johnston, make a dash for the Ohio, and reclaim Kentucky?

There were also, in Wilmington, women. Widows, many of them, or wives whose men were at war. Their very existence unstrung his nerves, made him frantic; he wrote them tempestuous letters and demanded their love in terms alternately peremptory and desperate. Sometimes, possibly because it seemed to mean so much to him, they surrendered. None of them seemed to mind that he snuffed all the candles, drew all the drapes. He told them he was concerned for their reputation, but he wanted darkness for his own purposes.

He was remaining faithful to Virginia.

Perhaps the letter-writing campaign did some good; perhaps it was just the constant attrition of experienced officers that mandated his reemployment. His hopes, at any rate, were justified. A brigade was free under George Pickett, and furthermore it was a lucky brigade, one that all three Confederate corps commanders had led at one time or another. Perhaps, Poe thought, that was an omen.

Poe was exultant. Lee was going north after whipping Hooker at Chancellorsville. Poe thought again of liberating Maryland, of riding on his thoroughbred charger to Shepherd's Rest, galloping to the heart of the place, to the white arabesque castle that gazed in perfect isolate splendor over the fabulous creation of his soul, his own water paradise. Once he fought for it, Shepherd's Rest would be *his;* he could dispossess the restless spirits that had made him so uneasy the last few years.

Determination entered his soul. He would be the perfect soldier. He would never complain, he would moderate his temper, he would offer his advice with diffidence. He had a reputation to disprove. The army, to his relief, welcomed him with open arms. Hugin and Munin appeared, delivered by grinning staff men who wore black feathers in their hats and chanted "Nevermore." His immediate superior, the perfumed cavalier George Pickett, was not a genius; but unlike many such he knew it, and happily accepted counsel from wiser heads. Longstreet, Poe's corps commander, was absolutely solid, completely reliable, the most un-Byronic officer imaginable but one that excited Poe's admiration. Poe enjoyed the society of his fellow brigadiers, white-haired Lo Armistead and melancholy Dick Garnett. The Southern officer corps was young, bright, and very well educated— riding north they traded Latin epigrams, quotations from *Lady of the Lake* or *The Corsair,* and made new rhymes based on those of their own literary celebrity, whose works had been read to many in childhood. *Of the rapture that runs,* quoth Lo Armistead, *To the banging and the clanging of the guns, guns, guns. Of the guns, guns, guns, guns, guns, guns, guns—To the roaring and the soaring of the guns!*

It was perfect. During the long summer marches into the heart of the North, Poe daydreamed of battle, of the wise gray father Lee hurling his stalwarts against the Yankees, breaking them forever, routing them from Washington, Baltimore, Shepherd's Rest. Lee was inspired, and so was his army. Invincible.

Poe could feel History looking over his shoulder. The world was holding its breath. This could be the last fight of the war. If he could participate in this, he thought, all the frustrating months in North Carolina, all the battles missed, would be as nothing.

Pickett's division, the army's rear guard, missed the first two days of the battle centered around the small crossroads town in Pennsylvania. Arriving that night, they made camp behind a sheltering ridge and were told that they would attack the next day in the assault that would shatter the Yankees for good and all. Pickett, who had been assigned elsewhere during Lee's last two victories, was delighted. At last he would have his opportunity for glory.

The next morning the officers of Pickett's division and the other two divisions that would make the attack were taken forward over the sheltering ridge to see the enemy positions. The attack would go *there*, said Lee, pointing with a gloved hand. Aiming for those umbrella-shaped trees on the enemy-held ridge, beneath which there was said to be a cemetery.

Standing in the stirrups of his white-socked thoroughbred, craning at the enemy ridge, Poe felt a darkness touching his heart. Across a half-mile of open ground, he thought, in plain sight of the enemy, an enemy who has had two days in which to dig in . . .

Was Lee serious? he thought. Was Lee mad?

No. It was not to be thought of. Lee hadn't lost a major battle in his entire career, Sharpsburg, of course, being a draw. There was method in this, he thought, and he could discern it through ratiocination. Perhaps the Yanks were weary, perhaps they were ready to give way. In any case, he had resolved not to complain.

Pickett left the ridge whistling, riding toward the Yanks to scout out the ground. Poe and the other brigadiers followed.

Longstreet remained behind. Poe discovered later that he had seen the same things that Poe had seen, and wanted a last chance to change Lee's mind. When time came to order the advance, Longstreet could not give the order. He just nodded, and then turned his head away.

Later that day Poe brought his men forward, marching with drawn sword at the head of the Ravens, Hugin and Munin crackling and fluffing their feathers on their perch just behind. He remembered with vivid intensity the wildflowers in the long grass, the hum of bees, the chaff rising from the marching feet, the absolute, uncharacteristic silence of the soldiers, seeing for the first time what was expected of them.

And then came the guns. There were two hundred cannon in the Northern lines, or so the Yankee papers boasted afterward, and there was not a one of them without an unobstructed target. In the last year Poe had forgotten what shell-fire was like, the nerve-shattering shriek like the fabric of the universe being torn apart, the way the shells seemed to hover in air forever, as if deliberately picking their targets, before plunging into the Confederate ranks to blossom yellow and black amid the sounds of buzzing steel and crying men.

The sound was staggering, the banging and the clanging of the guns, guns, guns, but fortunately Poe had nothing to do but keep his feet moving forward, one after another. The officers had been ordered to stay dismounted, and all had obeyed but one: Dick Garnett, commanding the brigade on Poe's left, was too ill to walk all that way, and had received special permission to ride.

Garnett, Poe knew, would die. The only mounted man in a group of twelve thousand, he was doomed and knew it.

Somehow there was an air of beauty about Garnett's sacrifice, something fragile and lovely. Like something in a poem.

The cemetery, their target, was way off on the division's left, and Pickett ordered a left oblique, the entire line of five thousand swinging like a gate toward the target. As the Ravens performed the operation, Poe felt a slowly mounting horror. To his amazement he saw that his brigade was on the absolute right of the army, nothing beyond him, and he realized that the oblique exposed his flank entirely to the Union batteries planted on a little rocky hill on the Yankee left.

Plans floated through his mind. Take the endmost regiment and face it toward Yankees? But that would take it out of the attack. Probably it was impossible anyway. But who could guard his flank?

In the meantime Pickett wanted everyone to hit at once, in a compact mass, and so he had the entire division dress its ranks. Five thousand men marked time in the long grass, each with his hand on the shoulder of the man next to him, a maneuver that normally took only a few seconds but that now seemed to take forever. The guns on the rocky hill were plowing their shot right along the length of the rebel line, each shell knocking down men like tenpins. Poe watched, his nerves wailing, as his men dropped by the score. The men couldn't finish dressing their ranks, Poe thought, because they were taking so many casualties they could never close the ranks fast enough, all from the roaring and the soaring of the guns, guns, guns. . . . He wanted to scream in protest. *Forward! Guide center!* But the evolution went on, men groping to their left and closing up as the shells knocked them down faster than they could close ranks.

Finally Pickett had enough and ordered the division onward. Poe nearly shrieked in relief. At least now the Yankees had a moving target.

But now they were closer, and the men on the Yankee ridge opened on Poe's flank with muskets. Poe felt his nerve cry at every volley.

Men seemed to drop by the platoon. How many had already gone? Did he even have half the brigade left?

The target was directly ahead, the little stand of trees on the gentle ridge, and between them was a little white Pennsylvania farmhouse, picture-book pretty. Somewhere around the house Poe and his men seemed to lose their sense of direction. They were still heading for the cemetery, but somehow Garnett had gotten in front of them. Poe could see Garnett's lonely figure, erect and defiant on his horse, still riding, floating really, like a poem above the battle.

The cemetery was closer, though, and he could see men crouched behind a stone wall, men in black hats. The Iron Brigade of Hancock's Corps, their muskets leveled on the stone wall, waiting for Garnett to approach . . .

And then suddenly the battle went silent, absolutely silent, and Poe was sitting upright on the ground and wondering how he got there. Some of his aides were mouthing at him, but he snatched off his hat and waved it, peremptory, pointing at the cemetery, ordering everyone forward. As he looked up he saw in that instant the Federal front blossom with smoke, and Dick Garnett pitch off his horse with perhaps a dozen bullets in him; and it struck Poe like a blow to the heart that there was no poetry in this, none whatever. . . .

His men were plowing on, following Garnett's. Poe tried to stand, but a bolt of pain flashed through him, and all he could do was follow the silent combat from his seated position. A shell had burst just over his head, deafening him and shattering his right thigh with a piece of shrapnel that hadn't even broken his skin.

Another line of men rushed past Poe, Armistead's, bayonets leveled. Poe could see Armistead in the lead, his black hat raised on saber-tip as a guide for his men, his mouth open in a silent cheer, his white mane flying. . . . And then the last of Pickett's division was past, into the smoke and dust that covered the ridge, charging for the enemy trees and the cemetery that claimed them, leaving Poe nothing to do but sit in the soft blossoming clover and watch the bees travel in silence from one flower to another. . . .

The first sound he heard, even over the tear of battle, was a voice saying "Nevermore." Hugin and Munin were croaking from the clover behind him, their standard-bearer having been killed by the same shell that had dropped Poe.

The sounds of battle gradually worked their way back into his head. Some of his men came back, and a few of them picked him up and carried him rearward, carried him along with the ravens back to the shelter of the ridge that marked the Confederate line. Poe insisted on facing the Yanks the entire way, so that if he died his wounds would be in the front. A pointless gesture, but it took away some of the pain. The agony from the shattered bone was only a foretaste of the soul-sickness that was to come during the long, bouncing, agonizing ambulance ride to the South as the army deserted Pennsylvania and the North and the hope of victory that had died forever there with Armistead, he had died on Cemetery Ridge, shot dead carrying his plumed hat aloft on the tip of his sword, his other hand placed triumphantly on the barrel of a Yankee gun.

"Law is dead, General Gregg is wounded," Poe reported. "Their men have given way entirely. Colonel Bowles reports he's lost half his men, half at least, and the remainder will not fight. They have also lost some guns, perhaps a dozen."

Robert Lee looked a hundred years dead. His intestinal complaint having struck him again, Lee was seated in the back of a closed ambulance that had been parked by the Starker house. He wore only a dressing gown, and his white hair fell over his forehead. Pain had drawn claws down his face, gouging deep tracks in his flesh.

"I have recalled the army," Lee said. "Rodes's division will soon be up." He gave a look to the man who had drawn his horse up beside the wagon. "Is that not correct, General Ewell?"

"I have told them to come quickly, General." Ewell was a bald man with pop eyes. He was strapped in the saddle, having lost a leg at Second Manassas—during a fight with those damned Black Hats. Now that Poe thought about it, perhaps the Black Hats were becoming a *leitmotiv* in all this shambles. Ewell's horse was enormous, a huge shambling creature, and the sight of it loping along with Ewell bobbing atop was considered by the soldiers to be a sight of pure high comedy.

Poe thought it pathetic. All that stands between Grant and Richmond, he thought, is a bunch of sick old men who cannot properly sit a horse. The thought made him angry.

"We must assemble," Lee said. His voice was faint. "We must assemble and strike those people."

Perhaps, Poe thought, Lee was a great man. Poe could not bring himself, any longer, to believe it. The others here had memories of Lee's greatness. Poe could only remember George Pickett, tears streaming down his face, screaming at Lee when the old man asked him to rally his command: *"General Lee, I have no division!"*

Poe looked from Ewell to Lee. "Gentlemen," he said, "I would suggest that Rodes be sent north to contain Hancock."

Lee nodded.

"The next division needs to be sent to Hanover Junction. If we lose the railroad, we will have to fall back to Richmond or attack Grant where he stands."

Lee nodded again. "Let it be so." A spasm passed across his face. His hands clutched at his abdomen and he bent over.

We may lose the war, Poe thought, because our commander has lost control of his bowels. And a case of the sniffles killed Byron, because his physician was a cretin.

The world will always destroy you, he thought. *And the world will make you ridiculous while it does so.*

General Lee's spasms passed. He looked up, his face hollow. Beads of sweat dotted his nose. "I will send an urgent message to General W.H.F. Lee," he said. "His cavalry division can reinforce that of General Fitzhugh Lee."

Bitter amusement passed through Poe at Lee's careful correctness. He would not call his son "Rooney," the way everyone else did; he referred to him formally, so there would be no hint of favoritism. Flattened by dysentery the man might be, and the Yankees might have stolen a day's march on him; but he would not drop his Southern courtesy.

Another spasm struck Lee. He bent over double. "Pardon me, gentlemen," he gasped. "I must retire for a moment."

His aides carefully drew the little rear doors of the ambulance to allow the commander-in-chief a little privacy. Ewell turned his head and spat.

Poe hobbled a few paces away and looked down at his own lines. Gregg and Law's brigades had given way an hour ago, on the fourth assault, but of the Yanks in the woods there had been no sign except for a few scouts peering at the Confederate trenches from the cover of the trees. Poe knew that the longer the Yankees took to prepare their attack, the harder it would be.

A four-wheel open carriage came up, drawn by a limping plow horse, probably the only horse the armies had spared the soberly dressed civilians who rode inside.

They were going to the funeral of the Starker girl. Battle or no, the funeral would go on. There was humor in this, somewhere; Poe wondered if the funeral was mocking the battle or the other way around.

He tipped his new hat to the ladies dismounting from the carriage and turned to study the woods with his field glasses.

Hancock had broken through to the north of the swampy stream, but hadn't moved much since then—victory had disorganized his formations as much as defeat had disorganized the losers. Hancock, when he moved, could either plunge straight ahead into the rear of Anderson's corps or pivot his whole command, like a barn door, to his left and into Poe's rear. In the latter case Poe would worry about him, but not till then. If Hancock chose to make that lumbering turn, a path which would take him through dense woods that would make the turn difficult to execute in any case, Poe would have plenty of warning from the remnants of Gregg and Law's wrecked brigades.

The immediate danger was to his front. What were Burnside and Wright waiting for? Perhaps they had got so badly confused by Poe's attack that they were taking forever to sort themselves out.

Perhaps they were just being thorough.

Poe limped to where his camp chair waited and was surprised that the short walk had taken his breath away. The Le Mats were just too heavy. He unbuckled his holsters, sat, and waited.

To the west, Rodes's division was a long cloud of dust. To the south, Rooney Lee's cavalry division was another.

Another long hour went by. A train moved tiredly east on the Virginia Central. Rooney Lee's men arrived and went into position on the right. Amid the clatter of reserve artillery battalions galloping up were more people arriving for the funeral: old men, women, children. The young men were either in the army or hiding from conscription. Soon Poe heard the singing of hymns.

Then the Yankees were there, quite suddenly and without preamble, the trees full of blue and silver, coming to the old Presbyterian melody rising from the Starker house. The bluecoats made no more noise on the approach than Pickett's men had on the march to Cemetery Ridge. Poe blinked in amazement. Where had they all come from?

Then suddenly the world was battle, filled with the tearing noise of musketry from the trenches, the boom of Napoleon guns, the eerie banshee wail of the hexagonal-shaped shells from the Whitworth rifled artillery fired over the heads of Poe's men into the enemy struggling through the abatis, then finally the scream and moan and animal sounds of men fighting hand to hand. . . .

Poe watched through his field glasses, mouth dry, nerves leaping with every cannon shot. There was nothing he could do, no reserves he could lead into the fight like a Walter Scott cavalier on horseback, no orders he could give that his own people in the trenches wouldn't know to give on their own. He was useless.

He watched flags stagger forward and back, the bluecoats breaking into his trenches at several points, being flung again into the abatis.

He felt a presence over his shoulder and turned to see Lee, hobbling forward in his dressing gown and slippers, an expression of helplessness on his face. Even army commanders were useless in these situations.

The fighting died down after Wright's first assault failed, and for the first time Poe could hear another fight off on his right, where the Lee cousins were holding off Burnside. The battle sounded sharp over there. Poe received reports from his commanders. Three of his colonels were wounded, one was dead, and Clingman had been trampled by both sides during a squabble over a trench but rose from the mud full of fight.

The Yankees came on again, still with that grim do-or-die silence, and this time they gained a lodgement between the Ravens and Corse, and the Confederates tried to fling them out but failed. "Tell them they must try again," Poe told his messengers. He had to shout over the sound of Whitworths firing point-blank into the Yankee salient. He looked at the sad figure of Lee standing there, motionless in his carpet slippers, his soft brown eyes gazing over the battlefield. "Tell the men," Poe said, "the eyes of General Lee are upon them."

Maybe it was Lee's name that did it. Poe could no longer believe in great men but the men of this army believed at least in Lee. The second counterattack drove the shattered Yankees from the works.

The Yankees paused again, but there was no lack of sound. The Confederate artillery kept firing blind into the trees, hoping to smash as many of the reassembling formations as they could.

What did a man mean in all this? Poe wondered. Goethe and Schiller and Shelley and Byron thought a man was all, that inspiration was everything, that divine intuition should overthrow dull reason—but what was inspiration against a Whitworth shell? The Whitworth shell would blow to shreds any inspiration it came up against.

Poe looked at Lee again.

A messenger came from Fitz Lee to tell the commanding general that the cavalry, being hard pressed, had been obliged by the enemy to retire. A fancy way, Poe assumed, for saying they were riding like hell for the rear. Now both Poe's flanks were gone.

Lee gave a series of quiet orders to his aides. Poe couldn't hear them. And then Lee bent over as another spasm took him, and his young men carried him away to his ambulance.

There was no more fighting for another hour. Eventually the rebel artillery fell silent as they ran short of ammunition. Reserve ammunition was brought up. Messages came to Poe: Hancock was moving, and Burnside was beginning a turning movement, rolling up onto

Poe's right flank. Poe ordered his right flank bent back, Clingman's men moving into Hanover Junction itself, making a fort of every house. His division now held a U-shaped front.

What did a man mean in all this? Poe wondered again. Nothing. Byron and Shelley were ego-struck madmen. All a man could do in this was die, die along with everything that gave his life meaning. And it was high time he did.

Poe rose from the chair, strapped on his pistols, and began to walk the quarter mile to his trenches. He'd give Walter Whitman a run for his money.

The fight exploded before Poe could quite walk half the distance. Wright's men poured out of the woods; Burnside, moving fast for once in his life, struck at Hanover Junction on the right; and unknown to anyone Hancock had hidden a few brigades in the swampy tributary of the North Anna, and these came screaming up out of the defile onto Poe's undermanned left flank.

The battle exploded. Poe began limping faster.

The battle ended before Poe could reach it. His men gave way everywhere, the Yankees firing massed volleys into their backs, then going after them with bayonets. Poe wanted to scream in rage. The world would not let him make even a futile gesture.

The shattered graybacks carried him back almost bodily, back to the Starker house where civilians were solemnly loading a coffin into a wagon, and there Poe collapsed on the lovely green lawn while the batteries opened up, trying to slow down the advance of Wright's triumphant men. Limbers were coming up, ready to drag the guns away. Lee's ambulance was already gone.

Poe found himself looking at the coffin. A dead girl was a poem, he thought as his head rang with gunfire, but no one had asked the girl if she wanted to be a poem. She would probably have chosen to live and become prose, healthy bouncing American prose, like his Evania. That was why he couldn't love her, he thought sadly; he couldn't love prose. And the world was becoming prose, and he couldn't love that either.

The artillery began pulling out. Poe could hear Yankee cheers. Poe's staff had vanished, lost in the whirlwind of the retreat, but there was Sextus, standing by the buggy, looking at the advancing Yankee line with a strange, intent expression. Poe dragged himself upright and walked toward the buggy.

"Come along, Sextus," he said. "We must go."

Sextus gave him a look. There was wildness in it.

Poe scowled. This was no time for the African to take fright. Bullets fluttered overhead. "Take the reins, Sextus. I'm too tired. We must leave this *champ du Mars.*"

At the sound of the French, Poe saw a strange comprehension in Sextus's eyes. Then Sextus was running, clutching his supposedly injured arm, running down the gentle hill as fast as his legs could carry him, toward the advancing Northern army. Poe looked after him in amazement.

"Sextus!" he called. "You fool! That's the wrong way!" The fighting had obviously turned the darky's wits.

Sextus gave no indication he had heard. "The wrong way! We're running *away* from the Yankees, not *toward* them!" Poe limped after him. *"Madman!"* he shrieked. *"Baboon! Animal!"* His nerves turned to blazing fire, and he clawed for one of his Le Mat revolvers. Holding the heavy thing two-handed, Poe drew the hammer back and sighted carefully. A few Yankee bullets whistled over his head.

Sextus kept running. The dark masses of Union men were just beyond him. The pistol's front sight wavered in Poe's vision.

Stupid, Poe thought.

He cocked his arm back and threw the revolver spinning after Sextus. There was a bang as the Le Mat went off on impact, but Poe didn't bother to look. He turned to the buggy and stepped into it; he whipped up the mare and followed the guns and the funeral procession through a cornfield toward the Confederate rear. Behind him he heard Yankee cheers as they swarmed up onto the deserted Starker lawn.

The corn was just sprouting. The buggy bounded over furrows. The field was covered with wounded Confederates staggering out of the way of the retreating guns. There was a cloud of dust on the border of the field.

On, no, Poe thought.

Men moved out of the dust, became two divisions of A. P. Hill's corps, moving in perfect battle formation. Marching to the rescue, like something out of Walter Scott.

Poe halted, examined the advancing Confederates through his field glasses, and then whipped up again once he found the man he wanted to see.

Little Powell Hill was riding in another buggy—another officer too sick to ride—but he was wearing the red flannel he called his "battle shirt," and his heavy beard, a contrasting shade of red, was veritably bristling with eagerness for battle.

Poe passed through Hill's lines, turned his buggy in a wide circle, and brought it on a parallel course to Hill. He and Hill exchanged salutes.

"I hope you've left some Yankees for us, General." Hill's voice was cheerful.

Poe looked at him. "Plenty of Yankees, sir," he said. "None of *my* men left, but plenty of Yankees."

Powell Hill grinned. "I'll reduce 'em for you."

"I hope you will."

"You should rally your men. I need your support."

Where were you when I needed your *support!* Poe wanted to say it, but he couldn't. Instead he just saluted, and brought the buggy to a halt.

His broken men gathered around him. Hill's marched on, into the swelling battle.

The battle died down at sunset. The blows and counterblows weren't clear to Poe, but Hanover Junction, after having changed hands several times, ended up back with the Confederacy, and Grant's army was safely penned in the bend of the North Anna. The burning Starker house was a bright glow on the horizon, a pillar of fire. Someone's shellfire had set it alight.

Among all the other dead was Hugin, shot by a Yankee bullet. The raven lay wrapped in a handkerchief at the foot of his tall perch. Munin moved from side to side on the perch, his head bobbing, mourning the loss of his mate.

Poe stood under the perch in the light of a campfire, listening to reports from his subordinates. Torn and dying men were lying around him in neat rows. The living, some distance off, were cooking meat; Poe could smell salt pork in the air. From the reports he gathered that he had lost about sixty percent of his men, killed, wounded, or missing. He had lost eighty percent of his officers the rank of captain or above. The figures were almost as bad as the attack at Gettysburg, last July.

A buggy moved carefully through the darkness and came to a halt. Walter Taylor helped Robert Lee out. Lee had apparently recovered somewhat; he was dressed carefully in a well-brushed uniform. Poe hobbled to him and saluted.

"General Lee."

Lee nodded. "This army owes you its thanks," he said. "You have saved Richmond."

"I have lost my division."

Lee was silent a moment. "That is hard," he said. "But you must tell your men how well they fought, how they have saved the capital. Perhaps it will make their sorrows easier to bear."

Poe nodded. "I will tell them." He looked at Lee. "What will I tell George Pickett? They were his men, not mine."

"You will tell him what you must."

Is this, Poe wondered, how Lee had got such a reputation for wisdom? Repeating these simple things with such utter sincerity?

Lee stepped forward, took Poe's arm. "Come. I would like to speak with you apart."

Poe allowed himself to be led off into the darkness. "Grant will move again," Lee said, "as soon as he gets his wounded to the rear and his cavalry comes back from the Yellow Tavern raid. There will be another battle, perhaps more than one. But sooner or later there will be a pause."

"Yes, sir."

"I would take advantage of that pause, General Poe. I would like to send a division to the Valley on this railroad you have saved us, to defeat the invaders there and strike at Washington. I would like to say, sir, that I am considering you for the command."

An independent Shenandoah Valley command, thought Poe. A chance for glory. The same command had been the making of Stonewall.

"My division is destroyed," Poe said. "I can't commit them to battle."

"Your division," gently, "is General Pickett's. When he recovers his health, he will return to command it. I refer to a new division, assembled with an eye to the Valley adventure."

"I see." Poe walked in silence for a moment, and stopped suddenly as his boots thudded against a wooden surface. He looked at it and realized it was the Starker girl's coffin, lying alone in the rutted cornfield. Apparently it had been thrown out of the wagon during the retreat.

Glory, he thought.

The Cause was lost. He couldn't believe in it anymore. That afternoon he'd told Moses one should fight for something noble, even if its time was gone. Now he no longer believed it. None of this was worth it.

He should have died, he thought savagely. He should have died on that last spree in Baltimore. It would have spared him all this. And perhaps spared his men, too.

If he hadn't anticipated Grant's maneuver, all this savagery might have been avoided. And the war would be over all that much sooner.

The one chance he had to change things, to become the great man, and all he'd done was prolong the nation's agony. Put more good men in their graves.

He thought of the lines of wounded and dying men, lying in the cornfield waiting for the morning, and he felt his heart crack. One fought for them, or nothing.

He straightened, took a breath. "I must decline the command, sir," he said. "My health and spirits are too poor."

Lee looked at him somberly. "You may wish to reconsider, General. It's been a hard day."

"I want to stay with my men, sir," Poe said.

Lee was silent for a long time. "I will speak to you again on this matter, General Poe," he said. He began walking back toward the raven standard. Poe followed.

"Your men shall be spared further fighting," Lee said. "Your men will be assigned to bury the dead."

For some reason this made Poe want to laugh. "Yes, sir," he said.

"I thank you for your part today."

Poe saluted. "Sir."

Walter Taylor snapped the reins, and Lee's buggy trotted away into the darkness.

He has left me in command of the dead, Poe thought. Sexton-general in charge of dead hopes, dead causes, dead ravens, dead verse, dead girls.

He looked at his officers, gathered under the standard for his instructions. Poe stepped to the perch and picked up Hugin's body.

"About fifty yards out there," he said, pointing, "there's a dead girl in a coffin. Find some men, find a wagon, and deliver her to the graveyard in New Market." He held out the dead raven. "Bury this poor bird with her," he said.

"Yes, sir."

He pulled his black cloak around him. He could hear the moans and muttering of the wounded. They were his responsibility when alive; now they were his, too, when they were in the grave.

In a quiet voice, he gave his instructions.

Above him the raven mourned, and said nothing.

ABOUT THE EDITORS

GREGORY BENFORD is the author of several acclaimed novels, including *Tides of Light*, *Great Sky River*, *Heart of the Comet* (with David Brin), *In the Ocean of Night*, *Across the Sea of Suns*, and *Timescape*, which won the Nebula Award, the British Science Fiction Award, the John W. Campbell Memorial Award, and the Australian Ditmar Award. Dr. Benford, a Woodrow Wilson Fellow, is a professor of physics at the University of California, Irvine. He and his wife live in Laguna Beach.

MARTIN H. GREENBERG is the editor or author of over 300 books, the majority of them anthologies in the science fiction, fantasy, horror, mystery, and western fields. He has collaborated editorially with such authors as Isaac Asimov, Robert Silverberg, Gregory Benford, and Frederik Pohl. A professor of political science at the University of Wisconsin, he lives with his wife and baby daughter in Green Bay.